BLAINE M. YORGASON

HEARTS AFIRE

BOOK ONE

At All Hazards

SHADOW MOUNTAIN®

Library of Congress Cataloging-in-Publication Data

Yorgason, Blaine M., 1942–
   At all hazards / Blaine M. Yorgason.
     p.   cm. — (Hearts afire ; bk. 1)
   ISBN 1-57345-321-8
   1. Mormons—History—Fiction. I. Title. II. Series: Yorgason,
Blaine M., 1942–   Hearts afire ; bk. 1.
PS3575.O57A8   1997
813'.54—DC21   97-32542
                                          CIP

Printed in the United States of America   72082

10 9 8 7 6 5 4 3 2 1

For Dad,
who has never allowed me
to forget my dream.

CONTENTS

Hole-in-the-Rock Route viii

Acknowledgments xi

Prologue 1

PART ONE: The Call 7

PART TWO: The Journey Begins 111

PART THREE: The Hole 169

PART FOUR: Cottonwood Canyon 309

PART FIVE: The Never-Ending Journey 395

Epilogue 618

Author's Note 623

Annotated Bibliography 625

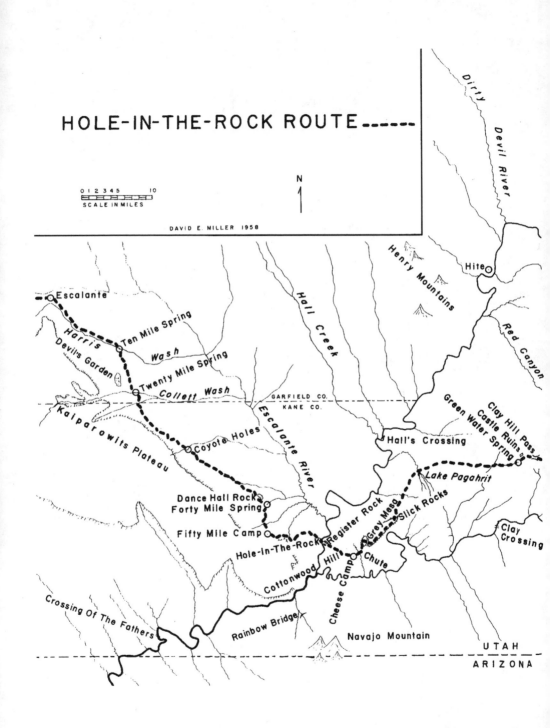

HOLE-IN-THE-ROCK ROUTE------

0 1 2 3 4 5   10
SCALE IN MILES

N

DAVID E. MILLER 1958

Dirty Devil River

Henry Mountains

Hite

Red Canyon

Escalante

Ten Mile Spring

Harris

Devils Garden

Wash

Twenty Mile Spring

Collett Wash

Hall Creek

GARFIELD CO.
KANE CO.

Clay Hill Pass

Castle Ruins

Green Water Spring

Kalparowits Plateau

Coyote Holes

Escalante River

Hall's Crossing

Lake Pagahrit

Clay Crossing

Dance Hall Rock
Forty Mile Spring

Fifty Mile Camp

Grey Mesa

Slick Rocks

Hole-In-The-Rock

Register Rock

Cheese Camp

Chute

Cottonwood Hill

Crossing Of The Fathers

Rainbow Bridge

Navajo Mountain

UTAH

ARIZONA

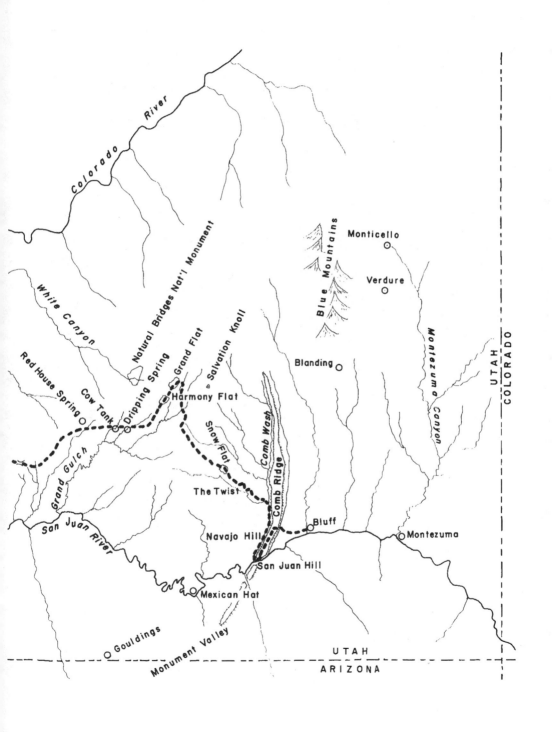

Acknowledgments

In a work of this scope, the list of contributors may be almost as long as the text, and in attempting to thank them some will be missed. For this I apologize and beg forgiveness. Nevertheless, certain individuals have given invaluable assistance that I must recognize. First is Albert R. Lyman, who came through Hole-in-the-Rock as a baby and spent his long and productive life gathering and recording the details of the San Juan's inhabitants. Years ago, in a personal visit that lasted less than an hour, he imparted to me an enthusiasm for *all* the inhabitants of the San Juan, as well as the amazing land that helped shape them, an enthusiasm that has never left me. Karl Lyman and his lovely wife, Edith, have enthusiastically shared with me their father Albert's writings as well as their own perspectives on the country. And when Michael Terry Hurst and Pearl Baker passed away, they kindly bequeathed me all their research on the same.

Karl Barton, his father Clyde, and DeVar Shumway have painstakingly—with horse, mule, and jeep—shown me the rocks and trees, the ruggedly beautiful mountains and valleys, the hidden arroyos and gulches that yet make up the San Juan country. With them and others I have traversed nearly every inch of the old trail except what is now beneath Lake Powell, and we have wondered together at the seemingly impassable road those Hole-in-the-Rockers managed to build and then use.

Under the auspices of the Utah State Historical Society and California State University, Fullerton, Gary Shumway has spent years directing the gathering and publishing of wonderful oral

xi

histories of San Juan's inhabitants. These he has unhesitatingly shared with me. And his sister Francine Shumway Sumner has never stopped waxing eloquent, through all the years of our friendship, about "her" land and its people.

My publishers and friends Ronald Millett and Sheri Dew have encouraged me from long before the actual onset of this project, and I express deep appreciation to them, as well as to their talented editorial, artistic, and marketing staff, for making this volume a reality.

Finally, I express heartfelt appreciation to my sons and daughters, who one after another accompanied me on my seemingly endless forays into the San Juan country; and to my eternal sweetheart, Kathy, who never once objected to the agonizingly long three years it took to finally pull this portion of the story together.

PROLOGUE

St. George, Utah Territory

For the better part of two days, the cold rain had fallen without letup, and now the street in front of the office was nine inches deep in red mud.

The shorter of the two elderly men in the front of the office watched a wagon slew around the corner and lumber past, the horses in the traces tossing huge globs of wet earth with each lifted hoof. "Well," he said, "I suppose it beats snow."

"Not by much," the other declared laconically. "Sort of makes a man wonder, though, whatever happened to sunny St. George. I marvel that the Lord doesn't see fit to spread these storms out a little, say back into January and February. Puts me in mind of deathbed repentance—a whole lot of activity at once, and not very effective."

Silently the two men stood, the only sound the drumming of the rain against the small panes of glass that made up the office windows—that, and the never-ending scratching of a pen coming from the back of the room. Finally the shorter of the two, a squarely-built man who, despite his age, gave the appearance of boundless energy, turned and moved slowly to the desk positioned against the wall at the rear of the room.

"Are these all that came, Billy?" he asked quietly.

"Yes, sir," the short, reed-thin man at the desk replied as he put down his pen and adjusted his wire spectacles. "I've put them in chronological order."

"Thank you." Taking the small stack of papers from his clerk,

1

the man glanced at them. Prophet, seer, revelator, and president of The Church of Jesus Christ of Latter-day Saints, Brigham Young was already familiar with the contents. "An express from Salt Lake brought these last evening," he said as he turned toward the man who had remained at the window.

"Reports on Indian depredations in the San Juan country?" Elder Erastus Snow of the Church's Quorum of Twelve Apostles asked.

"Partially. But besides Indians we have Gentiles moving westward from Colorado and taking up precious ground, and we have Texas trail herds and the outlaw element who follow them. And every bit of this activity seems to focus on the region of the San Juan."

"We don't know much about that country, Brigham."

"Not yet. We've had no one even near there since the Elk Mountain Mission was forced to close. But we need to learn. It's just as you said a year ago, Erastus. We need a buffer settlement in that country—a community of strong and faithful Saints who won't be deterred by lawless elements of any stripe but who will plant themselves deep and live their religion so well that the devil will be forced to pull up stakes and move elsewhere. Once such a community is entrenched, our converts from the Southern States will be more than pleased to join them."

"My son writes that there are many in Texas who are willing to emigrate if they can be assured that the country they come to will be similar to what they'll be leaving behind."

Brigham Young nodded. "It will be similar enough, you can count on that. But we mustn't lose sight of the real purpose of this mission, Erastus—for it will indeed be a mission. These brethren and sisters whom we send must develop positive relationships with the Indians of that area, the Navajos. In due time that people will be exposed to the uplifting principles of the gospel, and as they see the benefits of gospel living on the lives of the Church members who dwell among them, they will flock like doves to the stoop to the gospel standard. This is a divinely inspired plan and cannot fail of accomplishment."

"It'll be dangerous," Erastus Snow observed after a moment's contemplation. "The Navajos are still chafing from Kit Carson's roundup of the people and their subsequent poverty. Why, it's been less than three years since Jacob Hamblin nearly lost his life to them because of the murder of those two boys—"

"Murders committed by non-Mormons, Erastus. The courts have already proven that."

"Yes, that is true. And reports are that non-Mormons on or near the San Juan are waging continual warfare against the Indians in that country, killing all they can at the least provocation. This is especially true of the Pahutes—"

"There are Paiutes over there as well?"

Erastus Snow smiled. "There are, though I believe we're thinking of the name differently. From what Thales Haskell has learned, the Indians in the San Juan country aren't related to these western bands of Paiutes at all. Rather, they are Utes who have broken away from their main tribes and are called in the Ute language *Pah*, or water, because they won't leave the San Juan River to accept reservation life. Thales doesn't think there are many of them—maybe one or two hundred. But despite that, they have become a real scourge to the Navajos and the Gentile stockmen. If we establish a community in that region, they'll be a scourge to our people as well."

"Yes," Brigham Young said thoughtfully, "I can see it would be just as you say."

Again the men were silent, the falling rain making the only sound save for the ticking of the clock on the fireplace mantel. Suddenly there was a soft knock on the door, and a moment later a lean young man dressed in homespun was inside and removing the oilcloth cloak from his shoulders.

"Handy for keeping dry," Erastus said, nodding at the oilcloth.

"I picked it up during my last trip to Boston," the young man said as he removed his dripping, wide-brimmed hat. "How are you, Brother Snow?"

"Fair to middling, Will. You?"

"Fit as a fiddle and raring to go. And you, Father?"

"First-rate," Brigham Young replied. "Except for my lumbago, of course. That and the news from the San Juan."

"News?" Brigham Young's son John Willard, who served as a

3

counselor to his father in the First Presidency, glanced at the bundle of correspondence. "Is there trouble?"

"Not really. At least not so much that a community of good, faithful Saints set in the midst of it couldn't resolve."

"Are you thinking of placing a colony there, Father?"

"Have been for some time."

"Can we get them there?"

"We can get folks just about anywhere, once we know the way," Erastus Snow responded.

John Willard smiled thinly at the elderly apostle. "That's the point, isn't it."

"We'd need an exploring party," Brigham Young declared, speaking slowly to ease the slight tension in the room. It seemed that not all of the Brethren fully accepted his son as a member of the First Presidency. "What do you know of that country, Will?"

"I've never been there, of course. But from what Ira Hatch and Thales Haskell have told me, getting to the Colorado River, while difficult, is the easy part. After crossing it you get into wild desert country—little water, plenty of Indians—"

"Including the Navajo Peokon, who murdered young George A. Smith a few years back?"

"That's right, Father. But worse than Indians, far worse, is that the whole country seems to stand on end—huge masses of rock everywhere. Thales told me it may not be possible to take wagons into the San Juan country at all."

"An exploring party could tell us that," Elder Snow declared, "and maybe even blaze a road."

"Suppose they did," John Willard pressed. "What then? To send families off into that howling wilderness is tantamount to sending them off to suffer and maybe die. Is it worth it?"

Again the room was quiet. Even the scratching of his clerk's pen had ceased. Finally Brigham Young lowered himself into his chair. "Actually," he said quietly, his words measured, "I believe it is—worth it, I mean.

"Now don't get me wrong. I wish we could avoid such trials, Will. I truly do. But I'm finally beginning to see that suffering and even death don't mean the same thing to the Lord that they do to us.

Over the years I have felt impressed to promise, as an apostle of the Lord Jesus Christ, that the Lord would lead the faithful home to Zion, each and every one of them. But who is to say that those who perish along the way haven't obtained a better Zion than we who must tarry?

"And as for suffering, I've long proclaimed that suffering or persecution, no matter the source, is sanctifying. For instance, the Prophet Joseph Smith could not have been perfected, though he had lived a thousand years, if he had received no persecution. You may calculate when this people are called to go through scenes of affliction and suffering, are driven from their homes, and cast down, and scattered, and smitten, and peeled, that they are being sanctified, and the Almighty is rolling on his work with greater rapidity. If we had received no persecution in Nauvoo, would the gospel have spread as it now has? Would the elders have been scattered so widely as they now are, preaching the gospel? No, they would have been wedded to their farms, and the precious seed of the word would have been choked. 'Brother Joseph, or Brother Brigham, do not call upon me to go on a mission, for I have so much to do I cannot go,' would have been the general cry. 'I want to build a row of stores across this or that block, and place myself in a situation to make $100,000 a year, and then I can devote so much for the building up of the kingdom of God.' What utter and foolish nonsense! I'm telling you, brethren, the elders would have been so devoted to riches, they wouldn't have gone to preach when the Lord wanted them."

John Willard nodded. These were new thoughts to him, but he found himself agreeing with them wholeheartedly.

"Will," Brigham continued, "do you think persecution has done me good? Yes it has. I sit and laugh, and rejoice exceedingly when I see suffering and persecution. I care no more about it than I do about the whistling of the north wind, the croaking of the crane that flies over my head, or the crackling of the fire under the pot. The Lord has all things in his hand; therefore let it come, for it will give me experience. Do you suppose I should have known what I now know, had I not been persecuted?

"I only wish I was not so old and feeble as the years have rendered me. I would count it an honor to join a party of Saints in settling the San Juan country. Why, I'd reckon even Billy Foreman here would enjoy such a mission. Isn't that so, Billy?"

Nervously the small man adjusted the spectacles on his nose. "Yes, sir, I would, sir. Only, I . . . I wouldn't know the first thing—"

Without even hearing his clerk's meek voice, Brigham Young suddenly slapped his hand on the desk, causing Billy to actually jump. "Erastus," he ordered, still not noticing, "draw up a list of men you would recommend to head an exploring expedition into that country, and submit it to me as quickly as possible. Billy, once it's here, you get calls drafted for me to issue. I feel strongly that a colony must be planted and a mission established in the San Juan region, and it must be done soon.

"And Will, you begin making a list of families who could take such a mission—preferably younger families from this southern region—men and women who would be willing to go forth and do the work of the Lord, no matter the difficulties presented."

John Willard smiled sincerely. "Very well, Father. I'll start the list today. Billy, would you like me to put your name at the top as the first volunteer?"

Billy Foreman gulped and then nodded. "I would, yes. But—"

"Now hold on, Billy." Brigham Young looked concerned. "I do believe such a mission would be good for you. Very good, in fact! But you have never married, and we need families for such a mission. Besides, I have felt no impression that it is time for you to be released as my secretary. Do you understand?"

"I do, sir. Most certainly I do! That's what I've been trying to say."

"Good." Brigham Young turned again to his son. "When you're finished with your list, Will, give it to Elder Snow. He presides here in Utah's Dixie, and should something happen to me, he'll know what to do with it."

A look that spoke volumes passed between Brigham Young and Erastus Snow, and in the quiet that followed, all three of them realized that the rain had stopped. Perhaps it was going to turn into a sunny day in St. George, after all.

PART ONE

THE CALL

1

Thursday, September 25, 1879

Cedar City, Utah Territory

"You did what?"

Eliza Foreman, tall, thin, and even more ominous than usual because of the crutch she was leaning on, glared angrily at her cowering husband. She could not believe what she had just heard—could not believe the magnitude of it. Everything within her seemed to be shrinking, tightening up in fury, pain, and fear.

Anxiously adjusting his spectacles, Billy Foreman gulped as he tried to respond to this woman he had so recently married. "I . . . I volunteered to be part of this mission that's heading out for . . . for the San Juan country."

"Without saying one word to me, you volunteered us?" Eliza was almost shrieking, a terrible sound Billy had never heard in all their five months of marriage.

"Not us! It was me. I volunteered me."

"What?"

Frantically Billy searched for words. "This was going on three years ago, hon-bun, long before I ever knew you or even thought I might ever be getting married. I was in St. George with Brigham Young and Elder Snow, you know, when I was the president's clerk, and when Brigham Young proposed the mission, I said I . . . I should like very much to go with them."

"And all this time you've said nothing—"

"Until yesterday I'd forgotten all about it, Eliza. But when Elder Snow was going over the books at the co-op, he brought it up, reminding me that I'd volunteered and suggesting that I still consider going."

"And what did you say? You told him you were no longer interested, I hope!"

In anguish Billy shook his head. "I . . . I didn't say anything, hon-bun. I was too startled to know what to say."

Slowly Eliza lowered herself into one of the two chairs at the small, round oak table. "What an utter, sorry fool I've been," she breathed as she stared out through the window of the adobe home. "I should never have allowed you to talk me into coming into this horrible, God-forsaken country. No, Billy Foreman, I should never have allowed you to talk me into marrying you in the first place. That was my big mistake!"

"But hon-bun—"

"And stop calling me by that ridiculous name!" Eliza glared at her husband, a man twelve years younger than she was, three inches shorter, and with no more backbone than a garden worm. "My name is Eliza, and that is perfectly good enough for the likes of you."

Billy nodded. "A . . . all right, Eliza. But you felt the witness of the Lord that we were to marry every bit as strong as I did. I know it because you told me so."

"Lately," Eliza responded with a sigh, "I've concluded that all I felt was indigestion, which for five months has been getting worse by the day. It's growing late, Billy. Don't you have to open the co-op or something?"

Frantically reaching for his hat, Billy bolted for the door. "Don't forget that meeting up in Parowan tonight," he yelped as he stumbled off the stoop. "Be dressed by five, Eliza, for Elder Snow said we'd need to be there."

"Not if we aren't going on that insane mission!"

"Eliza—"

"You find Elder Snow, and you tell him we're not going, Billy Foreman!"

"If it's a call from the prophet, hon-bun, you know we can't turn it down!"

"Billy—"

"I love you, Eliza Foreman! You're beautiful!"
"Hummph!"

———◦—◦—◦———

As Billy unlocked the front door of the Cedar City Co-operative Store, swinging it wide for the day's business, he was troubled. Eliza wasn't happy, and it went a lot deeper than the possibility of a call to the San Juan. Of a truth she wasn't happy with him—not happy being married to him—and Billy had no idea what he could do about it.

Lifting his eyes, he gazed eastward toward the abruptly rising mountains, still blue with morning shadows. Billy loved the mountains and could spend hours just studying them, watching the shadows change and the colors go from cool to hot to cool again as the day progressed. The sun, an hour high, was already hot, and Billy adjusted his hat to shield his eyes as he gazed at the beauty of God's world.

The clopping of horses' hooves and the creaking and jingling of wagon boards and chains caused him to look to his left, and moments later he waved in friendly response to Hans Bogh and his wife Elsa.

Thank goodness, Billy thought, that Brother Bogh had greased his thimbles so that none of the wheels squeaked. There was no sound on earth, he thought, that grated on his ears more than squeaking, complaining wheels.

With embarrassment he remembered the rickety wagons he had bought in Salt Lake City just a few months before, and which he had used to haul himself and Eliza and all their belongings to their new home in Cedar City. The wheels had squeaked continually on both wagons, daily Eliza had stopped her ears with rag plugs, and Billy hadn't even known the horrible noise wasn't normal until a fellow in Kanosh had asked him why he hadn't greased the wheels. Billy's ears still burned red when he thought of the expression on Eliza's face, and of the laughter from the man and his sons when Billy had told them he hadn't known they'd needed it.

As he watched the fine dust raised by the passing wagon sift across the boards of the co-op porch and over his polished boots,

Billy adjusted his spectacles and thought about himself. Mercy, mercy! No wonder Eliza was fed up with him. If he lived to be a hundred, he'd never measure up to these hardened homesteaders who laughed at adversity and thrived on hardship. Why, it was nothing short of a miracle that he'd made it all the way to Cedar City, set up a home for himself and Eliza, and was putting the affairs of the co-operative store in order.

That was why it was sheer idiocy to even think of wanting to venture into the wilderness of the San Juan country. He lacked all the skills for a venture of that nature, as well as the basic physical strength so important to pioneers. He was way too small, too frail, too timid—

As he entered the store, Billy's nostrils were immediately assailed with the familiar, wonderfully musty aroma of the place. Hurrying down the aisle, he could identify the pungent smells of new leather, coal oil, garlic and onions, gunpowder, and several other items that were always in stock. To him the odor was merely comfortable, but Eliza had told him it put her in mind of the sutler's store at Fort Laramie, which she'd visited only once, more than twenty years before—and where she'd been unable to afford a desperately needed pair of shoes.

With a sigh Billy thought of Eliza again, and of how she'd suffered through the Wyoming blizzards during that horrible winter of 1856. A member of Edward Martin's handcart company, she and three other young, single girls had dragged their cart through the snows as far as Martin's Cove. There, during a blizzard that lasted days, her feet had frozen. And she would have lost them, too, but for the great faith of Brother Ephraim Hanks, who'd come with others to the rescue of the company. Brother Hanks had blessed her and then scraped the dead flesh from the bones of most of her toes. Then he'd cut off portions of both feet, including all her toes but one, and blessed her again, and she'd lost no more of her feet. In fact, though it was more than a month before she got to the Valley, and though all of that time was spent in frigid winter weather either riding in cold wagons or limping through knee-deep snow, she hadn't even experienced further frostbite.

Now, of course, she used a cane or crutch to walk because she couldn't keep her balance, and Billy knew that the cold weather bothered her a great deal, not only physically but also in her mind. For poor Eliza hated and feared snow and snowstorms, she truly did. And that was the other thing that troubled Billy about his desire to go to the San Juan. Eliza's fears were as real as her pain, and it would be absolutely wrong of him to drag her out of a comfortable home and subject her to a winter trek into the trackless San Juan country just because he'd once volunteered and now fancied going.

No, sir! Billy thought as he opened the books and placed the cash in the drawer. He wouldn't do it. His position at Cedar City was all a man should want, ever. No longer would he dream of a mission into the wilderness among the wild Texicans and even wilder Indians. No longer would he fancy himself becoming the kind of man to brave danger fearlessly while his wife looked adoringly on. No, sir! He'd just keep on being Billy Foreman the timid little clerk, and he'd satisfy himself with attempting for every hour of every day for the rest of his blessed life to give his beloved Eliza as much of the kind of life she so richly deserved.

Of course, he thought ruefully, if Elder Snow actually did bring him and Eliza a call to the San Juan Mission signed by President John Taylor, then he'd surely have to reconsider—

———o–o–o———

Parowan, Utah Territory

"I can't believe Kumen's home from their exploring expedition to the San Juan, Eliza. Or my brother Joseph, either. I didn't think the waiting would ever end."

Reaching over, Eliza patted the petite young woman on the back of her hand. Somehow she had become Eliza's friend, and despite age and other major differences, over the past summer the two had grown quite close. "We had a neighbor back in London," Eliza whispered in reply, "a widow lady who was absolutely full of proverbs. I heard them so often that some of them stuck with me. Listening to your joy, two come to mind: 'We may delay, but time will not' and 'One today is worth two tomorrows.'"

"They do fit, don't they." Now Mary wrung her hands. "And

13

they are back. But oh, Eliza, look how drawn both Kumen and Joseph look up there on the stand, how frail! I . . . I'm amazed they even had the strength to come back at all."

Though Eliza didn't know which man Joseph Nielson was, Kumen Jones did look drawn. In fact, Eliza thought, all the explorers looked much the worse for wear. Of course, they'd been gone a full six months, much of that time making their way across unchartered wilderness, building roads and living a very basic existence. No wonder they looked so fatigued.

Then, too, the room was exceptionally warm, and that didn't help much either. All day the wind had been hot and gusty out of the desert to the south, some said as a prelude to an approaching storm, and though the heat was uncomfortable, it was a relief for the assembled Saints to be out of the wind and the dust.

The meeting, presided over by Elder Erastus Snow, was the regular Thursday evening fast meeting, though with a good number of the explorers on the stand and the entire Parowan Stake invited, this promised to be a very irregular version of it.

Surreptitiously Eliza glanced to her other side where Billy sat. His face was impassive, which was unusual for him. But his eyes were moist as they practically devoured the men on the stand, one after another. And Eliza could almost read his thoughts as he dreamed his way to the same places they had been and saw the same things they had seen, and as he suffered the same ordeals these men had gone through.

The difference, Eliza thought as her eyes flicked back to the front, was that all of them had *done* it, while her husband never seemed able to get beyond his foolish dreams—

"Brothers and Sister," Erastus Snow said from the pulpit, interrupting Eliza's thoughts, "we bid you welcome. We will open this meeting by singing 'The Spirit of God Like a Fire Is Burning.' The invocation will be offered by Elder Lars Larsson, the sacrament of the Lord's Supper will be partaken of, and then I will introduce the discussion for tonight."

Quickly the opening ceremonies were concluded, after which Elder Snow again took the pulpit. "As you know," he said without preamble, "it was ever President Brigham Young's policy to colonize every habitable place in the territory. Thus we are building up the waste places of Zion and causing the desert, as Isaiah prophesied, to blossom as the rose! Many of you have been called to such endeavors in the past, and such missions can only be accomplished by men and women whose hearts are afire with the love of God, and who are filled with a determination to serve him at all hazards.

"To that end we have gathered this evening to discuss the mission to the San Juan country, to which we are presently calling missionaries whose hearts are afire. I had thought to immediately call upon Captain Silas Smith to discuss what the exploring party has learned about the San Juan. Instead, however, I feel impressed to share a few of my personal thoughts and feelings.

"In 1832, as a youth, I was introduced to the restored gospel of Jesus Christ, and since then difficulty and privation have assailed me on every hand. Yet would I wish my life to be different? Of course not! Once the Holy Spirit bore witness to my heart that the work was true and of God, I joined this fledgling church, The Church of Jesus Christ of Latter-day Saints, and committed myself to remain true and faithful no matter the difficulties that might follow.

"To my everlasting surprise, however, every trial I have endured has brought an even more glorious reward, blessings from God through the Holy Spirit that have strengthened and solidified my testimony until it has become rock-solid, an absolute assurance that the resurrected Christ lives and does in fact direct his work upon the earth. And that sure knowledge, which has led to my call to the holy apostleship, continues to give me peace as I stand as a special witness of Christ, issuing calls in his name that will literally change, and perhaps even end, the lives of you men and women who accept them.

"In my lifetime in this Church I have been directly involved in the establishment of more than two dozen communities like the one that will soon be established in the San Jan country. Kirtland, Ohio, was a frontier community, as were Far West and other Missouri communities established once Joseph Smith and the rest of us had been driven from Ohio to the western wilderness. Then came Nauvoo, which under the inspired vision of the Prophet Joseph arose from a

Mississippi River swamp to become in three years the greatest city in Illinois, if not the entire western United States.

"Vicious persecution against our people that began in New York took root in Ohio and grew rabidly in Missouri and finally reached full and evil bloom in Illinois, for there Joseph and his brother Hyrum were murdered by a mob of Christian militiamen whose hearts and minds had been filled by their sectarian ministers with secret, self-righteous oaths and instructions. Even after all these years I feel disgust at their motives, and I find it impossible to understand what sort of hatred could drive normally good men to such brutal crimes. Yet they were so driven, the deeds were done, and I will go to my grave feeling the sorrow of losing my beloved prophet and friend.

"After the martyrdom of Joseph and Hyrum, the Latter-day Saints were driven from their City Beautiful, and in the dead of winter we began the tortuous, fifteen-hundred-mile, two-year march that would lead us finally to the Valley of the Great Salt Lake.

"Brothers and Sisters, Orson Pratt and I were the first of our people to actually see the Valley, and I can still see clearly in my mind's eye how it appeared that July day in 1847. How beautiful it looked—tall waving grass, a vast lake shimmering in the afternoon sunlight, crystal-clear streams of cold water flowing from the mountains, and one single, solitary tree to give relief and emphasis to the view.

"Yes, it was beautiful, but oh, the work that lonely beauty represented, work that is still going forward as we labor with our might to subdue the earth and cause the desert to blossom as the rose.

"My call to the apostleship came in 1849," he continued, "and three years later came my call to travel to this southern country to establish the mission called the Deseret Iron Company. From then until now, except for occasional missions overseas, I"ve been directing Saints to establish communities throughout this far-flung desert territory: Cedar City, St. George, Grafton, Leeds, Harmony and New Harmony, Pinto, Panguitch, Snowflake, and a host of others.

"Through it all I've been blessed with the companionship and support of my wife Artemesia, a wonderful woman who is a true servant of God, quietly serving myself and a host of others no matter the difficulties. And there have been many of those, almost too many to mention, for it is she who has carried the burden of my life's work. Not alone the loss to mobs of homes and lands in Ohio, Missouri, and Illinois, but time and again here in the Territory of Utah she has pulled up stakes to follow me to new assignments or to go it alone when my work lay across the sea.

"Despite such obstacles, she has reared a fine family from a variety of homes: tents, wagon boxes, dugouts, log cabins, adobe homes, and even one or two brick mansions (as she describes them), caring little for worldly things as she seeks to worship and serve the Lord Jesus Christ.

"As with my dear wife, the true burden of this new expedition will fall upon you women, most of whom are enough to be my own daughters. Am I concerned about that? Of course I am. Yet compared to the glorious rewards awaiting each of you sisters who proves herself faithful, such trials and difficulties will be as nothing. More, they are to be welcomed, for they will temper the steel of your spirits faster and better than all the ease and luxury the world could provide.

"So by and large all of you who accept this calling will be up to it, and you will endure well the difficulties it represents. Yes, and through your sacrifices all will be blessed, from the least to the greatest, and in due time a community of God-fearing Latter-day Saints will be raised up in another portion of the wilderness, there to bear witness of Christ to all who come near.

"It is that certain understanding, brothers and sisters, that continues to set my own aging heart afire."

Erastus Snow concluded his remarks and then invited Silas S. Smith, the captain of the exploring expedition, to come to the pulpit. In clear and brief form Silas described the journey the men had made—about a thousand miles, it had been calculated—going south across the desert of Arizona, back north to the San Juan and across the mountains of Southern Utah, and then back south to Parowan and Cedar on the return home. Each half-circle leg was about five hundred miles, and each seemed equally difficult. Both routes would be passable, Captain Smith felt, though a third alternative might be better.

"To that end," he declared, "and with the authorization of Elder

Snow, I asked three men from the new community of Escalante, in Potato Valley, to spend the summer exploring the possibility of a more direct route than I knew we'd be taking, a shortcut, if you will, to the San Juan. These brethren performed their task admirably, and one of them, Bishop Andrew P. Schow, is here with us tonight. Bishop Schow, would you please take a few moments and tell us what you found?"

The bearded man made his way quickly to the pulpit. "The three of us who were called," he said without preliminaries, "were Charlie Hall, Reuben Collett, and myself. Charlie is a builder, and his explorations were with the view of finding a way to cross the river. Reuben, our town constable, is quite familiar with the country southeast toward the river, so we took a two-wheeled cart with a small wagon-box on it and traveled together.

"Shortly after reaching the Colorado, we found a cut in the cliff that could be widened into a roadway sufficient for a company of Saints to pass through. At present it's too steep and narrow to lower a boat through, so we traveled up the river about two miles to a point near where Escalante Creek empties into the Colorado. There we removed the wagon-box from the running gears of the cart and slid it over the face of the cliff to the levels below. First we lowered it to a narrow bench where there was considerable grass, and from there over another precipice and on down to the river.

"Having caulked the wagon-box, we climbed aboard and rowed to the other side. There we encountered another cliff, which we scaled without difficulty, to find ourselves in a fine, level valley with a clear stream of water flowing along it. We climbed this valley to a distance sufficient to see beyond it the San Juan River gorge.

"Having thus determined the passability of the route, we recrossed the river and beached the wagon-box for future use. Then we rescaled the cliffs and returned to our homes."

"Are there any questions?" Captain Smith asked as he stepped up beside his longtime friend and fellow scout.

"So the river can be crossed at that point?" someone called.

"Yes, without difficulty. And Brother Hall says he can build a ferry that will easily carry the wagons and livestock across."

"How far is it from the Colorado to our settlement on the San Juan?"

"Not far—I'd guess about a hundred and ten or fifteen miles. After talking with Brother Silas here, I wouldn't hesitate to say that the route we explored is far better than either of the trails these brethren explored, and it will cut months off your travel time."

"But you didn't go all the way?"

"No, we didn't. But from our vantage point we could see a vast distance, and the road beyond the river presented no real difficulties that we could discern."

"Based on this report," Captain Smith declared as he placed his hand on the bishop's shoulder, "we've determined to take this, the shortest of the routes, for our mission to the San Juan."

There was a stir of approval from the congregation, and after Bishop Schow had taken his seat, Captain Smith described the wonderful country along the San Juan. "I bear solemn witness," he concluded, "that the Lord wants our mission in that country, and he will not only prosper our journey, but he will prosper us in establishing our homes in that land."

Captain Smith took his seat, and Erastus Snow then opened the meeting to general questions.

"What about the Indians?" someone called out. "Word is that you had some close shaves."

"Parley Butt," Elder Snow directed, "will you respond to that?"

With a nod the young man, who had not yet turned twenty, came to the pulpit. "We saw plenty of Indians, all right," he drawled, "but mostly they seemed friendly. I reckon the only real close shave occurred after four of us went back to the Moencopi to bring the Davis family and our livestock back to Montezuma Creek, which is where we've determined to place our community.

"Three days north of the Moencopi we entered some very bad Indian country. A fellow by the name of Peokon came to our camp and caused a great deal of trouble. By the way, he's the man who caused the death of young George A. Smith, and we passed the head of the very wash where that happened. This Indian would kick the dirt on our food and strike our knives on the rocks. He'd draw his own knife across his throat to show Sister Davis and the children

19

what he'd do to them when he got help. Our boys acted like the time had come for them to kill or be killed, but we determined not to fire the first shot.

"Finally old Peokon left for help, and he didn't return by nightfall. When daylight came and Peokon and his followers hadn't returned, we felt much relieved and determined to prepare our breakfasts.

"About then an old Indian appeared in the distance, hurrying toward us. Ignoring our ready rifles, he told us to hitch up our horses as quickly as possible and to travel fast. We did so but were a little doubtful about the Indian's plans, fearing he might be leading us into a trap.

"The roads went through deep sand, so the horses had to stop often. This seemed to annoy the old Indian, who would stand on the spring seat and look far and wide, and then urge us to hurry. Finally, after a few hours of this, he told us we could stop as long as we liked and travel as slow as we wished.

"He then asked Brother Davis if he didn't know him, calling him by name and telling him where he'd come from. It seems he'd been in the Davis home many times and had always been well received. He told Jim that Peokon planned to kill and rob us as soon as he could find enough volunteers, and he'd come to save us by hurrying us out of their territory.

"As to his identity, I don't know it. But Thales Haskell, who hadn't returned to the Moencopi with us, said it sounded like Chief Dah-nish-uant, or Spaneshanks, as some call him. That's Peokon's own father, who was a friend of Ira Hatch and helped save the lives of Jacob Hamblin's expedition to the Hopi after George A. Smith's murder.

"As I said, that's the only close shave I know of on the whole expedition, and the Lord used friendly Indians to pull us through it. I reckon he'll do the same for the entire mission."

"I'd like to add something here," H. Joseph Nielson said as he stepped forward.

"That's him," Mary whispered as she gripped Eliza's arm. "That's my brother. He's only nineteen, but lawsy! Look how old he looks!"

"Go ahead, Joe," Erastus Snow urged.

"Thank you. I reckon I just wanted to add my two bits worth to Parley's testimony. Sure there are mean Indians out there, just as there are good ones like the old fellow who saved Parley's bacon. But if we do what we're asked, then God can protect us. He surely has that power, and I know it!"

As Brother Nielson turned back and took his seat, Parley Butt spoke again to the congregation. "Any more questions?"

"Are you planning on going back with the mission?" someone called out.

"I certainly am. That's a fine country, and my brother Willard and I intend to take our herd and build up a home there."

"Do you all feel the same?" a woman called out.

Erastus Snow looked around at the explorers. "Any of you men *don't* intend to go back?" he asked. When a half dozen or more raised their hands, he called Thomas Bladen to the pulpit. "All right, Brother Bladen, tell the folks why you don't intend to fill a mission to the San Juan country."

"I reckon," the man replied laconically, "that the country just isn't worth inhabiting."

Instantly the room grew still, and Mary Jones reached out and gripped Eliza's hand in her own.

"If you want specifics," the man continued, "I'll give them to you. The San Juan is a quicksand river, treacherous as can be. It also fluctuates a great deal in volume, meaning you can never tell if you'll have water in it or not. Our boys spent weeks helping build a ditch to irrigate some fields of corn, only to watch the water level drop so low that the ditch remained empty. The corn, of course, burned up.

"But that isn't all. The ground seems sandy and infertile, and the country is hot and desolate. Other than some Mormon haters named Mitchell on McElmo's Bend and a few cowboys up on the Blue Mountains, the nearest white folks are a hundred miles away in Colorado. To my way of thinking, the San Juan is no place to take women or children, and I wouldn't feel right subjecting my own family to such hardship and isolation. Questions?"

"How do the Mitchells live there?"

"They run a trading post. We saw no successful crops while we

21

were there. In my opinion folks on the San Juan could easily starve to death, beginning with the Davis and Harriman families and old Harv Dunton, who has stayed with them. Leastwise they sure won't be able to raise many cash crops in that country."

"More questions?" Erastus Snow asked, holding Thomas Bladen beside him.

"Is there wood for building?"

Bladen nodded. "Cottonwood and cedar or juniper, which as you know isn't worth a whole lot. High up on the Blues we saw pine and fir, but that's fifty, seventy-five miles from the river, with some mighty rough country in between. I didn't even see good clay for adobes, though some might be located if the time was taken."

"Any other questions? None? Good." Elder Snow then dismissed the man to return to his seat. "Any more of you explorers have anything to add?"

"I do," Kumen Jones said as he rose to his feet. "What Tom says is about right. The country is dry, hot, rough, and lonely. What he doesn't say, though, is that the Lord has called us to settle there, which means it most certainly can be done. He has also called us to take Christ's gospel of peace to the Indians, which means that can also be done. I for one look forward to returning, and I believe it will be a marvelous place to take my wife Mary and the little ones we hope to have."

"Amen!" George Hobbs shouted as he waved his hat in the air. "Amen to all Kumen has said!"

Amens echoed from among the explorers as well as throughout the room, after which several individuals rose to their feet and proclaimed either for the mission or against it, though the latter were few in number and had little to say.

"Thank you all," Erastus Snow said when the last person had finished. "We appreciate your attendance and your participation. For those of you who have been called to this mission, I ask that you remember two things. First, you are not required to go. Any of you may decline this mission with no fear of ridicule. Just let me know, and that will be the end of it.

"Second, for you who wish to accept your calls, we'd like to see you on the road as early in October as you can ready yourselves.

That gives you a month, preferably less, to be on your way. According to our calculations, that should put you on the San Juan before Christmas, which will give you plenty of time to construct homes and prepare the ground for spring planting.

"Finally, for you who haven't been called but would like to take up this mission, you're welcome to join. Simply let Captain Smith or me know, and then be ready to depart with the others."

And once again, as had happened that very morning when she'd confronted Billy, Eliza felt a terrible heaviness course through her, a premonition of something awful that would bring her pain and suffering far worse than anything she had ever endured.

2

---◦–◦–◦---

Friday, September 26, 1879

South of Bosque Bonito, Chihuahua, Mexico

"Sugar Bob" Hazelton, a mean-hearted soul with no imagination and hardly any more sense, was in an even uglier mood than usual. For three days he had been, as he put it, less than half the stride of a short heifer in front of a posse of Texas Rangers out of Fort Stockton. They'd run him mercilessly, day and night, with hardly a moment's rest except for a couple of hours at Van Horn's Wells, and the terror of being captured had about killed him. And when by sheer luck he'd made it across the Rio Grande into Mexico and paused to wave his hat at them in derision, one of the sons of devils had blown a hole through both his canteen and the belly of his horse with an old buffalo gun.

Cursing violently, Sugar Bob had whipped his entrails-dragging animal into a staggering lope that had carried him nearly a mile before the horse had died in midstride and collapsed hard against a huge stand of prickly pear. After an hour of pulling the fiery spines from his face, shoulder, and arm, Sugar Bob had stripped his rig from the dead horse. Then, venting his frustration by giving the animal a final, vicious kick, he'd set off in the safest direction he knew—southwest.

He didn't know for certain, because he'd lost his father's timepiece in a poker game with his sometime partner Fred "Dingle" Beston more than a year before, but to Sugar Bob the blazing sun seemed to be at about four o'clock. That meant he'd been walking five, maybe six hours, and every broiling inch of it had been over the driest, rockiest, thorniest, meanest country the devil had ever thrown together—and that with boots so shot full of holes from his long bout with poverty that his feet were oozing out like mush through a sieve. Worse, they were so fiery hot with pain that it took all the power of his will to keep from bawling like a baby. Instead he simply cursed, a continuous stream of profanity that would have turned the grass blue—had there been any grass in the country to turn any color at all.

And it was hot, too, hotter, as he put it to himself, than the back lot of hell in August, and Sugar Bob was positive he'd sweated out every last drop of water in his wasted body. Now his tongue was so swollen it filled his mouth, his lips were cracked and bleeding, and about all he could see through his red-hazed eyes were flashes of light. He couldn't tell if the flashes were out before him in the shimmering afternoon or simply exploding in his brain. But then, what by jingo did it matter? Those pings of light meant he was coming perilously close to dying of thirst, and it seemed to Sugar Bob that even the thought of dying had a certain attraction.

"Damnation," he muttered silently as he forced his feet to push him up the slope of a barren hill, "this country's strick dryer'n the whole state of Texas, and that ain't hardly possible!"

On top of the hill he staggered to a stop, unconsciously hiked his saddle higher onto his shoulder, lifted his hat with his free hand, and wiped his face on his grimy, tattered sleeve. Not often in his adult life had his choice of drinks been water, but with the afternoon hot enough to singe leather and his mouth dryer than a sack of Bull Durham, he was becoming somewhat less choosy. In fact, he thought gloomily as he started forward down the hill, right now he'd settle for the ooze in the bottom of a buffalo wallow, creepy-crawlies and all. Leastwise after that he wouldn't have to prime himself just to spit. No sir, by jingo, he'd drink about whatever he could get!

"Teach me to go shooting folks," he grumbled as he plodded forward. "No matter the fool needed killing. Like your pa once said, when killing's to be done, do it in private, and better yet, in the dark. But not you, Sugar Bob Hazelton! Oh, no. You got to go and plug that hombre in broad daylight in front of about fifty witnesses and some passing Texas Rangers on the main street of Fort Stockton. No wonder he up and called you dumb, Sugar Bob. You was, and that's a fact!"

Of course, the man who'd called him dumb hadn't been too bright either, Sugar Bob thought with what was left of his grin. Shooting off his mouth thataway when he hadn't even been heeled? Why, a man had to be either dumb or crazy not to pack a weapon, let alone to go mouthing off in front of a gunslick like himself! Served the sorry son of a devil right, it did. But it would have served him just as right a few hours later, in full darkness with nobody around and nobody the wiser, including those blamed rangers! Why—

"Buenos dias, señor."

"Well," Sugar Bob said to himself as he dragged his feet forward through the unbearable afternoon, "now you're hearing things, Sugar Bob. Next'll come the seeing, and maybe even the tasting of piddle-water from that same buffalo wallow you bin dreaming of—"

"Señor greengo, would you like a dreenk?"

"Huh?" Sugar Bob forced his mouth to work.

"The veellage, señor, it is not so far, and we have good water. But I have a leettle water here, also very good—"

Squinting, Sugar Bob could barely make out the form of a small man moving along beside him. Behind him plodded a heavily loaded burro, which Sugar Bob noted with more than passing interest. But it was the goatskin water bag in the man's outstretched hand that struck his immediate fancy.

"Here you go, señor—"

With an oath Sugar Bob snatched the goatskin bag from the Mexican, knocking him down in the process. He didn't know if the whole shebang was a hallucination or not, but even the dream of water beat the stuffing out of what he'd been wetting his whistle with lately. There, by jingo! Now he'd see—

Sugar Bob was actually surprised to find that the water was real. But it was, and he drank so heavily, ignoring the protesting Mexican, that he became ill and retched violently. Afterward he drank again, more slowly, and then he swept the piled sticks of firewood from the back of the burro and dragged himself and his rig aboard.

"Heeyah!" he shouted to the little animal as he dug his spurs into its ribs, "Geddup there!"

When the burro failed to move, he grew angry, and he stopped his tirade only when the Mexican fearfully took him by the arm.

"Eet ees a pet of my family, señor. Eet goes when I say go, and not otherwise."

Narrowly Sugar Bob regarded the small man, who had quickly pulled his hand away. "Then say go!" he growled menacingly.

"I . . . I weel, señor, but I must lead eet, too. Come, and I weel lead the burro and you to my veellage. There ees a cantina there, you know."

Cursing viciously but suddenly excited about the prospects of drinking something with a little hair on it, Sugar Bob allowed himself to be carried around the next bend in the wall of cactus, where, to his surprise, he found himself entering a small, adobe-walled village.

"Well, if it ain't old Sugar Bob Hazelton," a voice growled from the deep shade of a nearby veranda. "I ain't seen you in a sight longer than somewhat."

"And I ain't been looking to see you either," Sugar Bob said testily. "You still got my pa's watch, Dingle?"

"All but the fob," Fred "Dingle" Beston responded. "I give that to a soiled dove up El Paso way, and last I saw she was wearing it fer a necklace and thinking she was something. You look dirtier nor a Comanche's blanket, Sugar Bob. That there your regular hoss, or are you moving up in the world?"

"Not so's you'd notice," Sugar Bob replied as he swung up his leg and slid to the ground, contemptuously ignoring the small man who'd been his benefactor. "The man says there's a cantina hereabouts."

"He should know," Dingle Beston declared, inclining his head toward the open doorway beside him to indicate that Sugar Bob had found the water hole. "Trouble is, she's siesta time in this burg, and the barkeep won't serve no liquor nor anything else for maybe another hour."

"Won't he, now," Sugar Bob snarled as he tossed his rigging into the shade beside his erstwhile partner. "Well, I got a thirst big enough to wake up more'n a hundred sleeping Mexicans. What's he serving?"

"A few days ago he had some tarantula juice strong enough to draw blood blisters off'n a rawhide boot," Dingle Beston drawled as he drew himself to his feet to follow Sugar Bob into the dark room. "But since I drunk it all, he's reduced to a few bottles of mescal, which he colors now and again with a good spit of tobaccy juice."

"Mescal!" Sugar Bob thundered. "That's Apache liquor! And I ain't going to drink no Injun-made cactus juice."

"It's that or water from the trough down the way a piece." Dingle Beston was enjoying himself immensely, and it showed enough that Sugar Bob got even angrier than normal. What made it even better for Dingle was that he was telling the truth about the mescal. There was literally no other liquor in the village, for he'd looked, and looked good.

"You know who that Mex was who brought you in?"

"Yeah, a dirty little greaser."

"He's more'n that."

Sugar Bob Hazelton laughed harshly. "Not to me, he ain't!"

"As always," Dingle Beston grinned, "you're about as kind-hearted and sociable as an ulcerated back tooth. What sort of business did you say brought you here?"

"I didn't!" Sugar Bob growled as he looked around the small room. "Where's that blamed barkeep you was harping about?"

"Behind the bar, there. If you'd close your yap you could hear him snoring. Happen those ranger fellers are looking for you, I understand they can track a whisper through a high wind."

"Not across that river they can't!" Sugar Bob declared with another oath and a satisfied chuckle. "They got no jurisdiction here in Mexico, and you know it!"

Stepping to the plank bar, he leaned over and looked down. "Tarnation," he growled as he shook his head. "Are all these barkeeps fat? Where's he keep his red-eye?"

"Beside him. Two jugs, on the floor."

Without another word Sugar Bob stepped around the end of the bar, weighed in his hand the two jugs, took up the heavier one, pulled the cork with his teeth, and took a long swig.

"Yech," he spat as he lowered the bottle and took a deep breath.

"Stuff tastes worse'n I remembered!" And again he hoisted the jug to his lips.

Thirty minutes later, the jug nearly empty, Sugar Bob had grown more foolish but no less cantankerous. Dingle Beston, who despite being his partner now and again had never liked the man, was already thinking of some way to make himself scarce when with a loud snort the barkeep woke up, lay still for a moment, and then dragged himself to his feet.

"Oh, Señor Dingle," he said, looking surprised, "I deed not hear you come in."

"Which is some surprising, Julian, considering the racket old Sugar Bob made whilst he was rooting out your liquor. Fact, he was noisier'n an empty wagon on a hard-froze road, which frozen roads I don't reckon you know too much about."

"No, Señor Dingle," the heavy barkeep shook his head, looking sorrowful, "I do not. But I do know my jug was nearly full when I went to sleep, and now eet ees not."

"Yep," Dingle replied without enthusiasm, "I reckon he's about drunk it up, all right."

"Very well, Señor Sugar," the man called Julian said as he looked at Sugar Bob with more sorrow than ever, "that weel be two dollar American, por favor."

"Two dollars!" Sugar Bob growled. "That stuff ain't worth the stink off a dead coyote, let alone two American dollars!"

"Two dollar for the jug, Señor Sugar. Or six pesos, eet does not matter."

"I said—"

"Pay the man, Sugar Bob," Dingle Beston stated firmly and almost pleadingly.

"I ain't agoing to pay him nothing!"

"Sugar Bob, you ain't got the least notion of what you're messing with, but I'll tell you right now that Julian is younger brother to the feller what brought you in on his burro. And that feller is thorny as cactus. Was I you, I'd pay the man, pronto."

"Por favor," Julian pleaded, his hands lifted in supplication. "Señor Dingle is right, Señor Sugar. Because of my brother it is best that you pay—"

"You want pay," Sugar Bob snarled, "then I reckon I'll pay." And with a flick of his wrist his pistol was in his hand and spouting fire and lead. With a look that held only more sorrow, Julian looked down through the powder smoke as the stain of blood spread across the front of his shirt. For an instant then he lifted his gaze back up into the eyes of Sugar Bob Hazelton, and without another sound he finally crumpled to the hard-packed earthen floor.

"You shot him," Dingle Beston breathed in shocked amazement. "You done shot and kilt Julian Espinosa."

"And likely done the world a favor," Sugar Bob said as he holstered his pistol and reached once again for the jug.

Suddenly galvanized, Dingle Beston pushed himself from the bar. "You sorry, miserable fool," he practically shouted, his look one of growing terror, "you kilt more than poor old Julian Espinosa. You kilt the two of us sure as road apples ain't sweet. Now come on, we got to get out of here!"

"Whoa now," Sugar Bob remonstrated as he lowered the jug and gave another belch. "What you so het up about? He's only a fat, dirty greaser—"

"Who happens to be favorite baby brother to Felipe Nevio Espinosa, the bandito king who's kilt enough gringos on his raids into Texas, New Mexico, and Colorado to have him a reserved seat in hell!"

"Felipe Nevio Espinosa the *gunslinger?*" Sugar Bob Hazelton was suddenly feeling a little less secure, a little less confident. "He's that miserable, dirty little greaser what lent me his burro?"

"As ever!"

"But . . . but I heard he was kilt up in Colorado more'n ten years ago! Tom Tobin kilt him!"

"Then somebody forgot to tell Felipe, his mother, and poor Julian here."

Sugar Bob shook his head, trying to clear it. "But he . . . he was walking barefoot, hauling sticks!"

"Firewood for his mother," Dingle nodded. "He brings a load once a week, or so I hear. But being as how he's mean as a barrelful of rattlers to everybody but Julian and has forty riders busting their guts to be worse than him, I was some shocked to see him helping you into town. That's why I asked if you knew him."

Sugar Bob only stared, and from out in the street a dog began barking loudly.

"Come on!" Dingle shouted, ignoring Sugar Bob's stupefied stare. "Happen we don't scat and quick, afore Felipe gets here, we ain't neither one of us got the chance of a .22 cartridge in a ten-gauge goose gun!"

"Where . . . where'll we go?"

"As far as we can. I hear Mr. Lacey's moving his outfit up on the San Juan where life is high, wide, and lonesome. Despite what you did to his only daughter, maybe he'll hire us again. Leastwise that's where I'm heading!"

And without another word Dingle Beston ducked out the door of the adobe cantina and sprinted for the stables around back. And white-faced Sugar Bob Hazelton, who thought he was about to vomit again—only this time from fear—at least had the presence of mind to scoop up his rigging as he stumbled past. And with that in his benumbed hands, he did his best to wobble after.

3

Saturday, September 27, 1879

Cedar City

"It's wonderful of you to do this for me, Mary. I could never have dug all these cattails out by myself."

Snapping the reins to the little mare that was pulling the light spring wagon along the dusty track, Mary Jones laughed. "Fiddlesticks, Eliza, it was good for me to get out and do something besides worry about this upcoming mission. Besides, the weather has turned so hot that it felt wonderful squishing my feet in all that ooze. Are you going to try and replant these things?"

"No. I've widened a place in our irrigation ditch, and I'll just put them there until I get all the fronds used up. I don't really want them to grow back again next year."

"That means they probably will." Smiling, Mary glanced behind her into the bed of the wagon. "Lawsy, woman! With that many cattail fronds you'll be making fans from now until Christmas! Did you ever make hats from fronds like these?"

"Oh, a few bonnets many years ago, but no real hats. Ladies today want their millinery fancy—if possible, made of imported fabric and other materials. Did I tell you I owned a millinery shop?"

Mary smiled. "No, Billy did. He said one of your regular customers was Eliza R. Snow. Is that really true?"

"Sister Snow is a wonderful woman." Eliza smiled at the memory. "She was also my all-time favorite customer."

"Why?"

"I think because she's as plainspoken as I am. Sister Snow was very straightforward in her efforts to marry me off."

Mary giggled joyfully. "Truly?"

"Absolutely. 'Listen to me, sister,' she said practically the first time she came into my shop, 'a woman isn't made to live alone. Those who do become crotchety old things who aren't worth a pinch of snuff in a high wind. Now this is plain talk, but tall and homely as you are, that'll happen to you, too, happen you don't humble yourself and allow me to suggest your name to one of these good brethren. I know Abraham Hunsaker and a host of other hardworking, quiet men who would provide you with a wonderful home.'"

Mary was astounded. "She really spoke to you like that?"

Eliza nodded. "She did indeed. She's only a little bit of a woman who doesn't even come up to my shoulder, but she's filled with more energy and do-goodedness than anyone else I've ever known. And she's also filled with love—pure, Christ-like love—which washed over me with such force that it was impossible to take offense at her 'plain talk.'

"More, it inspired me to share with her, on a quiet day when we were alone together, why I wouldn't become some good brother's plural wife."

"You mean you actually considered entering into the 'principle?'"

Eliza smiled thinly. "Actually, Mary, I didn't. The whole idea of plural marriage seemed repulsive to me, and I ridiculed the principle and have scorned outright the proposals of at least a dozen potential often-married husbands. In turn, though, my attitude has brought scorn upon my own head, for many have been the matronly and saintly women—besides Sister Snow, I mean—who have solemnly wagged a warning finger in my face and prophesied my eternal, barren maidenhood. Yes, and there has even been a warning or two from well-meaning Church leaders, good men who did have my best interests at heart and wanted to see me cared for in time as well as eternity."

"And yet you resisted?"

"Of course I resisted. What none of them knew, at least until the day I confided in Sister Snow, was that I'd received a prophetic blessing under the hands of the elder who'd taught and baptized me a Latter-day Saint in far-off England so many years ago. I was promised that I alone would bear the responsibility of raising up a righteous posterity unto my husband."

"Lawsy, Eliza," Mary declared quietly, "but you are a woman of mighty faith. What would you have done if that elder hadn't been inspired?"

Eliza laughed. "That's exactly what Sister Snow said. And my reply was, 'He was inspired to teach me and baptize me. Why should his inspiration end there?'"

"And so you waited?"

"Yes, I waited." Eliza stared ahead as the wagon bounced along beneath her. "And as the years dragged by and no single man came to court me and carry me away to eternal bliss, I busied myself otherwise. I perfected my hand at millinery and opened a prosperous little shop only a few dozen rods south of where the temple is being constructed. Many patronized my business, from the lowliest emigrant woman struggling to feel presentable, to the wives of the noble and great who sometimes seemed to be struggling to feel better than each other. In a way, Mary, it has all made me laugh, for I've never liked hats, and have never been under the illusion that such tomfoolery could do much for my appearance. Still, I enjoyed my work, for through it I became friends with many wonderful people I never would have known otherwise. And," and Eliza smiled again, "through my work I managed to avoid becoming one of the city's few charity cases."

Mary nodded solemnly. "You've accomplished so many wonderful things, Eliza. You truly are a woman of great faith."

"I suppose some would say that." Eliza's tone was suddenly bitter, though if Mary noticed it she gave no sign. "Now I'm forty-four years old, and just look at where my faith has brought me!"

"You must have experienced times of great loneliness and discouragement," Mary declared, her voice still filled with awe, "and yet you've survived them by reminding yourself that the wait would be worth it, and that the man who was coming would be wondrous beyond belief. And he is, isn't he!"

In answer, Eliza could only stare bleakly ahead.

———◦—◦—◦———

The South Bank of the San Juan River,
across from Montezuma Creek

The Navajo called Peokon was angry and bitter. His horses were nearly gone, his sheep and goats had been decimated, and most of those who had followed him in the old days, the good days when wealth could be obtained just by taking it, were no longer around. Once he'd been a mighty chief and raider, a headman. But now no one was left to be a headman over, no one with the courage to be a man of the People, of the *Diné.* It was almost as if a *chinde,* a devil or witch, was—But no, he thought with scorn. He didn't believe in such foolishness. Peokon believed only in himself, and in the strength of his own good arm! It had been so always, and so it would always continue. Even if—

"The *belacani* people the Pahutes call mormonee have built only one hogan, my brother. It would be an easy thing to slay them all."

Following a moment of silence Peokon turned to look at the man who had spoken. He was called *Natanii nééz* because of his great height, but he was now using the *belacani* or white-man name of Frank, which Peokon detested. But he was also the only one of the old followers left, so Peokon was forced to tolerate much that might otherwise have been dealt with quickly.

The heat of the day was mostly past, and the two men were seated horseback atop the south bluff of the big river to which two families of Mormons had been brought by their exploring party the summer past—a vanguard of the coming San Juan Mission. The wind moved freely where the two Navajo warriors sat their horses, sliding up the bluff in the heat of morning and down it in the shadows of afternoon, keeping the bluff relatively cool except in the still heat when the sun was highest overhead. The wind was moving now, though, rattling the yellowing cottonwood leaves on the river bottoms below and lending a gentle coolness that the man called Frank found most welcome.

That Peokon found little joy in such things caused Frank no small amount of wonder. In fact, he often thought Peokon acted as if he had no relatives, which was a bad thing to think about anybody. And of course he did have relatives, for he had a woman in his *atchí'deezáhi,* his forked-stick hogan. This woman was of the Turning Mountain People from over east, and his father, now elderly, was Hosteen Dah-nish-uant, a great man among the People.

Nervously fingering his *jish,* the small bundle of supposedly sacred things tied around his neck, which he wore out of old habit, Frank found himself wondering about this man he'd known for so many long seasons—

"All *belacani* are coyotes," Peokon suddenly declared, his voice little more than a snarl as he unconsciously rubbed the scar that slashed across his cheek.

Surprised, Frank looked at his friend. To call anyone *maíi,* a coyote, was a hard insult among the *Diné,* for it implied not only bad conduct but also the evil of malice. To call a whole people by that name—well, that was either a very great thing or a very foolish thing. Coming as it had from Peokon, Frank concluded, it had to be a great thing.

"When I was small," Frank said, speaking quietly, "my father taught me that everything has two forms."

Peokon stared straight ahead, past the sage and bunchgrass, past the greasewood, past the cottonwoods and the river, past even the tiny *belacani* cabin. When he didn't respond, Frank continued. "The mountains have two forms—the outer forms we see, and the sacred inner forms that dwelt with the Holy People in the First World, the Dark World at the very beginning. And First Man brought them with him on his robe when he came. This is most especially so, my father told me, of the four sacred mountains that surround *Diné Tah,* the land of our ancestors, the land the Holy People gave us.

"All other things have two forms as well—the horse, the goat, even *wóó sitsíli,* the bedbug. All of them have the form of the *yei,* and they have the outer form that we see. According to the words of my father, you have two forms, my brother, as do I. Coyote also has two forms. But he is different, for there is no good in either of his forms."

Though Peokon still did not respond, Frank was certain he hadn't been speaking of *maíi,* the small wolf that occasionally vexed the sheep. Instead, he was sure his powerful friend had been speaking of *Asté Hashké,* the Trickster, who had also followed First Man out of the dark.

"They say Coyote is funny," Frank continued, his voice carefully respectful. "But my father did not think so. He said Coyote was always causing trouble. He was mean. He hurt people and was always causing hardship, making people die."

"The night the mormonee *belacani* called Ira Hatch came to our encampment on the Kaibab," Peokon suddenly declared, his voice filled with malice, "changing my father's thoughts and finally bringing to pass the death of my mother, I myself saw Coyote in the brush, laughing. I was only a youth then, but I saw him. The night before the mormonee *belacani* called Jacob Hamblin led the woman who had been my sister into this my own land to make a mockery of me in front of all my people, I saw Coyote laughing against the moon. The night before the *belacani* called Rope Thrower came and cut down my peach trees and burned my hogan and took so many of my neighbors on the Long Walk to the emptiness of *Bosque Redondo*, Coyote came and laughed among my sheep.

"Natanii nééz, I do not believe in the foolishness of these old traditions your father taught you. Nevertheless I do not like Coyote, for he is a *belacani*."

In the silence that followed, Frank thought about what Peokon had said. He didn't know whether he believed in the old traditions any more than Peokon did. Certainly since the days of his own youth Peokon had taught him not to believe. Yet there were times—and this was one of them—when the old ways seemed to be the good ways, and when the beliefs of his father were the only beliefs that seemed to make sense of the world.

So it was with Coyote, whom Frank liked no better than did Peokon. In fact, he feared him greatly, for whether one believed or not, Coyote had power that was not good. It was said that Coyote had transformed First Man into a witch, a skinwalker, by blowing his hide over him. After that, First Woman wouldn't sleep with First Man because he had all the evil ways of Coyote. He smelled like coyote urine, he licked himself and tried to lick her, and he did all the other dirty things that coyotes do. Only after the Holy People had removed Coyote's skin from First Man with their magic would First Woman sleep with him again.

But worst of all, before the Holy People had helped, First Man had run on four legs with the *yenaldolooshi,* the witches or skinwalkers. Frank shuddered just thinking about that, for despite his unbelief he greatly feared the skinwalkers. They were still around, here and there, hiding as normal people. Then at certain times they did vicious things to their neighbors and others. Was Peokon right in this thing, he wondered? Were the *belacani* truly *yenaldolooshi?*

"Natanii nééz," Peokon concluded, his hand still caressing the old scar that ran across his cheek, "evil is coming upon us, and it is coming soon." Then Peokon turned and looked straight at Frank, his eyes boring into him. "In the heat of summer, the night before these mormonee *belacani* passed by my hogan on their way to this place, I saw Coyote in the wash by my spring. And once again he was laughing!"

———o—o—o———

Cedar City

The wagon and its load of cattail fronds continued toward Cedar City. Both women had grown silent, and Eliza found herself feeling thankful for the wagon's springs, which were located beneath the seat. The road was nothing more than a dirt track, terribly bumpy, and the way Mary was driving she felt certain she would have been jarred practically to death if it weren't for the springs.

It was also dusty, for though clouds were finally building in preparation for the fall rains, the summer had been inordinately long and hot, and Mary's speed was, at least in part, an effort to keep ahead of the choking dust raised by the wheels and the mare's churning hooves. A breeze would have helped, but the air was still, so the only way to avoid the dust was to try and keep ahead of it.

Sort of like her life, Eliza thought without mirth. The only way to stand it was to keep ahead of it—to stay as busy as she possibly could. And that was what was so interesting about these silly fans she'd been selling. Probably anyone who wanted to could weave one. Yet folks were coming to her by the dozens, paying sometimes up to a dollar for a fan that she could weave and set aside to dry in thirty minutes. With so many orders she was kept busy from daylight to dark, giving her little time for the self-pity that seemed always on the edge of her thoughts.

To be truthful, though, despite Billy's . . . well, peculiarities, the two of them were getting along amazingly well. Back in London Widow Burnham had often said, "Search others for their virtues; thyself for thy vices," and the proverb had become Eliza's philosophy of marriage. Ever since her spectacular blowup two days before, she had kept a firm rein on herself, not even allowing her mind to criticize Billy. It seemed to be working, too, for though she wasn't exactly happy, she certainly wasn't miserable, and a woman like her had to be thankful for even the smallest of favors.

The trouble was, Billy was certain they were going to be called to the San Juan, and she simply didn't want to go! She didn't want to be mocked for her lack of skills on the trail or for Billy's ineptitude, either one. She didn't want to leave the home she'd spent the past five months fixing up and making lovely. And she absolutely didn't want to experience the unending pain a winter trek would cause her legs and feet.

Yet if they were actually called, how could she avoid going? In spite of her mounting disgust with Billy, he still seemed sincere about his adoration of her and was always finding ways to do little things for her. And Eliza appreciated it. It made it easier climbing into bed with him at night and facing each new day knowing she'd covenanted to spend the rest of her life married to him.

Besides, his kindness and love being so obvious and well-intentioned, how could she possibly divorce him? Divorce was rare and not well thought of except in the most extreme cases. And her case wasn't what anyone else might consider extreme. Besides the fact that she was miserable, she had no grounds for divorce at all. To push it would be to generate terrible stigmatism, both for herself and for Billy. And he, at least, didn't deserve that. As Widow Burnham used to put it, if she did what she should not, then she must bear what she would not. And Eliza Foreman wasn't about to bear, or even cause Billy to bear, the stigma of the entire community of Saints.

Of course, what the members of the Church thought of her was feeling less and less important, and almost daily she wondered at that. What was happening to her? What were her feelings, now, about the Saints—or rather, about the church she had joined so many years before?

How well she remembered her emotions when she'd first heard the message of the restored gospel. Young and idealistic, she had felt her entire body thrill to the news that God had called a modern prophet, an American named Joseph Smith, and through him had restored to earth Christ's true church in all its primitive, biblical glory.

Though her family had scorned her, she had diligently read a borrowed copy of the Book of Mormon and had believed the account fully, for over and over as she'd read, the Holy Spirit had borne witness that it was truly the word of God, and that the two missionaries who had brought it to her were authorized representatives of Christ.

Eagerly, therefore, the youthful Eliza had accepted baptism, and willingly she'd heeded the call to gather to Zion in Salt Lake City, knowing all the while that she'd never see any of her family again. But now twenty-six years had passed, twenty-six years spent on crutches because of the terrible journey through the snows of Wyoming, twenty-six years of loneliness, of never seeing a single member of her family. It was such a long time, and more and more Eliza found herself wondering if it had all been worth it.

What she didn't wonder about—what she knew with certainty— was that she could never return. There was simply nothing in England for her to go back to. During her years in Utah, her mother had died, she had lost all track of her father, and save for the briefest of notes sent after her mother's death, her two younger sisters had refused to contact her and wanted nothing to do with her. So for better or for worse, Eliza understood that her home must remain with the Latter-day Saints in the mountains of Utah.

But did she still believe? That was the question that had haunted her lately. Could Christ's true church really require such terrible sacrifices as she had been forced to make? Would a loving God truly demand such suffering as she had so willingly endured—as Mary Jones and the others called to the San Juan were about to endure?

Bleakly Eliza considered these things, knowing that answers that had once seemed so certain no longer were.

But why? How could things she had once known so surely— eternal things—possibly change? How could inner peace, the peace of the Holy Spirit, which had once given her such strength, vanish so completely? The reason, Eliza knew, was centered in her husband, Billy Foreman.

The reason, and the *only* reason, she had married him was not because he had enticed her or deceived her but because she had felt the power of the Holy Spirit when he'd proposed marriage—the same power she had felt when she'd read the Book of Mormon. And she *had* felt it. Overwhelmingly! But now, seeing that her marriage to the man had been such a terrible mistake, she was beginning to wonder if she had also deceived herself about the Church.

"A penny for your thoughts, Eliza."

Startled, Eliza avoided looking at the much younger woman. "It would be money wasted, Mary."

"I don't know. You looked like you were a million miles away."

"I . . . I was just thinking that . . . that it looks like it's going to rain, probably by tomorrow."

Mary laughed delightedly. "What a great fibber you are! You weren't thinking about rain at all, and you know it! Now come on, what were you really thinking?"

Eliza sighed with what she hoped Mary would consider resignation. "Very well, I was thinking that I think too much. That, and I was thinking what a sacrifice you and the others will be making when you leave for the San Juan. This probably sounds awful, but I'm glad it's you going rather than me. I truly don't believe I could make it."

"Oh, you could make it, all right," Mary stated confidently. "You have real strength in you, Eliza, strength that shows up plain as day. But much as I'll miss you, I'm also glad you won't have to take that journey. It's going to be a young person's expedition, requiring a young person's strengths. And it seems to me you've already sacrificed enough to prove yourself before the Lord."

Surprised, Eliza looked at her younger companion. "Why, what on earth can you mean? I've never thought of such a thing!"

"Well, I have. I told my father the same thing. Just like you, his ordeal with the handcarts in the snows of Wyoming back in '56 was sufficient to burn his faith clear into his heart. Now, whatever he's asked, he gives. 'A calling from an apostle iss a calling from my God,' he says, 'und I vill sacrifice everyting to be obedient.'"

"Jens Nielson is a remarkable man."

"Yes," Mary replied quietly, "just as you are a remarkable woman, Eliza Foreman. I reckon Father feels he's already sacrificed too much to turn back now, so he might as well keep on until the end. That's the same attitude that caused you to sell your store and accompany Billy here to Cedar, isn't it?"

"I suppose it is," Eliza responded quietly, her eyes once again fixed straight ahead. "More or less, I suppose it is."

——◇—◇—◇——

The South Bank of the San Juan River,
across from Montezuma Creek

It was only when the Navajo who called himself Frank realized that Peokon was no longer standing beside him that he saw they were not alone. He had heard nothing, seen nothing, sensed nothing. One moment he had been gazing across the river speaking of how easy it would be to raid these *belacani,* and the next he and the two ponies had been alone.

Turning in surprise, he discovered Peokon standing by a lone juniper some thirty feet away, silently facing a man who seemed to have appeared out of nowhere. The man, a *belacani* with long, white hair, sat his pony easily as a man of the People might do. And like a man of the People, he remained silent while he faced Peokon—a thing Frank found remarkable considering Peokon's fierce countenance and demeanor. Obviously the white man did not know the great warrior he faced.

For long moments there was no sound, no movement between the two. Peokon's stallion stomped a hoof impatiently, flies buzzed loudly in the still air, and *jeeshóó,* a buzzard, circled silently overhead. These things Frank noted without noticing, his entire attention on the warrior Peokon and the silent white man.

"It has been many seasons," the *belacani* signed with his hands after the necessary respectful silence had elapsed. And he signed it easily, fluidly, so that Frank understood that the man knew exactly who Peokon was and had seen him before.

"You are also remembered, *bináá dootízhi*," Peokon replied in the tongue of the *Diné*, calling the white man by his blue eyes.

When the *belacani* did not respond but stared at him without understanding, Peokon grunted with satisfaction. Then he repeated himself with the sign-talk of his hands, verbally adding the insult name of *maíi*, the coyote.

Again silence reigned. Frank, awed by Peokon's courage but feeling foolish because he'd been left behind, stepped carefully to the other side of the juniper. But even this movement did not distract the attention of the two men from each other.

"These people across the river," the *belacani* then signed, "are my friends. They are two men, two women, and several little children. They are here in peace and mean no one any harm. It would not be a good thing if they were to be thought of as enemies of the *Diné*."

For a moment Peokon stood still as if considering the *belacani's* words. "What is it you do here?" Peokon finally signed.

"I see to the well-being of my friends."

"Then I will consider your words." Peokon then stepped back, sat down beneath the juniper, and folded his arms. The white man nodded and turned his horse back to the top of the rise, only a few feet away, where he also waited. And Frank, still feeling unaccountably foolish, took up a position beside Peokon beneath the juniper.

"Do you recognize that one?" Peokon asked quietly. And then, without waiting for Frank's reply, he responded. "He was with the mormonee *belacani* Ira Hatch and Jacob Hamblin when they brought the one who was as my sister to shame me."

"Are you not concerned that he might hear you?" Frank asked as he glanced nervously at the nearby horseman, who sat with his back turned mostly toward them.

Peokon smiled thinly. "He does not understand the tongue of the People. I tried him and found it to be so."

Frank nodded with satisfaction. "No," he responded then, "I do not remember him."

"His hair was not white in those days, but I remember his eyes. They are without fear."

Frank considered that. "What will you do about the *belacani* across the river?"

Peokon chuckled, his hand caressing the old scar on his cheek. "I will tell him we will do nothing, and then return on another day and slay them all."

"Perhaps those *belacani* have many guns and will fight."

Again the Navajo headman chuckled. "I do not think so, my brother. It is as I have told you before. These mormonee *belacani,* they are all like old women—talk, talk, talk, but no fight. Like fools they wear their hearts on their faces, and so it is an easy matter to kill them." He chuckled again. "Perhaps we should ask this blue-eyed one to dismount and show us his gun."

Frank chuckled, remembering the young *belacani* who had been foolish enough to do that very thing so many seasons before. Truly Peokon was right—the mormonee were easy to kill.

"There is another thing to consider," Peokon declared, still rubbing his cheek. "If these fools have settled here, it means that many more will follow them to this place. That is good for us, not so good for them."

"But . . . we are no longer many," Frank questioned. "How can we make a raid with so few?"

"There are others, my old friend, not only among the *Diné* but also among the *Nóódái.* We will enlist them."

"But the Utes are our enemies! How can we accomplish such a thing?"

Peokon smiled. "You forget, brother, that my mother was a Paiute, and that I was raised among the Paiute on the Kaibab—on Buckskin Mountain."

"Buckskin Mountain is a long journey, my brother."

"True. But it is not those people we will enlist. Think instead of the ones called Water Utes, the dirty ones who have stolen a home from old Tsabekiss on Navajo Mountain. They are nearly the same people as those on the Kaibab, and their tongues are similar."

"That is also a long journey."

"Not if they come to us." Peokon chuckled again. "Do you not remember, brother, how the *Nóódái* like to cross the big river and ride down *Tsitah* Wash, thinking that it hides them? Then they leave the wash and go east of *Tohatin* Mountain to catch the Mud Clan People who live around Sweetwater, hoping to return to their homes with horses and women and children."

Frank nodded. "It is said, brother, that the *Nakai,* the Mexicans, will pay the Utes as much as a hundred silver dollars for a child of the *Diné*. It is said that such children make very fine slaves. I do not know how much the women will bring."

"Much more, especially since Rope Thrower caused so many of the People to die on the Long Walk. That is why we should have little difficulty finding some of these Water Utes to assist us. Unlike the *Diné,* who fear Rope Thrower and the white soldiers, the *Nóódái* are not afraid of raiding. With their help, brother, we shall become wealthy once again."

Abruptly Peokon arose and stepped from beneath the juniper.

"What is your decision?" the man on the horse signed as he turned back.

"It is good that those across the river come in peace," Peokon signed back. "We of the *Diné* will leave them in peace."

The man on the horse signed his pleasure, and Peokon, with a look of immense satisfaction, stepped back into the shade of the juniper.

"*Ásdzáán,*" Peokon snarled then, and that was all.

In amazement Frank watched as the white man on the pony sat still as death, not moving or reacting to the strong insult, not taking his eyes off the distant cabin. Finally, though, he turned his pony and again faced the two Navajo warriors.

"You are thanked for your kindness," he signed calmly. "May you return to your hogans with joy."

"*Maíi. Ásdzáán,*" Peokon said again with a sly smile, even as he made the sign of acceptance and farewell. "Coyote! Old woman! You would be easy to kill."

Nodding pleasantly, the white man turned his pony as if to go. But then, abruptly, he dismounted and, pulling his pistol from his belt, held it before him, butt forward, as he stepped toward the two surprised men.

"Take this weapon of mine, O Peokon," he said in the fluid tongue of the *Diné,* his voice so low that the two men had to strain to hear. "Then we will see who is the old woman. Then we will see if I am as easy to kill as the innocent boy you once murdered."

Too dumbfounded to move, Peokon and Frank simply stared. Neither man could believe this was happening. Neither man could believe that this *belacani* could so perfectly speak their tongue, could—

"*Ásdzáán,*" Thales Haskell suddenly spat, spinning the revolver and thrusting it back into his belt as he did so. "Peokon is the old woman! Peokon is also a liar, one who wishes to take the lives of my friends. As Ira Hatch once marked your face with his quirt as *nishjool,* a coward, so the mormonee God Jehovah has also marked you—as a murderer. Prepare, O fool Peokon, to *bi'niitsaah,* to begin to die. Prepare for all around you to begin to die as well. From this day the curse of our God, the Lord God of Israel, is upon you. Your death will not come quickly enough, and you will have no power to hasten it."

And without another word the white-haired *belacani,* who now seemed most assuredly to be *Asté Hashké,* Trickster Coyote, mounted his pony and rode slowly away.

4

○─○─○

Sunday, September 28, 1879

Cedar City

The rain beat steadily against the windows of the adobe home, chilling the air outside and making Eliza glad for her kitchen and its homey warmth. She sat now at the oak table, the cookstove behind her still radiating its welcome heat, and felt thankful that the meetings for the day were over. Lately they seemed such a trial to her, such a burden—

The coal-oil lamp on the table threw fitful shadows onto the walls and ceiling, but the lighting was sufficient for Billy to read to her from the old family Bible she had carried from England an eternity before. Of course, she told herself that she believed none of what he was reading, or ever would again. Yet truthfully Eliza looked forward all week long to reading with Billy. While he might be lacking in nearly every other way, her husband was an excellent reader and could make even the most difficult of words flow effortlessly from his lips. At the moment, however, he wasn't reading but was instead sitting silently, drumming his fingers on the table.

"Well?" Eliza asked impatiently. "Are we going to read tonight, or not?"

"Actually," Billy responded softly, "I've been thinking today about suffering, and the good it seems to do folks. I recollect once Brother Brigham telling Pa and me that suffering was sanctifying. Fact is, he used the Prophet Joseph Smith as an example, telling us that if he hadn't endured all his sufferings and persecutions, he might have lived a thousand years and not accomplished all he did in a mere thirty-eight."

"To me it seems like a perverse principle," Eliza murmured, "for I would rather not suffer at all. I'm not strong enough to endure such pains and difficulties."

"Eliza, hon-bun," Billy remonstrated gently, "you *are* strong! Mercy sakes, woman, look at you. In pain every waking moment of your life, you never complain. Torn from the bosom of your family for the gospel's sake, you smile and keep going." Billy paused and took a deep breath. "And . . . and now, being forced to stay married to a fool and a weakling like myself, you continue to hang on when others would have let go months ago."

Startled, Eliza looked directly into her husband's eyes. "Oh, Billy," she pleaded, "why do you say such a thing?"

"I'm speaking truth, Eliza, and you know it! I see it in your eyes every time you look at me, every time I open my mouth. Yet you endure, staying with me in spite of everything, allowing me to love you as best I'm able. Surely the Lord is sanctifying you for this."

"Billy, you mustn't . . . talk like this."

"But I must! Jesus said the truth would make us free, Eliza, and I am speaking the truth. I've thought about it and thought about it, and I haven't stopped praying about it in months. I love you, Eliza. From the moment I laid eyes on you I have loved you, and each day that passes I find myself loving you more. That's the truth, so help me God!

"It . . . it's also the truth that I can't bear hurting you an hour longer. Maybe this is what Jesus meant by being made free. I don't rightly know. But if you want, hon-bun—I mean, if it will give you even a moment's peace, I'll set you free this moment. More than that, I'll take you back to Salt Lake City and set you free there. I mean it, Eliza. What I'm saying is the truth!"

In the silence that followed, Eliza felt as though she were spinning in a huge circle. She didn't dare speak, didn't dare even to think. Yet there it was! Billy was setting her free! He was allowing her the right to walk away from all the sorrow, the regret, the humiliation. He was willingly giving up his stranglehold on her life, giving it back to her. She'd never dared dream of this, never dared hope—

"I reckon I'll read," Billy stated softly, "while you give some thought to what I said. You happen to recollect where we stopped?".

Numbly Eliza nodded. "It was in Paul's second epistle to the Corinthians, and we'd just come to chapter twelve," she responded absently while her mind raced with the joyous possibility Billy had presented her. It was so wonderful, so overwhelming for him to set her free!

Carefully Billy turned the pages, taking care of the old Bible the way Eliza had instructed him to, and appearing completely oblivious to her incomparable joy. Finally he began reading, and still Eliza paid him no mind. She couldn't, either, not when her entire life had just been opened back up to her. Billy was taking her back to Salt Lake City! He was returning her to her home and setting her free at the same time! It was almost as if . . . as if—

And suddenly, as Billy was reading verse seven, Eliza felt the power of the Spirit resting upon her. Startled, she sat still for a moment, wondering at the ecstasy, the feeling of warmth that cascaded over her body.

"Oh, no!" her mind screamed with a feeling of panic. "Not this again! I don't believe in this! I won't believe it! It's of my own making, I know it is! I know it!"

Yet despite Eliza's efforts to stop the sensation, to end it, the well-remembered and yet still overwhelming feeling only intensified, growing so strong that after another moment or so she began to wonder if she might be utterly consumed. But there was a difference this time, something to the feeling that she couldn't remember experiencing before. It wasn't so much pleasant, she suddenly realized, as it was painful, almost as though her entire being was being seared by one of her own hot irons.

"B-Billy," she whispered, pulling a handkerchief from the bosom of her dress and trying desperately to dry the unbidden tears that were coursing down her cheeks, "would . . . would you read those verses again?"

Looking up, Billy adjusted his spectacles and smiled. "Sure thing, Eliza. Starting where?"

"I . . . I don't know," Eliza responded, wondering that her husband couldn't tell what was happening to her. "Where it says something about being exalted, I think."

"That's . . . uh . . . verse seven. Paul says, 'And lest I should be exalted above measure through the abundance of the revelations, there was given to me a thorn in the flesh, the messenger of Satan to buffet me, lest I should be exalted above measure.' Do you want me to keep going?"

As the now terrifying feeling of heavenly fire continued to course through her trembling body, Eliza looked at her husband—at the messenger of Satan who had been sent to buffet her. And with a shudder of fear and terror she did her best to nod.

"Verse eight and continuing." Billy smiled. "'For this thing I besought the Lord thrice, that it might depart from me. And he said unto me, My grace is sufficient for thee: for my strength is made perfect in weakness. Most gladly therefore will I rather glory in my infirmities, that the power of Christ may rest upon me. Therefore I take pleasure in infirmities, in reproaches, in necessities, in persecutions, in distresses for Christ's sake: for when I am weak, then am I strong.'"

"That's enough," Eliza whispered. "What . . . what do you think it means, Billy?"

Finally aware that something was profoundly affecting his wife, Billy quickly reread the verses. "Lawsy, Eliza," he said when he'd finished, "it seems pretty straightforward. Paul was troubled by something he didn't want to suffer. But when he sought the Lord to remove it, the Lord told him that his strength was made perfect in weakness, and that he would be keeping his 'thorn.'

"And then, if you remember, Paul went on to have a hard life. Back in chapter eleven of this same epistle . . . let's see. Here, beginning at the twenty-third verse and continuing through the twenty-seventh, Paul writes, 'Are they ministers of Christ? (I speak as a fool) I am more; in labours more abundant, in stripes above measure, in prisons more frequent, in deaths oft. Of the Jews five times received I forty stripes save one. Thrice was I beaten with rods, once was I stoned, thrice I suffered shipwreck, a night and a day I have been in the deep; in journeyings often, in perils of waters, in perils of robbers, in perils by mine own countrymen, in perils by the heathen, in perils in the city, in perils in the wilderness, in perils in the sea, in perils among false brethren; in weariness and painfulness, in watchings often, in hunger and thirst, in fastings often, in cold and nakedness.'

"Eliza, darling, are you all right?"

Hardly daring to speak, Eliza merely nodded. She was not all right, not in the least. The prayers she had offered for relief from her marriage to Billy had just been answered, but not in the way she had either hoped for or expected. Nevertheless, the answer was clear, and she knew it had come directly from God and was not of her own manufacture.

Like Paul, she had been given a messenger from Satan, a thorn in the flesh, a burden she would have to carry throughout her life. She remembered once reading these same verses and feeling confident that her thorn was her nonbelieving family. A year later she had seen beyond that and concluded it was her crippled feet. But now she knew how shortsighted such ideas had been. Compared to the burden of being married to Billy, and feeling as she now did about him and his church, such thorns were in reality nothing. Like Paul, she seemed to be moving from one trial to another, each more difficult, each more demanding. But like the ancient apostle, she would surely be strengthened through endurance.

---o—o—o---

With a boom that echoed through the tiny home, the sound of someone knocking on their front door jarred Eliza from her sorrowful reverie.

"I'll get it," Billy said quietly, and taking the lantern he left Eliza sitting alone in the dark of her kitchen, still trying to understand what she had just experienced, what she had just felt. It was almost as if—

"Eliza," Billy called from the parlor, "would you mind stepping in here, please?"

Wondering whom Billy had ushered in, Eliza rose from her seat at the table, groped in the darkness for her crutch, and moved through the doorway. From the sound of the voice she knew it was a man, and knowing she would have no business with a man, she felt slightly irritated at being bothered.

51

"Yes?" she said as she passed through the doorway, forcing a smile as she maneuvered her crutch.

"Eliza," Billy said as he took his wife's arm, "this is Elder Erastus Snow. Elder Snow, my wife, Eliza."

With a smile the apostle extended his hand. "How do you do, Sister Foreman. I'm delighted to finally make your acquaintance."

With the familiar feeling of dread again filling her soul, Eliza took the proffered hand and curtsied slightly. "Likewise," she replied politely, at the same time fighting the feeling within her to turn and run. "Won't you please sit down?"

"Thank you." Elder Snow sat in the overstuffed wingback chair that, it was said, had come across the plains with Orson Pratt in the first wagon company in 1847, and that a dozen years later had, for two dollars and a straw bonnet, become Eliza's pride and joy. Together she and Billy sat on the divan facing him.

Elder Snow smiled. "You're probably wondering how I've heard of you, Sister Foreman. My cousin Eliza R. Snow has spoken of you often, and the last time I was in Salt Lake she asked if I'd seen you. According to her, now that you're gone, the millinery business will never be the same."

"She's very kind," Eliza responded. "I think a great deal of Sister Snow."

"As do we all. Then, too, I have in my possession a wonderful fan that keeps me comfortable during warm meetings. I'm told you are the artist who created it."

"I do make fans," Eliza acknowledged, wondering when this man would get to the issue that was making fear settle over her like a blanket. A glance at Billy showed that he was feeling the same, for he was perched on the edge of the chesterfield like a nervous little bird, his spectacles sitting askance on his nose, looking as if at the slightest noise he would startle and fly away.

"Well, it's a beautiful piece of work. Each time I use it now, it will be a delight for me to think of you."

Elder Snow sat back and looked closely at both Eliza and Billy. "Sister Foreman, recently as Billy and I worked together auditing the books at the Cedar City Co-operative Store, I reminded him of a request he made nearly three years ago as he sat clerking for

President Brigham Young and myself in the Church office in St. George.

"I'm certain he'd forgotten all about it. But I hadn't, and so I've taken the time to make some inquiries about him—and about you. Please allow me to explain.

"Billy has done a fine work for the Church since assuming his duties here in Cedar City. The ledger books are now in order, the co-op is organized and functioning wonderfully, and, for the first time, the shareholders may enjoy a small profit. All of this I attribute almost totally to the gifts and skills of your husband."

"Elder Snow . . ." Billy started to protest, though before he could go further the apostle held up his hand.

"Billy, I never say anything unless I mean it, and my compliments about your work are very sincere. I've made those same compliments in my reports to the brethren of the Quorum of the Twelve in Salt Lake City."

"Thank you," Billy said meekly.

"You have nothing to thank me for, my friend." Elder Snow smiled again as he turned his gaze to Eliza. "Knowing Billy as I did, Sister Foreman, it was only natural that I wondered what sort of woman would be the companion of such a fine man. I was delighted to discover that it was you—a woman I felt I had known for a long time."

Eliza was suddenly having difficulty breathing. If this man actually was inspired, he must surely know things had changed, that *she* had changed—

"And that brings me to the purpose of my visit." Elder Snow smiled again, reached into his pocket, and withdrew a folded, sealed paper. "You see," he said, holding the paper so that the gazes of both Billy and Eliza were riveted on it, "I had some strong impressions that day nearly three years ago when Billy made his request, some impressions that have been impossible for me to forget. I've learned through sad experience that it is best for me to always follow my impressions, so a few weeks ago I penned a letter about the two of you to Elder Taylor in Salt Lake City. As you know, he is president of the Quorum of the Twelve Apostles as well as acting president of

53

the Church, and when the time is right, he will be sustained as president.

"Apparently Elder Taylor agreed with my impressions, for yesterday I received a communication from him to that effect. Therefore, Billy, I'm here to release you from your assignment as clerk of the Cedar City Co-operative Association."

"Oh, Elder Snow," Billy responded, his voice hardly more than a whisper, "I . . . I thought—"

His radiant smile again bathing the room, Erastus Snow once more held up his hand. "I'm also authorized to extend a new calling to you, one that you and Eliza will share together."

Eliza's heart was pounding even more loudly than the rain that was beating against her windows, and it seemed to her that the room had grown very stuffy. A calling for the two of them, she knew, would absolutely negate Billy's having set her free. It would mean that the "thorn in the flesh" she'd been given, even "Satan's messenger," was about to be thrust impossibly deep into her heart.

"Now remember," Elder Snow was continuing, "any calling in the Church can be declined. If for any reason one or the other of you feels that you shouldn't accept this calling, we'll certainly understand, and other arrangements will be made.

"We hope, however, that you'll accept, for you both have a great deal to contribute to the work. Brother and Sister Foreman, acting in our office as members of the Quorum of the Twelve and presidency of this church, and acting under the inspiration of the Almighty, we hereby call the two of you to take up a mission to the San Juan country, and we ask that you be prepared to start within the month. You'll find the particulars detailed in this letter."

And with a smile of genuine satisfaction, Elder Snow held the sealed letter out toward a stunned and stricken Eliza.

5

Wednesday, October 1, 1879

Cedar City

Eliza, kneeling on the floor of the parlor, was bitterly wrapping what was left of the trinkets she'd carried away with her from far-off England. They weren't many, of course, for the handcart she'd shared when crossing the plains in 1856 had allowed few luxuries. Besides a few knickknacks there was the tiny blue china tea set made for children's tea parties that her father had purchased for her at the Potteries when she was but a child, and the two remaining place settings of exquisite bone china that had once belonged to her great-grandmother. These things she cherished, and so she was carefully wrapping and packing them in one of the two trunks she'd purchased in Salt Lake City a few months before.

This made the second time in less than a year that she'd packed them. But there was a difference this time, Eliza thought as she angrily swiped at her eyes with her sleeve, a vast and terrible difference. A few months ago she'd packed them with a heart filled with joy and hope, yes, and a heart filled with faith. Now, however, her heart held only bitterness. That, and complete despair.

Not only had she made a mistake in marrying Billy, she now knew, but she had made another one, perhaps worse, in accepting the call to go to the San Juan.

I can't do it! Eliza thought, fiercely blinking away her tears. She simply didn't have the stamina, the physical or emotional capability to go traipsing off on another winter wilderness trek—not at her age, not in her crippled condition! It wasn't fair of John Taylor or the

Lord either one to be asking it of her! And it certainly wasn't fair of Billy not to have taken a stand in her behalf and turned the calling down.

He had promised her—he had even *vowed*—that he would never ask her to go traipsing off into the wilderness again! More than that, he'd told her he would take her back to Salt Lake City so she could return to at least a few of the things she held most dear. Then, just like that, a letter from Salt Lake City had wiped it all out.

Of course, logically Eliza understood the situation perfectly. A calling was a calling and could usually be turned down with no serious ramifications. But when it was signed by the acting president of the Church and hand-delivered by a member of the Quorum of the Twelve Apostles, then it had better be accepted, at least it had if she or Billy wanted to live among these people and enjoy their continued respect and support.

Swiping at her eyes again, Eliza thought of that, but thought too of the fact that she simply couldn't make such a terrible journey! Despite what her mind said, her heart was furious with Billy for having accepted a call that would most certainly destroy her—

"Eliza, are you in here?"

Snapping her head around, Eliza glared as Mary Jones walked in unbidden, her face radiating a happy smile.

"I thought you might be packing," Mary declared as she looked around the room, "so I came to help. After all, the Brethren didn't give you much notice, and had it been me, I know I'd be needing help in the world's worst way."

"Humph!" Eliza grunted as she turned back to her trunk.

"Well," Mary responded, looking at Eliza out of the corner of her eye, "I see that I'm needed, all right. And since my own packing is about complete, I have oodles and oodles of free time. Kumen is bringing Billy in a little while so we can get your beans to drying, but I think until they get here, maybe I'll start upstairs." And like an irritating ray of sunshine, Eliza thought, Mary picked up her skirts and bounced up the stairs and out of sight.

"Lawsy, lawsy," Eliza muttered with further bitterness, "why can't I be more like her? In love with her husband, convinced that the gospel is true, and happy as a gooneybird to be heading out for the San Juan—"

And once again Eliza dissolved into tears.

———o—o—o———

"There it is, Billy. With the tarp catching the sun's heat, your beans should be dried and ready to bag within about a week."

"If it doesn't rain again," Billy said with a grin.

Reaching up, Kumen adjusted his hat. "It won't. We should have two or three weeks of good weather, maybe even a little more, and then the fall rains will hit us in earnest. Meanwhile, we'll help you folks ready yourselves for this journey in style."

Gratefully Billy smiled at his new friend. Kumen Jones, Mary's husband, was a small man like Billy, and he was also bookish and well-learned. Unlike Billy, however, he was also a farmer, scout, and frontiersman who had made the thousand-mile exploratory journey for the San Juan expedition, had dealt with wild Indians and every other sort of human being that frequented the wilderness, and was the kind of man Billy could only dream of being. Yet for all that he was kind, gentle, and affable, and had willingly come with his wife to help Billy and Eliza harvest their beans in preparation for the journey.

"So, Billy, where do you hail from?"

Straightening from where he had been spreading the beans Eliza and Mary were picking, Billy eased the crick in his back. "Mostly Salt Lake City, though I was born in Winter Quarters."

"You were?"

Billy nodded. "That first winter—November 1846."

"That makes you thirty-two?"

"That's right. Mother died as I was being born, so Father hired a woman to care for me, which she did until Father remarried in 1850. My stepmother died when I was ten, and she's the only mother I have any memories of. After her death it was just Father and me."

"Your father never remarried?"

"He didn't." Billy smiled ruefully. "By then he was clerking for Brigham Young, and when I asked him if he was going to get me another mother, he always said he was too busy."

Kumen's look was incredulous. "So who cared for you?"

"Father did. From age ten I was with him at the office or wherever else he went, learning ciphering and letters, making copies, doing whatever clerical jobs he couldn't get to. I was working fulltime as a clerk by the time I was fourteen or so, and that's all I've done ever since."

"You were Brigham Young's clerk?"

"Yes, for twenty years, until he died two years ago. After that I was hired by the Church to sort out the mess concerning what was the president's property and what belonged to the Church. I did that until I was called to come here and take charge of affairs at the Cedar City co-op."

Kumen looked at Billy with admiration. "Working so closely with the prophet, you must have had some wonderful experiences."

"I did." Billy smiled. "President Young was a man of amazing wit and wisdom, and it was a continual delight to be near him and the rest of the Brethren who have served as General Authorities."

"I imagine you learned a lot from them."

Billy nodded. "I learned, all right, more than I can say. The trouble is, Kumen, my education was lopsided. I can quote chapter and verse on most anything related to Church doctrine, but I'm still having a hard time learning how to milk old Hepsi, our cow. I can take dictation or solve most mathematical problems, but I haven't the least notion of how to plant and harvest a crop or put up a supply of food. I love to study the sciences and am fairly conversant with them, but Dick Butt and the other cowboys who come in and out of the co-op have laughed themselves silly watching me struggle to mount a horse or stay in the saddle.

"I have no idea how to shoot a gun or swing an ax, and even Eliza is a better hand at weeding and irrigating a garden than I am. Traveling here to Cedar last spring I never did determine how to properly harness the horses or drive them. And I've never once in my life even spoken with an Indian. So when it comes to living and making a valuable contribution in a frontier community, Kumen, I feel like I'm a mighty sorry specimen. I can't imagine why the Lord would see fit to call me to the San Juan."

Kumen smiled. "Maybe that's why."

"Excuse me?"

"So you'll learn. You mark my words, Billy Foreman. By the time we reach the San Juan you'll be a fair-to-middling hand at about anything the rest of us so-called frontiersmen ever thought of doing. More than that, you'll be amazed at the different ways you alone can contribute to the betterment of all our lives. Now, what say we go see if we can help the ladies finish harvesting those beans?"

———◇—◇—◇———

"Well, folks, that does it. Once they're dry you'll have two, maybe three good sacks of beans to haul to the San Juan country."

"Thanks, Kumen." Billy was truly grateful, though he doubted his words conveyed his depth of feeling. "Eliza and I appreciate what you and Mary have done for us."

"I'm just thrilled beyond words that you'll be coming on the mission," Mary Jones gushed. "Mercy sakes, Eliza, you can teach me things about etiquette and big city life the whole way there."

"When it comes to teaching, more likely the roles will be reversed," Eliza responded quietly as she looked at her husband. "I have no idea how we're going to do everything to get ready, especially when neither one of us knows a whit about such things."

"Those sorts of details have a way of working out," Kumen responded with a smile and a wink at Billy. "Why, before long, you'll be raising crops and children and proclaiming the gospel to the Navajos and Pahutes in your spare time."

"Did you meet any of the truly bad ones?" Billy asked quickly. "I mean, did you really meet some dangerous Indians?"

"Billy, for pity's sake! Stop pestering the poor man."

"It's all right, Eliza," Kumen responded with a grin. "I don't mind talking about those people. Yes, Billy, we ran into quite a few of the Lamanites who are dangerous—not so much because they are evil, for mostly they aren't, but because their culture is different than ours, and they don't understand what we're trying to accomplish. For that matter, we don't understand them—Navajo or Pahute either one. At least that's what Thales Haskell believes."

"And who is Thales Haskell?" Eliza asked in spite of herself.

"An Indian missionary and scout, Eliza. He's been in this country more than twenty years and in some ways is more of an Indian than they are. He's fluent in many different dialects, but he says his greatest skill is the ability to keep silent." Kumen smiled. "He says he can do that in any language."

"Meaning he can listen?"

"Partly I think that's so. But I saw him stare down old Peokon one afternoon without uttering a word. The silence was terrible, and none of us knew what would be the result. But Thales Haskell's silence ruled the day, and Peokon finally gave in and allowed us to dig for water on his land."

"Peokon," Eliza mused. "His name was mentioned at the meeting the other night."

Kumen nodded. "That's right, Eliza. And he's a bad one, too—dangerous as a stepped-on rattler and mean as can be. Fact is, he's the one who killed George A. Smith. It made the whole bunch of us mighty nervous knowing we were within a mile or so of where it happened and that Peokon was still in the neighborhood."

"George A. Smith the apostle?" Mary asked incredulously.

"No," Billy responded, "the apostle's son. I remember when it happened, but I don't remember any of the details."

"Neither Mary nor I were even born when it happened," Kumen declared. "But one night out in that desert Thales told us the whole story, and none of us slept well after that. I can see him now, standing tall and straight with the firelight playing off his flowing, snow-white hair. Thales Haskell is getting somewhat long in the tooth, but it hasn't seemed to slow him down any. For a fact he was up before any of the rest of us, rode more miles in a day, and was always the last man to set down to the evening meal. More than that he didn't seem to have much to say, and with his sky-blue eyes burning into a man like hot coals whenever he was asked a question, folks naturally shied a little away from him. But when he spoke we listened, I can tell you that.

"According to Thales, George A. Smith was young, about sixteen or seventeen, and a fine young man. When the Pony Express started—November 1860—Brother Brigham called Jacob Hamblin and several others on a mission to the Moquis—I mean, the Hopi, as they call themselves—and young George A. was a part of that mission."

"Who all was a part of it?" Billy asked.

"Well, let me see if I can remember what Thales said. There was Jacob Hamblin and his brother Francis. Amos Thornton went, and Isaac Riddle took a boat he had built. Ira Hatch took his Paiute wife, Sarah Maraboots, and she was accompanied by Jacob's adopted Paiute daughter, who I recollect was called Eliza. These two Indian women were specifically called by Brigham Young to spend a year with the Hopi, showing them that Indians could adapt to the ways of the Mormons. Of course, young George A. and Thales were there, and a couple of others whose names escape me.

"It wasn't an easy trip. In fact it was rough, for they never seemed to have enough to eat. Then, too, they had to abandon the boat before they ever got to the Colorado, which they found flooded and impassable. Apparently there were some Apaches at the river, and their Ute guide, a fellow they called Enos, told Thales they were waiting to cross and attack the Navajo, who were creating lots of trouble for everybody at the time. Of course, as you might suppose, that wasn't exactly the news the Mormons wanted to hear. Neither was the fact that Jacob Hamblin had been moping around for days with a heavy feeling in his heart, certain they were all headed for trouble."

As the afternoon sun settled toward the volcanic mountains to the west of Cedar City, Kumen Jones continued, his soft voice describing the missionaries' struggle to find water, the hunger of them all, Jacob Hamblin's growing sense of oppression, and the increasing fear of the two women that they would be abandoned by the missionaries and made slaves to the Navajos. This fear was especially real for Ira Hatch's wife Sarah Maraboots, who was half Navajo, and who fully understood her lack of status and what would happen if she was captured by them.

"They weren't yet to the Moencopi," Kumen continued, "when their party were set on by maybe thirty Navajo braves, all painted and rigged for war. Their leader was our old friend Peokon, then much younger, who as it turned out was brother to Sarah Maraboots, and who had a real hatred for her. More than anything else he seemed determined to capture her, and he had her up and thrown over his horse's withers before Brother Hatch could swing into action.

"But swing he did, using his quirt to lay open a gash on Peokon's face and forcing him to drop Sarah to the ground. Ira then took her up behind him, and all the Mormons made a break for a small mesa where they forted up as best they could."

"No one else was hurt in that fight?" Billy asked incredulously.

"Nary a one. But I've seen the scar on Peokon's face, and I can tell you he really took a quirting. From what Thales determined, the Navajos were fresh out of ammunition for their guns, and none of their arrows and spears connected, not even with the expedition's animals. Obviously the Saints were being protected by the Lord."

Kumen paused while his wife and Billy and Eliza visualized the situation. The afternoon was still, no wind, and even the dogs down toward town had stopped barking. Without thinking Mary tucked a loose strand of hair behind her ear, and then all were still. It was a time for visualizing, all right, a time for feeling that maybe the Navajo were out there still, a time for sucking in the breath and drawing close in the comfort of companions who would be making the coming journey together.

"If it hadn't been for Vittick," Kumen abruptly continued, "the company might have been all right. Vittick was young George A.'s horse, and he was a good one—a true thoroughbred. I guess George A. loved that black stallion, and when he saw it was thirsty after they had forted up and opened a parley with the Navajo, he decided against orders to take it to a nearby spring for a drink.

"Apparently that was all Peokon had been waiting for. He and another Navajo rode up to George A., who was a pure and trusting boy, and asked to see his revolver. In his innocence George A. handed the gun to Peokon, who instantly turned and fired several rounds directly into the boy's body. When he had fallen to the ground they pulled his shirt over his head, and Peokon put four arrows into him, all in his back. Then they left him for dead."

"But he wasn't?"

Kumen shook his head. "Not yet. After the Mormons found him, they got him on Vittick and made a break for it in the dark, and they got clean away. But from what Thales said, George A. truly suffered during that ride. He kept pleading to be allowed to stop and die in peace, but everyone else felt they needed to keep going. So the youth gritted his teeth and rode on, and sometime after daylight he just sort of slipped away and died.

"They put his body in a small ravine and covered it with rocks, which was the best they could do under the circumstances, and a year later Jacob and a few others went back and gathered his bones and sent them to Salt Lake for a proper burial.*

"Anyhow, that mesa where they made their stand and where George A. was shot was not more than a mile or so from where we were camped the night Thales told us the story."

"And this fellow Peokon is still around?" Eliza asked anxiously.

"He was this past summer. Somehow he and one or two of his warriors avoided Kit Carson's big roundup and stayed hidden while the rest of the Navajo people were forced on their Long Walk. From my own limited experience, I can tell you folks that he's still meaner'n a hydrophoby skunk and twice as testy. I have no doubt we'll be running into him again, once we get settled on the San Juan."

And with that disturbing thought planted in the minds of Billy and Eliza, Kumen Jones took his wife Mary and departed for his home.

---

* For a fictionalized account of this expedition and battle as well as the unusual courtship and marriage of Ira Hatch and Sarah Maraboots, see Blaine M. Yorgason, *To Soar with the Eagle,* Salt Lake City, Deseret Book Co., 1993.

6

Thursday, October 2, 1879

Cedar City

"Yo, the house! Anybody to home?"

"I . . . I'm home!" Eliza called as she took up her crutch and pulled herself to her feet. "Just a moment, please."

"You want me to get it?" Mary called from the top of the stairs. It was the second day in a row she had come around to help, and Eliza was starting to fear that maybe she would be ready to leave with the expedition.

"No," Eliza responded as she tucked a loose strand of hair behind her ear. "I'm already on my feet, Mary, but thank you."

Making her way through the mess of packing to the door, she found a young man seated on a horse out near the gate.

"Yes?" she asked, wondering why he hadn't dismounted and come to the door, and at the same time feeling thankful that he had not.

"Are you Sister Foreman?" he asked, awkwardly removing his hat as he spoke.

"I am."

The young man grinned. "Then I reckon I found me the right place. Billy said I was to put my mules in the corral out back, but that I was to mind your flowers and not let 'em get et or trampled, either one. Which way do you want me to go?"

"I . . . suppose there on the north side of the house," Eliza responded, wondering as she spoke why Billy was agreeing to hold the young man's mules. After all, they were scheduled to leave in the next few days, so they wouldn't be able to do much more than feed them once or twice.

"I'll do it, Sister Foreman, ma'am. And don't you worry none about your flowers."

Deftly reining his horse around, the young man rode to a clump of junipers that grew fifty yards south of the house, disappearing behind them. A moment later he reappeared with a rope in his hand and four large mules in tow, which he led at a trot toward her gate.

Surprised, Eliza watched as the animals were led into the yard, past her, and around the house. They weren't the small donkeys she had expected but were instead fine, large mules—Missouri mules, folks usually called them. They were prized possessions, and she wondered that anyone in Cedar City had two span so fine.

Turning, she made her way through the home and to the stoop at the back door. By the time she arrived, the young man had already loosed the mules into the corral with their cow and the glass-eyed mare Billy had purchased before they'd left Salt Lake City. Quickly he secured the gate, and soon he was forking some feed over the fence to them. That done, he took up the bucket and drew enough water from the well to fill the watering trough—a task Eliza had been putting off all day long. Only when all that was completed did he again approach Eliza.

"For October she's plenty warm," he said with a grin, pushing back his hat and wiping his forehead. "Anything else you'd like done before I go, ma'am?"

"No, thank you," Eliza answered, still feeling confused. "Uh . . . do I know you?"

The youth's grin grew wider. "I don't reckon so, ma'am. And I apologize for my lack of proper manners. My name's Willard—Willard George William Butt."

"And I'm called Eliza."

"Yes, ma'am. Billy told me. Pleased to make your acquaintance. Now, if there ain't anything else, I'd best be getting on."

"Willard, we'll be leaving here in the next few days with the San Juan Mission. I don't know what Billy told you, but we won't be here to care for your mules after that."

His mild expression not changing, Willard Butt nodded and

stepped into his saddle. His horse, a pretty black, snorted and tossed its head, but the young man paid it no mind. Instead he settled himself, then lifted his hat and ran his fingers through his hair, stopping to scratch at the back of his head.

"I don't reckon Billy's had time to tell you," he finally said. "He's been some busy, what with wrapping things up at the co-op and all. These mules are your teams, ma'am. They'll be pulling your wagon to the San Juan."

"Our teams? But we don't own any such animals. I don't—"

Willard Butt chuckled easily. "You still don't, Sister Foreman, ma'am—own 'em, I mean. These mules belong to my brother Parley and me, and we do treasure 'em. But I couldn't see any sense trailing 'em all the way to the San Juan with the rest of our critters when folks such as you have a need. Besides, there ain't nobody who'd give 'em better care nor Billy, ma'am."

"Billy Foreman?" Eliza was astounded. After all, what did her husband know of fine Missouri mules? Or anything else, for that matter.

"Yes, ma'am. That Billy's developing hisself a way with critters, and Parley and me ain't the only ones who've noticed it. And it don't matter the kind, neither. Horse, mule, cow, you name it. There ain't hardly been nothing brought into the co-op corrals all summer that Billy ain't been able to gentle down, including that old outlaw hoss called Hurricane what busted up so many good hands. Billy's good with livestock, ma'am. He truly is."

"But . . . but he can't be! He's never had a lick of experience!"

"Then I reckon it's a gift, Sister Foreman, ma'am. He takes good care of critters of all sorts, and I reckon they can sense kindness just the same as they can sense fear and meanness, and respond in kind. Take that old gray mare of yours. She follows your husband around just like a puppy. Why? I reckon it's because she knows he likes her and will always treat her good. Comes down to it, critters ain't much different nor human folks, ma'am. We all pretty much gravitate to the ones who treat us best and like us most."

With another wide smile the young man touched his fingers to his hat brim. "Be seeing you tomorrow, ma'am, when I bring the harnesses. Billy said he doesn't have any, and there ain't no sense ours sitting idle or getting sold for ten cents or two bits on the dollar, not when folks like you can be using them."

———o—o—o———

"Wasn't that Dick Butt out there?" Mary called from the top of the stairs after the youth had ridden away and Eliza had returned to her packing.

"Dick? I don't think so. He said his name was Willard something-or-other."

Mary Jones came down the stairs, her arms loaded with bedding and her face lit with a wide smile. "Willard George William Butt. But most everyone who knows him calls him Dick."

"And obviously you know him."

Setting the bedding down, Mary plopped herself onto the floor. "I should smile I know him. He's in love with my sister Julia, or Julie as we call her. He lives in Parowan. In fact, he manages their town herd for them. But three, maybe four times a week, he rides the twenty or so miles here to Cedar just to spark my sister. How he keeps up with all that riding and everything else he does, I'll never know."

Eliza put more packing in the trunk. "Sounds like you approve of him, anyway."

Mary's expression grew serious. "Dick Butt is a wonderful young man, Eliza, and I mean that. What he doesn't know about horses and cows wouldn't fill a thimble. And ride? Lawsy but that boy can make a horse do wondrous things. Julie says he'd rather be in a saddle than anywhere else, and that includes by her side. Fact is, she thinks he comes to see her just as an excuse to get some extra riding in. And folks up in Parowan swear he's honest as the day is long. So like I said, he's a fine young man."

"Are you trying to convince me or yourself?"

"Well, my parents are worried." Mary busied her hands refolding bedding. "You see, they've known Dick since he was a boy. They were neighbors over in Panguitch before the Indians drove them all out. Dick's father, Uriah Reed Butt, or Rye, as folks call him, is a shoemaker and does a fine business. He was converted to the Church in England, came here as a young man, and waited by every wagon train coming into the Valley for the girl he was certain he would recognize and marry."

"Had he seen this girl?"

"Never." Mary giggled. "Rye just felt certain that when he saw her, he'd recognize her. Turns out he did. Bridgit Rogerson was with one of the two handcart companies that got snowed in—"

"Bridgit Rogerson!" Eliza exclaimed. "I know her! She was with my company, the Martin Company—she and her whole family. Oh, but they suffered. Bridgit was a little older than me, but I watched how she cared for her suffering parents and younger brothers and sisters after the snows hit us, and it helped give me courage to go on. And she's this boy's mother?"

"One and the same. When Rye spotted her being carried into the Valley in one of the rescue wagons, that was it. He knew she was the one he'd been waiting for. I don't think it took them long to get married, either. Anyway, they're both wonderful people. And Dick and his younger brother Parley are good boys. But somewhere Dick picked up this awful habit of cursing—"

Eliza looked up, surprised. *"That's* what's bothering your parents?"

"That and the fact that he doesn't seem to want to change. Oh, he never curses around Julie or the folks, mind you. But they all know he does it, and he frankly admits it—says it's about the only way to communicate with some critters—and some people."

"Maybe he's right," Eliza declared as she thought of Billy. "But I'll tell you this, Mary Jones. If that was the only thing wrong with *my* husband, I wouldn't spend ten seconds worrying about it! No sir, I do believe a little cursing would be a relief."

Tenderly Mary reached out and took her friend's hand in her own. For a moment Eliza didn't respond. But then she began to squeeze, hard, and finally her pain and her anger tumbled forth. "Billy just isn't the man I thought him to be, Mary! He is so weak, so inept at everything manly. And he is so fastidious, so . . . so feminine-like. Everything about him must be neat and tidy. Worse, he won't fight with me, he won't stand up for himself. Whatever possessed me to marry him I'll never know. But I do know it was one of the two worst mistakes of my life—one that I'll be paying for the rest of my life."

For a moment Mary was silent, thinking. "You, uh . . . you're very much ashamed of him, aren't you," she finally breathed.

Eliza looked at her young friend. "Wouldn't you be? It shames me even to be seen with him! And I get so embarrassed by the foolish things he says."

"About you?"

"No . . . well, yes, but not only that. About everything. This isn't a good country for me, Mary. I'm not a frontierswoman. But it's a disastrous country for Billy. He belongs somewhere in a city, in a back office doing figures, not out in this raw, wild land of deserts and mountains and endless hardship. Here all his weaknesses are magnified into terrible foolishness, and he keeps stumbling blindly forward, trying and failing and showing the world his complete uselessness until I feel so ashamed of him I want to die!"

"If you're so miserable, Eliza, why don't you just divorce him?"

Eliza laughed harshly. "Are you serious? And do what afterward? No, Mary, for some reason God has cursed me to spend my life with that miserable little man, and so I have no choice but to follow him wherever in this awful wilderness he takes it into his addled head to go!"

Mary was silent for so long that Eliza thought she might not have heard. She was about to say something else when Mary abruptly withdrew her hand, rose to her feet, and walked to the window. For a long moment she simply stood, staring outward. Then, without looking at Eliza, she took a deep breath and leaned on the sill.

"Eliza, how much do you trust me?"

Startled at the question, Eliza shrugged her shoulders. "I don't know, Mary. A whole lot, I suppose, or I wouldn't have told you what I have."

"Then if I tell you a couple of things, and swear to you that I'm telling the truth, will you believe me?"

"Of course I will."

"Good." Mary turned to face her friend. "First, I know nothing about this curse you're speaking of, except to say that it doesn't sound like the way I believe God works. But whether it is or not, I believe that what you do about your marriage is your business, and yours alone. Only you know how you feel. The same applies to this mission. Whether or not you go, Eliza, has got to be your decision.

"Secondly, you should know that folks hereabouts, at least those who know him, think very highly of your husband."

"Oh, yes! For a diminutive little weakling he's managed to dupe a lot of people!"

"Eliza, my Kumen is about the same size and strength as Billy. More than that, he's neat and fastidious about his appearance, he prefers books to the great outdoors, and he absolutely refuses to argue or quarrel with me. If I want a fight, I have to argue with myself, for he won't participate at all. Interestingly, I've always seen those as his strengths, qualities of character that endear him to me."

"But Kumen's also a frontiersman, Mary, a scout of the first order, I believe Captain Smith said."

"Yes, because he's had to be, and because he's had the opportunity to learn such ways. Who's to say that, given the chance, Billy wouldn't be the same?

"More important, Billy doesn't have to be a wild frontiersman to make an important contribution in this desert land. Elder Snow told my father several weeks ago that Billy has brought order to the co-op a whole year faster than anyone in Salt Lake thought it could be done. That's a contribution, Eliza, an important one. My mother loves Billy's gentle manners, and I've heard other women say the same. That's a second contribution. And what Dick Butt said today about Billy having a way with livestock—"

"You were listening in?" Eliza was shocked.

Mary smiled sheepishly. "With the window open, Eliza, and feeling about Dick the way I do, I couldn't seem to help myself. Whether I should have been listening or not, you should know that Dick's told Julie and me the same things about Billy he said to you. And if Dick says it, you can bank on it.

"There, I've said my piece, and I've probably said way too much. But you're a dear friend, Eliza, and I wanted you to know there might be another way of looking at things, maybe even a better way." And with a bright smile Mary turned and headed back up the stairs.

7

Tuesday, October 7, 1879

Jornado del Muerto, New Mexico

"Doggone but it's dry!" Without varying the gait of his plodding mount, Curly Bill Jenkins lifted his hat and wiped his forehead on the grimy sleeve of his shirt. "Drier even than when I come through on my way south to fetch you boys. You'd think there'd be water somewheres along here!"

"Reckon that's how this here stretch of real estate got its moniker," Bill Ball replied as he glanced at the skeletal remains of hundreds of cattle that were strewn about the vast desert plain. "Journey of Death. Sure fits, all right."

And it did, too well. Flanked by the Caballo Mountains to the west and the San Andreas Mountains to the east, the nearly waterless desert known as the *Jornado del Muerto* stretched all the ninety miles from old Fort Thorn on the south to Fort Craig on the north. Practically treeless, the *Jornado del Muerto* was studded with the remains of both men and animals who hadn't been strong enough to make it without water. And there was none of the wet stuff in the whole ninety miles, Bill Ball knew, especially not in a drought year.

He and Curly Bill Jenkins and eighteen other men were riding drag on a herd of nearly four thousand head of gathered and branded range cattle being trailed north to the San Juan country for I. W. Lacy and his LC spread—all on the instructions carried from the San Juan by Curly Bill. Bill Ball was acting as *segundo* or foreman for the outfit and would have normally had a much better count of his charges, only the herd had stampeded three days before, and in the ensuing gathering had grown by somewhere between a hundred and a hundred and ten head. The strays needed to be cut out, Bill knew, but he wasn't about to do it until they were all the way across this ninety miles of New Mexican hell.

Without much hope the foreman lifted his head in an attempt to see beyond the perpetual cloud of alkali dust raised by the sluggish herd. He hated riding drag and eating dust all day, but neither would he order a man to do something he wouldn't do himself. Except for the dust, today wasn't bad, either, for the cattle were still moving forward. In another day, however, perhaps two, the cows would start going blind from lack of water, and then nothing he or any other hand could do would stop them from turning and heading back to where they had last found a drink.

Closing his eyes against the dust and the glare, Bill tried to imagine soaking in a cool pond of water. But his imagination ran funny on him, and he couldn't hold the image in his mind. All he could picture was alkali and polliwogs. With a sigh he gave it up, resisted an impulse to lick his cracked and bleeding lips, and turned to glance at the Cookie and his four-team, mule-drawn chuck wagons being pulled in tandem.

It was an unusual arrangement, Bill knew, especially for a trail herd. But with the second wagon filled exclusively with water barrels, exactly as I. W. Lacy had instructed, he had hoped it would make the difference and get them through. Now, though, with the day lost to the stampede—

Of course, even the water barrels wouldn't have helped the cattle much, but they could go as long as seven or eight days without water and still make it. Men couldn't do that, and neither could working horses.

In his mind Bill Ball thought of his men, misfits every one of them. At least half a dozen were riding the owlhoot trail, and one of them was a sure-enough bad'un. He was calling himself Jim Jones, but Bill had the feeling he was none other than Jim "Killer" Miller, the Neuces outlaw. More than half the boys were former Confederate soldiers, and at least Charlie Zimm had ridden with Quantril.

And weapons? Except for the Greenhorn Kid there wasn't a one of 'em that wasn't bristling like a porcupine, most of the guns

Confederate-manufactured cap-and-ball pistols like the .36-caliber Griswold and Gunnison he himself was carrying. One or two had actual Colts Revolvers, but most carried copies that were nowhere near so reliable. Most also carried either Spencer or Henry repeating rifles, he himself had an 1873 Winchester, and Curly Bill Jenkins packed an old .50-caliber Sharps single-shot buffalo gun that he swore could shoot a fly off a chippy's bare shoulder at 500 yards and leave her begging him to do it again.

And then there was the Greenhorn Kid. If he—

"How much water we got left in them barrels?" Curly Bill Jenkins asked suddenly.

"Not more'n a gallon, at the most two. No two ways about it, Curly. By tomorrow the whole shootin' match of us'll be drier'n Cookie's wooden leg."

"How's the Greenhorn Kid holding up?"

Bill Ball ran his tongue over his sticky teeth, doing his best to keep his lips closed as he did it. "He's on point with the Comanch. At least the air's cleaner up there."

"The Greenhorn Kid and the Comanch together?" Curly Bill sounded skeptical, and Bill didn't blame him. Maybe putting them together had been a fool thing to do. But the Greenhorn Kid was about done in, and right now point was the easiest job he had. As far as the Comanch, well, a feller could never tell about a bronco Injun. Tame ones, maybe, but not the wild ones. And this one was definitely wild.

As he thought about the Comanch, Bill would have smiled if it hadn't hurt so much. But still his mind went back to the day a year or so before when he had come on the old man sitting all alone in the middle of the *Llano Estacado,* practically dead from thirst. Bill had figured he'd been left by his tribe to die, which was a common enough thing, and he should have done the same. But no, he didn't have the heart to leave it alone. Not then, not still. So he'd climbed down from his horse and watered the old boy a few times, washing his face and so forth, and since then the old geezer had stuck closer to him than a burr on a buffalo's tail. He couldn't speak a word of English, but Bill knew a little sign talk, and it wasn't long before they got to communicating real well, sometimes just by looking at each other.

The Comanch was turning into a good cowhand, too, despite being seventy, maybe eighty years old. Fact is, even without a saddle he could outride most of the men, and he could stay horseback longer than anyone else Bill had ever known. He was no shakes at all with a rope, but he savvied cows as though he'd trailed them all his life, and he could get them to do about what he wanted just by yipping at them.

Since the Indian had lost most of his teeth, Cookie had to feed him special, and so the old man had taken a real shine to the cook. The Comanch had also taken a shine to the Greenhorn Kid, who was a sixteen-year-old boy from back East who still didn't have sense enough to spit downwind, but he never complained, and he busted his gut trying to please.

Tell the truth, that was why Bill had pardnered the two of them up. Not only was he giving the Greenhorn Kid a rest by making him point, but he wanted the Comanch to keep his eye on the boy. For Bill also liked the Greenhorn Kid and was doing his best to turn him into a top-notch cowhand. And he would, too, happen they managed to live through to the other side of this six-day furnace they were in the middle of wandering across.

Ahead of him the cattle plodded forward, their tongues hanging out and their slaver dried around their mouths. Bill noted that, knowing too that blindness was the next step. And there was still a good two days between them and Fort Craig and the muddy water of the Rio Grande.

"Say, boss, ain't that Brazos waving his hat?"

Looking up, Bill strained his burning eyes off to the right where he knew Brazos was riding swing. Through the dust he was finally able to make out the shape of a man standing in his stirrups and slowly waving his hat back and forth above his head.

"Reckon it is," he said, feeling suddenly tired. He'd told the men to use the hat signal, and carefully so as not to spook the cattle, only if something serious was going on.

"You hold the drag alone, Curly?"

"Long as the emergency ain't just some waddy feeling

lonesome," Curly Bill Jenkins replied. "Sides, since when did it take two to gobble up the teeny little bit of this here alkali dust them cow-critters are a-raising?"

Bill grunted and moved his horse off to the right, not hurrying but merely increasing his gait a little. He didn't think the cattle would be spooky, but all it had taken before was one of the hands throwing his hat at a rattler that had buzzed his horse. That had set them off, and the results hadn't been pretty. Fact is, they'd been devastating, costing all of one day and part of the next, which was why he'd run out of water despite Mr. Lacy's and his careful planning.

"What's up, Brazos?" he asked a little later when he'd caught the man who had signaled.

"Maybe I'm wrong, boss," the heavily mustached man declared sullenly, "but the sun ain't burning the same hunk of real estate on my face no more. Fact is, I reckon we've changed directions, maybe a little more than somewhat."

Surprised, Bill took stock, and for the first time he realized that the herd had veered considerably to the right. Another five, six miles and they'd be at the base of the San Andreas Mountains, a black ridge of ancient volcanic rock that had thrust up out of the desert floor.

Shaking his head, Bill thanked the cowboy and clucked his mount forward. "Durn fool thing to do," he muttered to himself as he did his best to hurry quietly, "putting the Comanch and the Greenhorn Kid on point. Curly Bill Jenkins is right, and Mr. Lacy had ought to give me my walking papers for pulling such a stunt. Both of 'em together don't know dung from wild honey, and I reckon I'm worse'n that!"

Not much later Bill was riding beside the Greenhorn Kid, with the Comanch nowhere in sight. "You shift directions a-purpose?" he asked bluntly as he cast his eyes about for sign of the old Indian.

"The Comanch said to follow his tracks," the youth replied, nodding forward. "That's them."

Bill Ball shook his head, wondering who was really *segundo* of this outfit. "And whereto is that sorry old Injun fixing to lead us?" he asked with only a little malice. After all, it wasn't really the boy's fault for trying to make the best decision he could. Bill shouldn't have put him on point in the first place. The Comanch, on the other hand, Bill was thinking of strangling with his own rope.

"I couldn't understand him very well," the Greenhorn Kid was answering. "But he made the sign as if he were drinking, so I think he's leading us to water."

"Water!" Bill ejaculated angrily, struggling to keep his voice low. "In this country? Not hardly he ain't. This is a desert, kid, besides which there's a drought a thousand miles wide and sixty foot deep covering the whole blamed world! Holy thunderin' blue blazes! I knowed that Injun should have worn a hat. Now he's gone and got hisself sunblistered on the brain, and he's gallivantin' all over creation looking for what ain't there.

"Ah, what's the use! Keep 'em coming the way they are, son, and I'll go find that durnfool old warrior and haul 'im back. Then we'll get these critters lined out the way they'd ought to be." And still moving quietly, Bill set off to track down and haul back to sensibility the old Comanche warrior.

He was still cussing when he came upon the Comanch's horse standing ground-hitched on the lip of a shallow wash maybe thirty minutes later. The wash, which headed fifty yards east where a rocky spur jutted out from the mountain, carried runoff from the San Andreas when there was any, but right now there wasn't. The wash was bone dry, shimmering in the afternoon heat.

The old man wasn't in sight, though his tracks were plain, seeming to stagger, and with a sinking feeling Bill clucked his mount forward, certain of what he would find.

And he was right, at least sort of. When he found the Comanch, the old man was down on the ground all right. But he wasn't dead, and he wasn't even lying still. Instead, he was on his blanket scooping sand out of a hole he had dug in the bottom of the wash, very wet sand, and Bill knew the old man had saved Mr. Lacy's herd.

"Ungh," the old man grunted with a toothless grin, at the same time signing that Bill should cross the wash and keep looking.

"What in tarnation fer?" Bill growled at the old Comanche. "You already done found the water—"

More insistently the old man signed Bill across the wash, so with a growl Bill kneed his horse and lunged up the bank and onto the far,

THE CALL

sloping side. There was nothing in sight, however, nothing but rocks and scattered brush, and Bill was about to turn back when a faint shout from the point of rocks caught his attention.

Kneeing his mount, he urged it forward, and in another three or four minutes he found himself staring down at the bloody wreck of what had once been a man.

"Dingle?" he said as he leaped to the ground. "Dingle Beston, is that you?"

"As . . . ever," the sunblistered, blood-covered man gasped as he tried to push himself up. "I . . . I seed you comin', Bill, just like I seed the old Injun, but I . . . I couldn't raise neither one of you—"

"You raised the Comanch," Bill said as he opened his nearly empty canteen and trickled a little water down Dingle's throat. "He's the one sicced me on you. Now I reckon he's saved old man Lacy's cattle *and* you."

"Then I . . . I owe 'im." Dingle was quiet as Bill trickled another swig down the man's throat. Finally sitting up a little, he took Bill by the arm. "Bill, I hate to do 'er, but I . . . I got some bad news."

"Oh?" Bill said, suddenly quiet. "What might that be?"

"I . . . I ain't alone. Yonder, round the other side of that big boulder, lies Sugar Bob Hazelton. He . . . he's in worse shape than me."

Slowly Bill Ball sat back on his haunches, his mind whirling. "Sugar Bob Hazelton?" he finally repeated. "He's alive?"

"Not by much he ain't. Unless I lost count, we ain't had water in four days, not since Felipe Nevio Espinosa kilt our hosses and put two bullet holes in Sugar Bob and this one in my arm."

"Espinosa? Is *everybody* comin' back to life? I heard Tom Tobin killed Espinosa eight, ten years ago."

Dingle shook his head. "Not hardly, though you ain't the only one who heard that. Two weeks back Sugar Bob kilt Julian Espinosa, Felipe's favorite younger brother, for two dollars worth of mescal. We cut and run, but Felipe caught up with us not more'n a mile from here and left us to die. Reckon we would have, too, if it hadn't been for the eyes of that old Injun."

"I heard somebody plugged Sugar Bob down in Abilene," Bill said, hardly paying attention to Dingle Beston's comments. "That's why I stopped gunning for 'im."

"I know," Dingle replied quietly. "I also know what Sugar Bob did to Mr. Lacy's daughter. He told me."

"Did he also tell you she went out and killed herself after she told her daddy?" Bill asked quietly.

The man on the ground shook his head.

"Well, she did! Threw herself off'n that rocky point south of the old home place. She . . . she left me a note, I reckon because she was too ashamed to tell me to my face. Wouldn't have mattered none to me, though. Hazelton's baby or not, I'd sure have married her anyway. Did you know we was fixin' on gettin' hitched, her and me? Afore Sugar Bob came along, that is."

"I heard. I was real sorry about the whole thing, Bill. You've always been square with me, and so has Mr. Lacy. I reckon this was one time I just sort of pardnered up with the wrong gent."

"I reckon." Bill reached down and, with hardly any effort, lifted Dingle Beston to the saddle of his horse. "Let 'im have his head, Dingle. The Comanch has dug hisself a well off there in the wash, maybe a hundred yards or so, and the hoss'll find it easy. After you get a little more water in you, you'll be fine."

"Thanks, Bill. Where . . . where you going?"

"I reckon I'm going after Sugar Bob," Bill replied, his voice sounding flat and dead.

"He . . . he's still my pardner, Bill."

"I know that."

"I . . . I'll take it hard if you kill him."

Bill Ball looked away. "Man deserves to die, Dingle, and I have as much right as anybody to kill 'im. Best way, I reckon, is leave him lay where he is and let the Good Lord save him or not, as He wishes. It's what Felipe Espinosa did, and it'd be worse by somewhat than putting a bullet through his brisket."

Bill Ball took a deep breath and then slowly let it out. "But I give you my word, Dingle, that I won't do it. Happen I'm able, I'll save that skunk's worthless hide. I'll even grubstake the both of you through to the San Juan. After that you can have a job if you want it. As for Sugar Bob, what happens to him will be up to Mr. Lacy. Laurie Yvonne was his daughter, so I reckon he and Mrs. Lacy'll have to be the judges of Sugar Bob Hazelton."

And with a bleak look on his usually amiable countenance, Bill Ball took his canteen and turned with measured tread toward the distant, foreboding boulder.

———◇—◇—◇———

Headwaters of Plateau Creek, Grand Mesa, Colorado

Wide-eyed, the two young half-brother sons of the Pahute known as old Chee stood at the fringe of the expectant throng, their eyes glued to the figures near the leaping fire in the center. The wind, which had been blowing fitfully all day, was in great measure gone, though the havoc it had wreaked in the boys' dark hair remained much in evidence. Yet neither Sowagerie, the older but smaller, nor Beogah paid their wild-looking hair much mind. Neither were they bothered by the well-worn and hole-infested buckskin shirts that only barely covered their nakedness. In their innocence such niceties meant nothing to them. Nor did it, apparently, to their provider.

In the cloudless dark a meteor streaked overhead but was noted by few. This was surprising to the youth called Sowagerie, especially since the People always took note when the great To-wats burned up a *poo-chit,* a star.

"Wagh," he breathed to his larger companion, "this is a night to be wondered at, Beogah. I am glad that Big-Mouth Mike brought us to this place."

"As am I, Sowagerie. Now stop all this foolish chattering, for I wish to hear what these men have to tell us."

"*Ick-in-nish,*" the youth called Sowagerie, or Green Hair, spat as he tossed his head derisively. "Perhaps I chatter a little, my younger brother, but I say you bray like *moo-rats,* the mule!"

"Ho!" Beogah snorted in instant anger, his chest swelling as he spoke. "And I say you make more noise than *o-bi-nunk,* the wild goose!"

"And I say—"

"Be silent, both of you!" ordered Chee. "Be silent, or *tangi,* I will see that you are kicked all the way back to the San Juan!"

Silenced more by the threat than because of it, for not within their memories had their father ever ordered them to do anything, the young men grew still and stared ahead to where the fire, replenished with more logs, was sending showers of sparks high into the night-time sky. That, at least, was a sight they were used to. But so many of the People gathered together in one place? That was another matter altogether, and despite their childish bickering both of the boys felt the sense of being part of something grand and important.

More significantly, they were in complete awe of the great men who sat nearest the fire, the men who had accomplished the won-drous deed they were about to hear of, and who at the moment were passing the pipe of friendship to each other.

Around them, scattered among the trees of this high-up forest in what were called the Shining Mountains, the wickiups of the People shown in the pale light of the moon. Here and there in these mostly leather lodges a baby cried, but other than that and the bleating of sheep and goats and the snorting of horses—sounds that were not even sounds to the boys they were so common—the night seemed infinitely still. The drums of the war dance had stopped, the laugh-ing and chattering of the women and children had grown still, and all eyes were on old Quinket, whose drooping gray mustaches marked him as a wise and venerable man.

"Ho," he finally declared after he had smoked the pipe and then held it to the four directions before laying it carefully beside him, "this is a day of the People."

The old man paused, and for the first time young Sowagerie real-ized that the chief was not happy. But before he had time to wonder about it, the old man lifted his head and continued.

"We have done a thing, a very big thing, and it is in my heart to wonder what will come of it."

There was instant, intense silence, almost as if the People about the fire were afraid to breathe. This too Sowagerie noted, and still he did not understand.

"What will come of it," a younger warrior who had been sitting next to Quinket declared fiercely as he rose to his feet, "is that now the whites will know we are men to be reckoned with!"

Instantly the air was rent with shrieking war cries, and the two young brothers were no less vocal than any about them. This man who had spoken was to be awed and feared, the People were whispering, for not only was he *Poowagudt,* a great medicine man, but he was very rich, owning more than a hundred horses, which everyone knew were the pride of his life.

"Killing the Indian agent called Meeker was right," the man continued, staring directly at the seated chief. "Hear these words, O Quinket, and believe them."

"I believe that you believe them," old Quinket replied with great heaviness of soul. "Perhaps even I believe them. But the problem is not convincing us, O Canalla. The problem will be to convince the Great Father in Washington and all the other whites who hate us because we will not leave the lands they desire for their own. I fear they will not be convinced of our rightness."

After a few seconds of silence the younger man crossed his arms after the manner of the wise among the People. "Then I, Canalla, would make a telling," he declared, his voice even and calm, forcing all the people to strain to hear his words. "I will tell you how the thing was, and I will tell you why the whites will see it our way. Wagh!

"The man Nathan Meeker was *katz-te-suah,* a fool! I went to him in a forthright manner and told him he was chewing up the ground of my best horse pasture with his evil machine. I told him he must leave my pasture and go away from that place before a bad thing happened to him. But the man was a fool. In his mouth was but one word, and it was the only word he could say. Work. Work! *Work!* He had to work, and so the People of the Shining Mountains had to work!

"Not so, I told him. The People don't like work. *To-wats,* God, doesn't work, and neither do the People work. *To-wats* doesn't like school, I told him. Neither do the People like school! Go away, I told him again, or a bad thing will happen.

"But the man Nathan Meeker was *katz-te-suah!* He told me I must shoot my horses, all but two or three of them, and learn to grub in the earth like *pah-rant,* the muskrat. In his head was one thought: Work! Work! *Work!* The man was a fool, so I threw him to the earth to show him that he had no strength against me!

"Now tell me, O Quinket, what reasonable man, even though his skin be white, will not understand a thing so plain as that?"

"Meeker was also *tu-wish-erer,* a liar," another warrior said as he arose. "I am called Nicaagat, my brothers, and in this thing I stand beside the man Canalla, who is now called Johnson. Meeker told us there would be no soldiers on our land so long as the grass grew and the water flowed. He showed us the writing of the white governor Pitkin, who promised us the same thing. Yet in a few days after Canalla had thrown Meeker to the earth to give him a little sense, word came to me that white soldiers were coming onto our land.

"Now brothers, you know I do not like war. I have lived with the whites called mormonee and have learned their language. I was even a scout for General Crook against the Sioux when I thought I could help them come together peacefully. I say truthfully that there is much about the way of these white people that I find good.

"So with Antelope and a few others, I rode fast and came to the chief soldier named Thornburgh as he was riding, and I asked him where he was going. It was in my mind that if he would hear my words he would be wise enough to stop and turn his soldiers back to where they came from. It was in my mind to believe that I could help him see the reasonableness of our position, so war could be avoided.

"My brothers, he told me he was taking his soldiers and his guns to the agency at White River, where Meeker had called him. I told him this was *katz-at,* a bad thing, and violated the words of the treaty. I told him to stop, think a little, and then go back to where he came from. Then I rode away to see what the man would do.

"But Thornburgh was as big a fool as the agent Meeker. He kept his men riding forward, so that night I rode alone into his camp and reminded him again of the words of the treaty. I told him his governor Pitkin had signed it, and that for him to go farther was a foolish thing indeed, for the People of the Shining Mountains would not allow it. Neither, I told him, was it necessary. I then suggested that he and four or five others leave the soldiers and go with me to the agency to see that Meeker was unharmed, and to work out the difficulty between Meeker and Canalla in an equitable manner.

"Thornburgh listened to my talk, but his scouts told him I was not to be trusted. And so in sadness I rode away a second time. In the morning he and his soldiers still did not turn back, and my mind began to be filled with the memory of what that devil Chivington and his soldiers had done to the women and children of the Cheyenne chief Black Kettle that morning on Sand Creek. As you well remember, none were spared, not even *tow-ats-en,* the little ones. I saw the dead, my brothers, and it was an evil that lives always in my mind.

"That is why, after they crossed the Milk River on the next day, many of us gathered to stop Thornburgh and his soldiers. I wished to do this with a show of force only, so I and a few others rode fast around the leaders of the whites, hoping to frighten them. It is an unfortunate thing, but someone then fired a gun at someone else, I do not know who, and before I could stop it there was much shooting. Major Thornburgh and many others of the soldiers died that day, and we will not speak again the names of the People who also crossed over."

Again war cries rent the still night air, and Sowagerie and Beogah, their young eyes glowing with pride and excitement, thought of the great battle they had already heard so much about. Major Thornburgh had been killed almost immediately, and then the battle had raged for days, the Utes keeping the leaderless soldiers pinned down behind their wagons and hastily thrown-up breastworks. Even the arrival of a company of black "buffalo" soldiers to reinforce the military had not turned the tide, and the soldiers had been forced to watch helplessly as their comrades died and hundreds of their animals were slain by the sharp-shooting warriors of the People.

"When I learned of the battle against Thornburgh," the *shaman* Canalla then declared, speaking again, "I took a few young men with me to the agency and told Meeker what his foolishness had done. When he denied sending for Thornburgh, I could see that the truth was not in him. So I shot him and drove a stake through his mouth and into his beloved earth so that I could stop his tongue from lying about us in the world of spirits. We then slew the seven others who worked with Meeker at the agency, for they were also liars. But we spared the women and children, who are with us now!"

At that, three bedraggled women, one clutching two small children, were thrust into the firelight, and again the war cries from all the People filled the night. Sowagerie and Beogah gaped openmouthed as the three, an older woman with stringy gray hair, Arvilla, the wife of Nathan Meeker; a much younger woman clutching two small children who would give her name only as Mrs. Price; and a girl not much older than themselves who had been the agent's daughter and was called Josephine, were pushed roughly about from one laughing warrior to another.

Their faces, arms, and legs were begrimed and dirty; they wore no shoes; and all had lost most of their clothing to the clawing warriors and angry squaws, leaving them woefully unclothed. And the faces of all of them were streaked with tears.

"Ho!" Canalla declared as he reached out to stop the laughing and shoving. "Here are the three *squaws* as well as *tow-ats-en,* the little ones. They are none of them good for much, I know, but it is the way of the People to care for even the slaves. The *tow-ats-en,* of course, will make fine People if they are taught carefully in all our ways." Slowly, proudly, he turned to look down at old Quinket. "It is because we have shown mercy and spared the lives of these three and have cared for them, O Quinket, that the whites will see that we are reasonable men."

"It is precisely for that reason," the old man murmured, "that the whites will wish us to be destroyed."

"You talk in riddles."

Rising, the old man pointed with his finger. "Look at these women, O Canalla. How many warriors have bedded them? How many women have beaten them? Will the whites think such treatment is reasonable, I ask you?"

Trembling with sudden anger, Canalla pointed back. "Then we will make them the same as our own women! What could be more reasonable than that?" Turning, he faced the silent throng. "Which of you, my brothers, will take any of these three and the little ones into your wickiups? Which of you will make them your wives and your children?"

"Wagh!" young Beogah breathed from beside Sowagerie, "I would take to wife that *nan-zitch,* that girl, if I were but a little older. It is in my mind to think that she would make a man many fine sons!"

Sowagerie snorted. "It is not in your mind at all, *moo-rats,* and you know it. In fact, I do not know that you even have a mind."

"What I think of is better by far than your foolish *no-ni-shee,* your dreams of being a great chief!" Beogah spat back, his anger evident. "You are so small and so poor in flesh that you could be chief over no one. The People would laugh you to scorn!"

"One day," Sowagerie seethed, his eyes hard with anger, "I will be your chief, my younger brother. And then we shall see which will laugh the other to scorn!"

The two half brothers glared at each other in the dim firelight, their lack of love obvious. But neither had their mothers, one quick and wiry, the other large and slow, ever shown affection for each other. After all, each had been in competition with the other for the few favors bestowed by old Chee, and none of this had been lost on the two growing boys.

Meanwhile, with much shouting and mocking, the three captives were unceremoniously pulled in one direction or another by the laughing warriors, the youngest going first and the eldest last. Only when that had been settled did old Quinket speak again.

"Perhaps this will turn into a good thing, brothers," he said as he gazed about him. "As has been spoken, we have done a big thing, a very big thing, and it will long be remembered around the campfires of our people. Only the passing of the seasons will give us understanding of whether it has been good or bad. For now, I have spoken. Wagh!"

"It will be a good thing," Canalla said with confidence, "for now we have been more than reasonable about it, as even the whites will see. But still, I send out my voice, my strong voice, that I do not think the pony soldiers will come after us into these shining mountains. No, it is in my heart to believe that they are now afraid.

"But should they be so foolish as to chase us here we will take up our guns and our bows, and with our sharp arrow points we will show them a thing they will never forget, not so long as the grass shall grow or the water flow! I, Canalla, have also spoken, and it is enough!"

Again the air was filled with the wild war cries of the People. Soon the drums were beating their haunting cadence, and the half-brother sons of Chee and his two wives watched in fascination as the stomping, swaying war dance began once more.

8

Thursday, October 9, 1879

Headwaters of Plateau Creek, Grand Mesa, Colorado

"Ho!" Beogah growled, doing his best to sound like a man, "this is the great warrior Canalla, lifting his weapon and shooting the fool Meeker! Boom! One shot and he falls, *puck-ki,* killed by a man of the People."

In his hand Beogah held a stick shaped roughly like a pistol, but now as he became Nathan Meeker, he allowed it to drop from apparently nerveless fingers. Then he slowly crumpled onto his back on the earth.

"And this is the great warrior Canalla," Sowagerie declared fiercely as he grabbed up another stick and stepped toward his brother, who was acting out death throes upon the ground, "driving the stake through the fool Meeker's lying tongue. Now *katz-te-suah,* you will never lie about the People in the afterworld. Wagh!"

"*Own-shump!*" Beogah sputtered as he felt Sowagerie's stick thrust into his mouth. "Enough!" Twisting his head he rolled away from his smaller brother and pushed himself to his feet. "*Pe-nun-ko,*" he snarled as he rubbed his cheek where the stick had scraped it, "in the future, Green Hair, you had better remember that I am not so big a fool as the man Meeker."

Sowagerie laughed at his younger brother. "Ho, *suck-ige,* it was a mistake, is all. For a moment I thought you really were the fool Meeker, you played his part so well. Now come, and I will show you how the brave Nicaagat shot the soldier Thornburgh out of his saddle with *pe-ap aukage,* his big rifle. That is the part I play best!"

And with a peal of laughter Sowagerie picked up a long stick to be his rifle, whipped his other hand behind him as if he were quirting a horse, and bounded away through the trees. Laughing again, Beogah was not far behind.

The October day was warm and clear, and as the boys came thundering out of the thick stand of fir and into a clearing not far from old Quinket's encampment, they took no time to notice the brilliant gold of the trembling quaking-aspen leaves. Neither did they note the sweet but pungent scents of crushed grasses and pasturing horses, nor hear the lazy buzz of insects or shrill cry of a red-tailed hawk as it wheeled slowly overhead. To the boys these things did not mean beauty so much as they meant normalcy, and so they passed unnoticed while their noisy play continued.

"Ho, *suck-ige,*" Sowagerie shouted as he paused atop a low hummock near the center of the meadow, "see how the great warrior Nicaagat raises his big rifle. He wastes no time; he does not even have to aim. He sees the soldier Thornburgh, his rifle is raised, and boom! The pony soldier is *e-i,* he is dead!" And with a wild cry Sowagerie threw himself from the hummock to roll unceremoniously to a dusty stop below.

"Ho!" Beogah shouted from above, "I think the pony soldier fell more in this manner!" And with a wild cry he, too, threw himself from the top of the hummock and rolled and flopped to a stop near the grotesquely postured and apparently lifeless Sowagerie.

For a few seconds the boys lay still, their performances continuing as they imagined themselves to be the dead Major Thornburgh. Abruptly, however, the afternoon air was filled with the sound of girlish giggles, and with great consternation the two half brothers leaped to their feet to stare around.

"*Poon-e-kee!* Look!" a girl's voice snickered. "Now we see how it is that little Pahute boys get so dirty."

And to the boys' amazement the bushes parted only a few feet away from where they stood, and they found themselves staring at three *nan-zitch* who could not have been much older than themselves.

Too surprised to react, Sowagerie and Beogah simply stared, and again all three girls broke into laughter. "Ugh," one of the girls said then, pulling an awful face, "they even smell *o-coomp!*"

"And they cannot talk," a second girl smirked.

"What they say about the Pahute people must be true," the third girl chimed in. "Their hair is filled with *poo-chump,* lice, their bodies *quan-na* in a horrid manner, and *tash-a ah-be-quy,* all day they lie around doing nothing."

At that last insult Beogah turned and fled, but defiantly Sowagerie held his ground.

"*Poon-e-kee!*" the girl who had first spoken continued as she pointed at Sowagerie, revealing herself by her actions to be the leader of the group, "his poor shirt does not even cover his nakedness! In all the wickiups of the People there is not enough sewing thread, *pan-shi-tam-mo,* to mend the holes in it."

Instantly self-conscious, Sowagerie looked down and for the first time in his life saw himself as another might see him. He also saw that, truly, much of his dusty body was exposed to view through the gaping holes in his worn leather shirt.

Self-consciously lifting his eyes, he glanced from one to the other of the girls, and also for the first time in his life he noted the neatness of the appearance of others. Each of these three, for instance, had her hair done neatly in braids, the ends tied with either ermine or otter fur. Their dresses, two of which were made of white mans' cloth while the third was of buckskin, were long and fringed, and they were elaborately decorated with beads or elks' teeth. Their feet, instead of being dusty and bare like his and Beogah's, were clean and clothed in carefully beaded buckskin moccasins. And their faces, he noted as his eyes lifted again, were also shiny with cleanliness. One especially had an appeal to him, though in his mind he could not understand why that would be so.

Truly these *nan-zitch* were a sight to behold, and young Sowagerie found himself feeling more awe than embarrassment as he gazed upon them.

"We are not Pahute," he declared at length, finally finding his tongue. "We are of the People, the same as you!"

Suddenly the girls were no longer smiling but had grown

indignant. "Ho!" one of them stated scornfully, the one he found strangely appealing, "you little *ipeds* and your fathers are not even fit to sit at the same fires with the warriors of the People. My father says you are water-Utes who stay off by your big river by yourselves instead of coming to our ancestral homeland here in the Shining Mountains and helping the People in our fight with the wicked *tsharr,* the whites. All of you are lazy and dirty and are not fit to be called the People!"

"Ho," Sowagerie replied with the same voice of indignation, "we would have fought had we been here, *me-poodg-e,* little one. But we had to come from *to-edg-mae,* a great way off." He had unconsciously used the name designating a small but well-beloved child as he had addressed the girl, and as her eyes flashed with sudden anger he realized too late his mistake.

"I am not your *me-poodg-e!*" she fumed. "I am Too-rah, a woman of the People."

"And I am called Soorowits," he declared, drawing himself to his full height, which was still much less than the girl's, "though because of what *tabby* the sun has done to my hair, I am more often called Sowagerie."

"Yes," the girl snickered, "it is not difficult to see why."

"My brother Beogah and I are warriors of the People," Sowagerie continued, lying easily. "Instead of fighting the whites behind us, we are kept more than busy defending the forepart of our land from the fierceness of the *Diné.*"

"Warriors?" the girl called Too-rah questioned, her scorn raking Sowagerie's ears like fire. "A true warrior is comely in his appearance. He cleanses his body with *nevaraga-nump* and then paints it carefully. His *tots-sib-a-wub* is braided and decorated manfully, and he would never be seen in such poor attire as you have chosen. Wagh! You are nothing more than a dirty little Pahute *ipeds,* Green Hair. I scorn you!"

Lifting her chin, the girl wheeled and marched away across the meadow, her two companions following silently after. And Sowagerie, too proud to admit to what the girl Too-rah had declared, shouted after her that she was no better than the white captives in the encampment, good for little more than preparing a man's meals and bearing his babies. A man, he added sullenly to her rapidly departing back, such as he, Sowagerie, was one day going to be!

———◦–◦–◦———

Cedar City

With a smile of satisfaction Eliza laid aside the paring knife and began spreading the bowl full of peach slices onto the drying tray. That done, she lifted the tray and carried it out the back door where she positioned it on some rocks to face the hot afternoon sun. Though late in the season for peaches, Billy had somehow obtained half a bushel from a trader who had stopped at the co-op the day before. And Eliza was thrilled beyond words to have them, for peaches were her favorite fruit. Of course she would have preferred them bottled in Mason jars, but dried fruit would ride so much more easily in a bouncing, shifting wagon.

Sighing deeply, Eliza stepped back inside, took up the knife and another peach, and began peeling away the skin. And she thought immediately—and bleakly—of herself. All her adult life she had believed herself to be one thing, and then a miserable marriage and a move to this desolate community had quickly peeled away the skin of her naiveté to reveal an entirely different woman. And now, with this move to the San Juan, she felt as though she were being sliced up and set out to dry just like the peaches.

"Lawsy," she muttered as she worked, "but you are truly making yourself miserable, woman! You're thinking too much, worrying too much!"

And she was, too. With most of their things packed into their newly refurbished wagon, she had learned the day before that there would be an indefinite delay in their departure. So now she and Billy were basically camping in their nearly empty home while they awaited word on the next scheduled date of departure. But waiting meant sitting around doing nothing, and that meant thinking and worrying. So for two days Eliza had been doing her best to keep busy, drying fruit, making candles, filling a last-minute order for fans—anything that would keep her mind occupied. Only nothing seemed to be working.

For days she had thought about Mary's comments regarding Billy, weighing them, trying to determine what she should do about them. As if there was anything, really, that she could do.

Spreading the last of the peaches, she stuck a slice in her mouth, savored its delicious flavor, and carried the tray out into the sun. Then, taking a seat on the stoop, she laid down her crutch and lowered her chin into her hands.

And that about summed things up, she thought gloomily as she watched a flock of magpies screeching about a nearby juniper. Since there was nothing else to do and nowhere else to go, she would be going with Billy to the San Juan, and there were no other decisions to be made.

Well, she thought guiltily, there *was* one. If she was going—and she was—then to preserve her sanity she had better be going with a plan. As Widow Burnham had often said, she who trusts all things to chance makes a lottery of her life. And Eliza was tired to death of living a lottery—and losing. No, sir, if she was going on this frighteningly insane mission, she was going with a positive attitude. The others in the company would have nothing but good to say about her, and it would be the same with Billy. Despite her previous failures, she would renew her efforts to make him feel loved and adored, singing his praises to everyone within earshot. She would renew them, and she would succeed!

And if she told such base lies for long enough, she thought grimly, well, perhaps she might even begin to convince herself that they were true.

———o—o—o———

Headwaters of Plateau Creek, Grand Mesa, Colorado

It was dark, the only light in the wickiup coming from two or three fingers of flame that still reached out from the coals of the fire. In the encampment round about all was still. Even the dogs had mostly stopped barking, and the only sound was the occasional wailing of the Meeker woman, the older one who continued to grieve over the loss of her foolish husband.

His eyes wide and sleepless, the boy Sowagerie lay staring

upward into the gloom. But it was not the darkness of the wickiup that he contemplated. Rather, his mind was troubled by the words of the young girl Too-rah, leaving him to worry them as *sar-ich* the dog worries a bone. It was these thoughts that left him sleepless, and it was the memory of the girl making a mockery of him in so many ways that filled young Green Hair's troubled vision.

Sighing, he closed his eyes tightly, trying to rid his mind of her face and the laughter of her scorn. But it was no use. Whether his eyes were open or closed, Too-Rah's comely face was always before them, the contempt of her voice ringing in his ears.

Perhaps, he thought, if he—

"My son, what is it that troubles you?"

"It is nothing, my mother." Sowagerie wanted to answer his mother in another way, by asking about himself and the Pahute name. There were also many other things he wanted to discuss, to understand. But he didn't want to offend his mother by suggesting that her only offspring might be inferior to others of the People. Thus he held his peace.

However, old Chee's favorite wife was not so easily dissuaded, and finally Sowagerie told her, in hushed and whispered tones, of his meeting with the three girls.

"What is it they are saying, my mother? They call me a Pahute, and they say that a Pahute is not worthy of the name of the People. Is this a true saying?"

Sowagerie's mother, whose name meant Little Wind in the language of the People, thought deeply about what she should say, and so it was many moments before she answered. And then, because she was stalling for time to think of the right way to respond, it was with another question.

"If you were different from the rest of the People, my Little One," she whispered, "would that be such a bad thing?"

But Sowagerie had not been born of this wise woman for nothing, nor had he lived in her wickiup nearly thirteen full circles of the seasons without learning a few things of his own.

"I will answer you," he responded carefully, lest again he show disrespect, "but not until my own question has been answered."

Chuckling at the cleverness of her son, the woman began her

telling, wondering as she did so if Sowagerie could truly understand things that seemed so elusive to her.

"*To-edg-e-tish,* my son. A long time ago the People were one in the Shining Mountains. They lived where they wished, they hunted where they wished, and if they tired of a place they simply packed their ponies and their dogs and went to another that seemed better. Not many lived in a band, but all were the same as all others, and when all the bands came together for *Queo-gand weep-pi,* the Bear Dance, or *Tabby weep-pi,* the Sun Dance, all considered themselves the same. These things I have been told, and I believe them.

"Then the white man came, first a few and then many, and it was not long before they wanted all of the Shining Mountains for their own. They wanted the People to sell what was not theirs to sell, and then go away to another place where the white man had not come.

"Many of the People were approached with this foolish idea, and none would hear of it. Instead, they lived as though the white man did not exist, secretly hoping he would one day go away. But the white man kept *pie-ka,* he kept coming and coming, and soon there were so many that they could no longer be ignored.

"Next, many people began dying at one another's hands, too many for a quiet telling such as this. But know this, my son, and believe it! Not all of the whites are bad, and not all of the People are good and wise. Thus there was *nah-oo-quey,* fighting, and blood was spilled by both the whites and the People. Much talking followed the bloodletting, and soon whites were finding men of the People who would take money in trade for parts of the Shining Mountains. Papers called treaties were made, and after that our small bands were made larger and told where we could go and where we could not. Some agreed to this and continue trying to live the ways of the white man where they are told they can live. The man Ouray is such a man, and he has become a big man among the People.

"Others, such as Chee and Mike and the other men of our band, do not agree with the treaties, and they are not so easy for the white man to throw a rope around. They will not be told where they may live. They will not be told how they may live. They will not be mocked and scorned for the darkness of their skin. They will not be ridiculed for their attire and their customs.

"To prevent these things, my son, Chee and Mike and many others refused to go to the white man's agency or to accept the white man's pay for our mountains. Instead they fled to the land of the big river, to the land of rocks and trees and deep canyons where only *quan-a-tich* the eagle may see the way of our passing.

"There are many who choose this path, my son, and we consider ourselves the true People. These others, the ones who stayed behind to take what little is left to us of the Shining Mountains, do not. They call us Pahutes because we like the land of the big river, and they speak evilly of us. Now, do you see why I answered your question with a question?"

"I see," Sowagerie replied softly, "that as eldest son of Chee I am different from these people. It is not for the reasons they think that I am different, but for my own reasons, and thus it is that I am content."

"It is well, little one," Sowagerie's mother whispered, reaching out to touch her only son. "Already you think like a man. One day you will be a great man indeed."

And his chest swelling with pride even while his mind continued to ply itself with questions, Sowagerie closed his eyes. At least, he thought as the vision of the girl Too-Rah came again to his mind, he would no longer be troubled with the name Pahute.

9

Tuesday, October 21, 1879

Shay Mesa, Blue Mountains, San Juan Country

"Thunderation but it's cold, Mr. Hudson! You sure grubbin' out this seep's gonna be worth it?"

A wet and bedraggled Joshua B. "Spud" Hudson looked up from where he stood knee-deep in the ooze created by the tiny seep. The wind off Shay Peak was raw and biting, and being wet from hocks to elbows didn't add much to a man's comfort.

"I ain't Mr. Hudson," he grumbled. "Not to nobody who works for me. From now on, Curly, you call me Spud."

"Yes, sir, Mr. Hudson, sir. I . . . I mean Spud, sir."

"And drop the sir while you're at it. As for grubbing out this spring being worth it," he admitted laconically, "it may not do much for you and me, Curly. But the wild critters'll like it, and cows grazing twixt Indian and North Cottonwood Creeks'll be tickled plumb to death not having to walk so far for a drink. I reckon maybe that makes it worth it."

"Not to mention it'll be a sign to old man Peters that this is your graze and not his?"

Spud Hudson grinned. "Well, he is a range-grabbing son, all right. He's built that spread below what he's now calling Peters' Hill, and he let me know in no uncertain terms that spring off thataway was his'n, too. Happen a feller doesn't claim things hereabouts quick, first thing you know this whole country'll be called Peters' this and Peters' that."

"Fools' names and fools' faces—"

95

"Amen, Curly. And you can bet I ain't calling this here seep Spud's Spring, neither!"

Curly Bill Jenkins chuckled. "Comes down to it, I wouldn't either. Sounds sort of riotess, I reckon."

"Riotess?" Spud Hudson planted his shovel firmly in the muck at his feet. "What in blue blazes is riotess supposed to mean?"

Wiping his grin from his face, Curly thrust his own shovel back into the ooze and began heaving it out to the side. He might be a lot of things, he thought, but one thing he wasn't was foolish. Not enough, anyhow, to get his new boss, who he'd been told had a temper a mile wide and a foot deep, riled up over nothing at all.

"Well?"

"Doggone it, Spud," he mumbled placatingly. "Riotess don't mean nothing, and you know it. I just made it up so's I'd sound as edicated as you do."

"What you sound, Curly, is nervier'n a busted tooth. Hell's tinkling hot brass bells! Out here edication is like a mother's love or a married lady's morals. Neither one is discussed in public, and you had ought to know that."

"Yes, sir, Spud, I reckon you're right."

"Course I'm right," Spud Hudson declared, waxing more eloquent by the moment. "You come out agin edication, Curly, and you ain't never going to get elected to nothing in this country."

"I never said I wanted to."

"It don't matter. You won't. Same with being a Mormon sky pilot. A wise man don't discuss them folks' religion, or come out agin it around these parts, either one. You'd be better off favoring horse thieves and giving free liquor and repeating rifles to the Pahutes. Why, I'd rather run on a ticket of drowning baby kittens and pistol-whipping little old ladies than utter a derogatory word agin edication or Mormon preaching."

"Yes, sir," Curly admitted, scraping at his chin and doing his best to look abashed.

"That's the trouble with old man Peters, too. A man who leaves his handle all over the place leaves trouble for certain. Either folks'll find out his weaknesses and mock him to scorn every time they have to say his name, or else he won't last and they'll say his name and wonder ever time who by jings the fool was who got so confounded lonesome he had to drop his handle ever which way just to hear the sound of it. Doing such a thing just don't pay, Curly, and in this country a man won't get elected on that ticket, neither."

"Yes, sir," Curly admitted again, wondering as he spoke why he'd ever made up that fool word in the first place. His boss was going now, hanging onto the topic like a drunk to his whiskey jug, and it'd be dark and maybe long past before he ran out of things to say. Of course it was humorous, in a way, and mighty entertaining. But happen a man didn't keep eating crow all the time and saying "Yes, sir" and "No, sir," old Spud would either tie into him with a string of words big enough to raise blisters on a rawhide boot or haul out his hog-leg and shoot him outright, which it was rumored he had done more than once.

Worse, when Spud Hudson got to talking he didn't work, and that left the mucking out of the seep to Curly's already overburdened and definitely chilled shoulders. Yes sir, by accidentally coming up with that word he had not just stepped into a common, ordinary cow chip. Rather, by tophet, he had lit with both boots square in the middle of the granddaddy pasture flapjack of them all!

"It's got me confusder'n a blind dog in a butcher shop," Spud was saying, "what's bringing all the fool people into this country in the first place. Water's bad, country's desolate, snakes are thicker'n flies and fleas, Indians are always on the warpath, summers are hotter'n hades with the bellows going, and days like this the thermometer drops faster'n a gut-shot elk. You'd think folks'd rather sign the deed to their baby sister's virtue than come to a country such as this.

"But no, some grub rider told me that Texas feller name of Lacy has brought two more herds of his cows down onto Montezuma Creek, trailing 'em all the way from Texas, by jings, and is fixing to bring his wife along in the spring. He calls his spread the LC, and I reckon he's even got more cows a-comin'."

Curly was amazed, being as how he was the same exact grub rider that had brought word of I. W. Lacy's growing spread. Fact of the matter was, he had ridden all the way from Texas with the second herd, Bill Ball segundoing, and had been told to slope once the herd was on LC range. Of course, he hadn't been alone. Half a dozen men had been let go, and all but him had hit the trail back. But there were a few folks in Texas he didn't want to meet up with, so he'd headed north instead of south and had the good fortune of running onto Spud Hudson's outfit when the forgetful old man was feeling good. But now he was beginning to wonder if maybe he had made the right choice.

"This shure ain't no good country to be dragging a woman into," Curly finally admitted, deciding to say nothing more.

"Not when there's human sidewinders such as Sweet-Tooth Hazelton or some such—"

Curly was startled. "You don't mean Sugar Bob Hazelton?"

"I reckon that's his moniker, all right. You know him?"

"I seen him once or twice, don't never want to again." Now Curly stopped working to look carefully around. Riding with Sugar Bob after Bill Ball and the Comanch had saved his life had been a nervous experience, for he was a naturally mean man made even worse by his festering bullet holes, and a man never knew where he stood with him. He was even worse than Jim "Killer" Miller, the Neuces outlaw.

Curly had been wondering, too, what had happened to Hazelton. One morning just before arriving at Lacy's cabins on Montezuma Creek, he had vanished, and nobody had even made mention of the fact. Of course, Curly understood why, too, and despised the man more for his cowardly churlishness than his meanness. But now, thinking that he might be hiding in the trees somewhere nearby, he felt a sudden chill that had nothing to do with the cold.

"Way I heard it," he declared, once again feeling as nervous as he'd felt the last part of the drive, "he's mean as poison and a sneak to boot. Folks end up dead around him, and not many of 'em have holes in the front."

"Then there'll likely be more." Spud Hudson shook his head. "Way the story goes, this Hazelton had his way with Lacy's daughter—raped her, I was told. When she started showing with child, he did the unmanly thing and left her, heading south. Strick with sorrow and humiliation the poor girl kilt herself, and Old Man Lacy vowed revenge."

"Don't say as I blame him," Curly snorted, stabbing his shovel into the mud and returning to work.

"Nor I. Trouble was, Lacy ain't been able to catch him, and Hazelton's traipsing around the country acting like there's a war on, shooting first and asking questions later. Like I said, Curly, the country's getting right dangerous.

"To make matters worse, I hear tell a whole passel of Mormons is heading for somewheres in this country—men, women, and kids alike. I ain't auguring nothing agin their religion, mind you. But folks what bring families into this wilderness seem plumb weak north of the ears. You hear me, Curly?"

"Yes, sir, Spud. Reckon I do." Now Curly's mind was really whirling. Mormon folks were coming, and with all their women, who he'd heard were the handsomest in the country? Why, it had been so long since he'd seen a real woman, let alone a handsome one, that he couldn't even remember the occasion. But with a whole passel of them coming, well, a brand new world of wondrous possibilities was suddenly opening up in Curly's mind—

"Why, they're crazier'n popcorn on a hot skillet," Spud was saying. "And only fifty, sixty miles away. Not only might they have to tangle with that crazy fool Hazelton, who could pick 'em off one by two and never be seen, but their coming don't leave a man like me no elbow room at all, and you know it! First thing you know I'll have to sell my outfit to one of 'em and go find someplace else where I can breath free again.

"Thunderation, Curly! Out here is wind and sun and the fresh rain in a man's face. Always there's more horses than a man can ride, more grass than a cow can eat, and more cows than a man can sell. At night there's the lonely, coyote-crying camps of the desert, by day the long passes and wolf-lonely, winding trails of the mountains, and always there's the high, sweet scent of pine, the wondrous odor of sagebrush, and the truly wonderful smells of woodsmoke, brewing coffee, and saddle blankets drying by the fire. And finally, by jings, there's the feel of a good horse under you and the long ride, far and fast.

"More folks coming in will foul all that, Curly, and you know it—foul it just as sure as a dead cow fouls a sweetwater spring!

Houses and bob-wire fences, churches and schools and picnic socials, and lots of purty girls sashaying about in frilly pink petticoats and taking a man's mind off'n his work! No sir, I ain't auguring agin their religion or their morals, either one. But I sure to high heaven wish the whole blamed shebang of 'em—the Mormon folks, Old Man Peters, and this Lacy feller and his wife—would've all stayed home and left me alone with the Indians.

"That's a ticket I'd run on, Curly! And in this country I'd win, sure as sulfur smells bad I would."

"Yes, sir," Curly admitted quietly, thinking of how amazing it would be to go to a real dance and actually sashay around with a frilly dressed, pink-petticoated, honest-to-goodness girl. And with a grunt and a sigh born of pure loneliness, he threw out another shovelful of ooze.

10

Wednesday, October 22, 1879

Cedar City

Billy could never remember feeling so excited. Not even his wedding day had filled him with such vim and vigor, as Brother Brigham might have put it. He and Eliza were finally on their way! Or soon would be, that is. The first wagons to leave Cedar for the mission to the San Juan were only a couple of blocks away and approaching fast, the dust of their coming already rising high in the cool morning air. He could even hear the people shouting instructions and farewells, and from where he stood it sounded like every dog in Cedar had joined the refrain. Soon he and Eliza would be part of the train, the dust and sounds of their leaving mingling with the others, and then the grandest adventure of their lives would begin.

Anxiously he began another tour around his single wagon, just to make sure that all was in place and nothing forgotten. Dick Butt's mules, both span, were restive and seemed as anxious as he did to be on their way. He'd had the devil's own time of it getting them harnessed in the early morning dark, and even the memory of the experience made him smile ruefully. Two hours it had taken—two hours to do a job a boy could have done in twenty minutes or so. Even the fitful light of the lantern hadn't helped much. But by daylight or a little after, each collar with its hames had been settled over each mule's head and against its withers, each bridle with blinders was in place on the head, each trace or tug was secured from the hames through the bellyband to the wagon tongue and singletrees at the end of each of the two doubletrees, and each of the eight rein straps was

101

threaded carefully back and looped around the wagon's brake handle. Additionally, for the wheeler span—the mules closest to the wagon—each harness included a backstrap and box britchen with croupier to hold the harness in place, and a neck yoke leading from the hames forward to the front doubletree, designed to keep the animal from stepping backward into the singletrees and wagon.

Hanging in his shed the past couple of weeks, the four sets of harness had looked like an impossible morass of collars, leather straps, chains, and buckles. In place on each of the mules, however, each part of the harness gave credence to the wisdom of the designers—however many of them there must have been.

So, too, with his wagon, Billy thought as he passed by the mules, patting each one on the rump as he walked by. One of the two wagons he had brought with him from Salt Lake City, it had been completely refurbished by a fellow named Buck Robison in trade for his second wagon. Of course, it had needed refurbishing, too. With new reaches and hounds in the running gear, new bolsters to hold the axles, as well as new thimbles on each axle, two new bows for the cover, half the wagon-box replaced, and new spokes, felloes, and iron tires on all the wheels, it seemed more like a brand-new wagon than the one he had nursed down from Salt Lake City only six months before.

The best part of the wagon, though, at least in Billy's opinion, was the door Buck Robison had built into the left-hand side of the wagon midway between the front and rear wheels. It was built so his crippled wife could more easily get in and out of the wagon-box, and Buck had designed the door so that little structural strength had been lost. Not alone did two iron hasps hold the door closed while traveling, but the blacksmith had designed it so that two heavy steel bars ran from front to back across the outside of the wagon. These bars, bolted through both timber and additional steel bars on the inside of the wagon, provided structural integrity when traveling and yet were quite simple to remove once camp was made. Then, should it prove necessary, Eliza would be able to gain access to the wagon without having to clamber up onto the high bench and scramble through the puckerhole in the canvas cover.

Billy smiled again as he remembered Eliza's pleased surprise when he had driven the wagon home. Not only had she seemed absolutely excited that he had been able to trade for the massive repairs, but she was also pleased that he had received two hundred and fifty dollars cash for the sale of their home.

"A cash sale?" she had asked, knowing as well as he that so much cash money was rare in Cedar, while empty houses were plentiful.

Naturally, all of it had gone into equipping them for their missionary journey, leaving them with no cash reserves whatsoever. But Billy didn't mind that, not when he knew they were about to embark on the most important event of their lives.

But what thrilled Billy as much as anything was that he'd made all the arrangements and all the purchases, not going to Eliza even once for help from her fan-making money. In fact, since their mission call, the subject of her money had never even come up, which was some surprising to Billy, for he'd thought his wife would have offered to help. But apparently she wanted her funds to remain hidden from him, which in the grand scheme of things hardly bothered him at all.

At the back of the wagon he inspected the chicken crate Kumen Jones had shown him how to build and mount on the endgate. In the slatted crate were two roosters and eight hens, a good source of eggs on the journey and a good start to a fine flock once they were settled on the San Juan. Their milk cow was also tied to the back of the wagon, her rope secured below and to the right of the chicken crate. On the left was the slightly shorter lead rope to the glass-eyed mare, who would follow anyway but who could thus be kept from getting in the way of other travelers. Billy knew there would be a company herd and herders once the missionaries were all together and organized. But for now, he reasoned, he would be wise to care for his own stock.

With Eliza making a final tour of the house, Billy checked off in his mind the amazing number of items he and his wife, with the help of Kumen and Mary Jones, had been able to pack into, on, or under the wagon. Besides the bags of seed grain and beans that filled the wagon-box directly behind and under the bench or seat, the dried food stored in and around the grub box, and the bedstead, rocking chair, table and chairs, small chest of drawers, and Eliza's trunks that were stacked throughout, the wagon was packed with bedding and ground cloths, a good riding saddle, cooking pots and utensils, two axes, and a hatchet.

There was also a single-action Colt's revolver; a Winchester model 1873 carbine with gunpowder, bullet molds, and lead; candle molds; and the basket containing Eliza's sewing needs. They also carried two lanterns with extra wicks, a small barrel of coal oil, two camp stools, a chamber pot, a washbowl, and a small wooden box filled with medicines, bandages, and other odds and ends. In the wagon were also all their extra clothing and a couple of good winter coats, and on the outside of the wagon-box were mounted a plow, a water-barrel, and a churn. In front, in the jockey box under their feet, was stored a good assortment of tools such as hammers, shovels, augers, a gimlet, assorted planes and chisels, nails and horse and mule shoes, an adz, and three good chains. Additionally, there was a supply of kingbolts and linchpins in case the wagon broke down, and underneath the wagon an extra axle and wagon tongue. There was also, of course, the grease bucket dangling from the back axle, which he would be sure and use this trip to keep his wheels from screeching in protest. And all this was in addition to the literally dozens of odds and ends that had been stuffed into every conceivable space within the wagon.

It was a good thing, Billy thought as he made his way back toward the front of the wagon, that Dick Butt had lent him the four good mules. It would take all they had, and then some, if his guess was right, to drag such a pile of gear all the way to the San Juan.

Even more satisfying, Billy thought with a smile, was the fact that at the co-op he had accurately anticipated the needs of the San Juan missionaries from the area and had ordered supplies appropriately. Thus at least the Cedar City contingent of missionaries were well equipped, not only for the six-week journey to the San Juan but also for establishing homesteads in that faraway place once they got there. Nor was the co-op left holding excessive merchandise that had not been purchased, which pleased Billy immensely.

"All set, hon-bun?" he asked as Eliza came out the door of their home for the last time.

"So far as I can tell," she responded. "All that's left inside is what we agreed to leave." Pausing on the stone walkway she turned and looked back. "This seems so final, Billy—much more final that it felt when we left Salt Lake City."

"Maybe it's because the house has been ours and now it isn't," Billy replied hopefully. "Neither of us ever owned a home in Salt Lake."

"Maybe. But I think it's more than that. Much more. Why are all the dogs barking?"

"Excitement, I reckon." Billy smiled widely. "Just like we feel. The first wagons'll be here in three, four minutes, you know, so we'd best be ready. You want I should help you up into the wagon?"

"What for? Do you disremember that I climbed up myself every day last spring?"

Surprised at the tone of Eliza's voice as much as by the words themselves, Billy stepped back as his wife clambered unaided to the wagonbench. Would he never understand women? Why, the week before, for the first time in . . . in goodness only knew how long, Eliza had been warm and affectionate every single day. And two nights before, when they had finally retired after Eliza had brushed her hair for most of an hour, it turned out that . . . that . . . well, she hadn't been as tired as he would have supposed.

Now, though, the warmth and intimacy he had reveled in for days seemed to have vanished like the mists of the night, leaving him as uncertain as ever about the woman he would gladly have died for.

With a last glance at his outfit, which was as packed and ready as he could make it, Billy scrambled onto the seat beside Eliza and unwound the reins from the brake handle.

"What are these rocks for?" Eliza asked abruptly, indicating nine riverbed stones Billy had placed on the dashboard atop the jockey box.

"To keep your feet warm on cold days," Billy replied easily.

"Well, I certainly don't need them today."

"No, I didn't reckon you would. That's why I didn't heat them through the night."

"Are you trying to say we have to carry these stones with us all the way to the San Juan?"

Billy smiled placatingly. "Jens Nielson, he picked them out special for you, hon-bun. He says such rocks have brought his frozen feet a world of comfort through the years."

"Humph! A body would think any old rock would do."

"I would have thought so too. But Brother Nielson, he says these rocks are harder than most others and will hold heat a great deal longer. They're flat so they won't roll around, and he says they won't crack as easily in the fire, either."

"Humph!"

Eliza seemed put out with everything this morning, though Billy guessed it had little to do with what she was fussing about. More likely it had to do with leaving Cedar City, which he knew she'd agreed to with great reluctance. In fact, he was also feeling troubled, though more from guilt than anything else. After all, he'd promised Eliza that he would return her to Salt Lake City only minutes before Elder Snow had brought their call to the San Juan. Though Eliza seemed resigned to the mission, Billy knew that one word from her would be enough to make him pull out and take her back to Salt Lake City. While it was never wise to turn down a call from the Lord's anointed, a man had to think of his wife—

"That's Brother Nielson's wagon," Billy said with another smile, "leading the train."

"So it is."

Tenderly Billy looked at his wife. "Eliza, hon-bun, I love you more than anything else on this earth, and I can't bear to see you miserable. Say the word and I'll climb down this very minute and unhitch these mules and send them on with the train to young Dick Butt. Then we'll make our way back to Salt Lake City as fast as we are able!"

Eliza, her eyes large, gazed back at the weak young man she had covenanted to love and cherish for time and all eternity, and whom she was now cursed to try and exist with. "Would you do that, Billy? Truly?"

"I would in a minute, and you know it!"

Eliza looked away as large tears broke free of her lashes. "I . . . I can't let you do it. I know I'm supposed to remain with you and to follow where you lead. It's just that I'm frightened, that's all. I'm terrified of leaving civilization so far behind. And I . . . I can't bear the thought of another trek through winter snows."

"It'll only be six weeks, Eliza." Billy reached over and took his wife by the hand. "According to the reports from the Potato Valley boys who were sent to scout our trail, we'll have no difficulty getting to the San Juan by Christmas. They do say it's warmer there, too. And besides, we'll have snug cabins put up in no time. And who knows? Maybe the weather will hold good the entire journey just like it is today."

Reaching up, Eliza brushed at her tears with the corner of her shawl. "It . . . is a beautiful day," she responded, doing her best to smile. "And I don't want us to turn back now, Billy. Since we've both been called, then I suppose the Lord truly does want us on this mission. I'll just have to tough it out as best I can."

"Sticky-to-ity," Billy replied as he squeezed Eliza's hand tenderly. "That's what Brother Nielson calls it. And we'll do it, hon-bun. Together we'll make it to the San Juan just fine."

And with all his heart, Billy believed that they would.

———o—o—o———

Headwaters of Plateau Creek, Grand Mesa, Colorado

"Who is it who comes?" Beogah asked as he strained his neck to see down the slope and through the trees.

"I do not know, *suck-ige*." Sowagerie, too, was trying to see without getting much closer. "I heard the dogs barking, saw some of the People *pun-ker-o*, making a run, and you know the rest. Why is it, Beogah, that you always think I know more about a thing than you?"

"I think no such thing," Beogah snapped defensively. "But you, well, since we came to this place you have changed, Sowagerie. It started with those three *nan-zitch* who stopped our games. After that you became a great thinker; that, and a great washer. Now everything about you must be washed clean, all the time. Then two suns back I saw you seated near the warrior Canalla and others, and only yesterday you ran right up to that old Meeker woman, the one who makes much water with her eyes even though she has gone to the lodge of patient old Nevarno to be his wife, and you spoke to her."

"I asked her if she was content," Sowagerie responded with a smirk. "Then I put my hand on her. I did it to mock her, and to show I was not afraid because she is white."

"Truly," Beogah breathed, "you do things I would not dare to do, my brother. Is the white *nan-zitch* content?"

"She told me in the tongue of the People, which surprised me, that she is not content, and that she expects the white soldiers to come and *wite-ung-i-nunk,* make us all captive and carry us away. I made a laughing at her foolishness."

"Perhaps she is right. Perhaps that is who comes yonder."

Sowagerie snickered. "Perhaps, *suck-ige.* But I do not think so. I have not heard the thunder of the man Canalla's big gun, nor have I heard the war cry of Nicaagat. It is in my mind to think it is a party of the People, and that there is no great cause for alarm.

"On the other hand, if they are white soldiers then the silence may be because our warriors have planned an ambush and do not yet wish their presence known. Wagh! If only I were a little older, a little larger in body."

Beogah stared. "You would dare to fight the white soldiers, my brother?"

"Of a certainty!" Sowagerie declared haughtily. "I would do it now, if I could."

"But . . . why?"

Sowagerie did not turn his head. "Because I have never seen a man *e-iqueay,* is why. Perhaps if these are foolish whites, then Canalla or another of our great warriors will take their lives. It is a thing I would like to see, or even better, to be a part of."

Awed by the power of Sowagerie's reasoning as well as the courage of his position, Beogah grew still. This one truly was a new brother, he knew, one whose heart had somehow changed and grown older.

Moments later, as the mounted men moved into sight, Beogah discovered that his older brother might well turn out to be right. It was indeed a band of warriors who appeared below. But with them, near the front of the group, was a white man who was riding as if he had no fear.

Beogah wondered at that and even thought of asking his brother's opinion of it. But when Sowagerie suddenly sped off down through the trees toward the approaching horsemen, he had no more time to wonder or to question. Not especially if he was going to keep up with him.

———o—o—o———

Cedar City

"Vell, Brudder und Sister Foreman, ve're off to de San Vaun. Are you ready?"

"As ever!" Billy called in response to Jens Nielson's booming greeting. At the same time, he was forced to rein in his mules, which seemed suddenly determined to commence the journey. And he was surprised at how difficult they were to hold back.

"Goot! Goot!" the tall old Danishman shouted as he pushed a long stick into the backs of his lumbering oxen. "Ve are all in fine spirits, by yimminy. Und I guess, ven ve yoin de udders in a day or so, dey vill feel de same."

Again he prodded with his stick, and Billy and Eliza watched in amazement as the two Nielson wagons, the second driven by Joseph, Jens' son who had been on the exploring expedition, rumbled past. Each of the two wagons was loaded to the hilt, and it was easy to see that Brother Nielson had moved more than once and was familiar with the process. Besides the wagons, several head of cattle and horses ranged alongside, and the younger Nielson children, either on foot or on horseback, kept them all moving.

Wagon after wagon followed the Nielsons—Sarah and Sammy Cox, George and Alice Urie, the Mackelprangs, and the families of the Perkins brothers, Benjamin and Hyrum. Lemuel Redd with his family, as well as his father, Lemuel Redd, Sr., whom everyone affectionately called Pap, came next, followed by old Isaac Haight and John and Harriet Jane Gower. And along with the wagons moved an astounding assortment of livestock—snorting horses, bellowing cattle, spare oxen, a couple of pigs that were roped to a wagon and being dragged squealing behind, dozens of barking dogs, and all sorts of caged or penned poultry that were adding to the general din. There were also the shouting and squealing of men, women, and children; the snapping of whips and rattling of chains; the screeching of wagons not adequately greased; and the constant protesting of iron tires being dragged across rocks and various other hardened road surfaces.

"Ho, Billy!" Kumen Jones shouted as his wagon came next. "Pull in front of Mary and me, and let's travel together!"

"I'm not sure I know what I'm doing!" Billy shouted back. "I've never driven mules before."

"They're just like horses," Kumen replied, reining in his teams. "Shake your lines a couple of times, and it'll be Ho! for the San Juan for you and Eliza."

With a wide grin Billy took his lines in both hands and, with Eliza gripping the side of the seat and expecting she knew not what, Billy shook.

"He-yaw!" he shouted gleefully as he shook the lines again, and without another hint the lead mules dug in, the wheelers leaned into their lines, and without a squeak or a groan the loaded wagon lurched forward and moved easily into the ruts created by those who had just passed by.

"He-yaw!" Billy shouted again, swinging his hat in the air as he did so. "We're off, Eliza, for sure and for good. Hold on tight, for like Kumen said, it's Ho! for the San Juan for the bunch of us!"

PART TWO

THE JOURNEY BEGINS

11

Paragonah Fields

"Eliza, hon-bun, you can't mean that."

"Oh, yes I can! And I do! Not one more step, Billy Foreman; not one more inch will I go on this fool's mission unless you agree."

The afternoon sun was high and hot, and the host of flies were sticky, as they became in the fall. The dust was an inch or more deep where Eliza was standing, and probably that deep everywhere else in the fenced fields. Worse, because of the churning wheels and hooves and feet of the pioneer company, it was now lifting in billowing clouds that hung like a pall above them all, drifting in the eddying air and finally settling down and sifting through every wagon, every article of clothing, every pot of water, every cooking kettle or pan, and every person in the encampment.

These fields were where the people of Paragonah raised their crops, and they were fenced to keep out the livestock that roamed freely, seeking pasture. But now that harvest was over, the members of the San Juan Mission had been given permission to camp in the fields and to bring their livestock in with them, thus corralling everything and everyone into one five-acre area. It was that close confinement with the hundreds of animals that was causing the dust, and it was the dust, after an entire day of trying to avoid breathing it and choking to death on it, that had finally become Eliza's last straw.

Dick and Parley Butt's four mules, finally freed of their burden of harnesses and wagon, were rolling in the dust nearby, raising clouds from under their bodies in every direction. Dogs and children

113

were barking and screaming and chasing each other willy-nilly around and around the wagons and raising more dust, animals were bawling and whinnying and braying and adding to the cacophony of sounds, and the smells—well, it was altogether more than a civilized woman should be expected to have to deal with! And for one, Eliza was through!

"Do you understand what I'm demanding?" she asked through the dainty kerchief she held before her nose and mouth. She was making the tone of her voice as icy as humanly possible, not only because she was seething with pent-up anger and frustration, but also because she didn't want any further arguments or conversations with this sorry little man who was already starting to think himself a pioneer.

"Yes, Eliza," Billy stated humbly as he fumbled with his hat. "You want the extra canvas thrown over the wagon and stretched out here to the side, with the tent poles at the corners to hold it up and give you shelter."

"To give *us* shelter, Billy, from all this fool dust, from the sun, and from rain and snow if we happen to run into them later on. Why, it took me two hours of brushing last night just to get the dust out of my hair! I want an awning for protection from the dust, and from every other element of nature. Do you understand?"

"Yes, hon-bun. But . . . stretching that big old canvas over the wagon every night is a pile of work, something I don't know if I have time to do, what with chores, gathering firewood, and all. I reckon we're talking an hour each time, making two hours a day. Folks aren't going to want to wait two hours extra for us. Besides, if I use the tent poles for your . . . I mean, our awning, then what will I use to put up the tent for sleeping?"

Eliza sighed in exasperation. "First of all, put the canvas in place and tie one side down to the wagon permanently—the side opposite from the door you built for me. That way it will always be in place, and all you'll have to do is stretch out the side above the door, place the poles under the corners, and tie it down. It should never take longer than five or ten minutes. Besides which, while we're traveling, it will give extra protection. Because it's so large, the sides will drape down and cover the puckerholes both front and rear, keeping out the elements.

"As for the tent, I will not be sleeping in it again. Last night was enough. I haven't slept on the hard ground since I crossed the plains—well, except for that miserable two weeks traveling into this wilderness with you last spring—and I won't sleep on it again. From now on my bed is going to be on the sacks of seed grain in the wagon, and you may join me as you wish."

Billy looked stunned. "The seed grain? But . . . but that's where our furniture—"

Smiling thinly, Eliza nodded. "Yes, and that brings up the rest of it. Once the canvas is in place each night, you will remove our table from the wagon and place it beneath the awning. We'll also need two of our four chairs, more if we should be expecting company, and my wooden rocker. Oh, yes, and the small cowhide trunk so I can properly complete my toilette each evening. That will clear the seed grain so we can make a proper bed on top of it."

"I . . . I'll do it for you, hon-bun." Billy sounded dazed. "Only, I don't hardly understand why—"

"Civilization, Billy! I am a civilized lady from a civilized nation. Even here in the wastes of Utah I've been a civilized woman of some substance and position for most of the past twenty-five years, and I have no intention of stopping and reverting to savagery just because I've agreed to accompany you on this fool mission! Therefore, each evening for the duration of this journey, I will set my table as a proper lady should. My lace tablecloth will cover it, and my serviettes will be folded and in place. My last two settings of my grandmother's china, which are all I could carry in that fool handcart I dragged across the plains, will be set out properly, with appropriate crystal and silver. We will not eat a meal unless we eat it at that table—unless we eat it in a proper and civilized manner."

Eliza was amused at Billy's expression, but she allowed no trace of her amusement to enter her voice. "No more sitting on wagon tongues trying to balance a plate on our laps," she continued, "no more squatting on rocks or logs near the fire like a couple of uncouth heathens. I will remain a proper, civilized lady for the duration of this expedition, Billy Foreman, or I will accompany you no further. Is that understood?"

And to Eliza's immense satisfaction, Billy humbly nodded. Then, settling his hat back on his head and adjusting his dust-clouded spectacles, the poor, bumbling man set to work to do her bidding.

———◇—◇—◇———

"Did you happen to notice the Foremans' wagon?"

The three women were standing on the bank of the irrigation ditch, their water pails filled for the evening and now resting on the earth at their feet. The sun had set, easing the heat, and the three were taking a brief rest before darkness settled over the camp and the bugle was blown calling them to prayers.

"I did!" one responded gleefully. "I watched it from my own wagon—Billy scrambling all over his wagon to stretch that huge canvas tarp and get it tied down the way he did. What on earth has gotten into him, do you suppose?"

"Him?" The third woman snorted. "It had nothing to do with him, and you can bet on it! It's that strange woman he married. She's the one behind all this, I swear it!"

"Why, what on earth do you mean?"

The woman smiled knowingly. "Well, you obviously didn't see what they put under that tarp once he got it stretched out."

"I couldn't believe my eyes!" the first woman chimed in, her voice filled with disgust. "There she was, just like some high-society prima donna, making her husband pull all that furniture out, and then setting her table all prim and fancy with lace cloth and china and crystal and everything else, just as if they were expecting the president of the Church to drop in for supper!"

"Or the king of England," another declared as they all snickered. "After all, she is a proper English lady, you know!"

"Oh, yes, that's right! What's her name again?"

"Eliza," one of the women replied, putting a harsh British accent to it. "Eliza the blooming Queen of England Foreman, is what I say she ought to be called."

Now the three were laughing outright, truly enjoying themselves.

"I feel sorry for her husband, though," one finally said after getting her breath again. "She'll work that poor man to death before we ever reach the San Juan. You mark my words and see if she doesn't!"

"If she does, it'll be his fault as much as hers. The little mouse ought to stand up to her, like any normal man would, and put a stop to her nonsense."

"Well, don't expect that from Billy Foreman. He's a nice enough fellow, I suppose, but he follows that wife of his around like a little whipped puppy. I declare, the way folks say she talks to him. Worse, I hear sometimes he even combs her hair out for her of an evening—"

"No!"

"Well, that's what they say!"

"Sometimes I wish my husband was a little more like that."

"Hush, woman! Don't even think such a thing! I thank God every day that my husband's a man, a real man!"

"But there's nothing wrong with a real man being kind and tender to his wife."

"There is in the way Billy Foreman does it. It's just as wrong as the way she rules and reigns over him. It's what comes of a short young man marrying a taller, older woman. I say it happens every time! They're a strange couple, I'm telling you, and I can't begin to imagine what they're doing with us on this expedition!"

"Well, the Lord has a reason for making the calls he does. It will surely be the same for Billy and Eliza Foreman. There's a reason why they're with us."

"Humph! To be the company clowns, I suppose. They're making a fine start at it, I'll tell you that."

The three all laughed again, more quietly this time. And then they picked up their pails of water and separated into the dusk.

12

Top of Little Creek Canyon

"One thing about . . . chopping wood," Billy panted as he lowered his ax for a moment to rest on the handle. "Of a cold morning, it does warm a body up."

It was early, only barely after daybreak, and fog shrouded the encampment of wagons, a chilling fog so thick that Billy could see no more than six or seven feet in any direction. The night before, after a hard day's push up steep and sidling switchback roads, his party of missionaries had finally reached the head of Little Creek Canyon. On a couple of acres of nearly level ground, the Parowan and Paragonah companies had already stopped for the night, and without hesitation old Jens Nielson had directed the Cedar and New Harmony companies to join them and begin the process of getting acquainted.

Billy smiled as he recalled the riotous good time of singing, dancing, and speechifying all had enjoyed. But now morning was here, too quickly, it seemed, and he and several others had gathered to chop firewood at a large blowdown of dead timber that lay nearby.

"Say, Billy," Kumen Jones's voice cut through the fog from no more than twenty unseen feet away. "You go to sleep over there?"

"Not hardly, though I admit the idea has merits."

Joe Nielson chuckled from a few feet away in another direction, where he, too, had paused in his chopping. "It was a short night, all right. But Pa says I'm young and hadn't ought to notice it."

118

"You are," Billy grunted as he toed the log he'd been cutting, rolling it so his axe could get a better bite.

"Not young enough, then," Joe grumbled. "Billy, if you don't mind my asking, what's this I hear about you and your wife setting out your furniture of a night?"

"Mary and I have been wondering about that, too," Kumen admitted. "Seems like a lot of extra work."

Billy swung with his ax and took a deep bite out of the dried log. "It is. But I'll tell you, boys, Eliza suffered a lot sleeping on the cold ground when she emigrated to Zion with the Martin Handcart Company, and the thought of doing it again is more than she can stand."

"A man can't much blame her for that."

"That's what I thought. So if it'll help her, I'm perfectly willing to clear the furniture off that seed grain every night of this expedition. And to tell the truth, those bags of grain do make a comfortable bed."

"But that extra canvas awning?" Kumen pressed. "Why that? And why the linen and china and the rest of that fancy fooferaw she sets out of an evening?"

Billy chuckled. "I married a civilized woman, boys, a true English lady. She told me she was perfectly willing to take up this mission into the wilderness with me, but not at the expense of her manners or her gentility. If she does nothing else for the next six weeks, she says those trappings of civilization will help her remember who she really is. The awning is merely to protect her while she's using them."

"Seems reasonable," Joe Nielson declared. "And I reckon in one way or another most of us are the same. Sammy Cox can't go to bed without at least a saw or two on his fiddle; every morning you can hear Ben Perkins singing the same Welsh song; and Will Goddard circles his camp with that big mastiff of his at least once every night. I know, because the durn thing wakes me up with its growling."

"We all have our peculiarities," Kumen agreed. "Does having a double canvas cover help much while you're traveling?"

"With the puckerholes covered front and back the way they are," Billy responded, "it does cut down on the dust we get inside. It may

119

also help a little if we run into any storms, though of course I'm not yet sure about that."

"Well, whether we do or not, Billy, you've rigged up an ingenious way of providing an effective shelter for you and your wife to enjoy whenever we're in camp. Mary and I may be visiting more often than you'd like."

"And me." Joe paused to drag another log into the clear. "In fact, Pa says that you . . . Say, do you fellers hear something?"

In the gray gloom, Billy, Kumen, and the others paused, their attention given totally to listening. Back at the camp Billy could hear subdued voices as the people stirred about their wagons. Here and there a child cried, women were either scolding young ones or singing softly at their chores, cattle and oxen were moving about and making their customary noises, chains jangled as men laid out their harnesses and other gear, and somewhere nearby a flock of song sparrows were trilling their greetings to the dawn. Other than that, Billy could hear nothing.

"There," Joe called again, his voice more urgent, "that's hoof-beats. Somebody's coming!"

"Not somebody," a man's voice muttered from the other side of the deadfall. "You listen, boys. That's a whole lot of somebodies out there, and you can bet they ain't coming slow."

Now Billy could hear the distant rumble, and even he could tell that a huge number of horses were coming toward them at a hard gallop.

"It's Indians, boys!" another voice shouted. "Grab your rifles or we'll all be slaughtered!"

"He's right," someone else called fearfully. "Take up your guns!"

Billy didn't move as the sound of scurrying feet moved away from the deadfall and in the direction of the road. "Kumen?" he called as the thundering of hundreds of hooves boomed nearer.

"I'm here, Billy. Don't get rattled."

"I won't. But I was worrying about young Joseph—"

"I'm right here," Joe Nielson replied. "Pa don't hold much with pointing guns at people, red or otherwise, and I don't have one with me anyway."

"Get your rifles up, boys," a man called softly from the road.

"We'll give 'em one warning shout, and then we'll let 'er rip with powder and ball. Ready?"

"We're ready," somebody growled.

"As ever," another responded.

"Good, because here those red sons come!"

And as Billy watched spellbound, the dim forms of running horses suddenly materialized out of the mist.

"Halt!" the man in the road shouted abruptly. "Halt there, or we shoot!"

There was an instant's pause, and then the voice of a young man came booming back from the fog. "You durn fools!" he shouted angrily. "It's me, George Decker, and I'm just bringing up your loose horses! Now quiet down or you'll spook 'em all!"

The fog thinned as the men in the road scrambled to get out of the way of the herd of horses, one hundred and fifty of them loose and one mounted. In minutes they were past and young Decker was slowing them to graze on the other side of the encampment. Abruptly Billy remembered his wood. Stooping, he gathered up an armful, and as he turned back toward camp, Kumen moved past him to stand in front of the man who'd done the shouting about taking up arms.

"I thought we'd been called on a mission to bring peace to the Indians," Kumen said quietly while Billy watched in amazement. "If you think you can do that at the end of your rifle, brother, you're on a different mission than I've been called to."

And without waiting for a response from the subdued and embarrassed fellow missionary, Kumen turned and strode purposefully toward his wagon.

13

Tuesday, October 28, 1879

Head of Bear Valley Creek

Eliza didn't believe she'd tasted anything better in her life. Kneeling again, she lowered a battered tin cup someone had left for that purpose into the icy water from the small stream, drinking cupful after cupful. Surely, she thought as she satisfied the thirst she'd accumulated during the grueling, dusty day, there could be no better water in all the world. If only she wasn't forced to drink it from such an abominably ugly cup—

Pulling herself to her feet, Eliza turned on her crutch and moved awkwardly back toward where Billy had placed the wagon, the filled water pail sloshing in her free hand. The high mountain valley where they were camped was beautiful, she had to admit, with dark green timber on the hills contrasting sharply with the brilliant yellow aspens and acres of grass and wild hay grown golden with autumn. Though the sun had not set, the air was already crisp, and, as on the morning before, Eliza expected that, come daylight, there would be ice on the water left in the pail. She didn't mind that. In fact, she expected it. But it would be a great relief to be on the San Juan and snug in a cabin before the full force of winter was upon them.

It was the start of their second week of traveling, and so she'd endured an entire week of dust and dirt, preposterous conditions for a woman of gentility and breeding such as herself—a woman who was simply not willing to perform her daily toilette in such primitive conditions! Still, for now she had little choice in the matter, not at least for the next five weeks.

Again Eliza glanced at the mountain peaks that surrounded her. Billy loved their beauty and seemed always to be waxing eloquent about it—a useless emotion, in her considered opinion. Still, the going thus far had been easier than she had expected. Partly that was due to the good roads they'd followed past Parowan and up Little Creek Canyon, and partly it was due to the wonderful animals Dick and Parley Butt had lent them for the journey.

Of course, if Mary were asked, she'd be quick to say that a tiny bit of the ease of Billy and Eliza's traveling was because Billy was actually starting to learn a bit about pioneering. What Mary didn't know, unfortunately, was that even though of a morning Eliza fed the chickens, milked the cow, and baited the glass-eyed mare and roped her to the wagon, it still took Billy longer than that to harness and hitch the mules. And every morning so far one or another of the men had "happened" to drop by just in time to help. It was all so humiliating to Eliza, who felt even more humiliated because Billy accepted their help eagerly, warmly, as though he were a child and not a man.

On the other hand, last night her husband had managed to properly hang the harnesses out on the rear of the wagon, and this morning Hansen Bayless, a young man from Paragonah who'd joined the company back in Little Creek Canyon, had praised him mightily for his layout. So he was learning, Eliza admitted candidly, and might someday pass for something less than a total fool.

Trouble was, Eliza also admitted candidly, her own plan to make Billy feel loved and to make the others in the company see that she loved him wasn't exactly working out. Oh, it had worked pretty well for a few days. Very well, as a matter of fact, for as long as they'd remained in Cedar. But now that they were on the road, Billy's foolishness and ineptness were bothering her more and more, and her mental criticisms were once again making their way into her vocabulary.

Of course, perhaps it was better that she was being honest—

"Mercy, woman," Mary Jones said as Eliza came around the end of the wagon, "you shouldn't be packing water that way. Here, let me carry it for you—"

"I can do it myself!" Eliza snapped, surprising herself as much as it surprised her friend. "I . . . I mean, there's no need, Mary. I've been carrying water all my life, and even though we're in the mountains, nothing has changed."

"I didn't mean it had," Mary replied as she fell into step. "My folks taught me that helping others is a virtue, and that we all need to look for ways to be virtuous. You're my friend, Eliza, and I just wanted to do something nice for you."

"Well, thank you for that. And I . . . I'm sorry I barked at you. Uh . . . is your wagon next to ours again?"

"Behind you." Mary's smile returned. "Shall we cook at the same fire again?"

"It does save firewood. I assume Billy will be dragging some in pretty soon."

"Kumen's out gathering fuel too. But with our party grown as large as it is, firewood might come a little more dearly. I declare, Eliza, the way folks are joining in, we're turning into a regular emigrant train."

Mary was right. As Eliza had counted wagons a little earlier, she'd been surprised to discover just under sixty, at least half of which had joined since they'd climbed into the mountains—wagons owned by folks primarily from Parowan and Paragonah. Each night since starting, Sammy Cox had blown his trumpet to call prayers, and it was in the assemblies that Eliza had been introduced to folks such as Joseph and Harriet Ann Barton, as well as Joe's brother Amasa, Hansen Bayless, and the entire Decker clan. Additionally, she'd heard about the large Dunton and Robb families; Samuel and Ann Rowley; Silas Smith, who'd been appointed captain of the company by Church authorities; George Hobbs; and Henry and Sarah Ann Holyoak. Of course, there were the Butt brothers, Dick and Parley, and in Bear Valley they'd been joined by Charlie Walton, his wife Jane, and their three little ones.

Of a truth she knew none of these people and didn't really want to know them. It was enough to know that the company seemed to be growing daily, and that others were expected to join them by the time they arrived at Escalante and the jumping-off point for the San Juan. In fact, Captain Smith had told them during assembly the night before that his assistant, Platte D. Lyman, was coming from the Oak

Creek settlement out west of Scipio, and his party would likely be one of the last to arrive.

At each gathering for evening prayer, hymns were sung, instructions given, and prayers offered, after which Sammy Cox and Charlie Walton laid down their trumpet and cornet in favor of fiddles, which they could saw with the best. And that brief hour of dancing, to Eliza's way of thinking, was the highlight of each day.

Despite the fact that she'd never learned to play any sort of instrument, Eliza loved music. Tunes filled her mind from daylight to dark, mostly nameless ditties that she made up as they progressed. Occasionally she even gave voice to them, though her spontaneous lyrics were worse than awful. Neither was she much of a singer, as any who sat beside her during meetings could attest.

On the other hand, she had a great sense of rhythm, and she had danced since she was old enough to walk. It was one of the things that had sustained her during the loneliness of her years in Salt Lake City, and the only thing she absolutely hated about being crippled. Still, she *could* dance, by herself with the aid of her crutch, or with a partner if he held her strongly enough. But Billy, she had quickly learned, was not adept enough at dancing, or coordinated enough, to keep up with her and support her. And she wasn't humble enough— at least she was sufficiently honest with herself to admit this—to dance in public with the aid of her crutch.

But the music still played in her head, and even on the sideline she could glory in the sweet-sounding fiddles—

"Mercy sakes, Eliza, where are you tonight? Off somewhere in dreamland?"

Blinking, Eliza smiled wearily. "I must be." Taking her skillet from the wagon, she sat in one of the chairs Billy had unloaded earlier and began slicing potatoes and an onion.

"Handy, having Billy unload your furniture like that."

"I find it helpful," Eliza acknowledged.

"Kumen says it's so you can sleep on your grain instead of in a tent on the ground."

"That's part of it," Eliza answered, wondering that Mary would even dare to make Eliza's private affairs a part of her business. "The other part of it is to keep me from becoming a savage even though I'm forced to live like one!"

Mary cocked an inquisitive eyebrow. "Are you implying something about the rest of us?"

"Only if the shoe fits," Eliza replied nastily.

After a second's hesitation, Mary laughed. "Well, whether it fits or not, I want you to know, Eliza Foreman, that I like your idea. I think your settings are beautiful, and it warms my heart of an evening to look toward your wagon and see your linens all spread out and everything so wonderfully organized."

"Thank you. Perhaps I'll be starting a trend."

"Perhaps." Mary was smiling sweetly. "But I won't be part of it, Eliza. In my opinion Kumen has enough to do in establishing camp each night. That would simply add too much to his burdens."

"Well," Eliza declared cattily, "he did come by a little earlier, you know. To help Billy unload."

"I know." Mary continued smiling. "I sent him."

With the air almost sparking between them, they dropped the subject, and in silence Mary mixed some dough by dropping a little water into a sack of flour. Deftly kneading it into a ball, she pulled it out, kneaded in salt and soda as it sat in the pan, and covered it.

"Well," she said brightly as Kumen and Billy walked up a few awkward moments later, their arms loaded with chopped wood, "here we sit, two cooks in need of a fire."

"And here we are," Kumen replied with a wink at his wife, "two flunkies in need of some grub. You hungry, Billy?"

"As ever," Billy smiled. "Like Pap Redd says, my stomach feels so shrunk up it wouldn't chamber a liver pill."

Kumen chuckled. "Or my tapeworm's hollerin' for fodder."

"Where do people come up with all those sayings?" Mary asked when she'd stopped giggling.

Billy was kneeling at a pile of twigs he'd built, a sulfur match in his hand. After he'd struck it and got the twigs burning, he leaned back on his heels. "I asked Pap that the other night, Mary, and he told me it came out by spontaneous combustion."

"The way some of our boys talk to their teams," Kumen acknowledged, "it ought to combust something or other. I declare, some of their language would sizzle bacon or peel the hide off a Gila monster."

"And that," Billy grinned as he rose to his feet and took up the milk pail, "is a perfect example of spontaneous combustion. Eliza, I'll be back after I've emptied Hepsi's udder."

"She ought to be udderly tickled by that," Kumen laughed as he followed Billy into the rapidly growing darkness.

"As much as walking through tall grass would udderly tickle her, I reckon." Billy chuckled. In another moment they were out of earshot.

"At least they seem to have become good friends," Eliza said as she fed the fire dried wood that would burn to a good bed of coals.

"Kumen thinks the world of Billy," Mary responded as she adjusted the lid on her dutch oven. "I do too. He always has a smile on his face, and he comes up with the most interesting ideas. Why, just this morning he was showing Kumen aspen leaves, some green and some yellow and some still in between. We've always been told that frost turns them yellow, but Billy thinks the yellow is always there and that after the first frosts the green just sort of withdraws down the stem, leaving them yellow."

"Fascinating," Eliza declared icily, recalling a similar pointless discussion when Billy had shown her his leaves, and her own abrupt ending of the same.

For a long moment Mary was silent. "Are . . . uh . . . are things any better with you?"

"Things are fine."

"Eliza, this is Mary speaking. Your friend."

Bleakly Eliza stared into the flames, knowing that her vow to fool the company had failed and was at an end. "I know, Mary," she finally replied, "and I'm sorry. It's just that, well, I don't know if anything will ever change. I certainly don't expect it to. I'm me and Billy's Billy, and that's that!"

"He's doing better and better on the trail, Eliza."

"Of course you'd say that. But he has no pride, no shame!"

"Is that a good thing, or a bad thing?"

Eliza pushed some burning limbs to the side of the fire with the end of her crutch and then placed her skillet, to which she had added some slices of bacon, atop the coals. "Oh, I know what the scriptures say about being prideful," she responded, "and I suppose that's bad. But lawsy sakes, Mary! A man needs a little spine to be a man. He needs to do for himself and not always be leaning on others!"

Mary, surprised as always at the anger in her friend's voice, kept her gaze on her dutch oven, which she had placed in the fire and upon which she was piling hot embers. "And you think that's what Billy does?" she finally asked.

"I know it is!"

In the silence that followed, the fire crackled and settled, sending showers of sparks high into the darkening mountain air. Around the two women, at other fires and at other wagons, people laughed and visited and enjoyed the friendship and even intimacy a warm fire seemed to bring to the missionary company. But at the fire between the two wagons, a troubled Mary Jones was not laughing, and a ramrod-straight Eliza Foreman gripped her crutch and stared into the flames, her anger and contempt as palpable in the night air as the sparks from the fire.

---o—o—o---

The Springs, Trout Water Canyon

Sowagerie sat without moving, his back against some brush, while his mind thought long thoughts about the past three weeks of his life. While the dark clouds of what promised to be a major storm churned overhead, his mother and the mother of his brother Beogah were both laboring tirelessly to establish what all hoped would be at least a semipermanent camp. A little way off the wives of Big-Mouth Mike were establishing a camp of their own, and fifty yards down the canyon the women of two other men were doing the same.

These four and perhaps sixty others, both Northern and Southern Utes, had defied and finally spurned old Quinket—these and their children, Sowagerie among them. Not many, the youth thought, who had not been cowards in the face of Ouray's threats or the foolish boasts of the white man Adams.

Still amazed that it had turned out so, Sowagerie thought back to the two days of councils as the lone white man had put at defiance the most powerful warriors of the entire Ute nation. Without even a weapon he had defied them, and in the end the warriors had handed over to him the three women and the children. Even more amazing to the youth was the fact that the warriors of Ouray had threatened to side with the whites and hunt down and put under the grass the men of the People who opposed them. Sowagerie could not comprehend such a thing, and he had been stunned when the warriors around the fire, one by one, had buried their blades in the earth.

"Let us all make a fleeing to the San Juan," Mike had fumed once the knives had been buried and the men removed to their wickiups. "The pony soldiers will never find us in that country, and Ouray and his warriors will not dare to follow us there."

"Humph!" Colorow had grunted. "That is not a good country. Even *te-ah* the deer gets lost in those canyons. As for these called the Pahutes, well, they are too *katz-te-suah* even to know they are lost."

"Not so," Chee had argued angrily while many around him had laughed. "Those rocks and canyons are our home. We know them as the pack rat knows his burrow, or *quan-a-tich* the eagle the sky-trails that lead to food. I tell you, brothers, there is freedom in that country that you will no longer enjoy in these shining mountains. More, the people called mormonee are coming to that country with more horses than a man can count. These mormonee are like women. They are filled with fear and will not fight. Soon that country will be fine for raiding!"

The mocking of the Utes, especially Colorow and Canalla, had become loud after that, and stung beyond words Chee and Mike and the others had fled from the encampment on Plateau Creek.

Traveling southwestward at a killing pace, the several families of Pahute rebels had crossed Geyser Pass south of Haystack Mountain in the La Sals. Skirting Boren Mesa, they had followed Brumley Ridge to where it dropped off into Spanish Valley and Pack Creek. Heading southwestward around the northernmost of the two mesas that would be named after the *shaman* Bridger Jack and past the natural arch at Kane Springs, they had crossed Muleshoe Canyon and the northern end of Flat Iron Mesa to descend by a precipitous and secret trail into Trout Water Canyon. Now they were camped in the head of the canyon with the dark and forbidding bulk of what would soon be called Hatch Point looming above them to the west.

But Sowagerie didn't worry about Hatch Point or any of the rest of the geographically forbidding landscape that yet lay between them and the San Juan. His father and Mike knew all the trails, all the passes, all the springs and seeps of water, all the seemingly dead-end canyons and impossibly steep bluffs and ridges that made up the land he and the others called home. More, he was coming to know these things as well. For truly Sowagerie loved the land, its harshness and its softness, and he knew that, if the Pahutes could just entice the pony soldiers, or even the warriors of the weakling Ouray, to enter this land to do battle, they could all be *puck-ki* with no trouble at all.

And he would do it, too! He, Sowagerie, would do battle with them all and be victorious! Only he was still considered a boy.

"My father," he asked later as all sat eating the meat from a dog his mother had killed and boiled into a stew, "why is it that so many of the People are taking upon themselves the names of whites?"

"Who knows such a thing?" old Chee grunted. "Perhaps you should ask Mike. It is a thing he has done."

Feeling intensely curious, young Sowagerie did just that and received a kick from the sullen warrior for his efforts. Mike was notorious for his bad temper, and Sowagerie and Beogah had in times past made a game for themselves by seeing just how far they could push him with their childish jibes. And so, far from being upset that he'd been kicked, Sowagerie accepted it as part of the process and refused to leave the area of Mike's wickiup until he received the information he'd come for.

A sudden rain squall swept over the canyon, and Sowagerie continued to huddle outside Mike's wickiup, shivering and waiting. Finally, taking pity, one of Mike's wives made the sign for him to enter, and with a secret smile Sowagerie did.

"Why is it you carry the white man's name?" he was finally allowed to ask after much more than an appropriate period of silence.

"It is better than *katz-ne-ate*," Big-Mouth Mike growled sullenly. "It is better than no name."

Not understanding this at all, Sowagerie stared into the flames of the small fire that sputtered and hissed just beyond the door opening. The man was a fool, he was thinking. Everyone had a name, and some, like himself, had two. And he knew for a fact that Mike had had a name, a good one, before calling himself Mike. So what did—

"The People have lost their power," Mike continued without warning. "The whites have become like fleas on a dog's back, crawling about our country wherever they wish, sucking all the blood out of the People and killing us without taking our lives. They have taken our power."

Surprised by such a thought, Sowagerie made the sign that he understood, though in fact that was not strictly true. Nevertheless, Mike accepted it and grunted.

"You will see. Those fools who gave back the women and children to the white man Adams think they will now be loved by the whites. Wagh! It will not be so but is only one more sign that they are already *e-i,* dead. Soon they will be driven from the Shining Mountains, and we and the few who are already in our country will be the only warriors of the People who will remain alive.

"This man," and Mike thumped himself in the chest as he spoke, "knows this thing, and so do many who were at the council-fire. It is why, when a white man gave me his name, I took it and kept it. Now I have a little of their power. It is why Canalla allows himself to be called Johnson, and old Quinket, Douglas. Even Sapiah, who is a chief, has taken the name Buckskin Charlie. In this small way we have taken a little something from the whites, and soon it will give us power to take more."

His eyes wide with sudden understanding, Sowagerie reached out and touched the white man's trousers and shirt that Big-Mouth Mike was wearing.

"Wagh!" Mike exclaimed with a massive grin. "You see how it is, boy? I wear the white man's *pe-mo,* his pants. I wear his shirt. I wear his *katz-oats,* his hat. I wear his boots. I carry *ankage,* his rifle. All these things give me his power. All these things tell me the white man will never suck out all my *pwap,* my blood, and kill me while I am still walking about and not knowing I am dead.

"Ungh! And whenever I can, little green hair, I wash my hands in the *pwap* of the white man. With his blood smeared on my hands and face, I know I am alive. I spill his blood, I take his things, and with each doing I grow with power. That is why I am called Mike and nothing else. That is why, if I was not called Mike, I would have no name at all."

14

Saturday, November 1, 1879

The Road near Panguitch

The further the San Juan missionaries traveled toward their destination, the more amazing Eliza found them to be. Rather than growing fearful or despondent, they seemed to become happier, more enthusiastic, more excited by the prospects that lay ahead. Though for her things were the opposite, the others' joy seemed almost catching. For a fact, if she'd only felt better, Eliza thought with a heavy sigh, she might have forced herself to join in their gaiety.

Traveling northward up Bear Valley, they'd made a large turn to the east and then south again, following the general course of the Sevier River. Not far ahead now lay the town of Panguitch, where both the Nielson and Butt families had once lived. Already she could hear a brass band playing in honor of the first wagons, and she could see the townspeople lining the single street, cheering them on.

Gripping her crutch more tightly, Eliza pressed forward, walking to see if she could get rid of the sickness that had come upon her the past two or three days. Normally the sound of such music and celebrating would have perked her up considerably, but something was wrong with her, something that caused nausea to come and go, something that she feared was ague or dyspepsia or maybe even bilious colic. Eliza didn't know a lot about medicine, but she'd seen folks die of such things, and that worried her. After all, their illness had always started, or so she remembered, with bouts of nausea. Worse, she'd seen folks die just from getting near the vapors of such sick people, and she feared contaminating the entire company.

That morning, when her nausea had seemed worse than ever, she'd stirred together a mixture of ginger and soda in hot water, for someone had once told her that such a toddy was good for bilious colic. But the awful-tasting concoction had made her feel even worse, and so for most of the day she'd been walking, hoping the exercise would drive from her body whatever might be ailing her.

It seemed to be working, too. Except for feeling absolutely exhausted, she was some better, and maybe after tomorrow and the day's rest they always took on the Sabbath, she'd be well again. At least she hoped so.

"Say, hon-bun, did I tell you these mules have names?"

Eliza looked up at her husband, at the smile that seemed to perpetually crease his face, and again she felt the revulsion that came with just looking at him. Could he never be normal? Could he never just curse and complain a little, especially when things were going wrong? Of course, he was getting better at trail work—at harnessing, milking, driving, chopping, building fires—he truly seemed to take to such things. But even when he didn't, even when he had bad luck or made stupid mistakes, his smile never left him. His idiotic smile—

"Dick Butt reminded me of their names, last night. The left wheeler here is Little Bit, the right wheeler is Lots, and the lead mules are called Sign and Wonder." Billy chuckled. "The names make sense, too. Little Bit here, he only does a little bit of work unless he's forced into it by Lots, who of course does lots of work. And Sign and Wonder got their names because both Dick and Parley took it as a sign and a wonder from heaven when they got two lead mules that weren't stubborn and mean."

"And I suppose you can tell them apart?" Eliza asked sarcastically.

"Sure can," Billy responded, not noticing his wife's dour humor. "They're as easy to tell apart as four different people, especially once you get to know them. I hear tell we've got more folks joining the company here in Panguitch."

"What a surprise!" Eliza declared, thinking as she said it what utter fools some people could be. Here this little community was, set on a fine stream and surrounded by thick stands of timber—whole mountains of it. According to Jens Nielson, it had been two or three years since they'd experienced any sort of Indian troubles; the growing season was good, especially for wheat and hay; and considering the altitude, the winters were usually mild. Why would folks want to leave such a home, she wondered? Especially to go wandering off into a wilderness filled with savages both red and white—

"Fellow by the name of Dan Barney, his wife Laura, and a whole passel of young'uns will be joining us. Supposedly Amasa Lyman's here, but I reckon he'll wait and join his brother Platte when he comes through in a few days, trying to catch us. Then there's a standing bishop, a fellow by the name of George Sevy, and his second wife Margaret, who Jens says folks call Maggie. His daughter Hannah is coming, too, and she's married to a fellow name of James Pace, who's related to the New Harmony Paces who travel up near the front of the company."

"How do you remember all these names?"

Billy's smile, if possible, grew wider. "I just listen when folks talk, Eliza. I reckon that's about all it takes."

Shaking her head, Eliza continued walking in silence, the wagon bumping and grinding beside her. Watching the front wheel, counting its revolutions by a flag she'd tied around one of the spokes, was a mesmerizing trick she'd learned crossing the plains with the handcart company, and it still helped keep her mind from her own miseries. But today her mind wouldn't stop wandering no matter what she tried, and time and again she came back to the pile of trouble she was in.

"Oh, lawsy," she breathed as she skirted a huge clump of sagebrush that grew beside the road, moving a little distance away from Billy and the wagon, "why ever did the Lord want me to marry him? Why couldn't he have given me an honest-to-goodness man—"

The sound of shuffling hoofbeats behind her caused Eliza to turn, and with a groan she saw that she was being followed by Billy's fool glass-eyed mare.

"Billy!" she called. "Your mare's out of the herd again."

Looking around the side of the wagon, Billy chuckled. "Sure enough. Reckon I'll have to rope her and take her back tonight."

Reckon you will, Eliza thought dourly, mimicking the man's

foolish western drawl in her mind. Too bad he hadn't roped the mare and tied her to a tree before they left Cedar—either that or just shot the fool thing. Now, no matter how many times they put her with the company herd, she always—

"Eliza?"

Turning, Eliza wasn't surprised to see Mary Jones walking toward her, the shawl over her shoulders wrapped tightly against the cool November air. Though definitely colder, thus far the weather had held fair, and so their traveling had been without any real difficulty.

"Are you feeling better?" Mary asked as she drew abreast of Eliza.

"Considerably, thank you. I imagine this walking helps."

"It should. And the rest tomorrow will do you good, too. Kumen says we'll be camping in Panguitch fields southeast of town. I guess the folks hereabouts are planning on throwing a shindig for us tonight, in honor of our mission. Tomorrow we'll worship together, and Kumen says we'll be able to stock up on supplies come Monday morning, before we leave."

"Well," Eliza declared, "I suppose I'll miss the shindig. But I am looking forward to Sunday." For a change, she added in her mind.

"Billy's turning into a regular trailhand, isn't he."

Not replying, Eliza stared straight ahead.

"Fact is," Mary continued with enthusiasm, "he got his mules harnessed so fast this morning he had time to come back and help Kumen yoke up those fool oxen of Pa's. And look how he handles his teams, Eliza. I'll bet you're proud as punch of how well he's doing."

"Oh, Billy's a wonder, all right."

Carefully Mary looked at the older woman. "Your feelings haven't changed at all, have they."

"Would yours have changed?" Eliza asked bitterly.

"Yes. Yes, they would have."

"Fine, Mary! Then go and have good feelings somewhere else. I'm tired of your childish efforts to bring Billy and me back together, and I don't wish to discuss it any further."

For a moment the two walked in silence. The music of the brass band was getting louder, although the sound of people cheering as the missionary company with their new wagons, fresh teams, and new gear passed by was beginning to drown it out.

Suddenly, ignoring the hubbub and ruckus of the Panguitchites whom they were quickly moving toward, Mary reached out and took Eliza by the arm. "Eliza," she declared, "I've been thinking and praying and studying on this, and in spite of what you say you want, I can't be still any longer. I'm your friend, and you know that. I love you like I'd love the older sister I never had. That's why all along I've been trying to see this your way, trying to feel sorry because you married up with a weakling who was less than you deserved.

"But he isn't a weakling, Eliza. Billy's a fine man, strong in his own way and willing to learn. That day while we were packing, you told me all the things he did that made you ashamed of him. Well, as soon as he stopped doing them, and he surely did, you found more things to be shamed by. That's still going on, Eliza, and you know it.

"What I'm saying, I suppose, is that the problem with Billy isn't Billy. It's with you."

Steeling her mind against the harsh words of her friend, Eliza stared ahead. She didn't have to listen to this! She didn't—

"The way I see it, Eliza, until you find out what you have against him, or whatever it is that's bothering you that you keep taking out on him, why, Billy Foreman will never be good enough for you. No, not even if he was suddenly turned into a mighty angel from heaven arrayed in all his glory would he be good enough for you.

"There! I've said my piece, and I hope you'll still consider me your friend. Fact is, I've never felt more love for you than I do right now."

"Friend?" Eliza questioned, still staring straight ahead. "Of course, Mary. Maybe sometime we can share a dinner fire again." And without a parting glance she turned and limped back toward the wagon, signaling to her husband that she wanted to clamber aboard.

After all, there was only so much a body should have to take.

15

Red Canyon

"That'll do 'er, Belt Dailey." Dick Butt tousled the young boy's hair. "You run home and tell your pa the shoe fits fine, and we'll settle for it later."

Smiling widely the boy thrust on his hat and scampered off toward camp, yipping like a wild Indian as he ran.

"Seems like a good lad," Billy said as he examined Wonder's forefoot where Dick had nailed the new shoe.

"He is." Dick Butt stooped and gathered up a couple of nails he had dropped. "Both Wilson and Lorana Dailey are fine folks, even though they ain't Mormons and ain't interested in becoming such. But outside of that, they're raising Belt right, and their girl Bade ain't only almighty sweet but she can also sit a hoss better'n any boy her age I ever saw."

"If they aren't Mormon, how come they're on this mission?"

"Reckon Wilson figured it was a safe way for him to get his family to Colorado." Dick patted the neck of the mule called Wonder. "Captain Smith was glad to have 'em, too, what with Wilson being a fine blacksmith with his own forge and bellows and a load of coal to boot."

For a moment the two were silent. Though the sky was not yet dark, the camp, half a mile behind them, was already settling in for the night, and only the soft lowing of cows waiting to be milked or suckled broke the silence.

Red Canyon, where they were camped, was aptly named, Billy

thought. Rock formations layered in all hues of red rose on both sides of the roadway, and even the soil was a bright red. In fact, someone had said there was a whole mountain of similar redrock formations just a few miles to the east, although Billy wondered at the truthfulness of such a claim.

But just the canyon was a beautiful sight, and through the day as the company had slowly climbed, he had found himself marveling again and again. Surely, he exclaimed to himself at each new wonder, God was a master builder to have set in motion the forces necessary to create such surpassing beauty.

Why, the very thought of it so filled his heart and soul with joy that it was all he could do to contain his emotions—something he was trying desperately to learn how to do. He knew Eliza didn't approve of a man's tears, nor of a man expressing sentiments and feelings. So it wasn't difficult to imagine that hard-bitten young men like Dick Butt would scorn him even more than had his wife. Thus Billy restrained himself and reined in as best he could the joy and wonder that seemed so naturally to fill his soul.

"Lots of livestock you boys are herding," he finally observed.

Dick Butt nodded. "Nearly fourteen hundred head, cows and hosses combined. The Robbs alone have close to five hundred hosses, all of 'em riding stock. And the way I hear it, the Lymans are trailing another four hundred head of cows and hosses with them, which they'll join to our herd once we get together."

"Eighteen hundred head of stock," Billy breathed in wonder. "Just keeping them all on feed will keep you and George Decker and the other stockmen busy."

"If we can do it at all. Word is, beyond Escalante feed gets scarce as hens' teeth, and what water can be scraped out of the seeps and potholes ain't fit for nothing but growing pollywogs nor chinking log walls. But I reckon, since this is the Lord's work, we'll do what we can and leave the rest to him.

"Billy," Dick then declared, abruptly changing the subject, "I'm right glad you noticed that Wonder was favoring his hoof a little. Most folks would've missed it."

Not knowing how to respond, Billy remained silent.

"Since you saved him from some real damage, and since I hadn't shod him right in the first place, I'd like to take care of Wilson's smithy fee."

"I wouldn't hear of it," Billy declared emphatically. "That mule's pulling my load, not yours, Dick. Comes down to it, I reckon I owe for a lot more than a shoe."

Dick Butt chuckled. "All right then, what say we share it fifty-fifty? By the way, Julie says she heard that Eliza is doing poorly. Anything I can do to help?"

"Not that I know of." Billy shook his head. "She wouldn't even let me help her. Or at least not much. I offered to ask Brother Jens Nielson to give her a priesthood blessing, but she says she isn't sick enough for that. I don't know, Dick. I don't reckon I'll ever understand womenfolk. Was it me, after just one day of feeling as poorly as she seems to have felt all week, I'd be wanting blessings from everyone who'd offer. But not Eliza. She figures to tough it out. And she is tough, I'll give her that."

"As boot leather," Dick agreed. "But withall, from what I've heard, as fine a woman as there is."

Billy smiled. "I'll say amen to that, and add the hope that she'll soon be feeling better."

Dick Butt nodded soberly, took up the reins of his horse, and stretched out his hand. "Give her my regards, Billy. And give a holler if you spot any more trouble with these here mules of mine. Adios."

"So long," Billy replied, and with absolute admiration he watched the young man ride easily away. Then, with heavy heart because of his own inability to help his beloved Eliza, who might even be dying she had grown so ill, he turned and hurried back toward the camp.

———◦–◦–◦———

Eliza, who had grown bitterly angry at Mary in the two days since their conversation, thrust more sticks into her own little cooking fire. What right did the little upstart have? her mind kept questioning as she endeavored to keep warm and prepare a little nourishment for whenever Billy might be coming back. Who did the child think she was, speaking that way to a woman almost twice her age? More, how could she possibly know Billy's multitude of weaknesses when she only saw him for brief moments on any given day? She didn't have to live with him, for pity's sake, so how could she possibly say such things? Why, the very idea made Eliza's blood boil!

So did Billy's tardiness, for that matter! All around her people were finishing their meals and preparing for assembly. But not her! Oh, no! Somewhere her husband was chattering his fool head off with some new friend or other, wasting time when he ought to be thinking of her and the battle she was having with her health.

And it was a battle, too! The lack of nourishment was having a dramatic impact on Eliza's strength, and it wouldn't be many more days until she would be unable to walk, let alone perform the chores that were so essential to daily survival. Of course, she didn't want folks in the company feeling sorry for her because of her health any more than she wanted their pity because she'd been cursed with Billy. And despite Mary's ridiculous contention, she was certain that some did feel sorry for her.

Sighing deeply, Eliza stared out into the gloom, hoping to see her husband and condemning him at the same time for being so thoughtless. Could she do it, she wondered? Could she actually endure the curse of remaining with Billy for the rest of her life? Truthfully she didn't know how, not when just being in his presence made her feel miserable.

And that was something she had noticed. Of late her misery seemed to be increasing daily, as though she were sliding down the side of a bottomless pit composed of nothing but pure unhappiness. It was amazing, she thought as she thrust another stick into the fire, that one little man could have such a dramatic impact. Oh, how she hoped a few others in the company could see this as clearly as she and stand as witnesses when . . . when . . .

Well, Eliza thought as she saw Billy finally trudging toward her, she was positive there would be! Witnesses, that is. She knew that when they came forward, the truth about Billy would finally come out, and the world—including Mary Jones—would know how much she had been forced to endure.

16

Brushy Basin, South Slope of
the Blue Mountains, San Juan Country

"Rider comin'."

It was a cold afternoon, with not a breath of wind stirring the oak clumps and scattered juniper and pinion on the long, sloping flat. Sugar Bob Hazelton, his bedroll spread near the small fire, didn't even lift his hat from his face, let alone get up and take a look.

"Sugar Bob, I said there was a rider coming at us, and he ain't more'n two, three hundred yards off."

Sugar Bob groaned. "Shut up, Dingle! You know these holes Espinosa put in me ain't never healed up just right. So can the palaver and let me sleep!"

Turning, Dingle Beston looked at the prone man whom the cruel hand of fate had made him partners with. "Your funeral," he said disgustedly. "Was it me, I'd stop complaining and disappear down the wash until I was sure it wasn't I. W. Lacy come a huntin' me."

"Oh, fer—" Sugar Bob growled as he pulled his dirty blanket higher around his neck. "Is he alone?"

"Yeah, one rider is all I can see."

"Any other dust?"

"No, I don't see any."

"Then stop acting like an old woman!" Sugar Bob growled. "Laurie Yvonne tolt me once that her old man never rides nowhere

141

alone, not since he got that sickness. Reckon he's so puny anymore he has to lean against a post just to spit."

"That ain't how he looked to me when we brought those cattle in from the *Jornado del Muerto*," Dingle Bob argued, never taking his eyes off the approaching rider. "I reckon it's a good thing you cut and ducked for cover afore we got to his cabin, Sugar Bob. Why, the look Old Man Lacy give me would've made an icicle feel feverish, and I didn't do nothing to his daughter 'cept be your pardner and friend."

For a moment there was silence, the only sound the cropping of grass by the two horses that were tethered close by.

"You're right," Dingle finally acknowledged after further scrutiny of the approaching rider. "I reckon now he's closer that it's Bill Ball riding in, not I. W. Lacy."

"See. I told you to stop worrying." Sugar Bob shifted positions with his hips for the hundredth time that afternoon, seeking in vain for a softer spot of ground on which to lie. "If Bill was going to shoot me, he'd have done it back on the desert where he found us."

"We hadn't been living off his beef back then," Dingle Beston declared as he hurriedly threw his saddle onto his horse and drew the cinch strap tight.

"Man's got to eat, ain't he?" Sugar Bob wriggled his toes, which were free of the boots he usually wore, if not of his holey socks. "'Sides, we've only kilt two or three, so it ain't like we're rustling up a whole herd. Speaking of which, you reckon it's true about there being a whole herd of Mormons down on Montezuma Creek?"

"I reckon it is." Dingle was working as he talked, slipping the bit into his horse's mouth and strapping on the bridle. "Ole Olafson heard that down to Mitchell's Trading Post and swore it was true. Said he'd of stopped in for a palaver with the Mormons 'cept he heard they had a marshal with 'em."

"Yeah, maybe. But if they was Mormons, Dingle, they also had women with 'em—probably lots of 'em, what with all their wives and harems and such. I tell you, Dingle, was it me I'd have braved twenty marshals for a chance at a lively little Mormon woman."

"You probably would've," Dingle declared as he hastily tied his bedroll onto his saddle. "Well, Sugar Bob, we've pardnered long enough. I'm takin' a paeser, for good this time."

Finally Sugar Bob Hazelton lifted his hat and sat up. "Why, Dingle, what're you saying?"

"I'm saying adios, is what. I like Bill Ball, and I wouldn't want 'im hauling out no hog-leg against me on account of a couple of dead beeves I happened to help eat. More than that, though, I like I. W. Lacy, and I think what you did to his daughter, not to mention what you likewise did to Bill Ball, ought to have earned you a hemp neck massage."

"Well," Sugar Bob chuckled as he scratched his head, "you always was too fine and upstanding for my tastes, old son. Reckon that's why you missed out on all the fun with Laurie Yvonne. By all odds she was the finest blanket companion I ever had—once I got her convinced she didn't have no choice. It's amazing what a knife'll do to a woman's willpower, especially if she thinks she's about to have her purty face carved up. Why, once Laurie Yvonne felt the edge of that blade, she was about as willing to surrender as a willow in a high wind."

"I swear," Dingle Beston growled disgustedly, "I ought to plug you myself for talking that way. But instead I'll leave you and those beef hides to Bill Ball, and—"

"Not so fast, pardner!" Sugar Bob snarled as he whipped his pistol up from under the blanket. "Bill Ball's still a hundred, maybe a hundred and fifty yards off, and likely he ain't seen us yet."

"He'll of seen us."

"Maybe, in which case he'll sure be pleased I was able to plug the hombre who was rustling his cattle. Too bad he was my pardner, I'll tell 'im. But when a feller goes bad, you just got to sever old ties and do the right thing. Now, get down off that cayuse—"

"Drop it, Hazelton! Or don't, if you feel lucky!"

Too startled to reply to the voice from out of the bushes behind him, Sugar Bob slowly lowered his pistol.

"Let go of it and raise your hands. High!"

Carefully the handsome man complied.

"All right, Dingle, you get down and kick it away from him.

That's right. Now his rifle. Toss it over there in those bushes the other side of your horse."

"Say, that's a good rifle—"

"Shut up, Hazelton, and don't move. I'm coming in."

And with hardly any sound at all, the bushes parted and I. W. Lacy stepped into the clearing, his rifle held steady. "All right, Bill," he shouted then, "stop dallying and get over here. I've got 'im."

"Mr. Lacy," Sugar Bob exclaimed, forcing a smile to his face, "am I glad to see you! Dingle here just got through confessing to—"

With a snap of his wrist I. W. Lacy smashed the barrel of his rifle into Sugar Bob's mouth, shattering teeth and in general rearranging the man's appearance.

"You might like to know," he said calmly as he stepped back from the shocked and frightened man, who was just starting to spit out teeth, "that I've been in those trees long enough to hear it all. You're a flannel-mouthed so-and-so, Hazelton, but maybe this'll bust up your talk box a little."

And with another vicious swing I. W. slammed Sugar Bob in the mouth again, this time with his rifle's butt, knocking the man to the ground.

"You all right, Mr. Lacy?" Bill Ball was just pulling rein in the clearing.

"I'm feeling better'n I have in most of two years," the older man replied as he stepped back from the groveling Sugar Bob Hazelton, allowing the man to stagger to his feet. "You were shore right, Bill. He admitted to everything about my Laurie Yvonne, and Dingle here is my witness. Put a rope around his neck afore I smash his face even worse than I already have."

"You . . . you ain't a going to . . . to hang me?" Sugar Bob mumbled through his smashed lips.

"If I do it ain't no worse than what you deserve," I. W. replied as he looked around the basin. "You see any trees here big enough to hang him, Bill?"

"Them ponderosa up on the hill."

"Yeah, but that'd mean we'd have to ride next to this skunk all the way there, and I'm already getting sick of his stench. Besides, after the hanging he'd be dead whilst you and me and Mrs. Lacy'd go on suffering, and that doesn't seem a bit fair. No, sir, I reckon he had ought to live and maybe do a little suffering of his own." I. W. Lacy glared at the cowering badman. "Especially considering something he just said about a knife."

Again I. W. Lacy swung his rifle, and again Sugar Bob was knocked onto his back in the dirt. "Eight, ten years ago," I. W. Lacy then growled, "I was crossing the *Llano Estacado* when I come across this hombre the Comanch had staked out and left to die. Course I give him a little water and saved his life. But I didn't do him no favors, for the Comanch had carved him up some, just like you threatened my daughter, and it wasn't long afore he kilt hisself just to get shut of his shame. Again just like my Laurie Yvonne, you see."

"Now see here, old man!" Sugar Bob scrambled to his knees, his fear livid. "You can't—"

Another smash with the rifle knocked Sugar Bob sprawling for the third time in as many minutes.

"I told you to shut up," the old man stated quietly, "and I meant it. Bill, tie him good, give me your knife, and then get out of here; and Dingle, you might as well slope it along with him. I don't think you'll want to see what's coming."

"You . . . you ain't a-goin' to . . . to—"

"What I do, Dingle, he'll deserve. Now adios, and don't come back."

Nervously Dingle Beston spurred his horse away, and he didn't even look back when, moments later, Bill Ball rode up behind him.

"It ain't right, Bill."

"Maybe. But happen it was *your* daughter he'd raped and kilt—"

A terrible scream from behind them cut Bill Ball's words short, and after that neither man spoke again. They just rode, and rode hard, trying to wipe the sound of Sugar Bob's horror from their ears.

East Fork of the Sevier River, the Riddle Ranch near Widtsoe

"It looks like rain's coming, hon-bun," Billy called from the wagon seat. "You sure you don't want to ride?"

Feeling irritated not only because her husband was still using that ridiculous name but also because he'd shouted loudly enough that a dozen other people could hear, Eliza shook her head but remained silent. Merciful heavens, she thought angrily. Did the man think she was deaf? Or so stupid that she couldn't see the approaching storm? Or maybe so dumb that she couldn't tell when to come in out of it? And what right was it of his, shouting that idiotic nickname to the whole world—

"Did you answer me, Eliza? I couldn't hear you."

"I heard you," she responded through gritted teeth, holding her voice level and no louder than it needed to be. After all, there were too many busybodies in the missionary company as it was, and she didn't need to create more by providing new gossip. Besides, her fool husband didn't deserve an answer, not at least until he learned to keep his voice at a proper level.

But Billy was right about one thing. Those were black clouds boiling around the mountains ahead of them and to their left, and already she could feel the increasing moisture in the air. It would be raining soon, probably before they reached Riddle's ranch, and if it got any colder, which it was bound to do, it would surely turn to snow.

Eliza shuddered at the thought of it. For several days, ever since the temperature had started to drop, her once-frostbitten feet had been throbbing horribly. She knew when the winter storms started that her feet would begin to chill in earnest, and after that, day and night, she would not be without pain. It happened even when she was living and laboring indoors. But now that she was outside, taking part in this insane winter trek, the pain would become unbearable.

Not that it would matter, she reminded herself gloomily. Every day she seemed to feel worse than the day before, with nausea and light-headedness afflicting her practically from morning until night. And nothing she did seemed to help. No medicinal concoctions, no stews, no hot drinks, nothing! She was wretched from whatever was ailing her, and chilled and throbbing feet couldn't possibly make things much worse.

With a sigh of resignation she pulled up the collar of the buffalo-skin coat Billy had ordered into the co-op for her. It was heavy as sin, but it did keep out the cold wind, and it was long enough that she was protected to below her knees. Of course, nothing could help her poor feet, not the coat, not wrappings and shoes, not even the rocks Billy was now lining their fire with each night. Yes, the rocks remained warm through a good part of each day, but with her long legs she had to hold her knees practically to her chest just to keep her feet on them. Only, for some reason being scrunched up made her nausea even worse, and so she walked in an effort to keep from being nauseated, taking every opportunity to let her husband know that his scheme for keeping her feet warm hadn't worked.

With a guilty start Eliza recalled Mary Jones's unkind remarks of a few days before that Eliza was the real problem in her marriage. What nonsense! Anyone could see what a fool Billy was, and no doubt many had. Oh, he was a genial fellow, all right, and a quick learner. But he was so weak, so inept, so . . . so, well, so unlike a real man—

"Hello."

Spinning in surprise, Eliza stumbled and would have fallen if her crutch hadn't stopped her. "Stupid child!" she snapped at the little girl who had spoken. "Look what you nearly made me do! Don't you know you shouldn't surprise folks like that?"

"I like it when my papa surprises me," the girl replied, falling into step beside Eliza and easily keeping up with her. "I like it when he tickles me, too. Do you like to be tickled?"

Eliza merely glared ahead, not answering.

"What's your name?" the child then asked, undaunted.

"Why? Who wants to know?"

The small girl looked up, her eyes wide and innocent. "I do. What's that thing?"

"It's a crutch, to keep me from falling over when silly little girls surprise me." Eliza smiled thinly. "What's *your* name?"

"Alice Louise Rowley. I'm five years old, and I'm going with my papa and mama and all my brothers and sisters to convert the Indians. But first we have to cross that mountain. Are you going to convert the Indians too?"

"Well, I suppose I am," Eliza responded, deciding it was easier to humor the child than try to shame her or teach her, either one. "I'm a part of this missionary company, aren't I?"

"I reckon so. Only, how come you're walking way out here in the sagebrush where Indians could grab you?"

Eliza looked at the child, wondering that anyone could be so full of questions. "Well, first of all there would have to be Indians around here, which there aren't. And second, this is the ladies' side to walk on, to . . . uh, well, you know, to do their private business." Which, she thought grimly, meant being doubled over with the dry heaves every little while all the horrid day long!

For a moment the little girl was silent, thinking. Then she broke into a wide smile. "Oh, you mean eliminate, don't you. That's what mama says we should say. But I don't have to eliminate very often—"

"What did you say your name was?" Eliza pressed, hoping to change the unpleasant subject.

"Alice Louise Rowley. And if that's a crutch, then I bet you're That Strange Eliza Foreman."

Too surprised to be hurt by the girl's words, Eliza stared down at her. "That strange Eliza Foreman?" she repeated.

"Uh-huh. Papa says that's your name. And when Hannah, that's my big sister, asked who you were, Papa said you were the one with the funny horse and the crutch. But Mama says you're an Odd Couple. What's an Odd Couple, That Strange Eliza Foreman? Is that another name?"

Shocked beyond belief, Eliza gripped her crutch fiercely and stared ahead. "First of all, Alice Louise Rowley," she snarled, "my name is not That Strange Eliza Foreman. That's a bad name! I'm just plain Eliza Foreman, and that's all."

"But my papa said—"

"I don't care what your papa said! My name is Eliza Foreman!" Eliza took a deep breath, forcing herself to relax. "But if you'd like, Alice Louise, you may call me Eliza. That's what my friends call me."

"Is Odd Couple a bad name too?"

"I'm not a couple, little girl, odd or otherwise. A couple means two. As you can plainly see, I'm only one person, all alone out here in the sagebrush. So it seems rather foolish to call me an odd couple, don't you think?"

Alice Louise shrugged her tiny shoulders. "I reckon if you say so. Are . . . are you afraid of Indians?"

"Should I be?"

"I reckon not. Not unless they tried to make you their little girl. Mama says that's what might happen to me if I wander too far away from our wagons. Are we too far away, Eliza?"

"No, child," Eliza replied confidently, "we're not. Do . . . uh, do your parents talk about me a lot?"

"Just sometimes. Mama says you don't like Billy very much. Is Billy your horse?"

"No." Eliza was staring straight ahead, her heart in her throat. "Billy is . . . my . . . husband."

"You mean like Mama and Papa?"

"That's right. Who told your mama I didn't like Billy very much? Has she been speaking with that wicked Mary Jones?"

"Who?"

"The woman in that wagon right back there, the one being pulled by the spotted oxen."

Alice Louise turned to look. "I don't reckon we know her," she finally said, turning back.

"Then who told your mama such awful things?"

"I . . . don't reckon anybody did," the child responded, looking suddenly fearful. "Mama says she can tell by the way you look at Billy, and by the way you sit beside him in meetings, that you don't like him. But Papa says we aren't supposed to talk about it because it's gossip. He says God doesn't like gossip. Eliza, what's gossip?"

"It's . . . it's saying bad things about people."

The child looked up at Eliza, her eyes wide. "Have I been saying bad things?"

"No, child," Eliza responded, forcing herself to remember the little girl's innocence, "you haven't. But remember, my name is just Eliza, and not all those other words. And Billy and I love each other just like your mama and papa love each other. We're a family, just like you."

"Do you have lots of children in your family? Like we do?"

149

"No," Eliza said softly as a pang of sadness shot through her, "we don't. Billy and I are alone, Alice Louise. But in some families that's enough, don't you think?"

Again the small girl looked up, her eyes wide. "I reckon so. But I'm glad our family has us. Papa says he and Mama would be terrible lonesome without us. It's starting to rain, Eliza. Mama says when it starts to rain, I'm to hurry to our wagon and climb inside."

"Then you'd better run, child, and not get wet!"

"Okay. Can I walk with you again sometime?"

"Of course. Any time you want."

As the girl ran ahead, Eliza wiped away water droplets that had begun coursing down her cheeks. Rain, she thought grimly as she pushed memories of loneliness back down inside herself, memories of years and years of waiting for the wonderful husband her blessing had promised her. It was funny, though, that so much rain would get on her face when she'd felt almost nothing on her hands.

Funny.

17

Sweetwater Spring

"Howdy! My name's Maggie—Maggie Sevy."

Looking up from where she sat watching the water roil out of the spring, Eliza nodded. "I'm pleased to make your acquaintance."

It was late afternoon, the rain had temporarily stopped, and the camp was setting up in the nearby flats on the western side of the Escalante Mountains. Wanting fresh water, Eliza had brought her pail to the very head of the spring. There she had been so overcome by the quiet beauty of the spot that she'd lingered, pondering the impossible circumstances of her life. Despite the things people—such as that little Rowley child—were obviously saying about her, the relationship between her and Billy had grown too difficult, too strained, to endure. Something had to be done, or said, that would wake him up enough to see what was going on—what his bumbling ineptitude was doing to his wife. After all, it was his problem—

"And your name is?" Maggie Sevy asked expectantly.

"Eliza Foreman." This woman, Eliza thought as she really looked at her, was young, hardly more than twenty years old. She was short, perhaps five feet tall, frail rather than plump, with dark brown hair and light blue eyes that gave one the curious impression that they sparkled. In addition to her water pail she had a child in her arms, a small boy, Eliza guessed, who was old enough to be walking but was instead clinging round his mother's neck with one arm and sucking his thumb contentedly.

151

Obviously, Eliza thought critically, this was the woman's first child, for only a mother of one would ever spoil him so thoroughly.

"Eliza Foreman," Maggie Sevy said thoughtfully. "You're the one who sets that delightful table under the awning every evening!"

Eliza smiled thinly. "I'm pleased that you find it . . . delightful."

"I do," the young woman said brightly. "I admire anyone's efforts to make things beautiful. I think everything God made he made beautiful, but if given half a chance men will mess up most of it first thing and make it ugly as sin. Not many see beauty and try to recreate it in their own lives, especially under difficult conditions, and I admire those who do—you included."

Now Eliza was paying attention, though for a brief second a proverb from her childhood neighbor flashed through her mind. "The best way to knock a chip from another's shoulder," Widow Burnham had said on numerous occasions, "is by patting her on the back." That was precisely what this woman had done, Eliza was thinking. More and more she was sounding like an ally, a friend who would understand why Eliza did what she did, why she suffered so sorely. "What did you say your name was?" she asked a little more eagerly.

"Maggie Sevy." The woman was positively beaming. "I'm George Washington Sevy's wife. He's the bishop of the Second Ward in Panguitch, and that's where we joined the company. This darling child is our son, George F. Sevy, and his older brother Reuben Warren Sevy is off with the livestock."

"Well, Maggie," Eliza said, realizing that the woman had two children rather than one, "what brought you and your two Georges and young Reuben Warren on this godforsaken journey?"

"We were called by the prophet," the young woman said as her smile diminished just a little, "and I don't think God has forsaken us at all! In fact, I believe he is blessing us remarkably. Have you tasted this water? I hear it's absolutely wonderful!"

Setting her son on a rock, Maggie leaned down and began, in a very unladylike manner, to scoop handfuls of water up to her mouth. "Ahhhh," she said as she dried her face on her apron a moment later, "it's every bit as good as they said. Don't you think so, Eliza?"

"I haven't tried it yet. I prefer to drink from a cup."

"Oh. Well, I . . . Say, you don't seem very happy," Maggie stated abruptly, her tone at once low and sincere. "Is something wrong?"

"Why, I declare—"

"There's no need to sound so pompous and offended," Maggie stated with a bright smile. "I have no wish to pry, but if something's wrong, I'd be happy to do what I can to help you."

For a long moment Eliza gazed at the young woman, wondering. She probably shouldn't expose herself by revealing the truth. On the other hand, since Mary had stabbed her in the back, it would be so nice to have at least one ally—

"Of a truth there's a great deal wrong, with my marriage and much else," Eliza finally replied with disgust. "But I don't believe that talking about it will do a bit of good."

"Why," Maggie exclaimed excitedly, "Mark Twain said that very thing! He said there was no point in talking about all our problems because eighty percent of the people we told wouldn't care anyway, and the other twenty percent would think we deserved them."

Eliza couldn't help but laugh.

"On the other hand," Maggie continued almost without pause, "Sister Phoebe says that—"

"Phoebe? Who's Sister Phoebe?"

Maggie looked surprised. "Why, she's Brother Sevy's first wife. It's her son Reuben Warren that's traveling with us. Everyone I've ever met knows Phoebe Butler Sevy, so I just assumed—"

"You . . . you're a polygamist?"

Maggie smiled. "Brother Sevy doesn't care for that term. Actually I'm a plural wife, sealed to Brother Sevy in the Endowment House in Salt Lake City."

"But . . . you seem so happy."

"Of course I'm happy, at least most of the time. Why? Aren't we plural wives supposed to be happy?"

"Well," Eliza stated, "I've known a great many who weren't!"

"You've known them?"

Eliza sneered. "Yes, I have. They're not happy because they aren't first in their husband's heart! Because they're always playing second or third or fourth fiddle, so to speak. Because they're trapped in a marriage system that the world has rightly rejected. Because—

because—Well, I ask you, Maggie Sevy, what woman could possibly be happy knowing she had to stand in line for everything she ever got from her husband, including his affections? Those are a few of the reasons why so many plural wives are unhappy!"

"Interesting." Maggie nodded thoughtfully. "Are you also a plural wife, then?"

"Me?" Eliza was shocked. "Of course not! Whatever gave you that foolish notion?"

Maggie smiled kindly. "Because you're miserable and unhappy, Eliza, and from what you said a moment ago you must feel trapped in a marriage you don't want to be a part of."

Stunned, Eliza gave a hard look at the younger woman, wondering once again. But she could detect no malice in Maggie's dancing blue eyes, no sarcasm in her laughter-prone voice. Instead she seemed perfectly sincere, and Eliza found herself thinking, as she struggled for a rebuttal, that the woman was as frank and forthright as the little Rowley child had been. It was almost as if—

"How do you know those things?" she finally snapped.

"George F. and I must be getting back," Maggie said abruptly as she rose to her tiny feet. "But before I go, Eliza, you should know that I've heard from several people about the difficulties between you and your husband. I don't much care for gossip, but sometimes it's difficult not to hear.

"More important, as my philosopher mother, Anna Eliza Cloward Imlay, used to say of my father, James Havens Imlay, 'A righteous husband is like a precious gem. The more righteous he is, the more luster he gives off. And the more luster he gives off, the more people are blessed by being in his presence—especially his wife. A woman should cling to such a husband and cherish him.'

"Eliza, Brother Sevy is a righteous man. Truly my desire is to cling to him always and to cherish him tomorrow as much as I do today. I'm honored not alone to be his wife and to bear his children but also just to be in his precious presence and to share in his luster—his Christlike love for all mankind."

Maggie smiled and then continued, her voice as soft as goosedown. "Folks say, Eliza, that your sweet husband is a lot like mine."

And without a backward glance the young woman turned, swept up her son, lifted her pail, and jauntily started back toward the encampment.

18

Saturday, November 8, 1879

Escalante Mountains

"You all right, Eliza?"

Numbly Eliza nodded. She was clinging to the wagon seat, hold-ing the reins, and doing her best to guide the teams. Billy, mean-while, was trudging upward through the knee-deep snow, pulling on the rope he'd tied to Sign's bridle. It was snowing so heavily that Eliza could barely see the wagon in front of them, but what she could see was frightening beyond belief. Not only was the snow up to the wagon's axles, but the steep dugout they were calling a road sidled terribly downward, making Eliza wonder how the wagon kept from sliding off and rolling sideways down into the gorge.

For herself, she was perched hard against the upper end of her own wagon seat and leaning as far uphill as she could, adding what little weight she had left to that side of the jolting, squeaking wagon. But the treacherous track up Sweetwater Canyon and over the Escalante Mountains seemed endless, and she was sure that she and everything she and Billy owned in the world was doomed to sudden destruction.

Eliza had long since lost what little nourishment she'd been able to force down that morning, and the jolting of the wagon had made her feel worse than ever. But maybe it would be good to die in a rollover, she was thinking. That way she could go quickly and coura-geously, instead of slowly with the debilitating illness she had some-how contracted.

Suddenly the wagon lurched to a stop. Peering through the

155

falling snow, Eliza saw that the wagon in front of theirs, driven by Mons Larson and his young plural wife Olivia, had also stopped. Olivia was growing large with child, and Eliza found herself wondering how the poor woman was enduring the grueling climb. Thank the Lord, at least, that she hadn't been called upon to endure that trial! Thank the Lord—

"Isn't this beautiful, hon-bun?" Billy exclaimed as he appeared out of the snow to stand beside her. "Everything is so quiet, so muffled. I swear a body can almost hear the snow falling! And look at how beautiful the trees look. These are mostly Engelmann spruce along here, but higher up along the ridge I saw what I think are bristlecone pines—twisted, scrubby things they say are tens of thousands of years old. And of course the copses of quaking aspen are scattered everywhere. I declare, Eliza, that besides yourself I never saw such unsurpassing beauty!"

"It's lovely," Eliza muttered with a sarcasm that was completely lost on her husband. "Why did we stop?"

"We've nearly reached the top. But it gets tolerable steep the last couple of hundred yards, so we're doubling teams and helping each other with the climb. Will you be all right if I take Sign and Wonder and go on up to help out?"

Eliza almost laughed. "All right? Of course I'll be all right. Why wouldn't I be?"

Billy looked confused. "Well, you know, with you feeling poorly and all—"

With a wave of her hand Eliza dismissed the thought. "Go. I'll just sit in the wagon and listen to the snow fall."

Smiling, Billy reached up and patted her hand. Then he pushed through the ever-deepening snow, unhooked the leaders' tugs from the singletrees, and soon both he and his team had vanished into the white gloom.

Being careful so she wouldn't slide down off the slanted seat, Eliza set the brake with her foot and wound the reins of Little Bit and Lots around the handle. Dusting what snow she could from her scarf and heavy coat, she stiffly and awkwardly clambered through the opening or puckerhole of the two wagon covers and onto the sacks of seed grain Billy expected to plant on the San Juan come spring, the sacks that for three weeks now had been their surprisingly comfortable bed.

With the furniture back in the wagon there was barely room enough for her, but Billy had found a way to stack things so she could sit and even stretch out when she needed to lay down.

Only, as she started working her feet back under the chairs Eliza's head began to spin terribly, and she felt as if she were going into a swoon. Had she been able she would have knelt with her head held low until it went away. But as it was, all she could do was lay with her eyes squeezed closed while the wagon and all the rest of the world swung in crazy circles around her.

"Lawsy," she gasped when the spinning began to slack into the dreaded nausea, "if you don't find a cure soon, woman . . . well, you can't live a whole lot longer without some sort of nourishment."

Struggling to sit again, she pushed her head under the double thickness of the canvas cover and over the side of the wagon, where she remained until the convulsions in her stomach had eased. Then, gasping for breath, she pulled herself back inside to lay sprawled on her bedding atop the feed sacks.

What idiocy! she thought as she contemplated the grain. What bullheaded optimism! How could Billy possibly imagine that he was going to turn himself into a farmer? Did he think the San Juan country was magic or something? Or did he expect that the Lord would simply touch him with his finger and perform a miracle? In continuing amazement at the thinking process of her husband—or lack thereof—Eliza shook her head. And she thought, abruptly, of Mary Jones's contention that, no matter how well Billy did at whatever he did, it would never be good enough for Eliza. She would always be looking for something new to criticize. The problem with their marriage, therefore, was of her making rather than Billy's. Or at least that was how Mary felt about it.

And that upstart Maggie Sevy, whatever business was it of hers? Imagine the woman, denouncing gossip while at the same time saying the gossipers felt that Billy was as fine a man as her husband the bishop. Humph!

But now, as she lay in misery while the snow tumbled silently out of the heavens to cover everything around her in robes of winter

157

white, and while the remains of her poor feet throbbed with their endless pain, Eliza found herself wondering for the first time if perhaps both Maggie and Mary had been right. Certainly she wasn't consciously looking for things about her husband to criticize. Yet she did criticize him, constantly. As a matter of fact, now that she thought of it, she couldn't remember the last time Billy had done something she hadn't managed to find fault with. Of course, he was such a strange little man, so odd and unusual—

Abruptly the words of five-year-old Alice Louise Rowley were in her mind again, calling her an Odd Couple and That Strange Eliza Foreman. Was it so obvious that she and Billy weren't well-matched? Or that she didn't love him? And were other people besides Mary and Kumen Jones and the Sevys and Alice Louise's folks talking about them? Even the thought of such a thing caused Eliza's face to burn with shame.

But what truly hurt, what amazed her more than she could say, was that the witnesses she had been expecting, the witnesses personified by young Mary Louise Rowley and Maggie Sevy, were not talking about and criticizing Billy. No, not even with his silly grin and inept ways in all things Eliza considered manly. Instead they were speaking of her, calling her strange, linking her with Billy as an odd couple, and whispering that she didn't love her husband. Which was true, of course. She didn't. But it didn't seem right that her emotions should be so noticeable to other folks, especially since she'd told Billy she intended to stay married to him and make the best of it.

Not that remaining with the little fool was her first choice. Rather it was her only choice; God had so witnessed to her, and she knew it.

"Oh, God," she pleaded as she lay in the badly tilted wagon, "You cursed me to stay with him. But if I don't have to, then help me to see it and to know what to do. I'm so tired of feeling sick and miserable, and I don't mean just this illness that is slowly killing me. Please, God, if you could just give me some idea—"

Suddenly the wagon lurched a little to the side, and an instant later Mary Jones's smiling face appeared in the opening of the wagon covers.

"Want company?" she asked brightly. And then, without waiting for a response from the startled Eliza, she dusted the snow from herself and climbed over the seat and into the cramped and gloomy interior of the wagon.

———o–o–o———

"I think we waited too long on the butter," Billy stated as he gazed into the churn that had been secured to the side of the wagon. "Looks to me like it's about frozen."

"At least you can drink the buttermilk," Eliza responded from her chair beside the wagon. Her voice was weak, almost a whisper, and Billy was surprised by it.

"Wouldn't you like any?" he asked, trying to encourage her a little.

Eliza shook her head. "I . . . don't think I could hold it down, Billy. I can't even hold down water anymore."

It had been a long and tiring day for everyone in the company, and Billy's legs were wobbly from tromping up and down the steep cut in the knee-deep snow. Yet all the wagons had been brought over the summit and into camp in the high mountain meadow that overlooked the frontier community of Escalante, and he felt good that he'd been able to help.

Unfortunately, he hadn't been able to do as much for his wife, who now sat bundled in the chair facing the fire, her feet extended toward the flames. Her face was pinched and drawn, her eyes were hollow, and Billy knew she was slowly starving to death. What he didn't know was what was wrong or what he could do about it. No matter what she tried to eat or drink, she lost it within minutes. And she was so weak and dizzy she could scarcely walk anymore. Yet she wouldn't even consider receiving a blessing, and no matter how hard he prayed for her, it seemed to do no good. He was losing his wife, he knew it, and it felt like his whole world was collapsing around him.

"I'll heat this buttermilk," he said tenderly as he poured it from the churn, still trying to be optimistic. "Warm buttermilk might be just the thing for you."

Eliza shook her head. "Thank you, Billy, but no. It will just make

159

me sick again, and I don't think I can take another bout of that tonight. Is . . . the butter too cold to paddle?"

"Probably." Billy scooped the hard mound of butter from the churn into a wooden bowl. "But I'll cover it and put it near the fire, and maybe in a little while I can paddle a little more buttermilk out of it."

"Don't forget to add the salt when you're through."

Billy grinned. "I won't. One time is all it takes to learn that lesson."

For a moment or so there was silence, and both could hear the nearby sound of a crying baby. It was probably little George Perkins, infant son of Hyrum and Rachel Perkins. When he didn't get fed on time, he let the world know how bad off he was, and his lusty crying was already a well-known sound in the camp. It was—

"Would you like me to comb out your hair for you?" Billy asked tenderly.

Briefly Eliza smiled. It would feel good to have her hair combed out, she thought. After all, it hadn't been done in almost a week. Of course, there hadn't been a whole lot of dust since the weather had turned bad, and she'd kept her head tightly covered with a bonnet most of the time anyway. But since she wasn't planning on washing it until the weather warmed up the following spring—to protect her from taking cold or coming down with pneumonia—she could surely wait another day or so for a combing.

Besides, she thought ruefully, all that tugging on her hair once it was let out of the bun would only make her head feel worse than it already did—

"Mary came to see me today," Eliza abruptly declared, putting Billy's offer out of her mind.

"I know. She told me when she brought me some supper a little while ago."

"Did . . . she tell you what we talked about?"

Billy shook his head. "All she said was that she was frightened for you."

"Frightened?"

"Yes, because you're so weak. She thinks maybe you're dying."

160

Eliza sighed. "I might be, but I don't think that's what is frightening her. And it certainly isn't what's frightening me."

Squatting near the fire with his hands outstretched, Billy looked up at his wife. "Oh?"

"I . . . uh—" Eliza paused, groping for words. "Billy," she finally stated, determining simply to plunge ahead, "did you know that folks were talking about us . . . about me, I mean?"

"Talking? What do you mean?"

"Saying things. Calling me things like 'that strange Eliza Foreman.' Or calling us an 'odd couple.'"

"Who's doing that?" Billy was already up on his feet, his face revealing how upset he was.

"Just . . . people," Eliza replied evasively. "But there's something worse than that, Billy. The word is being spread around, at least by some folks in the company, that I don't love you. I . . . I haven't said any such thing to a soul, and I want you to know that. But I suppose the expression on my face has been way too plain, and folks are hearing truths I'm not even speaking."

Feeling stricken, Billy sank back down on his haunches. A log in the fire popped, sending a shower of sparks upward into the gloom of the overcast sky. Though it was no longer snowing, the clouds remained low and threatening, and the decision had been made by big old Jens Nielson, who had been sustained as presiding elder back at Holyoak Spring, to push ahead in the morning even though it was the Sabbath. Until now that had seemed important to Billy, worth considering and discussing. But now—

"I only wish folks weren't such awful busybodies!" Eliza continued, surprising Billy with the anger in her voice. "What I think and feel is none of their business anyway!"

"No," Billy responded, poking a stick into the fire as he spoke, "that isn't exactly true, Eliza, and you ought to know it."

Surprised, for Billy had never argued with her, Eliza forgot for a moment how awful she was feeling. "Whatever do you mean, Billy Foreman? How could what I think and feel possibly be the business of another human soul?"

Billy took a deep breath. "Eliza, look around us. So far in this company you'll see about sixty wagons and considerable over a hundred people—men, women, and children—with more traveling from other places to join us. In other words, you'll see a community, put together and organized to tame a frontier and subdue a wilderness. Whether you've thought it through or not, everything we've learned tells us the San Juan country is raw, wild, and violent. A good many of the folks we'll find there have no regard for God nor man, and they will hurt or kill us or anyone else at the drop of a hat.

"Mark my words, Eliza. The success—no, the very survival—of us all depends on the thoughts, feelings, and actions of each one of us. I don't just mean that we all have to be wise and strong in the ways of the frontier, though that will be important. I also mean we must be as righteous as possible in every way, for our community, our very mission, won't survive without the blessings, protection, and even direct intervention of our Heavenly Father.

"That's why everything each of us thinks, feels, says, or does is the business of everyone else. In other words, no one of us is alone, and each of us is accountable both to and for everyone else.

"For example, think back to the people of Enoch the prophet, who also established his community in a violent, raw, and wild frontier where he was completely surrounded by enemies. Enoch was given the responsibility of teaching his followers to be pure in heart—in other words, to be Zion, so that they'd be worthy of being protected and preserved. He was so successful that the Lord not only protected them but ultimately lifted their entire city from the earth. But if even one of Enoch's followers had refused to become pure, it would have completely frustrated the hopes, dreams, desires, and goals of all the rest, Enoch and the Lord included. Do you understand what I'm saying?"

"Enoch could have asked such a person to leave."

"He could have. But would that have been the way of a man—or of a people—who had become pure in heart?"

Slowly Eliza shook her head. "I . . . hadn't thought of it like that."

Billy smiled. "That's why we're each the business of everyone else, Eliza. It has to do with perfect, righteous love, each of us for everyone else. That's what being pure in heart means. But it goes even further. If one of us misbehaves, then the rest of us, as a society, have the responsibility not only to know about it but also to help reeducate or even punish that person."

"Are you serious?"

"Yes. And if our efforts aren't enough to bring about the desired change, then we're all jeopardized by the outcome, just as the people of Enoch would have been."

Eliza was upset, and it showed. "But we're not trying to be translated!"

"How do you know we aren't? Wasn't it the goal of Joseph Smith, Brigham Young, and now President John Taylor to perfect us so we can be brought into the presence of the Lord—the Lord's rest, as he calls it in the scriptures? Isn't that the next step to being translated?"

"I . . . I don't know."

"Think about it, Eliza." Standing, Billy stepped to the wagon and took out his several volumes of scripture. "In the Book of Mormon, Alma called the wicked Zeezrom to repentance. Alma taught, 'God did call on men, in the name of his Son, (this being the plan of redemption which was laid) saying: If ye will repent, and harden not your hearts, then will I have mercy upon you, through mine Only Begotten Son; therefore, whosoever repenteth, and hardeneth not his heart, he shall have claim on mercy through mine Only Begotten Son, unto a remission of his sins; and these shall enter into my rest. And whosoever will harden his heart and will do iniquity, behold, I swear in my wrath that he shall not enter into my rest.'

"That's in the twelfth chapter of Alma. In the thirteenth chapter Alma goes on to say: 'Now they, after being sanctified by the Holy Ghost, having their garments made white, being pure and spotless before God, could not look upon sin save it were with abhorrence; and there were many, exceedingly great many, who were made pure and entered into the rest of the Lord their God. And now, my brethren, I would that ye should humble yourselves before God, and bring forth fruit meet for repentance, that ye may also enter into that rest.'"

"But . . . what does entering into the Lord's rest actually mean?"

Quickly Billy began turning more pages. "I think both Moses and Joseph Smith must have pondered the same question, for in the

163

eighty-fourth section of the Doctrine and Covenants, the Lord revealed that Moses had tried diligently to help the children of Israel become purified so they could enter into his rest. But apparently he failed, for verse twenty-four says, 'They hardened their hearts and could not endure his presence; therefore, the Lord in his wrath, for his anger was kindled against them, swore that they should not enter into his rest while in the wilderness, which rest is the fulness of his glory.'"

Eliza was astounded. "So Moses was actually trying to bring the children of Israel into the presence of God? In this life?"

"That's right—just as Enoch did with his people. And just as our prophets have been endeavoring to do with us. We may not be working toward translation, but we're certainly working toward entering into the Lord's rest. The thing is, Eliza, too many of us are like the children of Israel instead of the people of Enoch; we keep hardening our hearts—"

Eliza shook her head in frustration. "But . . . we're not talking about some horrible deed here, Billy! This is personal, private, between me and you alone."

Billy smiled. "Yes, it is certainly personal and private. But suppose we decide to separate from each other. Where do we go to do that? If we decide to leave the company, they'll be short of manpower, and if we leave once we're in the wilderness, they'll feel obligated to send men along to see that we get back to civilization safely, which shortens their manpower even more.

"On the other hand, if we separate but remain with the company, folks will sooner or later have to choose sides, which means they'll be divided instead of united. That means contention, Eliza, and you know as well as anyone that the spirit of contention is of the devil. And since we've been called as missionaries for the Lord and need his spirit and blessings if we're to succeed in his work, let alone survive—"

"I know, I know," Eliza declared quietly as she laid her head back against her chair. "It's conceivable that our—I mean *my*—actions could doom the entire mission to failure."

Placing his scriptures on the table, Billy walked around behind his wife, where he began gently massaging the muscles in her neck and shoulders. "It isn't just you, hon-bun," he declared quietly. "If I was just man enough to do things right—"

"Mary and I talked about that the other day."

"You did?" Billy felt his ears burning with sudden embarrassment. Why, oh, why hadn't he managed to learn—

"Mary's of the opinion that the problem isn't you, Billy. She . . . she says there's something in my head that will find a way to criticize you, no matter how much you learn or accomplish."

"Eliza, that just isn't so!"

"Well, I think it is. Leastwise when I consider it honestly, Mary does seem right. Every day I manage to find something new to pick at, something new to find fault with."

"That's because I'm just no good at this sort of life!"

"But you are, Billy! And you're getting better right along. Maybe that's . . . that's why I'm not. Getting better, I mean. Maybe because I've been so full of meanness toward you, or maybe because I'm affecting the whole entire company with the spirit of contention and meanness, God is smiting me."

"But God wouldn't do that, hon-bun. He's a God of love, not hate. And he loves you every bit as much as I do, and piles more besides. No, if he was going to curse anybody around here, it'd be me. Why, I was the one dragged you off from your friends and business—"

"Billy! I came with you because I chose to, and I don't want to hear any more about it." Eliza reached up, took her husband's hand in her own, and pulled him around to face her. "Mary's an interesting girl, you know. I'm easily old enough to be her mother. But she's been playing mother to me for some time now. After I'd told her a few days ago how miserable I was, she came today and showed me in that same Book of Mormon that it's Satan and not God who wants my misery. In fact, according to that scripture, the devil actively seeks to make me miserable.

"I asked Mary how he could have power to do that, and she reminded me of a few things—things she called sins of omission— that I'm certainly guilty of. For instance, the past two months I've been omitting prayer from my life, not just with you but personal prayer, too. I wasn't getting any answers, so I concluded, why pray?

I've also omitted studying the scriptures, I've omitted being kind and loving and forgiving, I've even been unwilling to accept a priesthood blessing for my illness, which means I've omitted the faith necessary to be blessed."

"Eliza, hon-bun, you don't—"

"Billy," Eliza said, stopping him, "I . . . I don't know that Mary is right, at least about why I'm miserable. But she's right that I am, and the course I've been following only seems to make it worse. So today I promised her I'd change course for a time, and at least see if it will make a difference. If . . . if you asked, do you suppose Brother Nielson would come and . . . give me a blessing?"

"Of course he would!"

"Then go fetch him, Billy." Eliza smiled wanly. "If I don't get better soon, I'll be dead, and I . . . I don't want to go before I know—"

"Don't you move from that chair, Eliza," Billy declared, joy filling his heart and lighting his face. "Brother Nielson and I will be back in hardly more than two shakes of a lamb's tail, and you'll have that blessing you've been needing for so long!"

19

Sunday, November 9, 1879

Escalante Mountain

Though it was well into the early hours of Sunday morning, Eliza found herself unable to sleep. The wind had picked up a little, and it was snowing again, the snow pelting the canvas covers of the wagon as the wind whipped it along. But inside the wagon there was shelter, and the warm rocks Billy had packed at the foot of their bedding were doing wonders for her throbbing feet.

Over and over she'd been rehearsing in her mind the conversations of the previous day, both with Mary Jones and her husband. They had been significant conversations, she felt, and there was a good possibility her life would change because of them. Or rather, her life could change because of the commitments those conversations, as well as the conversations with Maggie Sevy and little Alice Louise Rowley, had impelled her to make.

But more, Eliza was also pondering the words of the blessing pronounced on her head by the presiding elder of the missionary company, Jens Nielson. It had been a simple blessing, couched in broken English flavored with the man's heavy Danish accent.

"In de blessed name of de Lord Jesus," he had said, "ve rebuke de power of de sickness dat iss destroying you, und promise dat you vill get vell."

As yet that hadn't happened, for she was just as weak as ever. In her mind, though, was a difference, and Eliza was as certain she

167

would get well as she was that daylight would be upon them in another two or three hours.

In the darkness Billy stirred restlessly, and Eliza wondered for a moment that he could sleep, especially considering all that had happened. Yet she knew that the day's work had exhausted him, and that it was selfish for her to even think he should remain awake with her.

Her mind went back to the blessing. Besides promising her a restoration of health, it had also been spiritually powerful, Brother Nielson making promises he couldn't have known she needed, and referring to things he couldn't have known existed. In fact, in some ways it had been much like the blessing she'd received years before in England—the blessing wherein she'd been promised a wonderful husband for whom she alone would raise up a righteous posterity.

Had she ever shared that with anyone besides Mary and Eliza R. Snow, she wondered? Perhaps. But she'd certainly never shared all the details of it, not with anyone. So the fact that Brother Nielson had alluded directly to it in his blessing, and to the specific promises made therein, which promises would prove blessings to her rather than cursings, could be nothing more than inspiration or revelation. And that meant, Eliza knew, that the words of both blessings, the one ancient and the other recent, had come from God through the power of the Holy Ghost to a Church leader, and from him to her.

In other words, they were statements of truth granted from an eternal realm, and she had no choice but to believe them. Especially, she thought as a radiant smile creased her tired and worn face, she had to believe the moment when Brother Nielson had paused and then had begun to bless with good health and a long life the unborn son who he declared was even then growing within her womb.

In her womb! she thought exultantly as tears of joy suddenly streaked her cheeks and filled her ears. *In her womb!* She, cranky and homely old spinster woman Eliza Foreman, was going to have a baby, a son who would grow to be her husband's righteous posterity!

PART THREE

THE HOLE

20

Thursday, December 4, 1879

Top of Hole-in-the-Rock

Billy felt good as he climbed the gradually sloping rimrock. In fact, though the sky was heavy with clouds and threatening more snow and frigid winds, he couldn't imagine how a man could feel any better. Not only was he going to be a father, a fact he still couldn't comprehend, but except for her feet Eliza herself was finally feeling first rate, which was worth everything in the world to him.

Adjusting his spectacles on his nose, the young man thought about the month since Jens Nielson's sweet blessing of his wife. Though not recovering immediately, she had begun the next day to get over her nausea, and it was soon evident even to Eliza that she was indeed expecting a baby. And such an expectation was changing her, Billy thought; that, and doing the things she'd promised Mary she would do. She was growing more mellow, more tolerant, less inclined to criticize. She was also reading on her own again, from both the Bible and the Book of Mormon. Several times Billy had caught her at it, which had pleased him tremendously. She also responded willingly either night or morning when he asked her to take her turn in prayer. These things were having an effect for good on his wife, though in Billy's opinion none of them could touch the joy and obvious excitement in her countenance each time their unborn child was mentioned.

Now as he crossed the last few yards of the wind-swept cliff top, Billy offered a prayer of gratitude, thanking the Lord for the multitude of his blessings, and thanking him as well for the incredible wife he'd been given—

With a gasp of surprise and fear Billy dropped to his hands and knees, closing his eyes against the sudden vertigo that he felt might topple him over the edge of the huge sandstone lip. Directly in front of him, less than two yards away, was the narrow slit in the stone that was already being called the Hole-in-the-Rock. And only inches beyond that, not more than a few feet, the sandstone bulge dropped away into dizzying depths such as Billy had never even imagined.

"Oh, dear Father who art in heaven," he breathed fearfully as he forced his eyes to reopen and look outward into the teeth of the gale that was whipping out of the depths below, "I had no idea this was where they intended to go. Please give all of us the strength to face this awful task—"

Earlier in the day, in solemn meeting, he and Eliza had raised their hands with the rest of the company to sustain Captain Smith and Brother Nielson in their resolution to push a road over this incredible cliff and on to the San Juan. But now, as he viewed the awesome gorge into which they had voted to drive their wagons, Billy found his mind almost stupefied. The Hole would be too steep and would drop too far into the bowels of the earth—

Already six weeks into their journey—the amount of time originally estimated to reach the San Juan—the company had moved only sixty miles past the Escalante Mountains. And that last sixty miles had taken the better part of a month to accomplish.

It had been a horrific time of backbreaking labor, too. Leaving the mountains, the company had dropped rapidly down through what were called the Circle Cliffs and into the burgeoning little frontier community of Potato Valley or, as it was now being called, Escalante. There they had purchased as many additional supplies as they could afford and the people were willing to sell, after which they pressed on into the snow-covered wilderness known as the Escalante Desert.

Though appearing quite level, in reality this desert was cut across by numerous wicked gashes of canyons running from the looming Straight Cliffs of Fifty-Mile Mountain northeastward into the steep-walled canyon of the Escalante River. Interestingly, the largest of these cliff-sided canyons, which usually contained seeps or springs of water and some fairly good feed, showed up at almost exactly ten-mile intervals. Hence the first one, where they had waited several days until the Smith and Lyman parties had arrived to finish filling up their company, was called Ten-Mile Spring and Ten-Mile Camp, respectively.

While camped at Ten-Mile, Jens Nielson had sent exploring parties to scout a road southeastward to the Colorado River. Soon crews of men were ahead of the company, clearing and cutting the proposed road so the wagons could move forward, for this was new and wild country where wagons had never been taken. It was also desolate beyond belief, and while not deeply snow-covered like the mountains behind them, it afforded nothing for firewood save an occasional juniper and the fast-burning and almost useless black shadscale brush.

After Ten-Mile, the company had inched forward through numerous steep-walled gulches to Twenty-Mile Wash, where they found the feed good and the water bad. Here they had been forced to divide up the herd of livestock, which by all accounts had grown to nearly two thousand head of horses and cattle. Since then the young men assigned to herd duty had been hard-pressed to find adequate feed for the animals and were ranging them all over the vast, arid desert in search of it.

And the gray plain, smooth and easy to travel immediately out of Escalante, had become more difficult the farther they had moved into it, until finally company assistant captain Platte Lyman had called it the worst country he'd ever seen. Billy wholeheartedly agreed. It had taken days and days to push through the ravines and gulches from Twenty-Mile Wash to Thirty-Mile Hollow, and many more days to struggle from there to Forty-Mile Camp, which had been established near a huge sandstone cove or amphitheater they'd taken to calling Dance Hall Rock. There, after many a hard day's labor on the road, and despite the freezing temperatures, they had gathered to sing the songs of Zion and dance to the fiddles of Sammy Cox and Charlie Walton, dancing until their bodies were warmed, their troubles forgotten, and their spirits made light enough to continue.

Finally some of the company of missionaries, he and Eliza included, had straggled into camp at what was called Fifty-Mile Point. From there, the day before, to conclude the nearly month of backbreaking and time-consuming work it had taken to cross the Escalante Desert, he and the others of the contingent from Cedar City had moved eastward amid intermittent flurries of snow to camp at the actual edge of the cliff above the Colorado River.

Now Billy knelt alone on the windy ledge, his eyes watering from the cold as he gazed off into the distance, his stomach turning queasy at the view. Eliza was back at the wagon, trying to put together a little supper over a pitiful shadscale fire, and he had tracked down the cow to take what little milk she was producing. With the bucket only a third full, he had started back to camp, glanced at the rimrock that loomed nearby, and decided it was time to take a look at where he had so willingly agreed to go. Only, he thought with a gulp, he almost wished he hadn't.

Forcing his eyes away from the incredible depths of the Colorado River Gorge, Billy looked outward, trying to assess the country. Off to the south, rising out of a maze of deep gulches, impossible canyons, and barren sandstone buttes, rose the hulking blue of Navajo Mountain, which towered more than 10,000 feet into the air and was the single distinguishing feature on that distant horizon. Directly west of him but on the north of the Colorado River rose the Straight Cliffs of Fifty-Mile Mountain, which would one day be known as the Kaiparowits Plateau. Presenting an almost impenetrable wall that was layered like the pages of a book, the fifteen-hundred-foot abutments appeared almost level on top, which Billy assumed was just as deceptive as the "level" Escalante Desert they had crossed beneath them.

Turning more northwest, Billy gazed again at the huge walls of stone that jutted eastward from Fifty-Mile Mountain. There were two of these short "side mountains" in the ten miles between Fifty-Mile Spring and the Hole, and they stood straight out into the desert for a quarter to half a mile. There the sheer cliffs tumbled abruptly away to end in massive, bulging, rounded sandstone formations of hills and hollows that, to Billy, looked for all the world like the deformed feet and toes of a sleeping giant. He had been amazed by those formations when they had passed them, but now he could see that similar sandstone mounds stretched endlessly away to the southeast on the other side of the Colorado—where they would soon be making their way.

As he steeled his mind for another look directly downward, Billy once again examined the narrow crevice the company was calling the Hole. Actually it was merely a slit in the rock, a crevice that dropped a dizzying two thousand feet before it reached the Colorado River below. And it was narrow where it cut through the rimrock at Billy's feet, not even wide enough for a man to squeeze into. But, he reminded himself, the explorers from Escalante had sworn that it widened out somewhat below the initial bulge of sandstone and without too much labor could be made into a passable wagon road.

In his own mind Billy couldn't imagine such a thing, especially not now that he was looking at it. Nevertheless, he had faith in the others, and if they believed they could descend to and then cross the Colorado River at this point, well, who was he to disagree? Besides, he thought with a wide smile as he scrambled on all fours away from the terrible edge, neither could he imagine becoming a father. Yet in the spring that, too, was surely going to happen.

21

Saturday, December 6, 1879

Fort Lewis, Colorado

When I. W. Lacy reined his horse to a stop in front of the Gilded Slipper Saloon, he was still looking around in amazement. To his certain knowledge Fort Lewis, Colorado, had not existed two months before. Yet here was a whole community—mostly of tents, to be sure, but a community nonetheless—lying on the banks of the La Plata River not too many miles south of Animas City.

Two hundred yards away, the Sibley tents of the military were laid out in orderly rows, but here in the bursting community of camp followers there was no such order. The Gilded Slipper was a tent, and next to it were two more tents with slat-board sides identified as the hotel. Directly across the street—if that was what it could be called—were four tents that in a more orderly place would be called the cribs of the whores. And despite the primitive conditions and the daylight hour, I. W. could see that the chippies were doing a booming business.

So, too, was the whole of Fort Lewis. From what I. W. had been told by the grub rider who'd ridden through the San Juan country a couple of weeks before, the military had been sent here in response to the Thornburgh Massacre and the killing of Nathan Meeker. Hopefully they'd put a stop to any additional outbreak by the Utes.

So in two months a fort had sprung up, both officially and unofficially, and now it was wide open and running wild, with people scurrying every which way and every last one of them but the soldiers in a hurry and certain he or she was just one jump away from getting rich off government gold.

Well, I. W. thought as he climbed stiffly from his horse and stretched his back, that was just dandy with him. He'd be getting just as rich as the rest of them, and maybe more so if things turned out as he thought they would. Why? Because both soldiers and camp followers, no matter what their professions, needed to eat. And seeing as he was now running one of the biggest beef spreads in the country, it was only natural that he get here as fast as his horse could galvinate, and fill the demand for beef with supply.

Besides which, he thought with a grin, he was pretty sure he'd arrived in Fort Lewis before the other big rancher in the San Juan country, a feller by the name of Spud Hudson, could have gotten there. Likely as not old Spud, who, I. W. had been told, liked to hole up out in the hills with his cows for weeks at a time, hadn't even heard of Fort Lewis. And if he had, then just as likely I. W. could undercut him on the price of his beef, that on account of the fine shape Bill Ball had brought in his main herd from Texas a couple of months before. Why, with that many cows on the range already fat and growing fatter, a feller could sell them for just about anything and make a good profit.

Hitching up his trousers and gun belt, I. W. lifted his hat and slicked back his silver hair. Then he twirled his snow-white mustaches with a little beeswax he carried for the purpose, just to make certain they were even. Being now as presentable as he was likely to get, which was not much considering his complete aversion to icy stream bathing, he grinned slightly at the irony of things, pushed aside the tent flap, and ducked into the saloon.

If I. W. had expected to be immediately noticed, his hopes were dashed. The bar, a plank laid between two barrels at the rear of the tent, was crowded with laughing, jostling men, soldiers and civilians alike, lined up two or three deep. And they were apparently intent on only one thing—the whiskey they were drinking. In front of the bar were two tables, both of which were surrounded by men both playing cards and observing. And there were even men squatted along the tent walls, though what they were doing there I. W. had no idea. In short, the place was packed, and I. W. thought wryly that maybe he ought to give up running cows in the far lonesome and open up another saloon in this new fort. Of course, when she got wind of it, Mrs. I. W. Lacy would make short work of that little scheme.

"Well if it ain't I. W. Lacy, the LC cattle baron hisself!"

Turning, I. W. grinned at the long, cadaverous-looking man who had spoken. "Monk," he growled by way of reply, "I heard you got yourself killed down in the Nation."

"Practically," the man responded as he pushed himself away from where he'd been seated at a table. "Turns out the other feller was deader. I heard you'd moved the LC somewheres up into this country, I. W., but I didn't believe it. I didn't think they'd ever drag you outa Texas."

"Too much dry down thataway, Monk. I was losing more cows to drought than I was to Comanches, which since the buffalo all got killed has been considerable. Then I heard about the grass up here in the San Juan country, belly-deep to a tall horse even in the bad years, and I said to myself, I. W., if it's true, that's the country for you. Turns out it was, I was right, and here I am."

"So, where's your spread?"

"Place called Montezuma Creek, over west of here. Up near the head of the creek, directly under the Abajo or Blue Mountains, is where I built my place. Creek and everything else in that country drains into the San Juan, so I reckon that makes it San Juan country. But she's a paradise, Monk, a pure paradise!"

Monk nodded. "And Mrs. Lacy? She with you?"

"Nope. She's back on the home spread. We've still got ten, fifteen thousand cows there that she's keeping an eye on. Blamed if she ain't fattenin' 'em up, too, though how she does it without no grass nor water I can't hardly guess. That woman's got her a nose for the cow business, no two ways about it."

"And Laurie Yvonne? Is she here or back to Texas? Way I recollect, she ought to be about full growed and beautiful by now."

"She ought to be," I. W. replied sadly. "Only she ain't, on account of she's dead and buried."

Monk looked shocked. "I. W., I'm sorry. I hadn't heard."

"No harm done. And the man what done her dirt has been taken care of, too, so I reckon we're about even." I. W. glanced at Monk's pile of silver winnings and then quickly averted his eyes. "What you up to these days, old friend?"

Monk, too, glanced down at his cards and winnings, and then quickly he looked back up, feeling a little foolish. Gambling was, after all, a far cry from owning and running a hundred-thousand-acre cattle spread down on the Pecos River, and so it was embarrassing seeing his old neighbor like this. Still, maybe everything in life was just a big gamble.

"Oh, mostly just holding body and soul together, I reckon," he finally responded.

"You married again?"

The man shook his head. "Got nothing left to offer a woman, I. W., not since I lost my place. 'Sides, I'll never find another Abigail, and you know it."

"She was a good'un," I. W. acknowledged. "Purebred from the get-go. So were those two little gals of yours that died along with her. You hunting work, Monk? Bill Ball's fixing to go back to Texas for another four thousand head, which will give me somewhat more than thirty thousand here on the San Juan, and not nowheres near enough good men to run 'em. Happen you want it, you got yourself a job."

Monk smiled. "No, thanks, I. W. The cards have been treating me mighty nice lately, so I'll give 'em a chance to die on their own. Speaking of which, you want to set in on our game for a spell?"

I. W. Lacy shook his head. "Not hardly, Monk. Not yet, anyways. I'm here to sell a few cows, and after that, we'll see. Depends on how well I do. Besides maybe wetting my whistle, I came in here to learn who's the feller in charge of this fort. You happen to know?"

"Major Gruen, or Green, or some such as that. Seems like a nice enough feller. Quartermaster is an old Irishman name of Sergeant Tibble, and as of yesterday he had no beef contract with anybody. I know because he was in here grousing about it and wondering how he was going to feed all those soldiers once the few head they brought with 'em are gone."

"Then I'm his solution." I. W. grinned. "I can have him five hundred head by the end of next week, and as many more as—"

A sudden commotion behind him caused I. W. to turn, and as he

179

did so the crowd suddenly began scrambling to clear away. Caught in the press, the owner of the LC Cattle Company tried to push free, aware of chairs falling and tables crashing. Then directly inside the door-flaps appeared the angrily contorted and disfigured face of Sugar Bob Hazelton.

"I swore I'd get you," Sugar Bob snarled as he waved his pistol wildly at the elderly rancher. "Lacy, you lily-livered son-of-a-gun, there ain't nobody alive that can cut and geld Sugar Bob Hazelton and get away with it! Say your prayers, you miserable old galoot!"

And then, amid shouts of confusion and anger, the man leveled his pistol toward I. W. Lacy and began firing. Three gunshots echoed in the tent, sounding almost as one, and the air quickly filled with acrid blue powder smoke.

As fast as it had begun it was over, and the man called Monk, pulling himself out of the dust where he'd ducked, saw that the angry man, whose cut-off nose looked like nothing more than a huge, raw sore, was already backing out through the tent door-flaps, swinging his six-gun from side to side as he moved.

The instant the flaps closed after the murderer, Monk bounded to the side of the fallen I. W. Lacy. As he rolled him over, he saw that the old rancher had taken a bullet through the arm and at least one more through the chest, right over the heart. Now his breath was coming in ragged gasps, and Monk could see the signs.

"Oh, no, I. W. Not you!"

"Monk . . . I . . . reckon I should of killed him when I had the chance."

"Who was he, I. W.?"

"Su . . . Sugar Bob Hazelton. He's the one what . . . killed my Laurie Yvonne—"

"We'll get 'im, then."

Weakly I. W. Lacy shook his head. "No . . . no need, old friend. I . . . already did, and now I'm a goner, too. Must be justice in there somewheres, I reckon. Get word to . . . to Mrs. Lacy, will you? It's all hers now, the herds, the spread, everything—lock, stock, and barrel. And Monk, tell her I wasn't . . . I wasn't—"

"I'll tell her," Monk whispered brokenly, "and I'll tell her what you was, too, I. W., which is only the best blamed friend this man ever had!"

And then, amid the crowd that was already pushing their way past the body of the old rancher and back to the bar, the long, cadaverous man called Monk picked up his friend and ducked out through the door-flap of the tent. It was, he thought bitterly, a mighty lousy way to die.

——o—o—o——

Neskahi Wash

Tsabekiss, the Big Navajo, had a bad feeling. All day he had ridden through where the Wind People were moving, circling north from Jackrabbit Canyon to the breaks of the San Juan, east then to Neskahi Wash, and now back south toward his hogan in Jackrabbit Canyon. In all that riding he had seen no sign. No, nor had he seen sign the day before, when he had circled east and south from his home beneath the looming bulk of Navajo Mountain.

And that was why he was nursing a bad feeling. Those cursed *No'daá*, the Pahutes, had to be somewhere! And wherever they were, he was just as certain they were doing an evil thing.

He had lost several fine horses to the *No'daá* since his return from *Bosque Redondo*, and many fine sheep had been taken from his wife's flocks—the long-haired *churro* whose wool was so perfect for her weaving. The Pahutes had even taken a few of the sheep from the brush corral that was built near their hogan—the corral that had been designed to protect them—and no noise had been made at all. It was a constant drain on Tsabekiss's resources as well as his mind, and he could never tell when the hated *cliz bekigie*, the snake-skins, were coming to raid, nor how to defend himself from them.

Then not long ago the raids had stopped and the tracks had disappeared. Just like that. For more than thirty days Tsabekiss had watched uneasily, at first feeling relieved and then growing more and more concerned. After all, he knew the ways up and down past the cliffs of Navajo Mountain, and he knew the Pahutes could not simply vanish without leaving some sign. Yet that is what they had done, and the big Navajo was finally forced to conclude that there was a witch among the *No'daá*—a witch that had abandoned eating his horses and his wife's sheep and was now, since his son's visit to the empty encampment, eating up the mind of himself and his son.

Reining in on the lip of a low ridge, Tsabekiss surveyed the land before him. Earlier a curtain of rain had swept across the country, and for a moment he savored the rain smells it had left behind—dampened dust, wet sage, piñon resin, and buffalo grass. But then he pushed his mind past those things and sent his eyes to the small places where a man might leave his sign and not be aware of it. Yet again there was nothing, not a hoofprint, not a disturbed stone or broken branch of sage or juniper—nothing.

Breathing deeply the man dismounted and squatted beside his horse. Reaching under the serape his wife had woven and into the V neck of his shirt, he pulled out a leather pouch, took from it an odd-shaped piece of turquoise that had been worn smooth from much fingering, and laid it on the ground before him.

For a moment then he sang, his voice barely audible, only loud enough to be heard in the minds of his enemies.

> *No matter who would do evil to me,*
> *The evil shall not harm me.*

The words were part of the war chant, and Tsabekiss sang the rest of it without pausing, hoping he had got it right. Then he reached into his medicine bag again, took a pinch of corn pollen, touched a bit of it to his lips, threw a little upward to Sun and Sky, and put the remainder on the top of his head. Then he sang again, a short version of what a true singer would take much time to do.

Feeling some better, for now he had at least a little protection, the big man replaced the stone in his leather pouch and climbed back onto his horse. What he really needed, he knew, was a sing. Ever since his son Bitseel had found the empty camp of the Pahutes and had made the mistake of poking about it, things had not been right. Of course, the boy was not old enough to know all things, but even he should have known that to go into the place of an enemy, to touch his things, was to give the enemy power. Now, of course, he Tsabekiss would need to hire a singer—no, two singers and a scalp shooter, and hold an Enemy Way. At least he would if he wanted to take back the power Bitseel had given the *No'daá*. Though expensive, it would be a good thing for him and his family to be cleansed of the Pahutes' evil influence and within a year to be rid of them altogether. Yes, he thought, that would be a very good thing indeed!

Remounting, Tsabekiss nudged his horse down off the ridge and across the wide, nearly flat plain where his horses should have been grazing. That they weren't bothered him, for he did not have enough horses as it was. He was also bothered that Bitseel was not here with them, for the boy had been charged to keep an eye on the horses while his father was riding. Yet there were not even any tracks, and the rain had not been enough to wipe them away.

How he longed for his neighbors, the good people who had lived nearby before the Rope Thrower, Kit Carson, had come to drive them away. Tsabekiss thought of the Long Walk when he and thousands more of the *Diné* had been led to *Bosque Redondo*, The Grove, an arid and inadequate plain in New Mexico where the government of the *belacani* was supposed to feed them and care for them and teach them how to be farmers.

Yet never had their crops grown at Fort Sumner, never had the *belacani* government given them enough food or clothing, never had there been enough wood for fires or to build the hogans the People needed. Worse, sickness had raged at Fort Sumner, slaying many, and the People had not been able to get away from it.

Here in their own country between the four sacred mountains, the *Diné* understood the danger of such things and took measures to protect themselves. If one died, those left must abandon the hogan, either destroying it or at least closing the smoke-hole so others would know it was no longer a fit abode. But at *Bosque Redondo* there had been no place else to go, not with the *belacani* soldiers watching them all the time. And so many, including his own brother Tsa and many of his former neighbors, had died.

After four years of misery, the *Diné* had been sent home, first having sworn by treaty that they would never again raid the *belacani*, the whites. But they had been sent home in poverty, with one or two sheep and few horses, and with no way of increasing their wealth. Even their peach trees had been destroyed, for Rope Thrower had ordered his men to chop them down as they had gone through the country killing the livestock and burning the hogans and cornfields.

So how, they all asked themselves, could they increase their wealth again without raiding? No one seemed to have an answer to this, Tsabekiss included. Not unless they raided far to the north across the Big River, where dwelt the wealthy mormonee *belacani*. Many feared to do even this, for they did not want to be taken once again to *Bosque Redondo*. But the few who had made such raids had quickly learned that the white government did not think of the mormonee the same as it did the rest of its people. It was obvious that they were not so important, for after the raids no soldiers came, but only weak men bearing gifts and asking for peace.

Tsabekiss shifted uneasily on his pony as he thought this, for he knew it wasn't altogether true. Yes the mormonee came bearing gifts, and yes they did not want to fight. But there had been among them men of great power, men who did not blink at death, men who spoke quietly and slowly, without apparent weakness. These men, such as Jacob Hamblin, Ira Hatch, and Thales Haskell, bothered the big Navajo, for they could not be explained. And to the *Diné,* everything had to be in order, everything had to be understood, everything had to be explained.

Thus many things were spoken of these men, and many ideas put forth. Perhaps they too were children of First Man and First Woman. Or perhaps they had an understanding of Changing Woman and her hero twins, Monster Slayer and Child-of-the-Water. Perhaps they even had access to the Holy People. Or perhaps they were witches and got their power in dark ways.

Tsabekiss didn't know, but neither did he want much to do with them. And so he raided in the distant north rarely, preferring instead to breed his livestock and build his wealth closer to his homeland. And therein was his problem.

Upon his return from Fort Sumner and the *belacani* soldiers, Tsabekiss had been dumbfounded to find his homeland under the pleasing bulk of Navajo Mountain invaded and defiled by a small horde of filthy Pahutes, the *No'daá.* They were a lazy people of no industry who swarmed about the country like angry hornets, creating trouble where they could and taking whatever they managed to lay their hands on.

Of course, this was also raiding, but Tsabekiss didn't see it that way. For one thing, the *No'daá* raised no fine herds of livestock. Yes, they had their scraggly ponies and a few ugly goats. But whatever they stole they killed and ate immediately, taking no thought to what might be done with such a fine animal. Tsabekiss hated this wasting of precious animals, hated it nearly as much as he hated the Pahutes' abject poverty. For never did they have sufficient to make his raiding of them a worthwhile proposition, and with all his heart Tsabekiss wanted to raid them, to make them suffer just as he and his family had been made to suffer.

Still, he thought with a grim smile as he topped the next ridge and spotted his son and his horse herd in the distance, holding an Enemy Way sing to get rid of the *cliz bekigie,* the snake-skins, would be almost as good as raiding them. Then, at least, he and the few other *Diné* who had come back to Navajo Mountain could live in peace and prosperity.

With that thought big in his mind, Tsabekiss cantered his pony off the ridge, rode through a scattered grove of juniper, and gradually drew nearer to his young son and the horses that were slowly becoming his symbol of wealth.

22

Friday, December 12, 1879

Top of Hole-in-the-Rock

The first time Eliza looked down the narrow crevice that was supposed to continue the new wagon road to the San Juan country, which was more than a week after Billy had taken his first look, she wasn't even supposed to be there. But on account of chasing after their fool glass-eyed mare so she could drag in a little shadscale for firewood, she was. So she ignored the glances of the three men who were laboring on the rock nearby and stole a look—and immediately forgot for a moment the continual pain in her feet. For of an instant her knees grew wobbly, her head went light, and she was every bit as nauseated as she had been with her morning sickness more than a month before.

"Well," she whispered to herself, gripping her crutch and hobbling quickly back from the edge and not even noticing whether the men were watching her or not, "Billy warned you, woman. But no, you wanted a look for yourself. Serve you right if you lost your breakfast right here and embarrassed yourself further. Oh, dear Father, I ask thee to help me endure what I see is coming—"

Breathing deeply of the cold December air, Eliza willed her mind away from the Hole, refusing to think of the thin chasm the men were planning on turning into a road. Neither did she think of the three men who had been holding ropes in their hands, dangling something or other over the bulging edge of the cliff. Instead she thought for the hundredth time of the unlikely fact that she had now been involved in two desperate meetings in her lifetime, two life-

186

and-death decisions made by largely uninformed people who had chosen to go against reason and logic because of their faith.

Despite the fact that the first of these meetings had occurred more than twenty-three years before, Eliza could recall it as vividly as the one she had attended only a week ago. With more than a thousand others she had been seated on the side of a grassy swale outside Florence, Nebraska. While the late August sun had burned with unrelenting heat, the leaders of the two handcart companies—Captains Willie and Martin as well as a half-dozen other Church officials—had discussed the advisability of continuing to the Valley with so late a start or of establishing a winter camp somewhere nearby.

Clearly she could remember the lone dissenter to those who had advised going on—a man attached to the Willie Company whose name was Levi Savage. Boldly he had stood to declare that they could not cross the mountains with a mixed company of the aged, women, and little children so late in the season without much suffering, sickness, and death. He had therefore advised going into Winter Quarters without delay. Still wondering at it, Eliza could remember the hundreds and hundreds of people, herself included, enthusiastically voting against him—voting to go on.

"Brethren and sisters," Levi Savage had then added, his expression as bleakly clear in Eliza's mind as if she'd seen him only an hour before, "what I have said I know to be true; but seeing you are to go forward, I will go with you, will help you all I can, will work with you, will rest with you, will suffer with you, and, if necessary, I will die with you. May God in his mercy bless and preserve us."

Shuddering, Eliza tried to push from her mind the memories that followed, of ice-packed rivers, howling blizzards, broken handcarts, useless tents, and scant food and clothing that had proved completely insufficient to preserve life. Neither did she allow herself to remember the innumerable shallow graves, sometimes only beneath a thin layer of snow, that lined their bloody trail from the Platte River onward. Or the ghastly white skin on her feet and ankles that had denoted the irreparably damaging frostbite—

And now, twenty-three years later and still painfully crippled from the effects of that first decision, she was in the same situation again—part of a company of faithful but ignorant people who had voted to go forward on a winter march into unknown country for which they had not even begun to prepare. Why, after planning for a six-week journey from Cedar all the way through to the San Juan, they had already been out seven weeks and were only to the Colorado. Goodness only knew how much time it would take to cross the river and blaze a road through to the San Juan! Goodness only knew—

Yet still the company had voted to go on. And once again, Eliza thought in wonder, she had voted to go on with them!

Breathing deeply, Eliza rubbed at her eyes, physically wiping away the terrible vision that had been troubling her of late. Instead she thought of her own personal miracle, the pregnancy she had so recently been blessed with. For she was pregnant; more than half a lifetime older than almost every other woman in the party, far beyond the time any sensible woman would have stopped being fertile, her body was filled with new life. She was nearly three months along and already starting to show.

Despite that she was standing near the edge of a two-thousand-foot cliff facing the untold hardships of another winter expedition, Eliza almost smiled, not because it was practically embarrassing to be pregnant at forty-four, but because she felt so smug about it. Truth be known, in fact, she was proud as a peacock of herself. Trouble was, the scriptures taught that pride goeth before the fall. Should she continue feeling so blasted proud, she knew, she would get her comeuppance, and good! Only it felt so wondrous to be right about something for a change, exactly right, and to be so perfectly successful at a thing that really mattered—

Nearby the glass-eyed mare nickered from where she was munching some thin bunchgrass in a tiny swale between bulging sandstone humps, and Eliza glanced balefully at her. Ugly animal, with a knobby sway back and bony hip-shot rear and a huge round belly. Just like herself, Eliza thought with a little giggle—bony, angular, ugly as sin, and with a belly that was already starting to loom huge and round!

It was amazing that Billy could find her so lovable. Yet Eliza was positive that he did, not alone because of the things he was always saying but also because of the almost reverential way he acted whenever he was near.

Eliza laughed at that, thinking it was foolish for a grown man to act so. A month ago she would have scorned him for it, and in fact had scorned him time and time again. Yet in the last month something was growing within her, something besides an unborn baby. Somehow she was feeling more mellow toward Billy, more tolerant. Why, to her everlasting surprise, she even found herself looking forward to spending time with him, if that could be imagined. Oh, there were still things about him that bothered her—bothered her a great deal. And there were moments when the old shame returned. But all-in-all, things between them seemed to be improving. In fact, she had the sneaking suspicion that one day she would come to realize that Billy was a man who was like nothing she had ever expected, but who would turn out to be everything she had ever dreamed of.

As for herself, however, Eliza had no difficulty seeing that she was definitely more happy, more outgoing, more filled with an unreasonable hope for the future. Why, two of the sisters in the company had even made not-so-subtle comments about it. But instead of offending her as they might have in the past, their remarks had been welcome, and now fond friendships were growing where once had been only silence and a feeling of terrible distance. Why, she was even learning the names of the other folks in the company, and to her surprise had found several who had connections in one way or another to her past.

Of course, Eliza had pondered this change that seemed to be occurring within her. Both Mary and Billy would have stated emphatically that it was a blessing due completely to the fact that she was repenting. And she *was* doing her best in that regard—studying the scriptures and praying daily and usually many times more than that. But on purpose she wasn't asking the Lord to bring her and Billy closer together, and on purpose she wasn't telling either Billy or Mary about the changes she was beginning to feel. Instead she was keeping it all within herself, allowing the Lord to do whatever he had in mind with no further meddling from herself or any other mortals—

"You all right, Sister Foreman, ma'am?"

Looking up, Eliza smiled. The speaker was James W. Pace, who had, with his father-in-law George Sevy and a few others, joined the company in Panguitch. A quiet young man of probably twenty-five or twenty-six years, he had, with his sweet wife Hannah, already experienced more mortal grief than Eliza could even imagine. The parents of five children, they had lost the oldest four of them to sickness during the single month before starting on this mission to the San Juan. Think of it! Burying four precious children in a month's time. It was no wonder that Brother James was quiet, and that Sister Hannah clung so lovingly to her tiny Margaret Melinda.

Oh, if only they could see what lay ahead—

"I'm fine, thank you," Eliza replied with a forced smile. "I suppose I wasn't quite prepared for what I saw."

"No one is, ma'am." James Pace rubbed his hands where the rope had burned them, and then he and the two Perkins brothers stretched their aching muscles. "George Hobbs says the Hole's steeper than the slide into hades, and I reckon he's about right. Myself, I try not to look down it too much. Thoughts of driving a wagon down it scare the bejeebies out of me—pardon the language, ma'am—but it's a fact, nonetheless."

"Steepness up here isn't so much the problem," Hyrum Perkins declared in his rich Welsh voice. "What worries me is the place where our road will come out of the Hole. There's a fifty- or sixty-foot drop there that's practically straight down, with nowhere else to go. Now, that's steep!"

Ben Perkins, Hyrum's older brother, smiled. "That it is," he agreed quietly, his baritone voice even richer than his brother's. "But I've a bit of a solution in mind. I'll need to study on it some, but I'm thinking we can continue the road right to the bottom without too much trouble."

"What?" Hyrum asked, Eliza already forgotten.

"I'd rather not say yet, for I haven't studied it all the way through." With a smile, Ben Perkins turned again to Eliza. "If you listen carefully, Sister Eliza, you can hear the sound of the men building the road down below the Hole. I reckon that's where Billy is. If you need him, one of us will be delighted to rope on down and give him a holler."

"No, I . . . uh . . . " Eliza was immediately embarrassed. "I didn't mean to come and see Billy," she finally declared, adjusting her heavy shawl over her shoulders and smiling widely to hide her discomfiture. "I was just trying to catch that fool, glass-eyed mare of ours."

The men nodded, for the wandering mare had become a familiar sight to all in the company, and all knew the animal would respond willingly to no one but Billy.

"Jimmy," Ben Perkins called from his place by the rope, "someone needs to be hauled up."

Eliza was stunned. "You . . . haul people up . . . with that rope?"

"Some, ma'am, when they're in a tolerable hurry. They ride in half a barrel, built by Charlie Hall of Escalante."

"Does . . . Billy ride that way?"

"No, ma'am, at least not yet. Billy takes the trail like the rest of us sane folks, which is a couple of miles north of here, up the river. In another week we'll have a trail cut out right here, too, and that will save a sight of time."

Shuddering at the thought of anyone riding up or down that cliff in a barrel, Eliza turned and caught the end of the glass-eyed mare's rope with the tip of her crutch. Hobbling forward, she had to stoop twice before she was able to catch the rope in her hand.

"You need any help, Sister Foreman?"

Brother Pace was obviously concerned. "No, thank you, James." Eliza smiled as sweetly as she could, at the same time pulling at the mare's head to get her attention.

"Sometimes I seem to start dreaming, and when I do, somebody might as well come up and shoot me for all the good I get done. Maybe, though, if I can persuade this fool, glass-eyed mare to go where I want her to go, I can get some of this useless shadscale dragged up for the sisters who are assigned the cooking this week, and sometime tonight we can all have a bait of supper."

———o—o—o———

Jackrabbit Canyon

With the doorskin closed, it was dark inside the sweat lodge, dark and hot. Tsabekiss relished the steam for its cleansing power on

191

his body; he relished it more because he knew it was the first step in the ritual cleansing of his heart and mind.

Outside the tiny lodge, the day was calm and bright, with the first clear weather in many days, and the big Navajo felt good that Sun had at last driven the Wind People and the Rain People into hiding. His woman, he knew, would be seated at her loom outside his *atchí'deezáhi,* laboring to complete another blanket. These, he had learned, were becoming valuable to traders, and so the more she wove, the more she helped overcome their difficult condition.

Tsabekiss sighed and pulled his thoughts away from their wanderings. After all, this sweat was a cleansing of both body and mind, and he wanted to be cleansed in every particular. He thought of the good day showing outside the sweat lodge, and that was helpful.

Bitseel was again with the horses in a protected canyon nearby, and Tsabekiss's daughter Dawn Girl was with the sheep not far away either, thus allowing his wife the time to do her weaving. In the old days, Tsabekiss thought without much rancor, he had had enough Mexican slaves to watch both the sheep and the horses, leaving his children time to learn their duties in the Navajo Way, and his wife to weave all she wanted. But these were no longer the old days.

"Ho," he said to the sweat lodge's only other occupant, his wife's cousin's husband, Dagai Iletso, or Yellow Whiskers, "in my mind is the time when the mother of your wife's mother was carried away by the *No'daá.*"

"It was a bad time," Dagai Iletso admitted into the darkness. "The Utes took her for her skills at weaving."

"Not for themselves," Tsabekiss stated, knowing the story well but enjoying the conversation and wanting it to continue.

"That is a true saying. It was the *Nakai,* the Mexicans, who wanted her. They have never been very good weavers."

Tsabekiss chuckled. "But they are very good keepers of our flocks and herds. Especially the *Nakai* children."

Dagai Iletso agreed, thinking nostalgically of the slaves he himself had captured and owned. Without thought he poured a little more water from the round-bottomed pot onto the hot rocks, letting the increased steam flow over his naked body.

"The Red Foreheads held an Enemy Way ceremony after the

woman was taken," he declared after a moment or two. "Perhaps it was the last one."

"Not so," Tsabekiss disagreed gently. "Such a sing was held by some of the clan when Rope Thrower was rounding up the People for the *belacani* at *Bosque Redondo*. I was in attendance at that one."

"It did not bring the mother of my wife's mother back to her hogan."

"Neither did it stop Rope Thrower from taking most of us for slaying or to Fort Sumner." Tsabekiss thought for a moment. "Of course, the *No'daá* never again took a slave from the Red Foreheads. And now many of us are on our lands again, between the four sacred mountains, and *Bosque Redondo* is just a bad memory. Who is to say what powerful medicine may be found in the Enemy Way?"

"That is a true saying," Dagai Iletso concurred. "Did you have a star gazer come to Bitseel?" he asked after a few more moments of silence. "Or did you have a hand trembler come?"

"It was *hosteen* Bitsi who came," Tsabekiss acknowledged.

Dagai Iletso knew that *hosteen* Bitsi was a hand trembler. "He is very old."

"He is. And his medicine is good. He sang all the hand-trembling songs and held his hand out over the boy Bitseel, and it shook and shook. He said he thought it was a *No'daá* witch that was bothering him, causing all the bad things to happen and giving him bad dreams. Or maybe it was *chinde,* the ghost of a witch, that was doing it all."

Dagai Iletso grunted. "There are times when a hand trembler gets things wrong."

"That is so." Now Tsabekiss grunted. "To try the *chinde* we had a blackening; this was two darknesses past. Bitseel slept with ashes all over him, which made him invisible to the *chinde* so that he had no dreams."

"That is good, my cousin. *Nayenezgani,* Monster Slayer, blackened himself so evils would fear him, and it is a known thing that enemy ghosts fear the soot and will not stay near it. Do you have knowledge of *haáthali,* a singer who knows the Enemy Way?"

"I have been told that *hosteen* Yazzi has such an understanding." He paused, feeling the old concern creeping back into his mind. "My son Bitseel desires to be the scalp shooter."

Amazed, Dagai Iletso stared at his cousin through the gloom. "The boy is young," he said with wonder. "Very young."

Tsabekiss knew that this was so. He also knew that Bitseel had never had an Enemy Way sung over him. "He knows the way to the encampment of the *No'daá*," he finally said. "And he is very determined. He is a son to make a man proud."

"That is so. Who will teach him the Tracking Bear Song?"

"I myself have already taught him," Tsabekiss stated with some pride. Then, after pouring more water over the heated rocks, he rubbed his hands carefully over his arms, chest, and legs, softly chanting as he did so.

"In shoes of dark flint I track the Ute warrior," he began, and then his words spoke of tracking the Ute warriors with Big Snake Man, acting always as Tracking Bear, and slaying both them and the Ute women and taking their scalps.

In silence Dagai Iletso considered the powerful chant he had just heard.

"There is more, of course," Tsabekiss stated after a long pause. "Bitseel knows it all."

"You will need many sheep to pay for this sing and to feed the People."

Tsabekiss grunted his acknowledgment.

"In the clan of my wife there are starting to be many sheep. I will see what I can do."

"Well," Tsabekiss stated after more silence, "I think we should have this sing soon—in six days' time."

"That is very soon, but I think you are right. I will spread the word."

Tsabekiss indicated his gratitude for the burdens Dagai Iletso had willingly taken upon himself, and then throwing the doorskin back, he and his wife's cousin's husband crawled into the sunlight to rub their bodies clean. Truly, he thought as he squinted his eyes against Sun's glare, *hózhó,* balance in the universe, was going to come again.

23

Sunday, December 14, 1879

Top of Hole-in-the-Rock

"How are your legs feeling?"

From where he sat cross-legged on the sandstone, Billy smiled at his wife. "My legs are just dandy, Eliza."

"Billy, you tell me the truth now. You hear?"

Smiling at Eliza's concern, which was something else that was new about her, Billy reached over and took her hand. "I'm telling you the truth, hon-bun. They're fine, and by morning they'll be first-rate. Now stop worrying your pretty head on account of my legs."

And Billy's legs were fine—that despite the fact that he was wondering, as he sat there, if they would ever truly recover. Ten times he had been up the lower half of the Hole the day before, collecting dropped tools to send up in the half-barrel, and ten times he had scrambled back down again to get himself out of the "line of fire" of dropping tools, as Ben Perkins put it. And now, a whole day later, his legs were all a-tremble so that he walked like someone drunk, and there was so much pain in the front of his thighs that whenever he tried to step down, even if only a few inches, it about brought tears to his eyes.

Thank goodness this was Sunday, he thought wryly. A day's rest ought to be long enough to stop the pain, and by morning, with any luck at all, he should be able to crawl back down that trail and get on with the work he'd been assigned.

Before him now a large juniper fire burned, juniper some of the brethren had loaded in a wagon and hauled nearly twenty miles to

195

the camp, and as he sat on a folded quilt beside his beloved Eliza waiting for the others to gather to meeting, Billy adjusted his spectacles and thought how wonderful it felt to do nothing but sit.

"Who are those men?" Eliza whispered as two men strode into the firelight with Platte D. Lyman, assistant captain of the expedition.

"Two of the Escalante boys," Billy replied. "The one on the right is Bishop Andrew Schow, and the other, the man with one arm, is Reuben Collett. I understand he used to be a peace officer. They're the ones who did the first exploration and found the Hole."

Eliza shuddered. "I saw the Hole day before yesterday."

"You did?" Billy was astounded.

"You were right," Eliza stated through set teeth. "It was awful! I believe everyone must be crazy to think we can drive wagons down off that cliff. Why, it's worse than straight down!"

"It won't be, once we blast a bunch of that rock off the face and make a more gradual cut."

"There'll be blasting?"

"We hope so, once we get some powder."

"Do the men know how to do that?"

Billy grinned. "Well, the Perkins brothers surely do. They were Welsh coal miners before they emigrated to Zion. They've even been teaching me a little about it, or at least a little about drilling. Why, the one time I tried it yesterday they said I had a real knack for it. I didn't have a fitcher the whole time, and—"

"A what?"

"Fitcher—when the drill gets stuck in the hole. It's caused by not turning the bit regularly. I didn't have one, and if I hadn't hit the bit wrong with the singlejack that one time, I could have done a lot more than I did."

Billy could see that his wife was surprised by the pride in his voice. But then, so was he. It felt good learning to do such things, and it felt even better thinking that perhaps he might be making some sort of contribution to the success of the company. Come down to it, he thought with a secret smile, in time he might even turn into a real frontiersman.

"Well, you be careful—"

"Hon-bun, with you waiting at the wagon, and with the prospects of seeing my own firstborn looming larger and larger—" Billy reached over and gently patted his wife's tummy—"I'll never *ever* take a single desperate chance. You have my word on that."

Eliza smiled at him, and Billy, as fiercely determined to please her and make her proud of him as he had been the first day he'd seen her, renewed again his vows of eternal love and fidelity. Eliza was the most amazing thing that ever happened to him, and the wonder of her seemed to grow greater each day.

"Dear Lord," he breathed as he gazed into her lovely eyes, "I know I haven't ever done a thing to deserve her, but nonetheless I'm thankful as can be that you brought Eliza and me together—"

The meeting began then, Jens Nielson conducting, and after a song and brief prayer Platte Lyman stepped forward to speak.

"How many are living on parched corn and seed grain?" the man asked abruptly.

Billy looked around and was surprised to see the number of hands that went up. "Are we?" he asked quickly, quietly, of his wife.

"Not yet," she whispered back. "By the end of this next week, though, I expect we'll have to."

"Captain?" The speaker was Bishop Schow of Escalante, who now stepped forward. "We've got quite a bit of grain, beans, and squash at the storehouse, and wagons will have most of that here by the first of next week. I know Brother Hall has some molasses still on hand, made from his own sorghum, I might add, and he told me your party were welcome to it. Then for those of you with a little extra money, some of the folks in town have truck goods and pigs and other livestock they'd no doubt part with at a fair price. Maybe you could send wagons back for that. I do hope that'll be of help to you."

Platte Lyman nodded. "Thank you, Bishop. It will. Now, for those of you who are reduced to grinding your seed wheat in your coffee mills, I've been told that Wilson Dailey has rigged a more effi- cient handle to his coffee mill at Fifty-Mile Camp, and any and all are welcome to use it. I might add that in the morning Wilson will be moving his black-smithing forge here to the Hole, as will Brother George Lewis, who has joined us from Kanab. I expect that two forges will be enough to keep sharp the drills, chisels, and picks dulled by these blasters and blowers from Wales."

There was a chuckle from the congregation, for all knew that Brother Lyman was referring to Ben and Hyrum Perkins.

"Brother Decker," Platte Lyman asked, "would you give us a report on your labors?"

A quiet man, Cornelius Decker moved to the firelight and removed his floppy, wide-brimmed hat. "Well," he said, very serious, "us boys from Fifty-Mile Camp are doing fine."

"The dugway up out of the river to the east is progressing?"

The man smiled widely. "I'd tell a man, Brother Lyman. Why, I don't think I've ever seen a lot of men go to work with more of a will to do something than our crowd has. The way our boys make that dirt and rock fly is a caution, a pure-dee caution. We'll have our road made by the time the Cedar boys get that ledge above the Hole shot down, and that's a promise."

Some in the congregation laughed and applauded, and Platte Lyman joined with them. "We'll hold you to that, Brother Decker," he responded. "Sister Elizabeth, you keep prodding him, will you?"

"You bet I will," Elizabeth Decker answered from behind Billy and Eliza, and there was more good-natured laughter and bantering.

"All right, you Cedar boys, your turn. Ben Perkins, how goes work on the Hole?"

His boundless energy evident, Benjamin Perkins leaped to his feet and strode into the firelight, where he, too, removed his hat. "Ready we'll be to blast once we get some powder," he said with a twinkle in his eye. "I've a fine crew of drillmen, both up and down, and the boys we've thrown over the ledge have the first drift ready for powder. A fine seam there be down in the Hole at the base of the cliff, running straight out, and by widening it a mite we'll have tons of easy fill for the road below."

"Can you keep busy until the powder comes?"

Ben Perkins nodded his head. "Of course, Brother Lyman. Fact of the matter is, the boys about have the road completed from the river up to the cliff. Then, too, I've a bit of an idea that might provide a road out the bottom of the Hole without much blasting."

"Do tell."

"There be an angled cliff that runs left, or to the north, coming out of the Hole. I've cast my eye along it, and with a bit of drilling and some good oak staves of between three and four feet, I'm of the opinion that a good road may be tacked onto that cliff—a dugway, if you will, and nowhere near so steep as at the top."

"Where would it come off?"

"At the top of the sandhill. Simple it would be, I'm thinking, to lay the road from the river over to there."

Platte Lyman looked at Ben Perkins thoughtfully. "A dugway, is it? Wouldn't that take a lot of wood?"

"Mostly driftwood, I'm of the opinion, and brush. Beyond the oak staves, that is. We'd blast out a groove for the inside iron tires, and by bringing up the fill to that level, a tolerable road is what we'd have."

"Is he serious, Billy?" Eliza asked as she turned to her husband.

"Sounds like it, hon-bun. Anybody else I'd think they were crazy, but not Ben Perkins. That feller knows what he's about."

"How . . . how far would a person fall, happen the road didn't hold to the cliff?"

Billy shook his head. "Beats me, Eliza. Forty, fifty feet, maybe, if he means where I think he means. But the cliff isn't vertical, either. It slopes some, so a fall would be more of a skid, or a roll, and probably wouldn't be deadly."

"Unless you ended up with your head smashed like a melon against some boulder at the bottom! I'm telling you, Billy, that sounds scary to me."

Billy reached over and took Eliza's hand. "Have faith, Eliza." Billy was building his own bravado as much as Eliza's, and maybe more. "Remember, this is the Lord's work we've been called to do. If we perish, at least we perish unto him."

"Billy Foreman!" Eliza whispered fiercely, suddenly upset. "I didn't sell my shop in Salt Lake and drag myself into this howling wilderness just to put myself into a position of perishing 'unto the Lord.' Or marry you, either one! And I certainly didn't get with child for that purpose. So I'll thank you to stop talking like that."

Surprised, Billy nodded.

199

"Besides, I've waited a long time for this little one, more than anyone can begin to imagine—"

"Thank you, Ben," Platte Lyman was concluding. "I'll look at it with you tomorrow. Now, is Dick Butt or another of the herd-boys here?"

There was the scrape of boots, and young Willard Butt rose to his feet and moved to the front. "I'm here," he responded quietly.

"Good, Dick. What's the status of the livestock?"

Shyly the young man shuffled his feet. "I . . . uh . . . I reckon we have about twelve hundred head of cattle back on the Escalante Creek drainage, up west a mile or so from all those arches and such. They're some spread out, ranging from Ten-Mile Flat down past Coyote Holes and Dance Hall Rock all the way to Forty-Mile Spring. Most, I reckon, are nearer the spring. Tolerable feed, but nowhere near enough."

"Water?"

"No problem since this last snow. It's melted in every rock hollow from here to Escalante. With that and the springs and seeps, there's plenty of water."

"And the horses and mules?"

"Well, we took all eight hundred head of 'em down onto Jackass Mesa yesterday . . . no, day before yesterday, it was."

"Jackass Mesa?" somebody called from the congregation. "Where's that?"

Dick Butt grinned out into the darkness. "Couple miles north of here, and down off the rim. We named it that on account of only a jackass would be fool enough to take the trail down to it. Fact is, we lost eight animals going down, though I hope the boys will be able to salvage most of the meat. I reckon there's about a hundred acres of pretty good pasture there—enough at least for a few days."

"Any water there?"

The young man nodded his head. "Same as here—in every rock hollow on the mesa. Besides that, there's a hint of an old Indian trail that winds on down to the river. Happen we run shy of water in the hollows and tanks, we'll run them critters on down to the river whether they're thirsty or not."

"How come we don't make the road down off this Jackass Mesa instead of blasting through that fool hole?"

Platte Lyman turned to the one-armed man behind him. "Reuben, you want to answer that?"

Reuben Collett stepped forward. "We thought of it," he stated quietly. "But betwixt us and the head of that trail, the country's so scarred and cut up it'd take longer to build a road across it than to blast ahead down through the Hole. In short, the best route is the most direct one, so far as we can judge."

"She's rugged country between here and yonder," Dick Butt agreed, nodding his head toward the north. "The horses made it, but I'd hate to try wagons."

"I'm a little gun-shy about trying 'em down that Hole we're figuring on cutting," somebody called back sarcastically, and again there was a ripple of laughter, easing the tension.

Jens Nielson then hobbled forward, and Dick Butt made his way back to his seat next to Julie Nielson.

"Brudders and sisters," the large old man said in his broken English, "ve haff all of us been called by a prophet of God on dis mission to de San Juan, und derefore God iss over de vork. Ve are to plant a colony betwixt our people und de vild Indians of dat country, a buffer to der savagery, it has been called, und ve are to teach the whole of dem de gospel of Yesus Christ. It iss a noble undertaking, und a great vone.

"Even under present circumstances ve are much blessed, und der iss great unity in our camp, for vich I tank de Lord. But der iss much to do before ve can come to de country of our mission, und vithout great sticky-to-ity ve vill surely fail. Ya, I vill say it again. Vithout great sticky-to-ity und love for each other, ve vill surely fail. In de name of Christ Yesus I say it. Amen."

24

Wednesday, December 17, 1879

Top of Hole-in-the-Rock

"Mighty cold wind today." Platte Lyman pulled his collar tighter at the neck. "Hope it doesn't mean more snow."

Without answering or even looking up, George Sevy poked a stick into the small fire, hoping to scare out a little more heat. At his back the canvas of his wagon billowed and snapped in the wind, and he knew that his wife Maggie was inside, trying to keep warm and overhear the conversation at the same time.

"You want an expedition of the four of us to leave today?" Lemuel Redd, Sr., asked. A genial man, he was known far and wide simply as Pap Redd, which helped distinguish him from his son Lemuel Redd, Jr., who with his wife and daughter was also on the expedition. "Under the direction of George Sevy but led by George Hobbs," Pap Redd continued. "Is that what you're asking?"

"That's right, Pap."

"Well," the man said good-naturedly as he squatted on his heels, "the rest of you boys may be saltier than a late summer deer lick, but I'm not. I'm tired. Fact is, the whole idea hits me harder'n a heel-clod from the leader in a horse race. Or maybe a whippy branch slashing close behind the man I'm following through thick brush. I'm not sure I can keep up with you young sprouts on a winter trek."

"George Sevy's about your age, Pap."

"Maybe," the cattleman grinned wryly as he looked up at George Sevy, "but he looks to have wintered through better'n me."

The men chuckled, and Platte, glancing at the rest of them, con-

202

tinued. "Before our whole company gets across that river, boys, I want to make certain we can punch a road through to Montezuma Creek on the San Juan. That's where we've been called to settle. As you know, we've sent some others across to look at that country, and every one of them comes back with a different opinion. Well, I'm not interested in opinions. I want you boys to push all the way through to Montezuma Creek—or at least to push until you can go no further. That way, at least, we'll know."

"You planning on turning back if we can't?"

"Or at least trying a different tack, Brother Morrell. Right now the snow's too deep on the Escalante Mountain to turn back—five feet at the least. But we can't stay here on the plateau, either. She's way too exposed, and there's no way to feed our animals or keep warm. So you boys have got to find out if we can go ahead, or if we need to hole up for the winter someplace back near Escalante.

"Brother Hobbs, you look like you have a burr under your saddle."

"I don't hardly know if I do or not," George Hobbs grumbled as he toed a burning stick with his boot and then squatted down across the fire from Pap Redd. "I don't know these here fellers too well, 'cept for George Morrell. But the last bunch of hardy explorers I crossed the river with were too weakhearted to go more than a day to the east, and some not even that far. Tell the truth, Platte, I'd about as rather go exploring with Billy Foreman as tackle another exploring party like the last one."

"Brother Hobbs," George Sevy declared emphatically, "I can't speak for the others, but for myself, I'd rather you didn't speak disparagingly of Billy Foreman. He's become a friend of mine."

George Hobbs laughed easily. "I didn't mean that offensively, fellers. It's just that—well, you know what I mean."

"We all have our gifts, Brother Hobbs. Our weaknesses, too— you and Billy Foreman alike. And we won't be discussing this issue any further." Platte Lyman looked at the other three men. "What about it, boys? You feel up to George Hobbs's challenge?"

George Sevy squared his shoulders. "Brother Hobbs, you accompany us on this little jaunt we've been called to pursue, and I'll follow as far as you dare lead."

"I'm with Bishop Sevy," Pap Redd stated quietly as he rose to look down at the younger man, his ire apparent. "Today I may feel used up as a dance-hall gal come six o'clock of a Sunday morning. But wherever Hobbs leads once we get started, I'll be closer behind him than a bull snake's shadow. Fact is, Brother Lyman, and you can bank on this and burn the receipt, Hobbs here can go till hell freezes over and then camp on the crust, and he'll still find me standing in his most recent moccasin tracks."

"And I'm with the rest of you boys," George Morrell added with a grin that seemed to come naturally to his face no matter what he was feeling. "But Brother Pap Redd here has got me to wondering about something else that may come up. With three fellers named George among the four of us, ain't we likely to have a hard time telling each other apart?"

"No harder'n folks have calling everybody Brother all the time," George Hobbs groused in return. "I declare, some days I about get 'Brothered' out." Quickly he rose from where he'd been squatting before the fire. "Fellers, my camp's back at Fifty-Mile, so by the time I round up a few supplies and get back here, it ought to be two, maybe three o'clock. That give the rest of you enough time to get ready?"

"As ever, *Brother* Hobbs," George Morrell said with a sly grin.

"Humph!"

"Pack up supplies enough for eight days," Platte Lyman instructed. "That ought to be enough, hadn't it?"

"It ought to." George Hobbs's sarcasm suddenly erupted. "*Brother* Morrell, now you look like a man has something to say."

Again George Morrell smiled, this time almost sheepishly. "I was just thinking of the weight of an eight-day pack of supplies, is all."

"And?"

"Well, some of the fellers who crossed the river a few weeks back said it would take a thousand dollars appropriation from the legislature just to construct a burro trail through the first ten miles of that country. You hold with that view, Brother Hobbs?"

George Hobbs laughed outright. "Not hardly I don't. Fact is, I believe I could get a burro through with hardly any labor at all."

"Good," George Morrell said with satisfaction. "Because I've got the burro, and I'd like him to pack my supplies."

"Fair enough. Bring him along."

"That being the way the land lies," Pap Redd said with a twinkle in his eye, "I've got me a mule that's not much larger than Brother Morrell's burro. If you can get a burro through, Brother Hobbs, then I do believe I can get my mule through about as easily."

"And I've got a horse not much bigger than Pap's mule," George Sevy added with a chuckle. "If we can get the burro and the mule through, then I reckon I can get that horse through, too."

There was a little silence then, and Pap Redd started to chuckle. "I declare, Brother Hobbs. That slack-jawed look of your'n puts me to mind of the village idiot when he sees the purty young school-marm for the first time. Ain't you got nothing to say?"

George Hobbs glanced at the older man, his look baleful. "I don't hardly cotton to being poked fun at," he finally declared. "Or to being left odd man out." And then he chuckled easily. "Howsomever, Joseph Lillywhite's got him a horse about the same size as George Sevy's nag that I reckon he'd loan me, was I to ask him nice. Reckon I'd better, just to keep peace in this here new little family of ours."

"Four animals," Platte Lyman assented. "Two for packing, two for riding. Sounds to me like a mighty fine expedition."

"How far you figure to have gone by the time we get back?" Pap Redd asked quietly, changing the subject.

Platte Lyman looked off toward the Hole. "Nowhere, Pap. Fact is, we won't be going anywhere at all until Captain Smith gets us some blasting powder and some tools from the legislature, and that's no matter how long you're gone. Even with all the powder we can use, Ben Perkins thinks it'll take four to six weeks to blast down that Hole. So take your time, boys. Take your time."

"With eight days' worth of supplies?" George Hobbs laughed again. "Thank you, but no thank you, Brother Lyman. We intend to push this expedition right along. Now, if you girls are about through with all your gabbing—"

And with some good-natured shoving and laughter the men broke up to begin gathering their supplies.

25

Thursday, December 18, 1879

Jackrabbit Canyon

Natanii nééz, who had taken upon himself the *belacani* name of
Frank, sat beneath the boulder where the sun would warm the sand,
idly watching the members of his born-to clan, the Streams Come
Together people. The early morning air was cold, and he was glad
that he had dressed warmly. He was a tall man, barrel-chested and
muscular, and it pleased him that his size created both awe and fear
among those who gazed upon him. Over the years he had learned to
use his size, always to his own advantage, and he had come to
believe that he was pretty much invincible.

Except, that is, for the man Peokon, whom Frank feared with all
his soul. Frank was larger than Peokon, too, though it made not a
feather's weight of difference. When he was with Peokon he always
felt small, like *áwéé áshkii,* a boy-child. Still, Peokon had taught
Frank much concerning the getting of gain, and Frank looked upon
him as a close friend, a brother.

Now, though, something evil was happening to Peokon, something evil that Frank did not like to even think about. So, forcing
thoughts of the man from his mind, Frank gazed about the country
in Jackrabbit Canyon. It was the second day of the Enemy Way
ceremony, light but with no sun yet showing, and many of the
assembled *Diné* had already climbed the ridge to bless the rising sun
with prayer and a pinch of pollen. Like almost all others of the
Streams Come Together clan, the clan of his mother, he had gathered
upon invitation to the hogan of Tsabekiss. Unlike the others,

however, and despite the fact that he had been born for the Standing Rock people and so taught by his father in the ways of the *Diné,* Frank had learned to consider the ceremony foolish. In fact, under Peokon's careful tutelage, Frank had come to feel that the only thing that wasn't foolish about the old way, the way of the People, as they called it, was the raiding. Raids Frank both enjoyed and promoted. He always had and always would.

Frank considered the ceremony that was progressing within Tsabekiss's hogan. No doubt the sand painting would be completed by now, of Corn Beetle and Big Fly being surrounded on all but the east side by the Guardian, and the boy Bitseel crouching with hands and feet on the hands and feet of Corn Beetle. Four alternating lines of red and yellow sand, the Guardian's body would have been painted in a large square with his head to the north and his feet to the south. In the opening to the east Old Man Yazzi, the singer, would no doubt have placed Thunder with all his crooked arrows, for in the two other Enemy Way sings Frank had seen him do, it had been so.

And all the while Old Man Yazzi would have been singing the chants, about Corn Beetle telling Changing Woman that her sons the Twins were well and that Monster Slayer had slain the *Yeí.* Then would follow the chant of Big Fly telling the People that Black God and the warriors were returning from their victory against the Pueblos, and of the two girls taking food to the warriors.

Any minute now Bitseel and the rest of the family would come out of the hogan to vomit, having been given the powerful concoction that would bring it to pass. Such vomiting was supposed to rid them of the enemy that had got inside their bodies, but of course all it rid them of was the remnants of their previous meal.

Frank grinned knowingly, thinking about it, and he almost laughed when, just as the edge of the sun topped the mesa to the southeast, the boy Bitseel suddenly broke out the doorway of the lodge and stumbled hurriedly toward the sheep corral. He was followed immediately by the others, and last of all by Old Man Yazzi, who stopped and stood alone outside the east-facing door opening, breathing deeply of the cooler outside air.

In an hour or so the Stick Receivers would arrive for the Encounter between the Camps. That would be followed by some other rituals, including the gift giving, all of them leading to the scalp shooting. Already Old Man Yazzi had burned the required sticks, grasses, and feathers for the ash, which would be smeared over Bitseel before his attack on the enemy scalp. And of course in the evening everything would be followed by the Girl Dance, which would last until after dawn.

People came from all over for that, Frank knew, for it was a big celebration: girls looking for husbands, young men looking for girls, horse racing, and here and there some gambling and other noisy fun. And in fact, that was at least partially why Frank had come. Learning from Peokon, he had become more than proficient at gambling with cards, and he seldom lost. Unless, that is, he chose to. And then only at the beginning.

Smiling with his vast knowledge, Frank allowed his mind to continue rehearsing the ceremony called Enemy Way. Early in the morning of the third day, Old Man Yazzi would lead Tsabekiss and his family from the hogan. Then the Singer would sing the four First Songs and the Coyote Song, and Bitseel and his family would inhale the necessary four deep breaths of the Dawn People. Then the boy and his family would be cured, and the witch—in this case some poor, unsuspecting Pahute—would have his witchcraft turned against him. Also, he would have one year left in which to live.

If the Pahute were a witch, that is.

And if the foolish old ceremony had any power.

Still smiling, Frank kept his eyes on the gathering crowd, searching for those he wanted to entice with a little liquor and a game of cards. It wouldn't take much of either, he knew, to get the men where he wanted them, not with so many of them struggling in poverty and feeling overwhelmed by the *belacani* government's changing of their ways. And since *Bosque Redondo*, their ways had definitely changed.

Of course, Frank had not been rounded up by the one called Rope Thrower, and so he had little experience with the white soldiers. Instead he had hid out in the big canyon with the powerful Peokon, who was wise in many things, and who had known that the old ways of the People were foolish and ready to be discarded.

"Ho, Cousin."

Turning, Frank saw the scowling face of a man named

Hoskanini, and to his side the equally scowling face of his son Hoskanini Begay. But the scowls meant little, and Frank knew it, for both the older man and his son were *ana'dlohi,* filled with much laughter, at least when they weren't angry.

"Ho, Cousin," he responded in return, wondering if these men would do for his plans. For he did have a plan, one that was much larger than the mere gambling for possessions with cards. "Sit here beside me, if you wish."

Hoskanini nodded and took a place on Frank's sheepskin, while his son laid out another sheepskin and sat upon it at their feet.

After a respectable silence the two men began speaking of things that had little to do with anything. Finally, however, the conversation took the direction Frank had expected it would take since the moment they had begun talking.

"I heard that the boy Bitseel went and captured the scalp," Hoskanini declared, the pride in his voice evident.

"As did I," Frank admitted.

"It is said that he raided the encampment of the *Nóódái* and brought back something, I think a *cháh ditlóoi,* and this will be the scalp."

"Yes, I also heard of the cap, but I do not know how they know it belongs to the witch."

Hoskanini chuckled. "If they are Pahute does it matter? But the boy is very brave, don't you think?"

"He is," Frank agreed, feeling pleased with himself—with his plan. "There is little of such bravery left among the People, man or boy."

Hoskanini looked hard at him. "What is your meaning, Cousin?"

Frank stared straight ahead, ignoring the man's glare. "My meaning is that the People are afraid. Since Rope Thrower took us to Fort Sumner, we are all afraid of the whites."

"It was a hard time that no one wishes to repeat," Hoskanini replied, trying as he spoke to remember if the man who was calling himself Frank had actually been there. He couldn't remember it, but then, who would wish to claim it if it were not so.

"And so we will all wear out our lives in poverty?" Frank shook his head. "That does not sound like the way of bravery to me."

"Do you have some thoughts on this?" Hoskanini asked after a moment's consideration.

"Some. I have thought it might be time for more raids."

Hoskanini chuckled. "And who would you raid, Cousin? The *belacani* with their big guns and many soldiers? The *Nakai?* The Mexicans are even poorer than the *Diné.* Or the Pahutes, whose horses and goats are not worth taking? They raid even more quickly than we do. You see how it is, Cousin? We are in a bad place, it is true, but neither is there a good way out without great patience while our flocks and herds multiply."

"Well," Frank said softly, thinking of Peokon and his wisdom, "that may be so, Cousin. Still, I know of a people who are wealthy with many things but who are like women when it comes to fighting. They protect themselves poorly, and they die easily, and they want nothing more than to be friends with the *Diné.*"

"And who are these people?" Hoskanini questioned skeptically.

"The mormonee *belacani,*" Frank replied easily. "The people who dwell across the big river, on the other side of the Kaibab."

"It is a long way to make a raid." Hoskanini was thoughtful.

"Perhaps. But when their horses number many more than all the fingers on all the hands of this clan, and their cattle and sheep the same, and when there is no danger, the distance does not seem so great. But come, Cousin. Let us talk of such things no longer. I have cards as well as a little *tó likoni.* On a cold morning such as this, alcohol would taste very good, don't you think?"

Hoskanini nodded agreeably, and with a satisfied smile Frank led the man and his silent son to a secluded place in a nearby wash, a place already being warmed by the sun. Yes, he thought as he climbed down to where all had been carefully prepared for his guests, things were going just as he had expected they would. Soon he would begin gaining power and wealth, and it would grow until he was even greater than the feared Peokon. Truly it was going to be a good day, and just as truly was he thankful for the old way of the People, the Enemy Way.

<hr />

Mitchell's Trading Post, McElmo's Wash

"Don't look now, Mitchell, but there's an Indian at the window."

Young Ernest Mitchell didn't look up from his hand of cards. "I see him," he responded evenly, quietly. "Looks to be Pahute."

"What do we do?"

Mitchell smiled at the older man. "Do? This is a trading post Pa's running here, Jim. A trading post for Indians."

"I know," James Merrick stated nervously as he shifted his weight on the chair. "But he's just staring—"

"He's also just a kid, Jim. You've prospected this country for years and probably been around hundreds of Indians. Why you so nervous now?"

"I don't know," the man mumbled defensively. "I reckon I never did cotton to Indians staring at me."

"Me neither. But I guarantee this one's harmless, so stop worrying and play your hand. Maybe in a little while the kid'll get over his nerves and come in. Then we'll see if he has anything worth trading."

The December day was raw and cold, with an icy wind blowing down off the mountains to the north and east. Even on the north side of the San Juan, where the sun usually warmed the log trading post below the bluffs, it was colder than usual. Yet the fire in the mud-chinked fireplace was warm, and it did much to nullify the probing, chilling fingers of the wind.

Ernest Mitchell and James Merrick were alone in the trading post, Ernest's parents having been gone more than a week freighting supplies in from Mancos, in Colorado. It would be another week before the old man got back, Ernest knew, and maybe two. Especially if his mother and sisters had their say about sleeping in real beds and bathing in an honest-to-goodness bathtub. To them the place on the San Juan was primitive and isolated, and the longer they could stay away the better they liked it.

Of course, they had for neighbors John Brewer and George Clay and their families, the whole shebang of which had emigrated from Colorado. But they were clannish folks, standoffish and quiet, and seemed to shun the neighborly duties most folks took for granted.

Maybe that was why—

"I hope you have a gun handy."

Again Ernest Mitchell smiled. "Two of 'em, right over there. And they're both loaded."

"Not very close to hand, are they?"

"Don't want 'em to be. Scares the Indians, seeing Pa or me packing a gun." For a moment Ernest Mitchell studied his cards. "I was right. The boy outside's a Pahute. They love cards, call 'em *ducki*. Reckon what he's watching is this here game you've stopped playing."

"Sorry," James Merrick responded as he hurriedly played his hand. "Pahute or Navajo, makes no difference. I just don't cotton to Indians!"

"You're in the wrong country, then," Ernest Mitchell responded laconically. "And the wrong profession. Fact is, maybe we ought to cancel our little expedition."

"Not hardly," the grizzled man declared adamantly. "This is sure a new feeling, though. Ever since I stumbled on that Navajo silver mine, I've had me a case of the creepy-crawlies about Indians, Navajos especially. I'm telling you, Ernest, every time I think on that silver I get to feeling like somebody's stepping on my grave."

Laying down his cards, Mitchell stretched and then scratched his unshaven jaw, which because of his youth looked about the same as if he'd shaved that very morning.

"And I'm telling you," he responded evenly, "that we'd be crazy *not* to go after that silver. Howsomever, if you don't want to go, then a map to the place should about cover your losses, which are getting to be considerable. With or without you, Jim, I'm going!"

The older man looked squarely at his younger companion. "Well," he finally declared, "you ain't going without me, and that's final!"

Ernest Mitchell smiled. "Good for you. Why, you found *Peshlaki,* man, the sacred lost mine of the Navajo! Way I hear it, that stuff's practically pure silver and takes only a little smelting to draw it out. Jim, there's thousands and thousands of dollars there, and all of it's just waiting for us to go in and pack it out."

"I know, Ernest," the man stated pensively. "I've spent some of it. Remember? I know the silver's there waiting. But what I keep asking myself is, how many Indians are also waiting? You ain't been in that country, and I have. It's a land of haunts, I tell you—weird rock formations full of silence and echoes and danger so real you can feel it. Makes your skin crawl. You mark my words, Ernest. That *Peshlaki* is cursed, sure as you're born!"

Ernest Mitchell laughed. "You sound like a Navajo, Jim. They're the most gosh-awful superstitious people alive—them and the Mormons. Now stop worrying about such nonsense as curses and haunts. As soon as the folks get back, we'll cross the river and get us a little of that *Peshlaki* silver—"

Abruptly the door of the crude cabin was pulled open. Two young Pahute boys stepped inside and then stood silently, one slightly in front of the other, looking around. Their buckskin shirts, under old robes of buffalo hide, were ragged, and their moccasins and leg wrappings were patched and marred with holes.

But it was their hair the two white men noticed most, especially that of the smaller youth who stood closest to them. Besides being wild and unkempt, with no band of any sort to keep it in control, the sun had apparently bleached it to a strange green. Neither of the men had seen such a thing before, and they could hardly keep their eyes off it.

"How," Ernest Mitchell said in customary greeting as he raised his hand. "You come maybeso trade?"

The youth's eyes glinted as he stepped forward, his finger outstretched toward James Merrick's hat.

"Allthesame heap *katz-oats*," he said, not knowing the English word for hat. "Maybeso pike away, pike away."

"What kind of fool talk is that?" James Merrick questioned uneasily.

"I thought you'd been around Indians?"

"I have. Navajo, Apache, Zuñi. But I never heard anything like that before."

"Well, he's Pahute, and I reckon that's the best he can do with the King's English."

"You understand him?"

"Sure. And I was wrong. He isn't interested in *ducki*. Fact is, he wants your hat, and he wants it in a hurry. Right now!"

James Merrick looked startled. "My hat? Why, the dad-blamed young fool's crazier than a wall-eyed colt if he thinks I'm gonna give him my best and only—"

"Pike away! Pike away!"

Ernest Mitchell laughed. "Come on, Jim. Give the kid your hat. Pa'll fix you up with another one, and it'll likely save us trouble later on."

James Merrick wasn't convinced. "Well, of all the fool notions! What I ought to do is give him a bust over the head with the butt of my gun. That'd settle his milk in a hurry."

"Maybe. But much as I don't like the Mormons, their idea of feeding the Indians rather than fighting them is plumb wise. Now, give the boy your hat."

James Merrick hesitated, looked around the crowded room as if seeking some sort of alternative, and then with a curse took off his hat and slammed it to the earthen floor of the cabin.

Instantly the boy reached down, grabbed the hat, and jammed it onto his head. Several sizes too large, it settled over his eyes and pushed out his ears, causing the other, larger youth, the silent one, to cackle with merriment. But a well-aimed kick from the smaller one silenced the laughter, letting all in the room know who was in charge.

"You have trade?" Mitchell asked the boy, making the sign for trade as he spoke.

For a moment the boy's brow darkened. But then with a quick look of satisfaction, he pointed outside and made the sign for horse.

"Well, my friend, looks like you got yourself a horse."

"The deuce I did! I already got a horse, Ernest, and you know it. Five of 'em, as a matter of fact, and more where they came from."

"Then one more hadn't ought to hurt you. These Pahute ponies are tough little critters and ought to come in handy when we brace that Navajo country next week."

"Yeah, sure. And I reckon it'll be a skinny, sway-backed bag of bones, too. The only thing an Indian pony is good for, Ernest, is selling to another Indian."

"Happen you're right," Mitchell declared, still smiling, "then we'll take the animal with us when we go find your lost mine. We run into Navajos, maybeso it'll come in handy.

"Say, boy," he said then, signing as he spoke, "what's your name?"

The boy, preoccupied with fitting into his new hat, hardly even looked up. "I am called Sowagerie," he mumbled in Pahute.

"Green hair?" Ernest Mitchell guffawed. "Well, she fits, all right. Fact is, kid, your hair's so green you look like a blooming posey."

Instantly the young man's head jerked up. "Posey," he breathed, forming the word carefully with his mouth. "Posey. Maybeso allthe-same heap Posey!"

And thumping himself triumphantly on the chest the boy pushed back his hat and swaggered past the ogling form of his younger brother. "Posey," he declared as he strutted through the doorway and out into the cold of the November afternoon. "Heap ticaboo Posey!"

And with no hesitation at all he walked past his mount, took up the rope hackamore to Beogah's horse, led the animal back past his stunned brother, and handed the rope to James Merrick. Then, with another chest-thump and exclamation of his new name, the youth swung onto his own pony and jerked it around toward the willows that crowded the mouth of McElmo's Wash, leaving his brother to follow on foot as best he as was able.

26

Tuesday, December 23, 1879

Top of Hole-in-the-Rock

"Morning, Sarah."

Sarah Williams, eighteen and usually pretty as a picture, looked up from where she was futilely trying to pry loose a shadscale bush with her pitchfork. From her tear-streaked face Eliza could see she had been crying, and from her hollow cheeks and eyes it was obvious she had been neither eating nor sleeping—at least enough.

"Oh, g-good morning, Sister Foreman," the girl murmured, wiping at her face and doing her best to smile. "I . . . didn't hear you coming."

"It's the wind," Eliza replied as she wrapped the lead rope of the glass-eyed mare to the top of a bush. "Blowing the way it is, it's a wonder any of us can hear anything at all. Why don't you let me help you with that shadscale."

Without waiting for a reply, Eliza hobbled to the girl's side, reached down into the bush with her heavily protected hand and arm, and expertly twisted the brush loose from its brittle roots.

"Thank you," Sarah declared as Eliza pushed the bush against another the girl had already worked free. "I . . . I suppose I shouldn't even be out here, what with Mary Ann needing help with the children like she does. But lawsy, I get so blamed cold that all I can think about is building up a little fire for myself—"

"You do look cold," Eliza declared as she gazed at the shorter girl. "Here, why don't you wear this buffalo coat Billy got for me."

"But . . . I couldn't—"

216

"Sometimes it gets too heavy for me to even want to pack around." Eliza smiled and shrugged out of her coat, which she handed to the trembling girl. "Especially when I have to gather up as much of this useless shadscale as I do."

"Oh, this is warm!" Sarah breathed in wonder. "Th-thank you."

"Think nothing of it." Eliza steeled her mind against the bite of the frigid wind that was now cutting through her like a knife. "Besides that coat and my dress, I'm wearing about a dozen sweaters and so many petticoats and bloomers I can hardly move. Say, why don't you walk with me for a few minutes while I gather up a load of brush for this fool, glass-eyed mare to drag back to camp."

"I declare, I don't know how you walk anywhere," Sarah said as they moved from brush to brush, tearing up whatever they could and piling it on the rope drag Kumen had rigged behind the mare. "What with the snow and this sandstone being as slick as it is, well, I just can't hardly comprehend it."

Eliza didn't answer but continued to work, wondering as she did so how long she would be able to endure without her coat. But this girl, the younger sister of Mary Ann Perkins and the sister-in-law of Benjamin Perkins, needed it every bit as badly as she did. After all, even her lips were blue, and Eliza had seen enough folks freeze to death to recognize some of the symptoms. At least for the moment, therefore, she would simply do without that wonderful coat and get along as best she could.

"Don't your feet hurt in all this snow and cold?" Sarah asked. "Mine throb something terrible, and I'm not all crippled up like you are."

For a moment there was silence, and then Eliza, realizing with surprise that she hadn't been offended by the girl's blunt remarks, chuckled. "All right, Sarah, I'll admit it, but only to you. My feet are cold *all* the time. But more than that, they hurt terrible, I suppose from that old frostbite I got in Wyoming."

"Wyoming?"

"That's right. I was part of the Edward Martin Handcart Company that got caught in the snows of Wyoming; one of the lucky ones, I suppose. I lived."

Sarah gazed wonderingly at Eliza. "Jens Nielson told me about those people one night. He said the suffering was indescribable."

"He was with the Willie Company. Still, I suppose our experiences were similar."

"Is that what crippled you?"

Silently Eliza nodded.

"You went through that," Sarah breathed in awe, "and now you're willing to endure another winter trek that could be just as bad, or even worse?"

"Well," Eliza grunted as she pulled loose another brush, "so far it isn't anywhere near as bad. That winter of 1856 seemed far worse than this one, and I was far less prepared for it."

"In what way?"

"For one thing, back then I had no shoes after my only pair fell to pieces. Instead I wrapped my feet in rags that were almost always wet and frozen. For another, quite foolishly I burned my cloak and blankets when we were ordered to lighten our loads just a day or two before the last crossing of the Platte River."

"You burned them?"

"It was warm that day, Sarah. Hot, even. And we had no suspicion it was going to start snowing within a day or so and not let up for the next several months. So to lighten our loads we all burned what we thought we wouldn't need. And that left me, after the blizzards started a couple of days later, with virtually no warm clothing, not even a decent quilt.

"Another difference was that we handcarters knew no such comforts as the wonderful wagons and tents you and I have to ride and sleep in. A body stays so much warmer when it can get off the frozen ground and out of the snow and wind. And for a fourth difference, on this trek I have this wonderful, glass-eyed mare to follow about the desert gathering shadscale, and she keeps my circulation going pretty well. Tell the truth, Sarah, I can hardly comprehend my present blessings, and that's a fact."

And it was, too. Eliza was beginning to realize that she was far better off with this company than she had ever been with the handcarts. Especially she was thankful for the wagon—for the wonderful shelter it afforded her.

Like some of the others in the camp, when they had arrived at the Hole, she and Billy had emptied into a tent the contents of their wagon-box, removed it from the running gears, and placed it on the ground. Then they had piled sand and snow against it as a windbreak and roped down the extra canvas to better shut out the wind. Of course it wasn't heated with a cast-iron stove like the Decker wagon and some of the others, but with the two canvasses neither was it very drafty, which Eliza considered wonderful enough.

Why, even to have thought of such luxuries during that handcart trek would have been the height of folly, and would have made her more miserable than ever, they were so unattainable. Yet now such comforts were real, and more and more Eliza was feeling so much gratitude that she couldn't find words to express it. It was as if—

"I don't know about you Mormons," Sarah abruptly declared, shaking her head. "I sometimes think I will never understand you."

Eliza was stunned. "You aren't a Mormon?"

"Not hardly." Sarah shook her head. "When Mary Ann joined the Mormons and came west I was pretty young, but I tagged along because she was about my only family. As you see, I'm still tagging along, but more and more I find myself wondering what makes you people do the things you do, sacrificing yourselves for something that might just as well be false as true."

"It isn't always easy." Eliza's voice was quiet. "In fact, I've wavered and stumbled from time to time and even had my own doubts about things."

"Then why do you do it?"

Eliza stopped the mare and moved to her lee so that both she and young Sarah Williams would have a little protection from the wind. Then, taking a deep breath to bolster her courage, she leaned on her crutch and faced the younger woman. "We celebrate a man's birthday today, Sarah, and the birthday of another man day after tomorrow. It's all on account of those two men that I do what I do, and try always to do it better."

"Truly?" Sarah responded, looking confused. "I know it's Christmas day after tomorrow, Jesus' birthday. But I haven't heard about any birthday today—"

"Today is Joseph Smith's birthday, he who was called of God to

219

restore the fullness of the gospel and establish the Church of Jesus Christ on the earth in these latter days."

"But he's dead, Eliza!"

"That doesn't make him any less of a prophet. Had Joseph lived he would be . . . let's see, seventy-four years old today. But the fact that he didn't live can't change the fact that he was—and is—a prophet of the Living God. While he lived he was Christ's mouth-piece on this earth, restoring the fullness of the gospel and establish-ing the Lord's true church. Even though he is dead, he continues to preside over this dispensation. And before he died he passed the keys and powers of being a prophet to Brigham Young and others, and John Taylor holds them today."

"But . . . but how do you know all this? How can you know?"

Eliza struggled with the sudden tears that filled her eyes—tears and a sweet burning that pulsed like fire through her being. "I . . . I know all of this," she declared fervently, "because the Lord revealed it to me in perfect clarity way back in England when I was about your age."

"But . . . you said you had wavered, and even doubted."

Eliza wiped at her eyes. "I have. I'm human, Sarah, and I'm filled with far more weaknesses than I'd like to admit. Sometimes I succumb to them, and when I do the devil always gets the best of me."

Sarah giggled. "You? From what Mary Ann has told me, I can't imagine the devil or anyone else getting the best of you."

"Believe me, he has. Thank goodness for dear friends who had the nerve to remind me that I was the one giving Old Scratch power over me, and not him. Here I was blaming the devil and those who loved me for things I was struggling with, and all along I was the one who was accountable. And it wasn't that I was doing bad things, par-ticularly, but that I'd stopped doing good ones."

"Such as?" Sarah was deeply interested, and Eliza wondered at that.

"Such as not praying, not studying the scriptures each day, and so forth. Mary Jones calls them sins of omission, and I suppose she's right. I'd certainly omitted them from my life. And because I knew better, the devil was on me in a flash, and I stumbled."

Leading the glass-eyed mare again, Eliza turned and moved back toward camp—back into the teeth of the wind. She had taken longer than she should have to gather the brush, she knew, and without a coat she had grown dangerously cold. Somehow she had to force herself to hurry—

"Eliza," Sarah gasped as she struggled to keep up, "do . . . do those things really help? I mean praying, reading the Bible and Book of Mormon, and so forth?"

Eliza nodded without speaking. She was also farther away from camp than she had thought, and the wind—

"Because they . . . they're the very things Benjamin—I mean Brother Perkins—has been hounding me to do. Only, they seemed so simple that I . . . I thought, well, I haven't done them." Sarah paused as she made her way through a deep drift of snow, still trying to keep up with Eliza. "Maybe I should try it. I mean, maybe I should read the Book of Mormon and pray about it—"

"Sister Foreman, ma'am, what are you doing out here without a coat?"

Spinning, Eliza was startled to see Dick Butt, who had ridden up beside them without either woman being aware of his approach.

"Here," he declared forcefully, swinging out of the saddle and shrugging out of his coat, "throw on this rig of mine and let's get you mounted. Miss Williams, ma'am, I'm right sorry I don't have another hoss. But I'll be glad to leg you up on my cayuse behind Sister Foreman, that is, if you're of a mind."

"Thank you," Sarah mumbled, too surprised and cold to protest, as she normally would have done.

"I'm right sorry about those bulky saddlebags," Dick Butt said as he prepared to help Sarah. "Today I found some wide-open veins of what I reckon must be coal, over yonder against them high cliffs. If it is, and if that shadscale can get the stuff hot enough to burn, then I reckon maybe our fuel problems will be solved."

Another moment and both women were mounted in front of the bulging saddlebags, and Dick Butt was out in front breaking trail toward camp for his horse and the brush-laden, glass-eyed mare.

"Who is he?" Sarah whispered in Eliza's ear, the cold suddenly forgotten.

"W-Willard Butt." Eliza was shivering, but Dick's coat was warm and comfortable, and she was thankful for it. "Most folks call him Dick."

"He . . . he's a fine figure of a man."

Thinking of the dance that was coming the next night, Eliza smiled knowingly. "That he is. And a very fine dancer, too. Not as light and quick as your brother-in-law Ben Perkins, maybe, but overall he's smoother, more fluid or something. He never seems in a hurry, and he never wastes a movement. And yet—well, I swan if I know what I'm trying to say."

"I . . . I think I know. He seems very . . . likable."

"Oh, he's likable, all right. But Jens Nielson says his language is mighty course, especially for a Latter-day Saint. Of course, Julie Nielson thinks she's going to cure him of that habit. And who knows? Maybe she will."

"Julie Nielson, is it?" Sarah sounded disappointed. "Well, maybe she will and maybe she won't. But as for myself, Eliza, I don't know if I give a fiddle for a man's language. It's his actions I care about—the private things he does when no one's watching or making him do them. Like now, giving you his coat and letting us ride his horse while he walks. He didn't have to do that. And there's loads of others in this camp who wouldn't. I know, for they've passed me time and again with a wave and a saintly smile and a 'Howdy-do, Sarah,' and nary a thought for helping me with what I was doing, even for a minute."

"There is something deep in that boy," Eliza said by way of acknowledgment, "something deep and fine and so controlled that no one's truly seen it yet, including him, most likely."

And that was the way it was with Billy, she thought with sudden surprise. Like young Dick Butt, there was something in her husband, something deep and fine that no one had yet seen, most especially herself—

27

Wednesday, December 24, 1879

Davis Wash, near Fifty-Mile Camp

The snow had stopped falling, the wind had stopped blowing at least temporarily, and for the first time in days Eliza found herself laboring after firewood in a patch of sunlight. Of course, it was so bright it hurt her eyes, but the warmth felt good, and for that she felt grateful. Trouble now was, she'd led the glass-eyed mare down into Davis Gulch hoping to drag out some dead cottonwood for a truly warm fire that night, and she couldn't climb back out. The snow had drifted too deep during the night, and the sides were too steep for her and her crutch. Besides, the fool mare was acting more like a mule, stubborn as all get out, and it was all Eliza could do to keep the animal moving forward with the heavy cottonwood limb dragging behind.

With a sigh, Eliza shielded her eyes with her free hand and glanced westward to where the deep gulch headed out. Fifty-Mile Mountain loomed above her, its top still shrouded in cloud. But the lower part of the mountain was clear, and she knew that just to the west of where the gulch ended was Fifty-Mile Camp. Going in that direction to where the gulch was less deep was the only way Eliza could think of to clamber out.

"Well, woman," she breathed, "you got yourself into this fix, so now it's up to you to get yourself back out. Pick up those frozen limbs of yours and get moving!"

Setting her teeth against the exhaustion and pain in her legs and feet, the bedraggled woman tugged at the mare's rope and struggled forward through the snow. While it was less than six inches deep up on the level, here in the bottom of the gulch it was from one to three feet deep, depending on the drifts. In fact, it was so deep that even with her crutch Eliza had a difficult time keeping her balance.

Snorting, the mare lunged through the drifts behind Eliza, the heavy limb sledding after. Fortunately, the large end of the limb turned upward near where Eliza had tied the rope, and that made pulling it a little easier. But nevertheless it wasn't easy at all, and by the time she'd found a place where she thought she could make it up and out of the gulch, she felt ready to drop. Besides, the old glass-eyed mare was blowing and snorting and stomping her hooves in exhaustion, and Eliza knew she'd never make it out with that log in tow without a few moments rest.

Pausing and leaning on her crutch, Eliza thought again of the amazing experience she'd had with Sarah Williams the day before. Truthfully she had thought of little else in the hours since, for it had been so transcendent, so profound. Not only had she been able to bear testimony to the young woman about the truthfulness of the restored gospel of Jesus Christ, but she had felt the power of that conviction surging through her heart like waves of fire even as she'd mouthed the words. Even now the memory of that moment brought more fire and more tears, not so strongly as the day before, perhaps, but strong enough to cause her to know that God had once again born witness to her soul, just as he had back in England so many years before, that she had joined his church and was doing his work.

Even more amazing had been her realization—again accompanied by the powerful witness of the Holy Spirit—that Billy was in truth one of the finest and noblest men she would ever know. And more, that she had fulfilled God's holy will by marrying him—was fulfilling it even more by carrying his unborn child. Truly had she been blessed, and it was incredible to her how close she had come to destroying her marriage and throwing it all away.

These thoughts were engrossing to Eliza, so overwhelming that it was difficult for her to think of much else. Consequently it was the longest time before she became aware that she was hearing the distant singsong voices of playing children.

"Merciful heavens," she said with a surge of excitement, "you must be nearer Fifty-Mile than you thought, woman. Happen you can't make it up that bank yonder, at least you can holler up some help and feel reasonably certain of it coming."

With renewed vigor Eliza tackled the bank of the gulch, and to her surprise both she and the mare lunged up and onto the level on the first try. With another tug and a little maneuvering, she next dragged the limb over the lip of the wash, and then it was time for another breather, both for herself and the ganted-up old mare.

Resting on her crutch again, she hung her head to catch her breath, and she was leaning like that, her eyes closed, when some words from the children's chant first assailed her ears.

> *Billy Foreman has a mare,*
> *Bag of bones without no hair.*
> *One eye here and one eye there.*
> *That is Billy Foreman's mare.*

Stunned almost beyond belief, Eliza raised her head to see a group of small girls giggling and jumping rope on a bare patch of rock a short distance away. They were so engrossed in their chanting, and in their rope skipping, that none of them had noticed Eliza's emergence from the depths of the snow-filled gulch.

Straining, Eliza could make out Mary Lillywhite and Delia Mackelprang, two little girls about seven years old, and the best of friends. The others had their backs to her, so Eliza moved toward them in order to better identify the chanters.

Two or three times the girls got through the first stanza before they were stopped as the skipper missed her jump, and Eliza was nearly upon them before Lucinda Nielson, who was also seven, jumped well enough to get the group into the second and third stanzas.

> *Billy Foreman has a wife,*
> *Long and thin just like a knife.*
> *She'll stick him good for all his life.*
> *That is Billy Foreman's wife.*
>
> *Billy Foreman ain't much good*
> *For building road or hauling wood,*

Too weak to work the way he should.
That's why Billy ain't much good.

Trembling from the pain of what she was hearing, Eliza nearly fled away in tears. And then she nearly tore into the group with shrieking voice and flailing crutch. But no, she forcefully reminded herself as she stood near the mare, they were just innocent children who likely had no clear idea of what they were chanting. More, they probably had no idea at all of who she and Billy were. Instead they'd no doubt heard the rhyme somewhere and picked it up to use in their little games.

Oh, her poor darling Billy! He would be absolutely crushed if he ever heard such chanting as this. He'd want to defend her, of course, and Eliza knew it. But that would only make matters worse—horribly worse. As for herself, Eliza already had a fairly clear picture of who she really was. And so the description was humorously close to the gospel truth. The same was true of their fool, glass-eyed mare, the biggest equine bag of bones Eliza had ever seen. But what they were saying about her poor Billy was so patently false, so unrighteous and cruel—

"Hello, girls," she said, making her voice sound as cheerful as possible. "Classes out already today?"

"Uh-huh," Mary Lillywhite said with a bright smile. "Teacher said since it was Christmas we could go play."

"How fun! A long time ago I used to skip rope."

"Was that before you got hurt?" a little girl asked as she looked at Eliza's crutch.

"That's right, it was—long before. Now let me see. I don't believe I know your name, child."

"I'm Sarah Jane Rowley."

"Of course. Alice Louise is your little sister, isn't she."

"Uh-huh. And my daddy's name is Samuel, and my mommy is Ann."

Smiling, Eliza quickly learned the names of the other two girls— who turned out to be Lula Redd and Leona Walton—as well as the names of their parents. She also verified the identities of Lucinda or Lucy Nielson, Adelia Mackelprang, and Mary Lillywhite. As it turned out, the girls were all seven years old, and they came together every day to learn ciphering and their figures.

"What's your name?" Sarah Jane asked.

"Eliza. But I thought all of you knew that. You were just singing about me, weren't you?"

"We were?" The girls looked at each other, confusion on their faces, and Eliza knew it was real. Still, she wanted them to know—

"My whole name is Eliza Foreman, and I'm Billy Foreman's wife."

The children's looks of confusion turned to amazement, and they stared at Eliza in open-eyed, slack-jawed wonder. "Is that Billy Foreman's mare, too?" Delia Mackelprang asked after a minute of thought.

"Yes, it is."

"No, it isn't," Lula Redd argued abruptly. "She can't be Billy Foreman's mare! She has hair everywhere, all over her body!"

"That's right, Lula. She does. And that means your song is wrong. In fact, it means your song is a lie, doesn't it."

Soberly the girls nodded their heads.

"Should we sing songs that tell lies, do you think?"

This time the girls shook their heads.

"If we do, how do you think it makes our Heavenly Father feel?"

"Sad," Lucy Nielson answered simply.

"That's right, Lucy. Very sad. Now, do I look long and thin like a knife?"

At that one or two of the girls giggled shyly, but the others vigorously shook their heads again.

Eliza smiled. "I'm tall and thin, but because nobody can be thin as a knife, that's another lie. But the worst lie of all is the lie you were singing about my husband—about Billy being not much good. As a matter of fact, girls, Billy Foreman is wonderful! He's good at so many things that hardly anybody else can do. Why, did you know he was Brigham Young's personal clerk?"

"He was? What's that?"

"A clerk is a man who is so smart he can cipher and do figures really fast, sometimes all in his head. Billy doesn't even need a slate or chalk, he's so smart."

"Gosh," Sarah Rowley exclaimed with wide-eyed wonder, "I wish I was smart like that!"

"Study hard, and maybe you will be." Eliza's smile was now genuine, for she understood these little girls—had in fact been just like them a long time before. There was no malice in them, at least none that was intentional. They were simply playing, repeating things they'd heard others saying—

"Promise you won't sing any more lies about my husband or me?" she asked as she took up the reins of the mare.

"We promise, Eliza!"

Lucy Nielson's smile was genuine, and as Eliza looked at each of the others she saw the same sincerity.

"Oh, dear Lord," she breathed as she hobbled away with the glass-eyed mare and the cottonwood limb in tow, "once again I can see what terrible damage I've done to that poor man you gave me to marry. If only I hadn't . . . hadn't—well, I ask only that thou wilt please . . . forgive me, Father, and help me to know what to do to help my husband—"

———o—o—o———

Top of Hole-in-the-Rock

"Billy, are you awake?"

It was Christmas Eve, the wind had not let up, and the temperature had turned off so cold that even beneath the quilts and with hot rocks at her feet Eliza wasn't very warm. Oh, she'd warmed up some at the dance a little earlier, when Ben Perkins had finally got her to jigging with him to Sammy Cox's fiddle. But that hadn't lasted long, not after she'd stopped because of the pain in her feet. And now she was shivering again, not violently, but enough to keep sleep from her eyes.

Everybody was suffering from it, she knew, and most more than her. She'd learned at the dance that in the past few days little work had been done on the Hole or on the dugway climbing out of the far side of the river, for the men were too cold to hang onto their picks and hammers. In both camps the women and children were suffering, and even the animals were growing thinner and weak. Of a truth her cottonwood log had been a welcome respite from the fast but futile fires of shadscale everyone had grown accustomed to.

Of course Dick Butt's discovery, which had indeed turned out to be coal, was going to be a tremendous help to everyone, for fires could now be kept burning indefinitely. To that end two brethren had been assigned to take a wagon back to where Dick had discovered the exposed vein, to mine it and to make regular trips as long as the camp was stopped where they were.

But it wasn't the cold that was troubling her, and Eliza knew it. The fact was, it was Christmas Eve, and never in her life had it felt less like Christmas! There were no candle-lit trees, no strings of pop-corn, no warm cider, no cheery fireplaces and warm rooms filled with the pungent odor of burning logs and roasting apples and chicken-and-dumpling stew. Why, there wasn't even a gift she could give to Billy—

And that brought up the chant she'd heard earlier, the lying ditty that defamed her husband so horribly. She needed to apologize to him about her part in it, she knew, but she had to do it so that he didn't learn what the girls had been singing—or even that they had been singing. Oh, lawsy, she thought. The harder she tried, the harder things seemed to become. In fact, she truly didn't know if she could endure.

"Silly woman," she declared mentally, abruptly chiding herself for her attitude, "stop murmuring! You brought it all on yourself, and you know it. So look at the bright side of your life, for heaven's sake! You had a wonderful time at the dance, didn't you? Why, Ben Perkins and young Dick Butt and all four of the Robb brothers danced with you, and each of them gave you a delightful time.

"And wasn't the singing truly beautiful? Woman, you've never heard such a flock of good singers, and you know it! The Perkins men and their wives, that sweet little Sarah Williams, Sarah Jane Hunter, Kumen and Mary Jones, all the Deckers and their wives, Joe and Harriet Ann Barton, Hyrum Fielding and his wife Ellen, and on and on! Every one of them were singing like birds! Even Amasa Barton, Jesse Smith, Ross Mickelson, and George Decker—all of them bachelors—fairly made the cliffs ring with their Christmas hymns.

"More than that, you were with your husband! What greater Christmas gift could there be, woman, than to have a man such as Billy beside you, and to be carrying his son in your womb? Shame on you for murmuring! Shame on you for feeling so sorry for yourself—"

"I'm awake," Billy suddenly replied as he rolled onto his back. "It's a mite cold for sleeping, I reckon."

"I'm sorry," Eliza murmured as she snuggled closer to her husband. "I should be keeping you warmer."

"Or vice-versa," Billy responded as he slid his arm under his wife's neck, taking care not to smear axle grease onto her from his bandaged hands.

"How are your blisters? They feeling some better?"

Billy thought of the dull throb in his hands caused by the bone-deep blisters he'd raised picking and shoveling at the rock down in the Hole. One day they would be calluses, he knew, but not until they'd a chance to heal. And that chance seemed mighty long in coming—mighty long!

"They don't hurt at all," Billy finally replied with a tiny smile. "I just worry about getting that blamed axle grease all over you and the bedding."

"You stop worrying about axle grease, Billy Foreman. I can clean it up whenever I've a need to, or leastwise I will when we get to the San Juan."

Billy looked up into the darkness. "You sometimes wonder if we'll *ever* get there?"

Eliza giggled. "Billy, I'm surprised at you, saying such a thing. I thought I was the only one afflicted with a complaining soul."

"Well," Billy murmured thoughtfully, "this journey is taking far longer than I thought it would. More and more I'm sorry I brought you out here into this . . . this nightmare!"

Eliza sat bolt upright. "It isn't a nightmare, Billy Foreman! And don't you dare be sorry we're here! We were called by the Lord's prophet to settle on the San Juan, and I wouldn't miss one blessed minute of it, cold or not! You hear me?"

Billy chuckled. "I hear you, all right. So did most of the camp, I reckon."

"Good." Eliza snuggled back down against her husband, thankful for the warmth of his body. "Then they know how I feel. Now it's your turn, Billy. I want the truth about how you feel, and no holding back to try and impress me, either."

"All right," Billy said with a sigh. "I reckon my hands hurt a little, though that'll end as soon as the calluses form. But truthfully, Eliza, the cold's what gets to me. I can't ever seem to get the chill out of my bones. I spend all day out on those cliffs or down in the shadow of that notch, knee-deep in snow and the wind blowing through me like it'll never stop, and I swear I *never* get warm. Then I get back here and all we have is a bit of a fire burning that useless shadscale, and . . . well, I'm telling you, hon-bun, I'm more thankful than I can say about that vein of coal Dick discovered. And I don't see how any of you folks survived that handcart trek back in the winter of '56."

"I feel bad that you're so cold, Billy."

"It isn't really me I'm worrying about," Billy declared quietly. "I'm worried about you, Eliza, and the little one. Me, I can take it well enough, I reckon. But what does such cold do to a woman who's growing with child? Or to the wee one in her womb? That's what's worrying me, especially when I'm too confounded cold to warm you up at night."

Touched, Eliza reached up and kissed her husband in the tiny whiskerless spot just under his chin that she had only recently discovered. "You're sweet, Billy. But don't you worry about the baby and me. The child's fine, and I'm not that cold. Really, I'm not."

"Eliza," Billy chided softly, "I can feel you shivering."

"That's just from being held by you," she whispered coyly. And mostly, she thought, it was.

"Are you certain you're feeling all right, Eliza?"

"Of course. Why wouldn't I be?"

Billy closed his eyes tight against his worry. "All that dancing, I reckon," he replied with as much tenderness as he could muster. "I . . . I was real nervous when Ben Perkins got you out there doing those snappy Welsh jigs with him. And then all those other fellows— well, like I said, I was real nervous."

"Nervous?" Eliza giggled. "Why, Billy, were you jealous?"

Embarrassed, Billy shook his head. "Uh-uh, not at all. I was just, well, I was remembering what happened after the dance that night up in Escalante—with that sister who was expecting. I mean, I could hear her screaming a little later when her baby was coming. And the next day we had to bury the poor little child—"

"Oh, Billy," Eliza whispered emotionally, "I didn't understand why you were so worried."

"Our baby is important to me, Eliza, and so are you. I . . . I don't suppose I would even want to go on living if I lost you! Or the child either, for that matter."

"Billy, Billy, Billy," Eliza murmured as she drew herself even closer to her husband. "That sister had problems right along. But me? Merciful heavens, I'm big and strong as an ox. You know that. And I know this little one is going to be just fine. I promise you!"

Billy squeezed his wife more tightly. "But you've got to take care of yourself while I'm off down in the Hole, Eliza. Promise me you won't do any more dancing and such, at least until after the baby comes."

"All right." Eliza sighed. "I promise."

For a moment the two of them were silent. A gust of wind rattled the canvas covers over their wagon, bringing sleet that would soon turn to snow. And in the midst of that particular racket, Eliza started to giggle.

"What's so funny?" Billy asked, rising on his elbow and looking down at the dim form of his wife.

"Us," she laughed quietly in the darkness. "Here we are in the midst of a howling wilderness, both of us in danger of freezing or starving to death, and we're worrying about a little dancing."

"I reckon it does seem foolish," Billy agreed with a chuckle of his own. "But you know what, hon-bun? I love you more than I can say. And without ever seeing him, I love that little feller growing in your womb. I want us all to be together, and I'll do whatever it takes to see that blessed moment come to pass."

"So will I," Eliza agreed, her giggling suddenly over. "Merry Christmas, my darling Billy. And I . . . I hope you can forgive me for being so perfectly awful with you." And tenderly, her eyes wide and bright, Eliza reached out and drew her husband to her.

28

Tuesday, December 30, 1879

West of Montezuma Creek, near the San Juan River

"You boys do look some used up."

The speaker was James Merrick, the older of two well-supplied men who were riding the same westerly direction as the four bedraggled Mormon scouts and their new companion, Harvey Dunton. It had been more than two weeks since the four had left their camp at Hole-in-the-Rock, several days longer than their entire exploring journey was supposed to have taken, and they were just barely starting back. Worse, they'd seen nothing in that time but snow and storms, and only a series of miracles had brought them through to the San Juan. And now, they all knew, it would take more miracles, major ones, to get them back to the company at the Hole.

Pap Redd smiled wanly, rubbing his hand across the pinched and whisker-choked remnants of his face as he did so. "Food's been scarcer out here nor steam locomotives," he growled in response to James Merrick. "Going without eating leaves a man some ganted up, all right."

"Nor were circumstances better back there at Montezuma Fort with the Harrimans and Davises," George Hobbs added as he urged his mule up the side of the small wash they were then crossing. "My sister and the rest of 'em are living on seed wheat and hardly any meat. They'll be lucky to survive the next sixty days."

"And they're the advance of a whole company of Mormon

settlers, you say?" asked Ernest Mitchell, the second of the two. "How did the families back at the fort get there?"

"A whole passel of us brought 'em out through Moencopi and the Navajo country last spring, scouting a route to this country. And we found one, too. But thinking it was too long and dangerous, what with some of the Navajos none too friendly and hardly any water to speak of, our leaders and a few others decided on the Hole-in-the-Rock shortcut, which we all thought would be about seventy, seventy-five miles once we got to the Rio Colorado."

"And it's further?" Merrick pressed.

George Sevy chuckled. "More like a hundred and seventy-five. And that don't count the ups and downs and the backs and forths, which may double the distance. Twixt here and the Colorado is awful rough country, boys, and that's a fact! Another fact is that it isn't any shortcut!"

"Then why you are doing it?"

"Mormons are a mighty peculiar people," Pap Redd asserted as he kicked lightly the other of the two mules he'd purchased from the Harrimans back at the fort, which now gave the scouts four riding animals and two pack animals. "They believe they're led by a man called of God as a prophet. That man issued an inspired call to a bunch of folks to settle the San Juan country and bring peace to the Indians. And what Mormons have been called of God to do, they just naturally set out to accomplish."

"And pretty much *do* accomplish," George Morrell added with his customary smile.

"Peace to the Indians? You mean Navajos or Pahutes?"

"Both, we reckon."

"Well," James Merrick declared, thinking of the skinny Pahute boy who'd slicked him out of the best hat he'd ever worn, "I'd like to see such a peace. I surely would. But tell the truth, I don't reckon any of us ever will. Indians have their own way of doing things, and it ain't civilized, not even a little. They rob and steal for fun, and it means nothing to 'em to commit a murder here or there if it furthers their cause."

"They're not all like that," Ernest Mitchell declared quickly.

"Maybe not," Merrick argued, "but all it takes is one or two. And believe you me, there's more than one or two of the bad ones ranging this country. I know! I've seen 'em!"

"He's just old and nervous," Ernest Mitchell said with a disarming smile, doing his best to change the subject. "So you truly believe you folks will blast a road all the way through to here from the Colorado?"

"That we do, Mitchell. That we do."

For a time the seven men rode in silence, moving westward along the north bank of the San Juan River, their mounts slogging through mud from the recent rains.

As they rode, George Sevy glanced at the bulging packs of Merrick and Mitchell and found himself wondering about the men. They claimed to be hunting good range country for the opening of a new cattle spread, but something wasn't right about their story, and George knew it. For one thing, they hadn't shown the least excitement when he and the others had told them of the Lake Pahgarit country the scouts had discovered on their way out—a country that showed definite promise in terms of ranching. And for another, well, their story just didn't ring true. No sir, according to the whisperings of the Spirit, these two birds were up to something besides hunting a ranch, and George Sevy felt it strong!

"Snow looks mighty deep to the north," Ernest Mitchell observed as he swung his arm off toward Elk Mountain and the more distant Blues. "Didn't you boys say that's where your trail led?"

"We did, and it does," George Hobbs agreed. "And the snow's deep, too. Chest deep in places through that cedar and pinion forest. Coming this way, that's where we run out of food."

"And out of direction," George Sevy added. "Happen Brother Hobbs hadn't climbed a little knoll we called Salvation Knoll on Christmas Day, which is from where he finally sighted the Blue Mountains, we might have perished right there."

"I thought we'd perish two nights later when we got down in the Comb Wash, weak as four botflied calves, and didn't have the gumption to hunt a trail out," Pap Redd injected.

"That didn't bother me," George Morrell said. "Tell the truth, boys, I didn't lose hope until we was down in the Butler Wash and

Brother Hobbs here started scratching his epitaph on the rock above his head."

"It was only my name and the date," George Hobbs groused.

"Maybe." George Morrell grinned. "But I got so almighty sorrowful studying on it that I began composing an epitaph of my own—one to scratch a little higher on the rock. But when I realized I didn't have the strength to reach that high, well, then and there I felt ready to roll over, curl up in a little ball, and give up the ghost."

James Merrick nodded his understanding. "It sure sounds like you boys have had a hard time of it."

"You have no idea," Pap Redd declared solemnly. "You think we look like shabby cadavers today, but we're plumb healthy compared to three, four days ago. Why, hadn't the four of us slat-ribbed galoots stumbled on the Harris spread when we did, none of us would've had a leppy calf's chance of wintering through one more night."

"They was some hungry," Harvey Dunton admitted. "According to Sister Becky Warren, who was there and doing the cooking, the four of 'em sat down to a meal fixed for sixteen folks, and none of the four budged till that meal was cleaned up and stowed away to the last drop, bone, and crumb. Hobbs alone ate twenty-two biscuits, and the others weren't far behind."

"How long were you without food?" James Merrick asked incredulously.

"About ninety-six hours, give or take an eternity or two."

"No wonder you were so anxious to buy flour from that trapper fellow."

George Hobbs looked up. "Peter Shirts? He's Mormon, I hear, but he sure skinned us on that deal—forty-eight pounds of flour for twenty dollars. Pure robbery is what it is."

"I reckon he's scraping the bottom of the keg hisself," Pap Redd remonstrated quietly. "Happen you boys didn't notice, he was gaunt enough to look like he'd been wintering through on prickly pear and juniper berries. For a fact, as far away from a mill or general store as he was, when it came to selling his flour old Brother Shirts didn't have to be no more agreeable than an army mule or a cross-eyed woman at her stitching."

The men laughed, and for another hour or two they continued in

236

a generally westward direction along the river, riding and joking until at length they slid their mounts down the ledge and into the mouth of Comb Wash.

"Well, boys," George Sevy declared as the party drew rein, "here's where us Mormons turn north. You sure you don't want to take a look-see at that pretty little lake we told you about?"

"I don't think so," Ernest Mitchell said as he looked carefully at his older partner. "Reckon Jim and I'll be crossing the river here and checking out the country on south."

"Luck to you, then, especially with the Navajos. Fellers, let's move it on out—"

"One or two of you boys wouldn't want to ride with us, would you?" James Merrick suddenly asked, interrupting George Sevy's parting and completely surprising his partner. "Comes down to it, besides offering plenty of food we can make it worth your time in other ways, too."

"How's that?" George Sevy asked as the five Mormons turned back curiously. "We've told you; we've got all the ranching country we need right here on the San Juan, where we'll build our homes and raise our families."

"Jim," Ernest Mitchell said quietly, "I don't think these men—"

"Be still, Mitchell!" James Merrick was insistent. "This is *my* call!" Then he turned to the Mormon scouts. "We ... uh ... weren't exactly thinking of ranching."

The scouts stole glances at each other but remained silent, waiting for the man to continue.

"About a year ago," the older man said as he lowered his voice secretively, "I was passing from Fort Wingate in New Mexico on up to Lee's Ferry, crossing the Navajo nation, when I stumbled on three crude smelters where the Indians had been smelting silver from silver ore. Well, I poked around a little and then took a bit of that ore with me into Utah, and it assayed out at ninety percent silver—a rare find indeed. Boys, I don't think it would be too much trouble to locate the mines that ore came from. And it's rich enough that a couple of burro loads would make a tidy haul. Two, maybe three trips in and out again and a man would be set for life."

"That's Navajo country," George Morrell said quietly. "They've been crossed by white men before, and they're none too happy about it."

"George is right as rain," Pap Redd added. "Ever since Kit Carson herded 'em out of the country back in '64, messing with them fellers has been about as sporty as standing barefoot in front of a lightning-struck stampede. Yes, sir, boys, fooling with that there Navajo silver could lead to a mighty sudden case of rigor mortis."

"But . . . but you don't understand!" Ernest Mitchell was dumbfounded. "This isn't just any old silver mine we'll be working. This is *Peshlaki!* This is the Navajos' sacred silver mine. This is the big one!"

"All the more reason we should all travel north," George Hobbs declared with finality.

"But we could all be rich!"

"And dead." George Sevy looked at the other scouts and at Harvey Dunton. "Any of you boys want to go with these fellers and get yourselves rich?"

No one moved, no one spoke.

"Reckon you boys will have to go get rich on your own," he said with finality. "All of us have families at Hole-in-the-Rock, and they're counting on our imminent return. And Hobbs's sister back there at Montezuma Creek will surely miss his supplies if he doesn't return with them in less than sixty days."

"We could sure use your help," James Merrick declared with desperation.

"I reckon that's so. But since we've been called to a higher mission, about all the help we can give is encourage you not to try it."

"It's no good, boys," Ernest Mitchell stated with determination. "Jim and I are going to have that silver, and no two ways about it. So do us a favor. Send up a prayer for us, and don't tell no one else about the *Peshlaki.*"

"You have our word."

"Fair enough. Adios, then. And good luck in all that snow."

"Good luck to you with the Navajos," George Hobbs shot back. "You'd most especially do well to shy clear of an old fellow name of Peokon, who lives south and some west of here. He's got a mean streak in him a mile wide and twice as deep. Last summer we camped by him and another feller who calls hisself Frank on our scout out to this country, and had there been less of us, or all of us less ready, he'd have put us under the sand for sure. Thank goodness Thales Haskell was along to point him out and give us warning."

"Peokon, is it? We'll watch out for him, all right. Thanks for the warning!"

With that the two silver hunters turned and splashed their mounts and pack animals into the San Juan, heading south. And the Mormon scouts, after waiting until the two were safely across the river, waved and turned their own mounts north, already intent on finding a more direct trail back to the slowly widening gap in the rimrock above the Rio Colorado.

29

Top of Hole-in-the-Rock

"It does seem like we've been here a long time," Eliza admitted to the girl who'd walked from Fifty-Mile Camp to visit.

"A long time? The men have been working on that road more than three weeks now, and I can't even see what they've done!"

That was the truth, Eliza thought as she spooned wheat for grinding from one of the bags of seed grain. It had been most of a month since she'd first seen the Hole, and it certainly didn't look much different to her. Of course, with no blasting powder, and with the horrible winter weather, the men couldn't be expected to do much. And if the rest of them had hands that looked as awful as Billy's—

"Besides that," the girl continued as Eliza retied the bag and knelt with her grinder, "this desert is a horrid place to camp, perfectly horrid! Everything is cold and wet and miserable; the only time I'm ever warm is when I'm working myself to death. Now I'm so awful tired I can't even do that anymore! Oh, Eliza, don't you miss your shop and the heavenly comforts of Salt Lake City?"

Eliza, busy grinding the wheat in their small coffee mill, looked up and smiled. She'd known Sarah Ipson Riley for nearly four years, ever since she'd come into her shop at age fifteen on an errand for her mother. And never, in all that time, had the girl—or now woman, Eliza thought wryly—been a complainer.

"At least the Lord gave you a way to keep little Jimmy's feet warm," she finally said, not answering her young friend's question.

"Humph!" The woman patted her baby on the back. "As if that's what a woman's bosom is for. How would you like to go around all day with your child's cold feet stuck down the front of your dress? My arms ache from holding him all the time, my back aches, his toenails scratch me, and he cries whenever I wrap him up and lay him down."

Eliza smiled patiently. "I'm sure it's terribly inconvenient, but be thankful you're shaped like you and not like me. Why, the way my body's put together, all bones and angles, my baby'd likely die of cold feet no matter where I put them."

"Your baby?" Sarah Riley was all ears. "Eliza Foreman, are you in a motherly way?"

"I am," Eliza replied quietly. "In the spring."

"Well, be thankful for small favors. At least you don't have to worry about keeping a child warm through the winter here in this desolate desert." Sarah adjusted herself in Eliza's wooden rocking chair, trying to get more comfortable. "Aren't you a little nervous, having a baby when you're so . . . well—"

"Old?" Eliza laughed easily.

"I . . . I didn't mean exactly that. But I . . . well, how old are you?"

"I'm forty-four. And merciful heavens, child, why should I be nervous? If the Lord is kind enough to allow me to conceive a child at my ripe old age, then he must be intending to send Billy and me someone truly wonderful. Why on earth would I be nervous about that?"

"You honestly believe that, don't you."

"Of course I do, for many, many reasons. But I'm glad he isn't here now, because it *would* be difficult to keep him warm."

"He? Do you think it's a boy?"

Eliza nodded. "Brother Nielson blessed me more than two months ago, and in the blessing the baby was referred to as a boy. Of course only time will tell for certain—"

"It'll be a boy," Sarah Riley declared. "I absolutely believe in those things. Is Billy excited about becoming a father?"

"Lawsy, yes! About all he can talk about nights is his new son and all the things they'll be doing together."

Sarah nodded. "James is the same about little Jimmy Morton.

Honestly, some days a body would think it was him that had the baby!"

"Well, in a way, it was. I've seen James look at your baby while he's holding him, and you can't fake that look of love."

"I know. Trouble is, anymore he's not around long enough to love anybody. All week he's down in that awful gorge working on the road out the other side, and Sundays he's churching all day and half the night. It doesn't leave much time for us, I tell you! Some days I get so fed up with the Church—"

Eliza looked up, her eyebrows raised questioningly as she realized how Mary Jones must have felt when she'd made similar comments.

"Well, I do, Eliza," Sarah remonstrated forcefully, "and I'm not afraid to say it! Day in and day out the men are gone hither and yonder, scouting and building roads and chasing stock and who knows what other tomfoolery because the Church wants the San Juan settled. And all the time us poor womenfolk are left alone in this horrid wilderness to defend ourselves from who knows what. I mean, what if we were attacked by Indians or something? What would we do?"

Eliza laughed. "Offer them supper, I suppose. That's what we're counseled to do."

"Humph!" Sarah was scornful. "Parched corn, beans, and cracked seed wheat are supposed to stop bullets and arrows?"

Eliza stopped grinding and stretched her back, wondering as she did so if she'd ground enough wheat to last more than one day. She was also wondering, selfishly, how she was going to endure the entire afternoon with this unhappy young woman. Lawsy, she thought, was that what *she* had sounded like to Mary and the others?

"Sarah," she said then, smiling to disarm her, "this is a silly argument. How would Indians ever get to this remote place without the brethren knowing about it?"

"How should I know? How did Tom Box and his outfit get to Fifty-Mile Spring? Nobody knew about them until they showed up morning before yesterday."

Eliza said nothing.

"And speaking of Tom Box," Sarah continued with sudden

242

excitement, "can you believe that his wife and daughters-in-law, every long-legged one of them, were wearing men's trousers and riding regular, just like their husbands and father. It was positively mortifying to see!"

Stunned by such audacity, Eliza hardly knew what to say. Other than a few days earlier on Dick Butt's horse, she'd ridden man-style only once, when she'd been much younger and not too worried about decorum.

"They were actually wearing men's trousers?" she asked.

"I should smile! Leastwise that's what I was told. It was scandalous, too—perfectly scandalous! And that Tom Box and his grown sons are the hugest men I've seen in all my born days! Mercy, Eliza, any of them would make two of Billy, at least. They're even tons bigger than James or Jens Nielson. They say they're Texicans, and all I can say is, they sure breed them big down there."

"Sarah," Eliza frowned, "there's no need for such language."

"I'm sorry, Eliza. My mother taught me better, but lately I get to feeling so perverse that I say what I shouldn't. Way out here in this wilderness I sometimes get to wondering if it even matters."

"You wouldn't want little Jimmy to hear such things, would you?"

Sarah was almost scornful. "He can't understand, Eliza, and you know it. He's too little."

"Don't you bet on that, honey. His spirit's been alive as long as yours or mine, and it hears and remembers everything." Eliza could tell that she'd caused the younger woman to think, for her facial expression was suddenly very contemplative. Well, good. Maybe after a little pondering she'd realize that her negative attitude might indeed affect her son. After all, her own had surely affected Billy—

"Well anyway," Sarah declared sadly, "the Box family has moved along. They said feed for their stock was too much of a scratch in this country."

"It's a scratch, all right," Eliza declared as she looked around at the barren rock and scattered, sand-filled hollows where the scant forage and nearly useless black shadscale grew. "But at least this miserable rock is good for dancing."

"And I'm not even much interested in that," Sarah declared,

again dispirited. "Too much work in the cold and wet has made James as awkward as a day-old heifer, and I'm just too cold and miserable to feel like dancing."

"That's why we dance," Eliza said, rising to her feet and again stretching her back, which for some reason was hurting more with each passing day. "Look around you, Sarah, and take a minute to think about what other folks are going through. For instance, over there is Maggie Sevy. Her husband, George, is on that scout for Brother Lyman. He'll be gone for who knows how long, if he comes back at all, so Maggie is left with full responsibility for her family. Why, already those four scouts are two weeks overdue, and poor Maggie is fit to be tied. I wouldn't want to trade places with her. Would you?"

Slowly Sarah Riley shook her head.

"Practically everybody else is the same. Between the two camps we have about fifty women, eighty men, and ninety children, all crowded with all their belongings into eighty or so wagons, and not a one of them is as warm or as comfortable as they'd like to be. Everyone spends a good part of every day being wet and cold and muddy, everyone is more or less hungry and tired, and everyone's at least somewhat fearful of what lies betwixt here and the San Juan.

"Of a truth, Sarah, that's just too much misery for folks to endure very long. Knowing that, the Saints have always been counseled by our leaders to make ourselves merry at every opportunity. Why, even in the snows of Wyoming back in '56 the folks in the Martin Company danced and sang as much as they could. I recollect one sweet man dancing for hours with his wife to get her body warmed up, and when he was satisfied that she was enough improved to keep on living, he sat down on a rock, smiled at her, and died.

"Well, in this company we're all young and healthy—Kirsten Nielson and I are the two oldest women along—and we aren't going to die just because we get a little cold. But if we don't keep our spirits up we could have serious problems, so that's why we dance. Literally, Sarah, we make ourselves merry instead of miserable."

Slowly the younger woman shook her head. "You amaze me, Eliza. Mother told me I could learn a lot from you, but I thought she was just being a mother. Now I see, well, I don't rightly know what it is, but you seem to know something, or maybe feel something, that I don't. Tell the truth, I wish I could learn it."

"You will, Sarah, just like I am—one day at a time. But if you're interested, I do have a word of caution."

"Of course."

"I've been learning the hard way that complaining and being critical don't accomplish one thing besides giving the devil power to buffet you."

"You?" Sarah was astounded. "Complain and criticize?"

Eliza smiled. "I've learned a trick, though. If I feel like complaining, I keep it to myself until I'm alone with Billy's glass-eyed mare. Then I tell her. Either that, or if I'm feeling particularly courageous, I kneel down and tell God. He'll listen, but I can tell you he has a pretty interesting way of leading me to see things differently. Some of those lessons hurt, which is why I'm learning to limit my complaining to the glass-eyed mare."

Sarah smiled. "I think I'll stick to livestock too."

"I don't blame you. Another trick I've only recently learned is to picture in my mind Billy and me together, my arm around his shoulders and his about my waist, just walking along being lovers. That always gets me to smiling."

"It should," Sarah said with a giggle, "the way you tower over him. I can't imagine how you ever came to love such a shorty."

"Why, Sarah Riley, I swan! I can't imagine that you'd say such an awful thing!"

Not realizing she was being teased, Sarah had the good graces to blush. "Oh . . . uh . . . I didn't mean . . . I mean—"

"It's all right, Sarah," Eliza said as she took a chair across the table from the younger woman. "I was some surprised myself. I'd always imagined marrying a big fellow, or at least a tall one. Fact is, I'd never even given the time of day to a fellow shorter than I was. Or younger, for that matter. But when Billy walked into my shop and couldn't even talk in my presence he was so tongue-tied and nervous, I couldn't help myself. I reached out to him, just friendly-like, mind you, and tried to put him at ease. Practically the next thing I knew, we were married."

"Just like that? He seems so shy. I wonder what made him so bold?"

Eliza smiled. "He says the Spirit of the Lord rested upon him, and he knew he was to marry me."

"Really?"

"That's right. He says he was walking past my shop minding his own business when the feeling came over him that if he would go inside he would meet his future wife."

"So he did?"

"Not exactly," Eliza stated, shaking her head. "First he looked through the window, got scared, he says, and wouldn't come near my shop again for another two weeks. When his conscience got the best of him and he finally came back, I saw him there and for some silly reason motioned him inside. That isn't like me, either, but it's exactly what I did."

"And so Billy came right in?"

Eliza laughed. "He did. When I proved friendly, Billy's courage grew apace, and we began courting, going to the theater and such. First thing you know I realized I'd stopped noticing how short he was, or how young. And to tell the truth, I'm not certain he *ever* noticed I'm the tallest or the oldest." Eliza laughed self-consciously. "I also discovered that for some fool reason Billy is totally convinced that I'm beautiful. Now, I've always known better than that, and I assume everybody else has. But now that I know I have him fooled, I'll spend the rest of my life going out of my way to keep him that way."

"So you really are happy with him?"

"I . . . I am," Eliza declared as sudden tears sprang to her eyes. "Finally I am! Do you know that not once since we met, except for asking me not to dance until after the baby comes, has he ever faulted me, or criticized me, or looked at me crosswise, or even complained about some little thing I have or haven't done. Instead, he praises me all the time, tells me I'm the most beautiful woman on the face of God's green earth, and in general fills my head with such utterly sweet nonsense that I swan I believe him half the time and hope he's right the other half.

"Fact is, Sarah, I can honestly say I'm desperately trying to be the woman he already thinks I am. If I ever make it, then I'll be something to behold, you can bet your high-buttoned shoes on that!"

"You already are," Sarah said thoughtfully as she pulled herself to her feet, careful not to disturb her sleeping infant. "I just wish I could make myself feel the same. But . . . but I didn't expect this journey to be so long and hard, nor the country so godforsaken and lonely. Oh, Eliza, how my faith is being tested!"

"So is the faith of every man, woman, and child in this company, as well as many who have been left behind. Any time any of us embarks on an errand for the Lord, Sarah, by and by the devil will come along and get his licks in. And those temptations, or discouragements or whatever, turn our experiences into trials of our faith."

"Well, I certainly wish they were less intent or less frequent!"

"You know what to do about that, don't you?"

Sarah Riley smiled. "I can hear my mother saying it now: 'Put your trust in the Lord, Sarah, dear, and all will be well.' And I'm trying, Eliza. I truly am. I know the Lord loves me, and I know he won't give me greater trials than I can bear. Only, I don't understand God's interpretation of what I can bear. For a fact, some days my life gets harder than I think it ought to be."

Eliza reached out and placed her hand over the hand of the young woman. "I understand, Sarah."

"Yes," Sarah said finally, and very softly, "I truly believe you do." And with that she smiled, drew her shawl more tightly about her shoulders, adjusted her baby again, turned, and with head erect walked away toward the camp at Fifty-Mile Spring.

30

Friday, January 9, 1880

West Bank of the Colorado River, below the Hole

"Looks somewhat different from down here, doesn't it."

The speaker was Platte Lyman, and Billy, his hands held under his armpits to warm them, looked up and nodded. "I'll say. From this angle it looks practically perpendicular."

"Well, if it ain't perpendicular," twenty-three-year-old Alvin Decker groused, "it sure is slantindicular!" Then he threw another length of driftwood onto the drag behind the mules Sign and Wonder.

Both Platte and Billy laughed, and Billy stored it in his mind so he could repeat it to Eliza that night. Slantindicular! It was an apt description of the Hole, all right, as was Amasa Barton's commonly expressed joke that a man driving down it had better be able to duck so he wouldn't be killed by objects falling from the back of his wagon. Billy smiled remembering this, too, but his smile was tempered by the knowledge that it was the steepest trail he'd ever seen.

"I was told you've surveyed the Hole," he said to Platte Lyman. "Did you figure how steep it was?"

The company leader lifted his hat and brushed his fingers through his thinning hair, remembering. "All I had was a square and level, Billy, and terrible footing, so I may have been off a bit. I figure, though, that the grade will drop eight feet to the rod for the first third of the way down, then about five and a half feet to the rod the rest of the way here to the river. That makes the upper grade about fifty degrees, and from the landing on down, about forty-five degrees, which to my way of thinking is a mighty steep road. Slantindicular, as Alvin says."

Billy nodded. "I figured the top the same as you, but I thought the bottom was closer to forty-four degrees. But I just did it in my head, so I'm probably wrong."

"In your head?"

"Well, of course, I had no instruments," Billy declared, feeling embarrassed and wishing he'd said nothing. Though he'd been down and up what was going to become the wagon road through the Hole numerous times in the previous four weeks, this was the first time he'd been given an assignment that took him all the way down to the Colorado River. And now that he was here, the sight practically overwhelmed him. Looking to the west and back up the Hole, it was easy to see the steep sand hills rising to the first of the terraced sandstone cliffs, and to see where the roadway had been worked up across them. At the base of the cliffs the roadway ended at what was already being called Uncle Ben's Dugway, a fifty-foot stretch of road that was literally being tacked onto the cliff face to the north of the Hole. It was on this dugway that he'd been laboring before his present assignment.

Above the dugway, the road entered the notch of the Hole itself, which at that point was a narrow canyon twenty to thirty feet wide. Still climbing the north side, the road followed up the quickly narrowing canyon until it was actually no more than a notch, a slit in the rock barely wide enough for a wagon to pass through. Above that point, the notch narrowed and widened and narrowed again, leaving areas where teams of men were picking and chiseling away the sides of the gorge so wagons could get through. It was along this stretch that the Hole seemed to be in perpetual twilight, and a man almost had to lay on his back to see the narrow sliver of sky above. And it was also in this area that two small springs seeped water into the Hole, creating sheets and ribbons of ice that were proving particularly treacherous to the workers.

Finally came the looming bulge of the rimrock, forty-seven feet of perpendicular sandstone cliff through which a narrow slit wound to the top. Before they'd run out of powder, some of this rimrock had been laboriously chipped and blasted away by those going over the edge in their barrels, and now the seam was barely wide enough for a man to pass through. And there was still a massive amount of rock to move before they could open a channel wide enough and sloped back far enough for wagons to pass through. Silas Smith, leader of the San Juan expedition, was in Salt Lake City arranging for more blasting powder and other supplies to accomplish this, but so far he'd sent no word, and no supplies had been forthcoming.

Now Billy looked up, marveling. Though the rimrock seemed small and insignificant from this angle, it was anything but that, and he knew it. And though the Hole itself seemed an impossible route for a road, that too was deceiving. Despite its steepness, and despite the fact that the boulder-strewn bottom would need to be filled in places to a depth of more than twenty feet, and finally despite the impossible-looking stretch of cliff-face that was on its way to becoming Uncle Ben's Dugway, the day was coming when wagons, more than eighty of them, would be pulled down that road by teams of oxen, horses, and mules.

Once down, Billy thought as he turned slightly toward the east, they would cross this mighty river—which was about three hundred and fifty feet wide at this point—and then immediately begin the climb out of the river gorge and onto the more level ground in the bottom of Cottonwood Canyon. That climb up from the river, the snakelike dugway the Deckers, Joe Barton, and others from Fifty-Mile Camp were working on, angled up the face of a two-hundred-and-fifty-foot cliff that seemed almost insignificant when viewed from the rimrock above. Yet from this vantage point, looking across the river and upward, even that cliff seemed massive and nearly impassable.

"Well, whatever its steepness, it about takes your breath away, doesn't it?"

"It surely does," Billy agreed as he looked upward again. It was interesting how everything in this country was so layered, not at all like the volcanic cinder cones and lava flows near Cedar City or the granite mountains near Salt Lake. Here the country, including the ten-thousand-foot-high Escalante Mountains and the Fifty-Mile Mountain that ranged along the Escalante Desert, was laid out in seemingly endless layers of exposed rock that continually reminded him of the pages of a book, they were so uniform.

Now, looking upward, Billy realized that the entire two thousand feet of the river gorge was composed the same—of layer after layer and color after color of rock, some of sandstone, some of slate, and some of other forms of rock Billy couldn't even begin to identify. Why, even the cutbank he was standing beside was layered.

"Platte," Billy called as sudden excitement filled his voice, "would you mind stepping over here and looking at this?"

Platte Lyman, with Alvin Decker not far behind, walked to where Billy was standing.

"How do you think this cutbank was formed?" Billy asked without preamble.

"Why, I'd say the river laid it down when the water was high," Platte replied. "Then it rose again and cut part of it away. Why?"

"Do you see how it's layered?"

"I do."

"How do you suppose such layers formed?"

Platte looked thoughtful as he stretched out his hand to touch the bank. "Well, again I'd say that when the river was this high, it was carrying all this gravel along, and it got deposited here. In that level there," and now he pointed to a level that ran at about knee height, "it didn't have much gravel, but it must have been tolerable muddy, for it was mud the river deposited."

"Would the same be true for this layer?" Billy asked as he pointed to a foot-thick layer of mud and sand near his feet.

"If I'm right it would." Platte reached down and rubbed his hand across the cut. "This is a mixture of sand and gravel, mostly sand."

"Is one layer older than another?"

Platte smiled. "Of course. The bottom layer would most certainly have been laid down before the layers above it."

"What in tarnation are you fellers talking about?" Alvin Decker asked.

"Layers of earth," Billy responded. "For the first time in my life, Alvin, I think I'm starting to get a picture of how terribly old this earth must surely be."

"Yeah. Six thousand plus six thousand years is mighty old."

Billy looked at Platte, who shrugged the argument off. "Actually," Billy said, "I'm beginning to think it's much older than that, Alvin. Maybe millions of years."

"Not according to the scriptures." Alvin was adamant. "The Bible says the Lord created the world in six days and rested on the seventh day after he'd created Adam and Eve, and that each of his days is a thousand years of our time. Add to that the six thousand years since Adam and Eve, and you get twelve thousand years. Period."

"Alvin, you may be exactly right in your interpretation of that scripture. On the other hand, maybe there's a meaning in it that's eluding us. Time and again I've heard one authority or another say that the scriptures are like an onion, with layer upon layer of meaning hidden in every verse, each layer opening to our understanding only when we're spiritually prepared to receive it.

"For instance, Joseph Smith taught that the scriptural terms *world* and *earth* don't mean the same thing. According to what President Young told me, Joseph said that *earth* in the scriptures refers to this planet, and *world* refers to the human family. Once we understand that, scriptural verses with those terms take on entirely new meanings."

"What President Young are you talking about?" Alvin Decker asked scornfully. "And who are you to be telling me how to interpret the scriptures?"

"Billy spent a little more than twenty years working around or being clerk for President Brigham Young," Platte answered quietly.

"No fooling?" Alvin asked, surprised. "Well, shut my mouth! I didn't have any idea of that." He paused, thinking. "So, are you saying that if the scripture says the world was created in seven days, it isn't necessarily talking about the earth?"

"Well, if it said that, yes, that's what I'd be talking about. But I don't think the scriptures make the timing of the creation all that clear. Instead we just get hints and glimpses, enough to make us think and even gain a little understanding, but not enough to do away with the benefits of the veil."

Alvin nodded. "That makes sense. The Lord still wants us to walk by faith."

"And learn to think as he does," Billy agreed.

"All the same, we know he organized this earth using miraculous means—his priesthood, if you will."

Billy smiled his agreement. "True enough, Alvin. But how do we know God's miraculous means aren't the same things we mortals call natural processes."

"Like a baby being conceived, developing, and then being born a living, breathing human being," Platte declared. "That's a natural process, but it's also one of the greatest miracles any of us will ever see."

"Exactly," Billy declared while Alvin nodded his understanding. "Take this cutbank here as another example. If each of these layers represents a yearly high-water stage of the river, then in this four-foot bank you can see at least three years of flooding and layering, and most likely a fourth year of cutting away.

"Now, translate that information to the two thousand feet of layering between here and the rim of the gorge, and then on up the fifteen hundred feet of Fifty-Mile Mountain and all the way to the top of the Escalante Mountains, which as you'll recollect are layered in the same way as this cutbank. If the cutbank was laid down by natural processes, wouldn't it seem likely that the same would be true for everything else?"

Silently Alvin nodded.

"If that's so," Billy pressed, "then how many years do you suppose it would take to lay those layers down and then wear them away?"

Alvin looked perplexed. "If you're right, Billy, well, I can't even think in numbers like that."

"But the Lord can, Alvin, and apparently does. Years ago my father showed me a number of the *Times and Seasons,* published in Nauvoo. The editor, W. W. Phelps, wrote that the Prophet Joseph had told him that the particular eternity relative to the doings of the Lord Jesus Christ, according to the records found in the catacombs of Egypt, has been going on in this system—not this world, mind you, but this system, which I assume means at least everything we can see in the heavens—almost two thousand five hundred and fifty-five millions of years."

Softly Alvin whistled his amazement.

"My father, and according to him, some of the authorities he associated with, interpreted that to mean that the grand council in heaven occurred that long ago. If that's right, then there would certainly be enough time for the Lord to create this earth using the natural processes we're familiar with.

"In other words, that many thousands of millions of years would not only give the Lord time to create or organize this earth in the first place but would also provide ample time to allow an ancient sea or lake to layer this country out the way it is, and then to go dry and leave this mighty river behind to cut away the earth the way it has obviously done."

"Amazing," Alvin said as he shook his head. "I've never even thought of such things." For a moment he paused, looking upward. "So you think this country was originally laid out in these layers by a sea or lake? Why do you think that?"

Billy smiled. "Partly because I can see that water layered out this cutbank, and partly because of all the sandstone this country's filled with. From what I've read, seashores are generally made of sand."

"But sandstone is rock!"

"You're right, and that's another reason why I'm beginning to believe this earth is tremendously old. Think about it, Alvin. Over enough time these layers of sand and silt and mud and gravel were all laid down just like this cutbank here, and as other, newer layers covered them over, I'd guess they got squeezed down until they were somehow turned into rock—sandstone, slate, shale, and so forth, depending on what sorts of material ancient rivers carried into the water. Then for some reason the lake or ocean dried up and went away, and ever since then this river we call the Colorado has been cutting down through the layered rock, digging out our gorge for us."

"So you've concluded," Platte now asked, "that all those rocks up there, even to the top of Escalante Mountain, were once underwater? And were not rocks but silt and soil?"

Soberly Billy nodded. "I think so, Platte. Now that I think on it a little, it's the only thing that makes any sense to me. Besides which, this morning I found this while I was leading the mules down through those cliffs above Jackass Mesa."

Reaching into his pack, Billy withdrew a small, thin piece of creamy white sandstone, itself composed of several thinner layers only fractions of an inch thick. But more than the obvious layers, what arrested the attention of both Platte and Alvin was the perfectly clear, dark-colored imprint of a small fish in the top layer of the stone.

"What's this?" Alvin asked.

"It's called a fossil," Platte responded as he examined the stone. "I've read about them in the *Atlantic Monthly* and *Gody's Lady's Book.*"

"Is it a real fish?"

"It used to be," Billy replied. "The way it looks to me, it died and was buried when this rock was still soft silt, the mud filling in all around the fish and completely covering it. Years passed, many thousands or even millions of them, and the silt got squeezed down by more silt into these thin layers until it turned into this soft rock. Then the lake or sea disappeared and the river came along and started cutting away, digging down and down, and after many more years this rock was exposed, broke off from what was around it, and was just sitting there on the ledge when I climbed down past it."

"And you found this up above Jackass Mesa?"

"I did. Up near the rim."

"Well, I reckon I've heard of flying fish—" Alvin grinned as he looked upward once again. "How come it doesn't look like a real fish? I mean, this is more like a picture of a fish skeleton."

"According to what I read, the fossil isn't the actual fish," Platte responded. "That decayed and disappeared long ago. But the impression in the silt-turned-rock remained, and gradually it filled with other minerals until they took up the exact space left by the fish—which explains why this fossil is dark while the stone around it is mostly white. Isn't that right, Billy?"

"It makes sense, though I didn't read those articles you mentioned. The thing is, the more I look at this fish and the layered country we've been passing through the past few weeks, the more I have the feeling that we're perambulating about on the bottom of an ancient sea, and that the hole we're widening out for our road cuts down through a huge version of this little cutbank. That's why I'm beginning to feel that this earth and God's work on it have been going on far longer than we give him credit for."

"Amazing," Alvin Decker breathed as he turned the stone this way and that. "If we ever get a break, I'd like you to take me where you found this. Maybe there are more of them lying around."

"Be glad to do it," Billy responded easily, and with that the three returned to the search for the more urgently needed driftwood.

—◦—◦—◦—

"What's it like up in Cottonwood?" Billy asked as he and Platte moved along the bank. "I mean, does the country ever change?"

Platte chuckled. "It changes, all right, mostly from bad to worse. But Cottonwood Canyon is nice, Billy. Lots of trees and grass, fairly level ground, a clear stream—it's a wonderful place to camp. However, getting out of there will be a sure-enough job."

"Worse than the Hole?"

"Well, maybe not worse but not much better, either. I was there a month ago with Kumen Jones and a few others, and it looked so bad I didn't expect we'd come this way at all. We'll have to build a lot of steep road, and within a mile or two after we're out of Cotton-wood, the country gets so rough and broken and cut in two by deep gorges—two to three hundred feet deep with perpendicular sides of bare rock—that I thought it was impassable for a wagon road. Fact is, I thought the country was impassable even for a man on foot. It's the worst country for traveling I ever saw. But as old Brother Nielson says, with a little sticky-to-ity and the help of the Lord, we can turn even impassable places into good, well-used road."

"Maybe George Sevy and the other explorers will find a better route."

Platte's expression turned bleak. "Maybe," he responded grimly. "I certainly hope so. But they've been gone two weeks longer than they should have, Billy. Tell the truth, I just hope they're alive!"

Thinking of the loneliness of George's wife Maggie, Billy could do nothing but agree.

For a time the three men labored in silence, moving along the river and gathering a fairly good load of driftwood for the base of the dugway. These sticks and logs, laid side by side on the oak staves that would be pounded into the holes drilled along the route of Uncle Ben's Dugway, would support the brush, rocks, and dirt that would comprise the outer portion of the roadbed. The inner portion, the groove where the inner wheels of the wagons would run, would then be chiseled and blasted out of the sandstone cliff. And thus the dugway would have at least one firm, solid side.

However, Billy, whose hands hadn't callused but had become festered and raw, was beginning to think of the Hole not as a road but as a nightmare from which he would never awaken. Day after day it was the same thing—climb down in the dark, scratch and pick at the unyielding rock during every last minute of daylight no matter the condition of the weather or his hands, and then drag himself back up to the rim when darkness came again. Of course, it was midwinter, and the days were now extremely short, for which he was guiltily thankful. But Billy was beginning to wonder if the road through the Hole would ever be finished. Truly it seemed—

"Your hands doing any better, Billy?"

Looking at Platte Lyman, Billy shook his head. "Not much."

"Kumen says your blisters have festered and filled with pus."

"I . . . reckon he's right." Billy was discouraged, and it sounded in his voice. "Eliza's done what she can, and I've tried to keep them moist with grease and clean rags. But I can't hardly grip the tools with my hands all wrapped, and with them unwrapped things just get worse. Tell the truth, Platte, I'm feeling more useless all the time."

"Well, there are always things a man can do. I hoped gathering driftwood would be a little easier on you than swinging a pick or singlejack all day long. That's why I changed your assignment."

Feeling terrible that he was becoming more and more a liability to the company, Billy didn't respond. But he was so disappointed in himself, so mortified—

———◇—◇—◇———

"Hey, Charlie," Platte called as he, Billy, and Alvin Decker came around a sandy point and in sight of the camp of Charles Hall and his sons, who were busy putting together the ferry the expedition would use when they finally got their wagons down the Hole. "How's the boat-building enterprise coming along?"

Rising to his feet, Charles Hall waved. "Come and see for yourselves," he shouted above the roar of the river.

"Let's go take a look, boys," Platte said with a smile, and the three temporarily forgot driftwood and even fossils as they made their way across the wide sandbar to where the Halls were working.

"Well, ain't that something," Alvin declared. Charlie and his two sons, John and Reed, had gone into the Escalante Mountains before the snow hit and felled several large Ponderosa pines. These had been cut to Charlie's specifications at the mill in Escalante, hauled in wagons to the Hole, and then lowered by rope and hand-carried down to the river. Here Charlie and his sons, with the help of a few carpenters from camp, had laid the lumber out as planned, and now before Billy and the others lay a sixteen-by-sixteen foot flat-bottom ferry, which was quickly coming together.

"Vell, vat do you boys tink?" Mons Larson asked as he proudly surveyed his and the others' work.

"Mighty pretty," Alvin declared from beside Billy. "But will she float?"

"You'd best hope so," Charlie rejoined, and at that the men chuckled. "If she doesn't, my boys and me are in the clear. That's because we're the experts. We'll blame Brother Mons here, and Stanford Smith and Will Mackelprang. They're only carpenters. Oh, and we'd better add the name of Bishop Sevy, if he ever gets back from that scout of his! Since he's missed out on all the work, should she sink, we ought to put the whole blame on him."

There was more laughter, and while Charlie modestly explained to Platte and some of the others how he'd prefabricated the boat so it would assemble more easily, Billy wandered over to a small kiln the men had built nearby.

"It's for melting out pitch from wood we gathered back in the mountains," a young man standing nearby explained. "We'll caulk the joints with the pitch once the boat is together, and it shouldn't leak much after that."

"Good idea," Billy exclaimed. "Howdy. I'm Billy Foreman."

"Reed Hall," the tall youth said as he extended his hand. "Glad to meet you, Brother Foreman."

"Billy is just fine. You folks have a nice camp here."

Reed grinned. "Yeah, Pa's a stickler about that sort of thing. Fact is, Ma and the other womenfolk have green showing already in their gardens, and we've got grapevines and fruit trees planted up yonder by the spring. I reckon Pa figures on us staying awhile."

"What on earth for?" Billy asked.

"Why, this'll be the regular road to the San Juan once she's open," Reed replied. "Pa figures we can run the ferry practically year-round and make a pretty decent living. Most days it's been like spring down here, so comes to that, I won't mind staying myownself."

"It is comfortable here," Billy admitted as he glanced across the river. "How will you get the ferry across?"

"Pa designed it so one man can row it without much difficulty."

"One man?"

Reed nodded. "One man with a good oar sitting on the downstream side. That'll keep the bow pointed a little upstream, and because she's so light on the water, she'll cross pretty much straight. Even high water'll make little difference because the river won't get wider here, only deeper."

Billy nodded, impressed. In fact, he never stopped being amazed at the things men knew how to do, things that had never even entered his mind. "You going to build cabins?" he asked.

"I doubt it. Pa thinks we'd lose 'em in high water. Besides, warm as it is down here, tents do just fine. But it'll be home, nonetheless. What are you going to do over on the San Juan?"

"Me, you mean? Or the entire party?"

"You."

"Farm, I reckon." Billy grinned. "Of course, that should prove interesting, since I haven't farmed a day in my life."

"No kidding? What do you do normally?"

Billy was suddenly embarrassed, for despite his efforts otherwise, he still thought of his former work as less than manly. "Uh . . . I'm a clerk, I reckon. An accountant."

"You mean you can cipher?"

"Pretty well. I've been doing it since I was a youngster."

In awe, young Reed shook his head. "No kidding. I've been studying on ciphering ever since I can remember, but I can't hardly get the hang of it. Course, I ain't had much time in school, but I think on it pretty often. Seems to me, Brother Foreman, if a man knew figures he could keep himself too busy to ever follow a plow."

"You think so?"

"You bet I do. For instance," and Reed picked up a stick and began to scratch in the sand, "Pa wanted a boat big enough to haul two wagons and two teams at once, so it had to be sixteen feet by sixteen feet. But with joist-timbers every two feet, cross-braces every four feet, and inch-thick planks both over and under, as well as a removable, two-foot rail all around, it took real figuring to work out the amount of lumber we needed to harvest and have milled."

"How thick's the boat?" Billy asked as he squatted on the sand beside the youth.

"Oh, yeah," Reed grinned, "I forgot that. Twelve-inch joists and two inches of planking. Fourteen inches altogether."

Taking the stick, Billy began figuring in the sand. "Well," he said after a few moments, "that's about how many board feet of raw lumber you'd have needed before milling."

Reed stared open-mouthed. "That's within a hundred board feet of what Pa and I figured, but we figured high on purpose, and it took me two weeks to get to that, with Pa's help. See what I mean, Brother Foreman? Why, a fellow who can cipher the way you do shouldn't ever waste his time farming."

Billy chuckled. "Maybe you're right, Reed. But I had a bit of an advantage here. I used to do the books for President Brigham Young, and one of my jobs was figuring the board feet of lumber cut at a sawmill he owned and then billing accordingly. Something else and I might not be so fast."

"Maybe, maybe not. But the principles stay the same, Brother Foreman, and you know it. Figures are figures, I reckon."

"Usually," Billy acknowledged. "Do you know how to do equations, Reed?"

"Shoot, I can add, subtract, and even multiply a little. But I ain't never even heard of equations. What are they?"

"Ways of figuring things even when you don't know the exact numbers. For instance, there are geometric equations, algebraic equations, and so forth. Platte Lyman used geometric equations to figure the grade of the Hole, and I used a little algebra just now to figure the board feet of the ferry. If you'll do me a favor and call me Billy instead of Brother Foreman, you can come up to my camp of an evening and I'll show you a few things about them."

Reed was overjoyed. "Doggone it, Billy, that's fine of you to offer. Trouble is, there ain't much time left before you folks leave. If you were willing and able, I'd want to start tonight."

"Tonight'd be just fine." Billy rose to his feet. "If you have a slateboard and a bit of chalk—"

"Boat coming!" somebody shouted, and Billy and Reed Hall looked up to see the small rowboat coming from across the river.

"It's George Sevy," Alvin Decker shouted a moment later, the excitement in his voice noticeable. "The scouts are back, boys!"

"At least one of them is," Platte Lyman said quietly as he waded into the river to meet the boat. "You alone, Bishop?" he called across the water.

"We all made it," George Sevy responded as he drew abreast of Platte and stepped from the boat, "with Harvey Dunton and Dan Harris to boot. The others are too done in to cross today, but I'm not putting off the chance of seeing my family!"

As Billy drew nearer, he was startled by George's appearance. Normally thin anyway, the man's face was now gaunt and hollow, his eyes were sunken, and not even his beard could hide his haggard, starved appearance.

"We like to have given up on you boys," Henry Holyoak declared as he put his arm around the man and helped him onto the upper bank of the sandbar. "We thought all of you were goners."

"You came mighty near being right, Hank." George Sevy glanced around. "Howdy, Platte. Howdy, boys. Billy, good to see you. You still camped by Maggie?"

"I am, George, and she's fine. Or at least she was this morning. So are the boys."

George smiled, and the relief on his face was obvious. "I'm mighty pleased to hear that. Taking so long as we did, I've been some worried about them."

"Did you find a route through?"

"Barely, but it took more miracles than a man normally sees in

261

a lifetime." George Sevy sank onto the side of the ferry, patting it with his hand. "You boys have done a sight of work since we left."

"We'll do more now that you're here," Charlie Hall declared.

"I imagine."

"So, what's it like out there?" Alvin Decker questioned.

"Like Platte told us a month ago, she's rock solid and straight up and down." George Sevy closed his eyes. "Fact is, we only found our way down off the Slickrocks when George Hobbs tried to lasso a mountain sheep and ended up following it to the bottom."

"Slickrocks?"

"Yeah, that's what we called 'em. Same sandstone hills as here, actually. But they're so apple-slick and smooth we couldn't navigate 'em, not even on foot, until George followed that sheep. But that isn't all. There's a canyon twixt here and the Slickrocks so steep you won't believe it. But if we can get down, and there's some good pot-holes full of water in the bottom, then it looks like the Lord himself has blasted out a road for us up the other side. It's steep, though, and straight as an arrow. We called it the Chute.

"Beyond that there's a natural lake, miles of cedar timber so thick we'll have to ax our way through, canyons so deep we'll have no choice but to head 'em like we did twixt here and Escalante, a jagged ridge we'll have to find our way around that's so steep and straight it looks like a cock's comb sticking up out of the ground, and all of those things are held together with miles and miles of nothing but pure lonesomeness covered by deep snow. In short, boys, I call it the land of desolation, and we'll have us a real picnic crossing it.

"Now, if one or two of you fellers are heading back up the Hole, I'd appreciate you throwing a rope around me and giving me a tow. As Pap Redd might put it, I'm weak as a drowned kitten and hungry enough to chew the rattles off a teased snake."

Soon George Sevy was being towed up the Hole by both Alvin and Platte. Billy, left alone to drive the mules with their load of drift-wood up to Uncle Ben's Dugway, was thinking again of Reed Hall and his promise to teach him, wondering if maybe his head for fig-ures just might be good for something after all.

31

Sunday, January 11, 1880

Top of Hole-in-the-Rock

"I simply can't get over how bad Brother Sevy looks!"

Mary Jones turned her face away from the noxious smoke of the coal fire, which a shifting wind had blown in her direction. She was browning some small onions and the last of a ration of stringy beef they'd been given a few days before, while Billy stirred thickening flour into a pot of boiling potatoes that had been brought from Escalante. In a few moments the beef and onions would be added to the thick potato soup, and all would enjoy a wonderful Sabbath meal.

Kumen Jones, who'd already milked both cows because Billy's hands were too infected to do so, was seated under the canvas awning at the Foreman table next to Eliza's rocking chair, and both of them were contemplating the nearby Sevy wagon and tent.

"He looked rough, all right," Kumen admitted, "but hardly any worse than poor Pap Redd."

"I thought they all looked bad," Mary said. "But then, why shouldn't they, considering what they've been through."

"They certainly showed plenty of pluck." Billy squatted back on his heels as the smoke swirled in his direction and then under the canvas awning, where it briefly irritated both Kumen and Eliza. "Like Platte said, they were lost four or five days in deep snow and blinding snowstorms, ran out of provisions and nearly killed a mule to eat, and only reached the fort on the San Juan after twelve grueling days."

"A hundred and seventy-five miles." Eliza breathed deeply after the air under the awning had cleared from the smoke. "Just imagine."

Billy nodded. "And after one day's rest at Montezuma Creek, they started back and took twelve days to cover a hundred and thirty-six miles."

"Well, at least they found a passable route for our road." Rising, Mary took the skillet of browned meat and slowly added it to the soup. "But from what they said in meeting, only Heavenly Father could have led them so far in such conditions—and in such a broken and timbered country, all cut to pieces with deep gorges, without food, compass, or trail, and most of the time without sun, moon, or stars to help them keep their course."

Kumen nodded as he arose and removed the protective sheet Billy was now keeping over Eliza's carefully set table. "There's no doubt the Lord protected them. It wouldn't surprise me if their experience turns out to be the hardest of any connected with this mission.

"Obviously a kind Providence came to their assistance. Why, their twenty-four-day journey makes the travels of Father Escalante look like a picnic party."

Billy nodded in agreement. "Brother Sevy told Eliza and me that many times he and the others nearly gave up in despair."

"At one time or another," Kumen added, "I believe they all did. George Hobbs even scratched his name on a rock one night, figuring it would be his last resting place. They had other opposition, too. Did you hear about the two prospectors they met? Mitchell and Merrick, their names were."

"George mentioned them, but I don't know the details."

"They were looking for some lost Navajo silver mine—supposed to be very rich. They had plenty of provisions, and our starving brethren tried to get the miners to accompany them so they could share in their bounty. Of course, the miners would have none of that, but they wanted our boys to help them look for the mine. Had any one of our scouts succumbed to the temptation, not just for wealth but even for food, the others probably wouldn't have made it back alive, and we'd have no idea of which way to go once we cross the river."

"Satan never misses a trick," Eliza said thoughtfully as she stretched her throbbing feet toward the fire. "One way or another, he'll manage to tempt us wherever we're the weakest."

Kumen nodded. "What I find interesting is that our scouts' temptation was the same as Christ's—food, wealth, and power. I wonder if, in one way or another, we don't all face those same temptations."

Billy and the two women looked thoughtfully at Kumen. "Well," Billy responded, "President Young always said he feared the Saints' successes more than their failures. He was afraid that once our people got a taste of prosperity, we'd end up seeking more of it rather than the kingdom of God. To my way of thinking, that's the same thing."

Kumen laughed. "If this road of ours is the only way there, then we all ought to be safe on the San Juan. I've a feeling wealth and prosperity will be mighty thin in that country."

"You're probably right," Billy acknowledged. "On the other hand, if we have to waste and wear out our lives in that wilderness just trying to survive, won't that keep us from spiritual growth about as much as having too much prosperity?"

Kumen's eyes narrowed. "Now, that's an interesting thought."

"The scriptures call it the cares of the world," Billy went on. "It includes everything that's opposed to worldliness, which is lusting after wealth, power, and so forth, and other such sinful activities. Of course, being bogged down by the cares of the world could apply to other things as well."

"Such as?" Both women were now listening intently.

"Parents spending so much time caring for their children that they neglect their own growth, or people worrying so much about a certain part of their lives that they never lift up their eyes to see what's beyond it. You know, that sort of thing."

"You mean like feeling constantly discontented because you haven't achieved some great dream, when all along you might have found happiness and contentment in what you already had?"

"That's right."

"I have an aunt and uncle exactly like that, always counting on a great and glorious success that has never occurred. Honestly, I can never remember them being really happy."

"This is amazing," Kumen declared with a shake of his head. "In all my life I've never heard such an idea as this. Yet I can find nothing to fault it. Rather, everything you say rings crystal clear."

"It does," Mary stated. "But it raises a question in my mind, one I've thought quite a lot about. If the Lord wants us so badly to go to the San Juan, then why?"

"We're to be a buffer against the Indians and the outlaws. You know that."

"Of course I do. But that isn't what I mean. My question is more personal. Why does the Lord want me, Mary Nielson Jones, to go to the San Juan? What does he expect me to learn there? What does he expect me to accomplish, to do? My whole being aches with a longing to be there, and I keep wondering why."

"Those are good questions, Mary." Her husband looked thoughtful.

Mary smiled at him. "Well, they certainly plague me. What's out there that *you* long for, Billy?"

Surprised, Billy was at a loss for words. "I . . . I don't know. I am awed by the beauty of this country, I suppose. And its grandeur. And I'm afraid of it, too—more afraid than I want to admit. But you're right, Mary. There's something out there besides beauty that's calling me. I don't know what it is, but I know it's waiting—something grand and marvelous that I'm practically bursting to go off and discover."

Kumen chuckled. "You feel that way even after the report of our scouts in meeting this morning?"

Soberly Billy nodded. "I do. I hope for all our sakes that we don't have to suffer as those men did. But even if we do, I have a feeling it will be worth it. Besides, I'm positive God will protect us no matter what comes."

"I feel the same," Eliza declared, "but I believe I know why I'm going to the San Juan. Long ago I was promised in a blessing that I alone would raise up a righteous posterity to my husband. That blessed day is now almost at hand, and more and more I have the feeling that the best place on earth for me to do that is on the San Juan."

Smiling, Billy reached out and took his wife's hand. "Then no matter the cost, it will be a wonderful experience for us."

"It will, Billy darling, it will!"

32

Wednesday, January 14, 1880

Uncle Ben's Dugway, below the Hole-in-the-Rock

"Well, Billy, how goes the battle?"

Looking up from his pickwork, Billy wiped his brow with his neckscarf and leaned back against the rock, trying to ease his throbbing hands and aching back. To help keep his mind from his hands, he'd been thinking of his fossil-hunting expedition the previous Sunday morning with Alvin Decker. They had found a couple of fossils, too. And though they weren't as clear or perfect as the fish Billy had found previously, Alvin had been pleased mightily, and he couldn't stop talking about them and what they might mean.

The man climbing up the rock toward him now was Joseph Barton, one of the Paragonah boys who worked on the dugway across the river. Joe was a good man, warm and friendly, and he and his wife, Harriet Ann, sang as one of the better duets in the company.

"Not bad, Joseph," Billy replied with a smile. "How are you boys faring across the river?"

"The rocks and the gravel are still flying far and wide." Joseph Barton laughed. "Fact is, another week, maybe two, we'll have a sure-enough road up that cliff face. They figure you don't need help anymore?"

"Either that," Billy replied with amusement, "or they're trying to keep me from slowing down real progress."

"Oh, I doubt that, Billy. But if it's true, come on across the river, and we'll make you part of a real crew." Joseph Barton's eyes were dancing with friendliness, and Billy felt it like a warm glow. "Only

267

problem on that side of the river is the way we throw together those seed-wheat slapjacks we eat twice a day. Mighty poor eating is about the best I can say for them. You a hand at cooking, Billy?"

Billy shook his head. "Not hardly."

"Well, then, maybe you wouldn't even want to consider us." Joseph looked up into the mouth of the Hole. "One of the boys came down from camp this morning with word from Harriet Ann that both little Eliza and baby Mattie—I mean Mary Viola—were feeling poorly, so I thought I'd knock off early and go see how they are."

"I hope they're all right."

Joseph nodded. "Oh, they will be. Probably just need a hug or two from their pa. Or maybe it's me that needs a hug—and some decent slapjacks thrown in to boot. This blamed Hole never gets a bit less steep, does it."

"Not hardly. Nor feel it." Billy laughed. "But at least on this job I only have to climb it once a day."

"Blessings everywhere, huh? So this is Ben Perkins's dugway?"

"As ever." Billy smiled widely. "The warmest spot on the whole road. See? Even the snow's melted along here."

"It is a pleasant place." The young man was looking at Billy's heavily wrapped hands. "You . . . uh . . . going to pick that entire ledge?"

"If we don't get a little blasting powder." Billy kicked a small rock down the cliff, hoping to distract Joseph Barton's attention. He felt certain his hands would harden eventually. But so far they simply continued to bleed and peel and ooze with infection, and it was becoming more embarrassing than it was painful. "The entire project is sort of waiting on that powder," he added lamely. "Ben Perkins and the others have used what they had to widen the crevice up on top, so at least it's a passable walking trail."

"Yeah, some of the boys from Fifty-Mile came down it Monday morning. They said it beats Charlie Hall's barrels or trekking down and across Jackass Mesa."

Billy nodded. "It does. Now they're picking and drilling all along the face up there, getting ready for whenever Brother Smith gets that powder sent down to us. When it comes, Ben says he can blow the entire ledge in two, maybe three days."

"There'll be some sure-enough booming on the river then."
Joseph Barton took off his hat and wiped his brow while he looked
up through the Hole. "It doesn't look like much of a road, though,
does it."

Billy's gaze followed. "I don't see how we'll ever get wagons
and teams down it, Joe. Of course, I don't have much experience
with this sort of thing, but it looks to me like it would frighten draft
animals to death just looking down. To think of forcing them to pull
a wagon behind them—"

Joseph laughed. "Maybe we'd better use my team of white
mares to lead out, Billy. They went blind from the pinkeye last year,
so they've learned to trust me, and they'll go exactly where I tell
them. I don't reckon this Hole would even phase those old gals."

"That's fine for the horses," Billy chuckled. "But what about
us?"

"Amen," Joseph added. "Amen and amen! I expect we'll just
have to close our eyes and pray for the best. Speaking of which, have
you given any thought to getting a priesthood blessing for those
hands?"

Slightly embarrassed, Billy shook his head.

"Might be something to consider. Who's the captain of your
ten?"

"George Sevy."

Joseph nodded thoughtfully. "Not alone is he a standing bishop,
Billy; he's also a fine man with a lot of faith. Was it me, I think I'd
ask him for a blessing. No sense suffering if you don't need to."
Joseph paused again to view the dugway. "Good luck with the ledge.
Build 'er strong, for I've got a couple of heavy loads. And remember, any time you're ready to brave our slapjacks, just give a holler
and we'll have you over across the river lickity-split."

Billy watched as Joseph Barton scrambled up into the mouth of
the Hole. A large, muscular man, he had little difficulty with the
steepness, and in short order he was around the corner of a ledge and
out of sight. As the sounds of his climbing mingled with the sounds
of the larger crew of pickers and shovelers several hundred feet
above, Billy thoughtfully examined his mangled hands.

"Amazing," he thought as he readjusted the rag wrappings. "A blessing. Why in the world didn't I think of that?" And with a smile of determination, Billy took up his pick and hefted it for another swing at the rock.

—o—o—o—

Top of Hole-in-the-Rock

"You all right, Billy darling? You seem like you're a thousand miles away."

Billy looked up from where he sat hunched over the coals of the small fire. The oil lamp put out a fitful light that did little more than brighten the canvas side of the wagon, but by it Eliza had already scoured with sand the cooking pot, washed carefully with warm water her china and crystal, and placed the snow-filled coffee pot down in the coals where the heated rock might give them another half pot of warm water.

"I'm sorry, hon-bun," he said quietly. "I'm just thinking, I reckon."

"Must be important thoughts, then."

Billy smiled but didn't immediately respond. Far out on the mesa a coyote began yipping at the darkened sky, and soon its chorus was taken up by another, and then a third, this one much closer in. Soon the camp dogs were also barking, and away off in the distance a cow started bellering. Then somebody laughed over near the Wilson Dailey wagons. A woman—Mary Ellen Lillywhite, by the sound of her voice—called her children back to camp, their own red rooster crowed unexpectedly, and there was the clatter of metal utensils and quiet laughter from the Robb compound of wagons. And Eliza, somehow in tune with all the sounds of the evening, breathed deeply of the chilling air. It was amazing, she thought, that in such abnormal circumstances life could seem so normal.

"Did you work alone again today?" she finally asked, anxious about her husband's distance but not really willing to probe.

"Mostly. There isn't a lot left to do until we get powder, and my hands are in no condition for real pickwork."

After that the silence continued, and Eliza busied herself as best she could. Her two largest pots were filled with snow, covered, and placed on the hot coals. By morning they would be some melted, the breakfast fire would do the rest, and she would have warm water for her daily chores.

"I heard today that Platte Lyman took his sisters Ida and Lydia for a boat ride down on the river a couple of weeks ago."

Billy nodded. "Three weeks. And Nellie Lyman, Joseph Alvin's wife, went with them. It was that warm Sunday just before Christmas, as I recollect."

Eliza looked at her husband. "Well, I declare. And to think I'd not heard of it until now. From what I hear tell from Mary, young Joe Nielson is sparking Ida Lyman daylight to dark, driving both families to distraction. It's a wonder he didn't go sailing with them."

"Humph."

"I also found out why Platte didn't bring his wife Adelia with him on this trek. She's expecting a baby—in fact she may have already given birth—and he didn't want her doing it on the trail. If it's a boy, they're going to name him Albert—Albert Robinson Lyman."

"Sounds mighty distinguished," Billy responded, and that was all.

"Of course, that didn't slow down Jim and Anna Decker. And their brand-new baby daughter seems to be doing just fine." Eliza tried again. "Did you hear they named her Desert, I suppose on account of she was born here on the Escalante Desert?"

"It's Deseret that they named her, Eliza, not Desert."

"Oh. Well thank goodness she wasn't named after this horrid place. Talk is that this awful trek is young Josh and Elizabeth Stevens's honeymoon. Puts me in mind of ours, traveling from Salt Lake to Cedar, except that they have more folks about. Still, it wouldn't surprise me much if she was one of the next to start showing with child."

The silence dragged again, and Eliza was growing increasingly anxious. She'd never seen Billy this way, and she was certain his quiet introspection could only be caused by something dreadful. Had he heard about that horrid little ditty, she suddenly wondered? Oh, lawsy! If he had, how would she ever be able to apologize? On purpose she had never brought it up, but that didn't mean someone else hadn't. After all, both Mary and Maggie had known about it when she mentioned it to them, so likely most everyone in the camp had heard it. What would she do if some careless soul had started singing it around Billy? Or worse, started teasing him about it—

"Lizzie Decker stopped by today," she said then, feeling desperate. "She says that meat we got yesterday was from Platte Lyman's mule that was so weak it couldn't get out of a ravine. That's why Platte killed it. I didn't know we were eating mule meat."

"Me neither."

"I suppose it's a good thing we didn't know where it came from. Otherwise I might not have felt so hungry. But Lizzie says mule meat is a delicacy to some Indian tribes. Have you ever heard that, Billy?"

"No, ma'am," the man replied absentmindedly. And Eliza was almost struck dumb by the fact that her husband had called her ma'am.

"Lizzie also says there was a real rumpus last night between Nell Fielding and Ann Rowley. 'You bet it was fun,' she said, and both of us got a good laugh—"

"Eliza, do you have to talk so blamed much?"

"Why, Billy, I swan!" Eliza was too startled to say more, so she simply sat down in her rocking chair across the table from her husband and waited.

"I . . . I'm sorry," Billy murmured, looking up, and for the first time Eliza saw the anxiety on her husband's face.

"You've no call to be sorry, Billy darling. I was only chattering to make myself stop worrying about you, and I had no business carrying on so, none at all. I . . . I was sort of hoping you'd want to tell me what happened today that's troubling you so. But, of course, that isn't necessary, and I know it. Sometimes a man just needs—"

"Joseph Barton suggested that maybe I should get a blessing for my hands."

Eliza was surprised. "A blessing? Really?"

"I . . . uh . . . I hadn't thought of it myself, which seems mighty foolish."

"Then we're both foolish, Billy, because I hadn't thought of it either. Who would you ask?"

"Well, Brother Sevy is captain of our ten."

"Of course! Come on, darling. Let's get over to the Sevy camp before it gets any later."

Billy smiled widely. "We'll go, hon-bun, and it won't be too late, I promise. But not tonight. Before the blessing I'd like the two of us to kneel in a word of prayer and open up a twenty-four-hour fast—at least I'd like to fast. Being in a motherly way, you probably shouldn't do it. But that way we can unite our faith and do a little apologizing for our lack of faith while we're at it."

Humbly Eliza reached out and took her husband's hand. "You're right, Billy. Thank you for . . . for, well, for being wise enough to see the right way of things." And with complete adoration she followed her husband as he led her into the tight quarters of their wagon.

33

Thursday, January 15, 1880

Top of Hole-in-the-Rock

"George Washington Sevy, you cut that out!"

Leaning back from where he'd been tickling his wife, George Sevy, his gaunt face still chapped and peeling, smiled. "Now, Margaret, darling, don't you get to fretting yourself about a little tickle. You love it and you know it."

"I know nothing of the sort, and you can stop calling me Margaret darling, too. Every other day I'm Maggie, and no sudsy palaver from you is going to soft-soap me now."

"Well, you can't blame a man for trying."

George reached out and began tickling his wife again, but she firmly pushed his hands away.

"This mission bothers me, George. It surely does! I can't help wondering sometimes if we made a mistake leaving our place back in Panguitch."

"It was a call from the prophet, Maggie, and you know it."

"Some days I know it, George. Other days, well, I start to wonder. What call has the Lord got sending us off like this? What good am I going to do away off there in that howling wilderness that I couldn't have done better back in my own home and community? And how are little George Frances and I supposed to live without a husband and father the better part of each year?"

"I don't rightly know," George replied quietly. "By doing your best to build up a civilization, I reckon. By befriending the Indians and teaching them of the glory that was once theirs when the Savior

274

walked among them. By bringing peace and prosperity to the land. And by helping the folks around you raise up a righteous generation to the Lord. Those good things seem like pretty near enough to keep you busy for a little while, wouldn't you say?"

Maggie Sevy took her husband and held him close while tears streamed down her face. "Oh, glory be, George," she finally whispered while she wiped her cheeks on his sleeve. "I'm scared to death. I truly am! What will I ever do when you go back to Panguitch and Phoebe and your calling? And why does that horrid federal government have to meddle in our religion and call our marriage illegal?"

George looked tenderly at his beloved plural wife. "I don't know, Maggie, darling. I truly don't. Neither do I know what either of us will do without each other." George Sevy shook his head. "Fact is, I don't even know what to do about a problem I've just encountered among my ten. Seems at least one of 'em hasn't yet thrown a bridle on his tongue, and pretty much any of them might say something hurtful and bust this whole expedition into little pieces."

Maggie looked up. "Meaning the younger ones, of course. At twenty years of age the will reigns; at thirty, the wit; and at forty, the judgment."

"That sounds like another one of your mother's proverbs. For a fact, some unkind things are being said by one or two in this camp, and I mean to do what I can to put a stop to them."

"Are you referring to that cruel little ditty about Billy and Eliza Foreman?"

George Sevy glanced at his wife, surprised. "You know about it?"

"Eliza told me after she'd heard it. She put on a brave front, but I know it hurt her."

George sighed. "I imagine. Trouble is, it's still going on. One of the brethren told me he'd heard it today, and he was concerned. So am I."

"You should be, especially since it's so baseless. As my mother used to say, the proof of gold is fire, the proof of woman is gold, and the proof of man is his woman. Eliza Foreman's quite a woman to brave a trek like this all crippled up and pregnant too. That makes her husband a man to be reckoned with—you mark my words."

"Eliza Foreman's expecting a baby?" George was surprised for the second time in as many minutes.

"She's had the morning sickness right along, and if you weren't so blind you'd have noticed it. Thank the Lord Billy tries to take care of her."

"I thought that was how he always was."

"Humph!" Maggie adjusted herself on the makeshift bed in their tent, drawing her quilt more tightly around her legs. "If he is, more of you men ought to take notice and be likewise. I declare I never saw a man so in love with his wife as Billy Foreman, nor so solicitous of her welfare, neither."

"Well, like Brother Lyman said in meeting last Sunday, we all have our gifts."

"Yes, and yours is to be irritating, George Washington Sevy. What do you intend doing about that ditty?"

"I don't rightly know. I've been talking to the Lord about it all afternoon, and—Say! Eliza Foreman's a mite old to be having a baby, isn't she?"

"It's a little unusual, all right."

"Well then, hadn't somebody ought to be gathering her firewood for her, and things like that?"

"George, the lady isn't dying, you know. Besides, my mother used to tell me it takes a lean horse to win a long race."

George laughed. "What's that got to do with gathering firewood?"

"Exercise, George. Keep Eliza lean and fit, and she'll go the distance."

"She will anyway." George grinned wryly. "And remember, a soft answer turneth away wrath. That, and great spenders are bad lenders."

"What?" Maggie Sevy was absolutely confused. "That makes no sense at all!"

George grinned. "I never said it did, Margaret, darling. I was just trying to come up with a proverb or two to match the ones you're so good at tossing about."

"George Washington Sevy," Maggie stormed, pulling the quilt

even higher, "if you weren't so big and old, I'd throw you out of this tent without so much as a by-your-leave."

"Well, I am getting a mite old," George admitted laconically. "But it isn't slowing me down none, at least not so's you'd notice."

"Well, not so's *I* notice, at least," Maggie said with a sly smile. "Now, come here, you big—"

"Hello the tent!" a voice softly called from outside. "Brother Sevy, are you and Sister Sevy still awake? It's Billy and Eliza Foreman."

"Why, sure we are, Billy." Quickly George looked at his wife, a question in his eyes. Then, getting no answer from her own dumbfounded expression, he pulled on his shirt and lifted his galluses back over his shoulders. "We're decent, I reckon, so you and Eliza come on in here and tell us what we can do for you."

34

Friday, January 16, 1880

Down in the Hole-in-the-Rock

"Have you boys seen Ben Perkins today?"

Lowering their picks and shovels, the more than two dozen men assumed various positions of rest in their cold and gloomy retreat. They were laboring on the steep decline in the depths of the Hole, scratching at the cliffs both around and beneath them in a seemingly futile attempt to widen the notch and turn it into a roadway for their wagons. Above them the red and ochre walls loomed hundreds of feet into the air, in places bulging so close together that the sky wasn't visible at all. And around them in the notch itself were lodged huge boulders that the men hadn't a prayer of moving.

"Why, Brother Lyman, we wondered if you were coming to work today," Hanson Bayles teased.

"The way you fellers are slinging rock around," Platte Lyman responded with a grin, "I thought I'd take the day off and keep out of your way."

"You implying we're dangerous?" Dan Barney questioned.

"If he ain't," Pap Redd rejoined from a little farther down the Hole, "then I am! It may have been cold enough on that scout of ours to make a polar bear hunt for cover, but the way you boys are fixing to put me to bed permanent with your far-flung detritus, I'm beginning to wish I was still off in the far lonesome turning blue. I do believe it was safer."

"Our how much?" Joseph Stanford Smith questioned.

"Detritus. He means disassembled rock and other fragmentary

278

remains," Kumen Jones explained to the laughing group. "Most especially the airborne portion of the same."

Pap Redd lifted one eyebrow inquisitively. "Well, who edicated you, you young whippersnapper?"

"Oh, a feller I knew once. Most days he was filled with equal parts verbal lather and panther juice, so like cream the lather rose to the top and got blown about by his self-created breeze. Tell the truth, Brother Redd, he puts me somewhat to mind of you."

"Why, Kumen Jones, I ought to—"

Kumen Jones laughed. "No, you hadn't ought, Pap. Fact of the matter is that I let you off easy. I never did say the feller was so thick he couldn't cut a lame cow from the shade of a small tree."

"Or that he didn't have sense enough to spit downwind," Adam Robb tossed in with a chuckle.

"Or that he was so dumb he couldn't teach a setting hen to cluck," Dan Barney continued quickly.

"Fact is, Pap," Kumen Jones went on, "that feller's brains were skimpier than bees in a blizzard, which is a sure-enough fact. But not once did I imply that you were exactly the same."

Pap Redd sighed painfully. "Listen to that young feller crank the handle on his word mill," he complained, looking at Platte Lyman for support. "Hadn't we ought to call him Euphemistic Jones? Or at the very least, Windy? I'm telling you, Brother Lyman, I recollect a time when making fun of a feller's elders the way these boys do was about as safe as pulling sucking cubs off a sow grizzly. Or—"

"Or doing a Welsh jig in the middle of a rattlesnake convention," James Pace interjected laughingly.

"Or riding bareback in a porcupine rodeo," Hanson Bayles chimed in, bringing more laughter all around.

"Fact is," Kumen Jones declared straight-faced, "making fun of our elders is still about as dangerous as—"

"Now hold it right there!" Pap Redd thundered, working furiously to keep from laughing with the others. "Why, the way you young bucks is ganging up on a stove-up old feller like me, I'd say there was more sand in one of my daughter-in-law Eliza Ann's biscuits than in the craws of the whole flock of you."

"Or," somebody else hooted, "more innards hung on a fence after butchering one little hog than—"

"That's enough!" Platte Lyman shouted into the howling group of tired men. "You boys are welcome to continue this war after I'm gone, happen you can work, too. But me? I just want to know where Ben Perkins might be."

"Well," Sammy Cox put in with a wide and innocent smile, "he might be just about anywhere—"

Platte Lyman was disgusted. "All right, all right, I give in. Howl with each other all you want. And persecute, too, if you're of such a mind. But if Ben Perkins isn't somewhere down below, and you and I take the rest of this little hike for nothing, I'll make certain there'll be no warning from above when the powder blows."

"Powder?" David Hunter asked quickly. "Do we have powder, Platte?"

"No, but it's coming. A thousand pounds, to be exact. A courier just brought through a letter from President Silas Smith, and the powder is on its way."

"That being the case," Jim Lewis said after sending a wild whoop of joy echoing up and down the narrow defile, "you'll find Ben down at the dugway, working with Hy and Billy Foreman."

"Speaking of which," Kumen Jones interjected, "have you taken a look at Billy's hands?"

Platte shook his head. "I heard they were in mighty rough shape."

"They were, is right. But the way Billy tells it, he got a blessing for them last night—from George Sevy and Jens Nielson. And I'm here to tell you, Platte, that the day of miracles has not passed away."

"Do tell."

"We've all seen his hands today," James Pace declared quietly, "and we saw 'em yesterday, too. Billy's been healed, Platte. Completely. He says when he woke up this morning they weren't hurting, and when he took off the rags the sores were gone, covered by brand-new skin."

"Soft and pink as a baby's bottom," Pap Redd added. "Makes a man feel almighty humble, is what it does."

"Amen," two or three others responded immediately.

"That's wonderful," Platte Lyman declared quietly. And without another word, but with only a tip of his wide-brimmed hat, the company leader silently worked his way through the suddenly subdued men and continued his steep descent through the Hole. He'd heard of the blessing, all right, but not of its consequences. And somehow, he didn't have the feeling that he'd heard all of them even yet.

———o—o—o———

The Crossing of the Fathers

Though the nearly full moon was lighting the rocks and the undulating river well enough to show that no enemies lurked nearby, the Navajo known as Frank was apprehensive. He didn't understand this, for the raid against the mormonee *belacani* settlement across the Kaibab had gone well, very well. Now they were returning with more than *tsostsídiin*, seventy prize horses, the beginnings of a world of wealth for all of them. Truly it had been just as the great Peokon had said it would be when he had given instructions, a thing of such ease and simplicity that it had not even felt like a raid.

For many days Frank had ridden at the head of the raiders, giving instructions and showing in all ways that he was a man to be reckoned with. Yes, and all of the ones whom he had persuaded to follow him: his relatives Hoskanini and his son Hoskanini Begay, Taddytin the crafty horse-thief, his cousin Zon Kelli, Bitani, a man called Wolfkill, and even a *Nóódái*, an old Pahute headman named Peeagament, had been willing to listen and obey.

They had done all the right things, too—the old things that it was said made raiders strong and successful. Of course, Frank did not really believe in these things, but if they made the others feel good, then who was he to argue? So before the raid they had all gathered together for a sweat bath and to make offerings, after which all had made new moccasins and new strings for their bows.

That accomplished, each had then seen to his own equipment— his arrows tipped with poison and secured in a fine hide quiver, his shield of two thicknesses of buckskin dried hard and painted with power symbols, and his lance tipped either with stone or, if possible, with the end of a Spanish saber. Frank and two of the others also had

281

guns, old cap-and-ball weapons that could usually be fired just once in an actual battle. Still, owning such a weapon gave a man much honor, and so it was worthwhile to carry it no matter how useless it proved to be.

Each of them had also donned his shirt of armor—several thicknesses of buckskin glued together. And because it was the season of cold, they had wrapped themselves in woolen blankets woven by the women of the People.

At the hogan of Hoskanini, where they met for departure, Frank had sung his songs, chanted his prayers, and then told the others how they must behave. They must always be serious. They must not think of home. And they must use a special language, giving new names to themselves and their horses, names they must use until they arrived at the enemy settlement.

As they had departed all had heard a good omen, for all thought they heard the sound of horses trotting in the distance. This had relieved Frank, for had they heard an owl or coyote he wasn't sure he could have persuaded the superstitious fools to continue.

During the long days of riding, Frank had wisely continued to insist on the old ways, singing songs night and morning, watching always for signs of ill luck, and never thinking of home. Finally at the *belacani* settlement, he had performed a final ceremony. All of them had painted their bodies with magical signs of snakes or bears, and then all had waited in the chill air until the last hour before dawn when the *belacani* were sure to be asleep.

And then, without the least trouble, Frank had led the others into the meadows below the settlement. There they had successfully freed and led away the entire herd of fine horses. No one had shouted a warning, no one had fired a shot, and as far as Frank could tell, not one of the mormonee *belacani* was even following them. Truly it was as the man Peokon had told him it would be. The people called mormonee were like *ásdzáán,* old women—talk, talk, talk, but no fight.

Of course, Frank would not permit himself to think of the fearsome *belacani* Peokon had called *bináá dootízhi,* Blue Eyes—the mormonee Thales Haskell.

So now they were coming up to what the *Nakai,* the Mexicans, called *El Vado de los Padres,* the Crossing of the Fathers. Frank was relieved to have come so far without difficulty, and in his mind he was already enjoying his newfound wealth and prestige. But in his mind there was also that other thing, that *biyaa nahalyiz* or apprehension. Frank did not know what, but something was about to happen that was not a good thing—especially for him. And for some reason he could not keep his eyes from the faces of Taddytin the crafty horse-thief and his cousin Zon Kelli.

35

Thursday, January 22, 1880

Fifty-Mile Camp

"Brudders, ve are glad you vere able to gadder togeder tonight. Ve vill ask Brudder Holyoak to offer de invocation."

At Jens Nielson's request, Henry Holyoak stood and prayed quietly, asking the blessings of God upon himself and the other leaders of the San Juan expedition. As he prayed, the firelight played on the walls and roof of the canvas tent that surrounded them, a tent that had been erected so they might enjoy a little privacy. This measure had never before been taken, but at Platte's request three of the company's young bachelors had spent thirty minutes' easy labor at a spot some distance from the camp, and now the tent was up.

"Tank you," Jens Nielson said as the prayer ended and he rose unsteadily to his feet. "Ve know de hour iss late, Brudders, und so I vill set down purty quick und turn de meeting over to Brudder Lyman. He hass some tinks to discuss dat I tink vill prove interesting indeed."

Platte Lyman stood and surveyed the group of six captains over ten, meaning ten families within the camp. Besides Jens Nielson, they included George Sevy, Ben Perkins, Henry Holyoak, Zacharia Decker, Jr., and Samuel Bryson. Charles Walton, Sr., in his capacity as company clerk, was also in attendance.

"Brethren," Platte began with little fanfare, "two or three things have come up that we need to address. First, Arza Judd brought in twenty-five pounds of black powder today, as arranged by Captain Smith. More is supposedly coming, but Arza doesn't know when. Brother Ben, is twenty-five pounds enough to blast that hole?"

284

"Aye, if it needs to be," Ben Perkins replied. "Hyrum and I can put together the charges in the morning, and blasting we can start by afternoon."

"Wonderful. Use what you need, of course, but if there isn't enough powder to blast out a shallow road, then blast out a steep one, and we'll make do. How many days do you think you'll need?"

"Depends on how many men we have available. Blasting won't take long, I be thinking, not more than two or three days. What'll take the time is mucking the detritus down in the Hole, covering those boulders the boys have been working around, and in general grading a passable roadway for the wagons and teams."

"So the more men the merrier," Platte smiled.

"That be the truth."

"Good. Brother Zach, aren't you boys from Parowan close to finishing that road up the other side?"

Zachariah Decker nodded. "We'll be done tomorrow, Platte. I can have 'em back across the river and ready to muck the Hole by late afternoon."

Platte smiled. "That'll give us near fifty men, Ben. I'd say as fast as you and your brother can blast that rock down, fifty of us can easily grade it out."

"Two days, then, and it's a road you'll be having."

"Good. We're ready. The next issue concerns Brother Silas Smith, our company captain, who's been up with the legislature appropriating funds for our little trek. When Arza Judd brought the powder today, he also brought word that Captain Smith is laid up sick at Red Creek, and at least for now he can't continue. We must decide, then, whether or not to wait for him."

"He'd want us to go on," George Sevy declared with conviction.

"He would at that," Ben Perkins agreed.

"Whether he would or not," Henry Holyoak said quietly, "doesn't really matter. If our people are going to survive the rest of the winter, we've got to get moving!"

"Not to mention our stock," Samuel Bryson added. "There's no feed left for twenty miles around, and there isn't a critter among the two thousand that isn't showing ribs."

Zach Decker nodded his agreement. "I vote we move on."

"Do we have a second?"

"I second it."

"Thank you, Charlie. All in favor?"

A chorus of quiet ayes was heard.

Platte smiled knowingly. "Good. I'm pleased we're in agreement, for I already sent word to the captain about our decision. Two days ago Frank Rysert and James Dorrity started back for Kanosh, carrying a letter to Captain Smith. They met Arza on the trail, so they know he's at Red Creek. Two, three more days and he'll have my letter, and then he'll feel free to rest up and catch us when he can."

The men chuckled good-naturedly.

"That brings us to the final issue, brethren, which concerns morale within the camp. As you know, if we're to accomplish this mission we've been called of God to fulfill, we must be united in heart and mind—all of us. But right now there seems to be a bit of a problem. So, let's take a few minutes and discuss Billy and Eliza Foreman. I'd like each of you to tell me what's happening concerning these folks within your groups."

There was a moment or two of silence, and then Henry Holyoak spoke. "They are a strange-looking couple," he said quietly.

"Which of us isn't?" Platte smiled.

"True enough. But they're different enough that folks are just naturally going to talk."

"It be more dan talk," Jens Nielson growled. "Two veeks ago I heart my little girl Lucy skipping de rope, und she und de udders vere singing un awful song about Billy und his vife. You bet I made dem stop, und quick! Charlie, your daughter vas singing it, too."

Charles Walton nodded. "I know. Leona told me what you'd said. So I dug a little and found that Sister Eliza had heard them singing it sometime before that. She told them it was lies and not to do it anymore. I have no idea what got it started again the other day."

"So the Foremans know?" Platte looked from one to the other.

"Well, at least Eliza knows," George Sevy declared. "She mentioned it to Maggie a few days back."

"Bother! What a mess! Whoever came up with that thing ought to be horsewhipped! Charlie, do you remember the words?"

Without difficulty Charles Walton repeated the three stanzas.

"Well," Platte said with a sigh, "happen I heard that sort of clap-trap being sung about me by folks I'm supposed to be closer than family to, I'd—well, I don't know what I'd do. But here's the problem, brethren. What we're dealing with is gossip, pure and simple. Or in other words, the bearing of false witness against our neighbors. And we're just as guilty of gossip if we don't stop it when we hear it as we are when we spread it further abroad."

"What if it's true? Or at least part of it."

"What if it is?" Platte shot back. "Don't you brethren believe in the right of people to be individuals anymore? If we all have to be stamped from the same mold, then we're in deep trouble, because God certainly didn't create us that way, you and me included."

The men chuckled, and Platte went on. "Billy and I spent a day together gathering driftwood recently, and I learned a few things about him and Eliza that you boys might find interesting—some things that make them seem what some of us might call different.

"First, Eliza was with the Martin Handcart Company, and that's where she got crippled. Like Brother Nielson here, for her to have even accepted this mission tells me she's an uncommonly courageous and faithful woman. Until this past summer she never married, and for years she ran a successful millinery business in Salt Lake City. To be blunt, she has had a hard time adjusting to marriage. Now, though, from all I can find out, she pretty much thinks Billy is the cat's meow.

"Now, a little about Billy. His father was one of Brigham Young's personal secretaries. His mother died when Billy was born in Winter Quarters, and when his stepmother passed on when he was ten, there was nothing else for his father to do but take the boy to the office. From then until we left on our expedition Billy has worked at clerking, and when his father died, Billy also became one of Brother Brigham's personal secretaries. As you can imagine, brethren, in that occupation a man doesn't usually develop healthy muscles or pioneering skills, either one."

"So why is he on this expedition?"

Platte looked at the man who had spoken. "Same reason you are. President Taylor called him on it. He told him to go find a woman and marry her, outfit himself with a good wagon and so forth, and move to Cedar to bring a little order to the co-op. Billy had already whipped it into shape when he was called to come with us."

"But Platte, Billy lacks the very skills we'll need once we get to the San Juan."

"Maybe, if you're thinking of just physical things. But let me tell you a little something else. Billy's got the fastest head for figures I ever ran across, bar none! Charlie Hall told me Billy figured the board feet of lumber for that boat of theirs in two minutes flat, and got it more accurate than Charlie had. He's also calculated the steepness of our roadway down the Hole, in his head, mind you, and corrected me by about one degree. Out of curiosity I've since checked it more carefully, and he's right. Of a night he's also been teaching young Reed Hall about equations, he and Alvin Decker have been out hunting fossils, and I can tell you he's taught me some things about this country that have got me thinking some whole new thoughts about the nature of God and his handiwork.

"Now, brethren, I don't know how Billy and Eliza are supposed to fit in when we get to the San Juan any more than I know how you or I are supposed to fit in. But I'm more than willing to assume that the Lord knew what he was doing when he inspired his prophet to call them to join us."

"Ve all feel de same, Brudder Lyman."

Platte nodded. "Good. It's my testimony, brethren, that if we don't put a stop to such gossip as this wicked little ditty, as well as rude and unrighteous talk about anyone else that erupts among us, we'll never be blessed by God to accomplish our mission."

"There's something else, Platte."

"What's that?"

"Word is that Billy's . . . well, to put it bluntly, he acts like a coward."

In the complete silence that followed, Platte looked at the man squarely. "What do you mean?" he asked.

"I mean he somehow manages to avoid anything that might be the least bit dangerous, like going over the edge in one of Charlie Hall's barrels. That's being cowardly, ain't it?"

"Are you certain it's him that's doing the avoiding?"

"Well," the man chuckled, "who else would it be?"

"Me. Or whoever else is in charge."

The man squirmed uncomfortably. "Why in tarnation would you do that?"

Platte smiled patiently. "Do you want to explain, Brother Sevy? You're captain over Billy's family."

George Sevy kicked some sand with his boot, doing his best not to show disgust with the man's remark. "You bet I'll explain!" he growled. "Do you brethren know that Eliza Foreman is soon going to turn forty-five years old?"

"So?"

"Do you know she's also expecting their first child?"

"At her age?" Ben Perkins looked stunned. "No wonder Billy didn't want her dancing with me at Christmas."

"I reckon that's right, Ben. Billy's never been married before, either, and now that he's going to be a father, he's mighty protective of his wife and unborn child. Likewise is she protective of him. You would be, too, if the circumstances were the same and you and your spouse were both fearful of leaving the child orphaned."

"Fact is," Platte Lyman interjected, "having left my own wife home for the same reason, I'm overwhelmed by their faith and courage. Anyone who calls such people cowards is not only dead wrong but showing mighty poor judgment to boot."

George Sevy nodded. "I agree. Anyway, that and the bad shape of his hands is why both Platte and me have been protective of him. One other thing, brethren. Brother Jens and I gave Billy a blessing for his hands the other night. His faith was such that by the next day he'd been healed, and I mean completely. As far as I'm concerned, a man with that sort of faith is just the sort of man I want for a neighbor to my wife once I get her settled on the San Juan."

George Sevy clamped his hat back on his head as a gesture of finality, and Platte looked around the small group. "Well, brethren, can I count on you to see that this tragic situation is corrected within each of your tens?"

"Ve vill do vat ve can," Jens Nielson responded instantly. "But how vill ve change de attitudes of de udders?"

"Maybe by changing our own," Platte replied solemnly. And that was the end of the discussion.

36

Top of Hole-in-the-Rock

"I tink der be a storm coming, und soon. Dat vill not make Brudder Lyman happy."

The temperatures during the past week hadn't been particularly cold. The wind was gusting that day, but from no real direction, and the sky held only a few thin, wispy clouds. Still, Jens Nielson seemed to have a way of telling such things, something Billy just didn't understand.

"You sure?" he asked as he helped play out a little more rope to the men below.

"Ya, I be shure," Jens Nielson responded softly as he counted paper cartridges filled with black powder into a bucket in his lap. "In fact, I tink maybe it be a big vone. Last night de old rooster crowed two times und it vas not coming morning, our dog vas eating vat little grass he could find, und at sunrise de sky vas misty. Deese tings mean storm, I tink. But de vay my poor body aches, in all my yoints, I say ya, it vill be a big vone."

"For Eliza's sake," Billy said thoughtfully, "I hope not. Winter storms are real hard on her."

"Ya," Jens nodded, "dey be hard on all who ver vith de hand-carts. It vas a terrible time vith storms, for shure. You mustn't blame her for being afraid."

"Oh, I don't! But I don't understand what happened, either. Why did those companies keep coming west so late in the season?"

"Because it vas vere ve had been called to go." The tall old

290

Danishman smiled. "Yust like now, Billy. Ve go vere ve cannot, in de season ven ve should not, for turn around ve must not. Vhy, you ask? Yust because ve have been called."

"But lots of folks died in those handcart companies, Jens. How can that be right?"

Straightening but remaining seated on the rock, the older man worked the kinks from his joints and muscles. "Ve all die in our time," he finally responded, "und who iss to say dat it vas not der time? For my own son who perished, I tink it vas his time, und I have peace vid dat. For a fact, he came back in a dream und told me so. Shure und the suffering vas terrible, but all ver blessed und sanctified by de same, und I know dat dose who died, including my son, have reaped a glorious revard. It vill be de same for us after dis trek, I tink."

Wonderingly Billy looked at the old man, and just then Ben Perkins, coming up the slickrock toward them, called Jens's name.

"Brother Nielson, is Peter Mortensen around?"

"No, I tink he vent back to camp—to the blacksmit's, I tink he said. For more rope."

"Fiddle-dee-dee!" Ben exclaimed softly. "Well, Hannah said she hadn't seen him. And Hy's gone down below to check on the dugway." The man thought for a moment in silence. "Billy, now that we finally have a little powder, we need to get this done. Especially concerned I am that we do it before another storm hits. Do you feel up to going over the edge with me and becoming a blaster?"

"Me?" Billy's stomach immediately tightened with apprehension. He knew absolutely nothing about blasting. He'd hardly even fired a gun, let alone charges of blasting powder. And as for going over the edge? Truthfully, it looked to Billy like it might be a whole lot easier dying.

A furious gust of wind hit him, tossing his wispy, thinning hair, and as he adjusted his spectacles on his nose, Billy thought of Eliza, of what she would expect him to do—not what she'd say she wanted, but what she'd nonetheless expect.

"Well?" Ben pressed as he bent and examined the charges he and his brother Hyrum had made that morning, and that Jens had also been working on. "You want to go down with me, Billy? You're not

291

only lightweight and easy for the holders to lower and raise, but it's a fast learner you be. So it should be no trouble teaching you how to tamp in the charges and fire the hole. Be you willing?"

"You bet I am," Billy replied, taking a deep breath to still his quivering stomach.

"Good. Let's haul these boys up who have been finishing the drilling, and they can help lower us back down."

"Ben," Wilford Pace said a few moments later as the last driller was dragged to the top, "this rope's looking mighty rough."

"Will's right," Samuel Mackelprang declared, and all turned to see the rope he was holding up. It was frayed, Billy could see. In fact, it was frayed rather badly.

"Well, we haven't time to wait for more rope," Ben said softly. "So put a good knot in it, and I'll go in that barrel—"

"I'm lighter, Ben," Billy interjected, surprising himself as much as most everyone else. "Twenty, thirty pounds, easy. It'd be safer if I used it."

"You sure?"

Billy grinned reassuringly. "Sure as plumb pudding's sweet, as President Young used to say."

"Very well. Let's do it, then. And boys, you be careful with Billy's rope. You hear?"

Moments later the two men were over the edge and dangling some thirty-five feet below, with the drilled powder holes, fourteen in all, in the face of the rock before them. The wind, as strong as on top but growing more consistent, cut like icy knives through their clothing and quickly numbed their faces and uncovered fingers. Worse, it twisted and swung the barrels they rode in, rubbing the ropes against the cliff above and causing both men to approach their task with caution flayed by fear.

"Billy, is it all right you be?" Ben was reaching out and trying to snag the bucket filled with powder charges. Another bucket was being lowered closely behind, this one about half full of dampened sand.

"F-first-rate," Billy replied through teeth that were chattering only partially because of the cold.

"Good. Times like this, I'm more grateful than ever for our daily prayers for protection. We do need it."

Numbly Billy nodded, not telling the former miner that he hadn't stopped praying from the moment he'd agreed to go over the edge in the barrel.

"Now listen carefully, Billy, and I'll tell you what we're doing. See the pattern they've used in drilling? Seven holes on one face? We have two faces here, which means you have seven holes to charge, and I have seven; a triangle of three in the center, a 'reliever' hole at the top, 'edger' holes on each side, and a 'lifter' hole at the bottom. What we want to do is get the three center charges to blow first, making a cavity into which the slightly later blasts from the top and sides will squeeze the surrounding rock. Last to blow will be the 'lifter' charge, which will scatter the rubble up, out, and down into the Hole in a fairly even pattern. Then the brethren can muck it to where they want on the road without much trouble. Any questions?"

Billy nodded. "How . . . how do we get the center charges to blow first?"

"Shorter fuses, which I've cut to allow about fifteen seconds lighting time from them to the outer ones. Then you've got twenty more seconds to light them and get to the lifter, on the bottom. We're using Bickford Safety Fuse, Billy, a fine fuse which I've already fit into the powder cartridges. That makes it simply a matter of tamping the right cartridges into each hole with a handful of this wet sand, or mud, as we call it. The fuses will then hang out like rattails, which is what they're called.

"Now, the trick will be to touch our spitters—that's the short lengths of fuse we'll use to ignite the rattails—at exactly the same time. Once they're all lit, we'll have exactly two minutes to get hauled up out of here. If one of us gets off sequence, we'll have less time than that. You understand?"

His mind whirling with the impossibility of remembering all he'd just been told, Billy nonetheless nodded.

"Good. Insert your charges, fuse out. Then, using that drill in your barrel, tamp them gently with a bit of the mud in the bottom of your bucket. You ready? Good. Let's go to work!"

As quickly as he could, and avoiding looking off down the

dizzying, tumbling cliffs toward the ribbon-thin stretch of the Colorado River that wound below, Billy sorted through the seven cartridges in his bucket. "Shortest fuses in the center," he muttered to himself, "three of them. Then three a bit longer to the bottom— no, to the top and sides—and the longest fuse on the bottom. That's right. Now, push them in, gently, gently—

"Might these blow by accident, Ben?" he called into the wind.

"Not likely. Black powder this is. Very stable, though of course to pack the cartridges it was wooden spoons I used, to avoid sparks. How be you doing?"

"I've . . . uh—There!" Billy wiped his forehead with his sleeve, surprised that he could be sweating in such a cold wind. "I've got them all in the holes. Now I'll just tamp them—"

"Remember, Billy. Gentle as she goes. And it's careful you must be not to push the fuse in any further than it already is."

Shaking his head with wonder that he'd ever allowed himself to get into such a fix, Billy grabbed a handful of mud with his left hand and pushed it into the first hole. Then, steadying his swinging barrel with the muddy hand, he took up the drill with his other and carefully tamped the mud back against the cartridge. Starting toward the next hole, his mud-caked hand almost dropped the drill, and he realized it would be better to put the mud in all the holes before he tamped any of them.

Soon, in spite of the steadily worsening gale, all his charges were tamped and ready.

Holding his mud-covered hand under his arm to dry it and stop the chill from numbing his fingers any further, Billy turned to see what was next. "G-getting c-colder," he stammered weakly.

"And f-fast." Ben's teeth were chattering as hard as his own. "All r-right, Billy. It's in the bottom of the charge barrel that your spitter should be. Eighteen inches long it is, and you'll have to hunker down and shield your sulfur match after it's struck or it'll never burn long enough to light the spitter. Now, it shouldn't take the entire spitter to ignite your rattails. But if it does, and you feel that spitter burning your fingers before all your rattails are lit, then forget the others and let the boys pull you out of here. Linger too long, and it's likely you are to get mucked up with the rest of the rubble."

Billy gulped.

"You remember the signal to get hauled up?"

"S-sure. Two jerks on the bucket rope."

Ben nodded. "Now, s-starting with when we ignite our first rat-tail, I'll count out loud: one thousand one, one thousand two, one thousand three, and so forth. Each time I reach one thousand five, we should both be ready to touch off our next fuse. Qu-questions?"

"No," Billy replied as he steadied his barrel against a furious gust of wind. "I j-just hope I can keep this barrel under control."

"You will." Ben smiled widely, somehow reassuring the increasingly nervous Billy. "Fire in the hole!" he shouted both downward and upward, his rich voice booming in echoes through the gorge.

"Fire in the hole!"

Then, his voice once again quiet, Ben turned to Billy. "Now, take out your matches and let's get these spitters lit. It's a holler you should give when it's sputtering, and we'll start the count."

Nodding, Billy reached into his britches and pulled out the half-dozen sulfur matches he'd been given. Placing the ends of all but one of them into his mouth, just as Ben had done, Billy hunkered down into the barrel and, grasping the spitter tightly, struck the match on the rough wood beside him. Too hard, he thought with dismay as the head broke off and fell to the bottom of the barrel. Quickly taking another match he struck it and held the spurting flame against the end of the spitter. For a moment he thought it would take, but then the flame flickered and blew out and the fuse remained unlit.

"You lit?" Ben called.

"Not yet! But—"

"Don't hold the end of the match against the spitter, Billy! Just close is good enough!"

"Okay."

Quickly he lit another match and held it near the end of the fuse, and then another. Finally, with his fifth match, Billy was rewarded when fire began spitting and sputtering from the end of the fuse.

"I'm lit!" he shouted excitedly, realizing why the length of fuse was called a spitter.

"Good! Now, hold it right against your first rattail, the one in the center, and I'll start counting. Ready? One thousand one, one thousand two, one thousand—"

Working as quickly as he could, and steadying the swaying barrel against the cliff with his freezing left hand, Billy set to work igniting his rattails. Twice he fell behind the count, but two other fuses lit almost instantly, making things about even.

But the problem wasn't in getting the rattails lit. Instead it was the wind, which was buffeting and swinging his barrel until the fingers of his left hand were raw from scraping and grabbing at the rock. More troubling, he knew the already worn rope was taking even worse punishment than his hand, for he could feel it being dragged back and forth across the rough, bulging rock above him.

Miraculously, though, he somehow managed to keep even with Ben's count through the first six rattails. But then, as he wiped the sweat from his eyes and leaned over to ignite the 'lifter' rattail, a gust of wind caught him and swung his barrel completely around. Billy narrowly missed slamming his head against the rock, but he grabbed at the cliff, steadied himself, and found a tenuous grip.

"Billy," Ben shouted, watching from the side, "forget the lifter! Give the signal and get out of here!"

"I've . . . got it," Billy gasped as he leaned down again. "Another second and—"

"Billy, mine's been lit too long! It'll blow before yours. Now get!"

Grunting, Billy held a fraction of a second longer and saw the last rattail sputter to life. Then, dropping the spitter, he grabbed the bucket rope and gave two quick jerks.

Instantly he began moving upward in successive lurches that indicated the men on the upper end were pulling in unison, running with the rope. Grinning, he looked up to see Ben watching him from above, a relieved expression on his face. Billy waved, both men continued upward, and then Ben's barrel scraped against the bulge of the cliff. Instantly it swung slightly outward with Ben's well-practiced handthrust, and with a mighty heave on the rope from above, both the barrel and Ben disappeared above the bulge.

Abruptly alone, Billy thought the next few seconds seemed to drag on forever. Yet in that strange clarity of mind that comes in tense moments and seems to slow time, he found himself wondering not only how much of the two minutes had elapsed but also how much of the cliff would blow. It didn't really matter, though, for he'd done the job and was on his way up, the bulge only inches away—

Billy felt a sudden lurch. He looked up in surprise, and then for no reason that he could fathom, he discovered that he'd grabbed the rope above him and leaped to the lip of the barrel. An instant later, or even less, found him swinging up on the rope and lunging up and out for the upper edge of the bulge, at the same time pushing the barrel away with his feet.

Suddenly the rope above him parted and seemed to vanish, and Billy slammed face down on the steep upper edge of the bulge with such force that he thought for a second he would lose consciousness. But he didn't. His mind cleared, and he realized that his fingers had somehow found places to grip the stone. Relieved, he pressed with his legs, realized that his feet were dangling out in the air, started to draw one foot upward, and—

Billy didn't hear the explosions so much as he felt them. And they all seemed to take longer than they actually did. First the stone beneath his body quivered. Then it literally bucked, again and again, wrenching him from his perch with its violent heaves and tossing him upward. Next he felt a strange sort of pressure against his back that shoved him hard against the rock and wouldn't let him move. And finally a deafening *whumph* racked his ears, a noise that seemed one long explosion rather than several, leaving his ears ringing even when the silence had finally returned.

His eyes screwed tightly shut, Billy found himself wondering if he'd been killed. But the idea seemed silly, especially since he could feel the rough sandstone beneath his cheek. Somehow rough sandstone didn't fit in with his idea of the spirit world—

"Billy! Billy Foreman! Be you all right?"

Hearing the terror in Benjamin Perkins's voice caused Billy to finally open his eyes. Of course he was all right. Why shouldn't he be? Why, he'd been out of the line of the blast, and—

"Billy?"

Ben was nearer, and Billy finally lifted his head to see the blurry form of the man, as well as Kumen Jones and James Pace scooting

297

backward down the slope toward him. All three were securely tied with ropes, and all seemed thoroughly surprised to find him there.

"Wh . . . where're my spectacles?" Billy gasped, and he was startled at the weakness in his own voice.

"The Lord be praised!" Benjamin Perkins exclaimed, ignoring Billy's question. "We thought—" And without another word he reached out and took hold of Billy beneath his arms, his grip so tight that Billy almost cried out.

"Here," Kumen Jones said as he reached Billy's side and slipped a rope under him and around his body, "don't let go of the rock until I have this tied. Good. Okay, Billy, let go and we'll walk you—"

"He's not letting go," James Pace declared. "Billy—"

Surprised, Billy looked at his hands. He'd willed them to let go, but for some reason his whitened knuckles wouldn't relax."

"Would you look how he's clinging to that rock!" Kumen Jones exclaimed, suddenly aware of the strangeness of it. "I never saw the like! He has no handholds or footholds, and it's way too steep for him to just lie there the way he is—"

"Talk about sticky-to-ity!" James Pace breathed.

"Amen," Benjamin Perkins declared as his tears of relief and gratitude fell freely. "Boys, this is the Lord's protection that we prayed for this morning before we started. And to my way of thinking, it's one more example of this good brother's faith."

Soberly the men nodded. Gently they pried Billy's fingers loose, then led him up the bulge to safety. There they found his spectacles, undamaged and lying inexplicably on the top of the bulge.

It was a small incident, really, not even worth noting in their journals. More, as Ben and others were lowered immediately to begin drilling charge holes on the newly created face, Billy's experience was quickly forgotten. These men weren't stunned by miracles, they expected them. And when miracles occurred, they simply gave thanks to God and continued on their way.

And so it was with Billy, who remained on top helping with the ropes for the rest of the day. But he most certainly would have gone over the edge again, had he only been asked.

37

West Bank of the Colorado River, Bottom of the Hole

"I can hardly believe how much warmer it is here on the river." Eliza held her hands out to the flames that were leaping before her. "Of course, having a big wood fire certainly helps."

In the dancing light from the driftwood fire Billy smiled at his wife. "A fire helps, all right. But it *is* warmer here, too, because of the lower elevation. Besides, these cliffs absorb a lot of heat from the daytime sun that you can feel at night. Reed Hall—that's his family's camp over yonder, by the way—told me he figures a good sunny day boosts the nighttime temperature here on the river by as much as ten degrees."

Breathing deeply, Eliza looked past the mostly silent men and women who were gathered at the large fire, either preparing or eating their evening meals. They'd all been sobered by the day's events, just as she had been, and now all seemed more inclined to ponder than to rejoice.

Above her the looming cliffs cut off all but a narrow band of darkened sky. Looking upward, she felt almost claustrophobic, though she knew in the daylight the river gorge didn't seem anywhere near so close. Behind her the Hole was invisible in the darkness, which was just as well! Even now she shuddered when she thought of the perilous descent they'd made that afternoon, and with all her heart she hoped she'd never see the awful chasm again.

The sounds of restless oxen and horses assailed her ears, for there was scant feed for them on the riverbank. The herders were keeping them in tight bunches because of that, and many were bellowing their displeasure. Beside them the Colorado River ran smoothly and almost quietly, though the roar of rapids and falls a little more than a mile downstream reminded her of the pent-up power the river was always ready to unleash.

In the light from the fire Eliza could make out the ferry, tied now to large boulders and waiting for daylight before once again doing battle with the powerful current. Already that day, or so she'd been told, while twenty-six wagons had been ferried across, a gust of wind had also torn the ferry loose and swept it downstream, and it had come perilously close to the rapids and falls before the Halls had been able to stop it. And it had taken more than an hour for four horses pulling the corner ropes to drag it back to the landing.

Eliza thought of that and wondered if the river crossing would seem as insanely impossible on the morrow as the descent through the Hole had seemed only hours before. Of course, with the kind of faith Billy was slowly teaching her to have—

Abruptly she smiled, seeing in her mind the nearly square notch the men had cut in the rimrock that signaled the top of the Hole— the notch that was so obviously man-made and out of place in the rounded sandstone formations so prevalent in this impossible wilderness. But more than the notch, she was seeing her darling husband as he harnessed his teams and backed them against the singletrees on either side of the wagon tongue, hooked their tugs, and then gently clicked the animals forward toward that same terrifying notch.

Still smiling, Eliza pulled her shawl more tightly about her shoulders, remembering vividly the trembling that had suddenly taken control of her body. For she had been terrified to go down through the Hole-in-the-Rock, absolutely terrified. In fact, it had been all she could do to clamber up onto the wagon seat, deposit her crutch on the grain sacks behind her, and grab hold of the seat. Even Billy's comforting words and his own quiet courage hadn't seemed to help. She'd been so frightened she could hardly keep from bursting into tears.

She thought then of the four mules that had plunged down the abyss just barely ahead of the wagon. Their winter coats had grown so long during the six-week road-building delay that she had hardly even recognized them. And at least the wheelers had seemed unwilling to recognize their harnesses. As Billy had urged them forward up the gentle incline toward the notch, they'd been restive and balking, and Billy hadn't had an easy time with them. Yet up the incline they'd inched, each step drawing them nearer to the yawning chasm. As for herself, Eliza had sat rigidly, praying silently for the safety of themselves, the mules, the cow, and even the fool, glass-eyed mare who was inexplicably following of her own accord.

Both rear wheels of the wagon had been rough-locked, which meant that a heavy chain had been wrapped around the wheel felloes and iron-tires and then secured to the wagon's running-gears. This apparatus kept the wheels from turning and left the loops of chain on the bottom of the wheels to give traction. Of course, the scraping of the chains on the rock had created an enormous racket, and that, joined with the bellowing, snorting, and braying of the livestock and the shouting and screaming of the people had torn at her nerves like hooked fingers of fire, making everything feel even worse than it had probably been.

At Kumen Jones's suggestion, Billy had stopped the team so he and Eliza could tie themselves to the wagon by ropes that went from their waists back to the rear gate.

"Hon-bun," Billy had said as he was helping her with the rope, "we have nothing to fear. I feel to promise you that we'll get to the bottom okay."

In wonder Eliza had looked at her husband. The peace and serenity on his countenance was amazing to her. Of course he had told her about how he'd somehow clung to the rock during the explosion, and she'd wondered at it. Surely it must have been because of his faith, she thought, for with the healing of his hands she'd begun to understand the kind of faith her husband had been blessed with. But as far as applying that faith to herself, she hadn't the faintest notion of how to do it.

From the rocks ahead of them, Nell Fielding had begun softly singing a well-known hymn, and quickly Belle Smith, Hyrum Perkins, and others had joined in.

301

Come, come ye Saints, no toil nor labor
*   fear,*
But with joy, wend your way;
Though hard to you this journey may
*   appear,*
Grace shall be as your day.
'Tis better far for us to strive,
Our useless cares from us to drive;
Do this, and joy, your hearts will swell—
All is well! All is well!

With voices around her raising a quiet but joyful noise, Eliza had looked again at Billy. He'd been back on the wagon seat, tying himself with the rope, wrapping the reins about his hands, adjusting his feet against the dashboard where they'd kept the heated rocks—and smiling!

If only, she had thought, she could find a way to make herself feel the same—

Why should we mourn, or think our lot is
*   hard?*
'Tis not so; all is right!
Why should we think to earn a great
*   reward,*
If we now shun the fight?
Gird up your loins, fresh courage take,
Our God will never us forsake;
And soon we'll have this tale to tell—
All is well! All is well!

"Please, dear God," Eliza had whispered as the men and women around her continued to sing, "I don't want to shun the fight, but I'm so afraid of getting hurt or dying! I'm so awkward, and if I should fall from the wagon—Oh, dear Father, what will happen with our baby, with Billy's posterity? Please, oh please give me fresh courage—"

And should we die before our journey's
*   through,*

302

Happy day! All is well!
We then are free from toil and sorrow too;
With the just we shall dwell.

In an agony of fear, Eliza had closed her ears to the words. How could all be well if she died? Or if the baby died because of her clumsiness? How would her blessing be fulfilled? For it wasn't death that she feared, at least not death for herself. But she truly feared failing her husband, the wonderful man whom the dear Lord had given her and who was beginning to bring such peace and happiness to her life. What if she failed him? What if—

With a snap of the reins and a shouted "Giddup" Billy had once again shaken the mules into motion. Frantically Eliza had reached for the rope that was around her waist, felt that the knot was loose, and had started to undo and retie it. Suddenly Sign and Wonder had reached the top of the terrible incline, balked, and been whipped ahead by a couple of the brethren who were standing by the sides of the cut for that very purpose. Then, with squeals and snorts, the leaders had lunged over the edge, dragging the wheelers behind them.

With what had seemed to be amazing clarity, Eliza had watched the wagon tongue dip down with the mules. Then the wagon had jerked forward with their abrupt momentum, she had realized that the knot about her waist had not been retied, and then for a crazy second that seemed to last forever she, Billy, and their wagon had hung on the very lip of eternity.

"Oh, Billy!" she had wailed as they'd braced their feet against the wooden dashboard and she'd gripped the side and back of the seat. In the next instant they had all—rough-locked wagon, mules, mare, cow, she, Billy, their unborn child, and every single thing they owned in all the world, as well as the several men who were hanging onto ropes from behind—been sent careening down the shiny-slick, vertical-looking incline.

Instantly the noise and dust in the narrow defile had become suffocating, and the wagon had been jolted back and forth and up and down until Eliza had been certain she could no longer hang on. Yet somehow both she and Billy had managed the plunge to the bottom of the first incline just fine. She had held on for dear life, he had kept

303

the reins tight and the mules moving, and everything had apparently held together.

Taking a deep breath because they had leveled out, Eliza had just been starting to reach for the dangling rope when someone on the landing had yelled to keep moving. Instantly Billy had responded with another shout and snap of the reins, Eliza had screamed, the wagon had lurched forward again, and with more screeching and banging they had plunged down and into the choking clouds of dust that filled the rest of the Hole.

How Billy had seen to guide the teams Eliza would never know. Maybe the mules had guided themselves, for though the road down the Hole had been anything but straight, there were really no other options than to follow it. Yet other than the wheel hubs scraping the sandstone sides of the Hole at one curve, they had negotiated the road just fine, emerging from the Hole onto Uncle Ben's Dugway far sooner than Eliza had expected.

There the clouds of dust had dispersed to reveal the dizzying cliff to which the crazy-looking dugway had been attached. But the run down and across it to the top of the sand hill, which Eliza had expected to be absolutely terrifying, was over so quickly that she hardly had time to feel frightened at all.

Yet, meanwhile, she'd been gripping the wagon seat so hard that she was surprised her fingers hadn't crushed the wood. And her knees, locked straight as she'd frantically pushed her feet against the dashboard in a ridiculous attempt to keep from falling any faster, still ached from the tension.

In other words, while her husband had seemed calm and serene, she had been absolutely, bone-frozen terrified! She'd shown neither Billy's courage nor his marvelous willpower. Neither, when for an instant she'd stared from the wagon-seat down that terrible chasm, had she been able to see anything below her but death. That, and utter destruction. There had been no faith in her heart at all!

Thank the Lord that Billy had been beside her, Eliza thought with another smile as she watched their slapjacks cooking on the edge of the fire. Thank the Lord he'd given her such a wonderful man! Why, with Billy Foreman at her side she need never fear again, for he was a man of wisdom and courage who also knew the Lord, and who knew—

"Vell, brudders und sisters." Jens Nielson smiled as he limped into the firelight. "So far ve haff all survived de Hole. All but fifteen of de vagons from de first camp haff safely crossed de river, und in de morning—Vhy, Brudder Barton, ven dit you come down?"

Joseph Barton grinned. "About sundown, I reckon."

"But . . . I tought you vere vid de camp at Fifty-Mile."

"I was, but I got a little ahead of them, and here we are."

Jens Nielson shook his head. "Vell, at least de brudders vere dere to halp you down."

"Not hardly they weren't," Harriet Ann Barton spoke up, her eyes flashing. "Not for us or Joe and Belle Smith, either one! And Belle got hurt, too!"

"Vat? Sister Smith, I hadn't heard—"

"It's nothing," the twenty-seven-year-old woman declared softly. "Only a small cut—"

"Yeah, from her ankle practically to her hip," her husband, Joseph Stanford Smith, declared with some rancor. "Some of the brethren pushed our wagon back out of the way up on top while I was down here helping with the ferry, and by the time I discovered Belle wasn't here and had climbed back to the top to fetch her, we were alone. If I'd have known Joe Barton was close behind me I would have waited, but I didn't know. Besides, I was some steamed, and I figured if the brethren didn't want to help, then neither did I want it."

"I am so sorry, Brudder Yoseph, Sister Belle."

While Joe Smith remained silent, his wife Belle smiled sweetly. "I know you are, Brother Nielson. And I'm just fine, truly I am. Fact is, our horse was more beat up than me, and even he is all right."

"Goot! Does your leg need to be sewn? Because if it does, Brudder Pap Redd iss de man to do it."

Quickly Arabell Smith shook her head. "No, thank you, Brother Nielson. Joe washed and wrapped it real good, so I'm sure I'll be fine."

"Vell, you yust let us know if you need sewing. Billy, did you und Eliza haff any difficulty?"

"Tell the truth," Billy grinned, "we didn't. But you might be interested in knowing that Eliza rode the whole way without even a tie-down!"

"Vat? You *rode* down, Sister Eliza?"

Slowly she nodded. "I wasn't about to trust these feet of mine to that slope, or my crutch, either." Eliza then smiled. "But I'll admit I probably dented the boards of our wagon seat. I don't think I've ever squeezed anything so hard in my life!"

"Ya," Jens Nielson chuckled, "I yust bet you did! Und you, Sister Barton? Are you vell?"

"Of course," Harriet Ann Barton responded brightly. "I carried baby Mary, little Eliza walked beside me, and we slid right on down together. That rock is terribly slick, you know."

"Ya, ve know. It vas covered early on vith sand und small rocks, but each vagon going down dragged more to de landing until der vas notting but slickrock left."

"We had a little help from the Lord, too," Joseph Barton added softly. "After I'd surveyed the cavity I decided to rough-lock my wheels and come ahead and not wait for tomorrow. So I pushed my animals over the edge, and the next half minute landed the horses, the wagon, and me at the first station in a huge cloud of dust but still right side up. There I found that the chain to my rough-lock had broken, but through a providential act the chain had flipped a loop around the felloe in such a manner as to serve for a new lock."

"Had the chain not done that," Harriet Ann stated quietly, "my husband might well have perished."

"Well he might have," Milton Dailey agreed. "That first forty feet the wagons stood so straight in the air it was impossible to sit on the bench. Like the rest of you, I was actually standing on the dashboard with my head back in the puckerhole. And the chasm was so narrow we couldn't even leave the barrels secured to the sides of our wagons. All our women had to hold hands and slide down together—it was impossible to walk."

"Ya," Jens Nielson nodded, "it iss a steep road, und narrow. Ven Kumen Yones vas asked to drive Ben Perkins's vagon down as de first vone to scar de Hole, ve didn't tink of de barrels. Und dey vere bott smashed to smidereens by de rocks."

"All I know," Liz Decker said quietly, "is that even walking the descent about scared me to death. And if my folks ever come this way to pay us a visit, it'll scare them to death, too. And my poor little Willie. When we were walking and sliding down, he looked back and cried and asked me how we'd ever get home."

"I've been wondering that, too," Belle Smith stated to no one in particular. Suddenly tears started, and hurriedly she tried to wipe them away. "I . . . I suppose maybe we won't ever be going home."

"Ya, ve vill!" Jens Nielson declared brightly as he rose to his unsteady feet. "Fact of it iss, ve leaf for home in de morning—our new home, on de San Juan. Und ve can tank de Lord for de privilege!"

And Eliza, as she watched the big old man limping away to check on others of his charges, knew from the peace that was slowly filling her heart that he was right.

PART FOUR

COTTONWOOD CANYON

38

Friday, January 30, 1880

Oola Bikooh

When he knew he hadn't been followed by his young partner, James Merrick dropped to his stomach on the sand next to the cliff and began worming himself beneath the low sandstone overhang. He did this strictly by feel, for there was no light, but he did it quickly because he knew what he was doing.

In the canyon it was night, a black, moonless night of fitful breezes and stars so unnaturally bright they seemed to hang just feet above the looming, darker blackness of the cliffs. It was truly a night for haunts, and James Merrick was beginning to feel it.

For nearly a month he and Ernest Mitchell had been camped in the narrow, hidden canyon, working quietly and doing nothing that might reveal their presence to prying eyes. They'd even waited until after dark each evening to smelt the rich, silver-laden ore they'd found, knowing that in the daylight smoke could be seen for vast distances and followed without difficulty.

The vein of ore had been all he'd remembered, too—a twelve-inch-wide occlusion of silver-bearing quartz running vertically up the face of a massive sandstone ledge. When formed, the quartz had been fully contained or occluded within the sandstone, but an ancient earthquake or other shift in the earth's surface had split the sandstone open, leaving the silver lode exposed to any who happened upon it.

And he and Mitchell hadn't been the first to work the vein, James Merrick knew, not by any means. Not only did some of the Navajo know of it, which was evident by the crude, small smelters on the canyon floor, but centuries earlier the lode had been mined by the Spanish—inveterate treasure seekers who managed to find lodes of gold and silver in the most unlikely of places.

On the walls on both sides of the canyon, near the mouth where it closed to a narrow crevice before dumping into the Colorado River, were several chiseled inscriptions. Though time and weather had rendered unreadable parts of each of the two major inscriptions, one still proclaimed, "Junipero ano dom 1661," and the other, "de Julio 1796." Near them was a third bearing only the barely legible date, "1583," and beneath that inscription he and his partner had chiseled "Merrick and Mitchell 1880." It was a foolish thing to do, perhaps. But who was to say who might follow their footsteps in the years to come and want, as they did, to know who else had found wealth in the hidden canyon.

A few feet in from where he'd slid under the sandstone, the ground dropped away into an ancient tunnel, and this Merrick followed for about thirty feet until it abutted against the sandstone wall. Only then did he take out his candle, light it with a sulfur match, and place it on a small ledge someone had cut for that very purpose.

For a moment, as he did each time he entered the ancient mine, James Merrick stared at the wall before him, his heart pounding in his chest. All along the side of the tunnel was a horizontal ledge of rotten, purple-tinted quartz that measured about fourteen inches wide and was goodness-only-knew how deep. And laced throughout the quartz was bright, glittering gold, mostly of the wire type but interspersed occasionally with large nuggets that shown even more brightly than the wire.

It was a beautiful sight, and each time he gazed at it, James Merrick found himself almost overwhelmed. Had the ancient Spanish miners felt the same, he wondered? Or was it just a mission to them, an assignment to fulfill for their distant king? He didn't know, of course, but neither did he spend much time thinking about it. For himself, it was undreamed of wealth, a lifetime of ease spent doing all the things a man of vast means could think of to do.

Smiling at the thought, he took a deep breath, pulled free his stone hammer, and went eagerly to work.

And that work was amazingly easy. In fact, the quartz was so crumbly that it took no real effort to break any of the gold free. He had merely to pick a chunk loose from the ledge, hit it a couple of times with his hammer, and then pick out the gold. In that manner, working not more than an hour each night so that Mitchell wouldn't miss him, he'd nearly filled his saddlebags. This night would finish the job, he was certain, for the weight of the gold was amazing, and he didn't want to overburden his horse. Then and only then would he willingly leave, keeping the gold for himself and sharing the silver with the unsuspecting Mitchell.

For a moment he thought of how much gold he might have had if he'd been able to find the small "X" cut low in the sandstone wall a little sooner, for they'd been in the canyon a month, and he'd found it only five days before. He also wondered how much he might have had if he'd ignored the silver down the canyon, told Mitchell about the gold, and the two had mined it together. But no, that would have been more than foolish, and James Merrick didn't think himself a man who did foolish things.

An hour later, with his saddlebags, which he'd kept in the tunnel the entire time, so heavy with gold he could hardly lift them, the successful treasure hunter took a long, last look at the ledge of quartz. It seemed as though he'd hardly touched it, for the gold continued to glitter from every direction. It pulled at him, too, making him want to stay, to chip out just a bit more—

With a deep breath Merrick steeled his mind against the lure of the gold, blew out the candle, and made his way back to the sandstone overhang. Pushing the saddlebags ahead of him, he wormed his way out from under the rock and rose unsteadily to his feet.

Well, he thought to himself, so far so good. Now all he had to do—

Click!

The metallic cocking of the gun was accompanied by the cold feel of a gun barrel being pressed against the back of his neck. Freezing, James Merrick dropped the saddlebags and slowly lifted his hands. "Mitchell," he hissed into the darkness, "is that you?"

"*Peshlaki* is a myth," Ernest Mitchell replied conversationally, "a lie. Fact is, *Peshlaki* ain't even a Navajo word."

"It . . . it isn't?"

"Nope. Navajos call silver white iron, their word for it being *beesh ligai*."

"*Beesh ligai?*" James Merrick's mind was scrambling. "Th-that sounds a lot like *Peshlaki*."

Ernest Mitchell chuckled. "It does—might even be some fool *belacani's* way of saying it. Trouble is, Jim, I never heard from a single Navajo, nor has my father ever heard, of a fabulous Navajo silver mine, either lost or otherwise."

"Wh-what do you mean?

"I mean the Navajos call this place *Oola Bikooh*—Gold Canyon."

"How long have you known?" Merrick's voice was now just a whisper.

"Oh, I reckon I suspected it right along, but I wasn't certain until we had to cut logs to bridge that chasm so we could get into the canyon. I was some surprised at how long it took you to find the mine."

"I . . . I hid the 'X' last time I was here," Merrick mumbled. "Filled it with mud. And grass had grown up in front of it, too. So, what do we do now?"

Ernest Mitchell chuckled. "Do? Well, I could kill you for being such an underhanded, greedy snake—"

"It was my father!" Merrick abruptly declared, suddenly pleading. "He made me swear not to tell anybody about the gold!"

"Your father knows about this?"

"Actually, my uncle and some others found it first, following a map they copied from a mission church in Santa Fe. But Indians attacked them, and he had to leave all the gold behind just to escape. Neither he nor the two who escaped with him ever came back here."

"When was that?"

"About 1855. But he was old then, past sixty, and too weak to make a second try. So he went to my father and gave the secret to him."

"And your father's been here too?"

"That's right. About four years ago. He and his party took a lot of gold out, but again they were attacked by Indians, over on the Rio Virgin. They were all killed but my father, who was badly wounded.

But he plugged his bullet holes and arrow wounds with chewed cedar bark and made his way into the Mormon settlement of Santa Clara, and the folks there nursed him back to health."

"No wonder you've been so worried about haunts and curses. It sounds like the Navajos cursed this fool mine, or maybe it was the Spaniards. I wonder how many men have died over it since then."

"I . . . I don't rightly know. Too many, for certain."

"I reckon," Ernest Mitchell agreed. "So, how did you come to be here?"

"When Father finally returned to our home in California, he showed me the gold he had left—three beautiful nuggets and a handful of wire—and that was all it took. I knew I was destined to follow him here. But he made me swear I wouldn't mention the gold to a soul, not one. And I haven't, except to an assayer over in Mancos, who told me the gold would run $30,000 a ton. Do you have any idea how much money that is, Ernest?"

"I reckon I do, Jim. None, happen the curse is still intact and we don't get out of here alive."

"We? You . . . you mean—"

"I ain't a killer, Jim," Ernest Mitchell said as he lowered his pistol and thumbed the hammer off cock. "Never have been, never will be. And what with all the curses and haunts around here, I sure don't want to leave this canyon alone. You agree to a fifty-fifty split of everything we've found, including the gold, and I'd say we're partners again. That is, if you're willing to pack up come daylight and skedaddle on out of here."

"I'll do it!" James Merrick declared with relief, "and I'll still keep my word to my father."

"How's that?"

"I only promised him I wouldn't *tell* anyone about the gold. I never said a word about not sharing it."

Ernest Mitchell chuckled in his easy way, picked up the heavy saddlebags from where they lay on the ground, and together with his partner set off in the darkness for the lonely camp in *Oola Bikooh.*

39

Saturday, January 31, 1880

Cottonwood Canyon

"Look at it this way," the woman said as she wiped beads of sweat from her forehead. "At least it isn't as cold here."

The speaker was Olivia Larson, plural wife of Mons Larson, and now Eliza glanced at her. A woman who was always "sunny-side up," as Mary Jones put it, the smiling Olivia and her young family were not an official part of the mission to the San Juan. Mons had built her a home in Snowflake, Arizona, and they were on their way to it. Only they hadn't wanted to travel alone and slowly, and so they'd joined the expedition to the San Juan. Now, of course, instead of traveling slowly, they were practically at a standstill, and nowhere near Snowflake, Arizona. But at least, Eliza thought wryly, they weren't alone.

Reaching into the cold water of the pool around which she and several other women were kneeling at their wash, Eliza took another item of dirty clothing from her pile. Briskly rubbing lye soap into the fabric, she began drawing it up and then pushing it back down against the metal washboard she was holding with her chin against her chest. It was hard, sweaty work, and her arms and back were already aching—as much, she knew, from her pregnancy as from anything else.

And in Eliza's mind, that made Olivia Larson even more impressive. Not only was Olivia eight months pregnant and swollen in her legs and feet from carrying water, but she'd already washed more clothes than Eliza, was working faster, and was still smiling. She was an incredible woman, a description Eliza was beginning to feel aptly fit every woman in the company. They were all so courageous, so tenacious in fulfilling their duties in what seemed to Eliza like terrible adversity. And the men were no different, laboring without letup from daylight to dark six days a week and then doing their Church duties for most of the Sabbath.

Even Billy, she thought with pride. Every morning he was up and going before first light, and no task was too menial for him, or too strenuous. Despite the difficulties and challenges he continued to encounter, he never complained. He was like Olivia, always sunny-side up.

So why hadn't she been able to see that before now, she wondered? What on earth had possessed her to see only his weaknesses? Or worse, to malign and defame him before others? It was almost as if—

"It certainly isn't as cold as it was two days ago," Ann Rowley admitted, interrupting Eliza's thoughts. "I heard the river isn't even frozen over any longer."

"That's too bad." Olivia Larson smiled. "The other night when we were camped on the sandbar, there were otters and beavers everywhere, sliding around on the ice like it was what they were born for. I declare, I never saw such a sight, and it was all I could do to keep my little Moroni from going out and playing with them."

"I had the same trouble with Edison." Laura Barney shook her head. "Can you imagine, playing with otters and beaver on that thin ice? That's all I need is another child in that river! I thought I'd die when Alfred was knocked off the ferry in the middle of the river by those fool oxen. Why, I didn't even know he could swim."

"He did, though. And well." Eliza smiled at the woman who was herding nine children through this wilderness. "Who but Alfred would have thought to dive down and swim underwater to avoid those thrashing hooves? He must surely be a bright boy, Laura."

"He seems to be," Laura Barney stated modestly. "But probably no more than anyone else's fourteen-year-old son. I'm just thankful the Lord preserved his life."

"I believe he's preserved all our lives!" Mary Ann Perkins

317

paused in her washing. "Anyone who thinks that God didn't preserve us while we were driving all our wagons and livestock down through the Hole would have to be an infidel."

"And a fool!" Sarah Ellen Haight added. "The fact that there wasn't a single accident is to me a true miracle, as is the fact that God has brought us to this wonderful camp. My husband, Caleb, feels the same. I can't tell you how thrilled we are to be off that windy plateau and here under these gorgeous cottonwood trees! To us this canyon seems like heaven on earth."

"I agree." Rachel Perkins wrung out one of her husband's shirts and set it to the side. "And the feed for the livestock is excellent!"

"Not to mention all the wonderful firewood," Nellie Lyman exclaimed. "I expect we're all grateful for that."

Eliza smiled. "I certainly am! That coal smoke was dreadful, and I believe I gathered every scrap of shadscale on the entire Escalante Desert."

"All except for what I dragged in," Harriet Gower giggled. "Speaking of which, Eliza, where's that glass-eyed mare of yours?"

"She followed Billy today, so I expect she's back down by those huge rocks where all the men are chiseling their names."

"Fool's names and fool's faces," Rachel Perkins grinned, "and I'm sure my Hyrum has scratched his name into the highest place he can reach."

"Well, I know both Edward and Joseph were there day before yesterday," Nellie Lyman declared. "You'd think they'd get so tired of chiseling away at this wilderness of rock that they'd take a day off from it."

"You would," Ann Rowley agreed. "But I decided a long time ago there's just no telling how a man thinks."

"That may be so," Pauline Pace stated. "But I'm thankful I didn't have to do the thinking on how to build the road down through the Hole."

"Or the road that will take us out of this canyon, either one," Nellie Lyman agreed. "Have any of you walked up to the head of the canyon to see where we have to go next?"

None of the woman had.

"Well, I did, early this morning. Platte, Ben Perkins, my Joseph,

George Sevy, and Josh Stevens took a little scout to see the route Brother Sevy and the other scouts followed a few weeks ago, and I just sort of trailed along. Ladies, to me it looks every bit as bad as the Hole, only this time we'll be going up rather than down."

"Are you serious?"

"Dead serious, Harriet. There's a hill up there we'll have to climb that they're calling Cottonwood Hill. The bottom part isn't so bad—in fact, I climbed right up it. But then there's a whole hillside of drifting sand where I couldn't even make any headway. Somehow we have to drive teams and loaded wagons up through that horrid stuff. And then we come to a mountain of sandstone that Ben Perkins says we have to go up and over. Of course, the only way to do that is with another dugway, though Ben doesn't think this one can be tacked on. That means we're going to need more blasting powder, which Platte assured the men is coming soon."

"More blasting?" Ann Rowley questioned in dismay.

"I'll say. And that isn't the end, either. Beyond that sandstone mountain is another mountain almost as formidable. But at least there's a gash up the side, a ravine of sorts that with a lot of work we can turn into a road. Or at least that's what the men say."

"So, what do we have, Nellie? Another three weeks here, or four?"

Vigorously Nellie Lyman shook her head. "Not according to Platte. He thinks if we all work together, and if the powder comes and the weather holds good, we can be out of this canyon and up on the mesa in a week to ten days."

"That's a lot of 'ifs'," Harriet Ann Barton said softly. "I declare, tomorrow is February first, and it doesn't seem like we're any closer to the San Juan than we were last fall."

With that sobering assessment, the women around the rock pool became silent. Down the canyon toward the river a flock of crows grew raucous, and Eliza was wondering what might have disturbed them when she caught Ann Rowley's eyes on her. Flashing a quick smile, she was surprised when the woman instantly averted her gaze to her work, not smiling in return.

For a moment Eliza wondered at it, and then into her mind came the conversation she'd had months before with little Alice Louise

319

Rowley, Ann's daughter. Alice Louise had called Eliza strange, saying she'd got the words from her parents. Worse, she'd said her parents had also told her they could tell by the things Eliza said and did that she didn't like Billy very much.

Which had once been the truth, Eliza now admitted sadly as she dropped her gaze from Ann Rowley's downturned head. But no more! She could see now that she'd been wrong—wrong in so many ways. Billy was a wonderful man, a man who was worthy in every respect of a loving and decent wife. And she was trying to be that way, she truly was. Only how could folks like Ann Rowley know that? Or forgive her for the awful things she'd said and done? Billy had frankly forgiven her, or so he said. But how in the world could they?

Or worse, she thought as tears suddenly splashed from her eyes and into the sudsy pool, how could she ever forgive herself? How could she ever feel peace over the terrible things she'd said to the man she had covenanted to accept as her eternal companion; for the terrible things she had done? How could she have ever been so blind?

40

Sunday, February 1, 1880

Cottonwood Canyon

"There you go, hon-bun. Does that feel any better?"

Eliza's feet had been throbbing terribly since the Sabbath evening meeting, both from the cold and from the inactivity of sitting on the rock floor of the canyon for an hour or so. But for the past thirty minutes, almost from the moment they'd returned to their wagon, Billy had been gently rubbing them, restoring circulation and warming them with his own finally callused hands.

"Much better," she replied, smiling her relief. "I don't know how I'd get along without you."

"Most likely quite well." Billy grinned and adjusted his spectacles. "But I'm mighty grateful you don't have to." Slowly he straightened, stretched his back, and added more wood to the fire. Then he took a chair from the wagon, placed it next to his wife under the canvas awning where a little heat collected, and slowly sank into it. "I'm sorry your feet didn't do well, hon-bun, but in spite of the cold I surely did enjoy our worship services tonight. I reckon I especially enjoyed Kumen's remarks about the sisters being strengthened by the Lord for our journey."

"He must not have been thinking of me," Eliza declared with a sigh.

Billy smiled his understanding. "I don't know. Considering your condition and everything else, it seems to me you've been strengthened a great deal."

"By condition you mean my age?"

Eliza's voice was filled with discouragement, and Billy wondered at it. After all, in recent weeks she'd seemed so joyful, so positively happy about what was happening in her life. "Age doesn't mean a thing to the Lord, Eliza, and you know it. Nor does it mean any more than that to me. Fact is, I was thinking more of your pregnancy and the debilitating effects of the cold on your poor feet. Yet you've never once complained or slacked from your labors, and you've walked most of the way and kept up with the train just fine. I'm telling you, I believe that is clear evidence that the Lord has strengthened you just as he did those women Kumen was reading about in the Book of Mormon."

With a feeling almost of awe Eliza looked down at the worn leather book she was holding in her lap, the book her missionaries had presented her at her baptism a quarter of a century before. Wasn't it strange, she thought, that a little adversity had stopped her from partaking daily from the book's message of hope in Christ? And that lack of reading, in turn, had brought her to an almost complete abandonment of the divine witness she had once cherished beyond life itself. Worse, her lack of reading had somehow brought a nearly complete cessation of praying, and that had been followed quite rapidly by thoughts and actions she was now mortally ashamed of—horrible sins that had nearly destroyed her, her sweet husband, and the marriage she had waited all her life to enjoy.

Thank the Lord Mary Jones had called her wickedness to her attention, Maggie Sevy had seconded the motion, and Billy had been given the strength to endure—

"Look it up and read it, hon-bun. I think Kumen said he was quoting from the seventeenth chapter of First Nephi."

"He was." Eliza smiled as she opened her book. "In fact, I just read it the other day, and I was amazed at how similar our wilderness trek is to the journey of those ancient people. Of course, I don't think it was as cold for them in that part of the world, but—Here it is. Do you want me to read it?"

"Can you see it okay?"

Eliza nodded. "I can now that the fire's brighter. Let's see. Verse two reads: 'And so great were the blessings of the Lord upon us, that while we did live upon raw meat in the wilderness, our women did give plenty of suck for their children, and were strong, yea, even like unto the men; and they began to bear their journeyings without murmurings.'"

"That's it," Billy declared. "You see, Eliza, it's happening just like that for us! While we're not eating raw meat, everything else is about the same. Sister Lizzie Decker and the others who are nursing little children are doing just fine, as are their babies. And you and Olivia Larson and Emma Decker are strong and healthy as anyone else in the company. In spite of the fact that we face blizzards and swollen rivers and treacherous cliffs and who-knows-what-all-else that lies ahead, virtually everyone in the company is beginning to bear their journeyings without murmurings. To me these things are a marvelous manifestation of the Lord's love and power. And like Kumen, I feel like exclaiming all the day long, 'Praise to my Lord God Jehovah!'"

Eliza smiled at her husband's animation. "So do I, Billy. But even more than that verse, it's the next one that gives me pause. Listen to this: 'And thus we see that the commandments of God must be fulfilled. And if it so be that the children of men keep the commandments of God he doth nourish them, and strengthen them, and provide means whereby they can accomplish the thing which he has commanded them; wherefore, he did provide means for us while we did sojourn in the wilderness.'"

"In other words," Billy said when Eliza had finished, "if we keep the commandments, even if it takes us years and years, we'll finally be able to get through to the San Juan."

"Yes," Eliza declared as she lowered her book and gazed into the fire, "Of course that is so. But . . . well, what happens if we don't keep the commandments, Billy? What happens if . . . if somebody broke her eternal marriage covenants; if she slandered and defamed her husband and . . . and denied her testimony of the gospel?"

"Hon-bun, you didn't do those things. You just—"

"But I did do them, Billy! I did them as surely as I'm sitting here in front of the fire. And everyone in this company knows I did them, too. I loathed you, and I wanted the whole world to loathe you with me. Why, just yesterday I caught Jane Walton staring at me, thinking all those awful things she and Charlie first saw in me and told their kids, and when I smiled at her she dropped her gaze so fast it was shameful. Not that I blame her, mind you. After all, I'm guilty, and they were only being truthful."

"But you've stopped all that, Eliza. You truly have! More than that, the Lord has helped you change. You've become kind and loving, not just to me but to others. Your faith in the Lord has been restored, you love him, and you show it by your good works—"

Abruptly Eliza started to cry. "The Lord knows I've been trying, Billy darling. I have! Only, it isn't working! No matter how hard I pray, no matter how many scriptures I read, I feel no peace! Where is that Spirit I once felt? Where is the Holy Ghost that I can't be comforted? I . . . I'm afraid I went too far, Billy. I'm afraid my sins were so grievous that I'm doomed; that it has become impossible for Christ to comfort or forgive me through the power of his Spirit!"

Billy felt stricken. "Eliza, that isn't so, and you know it! Denying the Holy Ghost is the only sin that is unpardonable, and you certainly never did that. Merciful heavens, woman, the Lord knew we would all make mistakes and commit sins, even grievous ones. That's why he came, lived, suffered and then died for us—to pay or atone for such things through his grace. Here, let me read you something out of the Bible."

Quickly Billy took up Eliza's family Bible. "I believe this is in Isaiah, in the Old Testament. Yes, here it is. In verses four and five of chapter fifty-three it says: 'Surely he hath borne our griefs, and carried our sorrows: yet we did esteem him stricken, smitten of God, and afflicted. But he was wounded for our transgressions, he was bruised for our iniquities: the chastisement of our peace was upon him; and with his stripes we are healed.'

"There's another passage in the Book of Mormon that says very much the same thing, I think in Alma."

"How do you remember all these passages?" Eliza asked with wonder.

Billy smiled. "I don't know. They just sort of stick in my head, I reckon. Turn to the seventh chapter of Alma and start reading at verse eleven."

Eliza read: "And he shall go forth, suffering pains and afflictions and temptations of every kind; and this that the word might be fulfilled which saith he will take upon him the pains and the sicknesses of his people. And he will take upon him death, that he may loose the bands of death which bind his people; and he will take upon him their infirmities, that his bowels may be filled with mercy, according to the flesh, that he may know according to the flesh how to succor his people according to their infirmities. Now the Spirit knoweth all things; nevertheless the Son of God suffereth according to the flesh that he might take upon him the sins of his people, that he might blot out their transgressions according to the power of his deliverance; and now behold, this is the testimony which is in me."

"Do you see, hon-bun?" Billy asked when Eliza had finished reading. "The whole purpose of Christ's life and death seems to have been to redeem us from every one of our sorrows, including our sins."

"I . . . I don't understand."

"Well, think of it this way. The prophets say that Jesus Christ's atonement was both infinite and eternal. I believe it is eternal because its effect on mankind will be everlasting—without end. And I believe it is infinite because it covers the entire range of our mortal experiences. There is nothing we can go through in this life that our Savior didn't gain power over through his suffering, death, and resurrection. Thus my hands were healed through his power, your body was blessed to take in nourishment while your mind was enlightened with the knowledge of our unborn son, I was protected on the cliff, and so forth. The Atonement, being infinite, is to take away all our sorrows, afflictions, and sins, according to our faith, and give us eternal joy. There's just no way that he would ever exclude you from that glorious act of love and mercy!"

"Then . . . why hasn't it happened? Why don't I feel the peace of knowing that my sins are blotted out?"

Slowly Billy shook his head. "I don't know. Maybe . . . Wait a minute! When you were baptized and received the gift of the Holy Ghost, did you feel the peace of God's love? Did you feel that Christ had remitted your sins?"

Silently Eliza nodded.

"And you willingly gave up everything for him, didn't you. Your family, your friends and associates, your country—you sacrificed it all to gather with the Saints here in America. Did you feel peace about all of that, Eliza?"

"It . . . was a hard thing to do, Billy. But I was so much at peace that I'm at a loss about how to explain it."

Billy smiled. "There's no need to, hon-bun, for I believe I understand. Crossing the plains, where you sacrificed your body and almost your life for your new-found beliefs, did you ever feel bitterness toward the Lord?"

"Absolutely not!" Eliza was adamant. "I knew all along I was doing the right thing, and I felt complete peace about it. Of course, the physical pain was awful, and sometimes I still have nightmares about it. Yet the thought of dying held no terrors for me then, for I knew that, should it happen, I would be encircled eternally in the arms of God's love."

Billy's look was serious. "I believe I'm beginning to understand what you're dealing with, Eliza darling. Would you like me to explain?"

Blinking back sudden tears, Eliza nodded.

"All right. First, you need to understand that there's a difference between being forgiven of a sin and being redeemed from your sins. Anyone can be forgiven of any sin simply by repenting of it—feeling remorse or Godly sorrow, asking forgiveness, making retribution, and so on. The thing is, while being forgiven of one thing, a person may at the same time be sinning in another area, causing him to remain unclean."

"What? I . . . I don't understand."

"All right, suppose a person is a liar and an adulterer. If he completely repents of committing adultery, the Lord will forgive him for it, even though he continues to lie about other things. Do you see what I mean about such a person remaining unclean?"

Eliza nodded thoughtfully.

"Good. But to be redeemed from his sins, which means to be made clean of all of them and given Christ-like peace because he knows he has been pronounced clean, a person must repent of all of them. Turn to the twenty-seventh chapter of Third Nephi, Eliza, and read . . . uh . . . verse nineteen, I believe. These are the words the resurrected Christ spoke to the Nephites."

Turning to Billy's reference, Eliza read: "And no unclean thing can enter into his kingdom; therefore nothing entereth into his rest save it be those who have washed their garments in my blood, because of their faith, and the repentance of all their sins, and their faithfulness unto the end."

"There—repentance of *all* their sins, and faithfulness unto the end." Billy smiled kindly. "I'm certain that, as Christ told both Nicodemus and the Nephites, you repented of all your sins and were born again at the time of your baptism—born both of the water and of the Spirit, and redeemed from your sins through the precious blood of Christ. That's why you felt such peace. You became a daughter of Christ, adopted eternally into his family and lineage. In other words, you felt from day to day like singing the song of redeeming love, which led you to abhor sin as you practiced righteousness and did good for all around you."

"I . . . I did feel like that. But . . . but not anymore! What happened, Billy? What changed?"

"You changed," Billy replied softly. "God certainly didn't, for he is unchangeable from eternity to all eternity. So if a change occurred, it had to be you."

"But what did I do? I was always involved in the Church. I did charitable work, I gave to those less fortunate, I . . . Well, I don't know what I could have done that so blinded me to the truth—about you and everything else of value in my life."

"I don't either, hon-bun. But I do know that in section 93 of the Doctrine and Covenants the Lord revealed a couple of things to Joseph Smith that you might wish to consider." Quickly Billy turned the pages of Eliza's book and began scanning the verses of the noted section.

"Okay, Eliza," he said as he looked up, "I'm going to read a few scattered verses. Listen carefully and see if the Holy Ghost tells you anything about yourself: 'He that keepeth God's commandments receiveth truth and light, until he is glorified in truth and knoweth all things. . . . The glory of God is intelligence, or, in other words, light and truth. . . . Light and truth forsake that evil one. . . . But that wicked one cometh and taketh away light and truth, through disobedience, from the children of men, and because of the tradition of their

327

fathers. . . . What I say unto one I say unto all; pray always lest that wicked one have power in you, and remove you out of your place.'" Looking up again, Billy smiled tenderly. "Did anything come to mind?"

In anguish Eliza nodded. "M-Mary told me I'd been committing sins of omission—not keeping the commandments—by not praying and so on. Not only did that stop me from receiving new light and truth, but it . . . it allowed Satan to come into my heart—to have power in me, it says there—to take away even that light and truth which I had—Oh, Billy, how could I have been so foolish, so evil?"

"I can't answer that, Eliza. But I can tell you that the problem isn't unique to you. Remember when Alma was teaching the people in the Book of Mormon about being born again and receiving the image of Christ in their countenances?"

"I r-remember reading it, but I don't remember the details." Eliza was now weeping.

"It's in the fifth chapter of Alma. You should read the entire chapter when you get a chance. In general, though, the prophet was quizzing the people of the Church, reminding them of events in the past and asking them if they'd spiritually been born of God and experienced a mighty change of heart so that their focus was on spiritual things rather than worldly ones. You know, like what happened to you back in England.

"Then he asked a series of questions to help them formulate an answer in their own minds, so that each could know whether or not he or she had been born of God. At the time of your conversion, you would have answered every one of Alma's questions positively.

"Finally, and this goes to the heart of your question, Eliza, he asked, 'If ye have experienced a change of heart, and if ye have felt to sing the song of redeeming love, I would ask, can ye feel so now?' In other words, it is certainly possible to be born of the Spirit and then to lose it again."

Bleakly Eliza nodded. "By losing light and truth to Satan through not keeping the commandments until we become absolutely blinded. Like I have been the past few months!"

Billy smiled ruefully. "Alma specifically mentions that pride, envy, and mocking people and persecuting them are all ways to lose the Spirit of the Lord and become wrapped again in the bonds of iniquity."

"Oh, Billy!" Eliza looked at her husband, whose face glowed in the dancing firelight. "I . . . I certainly mocked and persecuted you."

Billy said nothing but waited.

"Only," his wife continued, her tears falling unheeded, "I've repented of those things! Or at least I've tried. And that's what I don't understand! Why isn't the Lord forgiving me and giving me peace?"

Setting the scriptures back on the table, Billy took up a handful of sand and let it trickle slowly through his fingers. "Maybe there's more," he finally replied.

"More?"

"Well, yes. More sin, I reckon. Maybe there are other things in your past that you haven't repented of, hon-bun, things that must be resolved before the Lord can give you the peace you desire."

Reaching out, Billy took his wife's hand. "Remember, to be born again, to have the peace that leads to singing the song of redeeming love, requires that we be willing to abandon *all* our sins, even the favorite little ones that nobody but us knows we enjoy."

"Favorite sins?"

Billy smiled. "The little ones we cherish and keep hidden from folks so we can commit them in secret—even while we're repenting of what we tend to think of as the big things. What I'm saying, Eliza, is that a person can't expect to step into the kingdom of God and be born of the Spirit if he's intentionally leaving one of his feet in Babylon. It's an all-or-nothing commitment that God is after. As Alma says, 'Lay aside *every* sin which easily doth beset you, which doth bind you down to destruction.' Do you see, hon-bun? This doctrine is taught again and again in the Book of Mormon. To be born again, and then to maintain that rebirth, we must repent of every sin and then endure to the end. Not just some sins, or even most, but every single one. And then we must keep repenting of the things we continue to do wrong, the mistakes we continue to make, every day thereafter. That's what I believe enduring to the end means, and if I'm going to be honest, that's what I feel is lacking in your life."

Glancing down, Eliza looked again at her copy of the Book of

329

Mormon. "I don't know," she declared softly as she stared without seeing. "I can't even remember all the things I'm certain I've done wrong—all the sins I'm sure I've committed. And I don't mean from before my baptism. I mean since."

Billy nodded knowingly. "I had the same problem. I think we all do. So one day I asked Elder Taylor about it, and he said to go to the Lord and ask that the sins I'd never repented of but that I'd committed be revealed to my mind. That way, he said, I could make amends and proceed forward."

"Did you *do* that?" Eliza was looking at her husband in wonder.

"I did. Mighty scary, too. I mean, until then I'd never thought about how God felt about my life. I'd been pretty much content with it and thought that was enough. But suddenly there I was, on my knees, brazenly asking God to show me who I really was—I mean in his opinion, not mine. 'I'm willing to give away all my sins,' I declared as boldly as King Lamoni's father, 'if thou wilt only remind me of which ones I haven't repented of.' I'll tell you, it was a humbling moment!"

"And . . . did he? Remind you, I mean?"

Billy smiled again and rose to his feet. Then he helped Eliza to hers. "Of course he did. Remember, 'Ask, and ye shall receive.' That's a promise he always fulfills.

"Now, it looks to me as if we're the only ones in this whole camp who are still awake. We even talked through the bugle and company prayer. Since we did, and since some of the men went and got that thousand pounds of blasting powder that the express from Panguitch left at Fifty-Mile, and since that means tomorrow begins another mighty big week of road-building, I reckon we ought to follow the others' example and get us a little shuteye."

"Billy!"

"It'll keep, hon-bun," Billy said with a grin. "Besides, I'm not about to go revealing my dark side to you, Eliza Foreman. At least not tonight. So into the wagon with you, and I'll be along directly."

—◇—◇—◇—

War God Spring

It was cold, colder than the green-haired boy who was now calling himself Posey could ever remember. Even in the wickiup with the fire before him it was cold, and he had drawn himself into the smallest shape he could so that his tattered blanket could better cover him. Now he sat shivering next to his half-brother Beogah and three smaller children while the two women who were not only his mothers but the first and second wives of Chee, his father, took turns stirring the pot.

Posey had no real idea what was in that pot, but he suspected—and the painful hollowness of his stomach confirmed this—that it contained little more than water. That was all it had contained the sun before this one, and the sun before that. On his hunts Chee had slain nothing but two rabbits, and everyone knew such meat was not enough to give a man true strength. Worse, Mike had slain nothing, and neither had the other Pahute braves who were part of the encampment. Thus all the Pahutes under Mike were hungry, and many were in danger of starving.

And that was why both Mike and Chee had left two suns before, going down the mountain to spy on the hogan of the enemy Tsabekiss in Jackrabbit Canyon. Somewhere near his hogan the wily Navajo kept hidden both his horses and his sheep and goats. If the Pahutes could somehow find them, it would be a simple matter to take a mutton or preferably a fat pony, drive it back up the mountain, and skin and butcher it before Tsabekiss and his son Bitseel would even know it was missing.

So now Posey sat in a tiny shivering ball while his anxious ears sorted through the sounds of the night—the moaning wind; the *yah-gi,* crying papooses; the rattling brush—listening for the first faint pounding of distant hooves. Once his father and Mike were back they would eat again, feasting as if there were no tomorrow—

On his head Posey felt the weight of the white man's *katz-oats,* the hat he had traded Beogah's pony for at the trading post across the big river. Already shapeless and smudged with dirt and grime, it was nevertheless sufficiently ennobling to make him feel the power of it whenever it was on his head. Thus it had become his most precious possession, so dear to him that he refused to remove it even in sleep. Of course, he still needed to get a white man's shirt and trousers before he would feel fully the power of the whites, but if they turned out to be as easy to obtain as the hat, then he knew it was only a matter of time.

In fact, only the night before he had *no-ni-shee,* dreamed a dream of taking the shirt and trousers from a white man. It had been an exciting though vaguely unsettling dream, for it seemed as though the white man had been familiar to him—*tig-a-boo,* a friend, who had watched helplessly as he removed the clothing. Of course, such a thought was foolish, for he had no friends among the whites. But still, he had dreamed what he had dreamed, and now he would have to wait and see what it all might mean.

A furious blast of winter wind slammed into the hide-covered wickiup of Chee and his families, sending icy fingers probing everywhere and bringing an even greater chill to the boy with the white man's hat on his head. It was a terrible time of cold and hunger, and Posey was certain he and all the others were close to dying—

"Wagh!" he suddenly breathed as a different sound whispered past his keen ears. "Listen, my brother."

For a moment the two boys strained, and then the sound came again, a little closer. And this time there was no mistaking the identity, the source.

Horses! At least two, and they were coming fast. That meant the news Mike and his father were bringing was good. Wagh! They had captured a fat pony from old Tsabekiss, or perhaps they had captured two! They would eat this night. All of them would eat, and then this terrible time of hunger would end.

Scrambling to their feet, Posey and the larger Beogah piled through the door-flap of the wickiup to wait expectantly beside their mothers. Others from the encampment quickly joined them— Suruipe, Wolf Tail, Tuvagutts, as well as their women and children. All were excited, for all had borne the pains of hunger longer than was desirable.

"*Pikey! Tooish apane!*" Mike ordered before his lathered mount was fully stopped. "Come on! Hurry up! We have found the tracks of horses, Mericat horses, mormonee horses! We counted *soos, so-use, wiuni, piuni, watso-wi-uni, nava-ga-uni*—yes, six big horses and only *so-use,* two, of the whites. They had a good outfit, too—new *carrinump,* saddles and pack saddles, many panniers full of flour and bacon and many other things to eat—things that should belong to the Pahutes. *Pikey, pikey!* Before that fool Tsabekiss makes us lose out!"

"Were these whites at the hogan of Tsabekiss?" Tuvagutts asked, not at all certain that he wanted to brave such a fortress.

"No!" Chee made the sign that it was not so. "They passed the hogan of Old Tsabekiss without stopping, but the tracks of two Navajo ponies followed after them."

For an instant all seemed frozen by the news. But then with wild whoops the three men beside Posey and his brother Beogah bolted for the brush. In short order they as well as Mike and Chee had gathered in five bony ponies. They saddled their mounts with the merciless boards and rawhide the Pahutes were forced by poverty to use as saddles, two threw sheepskins over their ponies' backs and tied them on, and one, old Wolf Tail, simply mounted bareback. Then, once the women had handed each his weapons, the five were off helter-skelter down the mountain, their whoops and yells rending the chill night air.

As the sounds of their pell-mell descent diminished into the distance, Posey suddenly realized that he had been left behind. He, who now wore a white man's hat as well as a white man's name, had been left with the women and children!

"Ho!" he shouted as he turned and sprinted for the brush against the cliff where the ragged ponies were kept, his hands holding his too-large hat and ragged blanket in place as he ran, "they think we are *tow-ats-en,* my brother. They think we are children! I am no child! I am no squaw. I am a man, and I will *nah-oo-quey,* I will fight with the men!"

"As will I!" Beogah shouted from not more than two or three steps behind. "But let us hope they have left us two ponies—"

And within another moment the agile brothers had found two extra ponies, thrown rope hackamores over their noses, gathered up their own puny weapons, and without benefit of saddles or even blankets or skins set off to follow the distant yipping of the men, the true warriors of their People.

41

─○─○─○─

Monday, February 2, 1880

Cottonwood Canyon

"Morning, Eliza."

"Good morning to you, Mary," Eliza responded with what she hoped looked like a happy smile. "Looks like a beautiful day for road-building!"

It did, too. Already the men were well along with the road out of the canyon. And since she was feeling particularly good physically, and also since she was determined not to spend the day dwelling on her past mistakes, it was Eliza's intention to join most of the other women from camp in helping carry rocks to work into the loose and sliding face of the sandhill.

"Lawsy sakes, woman," Mary Jones exclaimed as Eliza picked up a rock and began struggling up the newly cut dugway toward the sandhill. "What are you trying to do to yourself?"

"I'm trying to . . . to help build a road," Eliza grunted as she staggered under the weight of the rock, nearly losing her balance and her crutch at the same time.

"Eliza, this isn't very wise."

"And I'm tired of sitting around worrying!" Eliza declared as she renewed her effort to climb the steep slope with her one large rock. "Besides, Mary, everyone else is helping, and I feel like I should at least do something—"

Her comment cut short by her own yelp of surprise and fear, Eliza dropped both her rock and her crutch and would have tumbled

334

completely off the dugway if Mary Ann Perkins hadn't been there to catch her.

"Th-thank you," Eliza said with embarrassment.

Mary Ann smiled. "You're welcome. But I think Mary's right, Eliza. I don't think you should be doing this."

"Neither do I," Delia Mackelprang declared as she paused and dropped her load of several rocks so she could rest her arms. "If you fall, Eliza, we'll most likely be losing two of you, and that doesn't even count Billy, who I reckon would die of a broken heart if he lost you and the baby."

Knowing they were right, Eliza still felt heartsick. "But . . . I want to do *something!*"

"Glory be, sister. There's plenty to do in this camp without endangering life and limb!"

"Here," Mary said as she stepped to the side of her embarrassed friend, handing her the dropped crutch. "I'll walk back down with you, Eliza. We haven't talked for days and days anyway, and there's a sight of gossip I must catch you up on."

The nearby women laughed, Eliza smiled with them, and with Mary's help Eliza struggled back to the bottom of the draw, where the two stood in silence watching the work progressing above them.

"It's amazing," Eliza finally declared, "how united everyone has become."

Mary nodded. "Like vone big, happy family, as my father says."

"That's hard work, Mary. *Hard* work. Yet look how willing those sisters are to do it."

"No more than you, Eliza."

"Yes, if only I could! Are they making any headway across that sandhill?"

"Not much. No matter how many rocks we carry up for a foundation, or how deep we dig down to put them in place, they still shift and slide away the minute any weight is put on them." Mary's countenance brightened. "But there is hope. Early this morning Kirsten came up with the idea of pouring water into the sand to pack it as the rocks are being placed, and the results look promising."

"What an interesting idea!"

Mary nodded thoughtfully. "It is. Now if it will only work."

Of course, it was a job getting water from the creek up to the sandhill, Eliza thought as she watched people filling water barrels that had been strapped to the backs of their draught animals. But at least they had water sufficient to do it, and animals to carry the load.

Standing out of the way, she shaded her eyes and looked higher, up to the great slickrock mountain where Billy and the Perkins brothers and a few other men were drilling and blasting the rock. She was able to see them there, looking as small as ants while they crawled or hung on the rock face swinging their single- and double-jacks at the drills. From where she stood, it didn't seem like they were accomplishing much, but Billy had told her they would have a dugway blasted out by the time the road was finished across the sandhill, and she had no reason to doubt him.

On the canyon bottom near the beginning of the dugway, the two blacksmiths had set up their forges, using coal carried from across the river, and Eliza could hear the constant ringing of steel against steel as the men reshaped and sharpened the numerous drills being dulled by Billy and the others. It seemed an endless task the two men faced, but their work was invaluable, and there could be no progression without it.

As she watched the missionaries at their labors, Eliza thought again of the amazing unity of purpose among them—their great strength in numbers. Of course, they could progress in no other way, and she knew that all understood that. But still, even the smallest, most menial tasks seemed to contribute to the overall forward movement of the company. And so far as she knew, there was no one who felt that his or her task was unimportant. Unless, of course, it was her.

The entire upper canyon seemed a hive of activity, and after a few moments of leaning on her crutch simply watching, Eliza was already feeling useless and out of place. It was almost as if—

"Eliza, what's been happening in your life? It doesn't seem like we've talked in weeks!"

"Well, days anyway," Eliza responded with a smile.

Mary laughed. "All right. Days. But I still don't know what's happening in your life."

And Eliza, thinking of Billy's idea that old and perhaps forgotten little sins had given Satan power in her and were still holding her back, suddenly decided she didn't want Mary or anyone else to know that all morning she had been considering presenting herself before the Lord in the hopes that he would bring them to her remembrance. Not, at least, until she had tried it.

"You know, Mary," she replied, still smiling but now filled with renewed purpose, "nothing's happening in my life. It truly isn't. But if something does, you can bet you'll be the first, outside of Billy, to know."

———◇—◇—◇———

Begashinitani

Posey had never made such a ride in his entire young life. Neither had he ever been so happy to stop. When after many hours of hard riding Mike had finally given the order to halt, Posey had simply rolled from his pony, pulled his remnants-of-blanket more tightly around him, and collapsed on the ground where he was. Beogah had done the same, and as cold as it was the two boys had fallen almost instantly asleep. Now, though, *tash-a,* dawn, was creeping over the rocks of Nokai Mesa, and a rough kick in the ribs had awakened Posey to the realities of life on the war-trail.

"*Quir-i-ka!*" he of the big mouth ordered with a second kick. "Get up!"

Numb with cold and aching in every joint of his body, Posey staggered to his feet to discover almost immediately that their trail through the time of darkness had led them mostly eastward. They had circled the head of Jackrabbit Canyon, made their way down, through and then up the tortuous sides of Piute Canyon, and across Piute Mesa to a spring where they had paused only to water their ponies, and then in darkness they had ridden on. Down the treacherous slopes of Nokai Canyon they had forced their mounts, circling cliffs on narrow, winding trails and plunging down the sides of bluffs so steep Posey had no idea how he had kept astride his mount. Nor could he imagine that none of the warriors had plummeted to their deaths in the numerous yawning chasms of darkness they had encountered during their wild ride.

Now he could see that they had spent the last two or perhaps three hours of darkness in the head of a narrow canyon, and though he had no idea that the canyon was called *Begashinitani*, he could see easily that the location had protected them from the force of the winds on top of the mesa to the east. He could also see that Mike and the others had lost the tracks of the six big horses.

"Wagh," he muttered to Beogah as he wrapped his blanket more tightly about his shivering, emaciated form, "I did not know that this was the way of war-trails."

"It is *tin-zeer,* a hard way," his brother muttered in agreement. "Perhaps we should have stayed with the camp."

Posey gave his brother a strange look. "And miss this raid?" he asked, his voice filled with derision. "*Poo-suds-a-way-ah,* do you understand, my brother, that this is our chance to become true men? Do you understand that this is our chance to show our father and these others that we are no longer children—that we can ride as far and fight as bravely as any of them? Wagh! I do not fear these whites! I do not fear the cold! I do not fear the hunger! I do not fear the aching in my bones—"

"Do you fear being left behind again?" Beogah asked with a sly grin as he pulled himself onto the back of his pony and urged it up and over the rim of the hill. "*Pikey, tooish apane,*" he shouted gaily just before he disappeared, "or most certainly you will be!"

And Posey, dumbfounded, discovered that he was standing alone in the brush and rocks at the head of *Begashinitani.* Somehow the warriors had departed without his being aware of their going, and now Beogah had gone after them and he was alone with the bony *kuvah-u* he had been riding for what seemed all his mortal life. Worse, as he pulled his aching body back onto the horse and kicked the animal up the hill, he realized he had not taken time to relieve himself. Now he could not do so, and the new day stretching ahead of him suddenly took on draconian implications.

On top of Nokai Mesa, Posey was dismayed to see the others nearly a mile away to the southeast and already skirting the head of the west fork of Copper Canyon. He also saw that his father Chee was signaling to Beogah, who had nearly caught up with them, that they had found the tracks of the two white men, and to be silent in their pursuit.

Now the Pahutes would have the wealth of the two *tsharr,* the two whites; now he and the others would soon have powerful horses, white man's clothing, and all the food they could possibly stuff into their emaciated bodies.

With renewed enthusiasm Posey grabbed his precious hat and flailed his pony's rump with the end of the old hackamore. The bony old horse responded as best it could, quickening its pace and bringing the Pahute youth gradually closer to his brother and the others. But the gait of the pony was rough and getting worse, and each bone-jarring stride threw Posey into a renewed fit of personal agony.

Surely, he thought as his aching legs tightened around the pony's narrow girth in an effort to lessen the painful bouncing and jolting of his body, there had to be an easier way than this to bring wealth, honor, and glory upon himself and his hungry people.

42

Nokai Mesa

The Navajo called Bitseel, who was not very old but who since the Enemy Way sing called by his father had been thinking himself a man, stood and breathed deeply of the chill morning air. The little buckskin mare he had been riding stood behind him, waiting patiently as was her nature, while her grulla colt frolicked nearby. Bitseel had not especially wanted to bring the colt along, but as the colt's mother had been the only riding horse close to the hogan of Tsabekiss his father, he'd had little choice. After all, the colt was still nursing, and it did not do to separate such a fine animal from its mother. Besides, he thought with a smile, this was a day when he felt like the colt, full of life and joy and anxious to shout it to the world.

This was *hózhó,* he thought as the colt ran bucking past, this was balance in the universe. This was the beauty that Changing Woman had taught them to attain, the harmony with the world that his father had taught him to feel.

With his arms uplifted, Bitseel spoke his greeting to Dawn Boy, not shouting because those he followed might be close enough to hear but loudly enough that Dawn Boy would make no mistake about who was chanting. Next he greeted the sun, blessing the new day.

"Let beauty walk before me," he chanted. "Let beauty walk behind me. Let beauty walk all around me."

From the small medicine pouch that hung around his neck, Bitseel took a tiny pinch of corn pollen and tossed it into the clear desert air. "In beauty it is finished," he said quietly. And then with a last deep breath taken to savor the moment, he turned and pulled himself easily onto the back of the little buckskin mare.

This was his second day of following the tracks of the six big horses that wore iron shoes. Bitseel had stumbled on them two suns before when there had been only a little day left in the sky. Later in the hogan of his father he had described his discovery, and preparations had been made for him to take up the trail with the dawning. He had been counseled not to attack the white riders once he caught them, but to hang back and watch carefully, waiting for the proper time to raid the men, take from them their wealth of horses, and deliver that wealth back to his father.

With the first pink light of yesterday's dawn he had been on the trail, his excitement mounting as he saw that the whites were making no effort to hide their tracks. But then, with the sun scarcely two hours above the horizon, many additional tracks had merged upon the trail of the six big horses, smaller pony tracks that were unshod, and Bitseel had known abruptly that he was also following his father's enemies, the despised *No'daá,* the Pahutes, who had taken from his family their ancestral land on Navajo Mountain.

There were many *No'daá,* perhaps as many as eight, far too many for one such as himself, as yet untested in the ways of war, to fight. Such numbers also gave him less hope for the whites, for he now knew that there were only two of them, and four horses carrying heavy loads. These things he had learned after walking around a camp the whites had made, examining carefully the sign each man had made of his living. But now he feared that the *No'daá* would kill the whites before he could catch up to them, which meant that the Pahutes would take the wealth while the hogan of his father would remain empty and hungry.

"Step into the shoes of Monster Slayer," he now chanted as he rode, just as he had under the direction of Dagai Ileto during the Enemy Way sing held by his father. "Step into the shoes of him who lures the enemy to death."

Bitseel had wondered, at his first sight of the pony tracks, if they marked the leaving of the Pahutes. But by nightfall of the previous day he had known that all those he followed were men, which made this a raiding party and not a migration. Of course, he had felt disappointment at this, but even such a disappointment had not deterred him. He would follow as he had been counseled by his father, and perhaps the great *yei* spirit, Abalone Girl, who made her home on the top of Evening Twilight Mountain where the bow people had wounded the Sacred Bear of ancient *Diné* legend, would assist him in bringing wealth back to the hogan of his father.

Much later, above the steeps on the east side of Nokai Mesa, Bitseel stopped to survey the country. Copper Canyon dropped away below him, while off in the distance rose Hoskanini Mesa, where the man Hoskanini had his hogan. Of course, the dwelling of Hoskanini was not yet visible; only the grays and greens of distant sage, rabbit brush, juniper, cactus, gramma and bunch grass, mesquite, piñon, and, in the one or two places where water flowed, pine and spruce. It was a lonely country but beautiful, an important part of *Diné Tah,* where Changing Woman had taught the people to live in the beauty of the way she and the Holy People had taught them.

None of that was in the front of young Bitseel's mind, however. Instead he was thinking of the man Hoskanini, who was part of the crucial "born to" clan of his mother rather than the "born for" clan of his father. All the members of both clans were considered relatives, of course, but those of the "born to" clan carried a much greater responsibility, and because of that Bitseel knew he could turn to Hoskanini for advice and perhaps even assistance.

Besides, he thought with a wry grin as he urged the little buckskin forward, the well-trodden trail of both the shod horses and the unshod ponies also pointed toward the distant hogan of his cousin. Yes, he would stop there and enter in, being careful to do it properly as he had been taught, going sunwise from the entrance on the east toward the south, to the west, and finally to the north, being careful not to step over anyone, and finally taking his seat in the last place before the entrance.

Sunwise. That was the way everything worked when things were *hózhó,* in balance, and it was the way he would have to think from now on if he were ever going to bring wealth back to the hogan of his father. Sunwise. And he was certain that the cousin of his father would help him learn to do it.

———o—o—o———

Cottonwood Canyon

It was awful, Eliza thought as she made her way through the leafless cottonwoods toward what they were now calling the lower pools. Here she was, a thousand miles from anywhere, lost to the world in the midst of a howling wilderness, and still she could find no place where she felt alone. All about her she could hear children squealing and laughing. Women who weren't helping on the road were as apt to pop up one place or another as the children, and the boys who were on herd duty were busy riding here and there checking on the livestock. It was absolutely ridiculous that she could find no place to be alone with her Maker, no place where she could kneel and approach the heavens with her prayers.

Behind her the glass-eyed mare plodded softly through the sand, always friendly and always hopeful that Eliza would turn and give her a good scratching between the ears. Despite her appearance she was a good old nag, and to Eliza's surprise she'd grown quite fond of her. But the mare was old, too, and now Eliza had begun to worry that she would awaken some morning to find her dead. That would be very hard on Billy, and it would most likely be just as difficult for her.

Casting her eyes about, Eliza couldn't see a single place that looked secluded enough for the sort of prayer she felt was coming. Yet from the moment she had walked away from the upper canyon the day before, that is all she had thought of and even prepared for.

It was interesting that each time she had opened the scriptures in the hours since, additional evidence of her need to completely cleanse her life had been presented to her. That had to be more than coincidental! Surely the Lord was answering her pleas, speaking to her through his holy writ, confirming Billy's belief not only that she needed to repent of *all* her sins but also that He would reveal such sins to her when she was ready to ask.

Pondering Billy's idea of big versus little sins, Eliza had begun idly flipping pages and had suddenly found herself reading Nephi's prophecy that in the latter days "there shall also be many which shall say: Eat, drink, and be merry; nevertheless, fear God—he will justify in committing *a little sin;* yea, lie a little, take the advantage of one because of his words, dig a pit for thy neighbor; there is no harm in this; and do all these things, for tomorrow we die; and if it so be that we are guilty, God will beat us with a few stripes, and at last we shall be saved in the kingdom of God. Yea, and there shall be many which shall teach after this manner, false and vain and foolish doctrines, and shall be puffed up in their hearts, and shall seek deep to hide their counsels from the Lord; and their works shall be in the dark."

With a guilty start Eliza had realized she had been one of these people, proclaiming righteousness while secretly believing that God would understand and forgive the little sins she felt she was justified in committing—the poisonous words she had been spreading about Billy in an effort to get those around her to understand why she felt so miserable.

Of course, now she felt awful about it and was doing her best to repent. But were there other things in her past, sins committed so long ago or considered by herself to be so 'little' that she had no recollection of them?

"Apparently," Billy had said, "because of bad memory, faulty judgment, and so forth, we don't have the capacity to remember or see clearly our own sins and weaknesses. Therefore, the Lord has agreed to make them known to us by the power of the Holy Ghost, who as the spirit of truth communicates the truthfulness of all things directly to our spirits.

"Hon-bun," Billy had continued, opening the Doctrine and Covenants, "listen to this passage. 'Verily I say unto you . . . that you are clean, but not all; repent, therefore, of those things which are not pleasing in my sight, saith the Lord, for the Lord will show them unto you.' There, Eliza. Do you see how clear it is? If you have the courage and faith to ask, God will reveal to your mind the things you have never repented of."

The more Eliza thought about what Billy had told her, the clearer the idea seemed—the more right. And now that she had found scriptural verification, she would ask God and then see what sorts of things he actually revealed to her.

At length Eliza reached the lower pools, where the stream had worn a deep watercourse that had later been left dry. Now the old stream bed seemed to offer the privacy she craved, a small space where she could kneel in soft sand and be closely surrounded by the sandstone walls.

Once in the place she had chosen, Eliza stood still, making certain she was alone. There were no voices from nearby, no individuals that she could see. After taking a deep breath to calm her nerves, Eliza lowered herself and began to pray.

Almost immediately, however, a nearby noise distracted her, and she awkwardly pulled herself to her feet. "Fool mare," she muttered as she saw the swaybacked animal snuffing along the bank of the stream a dozen yards away. "This is hard enough as it is, so get on away from here and let me pray in peace!"

Lifting its head the mare nickered softly, and then, as if it had understood completely, it turned and shuffled back up the stream bank.

And Eliza, with a sense of wonder that for the first time ever the mare had willingly obeyed her, leaned on her crutch and once again lowered her knees to the sand.

—◇—◇—◇—

Hoskanini Mesa

As far as young Hoskanini Begay was concerned, the hogan of his father was not a happy place, nor was there *hózhó*, a sense of balance in his father's universe. More than usual he was angry, *tsádeeshnih,* and all who came near were feeling his wrath. Even the woman who was his father's wife and his own mother, one of infinite patience and great diplomacy, had abandoned the hogan to spend a few days with her sheep. Only he had stayed nearby, and he stayed only because he was of a troubled mind concerning his father.

With the good fortune of capturing the herd of *belacani* horses from across the Kaibab, one would have thought that old Hoskanini, whose name was derived from words meaning the Angry One, might better have been called *ana'dlohi,* the laugher. But no, in the cold of the big river at the place called *El Vado de Los Padres,* some *chinde,* some devil, had taken hold of the legs of both him and his cousin, who was calling himself Frank, and had bitten fiercely. Nor had the cramp gone away in the long days on the trail afterward, leaving both men so that they could hardly ride a horse and could not walk alone at all.

All that was bad enough, Hoskanini Begay knew. And yet it was not the worst part of the raid against the weak mormonee *belacani* that had been organized by Frank the day they had all played cards at the Enemy Way ceremony held by Tsabekiss. No, the worst part of the raid had occurred near the end of it, when the horses should have been divided evenly among the raiders.

Instead the man Taddytin, seeing the weakness of both Frank and Hoskanini, had seized control of all the animals by insisting that he alone knew of the best place to hide them. When Zon Kelli had backed him, there had been nothing for the others to do but *bee lá áshleeh*, agree to it. It would have been unseemly and not in the way of the *Diné* to do otherwise.

So the horses had vanished with the crafty Taddytin and his cousin Zon Kelli into the slickrock breaks south and west of the sacred Navajo Mountain, and Frank, Hoskanini Begay, and his father and the others had continued eastward empty-handed to their various places of dwelling. Now many days had passed, Frank had gone on to his own hogan, the *chinde* in old Hoskanini's leg had not released its hold, and no further word had been received from Tattydin and Zon Kelli. It was no wonder, Hoskanini Begay thought as he sat in the cold and watched the door of the hogan, that Tattydin was called the crafty horse thief. And it was no wonder that his father's laughter had died.

But now a new thing was happening, a development that promised to restore the balance that seemed to be lacking all around them. Not more than an hour before, young Bitseel had ridden up and sought counsel at the hand of his father. Hoskanini Begay had bid him enter the hogan, but when he himself would have stayed, his father had ordered him away, out to watch for the approach of others.

Of course, such an assignment was merely pretense—a way for his father to once again express his anger and frustration. Hoskanini

Begay understood this thing, for he understood the power of his father. He also understood that the counsel young Bitseel sought concerned horses—large *belacani* horses—for so the boy had declared before he, the son of Hoskanini, had been ordered out to hold watch. Now these things were big in his mind, and he felt certain that the way had come for his father to regain ownership of that which was rightfully his—the share of horses taken on the long raid to the north.

Hoskanini Begay had been thinking of these things, considering also the insults and wrongs suffered by himself and his father at the hands of Taddytin and Zon Kelli, when he realized that for some time he had been listening to the soft footfalls of approaching horses.

"*Hlohzho,*" the young man said by way of exclamation, for he was truly surprised. Six horses were coming toward him through the rocks and the grasses of the mesa top—not six of the little mustangs so common among his people, but six large *belacani* horses. And only two of them were ridden by *belacani.* The others carried pack-saddles and panniers, and from the way they moved, Hoskanini Begay could tell they were heavily loaded.

These, he realized instantly, were the very horses young Bitseel had been talking about. All along he had thought the youth was speaking of the horses taken on the raid. Instead—

And finally Hoskanini Begay understood that he had been sent out to watch not as a result of his father's anger, but because his father had understood that these two *belacani* would be coming quickly.

With fluid movements the young man rose from his place of seating and stepped into the open, into the teeth of the cold February wind. There he waited, certain he had been seen and wanting to be certain of what he himself was seeing.

And what it was puzzled him. These *belacani,* these white men, were coming from the west, from the direction of the rocky upthrust known from ancient times as *Nokai Cummenthi,* or "where the Mexicans were chased up." But they were also coming from the direction he and his father had taken following the raid. That meant, to young Hoskanini Begay, especially in light of their heavy panniers, that the two must have come from the mormonee settlements where he and the others had raided the horses. No doubt they were come to punish the raiders and take back their stolen animals. It was an uncomfortable moment for the young Navajo, and for the first time he felt glad that Tattydin and Zon Kelli had taken the horses and hidden them.

Now close in, the two men halted and sat for a moment in respectful silence. Finally the one in the rear signed the traditional greeting.

"You are welcome in the hogan of my father," Hoskanini Begay signed back. "We are a poor people, but all that we have belongs to you. Come inside, and I will care for your horses."

The *belacani* nodded his understanding but made no movement to dismount. And neither did the other. Instead they spoke with each other for a moment in their own tongue, speaking so lowly and rapidly that Hoskanini Begay could make nothing of what they were saying. Finally, though, the man made the signs of gratitude and appreciation.

"It has been many days since we have seen our own people," the *belacani* then signed, "and we would make haste to return to them. But our horses need water from your spring, and we would buy food if you have it to sell."

For a moment Hoskanini Begay considered these things. He felt certain that the white men were lying, that in reality they were look-ing for the stolen horses. But he could not deny them water and food without letting them know that he mistrusted them. On the other hand, the time spent by the *belacani* watering their horses could also be spent by himself conferring with his father. Yes, and if he sold them food that they might continue their search, there were always ways of getting the food back again.

"The spring is that way," he signed, indicating the direction with a traditional twitch of his lips. "I will gather a little food while you are giving your horses of our water."

"It is good," the *belacani* signed. Then, reaching into the near-est pannier, he brought forth a large chunk of *beesh ligai,* the white iron known by the whites as silver. "If it is sufficient, we will pay for the food with this."

The silver had no true form and had not been worked, but upon taking it the surprised young Hoskanini Begay knew its value. His face impassive, however, he made the sign of thanks and turned toward the hogan of his father.

"What is it the *belacani* want?" old Hoskanini growled after his son had entered and moved respectfully to the side of the door opening. The youth Bitseel remained silent on the opposite side of the door.

"They say water for their horses and food for themselves." Hoskanini Begay held out the chunk of metal. "They offer *beesh ligai* in trade."

The old man ignored the metal. "It is in your mind that they want more than this?"

"It is in my mind, my father, that they want our horses, the ones we raided from them. Yes, and perhaps they want our lives. It is in my mind that they have come from the mormonee *belacani* settlement and hunt for these things."

"*Chinde! Cliz bekigie!*" old Hoskanini hissed angrily. "Devils! Snake-skins!"

Hoskanini Begay waited patiently.

"Give them a little food," the old man finally declared. "Tell them it is all we have. Tell them we are happy to share it with them. But tell them these things only once or twice, my son, or at most, three times. To say a lie more than this is to lock yourself into the deceit, and you will no longer have *hózhó.*"

"I understand, my father."

"Once the *belacani* have gone, you are to join the son of my cousin in following after them. But as he has been doing, you are to go carefully so you will not be seen. Those fine horses now belong to Tsabekiss because Bitseel has laid claim to them, and because Tsabekiss has become a poor man and needs the wealth. It is up to you to help Bitseel find the best way to make the raid."

"And the panniers?"

Old Hoskanini made the sign of lack of concern. "Perhaps there may be something in them that Tsabekiss does not need. If so, bring it to me and I will decide."

"And what of the two *belacani?*"

"They are *gáagii,*" old Hoskanini declared by way of insult and

349

contempt. "They are crows, afraid of everything. Do with them as you wish."

In the silence that followed, Hoskanini Begay indicated again that he understood. Then, handing the silver to his father, he turned and began gathering a little food. He could not know that old Hoskanini, impressed by the size of the chunk of *beesh ligai,* had already determined, despite the *chinde* in his leg, to somehow follow the backtrail of the two *belacani* on the chance that he might determine where the metal had come from. Neither could he know that neither he nor Bitseel had any sort of a chance of fulfilling his father's wise instructions.

43

Wednesday, February 4, 1880

Cottonwood Canyon

"Eliza, are you feeling all right?"

Looking up at Elizabeth Decker, Eliza smiled wanly. "I'm fine, Lizzie, really I am." And she was, too, except for one or two little things that were praying on her mind.

"Well, it's a beautiful day for feeling good." Lizzie smiled. "Even warmer than yesterday!"

And it was beautiful, Eliza acknowledged to herself. The fire she, Lizzie, and the other women were working around had now been reduced largely to ashes, and each of them were preparing their cast-iron pots, filled mostly with ground-wheat gruel, to be covered by the ashes for an afternoon of slow cooking. That accomplished, all but two or three would climb back to the sandhill, where they would help in the road-building efforts of their husbands and others. The two or three who remained behind, of whom Eliza now accepted that she would usually be one, would turn to stitching and mending for the entire company while they kept their eyes on the food and little children, passing the hours of the afternoon in singing and pleasant conversation.

With the weather so good and wood so plentiful, it was the first time since leaving Escalante that the company had been able to experience such comfort, and Eliza absolutely loved it. Slow-cooked meals were also a real treat, as was the communal fire, for she was finally starting to relax around the others.

"There go those blowers and blasters from Wales again," Eliza

351

Ann Redd giggled as a booming, hollow explosion echoed from up the canyon. "My, but they raise a ruckus!"

"They do. Isn't Billy up there with them?"

Eliza nodded at Harriet Ann Barton and found herself trying to picture her husband working on the face of the sandstone cliff, hammering and drilling and blasting out a dugway that was supposed to resemble a road.

"Billy says it's nearly as bad as the Hole. Personally, I shudder to even think of driving a wagon up such a place, but Mary says it can't be any worse than the sandhill."

"That sandhill is awful," Lizzie Decker agreed. "Not only is it steep, but because of the depth of that loose sand it's turning into a nightmare as far as stabilizing a road across it is concerned."

"According to Lizzie's husband, Cornelius, and George Hobbs," Eliza Ann Redd added as she shooed her daughter Cula off to play, "neither the sandhill nor the dugway are as rough and foreboding as the country hidden beyond them. My father-in-law, Pap, agrees."

Lizzie Decker, who'd almost finished feeding her baby Eugene, nodded. "According to Cornelius, beyond the cliffs we can see, the sandstone lies like great smooth haystacks, filling a country that's already standing on edge so full of hills there's not a yard of level ground anywhere to be found."

"That's the country Platte Lyman considered impassable even for livestock when he first explored it." Harriet Ann Barton was also just finishing nursing her baby. "And now here we are, scratching and digging a roadway through the whole of it just as if it's the right thing to do."

"Which it probably is," Eliza said with a slight smile. "After all, as Platte is so fond of stating, the Prophet Joseph taught that a religion that doesn't require the sacrifice of all worldly things never will have the power to exalt a person in the celestial kingdom."

"Then to my way of thinking," Eliza Ann Redd declared emphatically, "that roadway—in fact this entire expedition—must surely be calculated by God as sufficient sacrifice to exalt the whole bunch of us!"

With that solemn pronouncement the women grew still, each absorbed with her own thoughts. Eliza, wondering anew if she could ever hope for any sort of eternal reward, suddenly found herself yawning. Instantly the focus was back upon her.

"Eliza Foreman," Lizzie Decker stated, "I don't care what you say! With those huge, dark circles under your eyes, you look absolutely exhausted."

"Lizzie's right," Harriet Ann Barton smiled. "Why don't you take the afternoon off, honey. We'll watch the food, and if you have any mending, why, Lizzie and me will do that, too. Meanwhile you skedaddle on back to your wagon and take yourself a long nap."

"And we'll keep those noisy little children away from there, too," Eliza Ann Redd declared knowingly. "Especially my Lula and her gang of friends."

"Honestly . . . I . . . I didn't sleep very well last night—" Eliza was embarrassed, not because she hadn't slept so much as why she hadn't slept. And with a reason like that, it seemed perfectly awful to allow these women to take over her chores—

"Don't you start fixing to argue with us," the normally shy Sarah Hunter stated as Eliza opened her mouth to protest, surprising everyone with her boldness.

"You listen to Sarah," Lizzie said quickly to cover their surprise. "After all, Eliza, you've two lives to care for now, not just one. And most of us know firsthand how difficult that can be. Now shoo, and let us gossip about you behind your back."

"Very well," Eliza smiled, "I'll go. But don't you be saying anything too awful about me. I'll know about it if you do."

The women laughed good-naturedly, and Eliza took up her crutch and made her way back toward her wagon. She felt vastly relieved, too, for she hadn't slept a wink all night long, not because she was remembering anything of past and forgotten sins, but because she had been worrying about what she might remember. Without her required sleep, she'd been feeling dizzy and faint all day, and she could think of nothing more appealing than to cuddle under the blankets in the wagon and sleep the afternoon away.

Why, instead of worrying, she should be counting her blessings! Here she was, surrounded by some of the finest women in the world, carrying the child of the man she loved, and engaged in a cause worthy of the attention of the very angels of heaven.

"Who would not envy me?" she muttered to herself as she opened the side door and pulled herself into the wagon. There she untied and pulled off her shoes, pulled the wonderfully warm quilts over her, and settled herself in the bed on top of the grain.

"Mercy sakes, woman," she muttered, "stop worrying. After all, you've gone and apologized to practically every soul in the company, and some of them more than once. If the Lord has something more to show you, he will, and then you can repent of it. But until then, just relax and go to sleep—"

———◦–◦–◦———

"Do any of you know what's going on with Eliza?"

Nonplussed, the women around the fire looked at each other, and then in the direction of the Foreman wagon.

"Three days ago she apologized to me for anything bad she might ever have said about Billy."

"She did the same with me."

"And me. And I don't think I'd ever spoken to her before in my life." The woman giggled. "Of course, I'd heard a few things—"

"Hadn't we all? Merciful heavens!"

"Well, I don't think what she's doing is right!"

"What isn't right?"

"You know, hanging out your personal troubles like a batch of laundered unmentionables, for everybody to see and gawk at."

"She's a strange one, too, all lifted up in her pride the way she is! I've said it since the beginning of this expedition, and I haven't changed my mind one whit."

"What on earth do you mean by her being lifted up in pride?"

The woman sneered. "I mean the way she has to have her table and chairs out and set up under that canvas awning, with her china and silver and crystal all perfectly set on that lacy tablecloth, like she was putting on the world's most elegant banquet, for heaven's sake!"

"Maybe she thinks she's too good to eat like the rest of us do!"

"Well, I shouldn't wonder if that was so. The way I hear it, she makes poor Billy take those things out of her wagon of an evening no matter if he's exhausted or not. Pride, I say! Pure and simple pride!"

"I don't know whether Eliza's prideful or not, and I've certainly never heard of Billy complaining. But I will say I enjoy seeing her table all set the way she does it. Somehow it helps me to remember home—to feel civilized in this desolate wilderness."

"I feel the same! And as for her going around apologizing to everyone, that seems like a mighty strange way of showing pride."

"Humph!"

Another woman smiled. "Mary Jones says Eliza is simply trying to repent of some personal things and put her life back in order."

"If they're personal, then she ought to keep them personal!"

"That's all well and good, unless you've offended someone. According to the scripture, you can't repent of that until you've gone to that person and made it right."

"But she didn't offend me! Like I said, I'd never spoken to the woman, and she'd certainly never spoken to me!"

"But you did listen to gossip. You just admitted that. And if you're anything like me, you most likely passed it on, at least to your husband."

"Now, see here—"

"I'm not condemning you, sister—I've done it, too." The woman's voice grew soft. "I just think we need to understand that Eliza feels responsible not alone for what she's said to a few of us about Billy but also for the gossip her remarks have stirred up throughout the company. Mary says that's why she's apologizing to everyone."

"That makes sense."

"It does."

"More than that, to my way of thinking it shows a *mountain* of courage, not to mention humility."

"That," someone muttered, "or stupidity—"

———o—o—o———

Eliza opened her eyes abruptly. It seemed only seconds that she'd been asleep, yet she knew from the shadows that several hours had passed. She had been dreaming, too, a vague sort of disquieting dream that she could almost, but not quite, remember.

"Dear Father in heaven," she prayed before she'd even moved, "if my dream is something I'm supposed to remember, something to do with my repentance, wilt thou please put it back into my mind—"

And then suddenly she did remember, and as she did, tears started from her eyes and flowed unchecked onto her pillow. Billy had been right. The Lord was revealing to her the sins she'd never repented of, the little things she'd long ago brushed off as mere annoyances to her conscience but that were apparently large enough to keep her from finding the inner peace she so desperately craved.

"Oh, dear God in heaven," she wept in anguish, "I . . . I didn't mean to say those things to her . . . Yes, yes, I did mean to say them, and I accept responsibility for them. But I'm so sorry, and I feel so ashamed. Wilt thou please forgive me, and wilt thou help me know what I must do to be cleansed through the precious blood of thy Son—"

Abruptly in her mind another thought formed, and with terrible energy Eliza threw back the quilts and scrambled across the grain toward the back of the wagon. There she found the small wooden secretary she had purchased in Salt Lake City so many years before. Squatting on the grain with the secretary on her lap, she opened the lid and removed paper, her ink bottle, and her beautiful pen, and with feverish haste she began to write:

Cottonwood Canyon, San Juan Mission, 1880, Febr. 4th

My Dear Sistr Jewall.

Perhaps you do not remember me, but with great shame and sorrow I recollect an encounter we had this summer past near the bank in Cedar City. If you will please remember, it had been raining—

———o–o–o———

"I'm telling you, hon-bun, this could turn out bad, mighty bad. Some of the boys are even talking about packing guns, they've grown so suspicious of each other."

It was late, and Billy had only barely come down off the cliff and finished milking their cow. Now he was wolfing down his supper as if he hadn't eaten in a week, doing his best to fill Eliza in on the news while he ate.

"It's the Robb boys and some of the others. They weren't called on this mission like some of the rest of us, and now it turns out they didn't join the company to be missionaries, either. Fact is, they've viewed it as a money-making proposition from the start, which according to some of the rest of the boys is contrary to the mind and will of the Lord. You can't serve God and mammon, you understand.

"As it turns out, however, the real issue is grass. Feed. All those hundreds of horses the Robbs are figuring on selling once they get into Colorado, well, they're eating circles around the rest of the livestock. At least that's what's being claimed. Now the Robbs, the Butt brothers, and those with them are talking about taking their horses and going on ahead once we get on top of the mesa, and that isn't setting very well with some of the rest of the company.

"Why? Precisely because of the feed issue. Some of the brethren feel that if those hundreds of horses go on ahead, they'll eat all the feed in the whole country, leaving barren ground for the rest of us when we finally get there. And that's why they're all talking about packing guns. Some of the brethren intend to stop them no matter what, and some of the others intend to break away and push ahead despite the consequences.

"I'm telling you, Eliza, it could turn into a real donnybrook. And the worst thing about it is that none of them on either side see that such contention is of the devil; it will drive out the Spirit of the Lord so fast we'll all be wondering what hit us. Why, it wouldn't surprise me if we started having accidents, serious ones, and illnesses, too. But worse than that, far worse, is the possibility that our entire mission will fail, and we'll all be ineffectual in our peacekeeping efforts once we get to the San Juan.

"Of course myself and Kumen and some of the others have been trying to say that, mostly to no avail. Now I've got a terrible feeling something bad is about to happen, something truly awful. I don't know who it will happen to, but there's murder in the air, and I can feel it. Something or someone connected to the success of this mission is filled with the spirit of murder—"

Billy stopped, for the first time realizing that his wife had not yet spoken. Looking at her in the lamplight he was surprised to see the evidence of tears on her face.

"Eliza, honey," he said as he put down his bowl and rose to his feet to put his arms about his wife, "what is it? What's happened to you?"

Her tears starting again, Eliza allowed herself to be embraced. "It's started, Billy," she whispered. "It truly has."

"What? What's started?"

"My memories, Billy. The Lord is bringing to my mind the memory of sins I've committed and not repented of, sins I'd completely forgotten about!"

"Oh, hon-bun, I'm sorry. Are there many of them?"

Drying her eyes, Eliza shook her head. "O-only one, at least so far."

Gently Billy stroked his wife's back. "Was it bad?"

"Terrible! Perfectly terrible! Do you remember Sister Jewall from back in Cedar? Well, one day after it had rained, she came hurrying along the street in her buggy, and when she rode through a puddle the wheels of her outfit sprayed me head to foot with water and that sticky mud.

"Of course, I gave her a piece of my mind, you can bet on that. But today I had a dream, and the Lord showed me how she had been in a desperate hurry to get to one of her children who had been terribly hurt, and how my harsh words had cut her so deeply that now she's stopped going to her Thursday and Sunday meetings, and—Oh, Billy, darling, what have . . . have I done?"

Billy, understanding fully how Eliza was feeling, could only hold her close and wait for her pain and her new flood of tears to subside. And for the first time that day, at least in his mind, the issues of horses and feed and the spirit of murder were forgotten.

44

Thursday, February 5, 1880

Mitchell Butte, Monument Valley

"Did you just hear something?"

It was breaking day over the distant Carrizo Mountains, and Ernest Mitchell was kneeling poised above the fire, a turning fork in his hand. This would be their sixth day since leaving Gold Canyon, and he felt well pleased for having talked the shrewd old Navajo Hoskanini into trading a bag of flour and some side meat for a small chunk of their silver ore. Had it not been for that, he and his partner might well have perished from hunger. But now they had enough to last through the three days yet required to get back to his folks at the trading post. And for some reason Ernest was feeling a deep desire to get there as soon as possible. He didn't know why, of course, for he'd always been of a wandering nature, leaving home at the slightest opportunity. But today he felt differently, willing to ride the rest of the way without stopping if only Jim Merrick and the horses had been able.

"I'm telling you, Ern, I heard something!"

Glancing around, Ernest saw that the older man was with the horses, which he'd only just started loading for the trail. Around him in all directions nothing else seemed to be moving, nothing at all. Near dark the night before, they'd climbed the steep, talus-strewn slope of one of the buttes this part of the Navajo country was famous for, looking for a secure camping site. And at the very base of the butte they'd found what they were seeking, a shallow cave surrounded by huge boulders that in ages past had crashed down from

359

above. In the area between the boulders and the cave had been sufficient grass for the horses, and a small fire just outside the mouth of the cave had warmed them without being visible to prying eyes. And they still had water from the spring called *Clee betow,* where they'd filled their canteens and watered the horses the afternoon before.

Of course, Ernest thought wryly, for those who might have been interested their tracks *were* visible—

"What did you hear?" he asked quietly.

"I don't rightly know. Something. But it wasn't natural, I can tell you that. I've got me a bad feeling, Ern, like we ain't alone up here."

"Well, act natural, Jim, and don't go looking scared. If we've got company it's likely because they're just curious. Sometimes some of these Navajo folk are like that. Most likely if we give them our breakfast, things'll be just fine."

"I don't know. My insides are all knotted up like they were that day at your pa's post when that Pahute kid was standing at the door—like folks was walking all over my grave. I'm telling you, Ern, something bad's going on around here, and I don't like it!"

In the silence that followed, Ernest rose slowly to his feet. His partner was right, as right as rain in the spring, and he could feel it too. There was no sound in the cold morning air, not even a breath of wind to moan around the rocks. Yet the six horses were standing still, their heads erect and nostrils distended, and that meant something or somebody was out there. Only nothing moved—not anywhere! Fact is, like that fellow Curly Bill somebody-or-other who was now cowboying for Spud Hudson up under the Blue Mountain might have put it, the whole situation was making him feel jumpy as a bit-up bull in fly time—

"How did we record those claims in the tin cans back in *Oola Bikooh?*" he asked quietly. "I mean, did we list us as you 'and' me, or you 'or' me?"

"It was 'or.'"

"Good. That means we don't both have to be there to file. If anything happens to me, Jim, you pile on that horse of yours and hightail it out of here—pronto! Get to Mancos and file those claims. Do that, and our trip won't have been wasted."

"I'd expect you to do the same," James Merrick stated as he

stooped and lifted the gold-filled saddle bags to place them on his horse.

"I will. And don't get to worrying about the gold and silver we've been hauling, you hear? Just leave it for now. Whatever it's worth, it can't match the value of our lives."

Guiltily James Merrick looked at his partner. But the young man hadn't been looking at him, couldn't have known that he was loading the gold even as he was speaking. So of course he was only expressing his opinion and not giving specific instructions. Besides, the gold was now loaded across the withers of his horse, and if he did have to make a run for it, he wasn't about to leave that much wealth behind! Not when—

"Jim, where's your rifle?" Ernest Mitchell was still looking away, studying the circle of rocks that surrounded them.

"Here under my saddle."

"Good. Don't pull it out, but keep it close to hand. Mine's stuffed in my soogans behind my saddle, so I reckon neither of us looks too awful threatening. I'm going to mosey on down to those rocks, see if maybe I can draw out whoever it is that's giving us the once-over. Keep an eye out, pardner, and give a holler happen you spot something I don't."

"You be careful, Ern!"

"I will," Ernest replied as he strode purposefully toward the circle of rocks he'd been watching. And he would, too. Why, most likely there was nothing ahead of him, at least nothing to be feared. After all, he'd seen no movement, heard no sound. And besides, the Navajos he'd met at his father's post had all been good folks—

And then, appearing as if by magic directly before him, was a man, a Pahute, with the widest, ugliest mouth Ernest Mitchell had ever seen. That was startling. But worse, and what truly caused young Ernest Mitchell's heart to begin pounding in his chest, what truly grabbed him by the throat and began squeezing, was that in the Pahute's hand was an old rifle that was pointed directly at him. And on the Pahute's face was a sneer, a horrid gash of a smirk that bode more evil than Ernest Mitchell had ever seen!

"*Oo-ah,*" the man growled in a guttural voice, threatening with the rifle as he spoke, "*mug-gi quap!*"

"What's he saying?" James Merrick whispered from behind.

"He . . . he wants us to give him tobacco," Ernest Mitchell breathed, not taking his eyes from the Pahute as he spoke—not taking his eyes from the gaping muzzle of the gun. "And since we don't have any, that's going to be a little difficult. You ready to ride?"

"Well, yeah, I reckon."

"O . . . kay." The young man gulped to steady his voice. "If for some reason I don't make it, leave your rifle alone. Just get out of here, fast! Head directly east past Gray Whiskers rock to that little butte just this side of the East Mitten. Go northeast from there until you hit the river, and was it me, I wouldn't stop for nothing till I got there."

"But Ern, I'm not going without you!"

Ernest smiled thinly. "And I ain't planning on going anywhere without you, either, Jim. But I am warning you to get ready, because there's no telling what this feller with the rifle is going to do."

"But . . . but there's only one."

"So far." Ernest took another deep breath. "I'll see if I can make a little medicine with him—"

In that instant, from all around them, more than a half dozen additional Pahutes rose to their feet, arrows nocked and bows drawn to the full as they stared without expression at the young man and his much older companion.

And in that same instant, without another word being spoken, something slammed hard against Ernest Mitchell's stomach, something that didn't exactly hurt but did about knock him over. As he caught his balance and saw the smoke billowing outward from the end of the Pahute's old rifle, the young man with the ready smile who was given to trusting all his Indian neighbors knew abruptly that he'd been murdered—that he'd never be going home again.

———o—o—o———

Mitchell Butte, Monument Valley

"Ho!" The young Pahute who was calling himself Posey grunted in surprise. The report from Mike's rifle was still reverberating in his ears, and he found himself staring in amazement as the man from the

362

trading post across the big river caught his balance, put his hands to his stomach, and then brought them upward again, finding them smeared bright red with *pwap.*

"*Ki yiii!*" one of the others shrieked, beginning his war chant. It sounded like maybe it was the warrior Suruipe, though Posey didn't turn to look. Instead he continued staring at the wounded white man, whose still-smiling expression was slowly turning to shocked disbelief.

Awkwardly the wounded one turned toward the other white man, the one whose hat Posey now wore, and took one or two steps in that direction.

"*Co-que!*" Mike ordered as he *to-wudge-ka,* as he hastily began reloading his rifle. "Shoot!"

And as Posey continued to watch in fascination, two arrows flew from around him to strike with solid thuds into the wounded man's side and back, knocking him forward onto his face in the dirt.

"Ri . . . ride, Jim! Ride!" the man screamed from where he lay. "D . . . don't forget my family—"

There was an instant clatter of hooves, and Posey and everyone else turned to see the other white man now mounted and leaning low over the neck of his horse, quirting it mercilessly through their ranks and down the steep slope of the butte. To their further chagrin the Pahutes next watched as all the other horses belonging to the white men, including the one with the empty riding saddle, followed after.

With grunts of surprise and admiration the Pahutes turned their weapons on the fleeing white man, sending a half-dozen arrows into both him and his big horse. But it wasn't until Mike finally fired his old rifle again that the man straightened abruptly in his saddle, seemed to ride fearlessly for a moment, and then gradually slumped forward to continue his wild ride down the eastern side of the butte.

"*In-e-to-ah! In-e-to-ah!*" Mike shouted angrily as he struggled to pour more powder into the barrel of his rifle. "He gets away!"

As one, all the warriors but Mike turned and sprinted toward where Beogah had been left to hold the horses. And it was only in the turning that Posey saw from the corner of his eye that the first white man, the one with the awful hole in his stomach, had somehow disappeared. Still, Mike and his rifle were there to bring *e-i,* death, to that one. Yes, and to do it in a hurry, too. Meanwhile, here was Beogah and his pony, and there were the others already pounding down the slope after the escaping white man.

Wagh! Yes! What more could a man ask than to join in such a chase? What more could a man hope for in life—

———○—○—○———

The Floor of Monument Valley

"Is the white man *e-i?*" Beogah shouted as he pounded along beside Posey, his wild hair and tattered blankets flying in the wind. "*Peshadny,* brother! Speak!"

"If that one is not dead," Posey responded, still thinking of the gory hole in the man's stomach that had appeared there so suddenly, "then he is very *puck-kon-gah,* my brother. Very sick."

"Did one of your arrows bury itself in his back?"

Startled, Posey thought back. And it was only then that he realized with chagrin that his hand still clutched the bow and single arrow he had managed to pull from his coyote-skin quiver—the arrow he had never even thought to fire.

"Of course I shot," he answered gruffly, trying desperately to hide his shame. "But in that same instant the man moved—"

"You did not hit him?" Beogah was stunned, for he well knew how close Posey had crept before standing to reveal himself.

"I did not say that!" Posey was growing more and more angry, more and more determined to declare his courage and so hide the awful truth. "I was about to say that I do not know if I hit him. It is the same with the one we now follow. Some did hit him. Perhaps I was one of them. But this much I saw today, brother. Arrows are worthless. Instead it is the round balls from the big gun of the man Mike that do the swiftest killing. Like *quan-a-tich* the eagle, those balls fly fast and true, faster even than a man can see. One day, my brother, I will have a big gun such as that one. *Wagh!* Yes! And then we will see how many of these weak and foolish whites I will put into the dust. *Oo-ah.* Then we will see—"

———○—○—○———

364

Merrick Butte, Monument Valley

When young Bitseel and Hoskanini Begay, as well as the colt that had followed Bitseel all the way from the hogan of Tsabekiss his father, finally came up with the Pahutes, at least one of the two *belacani* they had been sent to follow was dead. The other was nowhere to be seen, and so the two Navajo youth assumed—for the moment at least—that he had somehow escaped. But this one, alone on the arid floor of the valley beneath the little butte and surrounded by the exultant Pahutes, would never ride anywhere again.

Slowing their tired and lathered ponies to a walk, the two Navajo youths rode to within a few yards of where the Pahutes had already stripped the clothing from the dead *belacani*. Now they were shrieking victoriously and prancing around as they pulled various items of the man's clothing over their heads or atop their own rough wear.

One, however, remained apart from the celebrating, a young Pahute about Bitseel's own age who had not even dismounted from his pony. Now, as he glanced at Bitseel and Bitseel at him, seeing his ragged blanket and shapeless hat that had once belonged to a white man, the knowledge was somehow in Bitseel that this was the one whose cap he had stolen from the camp high on Navajo Mountain—this was the one against whom the Enemy Way ceremony had been performed!

"*Chinde! Cliz bekigie!*" Bitseel hissed venomously, his full hatred of these filthy Pahute marauders coming to the fore. After all, it was they who were ruining his father and who had somehow beaten him and Hoskanini Begay to the wealth of the two *belacani*. Yes, and it was this one especially who now seemed the most arrogant, the most haughty about his evil ways. "Devil!" Bitseel hissed again. "Snake-skin!"

Though the men on the ground ignored his name-calling, for a moment the Pahute youth on the pony looked his way. But his gaze was unwavering, and Bitseel could detect no fear in him. Instead of growing angry, however, the Navajo youth's mind was suddenly filled with part of the Enemy Way chant taught him by Dagai Iletso, the *haáthali,* the singer.

Step into the shoes of
Monster Slayer—
step into the shoes of
him who lures the enemy
to death.

"*Chinde! Chinde!*" Bitseel hissed again, this time directing all his power at the mounted youth. And then, thinking of the fact that because of the power of the chant this ragged one would somehow be lured to his death within less than a year, he grinned knowingly. "*Adókeedí,*" he smirked with perfect malice. "Beggar!"

And then, to Bitseel's dumbfounded horror, the Pahute boy's tongue flicked out of his mouth exactly as a snake's tongue did, running in and out, in and out, making an unthinkable mockery of Bitseel and all the people of the *Diné.*

In anger Bitseel lifted the rifle he had carried for so many days. But before he could even level it, all the Pahute warriors were suddenly facing him, their bows drawn and ready.

"*Cliz bekigie!*" he hissed again as he slowly backed the tired little buckskin pony back to where Hoskanini Begay was silently waiting. Then, with a twitch of his lips in the direction of the youth, Bitseel said with derision to his companion, "*Wóóseetsínii,* the grub worm."

Hoskanini Begay and Bitseel chuckled together, the Pahute on the pony disdainfully turned his attention back to what his companions were doing, and after that the two Navajo youth sat patiently, waiting to see what might yet develop that would be to their advantage.

Shortly from a nearby wash another young Pahute emerged, this one carrying a fine saddle, bridle, and bedroll. He was shouting happily, and though neither Bitseel nor his companion understood the Pahute tongue, both knew well enough that at least one of the fine horses belonging to the *belacani* lay dead in that wash.

There was a brief scuffle among all the Pahutes over the *belacani* belongings, and in an instant one of the older men had seized both saddle and bridle from the youth and was strapping them to his own scraggly pony. Proudly the youth then waved the blankets from the bedroll in the air, only to have another warrior seize one of them from him and throw it over his own pony. When the youth thought to complain, he was brought face-to-face with the man's *béésh,* his knife. Instantly silenced, he and all the others were staring angrily at each other when the mounted one, the one for whom Bitseel was feeling an intense personal hatred, suddenly wheeled his bone-thin pony and kicked it viciously in the ribs.

Dirt flew as the pony squealed and leaped away, and by the time the other Pahutes had mounted their own scraggly ponies and exploded like a covey of quail after him, the hated one was out of sight behind his own distant cloud of dust.

For a moment the two young Navajos watched them ride away. Then without a word to each other, they reined their own ponies toward the wash from which the Pahute had emerged.

Moments later they found the big horse, a bay, shot full of arrows and with its throat slit wide, lying in the sandy bottom of the wash. It was surrounded by blood and tracks, and it took only a moment for them to see that the *belacani* had crawled from the downed horse, pulled his way up the steep embankment, and apparently crawled to where the Pahutes had killed and stripped him.

Idly following the blood trail, Bitseel dismounted and pulled himself up the same bank the wounded white man had managed to climb. And it was near the top, in the shadow of a small brush growing from the side of the wash, that Bitseel found the recently disturbed badger hole.

Reaching into the hole, he felt around until his hand came upon what felt like leather. Surprised by its weight, he carefully dragged it out, and to his further surprise Bitseel found himself the new owner of a pair of finely tooled *belacani* saddlebags.

"What little thing did the *No'daá* crows miss?"

Bitseel looked up at Hoskanini Begay with a smile. "Ah, brother," he replied, "they missed these fine *belacani* bags. They are very heavy."

"Have you opened them?"

Bitseel made the sign that he had not. While his companion watched from horseback, he undid the buckles, lifted the leather flaps, and peered inside.

"*Oola,*" he said softly after he had examined both pouches.

"*Oola?* That is all they contain, brother? Gold?"

With only a little difficulty Bitseel dumped the gold from both bags onto the ground. "That is all," he declared sadly after again examining the pouches. "*Oola.*"

"Humph," Hoskanini Begay muttered. "This is a strange thing, that a man would think to hide gold when he might have hidden something that would help him escape the *No'daá,* the Pahutes—a rifle, perhaps. But then, there is no way to know the strange thoughts of the *belacani.*"

"Do you wish the bags?" Bitseel asked, making the sign that he understood and agreed with his companion's assessment.

"I have no need for them, brother. Nor has my father. Fill them with the gold and carry them to the hogan of Tsabekiss. Perhaps the bags and the *oola* within them will be of some use to him."

"Perhaps." Bitseel had great doubt about it, but he nevertheless did as he had been directed. And then slowly, for they were in no hurry, the two young Navajo warriors followed the trail left by the scurrying Pahute braves. Nor did they follow it exactly but crossed it back and forth, their keen eyes always watching for anything out of the ordinary.

By the time they had come to the foot of the steeps below the butte toward which the Pahutes had been riding, they had found another of the large *belacani* horses, broken packsaddle trees dragging behind it. And though they had not found James Merrick's fine rifle, which was buried in the sand back beneath the body of his dead horse, they had nevertheless found wealth. And thus they were content.

———o–o–o———

Mitchell Butte, Monument Valley

"Is it in your mind that the *No'daá* yet await us?" Hoskanini Begay asked, indicating with his lips the direction his thoughts were taking him.

Bitseel looked upward. "They seem to be a people of little patience, brother. Though the tracks of their ponies lead upward, my

368

thought is that they will also lead down in another place. I do not believe they await us."

Hoskanini Begay nodded, and then carefully and slowly both he and Bitseel urged their ponies up the boulder-strewn steeps of what would soon be known as Mitchell Butte. Already they had located two more of the *belacani* horses that the Pahutes had missed, one with empty panniers and the other carrying a saddle, a bedroll, and a fine rifle. Truly would they return to the hogan of Bitseel's father with the wealth that he deserved.

It was now very late in the afternoon, and even in the shade of the butte it was comfortably warm. Bitseel noted this, and he noted as well the calling of a flock of crows from off toward Gray Whisker Rock. The day was cloudless, a pleasant one, and the only movement anywhere in the vast valley was a dust devil—the Hard Flint Boys playing tricks on the Wind Children. It was a time, Bitseel thought as he urged his pony upward, for a man to be happy, to find *hózhó,* balance in his world. It was a time—

"Brother, we are not alone."

The soft voice of Hoskanini Begay urged caution, nothing more. But to Bitseel caution was an active thing, and in an instant he was off his pony and crouched low, looking around. Hoskanini Begay was also on the earth, and with a sign he indicated that he had heard something from above them, out of sight behind a rim of boulders.

Each choosing his own course, the two secured the horses and then ran soundlessly forward, dodging and weaving but encountering no opposition until they reached, within yards of each other, the rim of boulders Hoskanini Begay had indicated. There they paused, still saw and heard nothing, and so moved forward once again, through the rocks and into a small amphitheater of grass backed by a cave at the very base of the butte. And it was from that cave, now that they were close enough to tell, that a sound was issuing forth— the quiet sound of a chattering man.

"*Bizahaláanii,*" Hoskanini Begay breathed in awe, "that one is filled with many words."

Carefully the two young Navajo warriors moved forward, noting the indications of battle, the blood on the grass and rocks, the signs of the wounded *belacani* dragging himself forward, past the rocks that littered the mouth of the cave, and into the cave itself.

" . . . no use, Jim. I . . . should have seen it coming. I . . . That gold was too . . . heavy, Jim . . . slowed us . . . down—"

The sounds of talking, Bitseel and Hoskanini Begay could now tell, were coming from the cave. Carefully they inched forward, their weapons ready, until they could see clearly the shadowy interior.

"Jim? Is . . . that you, Jim?" the naked and badly wounded man gasped as he sensed their approach. "Why'd you come back? I . . . They got me, Jim! It was th . . . that kid, the one I give your hat to. The . . . ugly one shot me, . . . shot me good. But I . . . I was fixing on hiding until . . . until . . . He stole my britches, Jim. That kid . . . he stole . . . my . . . britches . . . I told him I was his friend . . . I did. But . . . didn't even wait until . . . I was . . . I was . . . I wrote my ma, Jim. Take my letter to Ma and ride . . . I hid it . . . under me . . . Roll me over and get it . . . Watch out for that kid with your hat, Jim. He ain't our friend no more! You know . . . the one we called . . . the one we called Posey—"

For a moment Bitseel and Hoskanini Begay stared at the naked man, trying to understand his gasping, halting words. Yet neither moved, neither inched one step closer to the dying man. After all, it was not a good thing for a man of the *Diné* to spend much time in a place of the dying or the dead, and both of them knew it. To do so would not please the *yei,* the Holy People, who might at any time vent their malice upon the earth and upon all who had offended them.

Therefore, as if on signal, the two stepped backward from the cave across the small meadow and through the ring of boulders, never once removing their gaze from the mouth of the cave. There they turned and hurried to their waiting horses, and within moments they were hurrying down the steep, talus-strewn slope.

Far off to the west the sun had set, and sunrays from below the horizon were lighting distant cloudbanks and reflecting red, converting the yellow hue of the universe into a vague pink tint. Shortly the two were riding hard together and leading their captured horses into that light, the man in the cave already forgotten as they considered with satisfaction the honor they were returning to the hogans of their people.

45

Monday, February 9, 1880

Cottonwood Canyon

"Platte, have you noticed how drawn and thin the folks are getting?"

Lowering the pickax he'd been using to chip away jagged parts of the sandstone wall on the south side of what they were calling the dugway, Platte Lyman nodded. "I have, Billy. Everyone's looking mighty ganted, all right, and I haven't seen a wagon that isn't being held together in one place or another with tied rags. Dick Butt and some of the other cowboys are calling us a rawhide outfit, and I don't think they're far wrong."

"Is everybody suffering from the dysentery?"

"Like you, you mean?" Platte smiled wisely, and Billy returned the smile.

"Yeah, like me."

Slowly the mission leader nodded. "Most everyone, at least so far as I've heard. Of course, it's the coarse food that's causing it. Not too many are used to a diet composed almost exclusively of ground wheat and oat bran, with now and then a little stringy beef tossed in." Platte sighed deeply. "I don't know, Billy. Some days I feel so tired and worn down it's all I can do even to crawl out of bed. We should have been on the San Juan weeks ago, and the way it's looking we won't get there for another couple of months. Just thinking on that gets a man discouraged."

Knowing what his leader was saying but not wanting to make it any worse, Billy looked up beyond the nearly finished dugway to

371

where a large crew of people were laboring in a steep, narrow ravine they were calling the Little Hole. It was nearly as steep as the notorious Hole-in-the-Rock across the river had been, with the added disadvantage of sharp drop-offs that had to be shored up with carefully stacked boulders. Virtually every able-bodied person in the company was now working to build up these areas, including the older children.

"It's good to have those Panguitch boys with us. They're fresh as daisies, so I reckon the rock is going to fly now."

"That it is." Platte grinned ruefully. "If those boys will give us a full week, we'll be out of Cottonwood and onto the top of Gray Mesa, maybe even through Wilson Canyon. According to George Sevy, that leaves just the Slickrocks to go down before we have pretty much level traveling ahead of us. You know, Billy, us putting a road through this country is nothing short of a miracle. Why, without the Lord opening the way for us to receive that thousand pounds of blasting powder, and without him inspiring these Panguitch boys to come to our assistance, we'd never in our lives be able to complete this roadway.

"Fact is, I sent both Captain Smith and Elder Snow letters today telling them those exact things—telling them we were all witnesses of a mighty miracle, and that every day of our lives we felt to thank the Lord."

Picking up a large chunk of sandstone to cart to the downhill side of the dugway, Billy smiled. "I believe that, too, Platte. I also believe that if God'll provide miracles for us on this road, he'll surely do the same with our food. Either he'll bless us with more, or, like he did with the ancient Nephites, he'll bless our bodies so we can thrive on what we have."

Lifting his pickax and laying it momentarily over his shoulder, Platte sighed. "Of course you're right, Billy, and I appreciate your pointing it out to me. It's just that, being acting captain, I feel a sense of burden I'd rather not feel. Especially I feel it when I look at folks like old Father Stevens, or Pap Redd or Emma Decker or Olivia Larson or, for that matter, your own dear Eliza. When I see those women big and awkward with child; when I see that aged veteran Roswell Stevens who fought so valiantly in the War between the

372

States, or Jens Nielson who got so crippled in the snows of Wyoming; or whenever I see any of the little children who are too young to understand why they have to be hungry, then my heart breaks, and it's all I can do to hold back the tears. I suppose that's the burden of leadership, Billy, but I would to God that he'd lighten it for me. Either that or somehow give all of us a little respite from this daily grind and toil."

As sudden tears splashed from Platte Lyman's eyes and disappeared into his beard, Billy felt his own heart going out to the man. Surely, he thought as he lifted another chunk of the rubble his captain had picked loose from the cliff, being a leader was nowhere near as glamorous as he'd always imagined.

"Don't you just love these dances?"

As Billy watched Eliza's smiling, gleaming face, he had to admit that he did. Not that he was worth a lick at dancing, or enjoyed it, either one. Rather, he loved them because of what the music did for his wife, for more than anything else it seemed to animate her, to fill her very being with joy.

Now he smiled just from watching her. "You do seem happier, hon-bun."

"Yes," she beamed as she gaily clapped hands to the lively schottische being played by expert fiddlers Charlie Walton, Sammy Cox, and Peter Mortenson. "For days and days I've felt in the midst of despair. But no memories today, Billy, darling. No memories!"

"Does that mean you've been completely forgiven, do you think?"

Eliza smiled without taking her eyes off the dancers. "Who knows? Probably I'm just being given a breather, like you have to give an old horse after he's climbed a long hill. And I'm certainly feeling like an old horse lately!" Eliza winked slyly. "But whatever it is, I'm more than thankful for it, and I intend to enjoy every blessed minute I'm being given."

"I just wish you could get out there and dance, hon-bun."

"Me, too!" Eliza continued clapping her hands to the tune, her face glowing at least as much from happiness as from the light of the fire. "I swan, Billy! I believe every young man in the company has come in from the herds tonight. They're ready for some serious dancing, too. Just look at them go!"

Finally turning to watch, Billy was amazed at the energy the young men of the company were expending. And as Eliza had said, most were there, too, dancing up a storm with whomever they could get as partners. Warren and Edmund Taylor, Albert Nelson, Caleb Haight, and George Westover were dancing with their partners near the large fire, and Onley Barney, John Robinson, and Stephen Smith were out there somewhere, though at the moment Billy couldn't see them.

Of all these men who at times worked with the herd, as well as John Topham, Alma Angell, Noah Barnes, Billy Eyre, Erasmus Mickelson, Joe Walker, Sid Goddard, Jens Peter Nielson, and a half dozen others Billy couldn't at the moment name, only Caleb Haight was married. The remainder were more or less bachelors, though a few were still too young to have received that distinguished title. And of them all, only Dick Butt seemed to have his eye on a particular young lady. The remainder, as well as one or two oldsters such as Isaac Haight and Roswell Stevens, seemed to be giving no serious thought to marriage, which Billy could easily understand. After all, he hadn't thought of marriage until well past thirty, and then he hadn't done a thing about it until he'd been directed to by President Taylor.

Now, though, he wouldn't change places with anyone in the world, single or otherwise. To simply stand by and see the joy on his beloved Eliza's face as she reveled in the music, to watch as the wee one in her womb grew larger and more active—well, he could imagine nothing that would make a man happier or more satisfied with his lot in life.

"How are your hands doing, Billy?"

Turning, Billy was pleased to see Joseph Barton standing behind his right shoulder. "Howdy, Joseph," he responded with a grin. "You always creep up on folks thataway?"

"Only when I can. You callused up yet?"

"I'll say." Billy stretched out his hands, which had the same rough and hardened look as those of practically every other member of the company. "They feel first-rate to me. Fact is, I hardly even notice the cold with them anymore."

"The human body's an amazing thing, the way it can adapt to extreme circumstances. And to my way of thinking, this winter trek is extreme. I hear tell the dugway's finished."

"You haven't been up there?" Billy asked in surprise.

Joseph shook his head. "Not until a little while ago, and then it was too dark to see much. A few days back, Platte sent me and Bill Goddard and Henry Holyoak back across the river to try and pick up a few supplies, but the snow was too deep, and we didn't even get to Escalante. Coming back we passed some of the boys who are going after the cattle, but I'll be surprised if they make it any farther than we did."

"Working in these warmer canyons I sort of forget how deep the snow can be up on that desert," Billy stated.

"I assume you mean warmer in a figurative rather than a literal sense." Joseph grinned. "When do you think the road out of Cottonwood will be finished, Billy?"

"We've been on the dugway ten days, and it's finally done. With good weather we'll be finished with the Little Hole by tomorrow night, and then we should all be able to pull onto the top of Gray Mesa."

"Is that what they're calling it up there?"

"Uh-huh, on account of all the gray brush. Of course, I haven't been on top yet, but George Hobbs says it stretches away gray as can be for miles and miles, so the name seems fitting."

"Well, one thing's for certain—this new road's mighty steep. Two days past I drove a wagon back up through the Hole. It took five teams to haul it up, and the wagon was empty. To me the dugway looks every bit as steep, and I hear the Little Hole is even worse. So I reckon we're going to be using a lot of teams."

Billy nodded. "Platte says the same thing. He thinks six, maybe seven teams to the wagon, and men with ropes to hold them on the sandhill and some of the other sidling places higher up. Fact is, he told me he expects some tipovers and maybe even rollovers, and he intends to warn the folks about them before we start. That way they can make certain their loads are packed and tied extra carefully."

"That's good," Joseph admitted, "but it probably won't do much good. Oh, some will listen, for they always do. But there'll be others who know too much to take such simple advice, and . . . and . . . Well, I don't suppose it does much good to say anything. But it'll be the same with this nonsense about one outfit's horses eating up the other outfit's graze, as if any of us owns any of it. From what I hear, Platte's been going around trying to pacify folks and remind them of who we are, but some are listening and some aren't. Happen they don't start—listening, I mean—this grazing affair will end in a shooting and that will be the end of our mission. Now I don't expect that, mind you, because Platte's a powerful man and a natural-born leader. But all it would take is one hot-headed so-and-so, and then everything we've sacrificed this entire winter for will come to naught."

Soberly Billy agreed. "I know Platte's worried about it, just like he's worried about food supplies and sickness and the overall condition of our company."

"And he needs to be, Billy, because we aren't in very good shape, any of us, and things are getting worse right along." Joseph shook his head ruefully. "I'll say this much: We'll be a mighty sorry outfit when we finally limp into the fort on Montezuma Creek."

"And hungry," Billy added quietly.

"Yes," Joseph agreed as he turned to look for his wife. "And hungry. Well, there's Harriet Ann! Reckon I'd better go cut in and give her a couple of spins before she figures out John Eyre's a better dancer than I'll ever be. Good talking to you, Billy. I'm glad there're one or two folks in this outfit a man can do that with."

"Me, too," Billy admitted quietly, and then he watched thoughtfully as Joseph Barton made his way across the rock to where his wife was dancing. And only when the couple had spun laughingly out of sight did Billy return his attention to his own beloved and still clapping companion.

—o—o—o—

"That was a fine benediction you offered tonight," Billy said as he and Eliza made their way back toward their wagon. "Praying does seem to come naturally to you."

Eliza chuckled softly. "Not hardly it doesn't, and you of all people ought to know that."

"I'm so pleased you haven't had any more memories come to you today."

"Amen!" Eliza declared with feeling. "Still, I wish the dance could have gone on all night—not just because of the music, but because with my mind focused on those fiddles and accordion and mouth harps, I can't possibly be reminded of any past sins I've never repented of. Now, though, with everything so still and quiet—"

"Do you think there might be more?"

"I . . . don't know." Eliza sighed deeply. "I certainly hope not, though. After all, I have nine letters traveling with Platte's express back to Escalante for posting, nine letters apologizing for things I did or said to people going back practically the whole twenty-five years I was in the Valley. They were difficult letters to write, too—necessary, but oh so humiliating. And those don't count the things I've had to repent of that were just between the Lord and me. I'm telling you, Billy, this has been the hardest thing I've ever endured! If I've committed any more sins that have been holding me back, I can't imagine what they were or when they might have happened."

Billy smiled tenderly. "Me neither, because to me you seem practically perfect just as you are."

"Billy!"

"Well, hon-bun, that's exactly how I feel! Is your heart at peace yet?"

In the darkness Eliza shook her head. "Not the way I thought it would be—not with a spiritual peace. But I certainly feel good about the progress I've been making." For a moment Eliza was quiet, thinking. "The interesting thing, Billy darling, is that every single one of my letters pertains to things I've said or done that weren't seemly—cruel or unkind things that must surely have devastated the poor folks I was speaking to. It's a wonder I had any friends or customers at all, the way I carried on."

Billy squeezed his wife's hand. "Well, you did, for since you and I became acquainted I've spoken with several of them, and they all swear by you."

"Who? Billy, you tell me. Please?"

Billy chuckled. "I wouldn't care to reveal such things at this time. But believe me, plenty of folks in the Valley loved you, and many was the person who spoke of your kindness and generosity, your unwavering honesty—"

And in that instant another memory flooded into Eliza's mind, a painful memory of a day when she had intentionally overcharged a woman whose catty remarks had brought the over-charge upon her. Or so Eliza had thought at the time. Now, though, as the Holy Ghost made her aware not only of her own dishonesty but also of the woman's reasons for her unkind behavior, a pained Eliza could see how wrong she had been—and how saddened the Lord had been by what she'd done.

"Oh, Billy," she whispered as she pulled her hand free to wipe at the new tears that were stinging her eyes, "I've been such a fool— such a consummate fool! Now I have another letter to write, and . . . and I'm beginning to believe that this horror will never end!"

And with heavy heart she hurried ahead of her husband toward their wagon, her well-used secretary, and her nearly empty bottle of ink.

46

The Dugway and Little-Hole-in-the-Rock

Eliza's heart felt as though it was stuck in her throat, choking her so that she could hardly breathe. As she stared up the hill that rose before her, she was absolutely terrified, and the longer they sat there, the worse it got. Going down through the Hole-in-the-Rock had been perfectly awful. But at least the Hole had been out of sight until she was in it, and then the descent had gone so fast a body didn't have time to think about it or hardly even be frightened until it was over. This was a different proposition altogether. Ahead of where Billy stood waiting with his two span of mules at the front of the wagon, the road stretched upward for a hundred yards. There it slammed into the sandhill, where the climb became impossibly steep, impossibly slanted, and impossibly slow for a little more than two hundred feet.

Beyond the sandhill, the road was fairly level for the next hundred yards, but after that it came abruptly to the first of two five-hundred-foot sandstone ledges, each of which they had to climb over. It was on the first one that Billy had been laboring, chipping and blasting out a steep and sloping track they were calling the dugway.

Above it, at least according to Billy, the road briefly leveled again before ascending more steep and rugged hills through a maze of massive sandstone monoliths until it came to the final five-hundred-foot ledge, with the trail up and over all of it so twisting, narrow, and steep that it had been given the name of Little-Hole-in-the-Rock.

Of course, from where she sat, Eliza couldn't see beyond the top

379

of Billy's dugway. But she had been forced to watch the first nine wagons laboriously negotiating the lower portion of the road, and the sight had filled her with absolute terror. Not only was it taking eight teams to pull each wagon, but a dozen men with ropes had to move along on the uphill side, doing their best to keep each outfit from rolling sideways down the steep slope.

One more wagon, Zachariah and Seraphine Decker's, stood ahead of them. Then it would be her and Billy's turn, and already Eliza's heart was pounding and she was feeling faint. Oh, if only she could walk! If only she could get on her own feet and make her way up the impossible grade—

"*Come, come, ye Saints,*" her mind began desperately singing, "*no toil nor labor fear, but with joy wend your way. Though hard to you this journey may appear—*"

Suddenly a rider came pounding down the road. Reining in near Platte Lyman, he delivered a quick and obviously unsettling message. Shaking his head, Platte walked first to the Deckers and then to Billy, and it didn't even take good ears for Eliza to hear him say that Henry and Sarah Ann Holyoak's wagon had tipped end-over-teakettle back down one of the upper inclines, landing upside down and scattering belongings from one end of the road to the other. Already folks were trying to clean the mess up, but everyone was being hampered by the Holyoak's hive of bees. Their winter slumber had been disturbed by the crash of their hive, and according to Brother Holyoak, they needed to be sacked up before his belongings or the major pieces of wagon could be carried to the top and reassembled.

"There'll be a slight delay," Billy called back as he patted Sign's restive neck. "Some sort of accident up the road a ways."

"I . . . heard."

Billy looked quickly at his wife. "No one was hurt, you know."

Abruptly all of Eliza's fears came rushing to the surface. "I don't even care!" she wailed. "I think this is crazy, Billy! Here we are, risking life and limb, and over what? A senseless trek across impassable country to accomplish an impossible mission in the face of overwhelming odds? I don't think we should go any further! I don't—"

"Eliza, hon-bun, where's your faith?"

"What? But I don't—"

"Yes, you do. You have great faith, and even this isn't going to keep you from what you know is right. Besides, soon we'll be on the top of Gray Mesa with everyone else, and you'll be thinking back and wondering what on earth you were so worried about."

Billy adjusted his spectacles and smiled then, his wonderful smile that seemed to light up the whole world, and immediately Eliza felt herself beginning to relax. It was amazing, she thought, that he could have such an effect on her. Amazing and perfectly wonderful.

"*Why should we mourn,*" her mind began singing in remonstration, "*or think our lot is hard? 'Tis not so; all is right! Why should we think to earn a great reward if we now shun the fight? Gird up your loins, fresh courage take, our God will never us forsake; and soon we'll have this tale to tell—All is well! all is well!*"

It seemed only moments later that the Decker wagon started up the grade, Zachariah walking at the head of the teams, and Seraphine, or Pheenie as folks had taken to calling her, on the wagon seat with the reins in her hands. Behind them trooped four of their five small children, seven-year-old Nat leading his brother and two sisters. The baby, tiny Jesse Moroni, was bundled and snuggled into the wagon behind his mother. According to Billy, Platte had offered to walk with the teams so Zach could drive and Pheenie walk with her children, but both the Deckers had refused.

Pheenie was a brave woman, Eliza thought as Platte and two other brethren started working with Billy to attach additional teams of horses ahead of Dick Butt's mules on their own wagon. Of course, Eliza knew how to drive the mule teams, but she wouldn't be caught dead doing it on a road like this. Too many things could go wrong, too many mistakes might be made—

Already the Deckers had reached the sandhill where the men had attached their ropes, and Eliza could see the teams laboring upward through the soft, deep sand. Quickly the wagon was also into the sand, the wheels sinking almost to the hubs as the men with ropes strained from above to keep the precariously balanced outfit from rolling over.

Her breath stilled, Eliza was watching the drama unfold above them when her own wagon creaked and Billy pulled himself onto the seat beside her.

"Looks mighty bad up there, doesn't it," he said as he took up the reins.

"Oh, Billy—"

"Don't worry, hon-bun. We'll be fine."

"All set, Billy?" Platte called from where he was standing at the head of the string of harnessed teams.

"As ever," Billy responded. Then with a wink at Eliza, he snapped the reins of the four mules, Platte shouted to the lead team of horses who lunged into their traces, forcing the teams behind them to do the same; the long chain from the wagon tongue to the lead team's singletrees pulled tight; and before Eliza could even think of more verses to the calming hymn they were on their way, moving up the slope toward that terrible sandhill.

"Billy, I'm glad you're driving—"

The pause before the sandhill was brief while the men with ropes attached them to the wagon, and Eliza was startled to see the exhaustion on their faces. The poor souls had been climbing up and down the sandhill all morning, and most of them looked as thought they had nothing left to give, let alone the strength to keep one more wagon from rolling over.

"Morning, Sister Eliza, ma'am."

Eliza was startled. "Mercy sakes, Dick Butt. Is that you? I've never seen you without a coat and hat. I swan, I didn't even recognize you!"

Dick grinned. "This is warm work, ma'am. Pardon my saying so, but I'd take off more'n my hat and coat if I thought I could get away with it."

In spite of her fears Eliza giggled. "Well, young man, you can't, so don't you be trying it."

"No, ma'am." Dick grinned, his grimy face revealing his humor. "You hold on tight now, and we'll do our best to see that you and Billy and the whole kit and caboodle of your outfit don't end up in a pile at the bottom of the sand hill. And ma'am, was I you I'd sit on the uphill side. It's a little less scary."

"Good idea," Billy grunted as he stood on the dash so Eliza

could slide under him. "Thanks, Dick. You boys don't lose those ropes now, you hear?"

Some of the men replied good-naturedly, and in another moment they'd scrambled back up the hill and braced themselves as best they could, their ropes tight and wrapped around their arms and bodies.

"All set!" one of them yelled to Platte, and then the wagon lurched forward again. At first nothing seemed different except that they were moving more slowly, but when the wagon hit the sand, Eliza knew they were in trouble. As the animals sank into the sand past their hocks they began squealing and lunging against their traces, and slowly the wagon skewed downhill at a crazy, tilted angle that Eliza didn't think it possible to maintain.

"Oh, Billy," she whimpered in terror as she gripped the wagon seat with stiff fingers and whitened knuckles. "Billy, darling, what have folks been doing for ten days? This isn't a road—"

"Hang on, Eliza!"

"I am hanging on! But oh, glory, this is insane! Look at those poor men being dragged down the hill on the ends of their ropes. They can't hold us, Billy! They can't—"

And then Eliza's mind was singing again, practically screaming the words of the hymn. *"We'll find the place which God for us prepared, far away, in the West. Where none shall come, to hurt nor make afraid: There the Saints will be blessed—"*

Suddenly, somehow, the teams were across the sand and onto firm ground, and seconds later the wagon followed, righting itself and nearly throwing Eliza off the seat to the side.

"You all right, hon-bun?" Billy asked as the whole outfit shuddered to a stop.

"I . . . think so. Why did we stop?"

"So the boys can remove their ropes. Besides, we can't start up the dugway until the Deckers are over the top. See? There they go, just as if that fool track we blasted out is a real road."

Looking up, Eliza was aghast. From below, the dugway had looked bad. But up close it looked perfectly awful, much worse than the tacked-on dugway Ben Perkins had designed back across the river at the Hole. It was narrow and slanted to the side, where it snaked around a huge sandstone monolith, and Eliza could see that one slip could mean the end for all of them. It was—

"Don't worry, ma'am," Dick Butt was saying from beside her where he was untying his rope. "Actually she's a good road Billy and the others built up that rock. You'll get over it just fine."

"Dick's right," Platte Lyman agreed as he paused before starting back down to help guide the next wagon over the sandhill. "Billy and the Perkins brothers did a good job on that dugway, good enough so that no one's had any trouble on it yet. The Lord will protect you and your little one, Sister Eliza, and you'll be fine."

Eliza did her best to smile a response. Then they were moving again, across the level ground and, with a lurch, up the crazy dugway her husband had helped build. Despite what Dick had said, it neither looked nor felt like a good road, and Eliza's knuckles went white again as her body was pitched back and forth and her mind cried out in frantic prayer. Loudly the iron tires scraped and grated against the rock, the teams were squealing again as they lunged against their traces, one of the horses slipped and fell to its knees and was dragged a short distance before it could scramble back to its feet, and for the first time Eliza noticed, in a glimpse that was hardly more than a blur as her head was snapped in another direction, the blood and hair on the rock from where other animals had fallen and lost patches of their hide. It was a terrible road, one that should never have been used—

"And should we die before our journey's through, Happy day! all is well! We then are free from toil and sorrow too; with the just we shall dwell—"

"There!" Billy exclaimed as the eight span of animals lunged over the top of the dugway, dragging the wagon behind them, "I knew that was a passable road!"

As George Ipson, who had been waiting at the top of the dugway, pulled the leader teams to a halt for a breather, Eliza looked around. Despite the feeling from the canyon bottom that this was the top of the mountain, she could now see that the illusion had been false. The country lying ahead was exactly as it had been described to her, rugged and broken, with huge boulders or sandstone formations lying like great stone haystacks in every direction. Worse, the lay of the land continued steeply upward until the next huge cliff rose out of the earth, a cliff every bit as steep and high as the one they had just climbed.

"My calculations are that we've climbed just over nine hundred feet in elevation," Billy was saying as he watched his wife. "By the time we get to the top of that next rise and onto Gray Mesa, the total climb will have been almost exactly sixteen hundred feet, only four hundred feet less than the drop through the Hole-in-the-Rock."

"Wh-where did Holyoak's wagon tip over?"

"Up there." Billy pointed toward the cliff, and for the first time Eliza could see that the road, after it emerged from the maze of massive stone formations, wound up through a narrow ravine. It was steep there, too, and Eliza could see places where someone had stacked rocks to build up the roadbed.

"The men built that up?" she asked in amazement.

"And some of the women and children. They've moved a lot of rock up here in the past week, and despite that it's steeper, Pap Redd says, than the price of rotgut whiskey in Salt Lake City, the road seems passable. By the way, I don't think you need to worry about tipping over backward like Hank Holyoak's wagon did. Apparently he made the mistake of putting all his weight at the rear of his wagon, whereas most of ours is at the front where Kumen advised me to put it."

"Is . . . is it a sidling road?"

"In a couple of places, yes. And there're three or four spots betwixt here and there where it gets a little dicey." Billy smiled. "But don't you worry, Eliza. We're not going to tip over sideways, either."

"I . . . I hope not. There go the Deckers."

"Yep. We'll give them a couple of minutes, and then we'll follow."

The Decker wagon had climbed out of sight around the first stone monolith when Billy finally signaled George Ipson to start the leaders. With a shout and a slap he did so, all the teams dug in, and with a jolt that snapped Billy and Eliza's necks even though they were prepared for it, the wagon was dragged into motion once again.

As they rounded the bend where the Decker wagon had vanished, they passed Will Hutchings and Bill Gurr, who were taking a set of teams back down to the bottom.

"They don't look much the worse for wear," Billy called from his seat.

"Maybe not these, but another horse skinned its knee pretty bad," Will called back. "Kumen is doctoring it up on top."

"Is the Holyoak wagon cleaned up?"

"It will be by the time you get there," Bill Gurr replied. "That was a sight, the way that tongue went straight up into the air before the whole affair keeled over backward. It's a wonder the Holyoaks got off safely, but they sure enough did."

"Was there a lot of damage?" Eliza questioned.

Will Hutchings grinned. "Oh, I reckon they lost a few dishes, but other than that, everything seems to be fine. They had their load tied down real well. The bees are pretty much all gathered up, and even the wagon will be fit as a fiddle come nightfall. Reckon the Lord's once again answering Brother Nielson's prayer for our safety."

Once Billy and Eliza had passed, the men waved and started their teams down the trail, and Eliza was just starting to relax when they climbed around another sandstone hummock and found themselves directly behind the Deckers.

It was immediately apparent that something was wrong. Whereas the road went along the upper edge of the steep sidehill that opened ahead of them, somehow the Deckers were off the road and maybe a dozen feet below it. Zach was out in front trying to get the teams to hurry, Pheenie was screaming and whipping her lines from the wagon seat, the children were huddled together on the road above them seemingly frozen in fear, and the wagon was tilted at an awful angle and continuing a slow but steady slide sideways down the hill.

"Oh-oh," Billy breathed as he reined in his teams.

"Billy—" Eliza whimpered as she clutched her husband's arm, her eyes wide with horror.

"Look out!" Will Pace, who was now at the head of Billy's teams, shouted frantically. "Give 'em the whip, Pheenie, ma'am, and get back on the road! Hurry—"

But all such warnings were far and away too late. With a slight jolt the wagon bumped against a low bush, stopped sliding, shuddered, and then slowly tipped to the side and rolled onto its top down the hill, crushing the bows and throwing Pheenie off and out of the way.

"My baby!" Pheenie screamed as she was falling, and before Eliza even realized what was happening Billy had tossed her the reins, leaped to the ground, and was literally bounding down the hill toward the sliding, overturned wagon.

With a groan of fear Eliza set the brakes and whipped the lines about the brake handle. George Ipson and Zach Decker were already hurrying down the slope, and Pheenie Decker had pulled herself to her feet and was frantically scrambling through the talus toward the overturned wagon. But because of their position Billy was ahead of all of them, and Eliza could see he would reach the wagon first.

"Oh, God in heaven," she prayed as the drama unfolded before her, "please protect my Billy—"

On the downhill side of the wagon Billy began clawing at the talus, quickly opening a hole. Seconds later, as the men heaved up the corner of the wagon-box, the faint sound of a whimpering baby could be heard from underneath. While a sobbing Pheenie knelt beside Billy, he was already arching his small, wiry body under the sideboards, feeling for movement.

"He . . . he's behind the seat," Pheenie screamed.

And Billy, groping in the confused jumble of belongings, suddenly felt movement. Carefully he pulled the dirt and small rocks of the talus away, and seconds later a well-wrapped little Jesse Moroni Decker was back in the arms of his mother, none the worse for wear.

Standing to dust himself off while the others moved away, Billy took a step to the side and immediately lost his balance. With a yelp he flailed his arms and fell backward, and in that instant the wagon broke loose and slid again, directly over where he'd been standing only seconds before.

As Billy fell and the wagon began sliding, Eliza wanted to scream but couldn't. In fact, she couldn't even breathe. All she could do was stare helplessly from her perch on the wagon seat while her mind repeated the terrible refrain from the hymn that had been on the edge of her tongue all day long. *"And should we die—And should we die—And should we die—"*

Seconds later, however, as Billy scrambled to his feet and emerged from behind the sliding, overturned wagon, Eliza stopped singing. There was no more need, for she knew that once again God had answered her prayer.

God had literally answered her prayer!

Perhaps he wasn't yet willing to give her peace of conscience, Eliza thought as a smile finally broke across her face, but at least he had allowed her to keep her sweet and wonderful husband—

47

The Edge of Gray Mesa

"I can't understand it, Billy. I don't think more than two or three minutes go by in a day but what I'm praying in one way or another, trying to find that inner peace I once knew. So why does God answer me in some ways but not in others?"

It was early morning, only just starting to show daylight, and Billy was preparing to take the two teams of mules and go back down into Cottonwood Canyon to help more of the company climb the grade. Already the cow had been milked of what little she was now giving, and the four mules had been harnessed and made ready. To her surprise, Eliza had found an egg in the chicken crate, and she had immediately boiled it for Billy's lunch. Then he'd finished his breakfast of cracked wheat that had been set to simmer by the fire the night before.

Unlike the previous week, it looked to be a cold day, for clouds had gathered during the night, and a frigid wind was whistling across the mostly unsheltered mesa where the company had established camp. Already Eliza could feel stinging droplets of moisture in the wind, and she was certain it would soon be snowing. But at least there were junipers scattered about, so firewood was plentiful, and it shouldn't be too difficult keeping warm.

"It isn't as though God doesn't answer me at all," Eliza continued, "for if you weren't protected by divine providence yesterday, I

389

don't know what that could be called. And it isn't as though he hasn't been revealing my sins to me, either."

"How many letters have you written now?" Billy asked as he looked up.

"Ten, nine of which have been sent out." Eliza winced. "And every one of them has been an apology for some aspect of my personal pride and vanity. Half of last night I lay awake wracking my brain, but try as I might I couldn't come up with the name of another soul I need to write. That being the case, why is the Lord delaying his response?"

"I don't know, hon-bun. Maybe it's just a matter of timing. He says he'll reveal himself in his own time and way, and I believe that means we're to be patient until he does. I know that's hard when we're suffering, but it's certainly how it worked with you."

Eliza was surprised. "With me? What on earth do you mean?"

Immediately embarrassed, Billy dropped his gaze. "I . . . uh . . . I didn't mean to say that."

"Billy Foreman, you look at me." Eliza was only partially upset. "Now, tell me what you mean."

Removing his spectacles, Billy rubbed his eyes. "I wasn't ever going to tell you this," he said softly as he placed them on his nose and adjusted the wires over his ears. "But I almost blurted it out a day or so ago, and now I've done it again. So I reckon I might as well tell you the whole thing and be done with it."

Almost fearful of what Billy might reveal, Eliza waited.

"And I'll do it tonight," Billy grinned mischievously, "after we get back from the canyon."

"You'll do no such thing, Billy Foreman. If you have something to say about me, I want to hear it now, before you leave." Eliza smiled then, letting Billy know she wasn't really upset. "Please, darling, no matter how bad it is, if it'll help me I really do want to hear it."

Hopelessly Billy looked toward the trail. "Well," he admitted reluctantly, "since no one's started down the road yet, I reckon I do have a couple of minutes. You recollect I told you how Brother Taylor told me I needed to pray about finding a wife before I took up my assignment to Cedar City?"

Eliza nodded. "Of course I remember. It was after you prayed that you saw me in my store."

"Actually, quite a while after, to tell the truth. You see, hon-bun, that's sort of how I knew what to tell you about repenting. I . . . well, I went through it too."

"You?" Eliza was astounded. "But . . . but you're practically perfect, Billy. I can't imagine that you ever did a serious thing wrong in your whole life."

Billy's smile was gone. "Apparently that isn't how the Lord felt, Eliza. Once I started praying in earnest to find you, it came to me in a mighty big hurry that the Lord wouldn't reveal you to me until I was worthy—until I'd repented of all my sins and been cleansed of them through the blood of Christ.

"So I tried for months to repent and didn't seem to be making much headway. That's when I went in and asked Brother Taylor what to do. He read me that verse on the last page in the Book of Mormon where the Lord promises to reveal all truth through the power of the Holy Ghost, and then several verses in Third Nephi where we're told to repent of all our sins. Then he told me to go home and ask the Lord to reveal the truth to me about all my sins—specifically the ones I'd never repented of.

"I did, and oh, lawsy, did I go through it after that! Just like you, I reckon, only maybe worse. For three solid weeks, every time I turned around or sat down or picked up the scriptures or ran into someone on the street, wham! There was something else I could see that I needed to repent of."

"Were they . . . awful things?"

Soberly Billy nodded. "They felt awful enough. I reckon, though, that they'd be considered little sins by most folks—little white lies, jealous acts of cruelty and unkindness, and that sort of nonsense. One fellow who worked with my father I didn't much like, so I was always thinking up mean tricks to play on him. Memories of those things shamed me terribly. But the real trouble was, from my baptism at age eight I'd not done much repenting. So once I asked, the Lord had a whole lot of remembering to put me through."

"Well, at least you didn't have to repent of any major sins such as trying to destroy your marriage."

Billy smiled, but Eliza could see the sadness in his eyes. "The single hardest thing for me to repent of," he said slowly as he looked away, "or what I now think of as my single most serious sin, was the giving up of my agency to others. That was such a blow to me, to realize that I'd willingly abdicated the very thing Christ had offered himself a ransom for—my right to make my own choices about my life."

"I . . . I don't understand."

His expression bleak, Billy looked back at his wife. "It . . . hurts to admit it, hon-bun, but I did it not because I was trying to be wicked, but because I was a lazy so-and-so. And I reckon my laziness turned into a terrible habit that wasn't pleasing to the Lord.

"You see, Father was mighty strict when I was a youngster, and he demanded that I do everything exactly as he told me—or else! I learned that lesson well enough that it became comfortable, so though I grew up I never—well, I reckon I never matured. Even after Father stopped giving me orders when he died, I let others take over and do the same thing. For instance, if someone said they thought I ought to take a room in a particular boarding house, I did it. Like I say, I was letting other folks do my thinking.

"One time I forgot to pay my rent, and in his anger my landlord said he ought to collect my pay and divvy out my money for me. Well, it was a real bother dealing with money anyway, so I told him that sounded fine, and I made the arrangements at the office. Mighty soon he was telling me what to wear, what to buy, and all sorts of things. He told me he couldn't imagine that I could ever be a hand with horses or any other sort of animal, so I just kept on avoiding them, and you know the consequences of that. One day he even told me I was no fit man for marriage, and I believed him again. That's why I never courted anyone or did any of the things young fellows generally do."

Eliza was astounded. "A man did this? To you? Who . . . who was he?"

"An elderly gentleman," Billy replied sadly. "A good man, too, with no more thought than I had about being inappropriate or taking away a body's agency. He thought he was helping, and so did I. That's why that sin has been the hardest for me to repent of. It was the last thing I expected to hear from the Lord, and it required a whole new way for me to look at things. I mean, who would have ever thought that not assuming responsibility for financial and other matters was in reality giving up the mental and emotional growth that agency promises? Or that not actively seeking out and courting a woman was actually denying both of us all the temporal and spiritual blessings granted through the exercise of agency."

"But I . . . I thought you felt I was the woman the Lord had prepared for you—"

"I do, Eliza. I absolutely know it!" Billy stood and walked to his wife and took her in his arms. "But think of the years I wasted because I let that man convince me I wasn't husband material—years you and I could have been together instead of alone, years when we might have been happy instead of—at least for me—miserable. But I willingly gave up my agency to that man, and I've paid a heavy price with what I've lost. Thank God He has been kind enough to allow me to repent, and to finally give me you and our little unborn son."

Eliza held Billy tightly, thinking as she did so of how much his love had come to mean to her. If only she hadn't—

"Was that it?" she asked abruptly. "When you repented of that, did the Lord give you the peace you so obviously feel?"

"No, not quite." Billy sighed deeply. "There was one more thing he wanted me to understand, to see clearly. So, he showed it to me."

"Showed?"

"Uh-huh. I'm not a visionary man, Eliza, and I reckon you know that. But if what the Lord showed me one morning during prayer wasn't an open vision, then I don't know what to call it. Surely it was the realest thing I've ever seen."

"Can you . . . tell me about it?"

Billy sighed. "I've never told this to a soul, but I reckon maybe it's time. While I was in my room praying one morning, I seemed to find myself on a hillside, surrounded by some bushes. As I looked around, I saw a couple of men doing something on the ground out in front of me. One of them was kneeling and the other was standing. I stepped forward to see what they were doing, and they had a man on

393

the ground between them, all stretched out on his back on top of this little log.

"One of the men took the man's hand, pulled it out straight, and put a spike of some sort against his palm. And that was when I realized that the man on the ground was Jesus Christ, and that these men were getting set to crucify him.

"With my heart in my throat I started hollering and yelling at them to stop, but they paid me no mind. Then I tried to rush them, to stop them, only I couldn't move beyond the bushes.

"By this time the man who was standing had started swinging his huge wooden mallet, and the sound of it driving the spike through the Savior's flesh was more than I could bear. I started sobbing and pleading for him to stop, and I . . . I reckon that was the first time I took a good look at him."

"At who?"

"At the man who was swinging the mallet."

"And you knew him?" Eliza asked, her voice hushed.

Billy dropped his embrace and turned away. "I should say I knew him," he responded sadly. "The man with the mallet, Eliza? The man who was driving that hated spike through the Savior's innocent flesh? It was *me*."

And in dumbfounded amazement, Eliza could only stare.

PART FIVE

THE NEVER-ENDING JOURNEY

48

Friday, February 13, 1880

Cheese Camp

"Eliza, come quick!" Harriet Ann Barton had rarely sounded so excited, and Eliza looked up in wonder. "Amasa Lyman has come with an express from the tithing office in Panguitch, and they've brought pork and cheese for us!"

Thrilled by the surprising news, Eliza pulled herself to her feet and started toward the central campfire, where everyone seemed to be heading.

That morning she and Billy had gone separate directions, he back with the mules one more time to help the last wagons out of Cottonwood Canyon, and she forward with Harriet Ann and some of the other women to help build the road ahead.

Past the camp the road had now been built up a small, dry canyon, to come at length to a series of ledges and buttes that had to be crossed before the next deep canyon was reached. There Eliza had spent the day seated on the cold slickrock in two narrow ravines stacking rocks and whatever else was dragged up as roadbed fill. Of course, now she was stiff and sore, and the biting wind and occasional snow flurries had thoroughly chilled her legs and feet. But finally she had been able to contribute some tangible effort to the road-building effort, and somehow that seemed to make her suffering worthwhile.

"Are you all right?" Mary Jones asked as she caught Eliza hobbling slowly toward the large fire.

"I'm sure I'll be fine." Eliza forced a smile.

"But Eliza, your condition!"

"Oh, pshaw, Mary. I worked all day beside Emma Decker, you know, and she's due about the same time as I am. If she can do it, I surely can."

Mary rolled her eyes in disgust. "Emma's twenty years old, Eliza Foreman, not forty-five, which you turned just last week. And she wasn't frostbit nearly to death on the plains of Wyoming, either. Lawsy, woman, I wish you'd keep in mind that there's plenty to do in camp where you can at least keep near a fire."

"True. But I suppose I needed a change." And that was true, Eliza thought. Of course, she wasn't telling Mary a change from what, but in fact it had to do with not wanting to think all day about the startling visionary experience Billy had shared with her the day before—the visionary experience that was now proving so troubling to her.

On the surface the message of his experience had seemed both obvious and ominous—all who sinned, especially knowingly, were contributing personally to the suffering and crucifixion of the Lord Jesus Christ. Eliza had never thought of sin quite like that, but now that she had, it made perfect sense. It was also terribly unsettling, especially in light of Billy's admission that after his vision he had felt he should not only go before the Lord and acknowledge his guilt but also apologize directly to the Savior for helping wound and crucify him.

For Billy it had been a terribly humiliating moment, a time when his own anguish had seemed overwhelming and unending. It was the moment when, at least in Billy's mind, his heart had finally broken sufficiently that he could be filled with godly sorrow—a requirement of complete repentance that he said the Apostle Paul had taught.

By lamplight Eliza had read the passage Billy had quoted from the seventh chapter of Second Corinthians, which declared, "Godly sorrow worketh repentance to salvation . . . but the sorrow of the world worketh death."

It made great sense to Eliza as she had thought about it afterward, and she was certain Billy was right. If Jesus Christ had truly suffered for all the sins of mankind, then it followed that anytime someone sinned he would be contributing to the Lord's suffering.

And if he sinned intentionally—well, it was no wonder Billy had felt compelled to apologize! So, she was now thinking, should everyone.

The trouble was, she didn't think she had the personal courage to do it. After all, knowing a little of what Christ had suffered in the Garden and again on Calvary, how could anyone bear the humiliation of willingly facing him and saying, "I helped drive the spikes through your flesh, and I knew what I was doing at the time." It would all be too horrible, too awful, too embarrassing, and Eliza was certain she couldn't deal with it.

But there was something else about Billy's experience that troubled her, the part where he'd felt so thoroughly condemned for willingly giving up his agency. There was a message in that for her, too, though it was deeply hidden, and as yet she hadn't quite grasped it. But it was there, something she was supposed to understand—

"Eliza, I asked you a question."

"I . . . I'm sorry, Mary. What was it?"

"While you were working on the road today, did you happen to get all the way to that awful canyon we have to cross next?"

Eliza shook her head. "You mean Wilson Canyon? I didn't see it, but I heard about it. I also heard that if we can cut a road through the rock to the bottom, the Lord has blasted a straight trail for us up and out the other side."

"It's true," Mary declared as she led Eliza to a wagon tongue where she could sit near the huge fire. "I saw it today. Folks are calling it the Chute, and it's a natural roadway straight up through that horrid slickrock out of the canyon. Even better, it's the perfect width for our wagons, it isn't sidling so there won't be tipovers—at least sideways—and it won't require a lick of work to make it a roadway. Kumen estimates that shooting the Chute, as he puts it, will save us a week's hard labor, and that's a miracle in itself."

"It would be," Eliza acknowledged thoughtfully. "It surely would be—"

——o–o–o——

"All right, Brothers and Sisters," Platte Lyman was shouting from where he stood on the tongue of a wagon, "if I can have your attention? I appreciate Brother Dan Barney's invocation, for we have a couple of hard issues to deal with this evening, and the Spirit of the Lord will be required if we are to solve them equitably."

There was a general murmuring of agreement. Platte Lyman raised his hands to regain the silence, and only when it was complete did he go on.

"But first, and in keeping with the fact that this is a body of Saints called to fulfill a spiritual mission pertaining to the salvation and exaltation of ourselves and others, I'm calling on Brother Jens Nielson to stand and proceed as the Holy Spirit directs he should. We need the Spirit of the Lord with us tonight, brothers and sisters, and Brother Nielson's calling is to direct us in obtaining it."

Slowly the elderly Danishman rose to his feet and hobbled to the place vacated by Platte Lyman. With help from Joseph Barton, he climbed to the tongue and gripped the wagon with one strong hand for balance. Then, for at least a minute and perhaps two, he gazed in silence upon the assembled crowd.

"Vell," he said when all had grown uneasy with his silence, "I yust don't know hardly vat to do—Ya, by golly, I do! Bishop George Vashington Sevy, de Spirit off de Lord has yust directed me dat you are to come forth und bear your testimony. Vill you do dat, speaking de vords de Lord puts into your mind?"

In the early evening silence the slight and bearded man from Panguitch, who was standing nearly at the rear of the assembly, nodded. With measured tread he stepped forward, making his way through the people until he, too, was on the wagon tongue that had become the evening's podium. Then, still moving calmly, his blue eyes scanned each and every face before him. Only then, when he had the attention of all present, did he begin.

"Brothers and sisters," he declared, his voice not loud so much as it was powerful, "A miracle converted me, but it hasn't taken a miracle to keep me converted. The testimony it left with me is my choicest possession and burns ever brighter as the days pass.

"I was born the 25th of February, 1832, in LeRoy, Genesee County, New York, the son of George Sevy and Hannah Libby— God-fearing people but not acquainted with the fullness of the restored gospel.

"After my father's passing in '49, I left my home and widowed mother to take part in the gold rush to California. Had my job as a teamster for a party of gold-seekers held out, I'd probably be there today among the discouraged and abandoned miners that fill the state. But the Lord intervened in a way that was hard to take at the time. I fell so sick that I couldn't continue with my party, nor could they wait for me to get well. They left me at a wayside camp and pushed on without me. I probably would have died, but a following party picked me up and carried me with them to Utah.

"Before reaching Salt Lake City I'd heard much of the Mormons, but nothing favorable, so naturally I was determined not to tarry among them. But being left stranded in Salt Lake City by the second party, I had no choice. I accepted work from one good Mormon brother who needed some teams taken to Palmyra, where a group of Saints were struggling to begin a new community. While waiting for a chance to return to Salt Lake City, I took board and lodgings with a good sister who taught me the gospel by the way she lived it. Under her influence my steeled heart softened, and favorable impressions of the Mormons and their teachings crept in, despite my resolves—though you may be sure I took elaborate care to let no one know of it."

A quiet chuckle rippled through the assembly, and then Bishop Sevy continued. "One night I went with them to a cottage meeting, more to please the good lady than because I was interested, and feeling sure my prejudice against the Mormons would never let them 'get me.' I listened to the talks indifferently, passive and undisturbed, until one brother arose and took my attention by speaking a strange language. The peculiar thing about it was that I understood him. I knew from the very start that he was speaking to me in tongues, telling me in a language no one else seemed to understand that I mustn't deny the voice trying to speak to me, nor be deaf to what it was trying to say. The plan of salvation was being shown to me, he said, and a way was being opened for me to accept it, and if I did I would be the means of taking the gospel to my widowed mother and being a savior to her.

"The idea shook me, left me so disturbed I wasn't even aware of his closing, not until the hush and quiet that followed could no longer be ignored. Then I came to with a start. The brother was asking who

401

in the room knew the interpretation. I was amazed that no one answered. I was sure they must know what I knew and that they were keeping still just to see what I'd do. When he pointedly asked me if I didn't have the interpretation, I kept still too, shaking my head vigorously, as much to convince myself that I hadn't understood as to deny I had. When the meeting broke up without any interpretation being given, I left the meeting feeling that every eye was boring me in the back, and that they were all wondering why I'd denied something I knew to be true. The uncomfortable remembrance of it kept me awake that night and tossed me about in my bed as I tried to make up my mind what to do. And not until I'd acknowledged the testimony and firm conviction that had come to me did I find rest. Then I went to sleep so soundly that I didn't wake until the noise of the family assembling for breakfast awoke me.

"I then satisfied my conscience by a confession I'd formulated during the night, and my heart rejoiced with the spirit of peace therein, and for the conviction that my search was over, that the thing for which I'd left my home had been found, and that it was something far more precious than the gold I had started out to find. I fulfilled the promise made to me and became the savior of my mother's soul. She followed me to Utah, with Pap Redd's wagon hauling her from the Mississippi River to my home in Panguitch. She lives there yet, a firm believer in the principles of the gospel I explained to her. She was a happy recipient of the ordinances that will ensure her salvation in the worlds to come."

Again Bishop Sevy looked calmly from one to another through the whole congregation, not one soul escaping his piercing view. "Brothers and sisters," he finally concluded, "that is the testimony I have lived with, and one day it will be the testimony I die with. I know that The Church of Jesus Christ of Latter-day Saints is the only true and living church upon the face of the earth today. I know the gospel we preach in this church is the Lord's true gospel—his pure and holy doctrine. I know that, when properly authorized, the sacred ordinances we perform by the power and authority of the Holy Melchizedek Priesthood are necessary for our salvation as well as our exaltation. I know these things, and I bear humble and solemn witness of them! In the name of the Lord Jesus Christ, amen."

"Thank you, Bishop Sevy." Platte Lyman stood again on the wagon tongue, surveying the throng. "I'm grateful for the spirit of peace your testimony has brought us."

Pausing, he again scanned the crowd, who were beginning to stir a little in the chill air. "Well, I reckon all of you have heard of the commodities my brother Amasa and his friends have brought on their pack animals from Panguitch. They are not only appreciated but desperately needed, and we will distribute them shortly.

"But first, we must discuss the rift that is growing among us because of the large horse herd and the feed it is consuming."

"Let 'em go ahead!" someone shouted, instantly changing the tenor of the meeting.

"We'll shoot the first one that tries!" someone else responded, and in that moment Billy and Kumen Jones stepped up behind their wives.

"Hi, hon-bun," Billy whispered as he leaned down and kissed Eliza's cheek. "What's going on?"

"The fireworks are about to begin," she whispered back. "This is awful, Billy, and I don't know how poor Platte is going to resolve it—"

"Nobody's going to be shooting anybody." Platte's voice remained amazingly calm. "Merciful heavens, brothers and sisters. Listen to yourselves! Most of you have been called of God to serve as missionaries to the Lamanites, and all of us are supposed to be brothers and sisters in the Lord. All of us are expected to have testimonies as firm as that of Bishop Sevy. For that to be true—for us to work successfully as we accomplish our divinely appointed mission, we must diligently foster a spirit of peace, harmony, and brotherhood, especially among ourselves. Is that possible when we're threatening to split apart, or to shoot each other on sight?"

The silence around the fire was again complete, and Eliza felt that no one was even breathing, herself included.

"This spirit of contention that has found place among us is so painful, so satanic, that I'm at a loss for words to describe my feelings about it. But I will say this; with my arm to the square I swear before God and all his holy angels that we will not disband tonight until every single issue is amicably resolved. As acting captain of this company I will no longer stand by and watch brethren in the gospel of Christ—the gospel of peace, I might add—packing cocked and loaded rifles as they go about their daily affairs. Such goings on are an affront to both man and God, and if they are not repented of immediately, I fear we will all be destroyed! Anyone disagree?"

In the silence Platte looked carefully about the company. "Very well," he finally continued, "if no one disagrees with my assessment, then I assume you all agree, and are willing to labor together to repent. So let's get to the solution.

"As I understand it, here is the issue. We have upwards of eight hundred head of horses with our livestock that have been brought along as a speculative venture to be used for stocking ranches or sold to the Indians or cowboys in the area of the San Juan. Primarily these horses are owned by the Robbs, the Duntons, the Butt brothers, Amasa Barton, and one or two others.

"As you know, we've learned the hard way that graze in this desert is scarce. Worse, because it's winter, nothing is growing, so the grass isn't replenishing itself.

"As a solution to this scarcity, these brethren have come to me and offered to drive their horses on ahead, pushing them through to the San Juan—"

"And giving them all the feed our teams are going to need along the way!" someone shouted. "Remember what you just said, Platte. The grass isn't growing yet, so it won't be replenishing itself!"

"That's true," Platte acknowledged, "it won't, not at least until spring. On the other hand, if we insist on keeping these folks and their horses with us, our own livestock will continue to starve and weaken on the insufficient feed. So tell me, brothers and sisters? What is the best course for us to pursue?"

"I say keep them behind us!" a man shouted. "Why give them such an unfair advantage?"

"And have all the animals starve?" another responded. "I say, send them on ahead and good riddance!"

Platte Lyman allowed echoes of the two arguments to bounce around for another minute or so, and then once again he held up his hand.

"You know," he said when silence had returned, "until a few

moments ago I thought we were dealing with the issue of feed for our livestock. I see now that I was wrong. The only issue being shouted about here tonight is selfishness—plain old greed. I reckon, what with the guns and that talk of killing, that I should have seen it sooner. But now that I do, the solution becomes crystal clear.

"The owners of the horses see a serious problem developing, and have come to me with a workable solution. They've even promised to push their animals as hard and fast as they can, thus leaving as much grass as possible for our livestock.

"The naysayers, however, have somehow developed the notion that God created that grass for the exclusive use of the missionaries, and that no one else has a right to any of it, particularly before they get to it. Frankly, that's where the greed is.

"My recommendation to you naysayers, then, as acting captain, is to repent. To you horsemen I say go and go quickly, sparing us as much feed as possible, and coming back once the horses are pastured on the San Juan so you can help us finish this road. All in favor of these recommendations, please signify by raising the right hand."

Eliza noted that all but one or two hands went into the air.

"All opposed, please make the same sign."

The remaining hands were raised.

"Very well," Platte Lyman concluded, "you who are opposed come one at a time and see me afterward. Meanwhile the voting is heavily in favor of the horses going ahead, so I would suggest, brethren, that you proceed with dispatch."

"Brother Lyman?" The speaker was George Hobbs.

"George, if this is about those horses—"

"It isn't."

"Very well. Then go ahead and speak."

"Thank you. As you know, myself and the three other explorers were on the San Juan the end of December, where we found the Davis and Harriman families in a state of near starvation. Obviously I didn't understand the true difficulties of pushing this road through, for I gave my sister and the others my word that if they could hold on for another sixty days, I'd return with fresh supplies.

"In less than two weeks that sixty days will be up, and our company will be nowhere near the San Juan and Montezuma Creek. I'd

405

like permission, therefore, to load some pack animals with provisions and push on ahead to the relief of our starving friends and relatives."

"You'll never make it," George Sevy said with genuine concern. "There's too much snow in that cedar forest, George. Even with strong animals you won't be able to push through."

"I'm willing to chance it!" George Hobbs declared. "I'd rather die myself than know that women and children are perishing for want of effort on my part."

Another vote was taken, and while no one seemed willing to accompany him, George Hobbs was given approval to leave for Montezuma Creek in the morning. Of course, as Billy was quick to point out to a worried Eliza, Dan Harris and some others had been gone more than three weeks trying to find a different route to Montezuma Creek for the same purpose, and the men with the horses would now be following the same trail George Hobbs would take.

"So," he concluded kindly, "George won't be alone on his journey, Eliza. And the families at Montezuma Creek will be sure to get more provisions even if for some reason George doesn't make it."

"That doesn't make me feel any better," Eliza declared. "Besides, it's a terrible shame that no one else volunteered to go with him."

"Would you like me to go?"

Eliza looked stunned. "But . . . you can't, Billy. We . . . I . . . need you here. I mean, I can't even drive the teams, let alone harness them."

"I reckon that's pretty much how everyone else feels, too. There were no other volunteers because none of us feels free enough of responsibility here with the company. Remember, George Hobbs has no wife or children, and he isn't closely associated with the herding like Dick and most of our other single men. That leaves him free to undertake such a venture, and to be a blessing to those at Montezuma Fort if he's successful."

———◦—◦—◦———

"All right, brothers and sisters," Platte was speaking again. "Last item of business is two hundred pounds of pork and forty pounds of cheese from the tithing office in Panguitch. There's enough pork for a meal or two for everyone, and we'll divide it that way. But I'm at a loss as to how to divide forty pounds of cheese among so many of us."

"Auction it off, Platte," someone shouted from the dark.

"Who is that?" Platte called as he tried to see past the fire and into the darkness.

"Bill Hutchings—from Beaver. I say we auction the cheese, use the proceeds to help defray expenses, and let those who have money remember those who do not."

Platte was thoughtful. "That seems like a fair idea," he finally agreed. "Pap Redd? As I recollect, you've done a little auctioneering. What say you climb up on this wagon tongue beside me and see how fast you can get rid of forty pounds of fine Panguitch cheese?"

With an agility that surprised no one, the man leaped to the wagon tongue and faced the company. "I dunno, Platte," he groused as he looked out over the now-smiling company. "To me the great majority of this outfit seem about as fire-headed, hard-eyed, and hog-poor as any citizens I ever encountered, with heads stuffed fifty-fifty with sawdust and cement. Given thirty days to do it, they couldn't figure out how to pour creek water out of a wet boot with the directions printed on the heel. And by jings, they're the smart ones among us."

Chuckling, Platte nodded. "You may be right, Pap. But let's auction some cheese and see if they're any better at that."

Pap Redd nodded. "All right, I'll do 'er. But first, a word about my friend Bishop Sevy. I've known him a long time. And he's right. I had the honor and the pleasure of his mother's company all the way from the Mississippi, and a finer, more upstanding woman I never met. Just so you'll know, she related to me everything George has testified to, and added some interesting details besides. This man speaks the truth, brothers and sisters, and any who harden their hearts against his words and witness—well, they've a hard life ahead of them is all I'm going to say."

Reaching down Pap took up one of the small cheeses. "The way I see it," he frowned, changing not only the subject but also his very way of talking, "this auction's got about as much chance of raising good money as a one-legged man in a kicking contest. Moreover, about the time the bids stop coming and I'm being stared at like an albino badger with two heads and a sweet disposition, you can have your job back. Now, which one of you anvil-headed so-and-sos will start the bidding for this cheese?"

"I'll go two bits!" Joshua Stevens shouted.

"And I'll go four!" declared Sam Rowley.

"Six bits!" Bill Hutchings called, after which Joshua Stevens bid again and got the cheese for a dollar.

And so it went. Over the next thirty minutes the various cheeses went for prices ranging up to five dollars, and Eliza noted that every last one of them were sold. She herself bid on several and got three, all of which she had Billy deliver to families whom she noted took no part in the bidding.

"You know," she said to Billy as the auction was nearing its conclusion, "Bill Hutchings has bid on every cheese, sometimes several times, and hasn't bought one."

"The poor man," Billy stated sympathetically.

Eliza looked at her husband in surprise. "Poor man? He doesn't want cheese, Billy. All he's doing is driving the prices up, playing a game at the expense of others. Under normal circumstances that wouldn't bother me. But out here, with our resources already so limited that it's frightening, I feel disgusted by it."

"How do you know he's not just missing bids?" Billy was still not convinced.

"Two things. I've been watching his face, and I've been watching the face of Pap Redd, who has also figured out what he's doing. I'm surprised Pap hasn't stopped the auction and called him on his shenanigans, and I'm thankful we have a little of that fan money with us, so folks who really need the cheese won't miss out."

Leaning down, Billy kissed his wife's cheek. "You're a good woman, Eliza. I hope you know that."

Eliza smiled briefly, sadly, and then Pap Redd spoke again, concluding the auction.

"Well, Platte," he declared, his eyes boring into those of a suddenly squirming Bill Hutchings, "despite that one or two of these folks you're leading is so crooked you could screw them into the ground like a corkscrew, or that most of 'em are so poor they burn their feet ever time they strike a match, the auction has worked. There ain't nary a cheese left in that bag, you have a little money for the public works fund, and most folks will have a taste or two of cheese by morning. And I allow I was wrong on another point, too. Comes down to it, there's more sand in some of their craws than there is in all the slapjacks in the whole blamed camp! And that's saying something, Brother Lyman! It truly is!"

49

Monday, February 16, 1880

Little Water Spring, Monument Valley

"You boys had enough water?" Spud Hudson was being pushy with the twenty men who were riding with him, and he knew it. But he also knew he'd been way too long in Navajo country, and the faster he had them all back across the San Juan and off the reservation, the happier he would feel. Besides that, he was chilled to the bone from the raw wind blowing down from the north, they were fresh out of coffee and most everything else that was edible, and he knew there'd be no warming fire until they were safely across the river and back at Mitchells' Trading Post.

It had been a tragic mission anyway, beginning as maybe a rescue of two white men and ending as a well-armed pony express bearing between all twenty-one so-called rescuers one half-written letter, some odds and ends of personal possessions, and a whole heartful of bad news. But how could anyone have known it would end that way? he thought as he watched the men, some of them his own, tightening saddle girths and climbing aboard their tired mounts. How could anyone have predicted that the Indians—Navajo or Pahute, depending on who was telling the story—would for no reason at all go on the warpath? And how could anyone have turned down the mother's plea of Mrs. Mitchell that somebody come down into this godforsaken country and find her missing son?

It couldn't have been done otherwise, and Spud Hudson knew it. And that was part of what made the whole blooming affair so doggone tragic. Despite the outcome, despite the two dead and mutilated bodies they had found and hastily buried in shallow graves, and despite the nearly two weeks he and twenty additional men had sacrificed in the doing of it, it would not be the end.

No siree, the deaths of Mitchell and Merrick would not be the last of it. Other white men would die in this country, maybe a whole lot more than a few. And other white men would just as certainly set out to try and rescue them and in the process maybe lose a few of their own, though in that at least he had been lucky. But he had not been lucky in finding all that silver spread about on the ground near Mitchell's cave; no, nor in having a bunch of the boys right there to find it with him. For now twenty men were riding with their hearts afire with dreams of instant wealth, twenty men who would have no more chance than snow in a hot skillet of finding the mine young Mitchell and Merrick had apparently found, and even less than that of getting silver out of it and bringing it home alive.

Of course, not all of these boys would be fool enough to try. But there would be a few, men who thought of nothing but instant wealth, sorry fools who went crazy as popcorn being shaken over a hot fire at the merest mention of lost or hidden treasure—

"The boys are ready, Spud."

The speaker was Bill Ball, the lanky Texican who was running the LC for Mrs. Lacy now that her husband had been bushwhacked by that miserable Sugar Bob Hazelton. Spud liked Bill Ball, liked the way he talked, liked the way he rode, liked the way he managed both men and cattle. It was a shame Mrs. Lacy needed him so doggone bad, for Spud would have hired him in a minute and turned the whole shooting match of his spread over to him so's he could retire and head out into the high lonesome to find a more remote country to settle. But Mrs. Lacy needed him too, so that was that.

Of course, with the country filling up and getting crowdeder'n fleas at a dog show, one of these days he might just pick up and go anyway, leaving the whole kit and caboodle of his outfit for Curly Bill Jenkins or whatever other sorry cowpoke was fool enough to settle down and work it—

For a time the men rode in silence, their trail the sandy wash that would ultimately spill into the San Juan. The country around them seemed bleak and empty, relieved only by occasional junipers and

411

the ever-present shadscale and sage. Behind them rose Hogan Mesa, and off to their right the looming bulk of Flat Top Mountain. At the moment there was little snow on the ground, but Spud could feel it in the air, and that made him all the more anxious to get across the river and on toward home.

"This ain't the way we came, Spud." The speaker was Parl Everett, a confirmed bachelor who'd become his *segundo*. He was a good man, too, though at times he didn't stop to think before he spoke, a trait Spud could hardly tolerate. Neither could he tolerate the man's penchant for being a pessimist.

"I reckon there must be some reason you're going this way, since it's longer by somewhat than the way we went out," Parl continued.

"There is."

"Well?"

Spud sighed at the weight of the burden he was forced to carry. "I want to get off the reservation," he said without looking at the man. "Place makes me feel about as welcome as a polecat at a Sunday picnic, and Montezuma Creek is the closest crossing I know of."

Parl nodded. "I reckon it is, happen the river ain't high and we don't get caught in no quicksand."

Now Spud did look at him. "You notice any spring thaws going on around here? Or turrible storms, either one? Parl, she's cold enough to make the cows give icicles and polar bears hunt for cover, and the whole blamed country's dryer than a sack of Bull Durham. I'm telling you, she's colder nor a Montana well-driller and drier'n a wooden leg, which means the river will be low and the ford good."

Parl nodded soberly. "I expect you're right, Spud. Course, a man can't never tell what might be going on in the high country."

"What do you mean, he can't?" Spud was absolutely disgusted. "Ain't you never noticed that the storms pass eastward across this country? And ain't you never noticed that the high country you're so dad-blasted worried about is out east of here? What that means, you chuckle-headed, addlebrained nincompoop, is that before some turrible storm stirs things up over in them San Juan Hills, she's got to first do a little stirring up in these parts. And since no storms have been stirring up these parts in quite a spell, and since she's too blamed cold to thaw what snow has been laid down in storms past, we'll cross that river with no trouble a-tall."

Spud glared at Parl then, just daring him to make another comment. But being of slightly more sound mind than Spud was willing to give him credit for, Parl didn't. Trouble was, Wax Wilson started up the chin music from another quarter, and Spud found his refrain even more distasteful than Parl's.

"This here silver is sure something," the man abruptly declared, holding a chunk of the metal in his hand and examining it carefully. "Practically pure just as she is. Those boys sure must have found that lost Navajo silver mine, all right."

"*Peshlaki,*" Ichabod 'Icky' Jones volunteered. "That's what I hear she's called. *Peshlaki.* It means silver in Navajo."

"How do you know that, Icky?" Spud growled, thinking the man had more lip than a muley cow. "You savvy Navajo or something?"

"Well, no. But that's what I've heard, and it does make sense."

"So does those two boys getting kilt for fooling around where they hadn't ought to have been. But that don't make it right!"

"You reckon that really is *Peshlaki* silver?" Bill Ball asked, his voice low.

"I don't hardly know." Spud was more amiable to Bill Ball than he had been to the others. "What I do know, Bill, is that what silver we gathered up had ought to go to the Mitchells. That, and every man-jack one of us had ought to take a solemn vow that we won't get no leaky mouths and go blabbing across all the rest of creation about what we found, nor turn chuckleheaded and greedy enough to sneak back into this Navajo country our own selves trying to find the mine it came from.

"*Peshlaki* or no," he declared then, speaking to the group as a whole, "that silver has blood on it, boys, probably lots more'n we can guess. And any man who wants to go add his own blood to the pot just ain't got the brains of a grasshopper. Besides which, I for one ain't got the least notion of a desire to come gallivanting down here again just to put a few more idjits to bed with a pick and a shovel."

The men grew silent then, thinking either of the two men they had buried and the undisputed wisdom of Spud Hudson, or of the incredibly pure silver they'd been smart enough to find. And they were still thinking when they rode out of the wash to look across the ford to the mouth of Montezuma Creek.

"Hell's tinkling hot brass bells!" Spud growled in surprise as he saw the low cabin and corrals built by the two Mormon missionary families who'd homesteaded the bottoms the previous summer. "I plumb forgot these folks was here." He had, too, and wouldn't have come this way had he remembered. Tarnation! Why couldn't such fools stay to home and leave the country—his country, he was fond of thinking—well enough alone. Now, by tophet, he'd for sure have to sell, for these folks would be just the beginning—

"Weren't a whole passel of others supposed to have joined them by now?" he asked as he looked both up and down the river.

"I heard by Christmas," Bill Ball replied quietly. "Reckon something turrible must have happened, Spud. Those folks yonder are sure-enough alone."

Spud sighed and nodded, knowing it would make no difference. The ones who were lost, or others just like them—it wouldn't matter. Shortly the country would be swarming with white folks—Mormon sky pilots out to save the world, no doubt—and his peace and solitude would be gone forever.

"Boys," he declared after another sigh of frustration and discouragement, speaking again to the entire group, "we'll stop at yonder cabin and warm up. But don't none of you go taking a fancy to nothing these Mormon folks have, food or otherwise. And by otherwise," he snarled fiercely, looking directly at Wax Wilson and one or two of the others, "I mean women!

"Now I reckon, what with no supplies coming in, that those folks yonder are going to be hungry enough to eat our wet saddle blankets. Course I know we're practically destitute ourselves, but if any of you miserable sons have anything extry in your saddlebags—a dab of flour, bacon, or anything else that can be chewed and swallowed, well, I'll just bet those folks yonder could use it."

"But . . . they're Mormons, Spud!"

"So?" Spud questioned, glaring at the man who'd spoken.

The man shifted uncomfortably in his saddle. "Way I hear it, Mormons have horns and are in league with the devil hisself!"

Spitting to the side and watching the wind carry his spittle away,

Spud showed his disgust. "That there's utter nonsense, Fin, and you'd best know I feel that way lest you make the mistake of saying it again. Mind you, I ain't auguring their religion, concerning which I admit to being plumb ignorant. What I am auguring is that they're human folks just like you and me, and any harebrained idjit what says they have horns or any other such tommyrot—well, somebody had ought to throw a dally around his tongue and snub it up afore he trips on it and breaks his neck. And as to Mormons being in league with the devil, I reckon some of you are a sight closer to that than those poor starving folks across the river. So I say we get over there and help out with whatever little we can.

"Any of you don't want to help," he concluded with finality, "that's fine. But don't expect a place at my table no more."

"Same goes for the LC," Bill Ball stated quietly.

There was a murmur of agreement among most of the twenty cowhands, and so with a nod to Bill Ball, who was smiling grimly, Spud kneed his horse toward the scarcely covered ford of the river.

The Desert Northeast of Moenkopi, Arizona Territory

It was cold where Frank sat in the *atchí'deezáhi,* the forked stick hogan of the man Peokon. In the place where the fire should have been burning there were only ashes, and Frank had been unable to find any firewood nearby with which to kindle a new flame. Neither could he look farther afield, for there was a great fear in the man Peokon's eyes that grew worse whenever Frank left the hogan.

Shivering in spite of the blanket he had wrapped about himself, Frank looked at his old friend and found himself filled with wonder. Had he not ridden to this place to report the theft of the mormonee *belacani* horses by Taddytin and Zon Kelli, and more important had he not known that this was indeed his old friend, Frank would never have believed what he was seeing, would never have recognized the man. Peokon's once-powerful chest had caved in, his back had grown stooped, his legs and arms looked like knobby sticks, and his gait had dwindled from a strong walk to an agonizingly slow shuffle. But it was the man's eyes that Frank could not stop himself from

415

staring at—the hollow, blood-shot eyes that no longer closed in sleep, did not even seem to *nischíl,* to blink. Instead the one called Peokon stared about him fearfully, his mouth open and drawn back across his teeth and his eyes darting here and there as if he were seeking the hiding place of an enemy no one else could see.

Nor could Frank wonder at the man's fear. Since his own departure for the hogan of his kinsman Tsabekiss to begin the raid across the Kaibab, the raid Peokon himself had envisioned and set in motion, much evil had come to pass in this place. Peokon's prize horses had begun dying, the large flock of sheep and goats belonging to his woman had also begun perishing at the rate of several a day, one of his two tall sons had been killed in a fall, and only the day before Frank's arrival Peokon's woman, weeping loudly that the spring had gone suddenly dry, stumbled and died just outside the entry to the hogan, her empty waterpot still gripped in her lifeless fingers.

Frank could not fathom such disaster, could not imagine what was causing it. And even as he was moving the woman's body and sending a runner to alert her clansmen of her passing, he was also fighting himself, forcing himself to return to Peokon's hogan, to this terrifying place of death, that he might further assist his ailing friend.

Now as he sat trying not to look at the staring, empty eyes, Frank began again to wonder what had brought this calamity upon the house of Peokon. Maybe the man had been fooling with wood that had been struck by lightning. Or maybe he had been around a grave too much. Or maybe he had a ghost sickness—a witch (which Frank didn't like to think about because Peokon had long ago convinced him they did not exist) had blown some bone from a dead person into him, which would also cause him to die.

Frank didn't know, and neither did he dare ask the man laid out on the ground beside him, the man who should have known. In fact, he dared not ask Peokon anything any longer. Each time he did, each time he even opened his mouth to speak of other things, the man's eyes would open wider than they already were, and he would begin wailing for *ázéé,* for death to come and take him. Truly, Frank thought as he sat on the dirty sheepskin beside Peokon in the frigid hogan, his old friend was *nihoneeláah,* he was dying a slow and painful death.

50

Tuesday, February 17, 1880

Wilson Canyon

"You all right, Billy?"

Looking up from where he was crouched against the rock, trying to shield himself for a moment from the wind and snow, Billy did his best to hide his pain. A toothache he'd been ignoring for several days was suddenly pounding in his lower jaw with a vengeance, and every time he swung his pick his entire face felt like it was going to explode. Of a truth, that was why he'd been crouching down, avoiding the wind while he pressed handfuls of snow against his jaw, trying to gain a little relief.

Still, that was his problem, not Platte's, and so quickly Billy rose and turned his chapped and bleeding lips into a smile. "I'm fine, Platte. I . . . I was just trying to warm my hands so I could hang onto this pick."

Nodding his understanding, Platte kicked some freshly fallen snow from the rough roadway Billy and others had been picking and drilling down the rock wall of the narrow defile known as Wilson Canyon.

Never more than a few hundred feet deep, the canyon nevertheless twisted for several miles across the face of the massive stone mountain the expedition was on, and it could be crossed only by picking and blasting out a roadway from the top to the bottom of the south side.

But that brought up an interesting point about Billy's thesis that they were crossing the bed of an ancient sea. It was now obvious to

417

him that the whole country from the upper end of the Escalante Desert to somewhere beyond where they now were, was nothing more than a huge mountain of sandstone that had been eroded into fantastic shapes and formations by wind and water and cut deeply by various rivers, including the Colorado and the San Juan. Even this relatively small canyon had been cut and eroded by water, for in the bottom were several large stone tanks, all kept full of water by a small seep or spring somewhere above where they were crossing.

He, Kumen, Platte, Alvin Decker, and some of the others in the company had discussed this sandstone formation endlessly, and now several agreed with Billy. Why, there were even places where the sandstone was rippled exactly as wind and water rippled regular sand along the banks of the Colorado. Such evidences of the sandstone's ancient origins seemed conclusive to Billy, though some remained unconvinced.

Of course, nothing he could think of explained the formation running up the north side of the canyon across from where he and Platte were standing—the formation the four explorers a couple of months before had dubbed the Chute. From the bottom of the canyon it ran practically straight up the north slope in a dizzying climb of between two and three hundred feet—a flat-bottomed cut whose perpendicular sides were exactly wide enough for the passage of wagons. In other words it was a steep but negotiable roadway up through an otherwise impassable cliff, a roadway that had been cut by the hand of nature—or the Lord, as many in the company were now saying. But whoever had cut it, Billy knew it was saving them three to four days of hard labor, and that was a blessing no matter what one believed.

"She's cold, all right," Platte finally acknowledged. "Folks say it isn't supposed to snow when it's this cold, but it seems they forgot to tell old Mother Nature."

"Or the Lord," Billy added. "Since he's promised to give us only good gifts, I've been trying all morning to see what possible good a foot of new snow will do us on this rocky trail. Unless he's trying to kill a few of us off by making the rock more slippery than usual, I can't come up with a thing."

Platte chuckled. "Well, since we've all been well preserved thus far, I don't think that's it. Rather I think it's just opposition, a little more of the vicissitudes of the flesh we're all called upon to pass through."

"Then this entire expedition is beginning to seem like one long vicissitude," Billy admitted quietly.

Looking off through the still-falling snow, Platte nodded. "I agree, Billy. I don't suppose any of us ever imagined anything quite like this."

"We *are* starting to look like a bunch of ragamuffins." Billy's grin was wider. "Most folks's boots are wearing mighty thin, and at least my britches have patches on their patches."

"You're not alone," Platte admitted. "Look at this hole in my coat. Half the back's hanging loose, and it's the only coat I have. Makes me wish I had my wife with me, for she's a real hand at stitching."

"Eliza'd be happy to mend it for you."

"So would either of my sisters, or Joe's wife Nellie. Trouble is, I don't take it off long enough to give any of them the chance. Too afraid of freezing to death, I reckon.

"But what amazes me, Billy, is the general good health of our company. In spite of the harsh winter weather and the snow and mud and other conditions we're forced to live with, and in spite of the fact that we're living on limited rations of ground seed grain and occasional stringy beef, there have been no major illnesses since we left our homes in October. Even the children are healthy. To me it's an absolute fact that the Lord is blessing us beyond belief—for which I find myself offering up continual thanksgiving.

"Speaking of which, how's Eliza feeling?"

"Like you said, remarkably well. Oh, she's starting to feel a little uncomfortable now that she's getting bigger, but the sisters who've been through it tell her that's normal. She has a lot of strength, and she's always keeping herself busy. Did you know she's been teaching some of the children how to weave?"

"Ann Rowley told me that. She said Eliza had gathered some cattail fronds while we were down in Cottonwood, and after only two or three lessons the Rowley children and maybe a dozen others are already making fans, baskets, bonnets, and all sorts of useful things. Eliza's a good woman, Billy. A very good woman!"

"I know that. I just wish she did."

Platte nodded his understanding. "Sometimes it takes awhile to discover things in ourselves that God and maybe a few others have seen all along. Sort of like you being a fine trail-hand, Billy. I dare-say six months ago you'd never have dreamed you'd be doing things that now come as naturally as breathing. Yet here you are, a good teamster, a fine hand with stock, according to Ben Perkins practically an expert in both single- and double-jacking, and above all a loving husband who has the respect and admiration of his wife. And that's in addition to the wonderful skills you had when you left Cedar City."

"Platte—"

"Oh, I know. Besides being modest you still don't see those things as clearly as I do, and you probably doubt all of them. Yet you wonder that Eliza doesn't see in herself the great qualities you and the rest of us marvel at."

Billy grinned crookedly. "I suppose we're all paradoxes, aren't we."

"For a fact. But I'll tell you one thing, Billy, and I mean this with all my heart. What Eliza has done, apologizing to folks, including me, and writing letters to people she fears she's offended in the past—well, I think it's a wonderful thing, extremely courageous because of the humility it's required. It's certain to bring the bless-ings of heaven not just on her but on the entire company. Now, I don't know when it will happen, but I feel certain that one day soon the Lord will give her the peace she's seeking. And then, Billy, when she's truly at peace with herself, God will start to reveal to her soul her own true identity."

"Do you feel we're all supposed to have such knowledge?"

"To one extent or another, yes, I do—and be comfortable with it, to boot." Platte smiled. "Do you suppose that God could be God, Billy, if he wasn't at peace about owning all the wonderful qualities of Godhood he possesses? And since Jesus commanded us to be like God, can we feel less about ourselves and still be obedient?

"The trouble is, in our inner souls it's far easier for most of us to acknowledge weaknesses and failures than it is to recognize goodness and strength. I believe we see this as humility, though in fact it may just be another manifestation of pride.

"However, when we humble ourselves as Eliza is doing, and seek diligently for the peace of the Holy Spirit, then God will surely reveal to us that our sins have been forgiven and remitted through the precious blood of Christ, making us clean before him. In that way only can we gain a correct understanding of the Atonement, and in that way only can we begin to attain inner peace.

"But that is only the beginning. Afterward, as we continue faithful, I believe that God will begin to reveal however much we need to know about our own eternal natures and identities. And he'll burn that knowledge into our hearts through the fire of the Holy Ghost until we can no longer doubt it. Such knowledge gives perfect peace, Billy, and it's part of what the Prophet Joseph called an anchor to the soul, making us sure and steadfast in our daily walk before the Lord."

Platte paused and looked up. "What do you know," he breathed. "The snow has stopped. That means we'll have to continue this discussion another time. If you and the rest of the boys are finished chipping this road out, Billy, then I think we'll have time to take a good portion of the company through here and up the Chute onto Gray Mesa before dark."

"Sounds good to me," Billy replied, his toothache practically forgotten. And with a will he bent to picking off the remainder of the small rock ledge that he thought might be a hindrance to the coming train of wagons.

———o—o—o———

Gray Mesa

Her eyes opening wide, Eliza was awake in an instant. Just as quickly she was aware that she was alone under the heavy quilts, and that Billy was gone. Was that what had awakened her? she wondered. Billy crawling out of the wagon? But no, she'd heard a sound of some sort, a small sound that had penetrated her slumber and instantly roused her into wakefulness. But what might it have been? What could have—

Pulling the quilts off her face she stared upward, listening intently. Above her the frosty cloud of her breath hung almost without motion, and only then was she aware that the terrible wind had stopped. Earlier several wagons, including their own, had been taken down the tortuous trail to the bottom of Wilson Canyon. There Eliza had watched as several teams had pulled each of the wagons up the amazing Chute.

By the time Kumen and James Pace had helped her hobble up after them, Billy had already driven ahead toward the camping place on the top of Gray Mesa. Leaning against the terrific wind, Eliza had followed after, and she would have been forced to walk the entire two miles if Francis Webster hadn't come along and offered her a ride on the wagon he was driving.

Of course, Billy had had no choice but to keep moving, for it wouldn't do for him to stop on the roadway and block the progression of the others. Eliza understood that. But then, neither had he realized how ferocious the wind actually was, or how dangerous the cold on top of the mesa might be for her in her delicate condition. Eliza knew that because she herself had been just as naive, insisting that she'd be able to walk after Billy as far as he could travel before dark.

Thank goodness the Lord had seen fit to help her! Thank goodness he'd sent Brother Webster with an empty space on his wagon seat where she might ride while shielded by two of his quilts—

Now they were camped next to one of the Lyman wagons, with Kumen and Mary on the other side of them and several others scattered nearby. And all of them were located on top of the barren mesa where they were absolutely without shelter save for each other. It wasn't a good camping spot, but then neither was anyplace else that she or Billy or the others could see. Up here there were no huge rocks, no trees, and no fuel for fires except the useless black shadscale. What there was, Eliza thought with discouragement, was the driving wind and clouds upon clouds of drifting, stinging snow.

Yet now the wind had stopped, the drifting snow had grown still, and Eliza was wide awake and listening. But for what? What had she heard? What—

There! The sound came again, barely audible in the stillness, and Eliza knew at once it was the sound of someone in great pain.

"Billy?" she whispered so as not to disturb the occupants of nearby wagons. "Billy, is that you?"

When her question was greeted by silence, Eliza rose to her knees, pushed aside the heavy canvas draped above the door, and peered out. For a moment she didn't see him, but when she did she knew immediately that her husband was having serious problems. He was seated below her on one of their chairs, bent over with his head held lower than the top of the table, and he was rocking back and forth in agony.

"Billy," she whispered as she grabbed a quilt and pushed it out to drape over his trembling shoulders. "Billy, darling, what is it? What's wrong?"

Without looking up or responding, Billy reached out and scooped another handful of snow, which he pressed against the side of his face. With the effort came a slight moaning, and now Eliza knew what she'd been hearing.

"Billy Foreman, speak to me!" she whispered sternly. "Tell me what the matter is!"

"M . . . my tooth," Billy mumbled in reply. "Something terrible's happened to it, Eliza, and I . . . I don't know what to do."

"Your tooth? Billy, darling, are you sure it's a tooth?"

Silently Billy nodded. "It . . . it's been aching off and on for a couple of weeks, maybe three."

"Why haven't you said something?"

"I don't know. I reckon I didn't want to burden you with it. Besides, it didn't really get bad until today. And then maybe an hour ago it felt like something in there popped, and now I feel like I . . . I want to die—"

"Well, you aren't dying, Billy Foreman!" Eliza was busy pulling on shoes and her buffalo coat. "If it's a tooth, we'll find someone who can pull it out."

"But . . . it's the middle of the night—"

"Which means nothing at all," she responded as she lowered herself into the snow. "Keep the cold on it, Billy, and I'll be back in a moment or so."

And without even thinking to take her crutch, Eliza hobbled away through the snow.

———o–o–o———

"Well, Billy, you look worse'n a leppy calf with the slobbers!" Gently Pap Redd pried Billy's hands away so he could better see the swollen jaw in the pale light from Eliza's lantern. "My, my," he declared softly. "You're either hiding a fresh goose egg in there, youngster, or you've got yourself a mighty bad tooth."

"It isn't an egg," Billy mumbled. "I can guarantee that. And right now, Pap, I don't feel like no youngster."

"And I don't feel like no dentist." The older man grinned in the lamplight. "Howsomever, Billy, I've got the forceps and somewhere between two and three hundred teeth in a jar back home on Ash Creek to prove I can use 'em. You game to add another to my collection?"

"I'm game for a doublejack in the forehead if it'll stop this pounding."

Pap Redd chuckled and straightened up. "I reckon we can do better than that. Why, I've set scores of broken bones and replaced dislocated joints, I've sewed folks back together when you'd have sworn they was torn asunder permanent, and two or three times I've even delivered babies. And all that with no more training than faith and reading a book on anatomy about a hundred times." Turning then he glanced at the sorry remains of their fire. "Eliza, ma'am, is that water in your kettle anywhere near close to boiling?"

"I don't think so—"

"Our water is still quite warm," Mary Jones declared. She and Kumen had arisen after Eliza had awakened them asking who in the company pulled teeth, and it had been Kumen who'd gone after Pap Redd. Now they, along with John and Pauline Pace and Ida Evelyn Lyman, stood by to offer whatever assistance they could.

"Good," Pap declared. "If you wouldn't mind, Mary, I'd appreciate you stoking your fire with whatever you've got to burn and boiling up a few half-inch wide strips of clean rag for me. And Ida, John, and Pauline, I'm going to need as many lanterns as I can get here so I can take a fair-to-middling look at what I'm doing."

"Why do you need boiled rags?" Eliza asked in wonder.

"I don't rightly know. But ever since I started boiling the rags I use to stuff into the hole after the tooth comes out, I haven't had any dry sockets. You know, holes filled with putrefaction. For some reason boiled rags seem to stop that."

While Eliza sat with her arm about her husband, and the others were hurrying after lanterns and fuel for the Jones's fire, Pap began washing his hands in Eliza's kettle of water.

"You remember the first time we met, Billy?" he asked as he scrubbed. "I know you ain't up to much talking, so I'll remind you. I was captain over the twenty-two men who guarded Brother Brigham during his last trip south back in the winter of '76-'77. You and me were practically companions all the way from Nephi to St. George."

"I . . . don't remember."

Pap chuckled. "I didn't imagine you would. Way I recollect, Brigham had you hopping pretty much from daylight to dark and then some, writing letters, scribing talks, doing books and such. Even when we was traveling, you sat in the back of his carriage with a desk on your lap, writing away to beat the band. Looked to me like you put out more documents in those two weeks than the whole blamed U.S. Congress in a year-long session."

"President Young had a lot of affairs to look after," Billy acknowledged.

"I reckon. Some of the boys and I talked about you after we got to St. George, and most of us were mighty envious of your education. Oh, I can cipher some. But I haven't seen the inside of a schoolroom since I drove our ox team out of Nauvoo and headed for the wild west in Father James Pace's wagon company back in '50."

"How old were you then?" Kumen asked as he walked back to the wagon.

"Fourteen. My folks had come out of North Carolina to Tennessee, where they joined the Church and emigrated to Nauvoo. There all of us met the Prophet Joseph and learned the gospel of Christ from him. Fact is, my folks both got their patriarchal blessings under the hands of Hyrum Smith, the Prophet's brother.

"Now Billy, I'm going to do a little tapping on those teeth, and it'll hurt some. But you've got to tell me which tooth hurts the worst so I'll know which one to yank out. You ready?"

Silently Billy nodded.

"Good. You folks with the lanterns hold them up so I can see into Billy's mouth. And don't none of you try looking in there with me, you hear? I cast a big enough shadow all by my lonesome."

Everyone but Billy chuckled, and soon Pap was tapping inside Billy's mouth with the handle of his forceps, searching out the bad tooth. It didn't take long to find it, either, for Billy let out a yelp of pain when a large molar was tapped.

"That the one?" Pap asked innocently.

"Yeah," Billy breathed, "it felt like it."

"Want me to tap it again, to make sure?"

Quickly Billy shook his head.

"All right, ol' hoss, but don't come whimpering to me if we get the wrong one. After all, the first one's free, but the second one's twice the price and has to be paid in advance afore I do the work."

During the laughter that followed, Pap Redd set about arranging Billy the way he wanted him. Eliza's rocker was moved and Billy placed in it so he could be leaned back against the side of the wagon. Those with lanterns were next placed according to Pap's instructions, and Eliza took her place beside Billy where she could help Kumen hold his head still.

"Tragedies and trials like this make me want to say it serves you folks right for coming on this fool mission in the first place," Pap grumbled as he puttered about, making certain of the boiling rags and inserting his forceps into the still-boiling kettle of water. "No sir, when I heard about this expedition I went home and said to my wives Keziah Jane and Sariah Louisa that only a fool would take up a mission like that. The next thing I knew, my son Lemuel and his sweetheart Eliza Ann and my granddaughter Lula had signed on, and you know what that made them. But there's no fool like an old fool, I hear, for when Elder Snow asked if I'd go along to make certain all you young folks made it to the San Juan in one piece, I found myself agreeing to do it. Course, if I'd known then what I know now—"

Carefully Pap leaned over Billy, pried his mouth open wide, and instructed him to keep it that way, and then he repositioned Mary and John Pace and the three lanterns they were holding.

"Billy, this is going to hurt something awful, and I may have to

426

put my knee on your chest just to get some leverage. You okay with that?"

"Uh-huh."

"Good. Then hang on, because here we go. And by the by, I'm pleased you've been packing snow against your jaw, for cold's the next best thing to whiskey for numbing things. Besides which, I'm fresh out of whiskey and wouldn't have give it to you if I had any."

Again Pap tapped, grinned with satisfaction when Billy grimaced and flinched, and without hesitation worked his forceps into Billy's mouth and began to search for the right hold.

"Yes, sir," he grumbled as he worked, gripping the tooth and starting to twist and pull, "a man leaves school like I did never does amount to much. About all I've done with my life is raise kids, punch cows, and chase wild horses, not well and not necessarily in that order, either one. About the onliest smart thing I ever did was marry them two women of mine. Course, they're both homely as a mud fence with no more wits nor a one-eyed quill-pig. Had to be that way, I reckon, or they wouldn't have married me. But they do keep the home place mucked out fairly well and the fires lit, and as long as I throw the both of them in the creek ever now and again to drown the gray-back nits and sort of keep 'em fumigated, we get along tolerable well."

"Pap Redd, I declare!" Mary stormed playfully, doing her best not to giggle at the man's dry humor. "They're both beautiful, wonderful women, and you know it! As for wits, Keziah Jane told me herself how she and her sister Charity worked up at Fort Bridger earning their keep and enough extra that she was able to hand you a ten-dollar gold piece on your wedding day. And as for Sariah Louisa, I know all about how she saved her invalid father from the floodwaters of the Santa Clara by dragging him into a tree and then holding him there all night until rescue came."

"Humph!" Pap grunted as he continued twisting and prying. "All poppycock. And you probably think younguns grow up to be a credit to their folks and other such nonsense, too. Here my pa was a wealthy sea captain and a natural leader of men, and look how I turned out. A cowpoke. And it just gets worse. Take a gander at young Lem, heading off on this fool mission with no more idea nor a mud turtle of how he'll make a living in the midst of a desert filled with hordes of outlaws and wild Indians. No, sir, you youngsters hang onto this like a drunk to a whiskey jug, and don't you forget it. This here journey's only the beginning of your tough times, and—"

"Aaaaaagh!"

"There, by jings," Pap chuckled as he held a large molar up to the light, "we got 'er out, Billy! We surely did. Now sit up and spit that blood and bile out pronto, and keep spitting until there's nothing left to spit."

Billy did as he was directed, and all waited silently while the bleeding eased and finally stopped.

"Mary," Pap declared then, "I'll need those strips of rag. Fish 'em out with a fork, and I'll take 'em one at a time until he's all plugged up."

"And while she's getting them," Kumen declared as Pap sat down on the tongue of the wagon, "I'm going to set the record straight concerning Brother Redd here."

"Kumen Jones, you young whippersnapper—"

Smiling, Kumen held up his hand. "Not now, Pap. I want Billy and Eliza and Ida to know who you really are. Folks, Pap's a stockman, all right, and a lot more besides. After helping his folks build up Spanish Fork, he was called to settle first in Las Vegas and then later in New Harmony. There he bought the John D. Lee spread out on Ash Creek, and in the years since he's been chairman of the board of trustees of the school district, justice of the peace, a member of the Kane County Court and Probate Judge, and first counselor to Bishop Wilson Pace.

"He's also a founding member of the Kanarra and Harmony Cattle Company and has served for many years as director and treasurer. He's qualified himself as both a doctor and a dentist, and I've never known a man, other than maybe Billy here, who reads as voraciously and thrives on knowledge the way Pap does. In other words, his colorful and countrified slang is only there because he wants it to be. Pap Redd is an educated man."

"Hummph!"

"He was an officer in the Black Hawk War who actually fought the Indians," Kumen continued with a satisfied smile, "and then he doctored the wounded on both sides after the battle was over. He's generous to a fault, and the real reason he didn't accept a call to this mission is because he feels a need to work in the new temple in St. George on behalf of his ancestors. That means he's also what I'd call a spiritual giant.

"There, Pap. Did I leave anything out?"

"Not a whole lot," the man groused as he rose to his feet to begin working again in Billy's mouth. "Not unless you plan on mentioning that I'm pie-eyed enough to think I can see the sun shining through a charcoal sack during an eclipse, and just plain fool enough to think all you young missionaries are going to pull this settlement idea off and do it proper, to boot. Fact is, Kumen, you're nervier'n Billy's bad tooth here and confuseder than a blind dog in a butcher shop. Why, just today one of my son's wheelers threw a shoe I didn't manage to notice until he came up lame. That's when I was forced to admit that my head's stuffed fifty-fifty with creek sand and lava rock, and that given a month of Sundays to do it, I wouldn't know how to find the north end of a southbound mule when he was standing still. That's who I really am.

"Now Billy, you keep spitting out all the blood and putrefaction you can. If that wad of rag comes out, you have Eliza boil it and put it back in again. Right away you should start feeling better, and in a couple of days you should be able to throw the rag away and be practically good as new.

"Oh, and one more thing. Forget all this nonsense Kumen's been spreading around and pay attention to me. I'm the feller what'll tell you the truth about where the bear crossed over the pass, so don't you forget it."

And with a wink and a wide smile Pap Redd took up his forceps and Billy's tooth and disappeared into the pre-dawn darkness, leaving Eliza and all the rest of them to wonder at the greatness of the people with whom they'd been called to serve.

51

Saturday, February 21, 1880

Gray Mesa

"Merciful heavens, please don't let it be snowing again!" Mary Jones, clinging to the seat of the lumbering, lurching wagon, looked up apprehensively.

"If that's a prayer," Kumen teased from beside her where he sat holding the reins, "then Mary, my sweet, I fear it will be wasted. Not alone is it starting to snow again—for the fifth day in a row, I might add—but now the wind is picking up. See how the horses' manes and tails are blowing? I'd say we're about to be caught in another blizzard."

Gray Mesa, as it neared its northeastern end, widened considerably while remaining fairly level, and so the members of the San Juan expedition had also fanned out, creating several parallel roads and often driving beside each other as they hurried toward the shelter of a few trees that grew at the top of the thousand-foot drop they faced at the edge of the mesa.

"Do you really think we'll have shelter at the top of the Slickrocks?" Mary asked as she tucked the quilts more tightly about herself and her husband.

"George Morrell says so, and he was here in December with the explorers. Platte, George and Maggie Sevy, and a couple of others got to the top of the Slickrocks yesterday, so I suppose they'll have some sort of camp already laid out. Then too, we've got folks strung all the way back to Cheese Camp, so we may not need a lot of shelter. Just some plentiful firewood would suit me."

"And me!" As Mary watched the snow, she realized it was falling more horizontally than otherwise. Then she sighed with resignation. "It'll be another blizzard, all right. Lawsy, but I'm getting tired of winter—nearly as tired as I'm getting of blazing this fool road. Neither of them ever seems to end!"

"That'll be so until one day both of them do." Kumen chuckled.

"They'll probably both come on the same day, too." Peering ahead through the strengthening storm, Mary sought in vain for the stand of junipers she'd been told marked the edge of the Slickrocks. "Aren't we coming to the route George Hobbs found when he was trying to rope that mountain sheep?"

Kumen smiled. "That's right. He says they couldn't find a way off the cliffs, but on account of chasing after that sheep Hobbs was led right to the bottom. I hear Platte followed it down again yesterday. So the route down the cliff face is there. All we need to do is turn it into a road, and things'll be just dandy!"

But Mary, feeling more and more alarmed, would have none of his optimism. "Kumen, look how this snow is starting to come down. How . . . how will we ever manage to build a road down those cliffs in this kind of weather?"

Under the quilts Kumen reached over and took his wife's hand. "I don't hardly know, Mary, my love. I reckon we'll just work one day at a time like we've been doing all along, and leave to the Lord the weather and other things we can't do much about. But the Perkins brothers tell me we've still got some blasting powder, and Amasa Lyman and the boys from Panguitch are going to stick with us until we can get that road cut through. So snow or no snow, we'll get the road built, and don't you worry about it.

"Look at that, would you? The snow's already so thick I can hardly even see the Barney kids, let alone their wagons. And yonder Nell Fielding's sure gathering her brood together. See that? Hyrum's pulled off to wait for her. And she's afeared of storms, too. Why, the poor woman was fit to be tied when her brother set off alone for the San Juan the other day. I—"

"Her brother?"

"Certainly. George Hobbs. I was told he's Nell Fielding's brother. I was also told their other sister is Sarah Elizabeth Harriman, who's already at Montezuma Creek and, according to all four of the explorers, likely starving by now. That's why George was in such a hurry to get there with some supplies.

"Billy?" Kumen called out toward the wagon bouncing along next to his, "does this look like another blizzard to you?"

"The way this wind's picking up," Billy called back as he wiped the snow out of his eyes, "I'm afraid it does."

"I hope George Hobbs and those folks with the horses don't run into it," Kumen shouted back. "We've at least got wagons for shelter, but those sorry fellows don't have a thing!"

Billy nodded. "It'll be rough if they get caught in it, all right. Fact is, I've been feeling a little anxious about Eliza."

"She's not in your wagon?" Mary asked, fear filling her voice.

"No." Billy leaned to the side and tried to look back, but he was forced to turn away from the driving snow. "Maybe an hour ago she got down to walk," he shouted as he again wiped his eyes. "Said the wagon was too bumpy, and besides, she wanted to see the Great Bend of the San Juan."

"Billy—"

Billy shrugged helplessly. "You know Eliza, Mary. If she's anything, she's a woman with a mind of her own. Besides, the sun had even come out—"

"That's when she started walking?" Mary was obviously frightened. "Oh, Kumen, what'll we do? What'll *she* do? That's surely two miles back. Now a blizzard's coming on, and she's big with child and all crippled besides. Maybe we should all turn around."

"Thank you, Mary," Billy said, suddenly taking charge, "but I don't think we should do that, not with the weather turning off like it is. Too dangerous for the animals, besides which Eliza wouldn't stand for it anyway. No, let's get into the shelter of the trees and get our teams out of their harnesses, and then if she hasn't caught us I'll head back and find her."

"But Billy—"

"Mary, Dick Butt told me an animal can suffocate if it's driven into the teeth of a heavy blizzard. This one's turning heavy!"

"Dick's right," Kumen agreed. "I've seen it."

"Besides which, Eliza's been here before, if you know what I mean. She'll know exactly what to do, Mary, and don't you doubt it for a minute."

"But . . . but what if she can't? What if she's hurt?"

"In that case I'll find her and bring her back!"

"And I'll help," Kumen declared quickly. "But remember, Mary, there are other wagons behind us, too, and one or two have pulled off the trail. Fact is, I saw one a little bit ago—it looked like the Larson outfit. Happen she needs it, Eliza could surely get shelter with them—"

---◦—◦—◦---

Along the Backbone of the San Juan

The snow was definitely worse, having quickly become a driving blizzard that felt as though it were sucking her very breath away. Ducking her head Eliza pressed on, knowing that it would do no good to rest, to sit down and curl up and wait for it to stop. Fact is, such a move could kill both herself and the baby, and she wasn't about to do that, not to the child, not to Billy. Thank the Lord the wind was coming from behind her. At least she could bury her face in the buffalo-skin coat and still keep breathing.

It had now been a week and a day since she and Billy had hitched Dick and Parley Butt's gaunt and shaggy mules to their wagon and pulled out of Cheese Camp, a week and a day of hard roads and agonizingly slow travel. Fact is, Eliza believed they'd covered less than ten miles. And within an hour or so they would be stopped again for another week, maybe more, while a road was chipped and blasted down the tumbling face of the Slickrocks.

Worse, in the days since leaving Cheese Camp, there had been little or no shelter, and day and night they'd been forced to deal with howling winds and fearful blizzards. Despite the prayers of practically the entire company, the storms seemed destined to continue. Fiercely the weather raged, and somehow the pioneers made their way before it, never stopping and never *ever* coming to the end of their journey!

At the moment, the snow was at least a foot deep on top of the Backbone, though in the gullies and other spots it had drifted much deeper. It was these, pockets of snow sometimes deeper than her head, that Eliza was doing her best to avoid.

A little earlier the snow had stopped and the clouds lifted, and for the first time she'd been able to see why the men were calling this stretch of Gray Mesa the backbone of the San Juan. Off to the left the mesa dropped gradually away to the Rincon and the Colorado River. To her right, though, the land dropped steeply and then plummeted more than a thousand feet practically straight down to where the San Juan had cut a huge bend out of the base of the mesa. It was an awe-inspiring sight, and Eliza had decided to leave Billy and the wagon and walk a little to the side of the road to get a better look.

But there had been more to her desire to be alone than a mere wish to see off the top of another cliff. For days she'd been pondering Billy's vision, as well as the story of his own repentance, doing her best to understand it. For she was certain her husband—or maybe the Lord through him—had been telling her something that had not yet been put into words.

She'd thought maybe the quiet of being away from the squeaking wagons and bellowing, braying livestock might allow her to think it through. Instead, however, Billy's vision of himself hammering the nails through Christ's outstretched hand continued to repeat itself in her mind, an excruciatingly brief and terrible panorama that would not leave her alone. Instead of being Billy's experience, therefore, it had become hers; constantly she could see the suffering Jesus lying on the ground at her feet, watching her eyes as *she* raised the heavy mallet to drive the spike through his quivering flesh.

Desperately she'd prayed that this terrible image be taken from her mind; in fact, she'd been praying for relief when she walked away from the wagon. But no respite had come, no release from the haunting view the Lord had somehow transposed from Billy's soul into her own.

When God had not removed the image, but had even seemed to make it more vivid than ever, Eliza had finally begun praying to know why. For far longer than she'd intended, she had pleaded for this information. Why was God forcing her to watch such a horrid view? Why would he give her no peace, no sense that she'd been forgiven and could be accepted back into his divine presence?

Now as she struggled through the snow, Eliza remained in ignorance, for no answer had come, at least none that she could discern. And though she would willingly have prayed longer, forcing herself to remain until the Lord responded, the clouds had lowered and the blizzard had hit again.

With sudden fear born of her long-ago experiences in Wyoming Eliza had struggled to her feet and turned back toward the road. That alone had taken her what seemed like hours, and now that she was on the track she had no idea how far ahead Billy and the others had gone. Billy likely wasn't worried, either, for Eliza had done this in the past, dropping out and then catching a ride with one of the wagons that was coming up behind. And the company was certainly spread out now, with the lead wagons sometimes two or three days ahead of the stragglers.

Since so many animals had been left behind on the Escalante Desert, several groups now had more wagons than they did teams. Thus they were forced to move one or two of their wagons into camp, unhitch their teams, trudge back to the previous camp, hitch up to their additional wagons, and take the trail all over again. Often this consumed two and even three days going the same distance she and Billy could travel in one, and it was part of the reason they were all moving so slowly—somewhat, she thought, like a giant organ grinder's accordion.

Steven Smith, son of Captain Silas Smith, had been doing this with his father's wagons. And Platte, Edward, Walter, and Joseph Lyman had also been traveling in this manner, relaying their several wagons with the use of just a few good teams. Combined with the necessary labor of building the road, it was an exhausting way to travel, but at least it had afforded Eliza a sufficiency of wagons in which to hitch a ride.

Until now, she thought bleakly. Until now.

Onward through the blowing and drifting snow she struggled, clutching her wooden crutch and hobbling as fast as she could. No longer was she feeling the cold, no longer was the image of herself

435

aiding in Jesus' crucifixion the only thought plaguing her mind. She was thinking now of Billy, aching to be in his arms or seated beside him on the wagon with her feet on the rocks he so painstakingly heated at every fire they ever kindled, aching further with the guilt of knowing that she might even perish, taking their unborn child with her and leaving Billy alone in this horrid wilderness.

And then, somehow, the road vanished. Or at least she lost it. The ruts left by the wagons had filled in with drifting snow, leaving her nothing to follow, no direction to go that felt right, and with great fear Eliza knew she was lost. Yet she had to keep moving! She had to find the company—

"Oh, dear Father in heaven," her mind screamed in panic, "don't let me do this to my poor darling Billy—"

When she bumped into the glass-eyed mare, Eliza was at first unaware of what animal it was. But as the fool animal nickered and nuzzled her, Eliza finally realized she had been found by Billy's unlikely pet.

Putting her arm around the mare's neck, she stood in its lee, feeling the snow swirl around her but being at least partially spared the force of the wind. For several moments she rested, wondering if she could possibly mount the animal and ride it to where Billy was. But then the mare, of its own accord, turned and plodded slowly away, leaving Eliza no choice but to follow. But at least its hooves had broken a trail through the snow, and when an exhausted Eliza reached out and grasped the mare's tail with her free hand, it paid no mind but continued forward, pulling her along at a gait perfectly suited to her own stumbling feet.

"Take me to Billy," Eliza found herself whispering as she moved, timing her words to the swishing of her feet through the snow. "Take me to Billy, you wonderful glass-eyed critter—"

The two wagons, when Eliza and the glass-eyed mare practically stumbled into them only a few moments later, were stopped. One had been there long enough for the ruts from its wheels to have filled with snow; the other must have arrived only a moment or so before, for the snow was still falling from where it had packed on the iron tires.

"This is one of the Smith wagons," Eliza muttered as she

released the mare's tail and limped past the newest arrival, recognizing the wagon as well as the gear packed on the side. "And this other one looks like Mons and Olivia Larson's—"

There was a sudden cry and some shouting, and as Eliza reached the front of the wagon, she was dumbfounded to see through the falling snow the youthful Olivia laid out on the spring seat of the wagon, alone except for her two small sons, just finishing the delivery of a tiny baby boy.

"Yust vone moment longer!" Mons was shouting from the other side of the wagon. "Yust a little bit more, Livvy, und Brother Smith und I vill have the tent erected—"

"Olivia?" Eliza questioned, still too surprised to truly comprehend.

"Oh, Eliza," Olivia gasped as she tried to cling to the wagon seat and wrap the baby at the same time. "Is . . . is that you? Thank goodness you've come! I've been praying for a woman to help me!"

"But . . . I don't know how to do this—"

"Just hold him, Eliza!" the young woman pleaded, wiping the combination of sweat and melting snow from her brow. "Climb up here and hold him close to my mouth so I can bite through the cord. Then wrap him in these blankets and keep him warm until I can take care of the afterbirth."

"Oh, dear," Eliza breathed as she clambered up the wheel and took the tiny infant from his mother and then held him out for her. "I don't know how to do this—"

With fumbling fingers the young mother tied a string around the umbilical cord near the baby's body. With one snap of her teeth she then severed the cord, and seconds later Eliza found herself back on the ground and around the corner of the wagon with her back to the wind, wrapping the child, holding him under her coat, and rubbing his tiny body vigorously with one of the flannel blankets she'd pulled from behind the seat. And as she rubbed, the infant began turning from a grayish-blue to pink, and his tiny mouth opened to emit a thin but piercing wail.

Weeping with joy, for Eliza had never felt so happy, she cuddled the baby to her breast and tenderly swayed her body back and forth. "Oh, dear Father who art in heaven," she sang softly, composing as she sang, "thank thee for sparing the life of this thy little son. Thank thee for bringing one such as me to help with his birth—"

"Brother Smith," Mons Larson was shouting, "hold the tent until I can get my Livvy into it!"

"I've got it, Brother Larson! Go get your wife—"

"Ho, the wagons!" someone suddenly called through the driving snow. "Is there a problem?"

"Is that you, Yim Decker?" Mons shouted. "My vife Livvy, she is having the baby!"

"Olivia?" Seraphine Decker shouted as she leaped from her wagon and hurried through the snow. "Is she in the tent?"

"Not yet! She vas on the vagon seat last I saw her."

"Oh, please help her—"

At that instant Olivia gave another thin cry, the afterbirth came, and with a great sob of relief the young mother sank back onto the seat. "He's here, Mons," she called weakly. "Our son is here!"

"Olivia?"

"It's all right, Pheenie," Olivia said as Seraphine Decker pushed past the teams and up to the wagon. "Eliza has the baby, and from the way he's yowling he sounds like he'll be just fine."

"Eliza Redd?"

"No, Eliza Foreman—"

Still smiling and weeping, Eliza stepped back around the wagon-box to the front. "I . . . I think he's fine, Pheenie. I've rubbed him all over until he's pink, but I haven't cleaned him at all. I . . . wasn't sure how to do it—"

"You did just right!" Seraphine Decker exclaimed as she took the child from Eliza's outstretched arms and peeked beneath the snow-covered blanket. "Why, a body'd think you've been doing this your whole life, woman. Oh, Olivia, he's darling! And everything looks just perfect, too!"

"We okay here?" Jim Decker asked as he pushed past the teams.

"We are now," Olivia breathed, "both of us, thanks to God and Eliza and all the rest of you wonderful people—"

52

Sunday, February 22, 1880

The Slickrocks

"You boys do look some used up." Platte Lyman stepped away from his early morning fire to greet the three men.

"Ought to," one of them grumbled good-naturedly as he broke some icicles from his beard. "Especially since we've been riding most of a day and a night without stopping."

"Too cold?"

"That," another answered as he slid wearily from his horse and began beating the snow and ice from his body, "and we didn't want to be late for church."

The others chuckled, for all knew the members of the expedition were now building roads and traveling seven days a week, trying desperately to get to the San Juan before they all starved or froze to death in the wilderness. Church services, therefore, were held on Sunday and Thursday evenings, and all in the company had voted for the extreme action.

The three men, all part of the expedition, had been sent back to Escalante a week before to deliver mail and round up all the loose livestock left behind on the Escalante Desert when the company had crossed the river in January, including the numerous missing teams. These animals, which most thought would be in fairly good condition after three months of rest, were sorely needed now that the expedition was moving again.

"You boys had any breakfast?" Platte asked as he stood back

439

from the fire so the three messengers could squat close and warm themselves.

"Not since yesterday morning," one answered.

"You haven't eaten since then?" Platte was incredulous.

"Sister Hall fed us last night afore her son Reed rowed us across the river. Except for a little jerky, that was the last we ate."

"Did you find our missing teams?" Platte asked hopefully.

"We didn't even look."

"You didn't? But boys, we're making double and even triple trips just trying to move all our wagons forward—"

The man looked up from where he was rubbing his hands over the flames. "You any idea how much snow is out on that desert, Platte?"

"I know we've got upwards of two feet across the whole top of this mesa."

"And two to three times that where she's drifted into the hollows," the man responded. "Of a truth, though, the snow's light here compared to the Escalante Desert."

"We like to have not even made it into town," another of the messengers agreed. "It was that deep. Like the man said, we didn't even try looking for livestock, Platte. We also found out there's probably six, seven feet on the level over the Escalante Mountains."

Platte shook his head. "What you're saying is the same thing we've been saying all along—the only direction this expedition's able to go, when it moves at all, is forward."

"As ever. You boys started building the road down the Slickrocks yet?"

Platte again stepped aside as Nellie, his brother Joseph's wife, slipped up to the fire with more slapjack batter. "A little was done yesterday before the blizzard got too bad and we had to quit. Today we hope to do better."

In the silence that followed, Nellie turned the slapjacks on the huge skillet and finally handed them one after another to the hungry travelers.

"Thank you, Sister Lyman, ma'am," one stated while the others nodded in agreement. "I never thought slapjacks would look good, but these do fit the bill."

Nellie smiled and kept working, and soon Ida Evelyn and Lydia May Lyman joined her. They were followed in short order by Edward, Amasa, Joseph, and young Walter, so that the whole Lyman clan had gathered around Platte, the fire, and the messengers.

"Did you find our teams?" young Walter asked, exactly echoing his brother's words of a few moments before.

"The snow was too deep," Platte responded while the messengers ate ravenously. "But we'll be all right a little longer, Walter, so don't fret about it. The best news is that now these boys are back we'll be able to put a whole crew of builders onto those rocks down below."

"Yeah, the never-ending road!"

"Well," Amasa Lyman said as he looked at his much younger brother, "like I told you yesterday, Bub, the Panguitch boys and I will give the company most of another week of road-building. After that we'll need to get back to Panguitch, no matter how deep the snow over that pass is. Besides which, Bishop Sevy says this is the last hard part of the road, so once you're off this mesa, life should get real easy and boring for the rest of the way."

"Ha! I'll bet that turns into a sorry joke, too."

"By the way, Platte," one of the messengers said as he rose to his feet, "we got a real bundle of mail this time—two saddlebags full. I also read an old copy of the *Deseret Evening News* that said Emma Smith, the Prophet Joseph's wife, died at Nauvoo, Illinois, last April 30th."

Platte's look was solemn. "So Sister Emma finally passed on, did she? Well, she and Brother Joseph have been waiting thirty-two years to be reunited, so I reckon it was a happy occasion."

"Some folks say she wasn't worthy to be with him."

"Some folks will say about anything," Platte stated grimly. "Personally I'll leave judgment to the Lord and Brother Joseph, who in this life certainly thought she was worthy of his love. Any other news in that paper?"

"Some. In July an Elder Joseph Standing was shot and killed by a mob while he was preaching in Georgia. The lawsuit Brigham Young's heirs filed against the Church has been settled for $75,000. California has passed a law that forbids the employment of Chinese.

And New York merchants are urging the Bell Telephone Company to open its exchange for telephone calls at five in the morning rather than eight, and to remain open later than six in the evening. Personally, I'd consider it enough just to *see* one of those newfangled telephones, let alone talk to somebody through it."

Platte chuckled. "Of a truth, so would I. What about the mail?"

"Well, I saw a couple of letters from Captain Smith, who I understand is still laid up at Red Creek, and there's a letter from Elder Erastus Snow marked from St. George. There're several other letters, but the thing I noticed most is a tied-together bundle of mail for Sister Foreman." The man paused, looking up at Platte. "You think she's been apologizing through the mail like she's done in person the past couple of months?"

"I'm certain of it."

Slowly the man shook his head. "I don't know about that. Was it me, I don't think I could be that humble."

"Then you couldn't enjoy the full blessings of the Atonement," Nellie Lyman declared, speaking for the first time that morning. "I believe Eliza's courage and humility are remarkable. I'll tell you something else I believe, and you men mark my words on it! The Lord's going to give that woman some incredible blessings in the next few years, wonderful blessings granted simply because she's been so willing to confess her sins and put forth the effort to turn her life around."

There was little wind for a change, and the day had grown lighter though the sun was still hidden by clouds. Someone nearby whistled once and then again, trying to herd some livestock. Two or three dogs were barking, and somewhere else a child squealed. But around the Lyman fire no one moved, no one spoke. Each of them was busy contemplating Nellie's statement, evaluating it, and ultimately either accepting or rejecting its implications for their own lives.

"I believe you're right, Nellie," Platte finally stated as he reached for the last slapjack. "But more, I'm convinced every member of this company will be blessed because of what Eliza's done. I've said as much to Billy, and now I'm saying it publicly. That woman's humility is helping to bring a spirit of repentance that's beginning to pass through this entire company, and we'll all be blessed because of it!"

Slowly Platte chewed the slapjack, enjoying every bite. "Where are the letters, brother?" he asked once he'd finished and put down his plate. "I'll deliver Eliza's packet to her right now. Meanwhile, I hope the three of you can get a little rest, because we've got a lot of road to build before we can get down off this frigid mesa."

———o–o–o———

"Sister Eliza? I've got some mail for you."

Eliza looked up from where she was trying to melt more snow so she could have warm water to clean with. "Mail?" she asked blankly. "For me?"

Platte smiled. "That's right. An express came in this morning from Escalante, and it looks to me like you have five, maybe six letters here."

Handing the string-tied bundle to the surprised woman, Platte looked around. "Billy doing chores?"

Slowly Eliza shook her head. "No. Hepsi's finally dried up, the mules are eating what they can find, and I feed the chickens a little grain each evening. So there are no chores. Billy's already gone with Hy Perkins down the Slickrocks."

"Ate early, did they?"

"You could say that." Eliza smiled. "They've been gone about half an hour."

"Billy's tooth doing okay?"

"He hasn't had another problem, so Pap knew what he was doing."

"He usually does." Platte smiled. "Thank you, Sister Foreman. Enjoy your letters."

As Platte walked away, Eliza looked again at the small bundle of letters in her hand. Though she hadn't looked at the others, the name on the front of the top one was that of one of the women she had penned an apology to nearly two months before.

Sitting down in the wooden rocker, Eliza took a deep breath. She was suddenly shaking, and for a change it wasn't from the cold.

Instead it was from fear, a cold fear of the anger she was certain she would encounter in the letters.

Still, she thought sternly, even that had to be faced if she expected the Lord to give her peace—

———o—o—o———

"Eliza, honey, what's wrong?"

It was dark when Billy was awakened by the sound of Eliza's sobs, though he was certain it was near dawn. The wind was blowing again, shaking the wagon as well as the two canvases that covered it, sending icy fingers through every crevice Billy hadn't managed to stuff closed. Snow was still rattling against the canvas, though it might have been drifting rather than falling fresh—Billy couldn't tell. And it was cold in the wagon, so cold it even hurt to breathe.

Thank the Lord for a bed made on warm sacks of grain, Billy thought as he rolled over and groped for a match. Thank the Lord Eliza had insisted from the start on sleeping in the wagon instead of in the tent as so many others were doing. And thank him too for the good thick quilts as well as Eliza's buffalo-skin coat they used to pile over top of them. It was such a blessing that they'd been given the means to procure such things before leaving Cedar, for without them they would certainly have suffered more than they were, perhaps even unto death.

Yes, Billy thought reverently, thank the good Lord for all things great and small—

Adjusting his sleeping cap out of his eyes, he struck the match, lifted the glass chimney of the coal-oil lantern, and lighted the wick. With the chimney back in place, the wick flared with light and even a little heat, and only then did Billy turn to see what was wrong with his beloved wife.

"I . . . I'm sorry," she whispered brokenly, doing her best to stop her weeping. "I didn't mean to awaken you—"

"I know that, hon-bun." Billy took Eliza's hand and began to comfort her, wondering as he did so that the steam of their breathing could be so thick in the almost still air of the wagon. It was truly a cold, cold morning!

"What happened? Can you tell me?"

"It . . . started with the baby. The Larson baby."

"He's all right, isn't he?" Billy's voice was instantly filled with concern.

"Yes, as far as I know he's doing fine."

"Good. I heard they were naming him John Rio on account of he was born practically overlooking the Rio San Juan."

Eliza nodded. "I heard that too. And it wasn't him, I mean, not exactly. I just started thinking—"

"Oh, Eliza," Billy interrupted, suddenly feeling that he understood, "are you afraid your baby might come in such awful conditions as Olivia's did?"

"No, I . . . well, I hadn't thought of that. I don't want to, either. It was more, well, I felt such peace while I was doing my little bit to help Olivia and the boy."

"I know you did." Billy smiled. "I could see it in your face. Despite all you'd gone through, being lost in the blizzard and all, you seemed supremely happy. It pleased me that the Lord had finally answered your prayers."

"I . . . thought he had, too." Taking a handkerchief, Eliza wiped her face, trying to stop the continuing flood of tears. "I mean, it's been days and days since I last thought of someone I've wronged. All my apologies have been made and my letters sent, and despite my pleading, nothing new in the way of my past sins has been made known to me.

"Trouble is, Billy, ever since you told me of your vision, I haven't been able to stop seeing it in my mind. Day and night it's always there, just like you saw except that it's me driving the stake through Jesus' hand, me helping to crucify Christ. Oh, Billy, that view has been haunting me, driving me insane trying to figure out what the Lord wants me to do about it.

"That's really why I left the wagon yesterday, to get off alone where I could plead with the Lord to take it away—either that or tell me why he wouldn't."

"And did he? Take it away, I mean?"

Slowly, tearfully, Eliza nodded. "From the moment I saw Olivia and realized she was in trouble, it was gone. And while I was holding that tiny child, I've never felt such joy, such indescribable happiness!

Somehow I even knew what to do with the baby to get him warm and breathing, and while I was doing it I knew perfectly well that the Lord was teaching me what to do.

"Even after I turned the baby over to Pheenie Decker and followed the glass-eyed mare here to camp, I was happy. I don't even remember the cold, and last night, though there was neither adequate warmth nor food, I was still happy. I was at peace. Honestly, Billy, I thought I was finally finished with my repentance, and all evening long I thanked God for the joy of mind and heart he had granted me.

"Then this morning Platte dropped by with some mail for me— replies to my letters of apology."

"You received some letters? But how—"

"Platte said an express came in this morning from Escalante, and they brought them."

"Were they . . . I mean, how did the women respond?"

Eliza blew her nose. "They were sweet, Billy. All five of them were so sweet and kind!"

"I'm pleased to hear that, hon-bun," Billy replied, feeling relieved.

"I've had the best day, too," Eliza continued, "bawling and carrying on like a big baby and feeling all good inside just like I felt when I was helping out a tiny bit with the Larson baby. Honestly, Billy, I've thought it was over, and that I'd been forgiven!"

"So why are you weeping now?"

"Because it . . . it happened again! An hour or so ago, just as I was going to sleep, I had another memory, something so displeasing to the Lord that I don't even know how to begin repenting of it!"

"Oh, hon-bun—"

"But at least," Eliza continued, not giving Billy the smallest chance to sympathize, "I see why God has kept showing me how I was . . . was the one driving those terrible spikes—Oh, Billy, what if this sin is one I can't repent of? It's so . . . horrid . . . I don't see how the Lord can ever forgive me."

Forgetting the cold, Billy sat upright. "Eliza, darling, nothing you've done could possibly be that bad."

"But it is, Billy!" Eliza was more animated than Billy had ever seen her, more determined to help him understand. "I remember it, or more accurately I understand it! That's why God gave me that peace yesterday and again today, to remind me that true peace and joy come only through service, in doing good things for others. But that isn't how I've lived. Not for twenty-five horrible years!

"Billy, darling, I've been so selfish, so greedy, and so arrogant about it! When I came to the Valley I was determined to make good, to prove to my family and everybody else I had made the right decision about joining the Church and coming to America. It was all I focused on. Right away I found work, and though no one had any money, I sustained myself and learned the millinery trade. By age twenty-two I had my own little shop, and I was shrewd, Billy, very shrewd. At the expense of others my shop grew and prospered, and as it did, my own sense of importance grew.

"As cash money became more available, I began focusing on acquiring and multiplying it—lending it out at interest. And it was so easy to make more money that way. You can tell by talking to people how desperate they are, and the more desperate they are, the more interest they're willing to pay. So by lending to the right people my fortune grew rapidly, and while I was pleasant to everyone, in my heart I mocked and scorned them all.

"Worse, I exulted in my own skillful management of my affairs. While taking advantage of peoples' sympathy for my feet or my lack of a husband, I could easily entice them to spend more than they'd planned in my shop, or to be extra generous with me when I made purchases of my own.

"I was so arrogant, Billy, so raised up in my pride, that I saw only good in all I was doing. Even the people I offended most, the ones I've been writing letters of apology to, seemed to deserve the way I treated them. Not once did I see that the problem was not theirs but mine. Not once did I recognize that I was envious of everyone who had anything I didn't have, and that in my pride I was mocking them as I stole from them in every way I could.

"Worse than that, I didn't change a particle after I met and married you. We're supposed to be one, Billy, sharing in all things good and bad. That's what I've come to believe eternal marriage means. Yet I have a sizable bank account with many thousands of dollars in Salt Lake City, a bank account you know nothing about. In other words, I've kept it hidden from you, not trusting you enough to even mention its existence. And every month it accrues more interest as my banker lends it out to others, usually at usurious rates.

"Oh, Billy, darling, I've been so arrogant, so perfectly filled with pride! Even in the past few weeks as I've been trying to repent of what I did to those few individuals, I've remained blind to the larger problem, these greater sins of pride, greed, and envy that have literally been my life! It's no wonder I stopped praying and reading the scriptures; it's no wonder I could see no good in you, even though we'd been sealed in the Endowment House by one of the Lord's anointed. Billy, darling, it's no wonder that God has kept that image of me assaulting Jesus so continually before my mind!

"I did it, Billy! For practically all of the past twenty-five years I pounded those stakes with practically everything I thought, everything I did! Worse, I still don't know how to stop—"

In anguish then Eliza buried her face in her hands. "Oh, dear Father," she sobbed in spontaneous prayer, "I . . . am so sorry! I'm so sorry for what I did to Jesus, for the mockery I've made of his suffering and sacrifice. I should have known better . . . No, I did know better! And I . . . I have no excuse. I am guilty, and I know that no amount of sorrow on my part can begin to make it right again. I'm lost forever, and I . . . I know that! But please, dear Father in heaven, please tell Jesus that I'm sorry—"

And Billy, too surprised to know what to say, could only watch as his beloved wife sobbed out her sorrow before the Lord.

53

<hr>

Thursday, February 26, 1880

Bottom of the Slickrocks

"Well, boys," the Escalante constable declared proudly, "we found both of 'em. They were in the herd of Jim Dunton and Amasa Barton."

George Sevy looked up from where he and Billy were shoveling sand into barrels strapped to the sides of Billy's borrowed mules. The snow, which had been falling off and on for better than ten days, had finally stopped, at least for an hour or so. But the wind was still blowing, and the temperature was hardly above freezing.

That's where it had hovered all week, while he and forty or fifty other weakened and chilled men had drilled and blasted and picked a semblance of a roadway down the steep and undulating Slickrocks.

Despite its roughness, the road was going to have to do, for the day before, the Perkins brothers had tamped and then blown the last of the thousand pounds of powder sent in January by the state legislature. Billy sighed, wondering that any of the men had been able to accomplish what they had—a road composed most frequently of stairs cut into the living rock, stairs on which he and George Sevy were now spreading sand.

The men had left their blood on the slickrock, too, for all were severely chapped and frostbitten wherever their skin had been exposed, and many had developed festering, bleeding sores. Yet not once had Billy heard a complaint; not once had any of his brethren expressed aloud his disappointment or discouragement over having undertaken the expedition. Each simply worked with a will and said nothing at all when things went wrong or their battered bodies temporarily gave out on them. This was even so of Jens Nielson and Father Stevens, who shouldn't have had to do any of the difficult labor each had been bearing. It was all so amazing, so admirable, that Billy couldn't stop thinking of it, couldn't stop admiring the men the good Lord had placed him in the midst of.

It had nevertheless been a grueling, exhausting week, and as each morning had rolled around, Billy had been amazed to discover enough strength to drag himself from his bed and return to his never-ending and heartrending labors.

Nor had the week been easy for Eliza and the rest of the women and smaller children. Because firewood had been scarce, there had been little warmth for any of them. Because it had been so cold, water had also been hard to come by, and a sense of filthiness was pervading the camp. This was particularly difficult for Eliza, Billy knew, for her fastidious English upbringing stressed neatness and cleanliness in all aspects of life—something severely lacking nearly every day since their departure from Cedar City the previous October. Neither did it seem she would ever grow used to it, for— and Billy smiled knowingly as he thought of it—right now if he were to return to his wagon, he would find the soiled lace tablecloth covering their table under the canvas awning and the two precious place-settings of Eliza's china and silverware, each set out in perfect order.

Some thought this behavior a bit strange, Billy knew, but he was proud as punch of his wife for sticking to her upbringing, as she called it. Yes, sir, they might end up living in a hole in the ground once they got to the San Juan country, but Billy felt peace in knowing that his son would still be taught the manners of proper civilization!

The Escalante constable and his three posse members were now stopped on the bank of the wash, pulling their collars higher against the chill and tightening the scarves under their chins that tied their hat brims down over their ears. From his position down in the warmer wash, which was actually the upper end of what they were calling Iceberg Canyon because of the amazingly deep snow the wind had packed into its steep-walled gulches, Billy sympathized with the chill they were obviously feeling.

"You going to charge either of them with horse stealing?" Bishop Sevy asked as he lifted his hat and wiped his brow, which was moist despite the cold.

The constable chuckled without much mirth. "Not hardly. Those two boys had no earthly idea these cayuses had joined their herd. Nor would I have, happen I was trailing so many animals through such terrible country in such gosh-awful weather as this is. No, these horses are just a couple of strays those boys accidentally picked up, and that's all there is to it. I just hope getting his animals back will settle the owner's milk enough so's he'll stop his foolish accusations. And maybe even convince him that Mormons—of which he's one hisownself, leastwise on Sundays—ain't such bad folks after all."

"That'd be a milestone, all right." George winked at Billy as he replaced his hat. "Fact is, it'd be nice if the whole world could get that attitude, though I don't expect to see it anywhere this side of eternity. Where'd you find the boys and their herds?"

The constable nodded the direction with his head. "Pushing their way through deep snow and heavy timber some fifty or sixty miles east of here, way off beyond that purty little lake you'll be coming to one of these days. Barton and Dunton and a couple of the Robb boys have joined that Hobbs feller, and from what they said they're all making a hard push to get supplies through to some folks on the San Juan."

"That'll be the Harriman and Davis families," George Sevy responded quietly. "They were left there last summer to start our settlement, and all of them were close to starving when the other explorers and me spent a night with them back in December."

"Then things aren't likely to have improved very much." The Constable lifted his gaze to the thousand-foot-high, steeply rising slickrock abutment just a few hundred feet away. "You boys actually think you'll be able to bring your wagons down that rock?"

"The road will most likely be finished and sanded come nightfall," Billy said, speaking for the first time. "We'll start bringing them down tomorrow."

"Even if it's snowing?"

"Especially if it's snowing. We've got to get down off that mesa!"

Shaking his head, the constable indicated the barrels George and Billy had already filled. "I reckon that sand's for better footing in all the ice and snow up there. But how you going to keep it on the rock?"

"We've cut steps or grooves in the dugways most of the way down," George responded. "Despite that this is the north face and steep as blue blazes, we'll come down without the loss of a single wagon or animal. You can mark my words on that."

The constable chuckled. "Having seen the rest of the road you folks have built, and finding no carcasses of livestock or broken-down wagons littering the trail, I'd say your words are already marked. What isn't so marked is why the whole bloomin' bunch of you would make such a trek in the first place. That I can't understand a-tall!"

"It has to do with following a prophet," Bishop Sevy declared evenly.

"So you say, and so I hear from the woman I married every day of my life. If only I could have the faith, as she puts it, to believe it. Well, adios, boys," the constable concluded abruptly. "I reckon we'll see you when we do."

George and Billy watched the posse and their two recovered horses drop into the wash and follow it toward the slickrock mountain, and only after they'd climbed the first bulging slope and moved out of sight did the two return to their shoveling.

"Horse stealing," George stated disgustedly. "Why anyone would think we'd steal two more horses to add to our two thousand starving animals is beyond me."

"It's an interesting idea, all right," Billy declared. "But horse stealing isn't unheard of, even in Salt Lake. More than once, I recollect, President Young had to deal with horse and cattle thieves. And most of them were Mormons, too."

George nodded. "I've run up against them in Panguitch, too. It's a shame that membership in the Lord's church doesn't guarantee a Christ-like life. In other words, not all Saints are saints. But in my years of bishoping I've had to learn that Mormons are about like everyone else—some good, some bad, and a whole bunch in the middle that seem mostly indifferent and ready to go whichever way the wind blows. That's a pity, when the Lord offers so much to all who will repent and give him their hearts and souls."

Billy nodded. "Thing is, repentance is a hard road, George. Mighty hard! It takes real grit to pay such a price and stick it out."

George topped the last barrel and then looked at Billy. "You're right, of course. But many in this company are doing it, your Eliza included."

"Many?" Billy asked, surprised that George knew about Eliza.

"I'll say. I reckon I've heard about or spoken with maybe three dozen people who are in one stage or another of cleaning up their lives. More than one has told me they're repenting on account of what Eliza's done. Your wife's set a fine example for all of us. Of course, I reckon this wilderness trek is helping some too. Like the ancient Nephite, Jaredite, Israelite, and Abrahamish Saints, the Lord seems to have led us into these harsh conditions at least partially so we'd be humbled enough to repent of our sins, learn to trust him, and become dependent on him. Leastwise that's what Kumen Jones has been preaching, which sounds about right to me. Those who will humbly take advantage of these circumstances, I believe, will one day see their promised land."

"Meaning the San Juan?"

George smiled. "I didn't say that at all, Billy." Clicking the mules into motion, the two men began leading them out of the canyon and toward the steeply rising road up the Slickrocks.

"Tell me," George Sevy continued a few moments later as they climbed the sharply inclined switchbacks of the zigzagging dugway, "now that Eliza's received all those letters, is she doing any better?"

Billy's expression turned bleak. "To my way of thinking, not at all. Oh, she had an afternoon of peace after she helped with the Larson baby's birth last week, and for a few hours the letters helped, too. But late Sunday night she awoke with the realization of a whole mess of sins she'd been committing over the past many years that had never been repented of—pride, envy, and so forth—and she's been mighty low ever since."

George nodded. "Puts me in mind of Sammy Cox's fiddle. It's interesting how, once we give him permission to begin tuning us, the Lord will draw our heartstrings to the same high, fine pitch Sammy uses. And he won't leave us stretched partway, either. Nothing less than a stretching to the absolute perfect pitch seems to do."

Two hundred feet above where the crew of pickers and chiselers were finishing a last segment of the steep road, the two men halted the animals and began pouring the sand into the freshly cut grooves. As Billy used his shovel to spread the sand across the nearly four-foot-wide track, he thought of George Sevy's analogy. Truly Eliza was being stretched by her memories, stretched tighter than he'd ever have supposed she might need. Trouble was, she seemed mighty close to being stretched to the breaking point—

"Is Eliza getting discouraged?" George Sevy suddenly asked.

"I'd tell a man! Not only does she feel like she'll never stop remembering additional sins, but she also believes the sins she has remembered are sufficiently awful to keep her suffering for the rest of this life and all eternity to boot."

"Keep *her* suffering?" George asked as he looked up, surprised.

"That's right."

"But that isn't what the atonement of Jesus Christ is all about, Billy. The Lord revealed to the Prophet Joseph, in what was first published as chapter sixteen in the Book of Commandments, that he'd already suffered beyond human comprehension for our sins so we wouldn't have to suffer. We can avoid that suffering by accepting him as our personal Savior and coming to him through complete repentance. Eternal suffering would only be our lot, Christ declared, if we would *not* repent, and it seems to me that no longer applies to your wife."

"As far as I'm concerned, you're right."

"Then you need to explain to her that God simply doesn't require such suffering from her or anybody else, not if she remains humble and repentant. To do so would negate the grace of Christ's own suffering—a thing no one has the power to do without intentionally remaining in his sins."

George dumped the last barrel of sand onto the roadway, and in silence he joined Billy in spreading it across the ice and snow that had packed into the grooves the men had chiseled during the previous few days. There was no doubt that this descent off the Slickrocks, which were mostly in shadow even on the rare occasions when the sun broke through the clouds, would be icy and dangerous. Billy could see it. And not only was it steep and slick, but some of the turns were hairpin, so that folks pulling wagons tandem—one wagon hooked immediately behind another the way he'd traveled from Salt Lake to Cedar City—would find negotiating such turns extremely difficult. Once again Billy was thankful he and Eliza had chosen to bring only one wagon. And once again he was thankful for the generosity of the Butt brothers who had loaned him their sure-footed mules—

"Another thing folks generally don't understand about the Atonement," George Sevy continued as he and Billy gathered up the ropes to the pack animals for their return to the wash in the canyon below, "is that Jesus didn't suffer, say, an ounce of suffering for each sin committed by a mortal being. In other words, there isn't a direct correlation between Christ's suffering and the amount or number of sins committed by the human family."

"I hadn't ever thought of that."

George smiled. "You need to, Billy, and you need to teach it to Eliza. As you no doubt know, the Book of Mormon declares that the suffering of Christ was infinite. However many sins have or will be committed—and only God knows that number—is immaterial. Christ's suffering went beyond that, so far beyond that it became infinite or endless or boundless—beyond anything measurable. Our sins are numbered, but Christ's suffering can't be. It was infinite—it had to be infinite—or it would never have had the power to overcome the demands of justice and bring to pass the law of mercy. At least that's what the prophet Amulek says in the Book of Mormon."

"I remember Brigham Young talking about that to my father," Billy mused, "but I've never really thought much about this aspect of it."

George Sevy reached into the pocket of his greatcoat. "Here," he said, pulling out a worn copy of the Book of Mormon, "read it while we're on our way back down for more sand. Sit on one of the animals so you won't fall, and I'll do the leading."

Billy smiled. "It's a deal," he declared, and a moment later he was astride one of the animals directly behind the empty barrels, his spectacles adjusted and the book of scripture open in his hands.

54

Sunday, February 29, 1880

The Slickrocks

"Who'd have ever thought we'd spend leap year day like this, risking our fool necks trying to get down off Harry's Slideoff? Especially since it's a Sabbath!"

It was a gloomy morning, and though the wind had finally stopped blowing, the weather had warmed, and now it was raining, turning the snow treacherously slick. Standing beneath her rapidly deteriorating parasol that was shedding rain instead of the sunshine it had been designed to shed, Eliza worried about that—worried about getting down off these cliffs and into the desert below.

But at least the company was starting to move again, Eliza reminded herself as she made an effort to look at the positive side of things. Or anyway some of them were starting to move. Of a truth, the whole expedition seemed no longer able to move anywhere all at once. They'd become too spread out for that, with too many obstacles, too many wagons, and with so many teams left on the Escalante Desert, not enough teams or manpower to travel all together.

Thank goodness, she thought as she looked down off the mesa and across the broken country a thousand feet below, Billy liked to be going as much as she did. When it was time to be moving, he was always one of the first to be ready, and so far they'd been spared the sorts of accidents or disasters that might hold them back.

This upcoming descent, however, made her nervous, for the new roadway was covered with ice and snow made even more treacherous because of the rain, and so Billy didn't want her riding down in

456

the wagon. Too dangerous, he'd said. Too much chance of accident. As if it didn't matter that he himself might be hurt—

Slowly somebody's wagon made its way past where she was standing on the rim above it, already started on the first leg of the road down the Slickrocks. Though she could see only the very top of the wagon's canvas above the bulging cliff, Eliza knew that all four wheels had been roughlocked, and that it was now sliding down the trail, carried along as much by its own weight as by the teams pulling in their harness.

Fifty yards away, where the road actually started down, a group of men were already wrapping chains around the wheels of the next wagon, roughlocking them in place. Other men were attaching ropes to the rear of the wagon, and two or three of these men would walk behind, helping to hold the rear of the wagon to the road. Still others had gone ahead doing the same thing with the wagon that had just passed beneath her, and Eliza could hear their shouts of instruction or warning echoing up from below. To her it was an amazing process of brotherhood, men and women willingly exhausting themselves while risking life and limb simply for the sake of helping each other. It was—

"Harry's *what?*" Eliza abruptly asked, her brain finally registering what Lizzie Decker had said. "What did you call this place?"

"Slideoff." Lizzie Decker, trying to hold her baby Eugene and keep her toddler Willie from getting too close to the edge of the cliff, looked confused. "Isn't that what it's called? Harry's Slideoff?"

Soberly Eliza shook her head. "If it is, Lizzie, I've never heard about it. Billy, Platte, Kumen, and everyone else calls it the Slickrocks, on account of the four explorers found the rocks too slick to climb down when they were searching out a road through here last December. So far as I know, it was them that named it."

Lizzie was instantly irate. "That doggone Cornelius Decker, fooling me the way he does! I declare! That man can talk me into believing anything! Sometimes I wonder why I even married him."

"Why, what on earth do you mean?" Eliza smiled widely at Lizzie's way of showing embarrassment. "What exactly did that sweet boy tell you?"

"Sweet boy, my foot! Sunday week ago I was ciphering a letter home, and I simply asked what this place was called. Well, that perverse and deceiving *man,* with as straight a face as you ever saw, told me some fool tale of a fellow name of Harry somebody-or-other who slid off these rocks a year or two back trying to get away from wild Indians. But they slid just as fast as him and caught him down at the bottom, and that was the end of poor Harry. Cornelius said the spot was famous for that, and that everybody back in the settlements would know right where we were if I just wrote the name at the top of my letter home. So even though I personally hadn't heard of it, like a complete fool I believed him and did! Lawsy, Eliza! Why am I so gullible? What'll the folks think when they see 'Harry's Slideoff' on my letter?"

"They won't know any different," Eliza replied, doing her best not to laugh at the young woman. "They'll think it's just another of our colorful names, like Hole-in-the-Rock, Shoot the Chute, Uncle Ben's Dugway, and so forth."

Lizzie shook her head. "I suppose you're right. But oooh, that Cornelius Decker! Somehow I'm going to get back at him—Willie, you stay away from the edge of that cliff! You hear me? You fall off of there and you'll be on your own, and I mean it!"

Mischievously the three-year-old boy looked up. "I not fall, Ma. I be careful."

"Willie, the day you learn to be careful—"

"See my valemtine, Eliza?" the boy asked, abruptly pulling a smudged paper from his layered clothing. "Gamma and Gampa from the semmelments sended it to me."

Lizzie sighed in frustration. "Willie, Eliza's name is Sister Foreman, not Eliza. You be respectful of her. It's settlements, not semmelments, that paper in your hand is a vale*n*tine, and Grandpa and Grandma sent it, not sended it. Besides which, young man, you've already shown it to Eliza at least three times in the past hour, not to mention everybody else in all of creation. So stop pestering folks with it!"

"Where's creation?" Willie asked, apparently paying not a word of attention to his mother's directions. "Eliza, is you in creation—"

"Willie Decker," Lizzie snapped, "that's enough!"

"Lizzie," Eliza laid her hand on her friend's arm, "it's just fine—"

"No, it isn't! Wilderness or no wilderness, this child of mine is going to learn some manners if they're the last thing I ever teach him! I swan but he does frustrate me! I . . . Look, Willie! Here comes your pa with his wagons!"

Looking up from the child, who was now standing at her feet, Eliza watched as Cornelius Decker, a humor-filled young man of twenty-four, guided his six horses and two wagons toward where the road started down off the cliff.

"Lizzie," she asked apprehensively as Willie started through the snow toward the oncoming teams, "Billy says there are some terrible sharp turns down below, hairpin turns he calls them. Can your husband manage such turns with the two wagons attached to each other that way?"

"Trailing the second one, you mean? I reckon he thinks he can, and that's usually good enough. Cornelius has been up and down the roadway so many times by now that he ought to know."

"It's amazing that just six horses can pull that entire load."

Lizzie nodded. "Our teams've done well, Eliza. Real well. We got the four lead horses when we traded our home in Parowan to Mrs. Pickering. She gave us the horses, seven cows, and that second wagon. Then Cornelius's pa gave him two green mares, which he broke to the harness back in October, just before we left. In all the months since then, none of them have given us a lick of trouble. Oh, they're some ganted up, all right, what with poor feed and melted snow for their only water. But the Lord has truly blessed us—"

"Pa," Willie shouted from near the front wheels of the wagon, "can I ride, Pa? Can I?"

Drawing rein, Cornelius looked down at his son with a quick smile. "You could, Willie, and I'd like that. Trouble is, I reckon your ma needs your help. With all this rain, that's a dangerous trail up yonder, and since I can't be there it'll be up to you to be the man and help her down."

"Does Eliza need my help too?"

"Willie," his mother fumed, "for the last time, she is Sister Foreman—"

Cornelius nodded. "I reckon Sister Foreman would appreciate a helping hand from a big boy like you." The man then lifted his eyes to Eliza, smiling again. "Billy'll be along shortly, ma'am. He and Kumen are helping poor old Brother Mons Larson."

"Are Olivia and the baby alright?"

"They're fine. But a bit ago while Olivia was nursing and Mons was trying to feed a bait of breakfast to their sons Moroni and Lars, something spooked his teams, which according to Mons have been fractious as cherubs in hades right from the get-go. Anyhow, they got rambunctious and somehow got their harnesses all fouled up and trampled in the snow. As you can guess, this rain didn't help much, so Mons is in a real mess. But I reckon with Billy's and Kumen's help they'll get it sorted out, and Billy'll be along directly. He's the one that suggested I come ahead and get this outfit to the bottom before the weather turns any worse."

Eliza smiled. "Thank you, Cornelius. I'll just wait here, then."

"Well, ma'am," Cornelius pushed his hat back and scratched his head, "Billy didn't want you to wait for him, neither. Delia Mackelprang and her brood, and Pauline Pace and her baby are walking not too far behind me, and I passed Sarah Riley and Eliza and Lula Redd just before them. Billy said he'd talked with you about going down with the help of others, and I reckon those women'll do just fine—all of you helping each other."

"Yes, my dear," Lizzie declared as she laid her hand on Eliza's arm, her voice wickedly sarcastic, "we must all work together if we expect to get safely down off *Harry's Slideoff!*"

Smart enough after one quick look at his suddenly knowledgeable wife to know that the trail down the Slickrocks was altogether less dangerous than lingering in her presence, Cornelius Decker tipped his hat, snapped the lines above his shaggy teams, and pulled out with a grin of mischievous satisfaction.

———◦–◦–◦———

"Mercy!" Mary Dailey breathed as she inched her way down the steep, slush-covered roadway, her grip tight on the hands of three-year-old Marian and two-year-old Madalene. "This makes a body wonder what we're doing here in the first place."

"You know very well what we're doing here," Hannah Mortensen declared from behind her, working to keep tight the rope that had been tied between them. "We've been called by the Lord to do this, and so we are."

"Do you think the Lord wanted us to risk life and limb going down this cliff? Or to risk the lives of our children?"

"That's right!" another agreed. "Look at Delia down there, with five children all roped together. What an awful thing it would be—"

"Don't you even think such a thing!" Delia Mackelprang called back from where she was carrying her baby Minerva and at the same time helping tiny Lydia Cornelia down a particularly high step. "I'm here because this is where Samuel and I have been called to be, and each and every one of my children will be just fine!"

"Delia's right," Sarah Riley stated as she, too, inched forward, leaning backward a little to balance her son in her arms. "This is the Lord's work, and I know it. After Eliza bore witness to me one day back at the Hole, I went out and got a witness of my own—Hannah, please don't pull. I can't go that fast!"

With concern Hannah Mortensen looked back. "Sorry, Sarah. These steps are slick, and without meaning to I went down two at once—"

Sarah Riley smiled quickly. "That's okay, Hannah. I reckon that's what these ropes are for—so we can all keep each other from sliding farther than we want."

"At least the brethren carved out steps for us," Pauline Pace declared as she, too, struggled to balance herself and her baby.

"And sanded them," Lizzie Decker added. "Billy and Bishop Sevy did most of that work, for which I will thank them forever!"

"Billy says the steps are as much to give the animals footing as us," Eliza muttered softly.

"And to shake all our earthly possessions to smithereens," seven-year-old Lula Redd called out. "Leastwise that's what Ma says!"

"Lula!" Eliza Redd exclaimed in horror as the rest of the women laughed delightedly. "Must you always repeat everything you hear?"

"Well, she's sure-enough right," Delia Mackelprang called back, feeling thankful that her own children had not repeated all the idle words she might have uttered. "Look yonder at how Cornelius Decker's wagons are shaking, just as if he were driving down the

461

parlor-room stairs. Glory be, Lizzie, I hope you packed things good this morning!"

Lizzie Decker chuckled. "So do I, Delia. So do I. But maybe it'll give that darn Cornelius a good shaking for me. Heaven knows he needs it! I . . . Oh!"

"You be careful, Lizzie," Eliza warned, "or this place will be known forever as Lizzie's Slideoff instead of Harry's."

"Hummph!"

"Harry's Slideoff? What's all this about?"

"Never you mind," Lizzie Decker declared sternly. "Eliza Foreman, if you breathe another word—"

Eliza laughed and quite happily told Lizzie's story, and for the next few moment everyone enjoyed a good chuckle.

"I don't know which is worse," Mary Dailey said a few moments later as she slipped and then caught her balance. "This slideoff, as Lizzie calls it, or the Hole."

"The Hole was worse by a mile," nine-year-old William Mackelprang shouted back authoritatively.

"My Willie would agree." Lizzie Decker, thankful to turn the subject another direction, guided her children down a particularly treacherous stretch of road. "When we came down the Hole, Willie looked back up and cried and asked me how we'd ever get back home. I reckon now he's starting to think this *is* home."

"I hope not!" Pauline Pace laughed.

"So do I. In a letter I wrote the folks last week, I told them this was the roughest country them or anybody else had ever seen; that it was nothing in the world but rocks and holes, hills and hollows. I told them the mountains are just one solid rock as smooth as an apple, and that the road to Dixie is a good one to the side of this."

"Well, Lizzie, at least that wasn't an exaggeration."

"No, not even if it had come from Cornelius, which it didn't!" Lizzie shook her head disgustedly. "My sister Emma tried to warn me Cornelius was fooling me, but I didn't listen. Oh, no! I had to believe his perverse prevarications. Harry's Slideoff, my foot!"

"Well, I'd rather laugh my way down this rock than weep," Eliza Redd said after everyone had chuckled again at Lizzie's story. "If

Cornelius and you can keep us laughing, Lizzie, then I say more power to the both of you!"

"Amen!" Hannah Mortensen breathed. "It sure beats the stuffing out of starving and freezing and feeling sorry for yourself from daylight to dark!"

"Or," Pauline Pace added with a wry grin, "standing together in the wind and snow and singing for the thousandth time all three verses of "Come Let Us Anew Our Journey Pursue."

And with more laughter combined with good-natured poking fun at themselves, their men, and their situation, the women and children of the San Juan Mission continued their way down the treacherous road off the Slickrocks.

55

Tuesday, March 2, 1880

Lake Pagahrit

"Can you believe how beautiful this place is?"

Ann Rowley was kneeling in the sand beside Eliza, a pile of wet laundry on a rock beside her. Now she was leaning back on her heels, the sun full in her face as she gazed across the small lake where the missionary company was camped.

The lake, which some were calling Pagahrit and others Hermit, was a J-shaped body of spring-fed water approximately half a mile long and a quarter of a mile wide at its widest point. The water filled a large, sandstone-walled gulch and was held in check by a natural sand dam over which the company had built their road. It was surrounded by vegetation, birds were everywhere, and the cold and desert-weary missionaries hadn't been able to resist stopping on its shore for a few days of rest.

"Just think of it," Ann breathed as her wonderment continued. "For two days in a row now the Lord has allowed the sun to shine, water here along the shore is warm—" Abruptly she giggled. "Did you hear what Hanson Bayles said this morning after he dived off those rocks over yonder where the men were bathing? I hear he came up all blue and sputtering and teeth chattering, and when he could finally talk he said the water down a few inches was liquid ice and colder than Job's turkey, whatever that means." She giggled again. "I know when I waded out past my knees my feet got so cold I could hardly stand it!"

Eliza nodded in agreement. It had felt so good to get behind that canvas curtain the men had erected and finally take a bath. But she, too, had noted how cold the water was down just a few inches, and so her bath had consisted more of careful splashing than actual bathing. Nevertheless, it had felt wonderful washing off some of the grime and soot that had been a continual affliction since Cottonwood Canyon, just as it did now as she busied herself in the warm sun scrubbing the accumulated grime from her and Billy's clothing.

Oh, but it was a trial for Eliza to feel dirty! Of a truth that was most of the reason she had never enjoyed camping, traveling away from civilization. On the trail everything became so primitive, so grimy and filthy. In England, even way back in the 1850s, her limited travel had been by comfortable coach and train, and inns provided more than pleasant accommodations. Such progress had slowly followed her west, so that within the past few years coaches and rails had even become common in Salt Lake City. The homes and buildings now being built there were lovely, and her lifestyle in the city had become so comfortable—

With a start Eliza realized what was happening—she was complaining again. With a quick mental apology sent heavenward, she brought her mind back and began thinking instead of the good things in her present situation. She was surrounded by wonderful people, she and the children of the company were beginning to become true friends, she was starting to find little ways to be of service to others, she was being obedient not only to God but also to his mortal servants, she was actually carrying a baby within her womb preparatory to becoming a mother in Zion—

But the greatest good of all was being with Billy. Of a truth she had finally come to realize that only by being with her husband— loving him, serving him, and being served by him, laughing and weeping with him, bearing his child and his name—could she experience the true happiness she had always sought.

With wonderment she had also come to understand that the same closeness gave Billy happiness and led to the continual praises he heaped upon her—praises that had once embarrassed her so deeply. But as she'd tried to explain to Sarah Riley that day when they were camped above the Hole, Eliza now knew that Billy truly did find joy in her presence, and speaking of her as he did was only his method of trying to share his happiness, his joy, with others.

Besides, Eliza acknowledged as she, too, looked around, there was beauty in this place, too. She'd have to agree with Ann Rowley on that. Oh, not the beauty of stately homes, wide verandas, and well-ordered streets and communities. But there was a God-given natural beauty here that could be even more appealing than civilization. In fact, Billy had said at least half a dozen times that this wild lake country would make a wonderful site for a cattle ranch, with plenty of feed and water for the stock and with cottonwoods for building and fuel, and for shade in what would surely be the hot summer months.

Of course, it was also a long way from Montezuma Creek and the San Juan, and thus an idle dream. But still—

"Do you think the bulrushes where Pharaoh's daughter found Moses looked anything like all these cattails?" Ann Rowley, still looking around, hadn't seemed to notice Eliza's silence. "I'll just bet they did. I waded out in them a little while ago, and I must have found a dozen birds' nests. Sammy and some of the others shot a brace of ducks last evening near where the water leaves the lake, so I'll wager they were ducks' nests I found, don't you think?

"Something else that's interesting," the woman continued almost without pause. "Did you realize it was leap year day when we drove off the Slickrocks and set up camp? And in spite of the roughness of the country, yesterday's drive here to the lake seemed easy, not more than six, seven miles. It was almost like the Lord gave us that extra day to get here so we could rest up a little. And was I ever thankful when Platte Lyman gave the order to march on the Sabbath! Getting down off those awful Slickrocks and coming to this . . . this paradise, must surely be pleasing to the Lord, no matter how hard we had to work on his holy day.

"And did you see those wild flags they found yesterday? Some of them, down in the rocks where they were protected from the weather and warmed by the sun, are already in bloom. Gorgeous things! Besides that, the willows are all yellow-green and starting to leaf out, the hills where the snow has melted are already green with grass, and even the cottonwoods are budding out. Mercy sakes, Eliza. It's practically spring here!

"Have you been to see the ruins of that old fortification on the rocks over yonder where they jut out into the lake?" Ann continued without hardly taking a breath. "I haven't, but those who have say it must be hundreds of years old. Father Roswell Stevens said he thought it might even be Nephite, but most everyone else thinks the ruins are just Lamanitish.

"By the by, was Lewellyn Harris carrying any letters for you when he came from the settlements yesterday? He was for us! Two wonderful letters from the folks in Parowan, and a letter that had been forwarded from my family. And poor Brother Harris. He's got to plunge on ahead now, braving this wilderness alone as he makes his way to his missionary labors in Mexico. I swan, but that seems like a terrible frightful journey. I don't believe I could ever do a mission like that, all alone and facing goodness knows what sorts of terrible dangers betwixt here and his field of labor.

"And Platte Lyman has gone ahead himself, this morning. He and Bishop Sevy and a couple of others hitched their wagons and away they went, seeing how far they could go without more serious road building. I thought we'd go, too, but Sammy decided to lay over another day to give me time to do the wash while he shoed our horse and the oxen. I noticed that Billy was shoeing your mules, too. I didn't know he could do that, but he seemed to know what he was about.

"Jim Riley was doing the same, and—"

Abruptly Ann Rowley stopped. "Eliza, have you lost your tongue? You haven't said a word in practically a coon's age, and all the while I'm blabbering on like a calf with the slobbers. Mercy sakes, sister! What's troubling you?"

Guiltily Eliza looked up. "I . . . I'm just thinking, I suppose."

"Did you get bad news? In a letter from home, I mean?"

Eliza smiled. "No, Ann, I didn't. I received two letters, and while one was more pleasant to read than the other, neither of them contained bad news."

"Are you feeling well, then? Is your baby giving you any problems—"

Now Eliza laughed. "Ann, I feel first rate, and so far as I know, so does my unborn son. Lately I . . . well, I've been trying to sort through some things, and sometimes I get to thinking so much that I lose track of what's going on around me. I'm sorry if I wasn't paying attention. I believe you were speaking of the beauty of this country?"

With a look of complete exasperation Ann shook her head, and together the two women returned to their laundry.

———◇—◇—◇———

The sun was just setting behind the slickrock mountains to the west when Ann Rowley surprised Eliza by walking up to her beautifully set dinner table.

"Eliza," she asked as she took one of the two chairs Billy had placed there, "may I please speak with you? Privately, I mean?"

For a moment Eliza could only stare. She'd been relaxing in her rocker, reading from the Book of Mormon, and waiting for Billy to return for supper. The cracked-wheat gruel had been simmering most of the day, so it was now well done, and with a little milk Belle Smith had given her, it looked to be a satisfying meal.

Around them the quiet sounds of the encampment continued— distant cries and laughter, the bellowing and lowing of contented livestock, the sounds of her own chickens clucking and preparing themselves to roost, the crackling of the logs in the fire—all these were peaceful sounds. Yet of a sudden Eliza felt fear, for the look on this woman's face was not one to inspire peace.

For some reason Ann's look brought to mind the letter Eliza had received the day before, the letter from a woman in Salt Lake City to whom she had written and apologized. Unfortunately, the woman's response had not been kind, and the things she had written to Eliza, while certainly deserved, had hurt deeply.

And now here was this woman who a few months before had said such unkind things about her and Billy—

"Sit down," Eliza finally replied, doing her best to control the tremor in her voice. "I don't know when Billy will return, but until then we may speak in private."

"Thank you." Carefully Ann Rowley regarded her. "You know, Eliza," she finally said, her voice and demeanor more confidential, more sober than Eliza had ever heard it, "you've changed. You truly have. There was a time I didn't like you very much, you know."

Eliza smiled ruefully. "I know. Alice Louise told me."

"So she's the one!" Ann Rowley giggled with embarrassment. "The little scamp, telling tales out of school like that. But what can you expect from a five-year-old except complete honesty?"

Eliza nodded.

"That night you came and apologized to Sammy and me, though, absolutely amazed me. Besides being embarrassed nearly to tears, just like I am now, I couldn't imagine how anyone would have the nerve to come to us like that."

"I very nearly didn't."

Ann smiled. "But you did, Eliza, and there hasn't been a day since then that I haven't thought about it. Fact is, I . . . well, I need to apologize to you, too. As you know, I said some awful things about you, and right or wrong I shouldn't have been saying them. I didn't even have any right thinking them, and I'm sorry for it. I truly am."

"Apology accepted," Eliza said quietly.

"Is . . . is that what your silence was all about this afternoon?" Ann finally asked. "I mean, not that I blame you, but are you still upset with me?"

Surprised, Eliza looked at the younger woman. "Mercy, no!"

"Are you certain? I mean, if I've done something else—"

Eliza held up her hand. "You haven't, Ann. Besides which, it isn't you I'm troubled about, but me. You see, I . . . I'm still trying to clean up my life, trying to repent of everything I've ever done wrong. I'm finding there's much more to repent of than I'd expected, and also that it's far more difficult than I'd ever supposed."

"Really?"

Soberly Eliza nodded her confirmation.

"But . . . why?"

"Have you ever thought about how Christ suffered for us?" Eliza asked after taking a deep breath. "I mean, really thought about it?"

Thoughtfully Ann shook her head.

"Except to believe in it, I hadn't either, not until the other night when Billy told me some things he and Bishop Sevy had talked about. Since then I've thought of little else, and I'm discovering that the atonement of Jesus Christ is a doctrine that runs more deeply than my feeble mind had ever bothered to dig."

"Is that right?" Ann appeared sincerely interested. "What have you learned?"

"Well, first of all, Jesus suffered for far more than just sins. According to the Book of Mormon, he suffered pains and afflictions and temptations of every kind so he could take upon him the pains and the sicknesses of his people. He also took death upon himself so he could loose the bands of death that bind us all. Then he took upon himself our infirmities so he could be filled with mercy and know how to help us in them. And finally, of course, he took upon himself our sins."

"So you're saying that Christ's suffering was for pain, sickness, and death as well as sin?" Ann's expression was completely sober.

Eliza nodded. "Yes, and infirmities, which I believe mean things like my crippled feet. Jesus has truly felt and therefore understands everything about the difficulties we experience in mortality."

"Amazing. I'd never thought of that."

"I hadn't either, not until the other night. But I believe that's why when we suffer for whatever reasons, including headaches, labor pains, loneliness, or even remorse at sins from our own stupidity, we can go to him and obtain peace—at least eventually. It's why we can be blessed to be healed. It's why we can obtain a better understanding of our circumstances as well as our natures. In other words, I believe it is because Jesus suffered beyond our comprehension in all ways and in all things that he gained power to become our Savior and Redeemer.

"I'd always thought Jesus suffered for each sin ever committed or yet to be committed—something that seemed almost comprehensible. But Billy showed me that Jesus' suffering was far greater than that—an infinite and eternal suffering that went so far beyond what I was thinking as to be unimaginable.

"Here," she continued, quickly flipping through the pages of the book in her lap, "let me read you the words of Amulek, Alma's missionary companion to the Zoramites."

Eliza then read Amulek's declaration that Billy had shown her about the infinite and eternal sacrifice of Jesus Christ.

"But here's the sobering part," she continued, "the part I've wrestled with for days, trying to understand. Amulek says: 'And thus he shall bring salvation to all those who shall believe on his name; this being the intent of this last sacrifice, to bring about the bowels of mercy, which overpowereth justice, and bringeth about means unto men that they may have faith unto repentance. And thus mercy can satisfy the demands of justice, and encircles them in the arms of safety, while he that exercises no faith unto repentance is exposed to the whole law of the demands of justice; therefore only unto him that has faith unto repentance is brought about the great and eternal plan of redemption.'"

"So the atonement for sins, at least, doesn't automatically cover everybody?" Ann's voice had grown very quiet.

"Apparently not unless they accept Christ as their personal Savior, which according to this scripture means exercising faith unto complete repentance." Eliza paused, looking deeply into the eyes of the younger woman. "That's what I've been trying to do these past weeks, Ann. But there's something here that has bothered me, something I've been praying about for days, trying to understand. It has to do with mercy overcoming the demands of justice."

"Is that . . . significant?"

Eliza nodded. "It must be, or Amulek wouldn't have dwelt on it so strongly. Still, its meaning has eluded me. Then last night Billy and I were reading the forty-second chapter of Alma, and suddenly the whole issue made a little more sense.

"According to Alma, once we sin—and all of us sin at some point—that sin forever makes us unclean. As it states here, it makes us 'carnal, sensual and devilish.' In such a state we become unworthy to return to the presence of God. Thus we are kept out, or damned. This is the law of justice, an eternal law that even God cannot break.

"As Alma puts it, and this is what I was reading when you came, 'There was no means to reclaim men from this fallen state, which man had brought upon himself because of his own disobedience. . . . And thus we see that all mankind were fallen, and they were in the grasp of justice; yea, the justice of God, which consigned them forever to be cut off from his presence.'"

"And Christ's atonement breaks that law?"

471

Quickly Eliza shook her head. "No, not breaks. It overcomes it by something the Lord calls the law of Mercy. Alma said, 'And now, the plan of mercy could not be brought about except an atonement should be made; therefore God himself atoneth for the sins of the world, to bring about the plan of mercy, to appease the demands of justice, that God might be a perfect, just God, and a merciful God also.'"

"And in order to do this," Ann questioned, "it had to be an infinite atonement—one not limited in any way?"

Eliza nodded. "I believe that's right. Anything less couldn't have had the power to change the eternal order of things. Having sinned and become eternally unclean, and having no ability ourselves to return to a state of purity, we're doomed to an eternal punishment. Alma says this punishment is as 'eternal as the life of the soul . . . affixed opposite to the plan of happiness, which was as eternal also as the life of the soul.'"

"So where is the hope in life? How can we possibly be redeemed?"

Eliza smiled. "You know the answer to that, Ann. It's what I've been working on with my apologies, and what you were working on a few moments ago when you apologized to me."

"Repentance." Ann sighed.

"That's right. Complete and honest repentance for every one of our sins. Listen to these words of Alma: 'Therefore, according to justice, the plan of redemption could not be brought about, only on conditions of repentance of men in his probationary state, yea, this preparatory state; for except it were for these conditions, mercy could not take effect except it should destroy the work of justice. Now the work of justice could not be destroyed; if so, God would cease to be God. But there is a law given, and a punishment affixed, and a repentance granted; which repentance mercy claimeth; otherwise, justice claimeth the creature and executeth the law, and the law inflicteth the punishment; if not so, the works of justice would be destroyed, and God would cease to be God. But God ceaseth not to be God, and mercy claimeth the penitent, and mercy cometh because of the atonement; and the atonement bringeth to pass the resurrection of the dead; and the resurrection of the dead bringeth back men into the presence of God; and thus they are restored into his presence, to be judged according to their works, according to the law and justice. For behold, justice exerciseth all his demands, and also mercy claimeth all which is her own; and thus, none but the truly penitent are saved.'"

"The truly penitent?"

"Yes." Eliza smiled. "Those who are willing to give up *all* their sins—not just once but as often as they might sin, all the rest of their days."

"Amazing."

Eliza nodded. "Yes, it is. And then comes this final, ultimate reminder. 'What,' Alma asks, 'do ye suppose that mercy can rob justice? I say unto you, Nay; not one whit. If so, God would cease to be God.'"

Eliza closed her book and gazed off into the gathering darkness, a distant look in her eyes. "The way I see it, Ann," she finally said, her voice pensive and subdued, "is that as the Apostle Paul taught, I've sinned, probably hundreds of times, and fallen short of the glory of God. According to the justice of God, I've made myself unworthy to ever be in his presence again.

"Knowing that, the sinless Savior came into mortality and suffered for me in an infinite way, enticing God the Father, through his infinite compassion for the Savior's infinite suffering, to set aside the demands of justice and allow mercy to reclaim me and bring me back into God's presence. The only condition for this merciful reclamation is that I accept Christ's offering by acknowledging and apologizing for my sins and then sincerely trying to avoid them in the future. In other words, I must exercise faith unto repentance. Then I will have peace."

"And have you done that, Eliza?" Ann asked quietly. "Have you felt God's peace?"

Abruptly Eliza set her book on the table and pulled herself to her feet. "Not yet," she responded quietly as she stared into the dwindling fire. "At least not fully. However, I'm trying to change my behavior, and with all my heart and soul I have apologized, not only to you and many others but also to the Savior himself. Day and night I cry that he will have mercy on my soul and give me peace. Beyond that I can only wait to see when—or even if—he will."

56

Friday, March 5, 1880

The Desert Northeast of Moencopi, Territory of Arizona

Except for the crows, it was quiet where the Navajo sat on the rimrock—the crows and the few dry cottonwood leaves left on the brush arbor behind him. The leaves were rattling in the chill wind, and the crows were circling below him off the bluff where the spring had once been, calling noisily to one another that the place had become dry. Now, silent and alone, Frank sat on the rimrock doing some serious thinking.

Called by the People *Natanii nééz* because of his great height, for the first time since he had come into his manhood Frank was thinking that being tall could not help him in this thing he was facing. Neither could he turn to Peokon for wisdom or understanding, the man who had helped shape his thoughts for so many cycles of the seasons that Frank could not remember when it had not been so.

Below him the crows were still calling as they drifted on sleek black wings from rock to brush to implanted post above the now-dead spring. Near them thin wisps of smoke drifted skyward from what had been the *atchí'deezáhi,* the forked stick hogan of Peokon and his woman. Now a small wind eddied the ashes that alone remained of the hogan, sending them upward with the smoke.

Nervously Frank fingered his *jish,* the medicine bundle that hung by a buckskin thong about his neck. He did not think of the cold. He did not think of the fact that the Turning Mountain People who had come to burn the hogan, the born-to clan of Peokon's woman, were now gone over east again as quickly as they could go. He did not think of the fact that he was now alone near this place of death, a thing no man of the *Diné* would intentionally do. Of a truth he did not even think of the fact that his friend Peokon was now *áníshdin,* dead. Instead Frank was still trying to see the big picture, to understand all that had happened in this place so that he might more adequately know what to do with himself.

Peokon had enjoyed no *hózhó,* no balance in his life, and Frank could now see clearly that it was so. Although of the People, he had always scorned their ways, making a mock of anything he could not see, taste, touch, hear, or smell. His favorite word for any who believed in more than these things, who believed in the inner form of the *yei* as well as the outer, visible form, had been *ásdzáán,* old woman, and often he had called Frank by that very term, causing him to be of two minds about the old ways of the People.

But now Peokon was *áníshdin.* So, too, was his woman and both of his strong sons, one killed in a fall and the other dead without apparent cause. The same might also be said of his daughter, though Frank had heard no word of that and so remained uncertain. What he was certain of was that Peokon's fine, strong horses had also died, every one of them. His wife's entire flock of long-haired sheep and goats had died. Even the great spring near which the man had dwelt, the spring that had never gone dry even during the seasons of great dryness—it, too, had dried up and died.

In fact, the only things left living in all of what had once been Peokon's wide circle of possessions were the three rock-walled seeps given him by the *belacani* Thales Haskell, whom Peokon had called an old woman, a coyote, and *bináá dootízhi* because of his pale blue eyes. Those three seeps, dug by the mormonee explorers the summer before when they had passed through the country on their way to the big river, yet contained sweet water, and it was to them that Frank had been forced to go each time he had tried to slack the thirst of his dying friend.

The question now was, who or what had held the power to *yishhá naastseed,* to kill Peokon and all his possessions in such a devastatingly efficient manner? Rather, that was the first question. The second was, if he could find an answer, what was Frank to do about it?

For long moments the tall Navajo sat upon the rock, pondering. Into his mind, for some reason, had come again the image of the reed-thin *belacani* mormonee with the long white hair and pale eyes. Though Peokon had said Frank should have remembered him from before, from the old days, Frank could not do so. Many times since their encounter near the big river he had cast his mind backward across the seasons, but nowhere did the image of the *belacani* make an appearance.

There was another long-ago image, however, that did—the memory of a *belacani* youth who had ridden a fine black stallion. Frank could still see him as he sat fearlessly on his horse while Peokon and he, who had been hardly more than a boy, had ridden up to walk their ponies beside him. Signing and speaking a little of the *belacani* tongue, Peokon had asked to see the youth's pistol, which he carried in a pocket of his coat. Without fear the youth had handed it over, and with no hesitation whatsoever Peokon had turned the pistol, smiled, and fired more than once into the body of the youth.

In his mind Frank could still see the surprise on the boy's face, the bewilderment as he had slid slowly from his saddle and into the rocks and dust of the trail.

Frank, assuming Peokon had shot the youth in order to have his fine horse, had reached immediately for the bridle. To his surprise Peokon had ordered him to drop it and to dismount and pull up the shirt of the wounded boy. Wonderingly he had done so, exposing the startlingly white skin of the boy's back. Then, still smiling but not with the joy usually associated with such an expression, Peokon had methodically driven four arrows from his bow, one after the other, into the young man's bare back.

With a harsh laugh he had then kicked the still-living youth from Frank's arms and into the brush and rocks beside the trail. Afterward he had mounted, ordered Frank to do the same, and without even a glance at the fine black stallion had turned and ridden away. And Frank, unable to catch the horse by himself, had been forced to follow after.

Perhaps twenty-five cycles of the seasons had passed since that day, and the image in Frank's mind remained as fresh as though it had been placed there the day before. More important, he now had *ákí'diishtih,* an understanding of the image, or rather the event, an understanding he had not had at the time.

The young *belacani,* Frank now knew, had been killed by Peokon strictly because of anger, because of hatred. Had he been killed because there was a raid being made and a fine black stallion being obtained that would bring much good blood into a man's own herd of ponies in the years to come, well, that would have been one thing. Or had he been killed because he was an enemy of the People come to make war, it would have been the same.

But that young *belacani* had died not because of raiding or of war but because a blackness seethed within Peokon, a dark wind that was not the way of a true man of the *Diné.* Thus the killing was something else altogether, *doo yááteeh da,* a bad thing that Peokon had done. And that was why Frank believed the man had had no *hózhó.*

Now, as he sat upon the rimrock ignoring the cold wind that was blowing out of the vast reaches of Monument Valley, Frank knew that lack of balance had been what had taken the life of the man who had been his friend. Or rather, he knew Peokon's lack of balance had been what had given another the power to take it.

And, he thought nervously as the dry leaves on the old arbor behind him rattled even more loudly, he also knew the name of the one who had held the power to slay Peokon.

"It was . . . the white-haired *mormonee belacani,*" his dying friend had coughed and wheezed just the night before. "The one with the *chinde,* the devil eyes, the white man who calls himself Thales Haskell. He . . . cursed me! When I wasn't looking he blew a bone into me."

Of course, Frank had understood what his friend was saying. Long ago his father had told him that Coyote, not *maii* the small wolf but *Asté Hashké* the evil Trickster, had transformed First Man into a witch, a skinwalker, by blowing his hide over him. After that, until the Holy People helped restore him, First Man had run on four legs with the *yenaldolooshi,* the witches or skinwalkers, blowing the bones of corpses into his neighbors to kill them, and doing other terrible things. These *yenaldolooshi* were still around, Frank's father had told him, hiding as normal people until they chose to appear otherwise.

"And . . . did the mormonee *belacani* also blow a bone into these others?" Frank had asked pensively as he thought of everything about the man Peokon that had also died.

But there had been no answer to that question, no response but the wild staring about the darkness of the hogan that was so unnerving. Therefore, as he had each day since his arrival, Frank had suggested that he be allowed to bring in a *yataalii* to do a sing to cure Peokon, an Enemy Way just as Tsabekiss had done for his son Bitseel. But Peokon, who had already withered away like a dried reed in the season of cold, had continued to stare about him, his entire body trembling and writhing with an ever-increasing fear, his only response to Frank's suggestion a continuing plea to be allowed to die.

And then, after many days of suffering and in a moment when Frank had least expected it, Peokon had finally stiffened in death, leaving Frank to deal with the *chinde* in the hogan himself.

Relieved that the hogan had now been burned and the *chinde* driven off, Frank sat in silence on the rimrock, deep in thought. In the distance a rider had appeared, and almost without conscious thought Frank had identified him as Peeagament, the old *Nóódái* headman who had accompanied him on the raid across the Kaibab. Soon he would arrive and begin asking questions. But not yet, not for a few minutes more. Not, Frank hoped fervently, until he had finished his fearful line of thinking.

Though he had not thought that he believed in curses, Frank had certainly heard one pronounced by the white-haired Thales Haskell, and now his dreaded friend Peokon was dead. Of course, it might not have been the mormonee *belacani's* power that had done it, but certainly the one who had died had thought otherwise. So, too, Frank now admitted with a shudder, did he.

Besides, without difficulty he could remember the *chinde* eyes of the man Thales Haskell, and he could remember the feeling of power when that curse was pronounced. And contrary to what Peokon had claimed, Peokon *had* been looking at the *belacani* the whole time they had been together. If a bone had indeed been blown,

Peokon should certainly have seen it coming. That he hadn't was further proof of the evil power of the white-haired *belacani,* a power any man should have been able to see, any man with *hózhó* should have been able to avoid—

And that, Frank's mind continued almost of its own volition, brought up himself! Again he fingered his *jish,* thinking as he did so of the raid he and others had recently made on the mormonee *belacani* village far away to the north of the Kaibab. It had been a good raid, too, with many horses being taken and much wealth brought back to the sacred land of *Diné Tah.* That did not bother him, and in fact Frank looked forward to more successful raids in the future, perhaps many of them, especially after the mormonee *belacani* came with their families and their wealth to settle on the big river. It was the old way of his People, the good way, and he intended to continue it.

No, what bothered Frank was that when the crafty horse thief Taddytin and his cousin Zon Kelli had taken all of the *belacani* horses and hidden them somewhere in the maze of canyons near Navajo Mountain, giving nothing to Frank or his cousin or any of the other raiders, the theft had turned Frank's heart into a stone. That bothered him.

Now, of course, he could see that his hard-hearted feeling against the two was not right—not, at least if he wanted *hózhó.* And more than anything else Frank suddenly realized that he wanted *hózhó,* he wanted to be in balance with the universe!

He should have known this thing, too, for long ago his father had carefully taught it to him. Since childhood he had known it was wrong to have more than he needed. Since almost before he could remember he had known it was wrong not to take care of the needs of his people before his own wants were considered.

Make three successful raids in a row, his father had told him many times, and then he had better stop for a time. Win three races on his fastest pony, and then it was time to let someone else win. Or, and this was why Frank felt so uneasy, when somebody wronged him or stole from him, his father had carefully explained, it was not a time to be angry or to feel malice. Rather it was time to hold a sing for that man to cure him of the *chinde,* the devil that had gained so much power over him.

With his fingers on his *jish,* Frank's mind continued to ponder Taddytin and his cousin Zon Kelli and the stolen *belacani* horses, and with his thoughts came the abrupt conviction that he did indeed lack *hózhó*. He, *Natanii nééz* who was now called by the *belacani* name of Frank, was no different than the man Peokon! Filled with malice, he had been thinking of revenge against the two horse thieves, even dreaming of it, when all along—

With a grunt of anxiety Frank rose to his feet and turned toward his pony, intent on riding to intercept the old Pahute called Peeagament before he rode too near this place of death. Of course, Frank knew the man who had been *yenaldolooshi,* who had somehow managed to blow the bone of a dead person into Peokon, giving him the corpse sickness that had killed him. It was Thales Haskell, the Trickster, *Asté Hashké,* the evil Coyote. And somehow, though Frank could not begin to imagine how, that same *yenaldolooshi* had also managed to blow the corpse sickness into every living thing Peokon had possessed.

What, Frank wondered as he looked anxiously around, if that same *belacani* witch had also blown a bone into him because he, too, had lacked the *hózhó* so important to his People—

—◦—◦—◦—

Castle Wash

"Hi, Eliza. Are we going to weave fronds today? I cut a whole bunch back at the lake, you know."

"Hello, Lula," Eliza responded as she looked over to where the young girl sat on the huge, bareback horse. "You ride that horse very well."

"Pa taught me. He says girls ought to learn to ride while we're still little. Then when we're grown and it isn't so prim and proper, at least we'll know how if we have to." The seven-year-old smiled. "Where's Brother Foreman? How come he ain't driving your teams today?"

"Remember, Lula, we don't say *ain't.* We say *isn't.*"

"I'm sorry, Eliza. How come Brother Foreman *isn't* driving?"

"That's much better! My husband has gone ahead to work on the road down the Clay Hill. I suppose he thought I could handle this easy wash by myself today."

The child looked disappointed, and Eliza noted it. Though Lula and most all the others called Billy Brother Foreman, it was amazing how much they all seemed to love him and gravitate to him. Billy had such a way with people, and their ages seemed to matter not at all.

Of course, a lot of the children loved her, too, and Eliza knew it. She could see it in their eyes each time they gathered around her table to weave hats, fans, dolls, and so forth. To them her weaving must have seemed like magic, for all the girls and even some of the boys clamored for the privilege of doing it, sitting enraptured each time she showed them something new.

She had also asked them to call her Eliza instead of the more formal Sister Foreman, and she was pleased that most of them did. Most of the time every one of them seemed like such sweet children—

"Are we gonna—I mean, *going to* weave today, Eliza? Are we?"

Eliza smiled as she guided the teams of mules around a large boulder and up a small sandstone ledge that crossed the bottom of the wash. Then she held tightly to the seat as the wagon groaned and lurched up the same incline. "Can you round up the others?" she asked after Lula had again caught up with her.

"You bet I can! Most of them, anyway."

"Good. Then go do it, for we'll be stopping soon. Oh, Lula? Tell everyone I have a surprise for them today. We won't be weaving, so don't bring your fronds. I have in mind that we'll be doing something even better!"

Lula Redd's eyes grew large. "Better than weaving? Golly, Eliza, what is it?"

"A surprise! Now skedaddle, and hurry back as soon as you can."

With a squeal of delight, Lula kicked her feet against the wide ribs of the old horse, and a moment later Eliza was alone again, wishing Billy was seated beside her but nevertheless doing her best to guide the teams and wagon through the heavy sand and scattered boulders of the upper reaches of Castle Wash.

———o–o–o———

"Is *that* the castle somebody named this wash after?" eleven-year-old Francis Magnolia Walton asked incredulously as she stared toward the high-walled north bank of the wide ravine.

"It sure isn't much of a castle," Laura Mae Barney agreed. Laura Mae was also eleven, and she and Francis were the oldest girls in Eliza's weaving class.

Now Eliza stood with them and more than a dozen other children near where she'd stopped her wagon, gazing northward. Since Billy hadn't returned, Kumen Jones had come back and unhitched the mules, and with eleven-year-old Samuel James Rowley's help he had unloaded Eliza's table and chairs and stretched out on its posts the canvas awning that became Eliza's ceiling each time the wagon was parked. Kumen was now gone again, taking the mules to water, and Eliza was alone with the children.

"Have any of you ever seen a real castle?" she asked quietly.

Almost in unison the children shook their heads.

"I have, back in England. In fact, I've seen two castles, and our king and queen live in both of them."

"Really?"

"Yes. And Laura and Franny are both right. Compared to the castles in Europe, this old Indian cliff-dwelling isn't much of a castle at all. Of course, since it's the best we have out here, then I suppose it'll have to do."

It wasn't a castle, either, Eliza thought as she looked across the wash and upward. Built from floor to ceiling in a small cave maybe thirty yards up and back from where they all stood, the old ruin consisted of three or four small rooms walled by flat rocks stacked atop one another and bonded together with ancient mortar. Some of the walls had partially collapsed, but two windows and a door were still obvious in the walls that remained intact, and the blackened ceiling of the cave gave mute evidence of the many fires that had once burned therein.

"One thing about this little castle, though," Eliza said. "Brother

Lyman and my husband Brother Foreman believe it is many hundreds of years old, far older than most of our castles in Europe."

"Who built it?" Nine-year-old William Samuel Mackelprang was always a curious lad.

"I asked Brother John Gower that same question last evening, Willy, and apparently Thales Haskell explained to the explorers this summer past that the Navajos, who Brother Haskell thinks came here long after these people were gone, have two names for the people who built it. One is *Moqui,* which is an insult name meaning those who are afraid to come out and fight. The other, *Anasazi,* is a nicer name, meaning simply the old ones."

"*Anasazi,*" nine-year-old John Henry Holyoak repeated. "*Anasazi.* That's a funny word."

"But it has a good sound to it, doesn't it. Brother Lyman told me he thinks the people who built this little castle may have been direct descendants of the people in the Book of Mormon."

"Wow!" Willy Mackelprang's younger sister Adelia breathed. "That's *really* old!"

For a moment longer the children, gathered loosely around Eliza, stared at the old ruin. And she, in turn, watched them. The six little girls she had caught singing the infamous ditty back at Fifty-Mile Camp were among the group, and they were now some of Eliza's closest friends. In fact, they were the ones she had started her weaving class with—and young Hy Fielding and Nate Decker, who were their same age.

Eliza had started the group to occupy the children's time and make herself useful when the others were doing work she herself couldn't do. But the group had taken on a life of its own, and now sometimes as many as twenty-five youngsters, ages five to eleven, would cluster around Eliza's table and wagon. Now as they talked, Eliza could see that more and more of them were gathering in response to Lula Redd's call.

"Say," Joseph Lillywhite suddenly shouted as he pointed upward, "there's smoke coming out of that castle! Maybe somebody still lives there."

"I see it!"

"Me, too!"

"Eliza, what sort of surprise is this? Are we going to fight the people in the castle?"

Eliza smiled at the boy. "No, we don't have to. The people up there are part of our company—"

"Well, Eliza," Mary Jones declared as she suddenly emerged from the rocks and bushes below the old ruin, flour spread about on her apron, "looks like you're going to have plenty of help."

"Hi, Mary. We have a crew to take up there, all right."

"A crew?" one of the children whined while the others looked pained. "Are we going to have to work today?"

"Not work," Eliza declared happily. "As a matter of fact, children, today is treat day. Since I'm from England, I've decided it's high time we all enjoyed a fine English brunch of tea and crumpets."

"Tea and crumpets?" Five-year-old Maggie Mackelprang pulled a face. "What are tea and crumpets?"

"Why, Maggie, I'm surprised! Tea and crumpets are what all proper Englishmen and all fine English ladies dine on, every single afternoon. But ours will be even more special. Our tea will be fresh water from that fine mossy spring we passed a little while ago, and our crumpets will be fresh, warm, oven-baked bread spread with molasses."

There were gasps of surprise, and then Francis Walton asked how they would do that, since no one in the company had an oven.

"That's what the castle is for, Franny," Eliza beamed. "Those old ones who built it left us a wonderful oven. The sisters in our company have been baking bread in it most of the day, and in a little while it will be our turn. Sammy, you, Joe, Charlie, and Willy need to spread out and find us some very dry firewood and drag it up there to the castle."

"Can we help?" the Decker and Fielding boys pleaded anxiously.

"Of course. Tommy, you and Benjamin can help too. All the boys may help with the firewood! Now, while you boys are out gathering, we girls are going to mix up a big batch of flour and saleratus, set it to raise, and get out my big jug of molasses, and by the time you boys have the oven stoked up and hot, we'll have the bread ready to bake. Any questions?"

"Eliza, my ma makes real tea out of the Brigham brush. I'll bet we could find some of that."

Eliza blanched, thinking of the bitter but popular drink folks were calling Brigham Tea, and of how it turned her stomach since she had become pregnant. "Thank you, Franny," she smiled, "but I think cold water will do just fine today. Now, you boys get busy gathering firewood, and we'll all have a race to see who can be ready first—the oven-stokers or the bakers."

With squeals and shouts the boys scattered, and after giving the still-smiling Mary Jones a broad wink, Eliza turned and led the excited girls around her wagon and to her table, which she had already set with her large wooden mixing bowl, a pot full of fine flour donated in the last hour by various members of the company, a tin of saleratus, and a pail of water. And, of course, her precious, nearly empty jug of molasses.

Today, Eliza thought happily as the little girls all crowded around, these poor children were going to enjoy a treat they would likely never forget!

57

Wednesday, March 10, 1880

Clay Hill Pass

"Eliza, is everything all right?"

Smiling, Eliza glanced at her husband. "All right? Of course it is, darling. Why do you ask?"

Billy scratched his head. "I . . . I don't know. Somehow you seem . . . well, different, I reckon. Happy. I mean, if I didn't know better I'd say you were glowing, only of course that isn't so. I . . . I have no idea at all what I'm trying to say. Except that whatever it is, I like it. I truly do."

Smiling again, Eliza moved the lantern and continued her task of stuffing whatever rags she could find into the openings around the wagon cover, trying to stop the frigid wind from finding its way inside. It had turned cold again, terribly cold and windy, and if it also started snowing again—and for some reason she was certain it would—Eliza was hoping to be ready.

"I hope the snow holds off until we can get all the wagons down the hill tomorrow," Billy declared, noting Eliza's task. "When it's wet, you just can't imagine how slippery that clay on the pass is, hon-bun. Snow would only make it worse."

"The road to the bottom is finished?"

"Pretty much. In spite of its slipperiness, thank the Lord this mountain is clay instead of rock. Between our shovels and a dozen teams and scrapers, we've built a good road down it, all in less than a week. Not bad for a thousand-foot drop, I'd say."

"Did you hear that Platte was back with Bishop Sevy and Samuel Bryson from their exploration of the road ahead?"

Billy nodded. "I did. The boys and I visited with them as they were coming up the hill. Mostly they talked about the thirty-mile forest of juniper and piñon up ahead we'll have to chop a road through—trees so thick there are places where they can't even be ridden through."

"Can't we go around them?"

"Actually, that's about what we'll be doing. The forest runs all the way from Elk Ridge down to the San Juan, and we'll be swinging way north up against the mountain and skirting the upper end of it, following an old Indian trail they found. Several places Platte says they tried a more direct route, but there's a huge canyon running up out of the San Juan practically all the way to Elk Ridge—Grand Gulch, they called it on account of how wide and deep it is. According to Samuel, the sides of that Gulch—and from what they say it has miles and miles of tributaries reaching out like crooked fingers—are straight down and drop a thousand feet or more. So the only way past it is around it, right up against the mountains. Bishop Sevy says it's a miracle he and the other explorers didn't stumble into it last winter, but he feels they were led by the Spirit to head it on their first try. Otherwise they wouldn't have had the strength to backtrack and still make it to Montezuma Creek."

"I'm thankful we're not going to try and blast a road down through it."

Billy nodded. "We couldn't do it, Eliza. We're completely out of blasting powder, but we're also too tired to make such an effort, both man and beast. We might get down, but I don't think we'd ever get back out again. No, chopping through those trees is our only recourse, and compared to that gulch it seems like a good one.

"Fact is, Eliza, I was asked if I thought you could handle the teams for a few days if I was sent on ahead to chop."

"Me?" Eliza was stunned. "Billy, I . . . I'd have no trouble driving them. Those mules are wonderful to handle. But I . . . well, I don't know if I could harness them by myself. I could certainly try, though, and learn by experience, just as you did."

"I know you could, Eliza. Hard as it might be, I know you would do it, for that's the sort of woman you are. But don't worry; I don't think they'll send me, not with you having bad feet and growing so large with child. Happen they do, why, we'll just find someone who'll harness and hitch the teams every morning and undo them every night—someone more than tolerably ugly and blind to boot."

"Billy!" Eliza scoffed. "I swan!"

Billy chuckled. "I mean it. I don't want some handsome feller looking at you and getting any ideas on account of your radiant beauty."

"Beauty? Why, I'm bigger than a barn, you silly man. No one would take more than a passing glance at me, and then only out of idle, sideshow curiosity—except maybe a blind man who was also more than tolerably ugly himself. He might find me of at least passing interest. Yes, that's the sort of fellow you'd better send, all right."

Scowling, Billy reached out and pulled Eliza over to him, and for a few moments they simply snuggled together in silence, Billy's hand on his wife's protruding stomach. Outside, the wind howled fiercely, shaking the wagon and reminding them that the springlike days at Lake Pagahrit and since had not meant winter was over. It wasn't, and the intensity of the cold was the exclamation point to their reminder.

"I can feel him kicking all the time now."

Pulling the quilts back, Eliza sighed. "*You* can feel him. This is one active little boy, William Foreman. I hope you're ready for him."

Billy grinned. "I am. Let's see now. It must have been something in that bread you've been baking in that Indian ruin."

"What was?"

"Whatever it is that's been making you so happy. Maybe it was something about that ancient oven—"

Thinking of the children and her baking experiences with them, Eliza couldn't help but smile. "Do you realize those children have hounded me to go back to that ruin with them three different days now?" she asked. "Altogether we've baked more than a dozen large loaves of bread, and it wouldn't surprise me if we've used half of what little was left of our jug of molasses."

"The word on the road crew is all about tea and crumpets," Billy chuckled. "Seems like that's all the kids have been talking about.

That, the two settings of your grandmother's china, and the miniature tea set your father gave you when you were a child. It sounds
like the children love that miniature tea set."

"They seem to."

Billy smiled. "I . . . uh . . . I even heard you'd been riding that
glass-eyed mare back to the ruin."

"Can't a woman get away with anything around here?"

"Eliza, you just be careful."

"Billy, darling, she's a good old mare, patient and slow and with
a surprisingly smooth gait. And the way her back sways down,
there's no way I could fall off." Eliza chuckled again. "It's much easier on me than walking, but I admit I haven't been riding sidesad-
dle."

"I've heard that, too."

"Well, Billy—"

"Hon-bun, no one cares, leastwise that I've heard. Folks are just
thrilled to no end that their children are happy. And Dan Barney says
his wife Laura has even started setting up her table the way you do,
with the serviettes and silverware and so forth, and demanding the
same table manners from her children that you've been teaching them.

"So, was it the children? Or maybe it was something in the
flour—weevil or something?"

Perplexed, Eliza looked at her husband. "What are you talking
about, Billy? We don't have weevil—not yet, at least."

"All right then, you tell me. Was it the water you got at Green
Water Spring that's been making you so happy the past two or three
days, or at that little seep in Mule Shoe Gulch?"

"It wasn't any of those things," Eliza replied with a grin, "and
you know it, Billy Foreman."

In the light from the coal-oil lantern Billy grew suddenly serious. "You're right, hon-bun, I know. You finally got your answer,
didn't you. The Lord has finally taken away your guilt and given you
peace."

Silently, as big tears formed and slid down her cheeks, Eliza
nodded.

"That's wonderful!" Billy's voice was more tender than Eliza
had ever heard it. "I can't tell you how thrilled I am for you."

"It . . . it wasn't like I thought it would be," she whispered after a moment more of silence. "That's why I haven't said anything, because it was so much more than I'd ever expected, ever hoped! And I just didn't know how I could possibly share it with anyone—even you." And again Eliza dissolved into tears.

"Hon-bun," Billy said as he held her tightly, "you don't have to tell me anything. Just seeing the happiness in your face is all I'll ever need to know."

"But I want to tell you, Billy darling. I do! You were so much a part of it that I can't not tell you."

"I was . . . a part of it?"

Eliza nodded. "It was a dream, Billy. The Lord gave me the most incredible dream! Or at least I think it was a dream. But he showed me things, and said things to me, that I can't even describe. In fact, some of them are so sacred that I can't repeat them, even to you. And already I'm starting to forget those things, which breaks my heart. But most of it I remember vividly, and if you'd like to hear, I'll tell you about it."

Soberly Billy nodded. "I would, Eliza. I want to know everything about you. I always have. I hope you know that."

"I do." Eliza took a deep breath and waited until a furious gust of wind had stopped shaking the wagon. Thank the Lord, she thought briefly, that she had shelter this time, and comfortable bags of grain to sleep on, and a dear, sweet husband to comfort and hold her—

"There were three parts to the dream, Billy—at least three I distinctly remember. In the first part I was on a wooden platform with . . . with the Lord, standing in front of him. He was surrounded by flames of glory, and as I gazed through this amazing, fiery brightness and into his eyes, someone spoke, telling me this was a transfiguration. I'd never seen such glory, such light, and I'd never felt such warmth and love. I knew how Jesus felt about me, how very much he loved me, and I didn't even know such love was possible! It seemed as though I was being enveloped in it, and I remember thinking that I never wanted it to end.

"The Lord never spoke a word during this part of my dream. Neither did I. Yet through it all I knew I'd been forgiven of every cruel or unkind word or thought or deed I'd ever committed. I knew

490

I'd also been forgiven of my pride, and so my guilt was swept away! Truthfully, Billy, I felt practically consumed by his overwhelming love, and it was that love which had cleansed me. It was more powerful than anything I've ever felt or even imagined. It was so powerful that I feel it yet, and when I think about it I find myself weeping with joy."

"That's what's making you so happy," Billy said as he held Eliza close.

"It . . . is. I feel like I'm practically floating every minute. I don't feel the cold or the pain, difficulties hardly seem to bother me, and I . . . Well, bother!" In exasperation Eliza wiped at the tears streaming down her cheeks. "I can't begin to explain it, but it's a wonderful feeling. And would you suppose it, Billy? I finally realized, as I stood there in my dream, that the peace I've been seeking for so long is nothing more than the love of Christ being made manifest in my life."

Billy nodded his understanding. "That is interesting, isn't it."

Quickly Eliza looked at her husband. "You knew that already, didn't you."

Billy smiled but said nothing, so with a smile of her own, Eliza continued. "In the next part of my dream I was again standing in front of the Lord, though we were no longer on that platform. In fact, I don't know where we were. He had two small vials in his hands, each filled with blood. As I watched, he began mixing the blood from the separate vials together, pouring the contents back and forth. I don't know how he did this, but nothing spilled, nothing overflowed. Somehow the one full vial fit perfectly into the other full vial, and vice versa. Though Jesus again said nothing, I knew that the vials represented you and me, or your blood and my blood."

"Our marriage?"

With new tears in her eyes, Eliza nodded. "You were right all along, Billy. In the dream I knew that our marriage had been sanctioned by God. We're becoming perfectly matched, and now that we've made eternal covenants with each other, we must do everything in our power to preserve them."

"We will, hon-bun, don't you worry about that."

"I'm not worrying, darling. I haven't for months. But it was so nice receiving that confirmation from the Lord.

"In the third part of the dream, we were outdoors, on a street somewhere, and a big crowd of people was standing around. In fact, there were so many I couldn't even see them all. Jesus had been on a wooden stand in the middle of the road, but it had tipped or been pushed over, and he was lying in the dirt. I was on the side of the road, holding our son—he seemed about two years. I was explaining to him—we'd named him William Foreman II, but I was calling him Will—that this was the Savior of all mankind.

"Meanwhile, though everyone else was ignoring him or perhaps couldn't even see him, you had come from somewhere and started repairing the stand and helping Jesus to his feet and back onto it. I explained to our son all you were doing to help the Savior in his work. I also explained the love Christ had for him, myself, and you, and I spent quite a bit of time teaching him all I had learned of Christ and his love for all mankind—even though most of the people were ridiculing him, mocking him, or at the least ignoring him."

Eliza paused, her gaze distant.

"Is that all?" Billy asked gently.

"Well." Eliza was suddenly embarrassed. "There was one more thing."

"If you don't want to tell me, Eliza, you certainly don't have to."

Eliza smiled. "I . . . I think I should. I . . . well, in all three parts of the dream Jesus was dressed in a long, white robe. When you were helping him to his feet and back onto the stand in the road, I realized that his robe was all he was wearing. I was embarrassed because I'd noticed such a thing, and then the same unseen person who'd spoken to me before explained that in the realms of glory, such feelings as I was having didn't exist. In other words, I was worrying about things that were totally unimportant. After that I was again at ease."

"Very interesting," Billy said quietly, "and very profound. And you say there was even more than this?"

Slowly Eliza nodded. "Quite a bit, actually—things that were said to me, wonderful things about my past and about what is to come that I've been trying for days to hold in my heart." Eliza's tears started again. "Almost instantly I forgot some of it, though, so I decided to write down the rest. But when I tried, I could remember nothing to write down. Then as soon as I put my writing materials away, almost all the words came back. But now they're going again—Oh, Billy, why am I forgetting such wonderful things?"

Tenderly Billy stroked his wife's arm. "I don't know, hon-bun, unless it's to protect you. But I don't think you should worry about it. President Young once told me that every word ever uttered by Christ has been recorded eternally. So all that was said to you is written down already, and when it's time, it will be given back."

"Do you . . . truly think so?"

Billy smiled. "Of course I do! Meanwhile, he's given you the gift of his love in a way few of us ever feel. What a great blessing!"

"But . . . why would I see such a sight, Billy? I'm no one of importance in this church, no one at all. Why would the Lord show himself to one such as me?"

In answer Billy reached over and lifted the book of Doctrine and Covenants. "Here," he said softly as he turned the pages, "this is the first verse of the ninety-third section. See what you think."

"Verily, thus saith the Lord," Eliza read softly, "It shall come to pass that every soul who forsaketh his sins and cometh unto me, and calleth on my name, and obeyeth my voice, and keepeth my commandments, shall see my face and know that I am."

Wonderingly Eliza looked up. "But . . . I . . . I didn't think that meant in this life—"

"For you, at least, and to this extent, it must." Billy smiled tenderly. "Think of it, hon-bun. In that verse Christ listed five conditions that had to be complied with before he would reveal his face, and you have met them all. You forsook all your sins by repenting of them and apologizing to others for them; you went to Christ in total humility to apologize personally for wounding him; you've called on his name continually for months; you've done everything the Holy Ghost—his voice, if you will—has directed you to do by way of repentance and obedience; and you're diligently trying to keep all his commandments. To me it's perfectly reasonable that he has revealed his face to you in the wonderful manner he has."

"Oh, Billy," Eliza breathed as joy and a measure of understanding swept across her countenance. "It's so good to feel peace, to know that I've been forgiven and once again redeemed from my sins—"

58

Monday, March 15, 1880

Whirlwind Bench

"Billy, wake up! Hurry!"

"What . . . is it?" Billy asked as he struggled to open his eyes.

"The noise, Billy. Can you hear it? That terrible moaning and whining, like the banshees my mother used to tell me about, coming to screech away our souls. Listen to it. It's coming closer—"

Sitting up, Billy fumbled with a match, got it to flame, and then lit the wick of the lantern. As he lowered the glass chimney, he became aware that there was no wind, and that the canvas over their heads was limp and still. Then, off in the distance, he finally heard the awful moaning—

For two days the company had been descending the three-mile dugway down the north side of what they were calling Clay Hill Pass. Though difficult, the road hadn't been overly treacherous, and in meeting the night before Jens Nielson had led the company in giving thanks to the Lord for holding off all but a slight skiff of snow until all were safely at the bottom.

Now nearly seven miles from the base of the pass, they were all encamped on an open bench that was rimmed to the north by what they were calling the Red House Cliffs. Someone had pronounced the name because the massive red rocks of the cliffs were as straight up and down as the walls of a house, and the name had stuck. The campsite itself was a fairly good one, Billy felt, because the feed for the livestock was sufficient and there had been plenty of water on the rocks and in the shallow washes and gullies they'd crossed over. All that was lacking was shelter and fuel, and there had even been a little of that, though not enough to make everyone comfortable.

The only thing worth worrying about now that all were down the pass, Billy had thought, was that some in the company had grown ill. Therefore, after Sunday evening meeting, he and Eliza had spent a couple of hours out visiting. Most of that time had been spent with Mary Jones, who'd taken a bad cold but was still up and about, and both John and Pauline Pace, who were so weak from chills and fever they could hardly take care of their baby Elizabeth.

Harriet Ann Barton had also dropped by to help, and between her and Eliza the child had been cleaned and fed and rocked to sleep without difficulty. The parents had also been fed, and once Billy had pitched and secured their tent and placed their bedding inside, the entire little family had been put to bed.

Platte and Jens Nielson had also been around visiting, Platte telling folks of his adventures the past two days as he, his brother Edward, and Joseph Lillywhite had ridden southward to strike the San Juan. There they had found about two hundred acres of level bottomland lying just six feet above the river. The trouble was that two hundred acres weren't enough for an entire community to settle on, besides which it was so thickly covered with cottonwood trees that they could hardly ride through. On their return trip, darkness had overtaken the three, and they'd been forced to spend the night in a cave, huddled over a fire and trying to sleep without any sort of bedding. It was, Platte had told everyone, one of the coldest nights he'd spent in his life.

Now, as Billy sat in his wagon listening to the distant moaning, he realized the weather had grown cold again, bitterly so. In fact, it was—

"Billy," Eliza whispered frantically, "the noise is much closer. I know it is!"

Silently Billy nodded. "You're right, hon-bun. If I didn't know better, I'd swear it was an approaching train. What on earth?" Abruptly Billy's eyes grew wide with understanding. "Eliza, that's wind! We've got a windstorm blowing straight at us. Roll up in those quilts and don't move. Hurry! I'll put on your buffalo coat and go warn the others—"

495

But Billy had no chance to warn anyone. Even before he could pull on Eliza's coat, the canvas cover of the wagon began whipping furiously, and seconds later it felt as if a wall of noise had slammed directly into the side of the wagon.

For a moment the wagon teetered as if it would blow over, and then with a snap two of the overhead bows broke, the canvas top caved partly in, and the pressure was reduced enough to allow the wagon to remain upright.

"Eliza?" Billy shouted against the terrible roaring, "are you okay?"

"I'm f . . . fine," her muffled voice replied from beneath the quilts. "Hadn't we better put out the lantern?"

"No need to . . . worry." Billy was scrambling to get beneath the quilts beside Eliza, to hold her and try to protect her from the fury of the storm. "I reckon the wind sucked the flame out already, because of a sudden she's blacker'n midnight out here."

"What . . . what sort of storm can it be?"

"Beats me," Billy mumbled as he struggled to roll himself on top of the quilt edges without pulling them from his wife. "It's got snow or sleet with it, though. Hear it hitting against the canvas?"

"I hear it. But what's that other sound, the pounding coming from right under us?"

"I don't know, hon-bun. Something's sure enough banging around under there. I . . . Wait a minute! I'll bet that's our canvas awning! Sounds like it, anyway. Most likely it's been torn off the poles and has somehow wrapped itself around the wagon. Eliza, hold onto the quilts! The wind'll suck them right off us!"

"Billy, what is this?"

"I don't know! Some sort of cyclone or something. Listen, Eliza, is that people screaming?"

"Where? All I can hear is the creaking of this poor old wagon— that and whatever it is that's pounding on the running gear under- neath us—Wait, that *is* screaming! Oh, Billy—"

"Those are animals, Eliza. Horses! But that . . . that's human. Women or children, I can't tell. Glory be. Somebody sounds like they're getting killed out there. Oh, dear God in heaven, please pro- tect the folks in our company—"

———o–o–o———

"Is . . . it over?"

Holding his trembling wife beneath the quilts, Billy listened intently. "Sounds like it," he responded as he pulled back their covering to stare into the inky darkness. "See? The roaring is definitely lessened."

"But the wind's still blowing."

"I'll say it is. And listen to the snow hitting the canvas. That's a blizzard out there, hon-bun. No doubt about it. But at least your banshees have gone on their way."

Finding the lantern, Billy again struck a light, and a moment later he was examining the two broken bows. "Well," he said as he sat shivering in the bitterly cold air, "Those can be fixed without much trouble, but I'm not going to try it until morning. Eliza, you stay here and keep yourself and the baby warm. I think I'd best go check on the Paces, for I'll bet they'll be laying in the snow without any sort of tent remaining to shelter them."

"Check on Kumen and Mary, too, Billy."

"I will. I just need to finish getting into this buffalo coat of yours, and then get on what's left of my boots—"

———o–o–o———

"You and Eliza all right, Billy?"

In the dim lantern light Billy nodded. "We're fine, Bishop. Two of my bows broke, and there's quite a tear in the outer canvas. The worst damage, though, was sustained by the china Eliza had left set on the table. That's broken and scattered all over the place."

"I'm sorry to hear that. Maggie told me how much store Eliza sets by that china."

Holding his lantern high, Billy looked toward the Sevy wagon. "Are you and Maggie and little George all right?"

George Sevy nodded grimly. "We're fine. We lost our tent, though, so I'm worried about the rest of the folks in tents. That was too much wind for a tent to handle."

"It was something, all right. Fact is, I was on my way to check out John and Pauline Pace and their daughter."

"Good. It's hard to tell in all this snow, but I think I see a lantern over that direction. That's comforting. Billy, check on Jim Pace and my daughter Hannah whilst you're over there, will you? She and the baby haven't been feeling well of late, and if they're without a tent now—" George looked bleak. "I'm worried about the Goddards and Duntons and Gowers, too, since they were camped off that way alone with no other wagons to shelter them. Reckon I'd better go check on them—"

"Billy? George? You folks all right?"

"We are, Platte."

"Glad to hear it." Huffing and puffing, Platte Lyman stomped through the snow until he was in the lee of Billy's wagon. "For a few minutes that was a wild one, and the way this snow's coming down, I'm not altogether sure it's over."

"How did your folks weather it?" Billy asked.

"Pretty well. Joseph's wife Nellie was some frightened—well, for that matter so was I. A wind like that's enough to frighten any-body! Mickelsons and Waltons both lost their tents, and Peter Mortensen lost his wagon cover, but so far I haven't found a single injury. To me that seems like a mighty miracle.

"I also checked on the Mickelsons, and Erasmus is rigging some canvas around Peter's wagon wheels. They have piles of bedding, and he seems to think they'll all be fine underneath the wagon once the wind is cut off. For Harriet and her baby's sake, I hope so."

Platte stamped his feet in the snow, trying to restore warmth. "I've also got my three brothers out gathering wood for a big fire, so if you find folks who've lost their shelter, tell them to gather at my wagons. In spite of this snow, we'll rig up some sort of covering, and between it and the fire we'll make it through until morning."

"A big fire sounds wonderful!" George Sevy declared. "I just hope your brothers don't get lost in this blizzard."

Platte nodded. "They might, but their horses won't. You boys going any particular direction?"

Quickly Billy explained their plan.

"That's good. I'll go this way, then, and check on Sammy Cox and both Dailey families, and then David and Sarah Jane Hunter. From where we start we'll all go clockwise from one camp to the next until everybody's been accounted for. Oh, I also saw Cornelius and Lizzy Decker. Their wagon cover's torn some, but their tent held, and the two children didn't even wake up. I don't reckon there's much need of bothering them again before daylight."

Both Billy and George Sevy nodded.

"All right. Give a holler or come running if you find somebody injured. I don't want anyone—Well, lookee there! In spite of this blizzard someone's got a fire going. I reckon that's the Decker camp, boys. Leastwise that's where they were before that whirlwind hit." Platte grinned. "Now I suppose they could be anywhere."

For a moment the three men stood in silence, their backs to the blizzard as they watched the distant flames. "Amazing how cheerful that tiny bit of fire looks," Platte declared softly. "I just hope they can keep it going, what with all this wind and snow.

"Well, let's go, brethren, and let's pray whilst we're at it that the Lord's protected everybody else as well as he has us and ours."

59

Thursday, March 18, 1880

Near Harmony Flat

"Hyaah!" Eliza shouted as she shook the reins over the backs of the two teams of mules. "Giddup there, Sign. You too, Wonder. You're supposed to be the leaders of this outfit, so get along there! Hyaah!"

Self-consciously Eliza giggled, for she wasn't used to hearing such language or even such volume coming from her own mouth. But then, as she shook the reins again and the mules lunged up a three-foot embankment of sand, pulling the wagon up behind them, her giggle turned into a wide smile. They were good animals, she knew, as good as any in the company. But like Dick Butt had told her several times since his return from delivering his horses to the San Juan country two days before, a person had to know how to talk to them before they would do the work they needed to do.

"Hyaagh!" she shouted as she snapped the reins again, "good job, mules. Now, let's not allow this little bit of snow to slow us down! Giddup there! Hyaagh! Hyaagh!"

"Say, Eliza! You sound like a regular muleskinner!"

Smiling, Eliza waved at Nathaniel Decker, who was trudging through the snow with two teams of horses in tow, apparently heading back to hook up to another of the Decker family wagons. "Even with my accent?" she called back.

"Feller wouldn't even know you had one." He grinned. "You ever want a job skinning mules, give us a holler."

"I'll keep that in mind. How are Emma and little Sarah Jane?"

Nathaniel paused, checking the horses behind him. "Sarah Jane doesn't like all this snow because she can't stand up in it, and Emma's just like you, I reckon—mighty uncomfortable. I know she'll be pleased when her baby finally arrives."

Eliza placed her hand on her swelling abdomen. "I know how she feels, all right. It's difficult doing anything anymore. I was going to come visit before that whirlwind hit, but since then things have been too hectic, and I'm not good at standing up in the snow, either. But give Emma my love and tell her I'm thinking of her."

"I'll do that. You need any help unhitching at night? Or harnessing up in the mornings?"

"Thank you, no. Dick Butt's been doing it since Billy left to go chopping. And since they're his mules anyway—"

Nathaniel laughed. "Far be it from me to get between a man and his mules. You take care, Eliza, and if you need anything, give us a holler. I—Oh, by-the-by, the Goddards and the Redds and some others from New Harmony have established a camp maybe two miles ahead in a huge sagebrush flat. It might surprise you to know they're calling it Harmony Flat."

"Are we without harmony invited?" Eliza asked mischievously.

Again the man chuckled. "You have harmony, Eliza, plenty of it, so I'm sure you'd be welcome. But be sure and pick a good spot to put your wagon. You just never know when another big wind might come swooping down on us."

With a wave the man was gone out of sight behind her wagon, and as Eliza snapped the reins again, she thought of the wind that had so quickly devastated the camp three days before. No one knew exactly what it was, but two or three in the company, having survived tornadoes on the Great Plains, claimed the terrible howling had been the same. So they'd decided it was a massive whirlwind, called the place of devastation Whirlwind Bench, and spent an extra day gathering livestock and repairing tents and wagons. Pap Redd had a bunch of large needles that his father had used to repair sails when he'd been a sea captain, and these were passed about freely as both men and women went to work sewing.

The carpenters had also been busy, as had both blacksmiths. George Lewis of Kanab, a young blacksmith who was traveling with his father James, had been the one who'd come to repair their wagon bows. Eliza had been certain the fractured wood was no good for anything but firewood, but in a short time George had forged several permanent clamps for both bows, and now they seemed as sound as ever.

What couldn't be repaired, Eliza thought with a twinge of sadness, were the two precious settings of china she'd managed to pull across the plains in her handcart—the china handed down from her grandmother. Thank goodness the miniature tea set her father had bought her had been packed away and was safe. But those two settings, which she and Billy had used every night but one since their marriage, had been so precious to her.

Still, she thought with a wry smile, it was silly to feel such emotion over *things*—

———◦─◦─◦———

"Are you warm enough, Eliza?"

"Hello, Mary." Eliza pulled her mules to a halt to give them a breather. "Whose team is that you're transporting?"

Mary Jones paused, reached up, and placed a hand on the muzzle of one of the horses, bringing the two teams to a halt. "Two are father's," she replied, "and the others belong to Hy and Ellen Fielding. The team they've been using on their second wagon is so ganted up for want of forage they couldn't pull it anymore."

"I saw the wagon parked in that little flat earlier, and I wondered."

"That's why they had to leave it. And Hy's still not well, you know. But Kumen and Father gave him a blessing last night, so I'm sure he'll be fine. Anyhow, I told him and Ellen I'd go back and haul their wagon up to camp for them. With their four little ones, Ellen has her hands full, and since Kumen was setting up our camp and helping Caleb and Sarah Haight with the broken wagon wheel they got hitting that stump, I have little to do but sit around trying to keep warm. So, are *you* keeping warm, Eliza Foreman?"

Eliza laughed. "Mary, for a woman less than half my age you continue to sound very much like my mother."

Mary grinned teasingly. "It's a thankless job, but someone has to do it. Now, are you going to answer my question?"

"All right, I'm fine." Eliza reached up and tucked a lock of hair back behind her ear. "Fact is, Mary, sometimes I'm too warm! These rocks Brother Nielson gathered and Billy insisted on hauling along have been wonderful. It shames me thinking of the fuss I made over them."

"They help, then, while you're traveling?"

"They certainly do! Of a morning I gather them from around my fire and load them, put a piece of old blanket over them, place these sorry old feet of mine on top of the blanket, wrap a quilt around my legs and spread it out over the rocks, and pull this buffalo coat over the top of everything, and the only thing that gets cold after that is my nose. And that's because of my old frostbite, not because it's cold."

"But it is cold!" Mary declared as she wrapped her arms about herself, shivering. "I swan, it's colder now than it was back in January! Some nights my legs never do warm up."

"If you'd get up out of the snow, Mary Jones, it would help."

"Yes," the young woman smiled, "but then who'd help the Fieldings?"

"You could always ride one of the horses, you know."

Reaching back, Mary patted the neck of the closest animal. "I could, all right. Kumen suggested it, too. But these poor dears have to work so hard anyway, Eliza, that I can't bear the thought of adding to their burdens. Have you heard anything from Billy?"

"Just through Platte. He says the whole bunch of them are moving right along, chopping up a storm. Apparently they've about headed the Grand Gulch and will be turning south again, down off this mountain we're all so tired of climbing. But Platte says the snow's a lot deeper where they are, and the work is slower because of it.

"Some of the company are stopping up ahead at Harmony Flat for a day or two to rest up. But according to Platte, there's another camping place up nearer where Billy is, an open area he's called Grand Flat. If my mules are up to it, and if Dick's still around to help

503

me harness up, I believe I'll try and push on to Grand Flat tomorrow."

"Kumen says that's what we'll be doing, too."

"Wonderful! Then I won't be alone."

Mary laughed. "You never are, woman. The way the children in this company flock around you, you'll never be alone again. Why, I never saw the like!"

"They're fun, all right. I've certainly grown to love them."

"And them you!" With a wave Mary started her teams moving forward again, and Eliza watched until she'd gone behind the wagon, out of sight. Then, breathing a small prayer of gratitude for the young woman's friendship, she snapped the reins above the backs of the mules.

"Hyaagh!" she shouted as the animals lunged into their traces. "Hyaagh, mules! Get along there—"

———◇—◇—◇———

Grand Gulch Plateau

"You getting that one, Billy?

"You bet, Joseph!" Scraping a couple of feet of snow back from the trunk of the large cedar, Billy dropped to one knee, drew back his ax, and began chopping. He was getting more proficient at this, he knew, for with almost every double-stroke of his ax a large chip of wood flew free. Yet he was still not as fast as some of the others, such as John Eyre, George Ipson, and Sidney Goddard. These and the others of the crew seemed able to chop all day, hardly resting at all, and they could chop down two or three trees while he was felling one.

Partly, Billy knew, his slowness was from inexperience with this type of chopping—sideways from on his knees. But partly it was caused by the strain in his back from swinging his ax from such an awkward position—that and the fact that everything from his waist down had gone numb from walking and kneeling and scuffling around in the snow. His upper body was cold and wet too, not just from snow but from sweating and chilling with the starting and completing of each tree.

Surely, he thought as he swung and swung again, trying to work past the chill in his body, the others must be suffering too. But none complained, none even slowed down as they moved from tree to tree with their single- and double-bladed axes, leveling a ten-to twelve-foot roadway through the never-ending forest of juniper and piñon.

So he wouldn't complain either, Billy vowed as he shifted position and twisted himself to swing again. In fact, he wouldn't even speak of what must surely be their mutual suffering lest he be seen as weak—not able to do his part for the mission.

"Are we still on that old Indian trail?" Joseph Lyman asked from nearby, where he'd just felled another tree. Now he was hooking his blade above the lower boughs and turning the trunk into the roadway so the teamsters, seventeen-year-old Stephen A. Smith, fifteen-year-old Billy Eyre, and fourteen-year-old George Henry Westover could more easily hook their horses to the trees and drag them out of the way.

"I believe so," Billy grunted as his ax took another bite out of the wood. "Least that's what George Morrell said an hour or so ago. Sure interesting how those Indians have figured this country out."

Joseph nodded. "It is. But then, they've had plenty of time to do it, too. And Platte says we aren't exactly following their trail anyway. An Indian on foot or even on a pony can go up and down and wind and twist about as he wants. A wagon and team, on the other hand, is more limited and has to travel a straighter path."

"Well," Billy responded as he looked back at the aisle of snow and short stumps that stretched away northward between the walls of trees, "this road of ours is straighter than a twisty trail, all right. I just hope all our stumps are short enough for the wagons to clear them."

"With three to four feet of snow," Joseph admitted with a smile, "it can be mighty hard to tell. It's terrible cold, too, don't you think?"

Grinning, Billy nodded. "But then we've climbed, Joseph. We're on a mountain here, and I'm certain our elevation is even higher than the top of Clay Hill Pass. It's no wonder the trees are so thick and the snow and cold so bad."

Once Billy's tree had fallen, the two men moved forward in silence, laboriously making their way through the deep snow. All around them sounds of chopping shattered the winter stillness as young men such as Alma Angell, Peter Mortensen, Jens Nielson, Jr.,

Walter C. Lyman, John A. Smith, and half a dozen others moved steadily forward, felling trees. They were an amazing group, Billy thought, each of them ignoring the cold, hunger, and other physical discomforts as they moved tree by tree, rod by rod, mile by mile, laboring practically without ceasing to open up a roadway through the timber. What courage they all had! What incredible faith, to subject themselves and their families to such trials and privations simply because a prophet had called them to take the message of peace—of the love of the Lord—to a couple of tribes of warlike Indians. It was almost incomprehensible that he, Billy Foreman, clerk and accountant, had been allowed to join such a group, to help them fulfill their mission—

"Billy," Joseph said as he paused to size up a tree that hadn't been cut, "my little brother Walter tells me you have a head for figures and other stuff and that you've been showing him a few things. Would you mind if I sit in the next time you and he get together?"

In surprise Billy, who'd just wiped his spectacles and knelt beneath a tree of his own, looked up. "Of course not, Joseph. But remember, I'm not much of a teacher—not like your brother Platte, for instance."

"He's not much of one either, not when he gets too much on his mind. Lately I hate to even trouble him about anything, let alone figures. He's just too busy with all the problems everyone is having. But I thought since you were already talking of a night with Walt—"

"Joseph, you're welcome at my fire any time, and don't you forget it." Billy grinned. "For now, though, I figure I can drop this tree before you can drop that one!"

"And I figure otherwise," Joseph growled happily, and seconds later two more axes were adding to the cacophony of sound already echoing across and down the mountain.

———◦—◦—◦———

Harmony Flat

"Those red cliffs are beautiful, aren't they. With the setting sun turning them bright red like that, they remind me of the cliffs near home."

Eliza looked up from the mending she was trying to finish before dark. "Yes, I remember those cliffs in Red Canyon. Amazing shapes."

Maggie Sevy laughed. "I didn't mean those. I meant the cliffs between New Harmony and Santa Clara and St. George. That's where I lived until I married Brother Sevy and moved to Panguitch."

"You were born there?"

"Actually," Maggie said as she built up Eliza's fire, "I was born on the Plains while my parents were coming to Zion. I was born and my older sister Rachel died, almost at the same time. From what I was told, Rachel was buried in a shallow grave beside the trail, and the rest of us kept on. I . . . I think my mother was a very courageous woman to keep going—to leave her baby that way and just walk on. More amazing to me is that I can never remember in later years when she wasn't smiling, wasn't happy."

Lowering her mending, Eliza looked up, studying George Sevy's young second wife. Her voice had been so filled with emotion that it was obvious to Eliza that something was on her mind, troubling her. What it might happen to be, however, was something else altogether. Perhaps if she—

"The farther we get from Panguitch, Eliza, the more terrible I feel. I . . . can hardly bear getting so far away from my babies!"

"But little George F. is with you, Maggie, in your tent, asleep."

Maggie's face was filled with anguish. "N . . . not him, Eliza. My first three. All of them lie buried back in Panguitch in their tiny little graves. And I miss them so terrible much I don't know what to do!"

"Oh, Maggie, I didn't know. I didn't realize—"

"Afternoon, Eliza."

Turning in surprise, Eliza was startled to see two of her little girls. "Why, hello, Sarah Jane. Lucinda," she said while Maggie composed herself. "What brings you girls out when it's getting so near dark?"

"We have a present for you!" Lucinda Nielson declared proudly. "From us and Sarah Jane's mother."

"A present? For me?"

"Yes siree, ma'am!" Sarah Jane Rowley was beaming. "That's

what Pa says. Ma said to get over here with it quick, as you'd be having need for it tonight."

"Mercy! What on earth can it be?"

"Here," Sarah Jane declared, her face still aglow as she held out
a cloth-covered bundle. "Open it and see. But Ma says to be careful,
Eliza, so they don't break on you."

Carefully Eliza reached out and took the bundle from Sarah Jane
and drew it to her. It was surprisingly heavy—or at least it was heavier than she had expected it to be. It was also round and hard—

"Hurry, Eliza!" Lucinda urged, her voice filled with excitement.
"You're really going to like them!"

"Yes," Maggie Sevy urged as she stepped up behind the two
girls, her happy countenance renewed, "let's see what they've given
you."

With a sinking sensation Eliza realized that she already knew.
She knew, and she could not accept the gift. Why, there was no
need—

"Come on, Eliza. Hurry!"

Forcing her smile to remain intact, Eliza fumbled at the knot
holding the corners of the cloth, undid it, and folded it back. Then
she stared in awe at what was lying in her lap.

"They're part of Ma's china that came all the way from
England," Sarah Jane said. "See, Eliza? They're just like yours that
got smashed in the whirlwind."

"But . . . I can't . . . " Eliza stammered. "I mean . . . your mother
will want these, Sarah Jane. Once we get settled in Montezuma Fort,
she'll need them!"

"No she won't." The seven-year-old girl was emphatic. "Ma had
twelve settings in that big old trunk of hers, and she told Pa she'd
never on this green earth use more than ten of them at a time.
Besides, she said she couldn't bear going past your wagon of an
evening and not seeing your table all set and pretty with your grandmother's china. She says it helps her feel civilized."

"It helps all of us feel that way," Maggie stated softly.

"But . . . I'll be just fine—"

"There's a note from Ma under the top plate," Sarah Jane interrupted. "I saw her put it there. I reckon it's for you."

Carefully Eliza lifted the dainty-thin piece of china and pulled out the note. Unfolding it, she read:

My dear Eliza:

How can I ever thank you for all you have taught me, all you have shown me. Especially I think of us seated together at your table near the lake while you taught me things about our Lord that I had never known. Such a change you have made in my thinking and feeling. If for nothing else I will love you forever for bringing me closer to my Savior. When the girls told me you had lost the last two settings of your precious china, I thought immediately of my own. In the future, as you gaze upon these pieces of an evening and think of your dear family in far-off England, perhaps you will also take a moment and remember me—your friend forever.

Ann Rowley

"It was great fun," Lucinda was saying, wanting to share her own part in the gift and not noticing at all that Eliza was quietly weeping. "I went with Sarah Jane and her mother to your camp on Whirlwind Bench after you and Billy—I mean Brother Foreman— had pulled out. We found two really big pieces of your china, and that was when Sister Rowley told us she had a set she thought was just like yours but wanted the pieces to make sure."

"And they *were* the same!" Sarah Jane was still beaming. "When we finally got that old trunk dug out of the wagon this afternoon, Ma compared 'em. See, Eliza? Ma didn't want you feeling bad about losing the only china left of your grandma's set. Neither did me or Lucinda or any of the others. Besides, that's part of what's fun about having tea and crumpets with you. We pull straws to see who gets to use your grandma's china, you know."

"You do what?"

"We pull straws," Lucinda confirmed. "I've won two times, Eliza. *Everybody* wants to use your grandma's china."

"That's very sweet," Eliza said as she gently caressed the edges of the elegant plates, saucers, and cups. "I thank you with all my heart. And Sarah Jane, your mother is wonderful! But I can't—"

"Eliza?"

"Yes, Maggie?" she responded, looking up. And to her surprise she realized that her younger friend was holding a finger over her lips, signaling silence.

"Eliza's a little overcome," Maggie said then as she hugged each of the girls to her. "So run along to your families, and Sarah Jane, you tell your mother thank you. I promise I'll help Eliza set her table with your beautiful china before I leave."

Happily the two young girls turned and ran, and only when they were out of sight did Maggie turn back.

"I can't keep these, Maggie, and you know it." Eliza was still caressing the sides of the top plate. "It isn't fair for Ann Rowley to break up a set this way, and besides, I'll be able to get more. I'm certain it won't be this same pattern, but—"

"Eliza?"

"Yes?"

"Brother Sevy tells folks we must be terribly careful about refusing gifts, that ninety-nine times out of a hundred it's best to accept them graciously, no questions asked. He's always quoting that scripture where the Lord asks what it profits a man who refuses a gift. 'Behold,' the Lord says, such a person 'rejoices not in that which is given unto him, neither rejoices in him who is the giver of the gift.'"

Eliza was dumbfounded. "A scripture says that?"

"It does. In the Doctrine and Covenants, section eighty-eight. I've heard it so many times I've memorized it. The thing is, Eliza, I don't think you have any idea how much those little girls love you. Or Ann Rowley either, for that matter. If you refuse this china, no matter how logical your reasons, it will only hurt their feelings and take away the blessings they might be earning besides. So, let's put these on your table here—"

"I can't accept them, Maggie. I just can't do it!"

"Why not?"

"Because . . . because it isn't right! I just don't need that china—"

Maggie Sevy smiled patiently. "Since when is physical need a prerequisite for receiving? Think about it, Eliza. If a giver is motivated by love and yearns to share that love through a gift, then isn't that yearning an emotional need that the recipient should be bound to honor?"

Carefully Eliza gazed at her younger friend. "Emotional need?"

"That's right. I'm talking about the need to allow the giver to give—which I believe is on a higher level than a physical need. The giver has a need, which creates a supporting need in the receiver. Bishop Sevy's taught me this. He calls it a more selfless receiving, and he says it requires a greater level of maturity. He also says such selflessness leads to the highest receiving of all, which is spiritual."

"How can receiving be spiritual?" Eliza pressed.

"Whenever we receive the Atonement," Maggie replied quietly, "we become spiritual receivers. Though the need exists, worthiness on our part doesn't. Nevertheless, the gift is offered, and receiving it requires great spiritual maturity. It requires that we become comfortable enough, through our love for Christ, to accept without hesitation his grace—his love for us. That's what all giving and all receiving leads to, Eliza. Christ's atonement is *the* infinite and eternal gift, and learning to receive these lesser gifts leads to it."

Sighing deeply, Eliza stared off into the distance. "Maggie," she finally said, "thank you. I think I can see what you're saying, and it appears that you're right again."

"Again?" The young woman looked perplexed.

"Yes." Eliza smiled as she pulled herself to her feet. "You were right that day at Sweetwater Spring when you told me what a precious gift a righteous husband was, and that I was destroying mine. Don't you remember?"

"I remember speaking with you, Eliza, because that was the first day we ever met. But I don't—"

The sound of crying suddenly erupted from the nearby Sevy tent, and Maggie turned and hurried inside. Eliza busied herself setting the china on her table, folding the serviettes and laying the silver on top of them. She was gazing at the table with a lump of emotion in her throat when Maggie returned, her small son bundled in her arms.

"Little George F. kicks so much when he sleeps that he loses all his covers," Maggie said as she comforted her child. "Then he wakes up freezing and bellering about it. I declare, Eliza, if I didn't love him so much I'd wonder if having children was worth—"

Abruptly Maggie stopped, her eyes wide. "My goodness," she said softly. "Now I think you're teaching me, Eliza. I mean, watching you calmly agree to accept that china even though you didn't want to, I finally understand what my mother knew—what kept her going even after she buried my sister."

Eliza remained silent, waiting.

"Before the Lord took Rachel from my mother, he gave her another gift—me. And though it must have been painful for Mother to leave Rachel behind in her grave, she was wise enough to understand that she mustn't refuse the Lord's second gift to her. To pine away her life beside that shallow grave, where I'm sure she wanted to remain, or to live anywhere else with constant sorrow and distress and grief would have been denying God's gift—it would have been denying me the happy childhood that every child of God deserves."

Slowly Maggie walked over and sat in the rocker that Eliza had vacated earlier. Tenderly, then, she began rocking her tiny son.

"Little George F. deserves my happiness every bit as much as I enjoyed my mother's," she breathed. "He is my gift from God, my precious, sweet, fourth little gift."

"Your fifth," Eliza corrected softly. "Dear Bishop Sevy was your first."

Maggie caught her breath and then struggled with her emotions. Finally, swiping at her eyes with the edge of little George F.'s blanket, she continued.

"Of course you're right, Eliza. And I . . . I'm honored to be sealed to Brother Sevy for time and all eternity, to be going with him to the San Juan, and to build up a home there in his name. More, I'm so very thankful for little George F.—that the Lord has allowed him to live." Abruptly the young woman burst again into tears. "But how," she finally continued, "how can I be happy when I've left my three little darlings behind me? How can I rid myself of all this pain, this emptiness? You know the answer, Eliza. I know you do, for I've seen your joy in spite of all you suffer. Please help me learn how to be happy again—"

60

Saturday, March 20, 1880

Montezuma Fort

"Hello the fort! Jim Davis? Henry Harriman? Hello in there! You folks at home?"

Mormon missionary Lewellyn Harris was feeling anxious. In fact, he'd been feeling anxious since the day before, when he'd run onto George Hobbs and the two Robb brothers in the bottom of Butler Wash. They'd told him of the Ute uprising on the White River as well as the warning from both a cowboy and an apparently friendly Navajo that the Pahutes were involved. Since then, though he'd seen nothing to indicate it, Lewellyn Harris had felt watched. The feeling had grown stronger the closer to Montezuma Fort he had ridden, and now that he was there —well, he was jumpy, and that was all there was to it.

So now he sat nervously in his saddle, surveying his surroundings. What he was seeing wasn't much, either. Built on the sandy bottomland where Montezuma Creek churned into the San Juan, the fort was actually two one-room cabins joined by a common roof and a breezeway into which both cabins opened. Nearby was a brush corral, presently empty, and beyond it were two or three acres of tilled ground. Several large cottonwoods were growing in the area, and some distance away thick stands of willows marked the present boundaries of the creek. Other than that, he could see and hear nothing, and the silence was oppressive.

"Hello the fort!" he called again as he nervously reined his horse in a tight circle, still looking around. No smoke came from the mud

513

and willow chimneys, either one of them. And he could see only darkness beyond the two small windows. "Is anybody to home here?"

Slowly the door of one of the cabins opened a few inches. "Identify yourself, please," a woman's voice called out. "Tell us who you are."

"I'm Lewellyn Harris, ma'am. I'm a missionary, on my way to preach the restored gospel in the land of Mexico. Are you Mary Davis or Sarah Harriman?"

Now the door swung wide, and two women stepped out, followed instantly by several small children and three large dogs. "I'm Mary Davis," the older of the two women declared, "and this is Sarah Harriman. Our husbands are on a scout with Thales Haskell and will be back directly. My son Eddie is with our livestock, guarding it. We've been warned about Indians and outlaws, so excuse us if we seem unneighborly. Are you related to the Harrises down on Harris Bottoms?"

"Yes, ma'am, I am."

"Are they well?"

Lewellyn Harris lifted his hat and scratched his head. "I've heard they are, ma'am, but to tell the truth I didn't stop to check. One, it was out of my way; and two, I'm in need of some decent cooked food. The way I recollect, neither of those Harris boys can cook a lick. George Hobbs, however, says the two of you are the best cooks on the frontier." Lewellyn Harris smiled. "Which is why I came directly here."

Both women smiled in return. "You're welcome here, Brother Harris. But did George also tell you we're running mighty short on food?"

"He did mention something to that effect," the missionary replied. "May I put my horse in the corral?"

"Certainly. Jimmy, will you see to Brother Harris's mount? See that it's fed and rubbed down, please."

A small boy of perhaps eight hurried out and took the reins of his horse, and so with a sigh Lewellyn Harris stepped to the ground. For a moment he simply stretched. Then, after lifting his bags and bedroll from behind his saddle, he slapped the horse on the rump and sent it following after the boy. Finally he sighed, stretched again, turned, and with a peaceful feeling settling over him at last, walked stiffly toward the cabins and the two waiting families.

———◦—◦—◦———

"Was George Hobbs all right?" Sarah asked once all had entered the cabin. "He's kin, you know."

"Yes, ma'am, I do know. And except for being a mite hungry, he was." Slowly Lewellyn Harris lowered himself into one of the two chairs in the room, a high-backed rocker. The only other furniture, he noted, was a table and two benches, and, against the rough-hewn wall, a bed. At the far end of the room a fireplace was filled only with embers; there was no firewood in the box, and so now he knew why he'd seen no smoke.

"You show me the woodpile after I've had a few minutes rest," he said then, "and I'll fill both your woodboxes for you."

"Thank you. That would be much appreciated. Since the Indian scare, we've let a few things slide."

"Yes, ma'am. Have they bothered you much? The Pahutes, I mean?"

"Not at all," Sarah Harriman said softly. "Nothing more than scare the dogs and us half to death one night when they rode past and crossed the river. That's why we brought the dogs in when they first spotted you. We didn't need their barking to warn us, and we didn't want to advertise our presence too much, either."

"Good thinking. Has Brother Haskell been working with the Indians very much?"

"Well, with the Navajo down at the Moencopi, he has. So far as I know, though, he's done nothing with the Pahutes. President Snow sent him here a few days back after he'd heard we'd all been killed. Brother Haskell's mission was to see if it was true, and if it was, to give us all as decent a burial as possible. If it wasn't true, he was to stay with us until the company from Cedar City arrived."

Lewellyn Harris nodded. "Then he'll be here about ten days longer, I expect."

"Ten days?" Mary Davis looked stunned.

515

"Yes, ma'am. Of course, I might be off a day or two either way, as you well know."

For a moment the two women looked at each other. On the bed one of two babies began fussing, and immediately Mary Davis picked it up. "This is Ethel Olive," she said softly as she placed the child over her shoulder and began patting. "First white child born on the San Juan."

"That's a mighty proud thing to say, ma'am, and to be."

Mary Davis smiled. "I hope so. The other baby is Lizzy Constance, Sarah's daughter. She sleeps better than my baby. James Henry is with your horse, this is Emily Ellen, Henry George, and Mary C., and the two little boys on the ground are John Orson and John A. As I said, my eldest son Eddie—Edward Fretwell—is guarding our livestock."

"I'm pleased to make the acquaintance of each of you," Lewellyn Harris declared as he reached out and shook the hands of each of the children. "Your politeness does your parents proud."

"Brother Harris," Sarah Harriman asked then, "how long do you plan on staying?"

"Three days, ma'am. If I can eat a bit and rest for three days, and the same for my horse, then we'll both be strong enough to make it to Mexico even if neither of us has another meal until we get there. Speaking of which, once I get your firewood I'd surely appreciate a bite to eat. It's been long enough since my last bite that my stomach probably thinks I've starved to death and forgot to tell it."

Again the women looked at each other, not smiling. The six children, completely silent, stood or sat in the corner either listening or scratching designs in the dirt floor. And the dogs, all three of them, lay quietly by the door missing nothing. Finally Sarah walked to the table and lifted a sack in which remained five or six pounds of flour.

"Brother Harris," she said as she gazed at the bag, "this is all that remains of our food. All of it! We've eaten what my brother George and the others from the camp managed to bring us, and so Harvey Dunton gave this to us two days ago when he left to try and live off wild game. A few moments before you came, Mary and I calculated that if we all ate sparingly, and then only twice a day, we might have enough in this sack to last two, maybe three more days. Certainly not ten! Now that you're here, well—We know how hungry you are, but we're both at a loss as to what to give you to eat."

"So the men-folks are actually out hunting instead of scouting?"

"They are. That's all they've done for most of a week now. But we've seen no wild game all winter, and it doesn't seem likely that they'll find anything today. Of course, we have our teams of oxen out to pasture, and we could butcher one of them. But it seems foolish to kill the livestock we'll need so badly for farming once it warms up."

Silently Lewellyn Harris rocked back and forth, his mind busy as he plied the heavens with prayer. Abruptly, however, he smiled and stood up. "Be of good cheer, Sisters," he declared as he clamped his hat on his head and turned toward the door. "Fix me up the best cake you can, for in the name of the Lord God of Israel, I promise that your worst days are over. That bag of flour will not fail, and none of you will go hungry no matter how long it takes the company to reach you."

That said, and with the power of the words he'd just spoken ringing in the minds of the two women, Lewellyn Harris went out to find the woodpile.

61

Sunday, March 21, 1880

Elk Ridge Near Grand Flat

The old Pahute known as Peeagament could not remember feeling more miserable. Not only was the snow melting on the southwest slopes and the ground too muddy for good footing, but the bag of bones he was forced to call a pony was worse gaited than any other animal he had ever ridden. Because of it, his back ached and his neck snapped with every step the animal took, and more than once he had been forced to restrain himself from leaning forward and slashing its throat even as it was carrying him forward. Of course, that would have put him afoot, and no self-respecting man of the People was ever that foolish. Nevertheless, with each step of the scruffy horse, the thought and the temptation persisted.

Unfortunately the old man had other problems than his pony, almost too many to consider. For one he was hungry. Not for three suns had he eaten more than snow and juniper berries, and he was starting to feel the effects of his long fast. Worse than that, he had lost his people. In his absence—admittedly too long—to visit the Navajo Peokon, they had simply packed up and *katz-kar-ra,* gone away, leaving him nothing but the decrepit pony upon which he presently rode. Not even his old wife or the two fine young *nan-zitch* who had been his other wives had waited. None of them! They were gone as well, no doubt already warming the beds of Prairie Dog or some other of the younger braves who had spent so much time huffing and puffing around his wickiup.

Viciously Peeagament lashed the pony's withers, letting his

518

anger at the world be taken out on his hapless mount. In response the animal stumbled and then lunged to churn its way up the steep side of a juniper-covered hill, and the old man very nearly found himself unhorsed, dumped face down in the ice and mud. Angrily he lashed the animal again and again, stopping only when his arm tired and he could no longer muster strength for more blows.

Where had he gone wrong? he asked himself as his mount crested a small ridge and began its bone-jarring slide down the far slope. To what did he owe the great evil that had befallen him? In less than one cycle of the seasons he had gone from being a great chief, feared and respected, to . . . to . . . *Ungh,* Peeagament thought with resignation, whatever he now was, at least he wasn't *e-i,* like the great and terrible Peokon—

Wonderingly the old man thought again of the feared Navajo's death, his worries about himself for the moment forgotten. In his mind he could see Peokon as the tall Navajo called Frank had described him, his large frame wasted away as he lay in his hogan with the smell and look of death hanging everywhere about him. Nor was that all. According to the one called Frank, Peokon's woman was also dead, his two tall sons were dead, perhaps his daughter was dead, and even the Navajo warrior's land was dying as his springs had dried up and his once-rich pastures had become the home of *o-coomp,* the dust.

Such a deadly reminder caused Peeagament to shudder, for large in his mind was the image of the *tshar-tots-sib-i-wub,* the white-haired mormonee called Thales Haskell. According to Frank it was he who had spoken the curse upon the feared Peokon. Yes, and he, Peeagament, could believe it, for large also was the memory of the day when he had been made a fool in the eyes of his people by the same white-haired mormonee who had cursed Peokon. From that never-to-be-forgotten day the old man had feared and respected the power of these strange whites who were coming—the power especially of the one called Thales Haskell.

Especially did old Peeagament fear that power now—now that he had seen the ashes of Peokon's hogan, the carcasses of his animals, and the dried-up place where once a good spring had flowed. With a shudder the old man remembered the tall one called Frank, the one who had shown him the places of death, telling him how Peokon had at first scorned the curse, many times making a *kee-en*, a laugh out of it. Then abruptly he had sickened and been left *nan-me-que*, confined to his bed. In that condition, and these were the words of the one called Frank, Peokon had watched with growing fear as one after another of those around him died.

Peeagament shuddered again as he thought of this terrible power owned by the man Thales Haskell and the people called mormonee. At first he had been like many of the others, both Navajo and Pahute, disdaining the curse that had been spoken upon Peokon. He and they had vowed to strip the mormonee of their wealth and leave more than one of them *paquy-nary*, stinking in the grass.

But he, Peeagament, now knew better than to even think such things. After all, when he had helped make a raid against the mormonee village across the Kaibab, hadn't he lost the horses that were due him? When he had intended to ally himself with Peokon, hadn't the Navajo grown weak and then died? When he had intended to lead his people against the mormonee himself, hadn't his people left him? When he had intended to ride hard after them, hadn't his *kuvah-u*, his fine pony, also died? And when on this awful-gaited old bag of bones he had gone to warn the mormonee who had gathered to Montezuma Creek, hadn't he found the place empty?

Oo-ah, yes! Of course, the two very poor families who had spent the season of cold were still there. But not the main band, not those with their great wealth of horses and cattle that his people intended to take for themselves. Neither were they anywhere else in the country, for he had spent many painful days on horseback trying to find them.

So now old Peeagament was *shu-mi*, he was thinking. Had the white-haired mormonee also spoken a curse upon him? Had he?

Peeagament did not know, but *hah-van*, many strange things had certainly been happening. And that was why he was riding westward now, making his way by an ancient trail to the mountain where the Pahute who called himself Mike was keeping his band.

Peeagament did not know Mike well. In fact, he hardly knew him at all, except that he was the cousin of his mother and therefore kin. Yet the *at-am-bar*, the talk, was that Mike was one of the few who had great power over the whites. Had he not killed two of them only lately down in the tall rock country, and had he not done it without fear? *Oo-ah,* yes! And did he not ride with a youth of even greater power, a youth who had taken the clothes from a white man while he yet lived, a youth who called himself the white-man name of Posey? All this was so, and Peeagament knew it.

Therefore he was suffering on the bony back of the aged horse, pushing himself as rapidly as he could toward the place where Mike and his band dwelt in the distant blue of Navajo Mountain, hoping to warn them that the mormonee were not the same as other whites—

With a horrified gasp the old man pulled rein and stared about him, gawking at the scattered wagons, the hobbled teams, and the many whites into whose midst he had suddenly and inadvertently ridden. He had been so deep in thought, so consumed with his worries, that he had not seen them, had not even heard them as he came down out of the trees and into the snow and sage-filled clearing where they were camped.

"*Ungh!*" he grunted in shocked surprise. He had never been around so many whites at once, and as his gaze swept from a heavily muscled old man to a tall thin woman who was big with child to a group of small girls and on to several other men and women who were moving snow or building fires, the thought of the curse returned.

He was surrounded! He was a captive, and soon these whites would take him—

"*Mike-tigaboo!*" one of the whites said in the old warrior's own tongue as he stepped forward, his hand held forward in the air.

Again surprised, Peeagament looked at the young man who had spoken. He held no weapons in his hands, his bearded face appeared gaunt and tired, and to the old man's further surprise he appeared to be making no move to take Peeagament captive. Instead, his tone was mild, even submissive, and instantly the old man's fear grew large.

These were not whites who would take him captive. These were mormonee! These were the very ones for whom he had been hunting, the ones who could make a man and his family *e-i* without weapons, with only words of power from their mouths. These were the people who had spoken the curse upon Peokon! These were the ones he needed to warn his people against harming—

Abruptly the old man scanned the crowd again, seeking the face of *tshar-tots-sib-i-wub,* the fearsome white-haired one called Thales Haskell. But he was not there, and much relieved, Peeagament sat more upright in his saddle.

"Where come from?" he asked in the broken English he was finally mastering.

"Across the Colorado."

Peeagament was nonplussed. "*Oo-ah,* yes, that so. But where you cross?"

"From Hole-in-the-Rock," the man replied, though these words meant nothing to Peeagament.

"Where you cross?" he demanded again, this time more insistent. And then he listened in stupefied amazement as the mormonee explained with many gestures where they had crossed the Colorado and the direction they had come since the crossing.

For a long moment Peeagament stared at the white man who had spoken. "You lie!" he finally breathed, not imagining in his wildest dreams that any people, even mormonee, could muster such power as that. "Bad country! Ver, ver bad! No road that country. Not now, not ever."

Yet in the silence that followed, as Peeagament continued to stare about him, he finally noticed the road that had been chopped through the trees, the road over which these mormonee had come, the road that stretched off toward the south and west in the direction the white mormonee had pointed.

With an exclamation of stark terror the old man kicked his sorry pony's ribs, suddenly pushing ahead through the startled encampment. It didn't matter what his people thought of him, he determined as he kept his gaze from falling on any of the scattered whites lest one should speak another curse upon him. These mormonee had power, great and terrible power. Now they had finally come into this country as they had promised, by a way that was not possible, and with Peokon dead, only he was left to spread the warning—

And with a look of grim determination already creasing his tired old face, the ancient warrior known as Peeagament lashed his pony

522

again and again, more anxious than ever to reach the distant blue of Navajo Mountain.

———◦—◦—◦———

Grand Flat

"Who was that?" Mary asked Kumen Jones as people came hurrying from all directions to look after the now-distant Pahute.

"That was old Peeagament," the young man answered thoughtfully as he, too, watched the retreating figure. "Or at least I think it was. Hanson, John, did you get a look at that old man?"

Hanson Bayless and John Gower looked at each other and nodded. "It was Peeagament, all right," John Gower replied. "He's the old Pahute chief that Captain Smith wouldn't feed last spring because he was trying to charge us that atrocious toll."

"That's right," Hanson Bayless agreed, smiling at the memory. "We fed all his people but him and then let him stew in his own juices while he watched everyone else eat. That was the last we heard of the toll, I can tell you that."

"Five hundred dollars, wasn't it?"

"It was. As if any of us might be carrying that much cash across the desert."

"That old man was a chief?" Harrict Jane Gower asked incredulously as she looked up at her husband.

"Yeah." John Gower nodded. "Of quite a large band, as I remember."

"But . . . but he's so ragged! And starved-looking! And that poor horse he was riding looked like it was on its last legs."

"He didn't look like he was doing very well," Joshua Stevens admitted.

"Like I've said before," Pap Redd said with a sly grin, "the fellow looked like he was wintering through on prickly pear and catalogue paper. Course it might be enlightening to hear what he's saying about us right now, too. For one, I've got patches on my patches— where I have any at all—and the way I've been taking in my belt notches I doubt I've got flesh enough left to waste away. Fact, if I were to return home tomorrow, I doubt either Keziah Jane or Sariah Louisa would recognize me—especially if I shaved."

"Or want you, either one," Kumen grinned. "Any man who'd leave two wives and five little ones to spend an entire winter off gallivanting in some snowy wilderness—"

"If this is what it means to go off gallivanting," Pap stated as he disgustedly kicked at the snow and turned back to the repairs he'd been making on his son's wagon, "then I'm thankfuller'n somewhat I haven't done any more of it."

With smiles and nods of agreement the company began dispersing to whatever tasks they had all been interrupted in, and only when most were out of earshot did Kumen turn to Jens Nielson.

"You know, Jens, that old man may not have been alone."

"Ya, I taught off dat." The spiritual leader of the company gazed up into the steeps of Elk Mountain. "But he vas some surprised to see us, I tink, for I saw his eyes. I also saw dat der vas no vone behint him. I vas looking."

"Glad to hear it. Still, it might not hurt to put out a guard or two."

"Ya. I vill talk vith Brudder Lyman about it." The old man paused a moment, then continued. "Der be some, I tink, who may doubt de need for guards yust because ve are on a mission of peace. But I say put out de guards und be careful, for vat good are dead missionaries. Ya?"

"Ya!" Kumen agreed. "By the way, when Dick Butt got back the other day, he said we should expect to see George Hobbs and the Robbs boys back from Montezuma Fort no later than today."

Jens Nielson looked up at the sky. "Vell, de day iss not over yet."

"No. But seeing that ornery old Pahute makes me a mite nervous. He was none too friendly to our exploring party last spring, and his disposition didn't seem much improved today. He seemed to be pushing that bony old horse of his mighty hard, and I just hope he wasn't running from a bloody murder!"

"Ya, dat vould be a tragedy, I tink—for us und for him as vell."

Kumen sighed. "I wish Platte was here. Since he isn't, I reckon we'll just have to wait and see. Jens, when the chopping crew made it back last night, I talked privately with a few of them. This sudden warmer weather feels good, but it had them all worried. Billy Foreman said where the snow was melting the mud was awful, and both John Eyre and George Morrell agreed. Since Platte and Edward aren't back with that other wagon of theirs, I'm thinking you should announce tonight at meeting that all who can should plan on pulling out come first light."

"Dat vould be goot, all right. Und Kumen, vould you gadder und lead anudder crew off choppers? Gadder young men if you can, men vidout families, und haff dem on der vay as soon as dey can depart. Und Kumen, ve vill take care off Mary."

"I'll do it," Kumen declared without hesitation. Yet he couldn't help thinking, even as he was mentally listing those he might ask, of the terrible condition of Billy and the others who'd returned the night before. The constant cold and wet of so many days and nights in that forest had taken an awful toll on their bodies, and Kumen wondered if any of them would have the strength to start again in the morning. Or if he would have any remaining strength at the end of another week.

Truly, he thought as he started toward John Robinson's tent to begin his recruiting with him and his tentmates, John Topham and Thomas Williams, Billy and the other choppers, including the three young teamsters, had to be some of the most courageous men he had ever known!

62

Kane Gulch

"Billy, darling, are you certain you're all right?"

With a crooked smile Billy looked up from his seat in the oak rocker. Naked except for his undergarments, he was wrapped in a quilt, soaking his feet while Eliza did her best to dry the caked-on mud on his shirt, trousers, and coat so it could be knocked off. As for his boots and knit wool socks, Eliza thought sorrowfully, she could see no hope for them whether they dried off or not. The boots were more holes than leather, the socks more darned patches than original wool, and even placed as they were between the two fires she had blazing—

"Never felt better," Billy was replying quite happily, "especially since I got these old feet of mine planted in this kettle of warm water."

"It was easy to get, too," Eliza said as she watched her husband, wondering at how disheveled and bedraggled he looked—how thin and gaunt. "Melting snow or scooping snow-melt out of puddles and rock tanks is fine when necessary, but a good spring like we have here is a thing to be cherished. This one's most as good as the one we found back in Dripping Spring Canyon, though the water isn't quite as sweet."

"You didn't like the water we found in Cow Tank?" Billy teased. "After all, there was lots of it—"

"Filled with creepy-crawlies even in the winter," Eliza said with disgust. "Billy, I swan! You look worse than that old Pahute who rode through our camp late yesterday!"

"I look that bad, huh? Now I wish I'd seen him. That would have been something to behold."

"Billy, I'm not making fun. You look positively awful!"

"That's only because I finally decided to shave and get rid of all the lice and bed-bugs." Billy was grinning again.

"Shaving and bugs have nothing to do with it!" Eliza was getting upset. "Look at you! Your legs, your arms, your hands and feet, your poor face—everything about you is raw and chapped and bleeding, and that open wound on your calf has me very worried!"

"It's starting to heal, Eliza—"

"It is not! When I cleaned the mud out of it a little bit ago it was filled with yellow-green putrefaction. I saw that on the plains, Billy, and folks lost limbs to such open sores!"

"Well, hon-bun, we aren't on the plains, and besides, none of them had you to take care of 'em like I do."

"Billy Foreman!"

Laughing, Billy held up his hands in mock surrender. "All right, Eliza, I give up. If it'll make you feel any better, I'll let you put axle-grease in it tonight and wrap it."

"Not until we have one of the sisters put some sulfur or something in it first."

"Medicine?" Now Billy was serious. "There's no sense in that, Eliza, not as long as we're still in snow and mud practically up to our eyebrows. That was heavy wheeling today, mud up to the hubs with me pushing and those mules pulling every soggy inch of the way. It'll likely be as bad or worse tomorrow, so there's no point wasting medicine when the mud and water'll just clean it out come daylight."

"You truly think so?"

"I do. After all, hon-bun, I've seen the road down around Cedar Mesa and across Todie Flat to where it turns east at Brushy Flat. We did a little chopping beyond that, but one of the boys pushed ahead nearly to what he called Snow Flat, and he said the snow's deeper in those thick trees than anywhere else we've been. If it's melting there as much as it is here, then we're in for more heavy wheeling, no doubt about it."

"Then that does it," Eliza said as she pulled herself to her feet.

"I won't ride another inch forcing those poor mules to pull my weight along with everything else!"

"Eliza, you can't walk!"

But Eliza was suddenly paying no more attention to her husband. Instead she was staring off beyond the wagon, her attention fixed. "Billy," she said, her voice low, "there's another Indian right over there, a woman. She's just standing there, watching us. Oh, Billy, she looks more ragged and decrepit than the old man looked yesterday."

And then, almost like an explosion, every dog in camp began to bark.

———o—o—o———

"Is she Pahute?" Jane Walton asked quietly.

"George Morrell says so," Charlie Walton answered from beside his wife. "He says Navajos dress differently."

Olivia Larson, standing next to them with her baby in her arms and her two little ones clinging to her dress, nodded. "Well, whatever she is, this woman's also hungry. Look how she's going down on Kirsten Nielson's slapjacks. I'll bet the poor thing hasn't eaten in a week!"

"Is she alone?" Mary Ellen Lillywhite asked as she looked around.

"Appears to be."

"No she ain't!" Noah Barnes declared. "Jim Dunton saw some movement out in the trees right after Eliza spotted this one. You can bet it weren't no deer."

"If it was, it'll be the first one we've seen since the Escalante Desert."

"And the last one, you can bet, the way our luck's been going."

There were a few low chuckles. The Pahute woman stopped eating to look nervously around, and seventeen-year-old Margaret Nielson stepped from the fire with more of her mother's slapjacks.

"Here," she said softly as she placed the slapjacks in the woman's lap. "Don't you be worrying about these folks. They mean you no harm. You just keep eating until you can't hold another thing."

After a moment the woman did just that, and Margaret stood beside her, smiling.

"You see how she's dressed?" Laura Barney asked. "The poor thing's got to be cold!"

"With more of her own skin showing than the rags and rabbit hides she's wearing, you're probably right."

"Well," Maggie Sevy declared forcefully, "I can fix that! I have four dresses in that wagon, and no decent woman ought to own more than three! I'll be right back—"

"Well, boys, this squaw wasn't alone after all!" Zachariah Decker was looking off toward the trees. "Here come two more. No, better make that four—"

"Five," Anna Gurr stated emphatically as the various dogs began barking again. "And six. Five men and two women, and that one has a child she's carrying."

"Lawsy," Margaret Nielson breathed, "I hope they aren't all as hungry as this one was. Ma, you have any more batter mixed?"

"I have some," Sarah Haight called from nearby. "I'll fetch it for you, Margaret."

"I have half a bowl," Hannah Pace stated, "and a little molasses we've been saving."

"Bring it," Margaret Nielson smiled mischievously, "and let's see what they think."

"And we'd better round up some more clothing of all sorts," Lorane Dailey added. "How they haven't all frozen to death is beyond me."

Nervously the Pahutes clustered around, and soon they were all eating slapjacks as fast as Kirsten, Emily Dunton, and Jane Eyre could cook. There was no care to their eating, and even the hottest slapjack seemed to present no obstacle to its immediate and total consumption.

"Heap good!" one of the men grunted at the taste of molasses Hannah Pace had just given him. "Heap ver good!"

"Maybeso more," another added as he smacked his wide mouth noisily. "Allthesame maybeso heap more!"

There was laughing amongst the Pahutes then, but when the woman with the child handed it to Eliza so she could eat more readily, the wide-mouthed man looked hard at Eliza before they all turned back to their food.

"Billy, did you see that?" Eliza whispered, forcing her thoughts away from the looks of the men. "Did you see how she just handed me her baby?"

Billy, standing in the snow in his bare feet and still wrapped in his blanket, nodded. "I did, hon-bun, but I also saw the look that fellow there gave you. You be careful, you hear? These are wild folks, not civilized like over to Cedar. They're probably swarming with lice, which wouldn't help us much at all right now. I've had lice a few times, and I don't like them. Worse, if you start looking soft-eyed at that baby, there's no telling what its mother or father might do."

"But what if it's hungry?"

"That baby's young enough to still be living on its mother's milk, Eliza. You couldn't feed it if you wanted. Now, what say you hand the child back—right now!"

Amazed at the firm tone of Billy's voice, Eliza did as she was bidden. She was just stepping back beside her husband when Platte Lyman strode up to the group.

"You speak any English?" he asked without preamble.

"Heap good!" the largest of the men answered with a wide smile as he held up a slapjack.

Now that Billy got a better look at him, the Pahute who had looked so hard at Eliza proved to have one of the most arresting faces he'd ever seen. While the man's head was extremely wide and seemed far out of proportion to his body, the features that grabbed a man's attention were the eyes and the mouth. The eyes, dark brown, seemed to flash with an anger that couldn't be hidden by smiles and laughing words—anger and an above-normal intelligence. And the Pahute's mouth, a cavernous gash outlined with extraordinarily thick lips that cut across his face almost from one ear to the other, gave one the feeling of great evil. Perhaps it was because the corners of the mouth turned perpetually downward, though Billy doubted that. There was something else, something—

Well, smiles or not, complimentary words or not, this man was not just extremely intelligent, Billy thought, but also highly dangerous. This was a man he intended to keep Eliza away from!

"Yes," Platte Lyman was saying in response to the wide-mouthed man's compliment about the slapjacks, "I know they're heap good. Now, listen to me. We're looking for three men—white men, hats, long beards, riding horseback. Have you seen these men?"

In the quiet that had settled over everyone, the Pahutes looked from one to another, their expressions blank. "Heap no see'um," the wide-mouthed man finally answered with a huge smile. "No see'um one, no see'um two, no see'um three." And as he spoke he held up one, two and then three fingers to signify the number he was counting.

"He's a mighty educated Pahute," someone growled from the back of the crowd.

"And that's a white man's hat he's wearing, too."

"Platte, you figure these fellows killed George Hobbs and the Robb boys?"

Platte shook his head. "I don't know. They might have, for the boys are way overdue."

"Shall we hold 'em? Tie 'em up?"

"No sense doing that. Not yet, anyway. You agree, Jens?"

The old Danishman nodded. "Ya, I agree, Brudder Lyman. After all, ve are missionaries, not Indian fighters. But I tink ve should send some men on a search off de trail off dese Pahutes. Ya, und I tink vone or two men vid rifles should start guarding us, dark or no dark, so dese folks can see ve are armed."

"Good suggestions. Any volunteers for the search, boys?"

Immediately several hands went into the air, and a short time later half a dozen men rode into the trees, searching out the backtrail of the Pahutes.

"Well," Billy said as he placed his freezing feet back into the now cool kettle of water, "do you think they did it, Eliza? Do you think these folks killed Hobbs and the others?"

"I do not!" Eliza's voice was as firm as Billy's had been earlier. "I also think it's silly to send out a search party just at dark. And one more thing, William Foreman! Lice don't bother me even a little, not if I'm called to be a missionary, they don't. And after this, I'll hold any woman's baby I choose, and thank you kindly to not interfere."

Surprised, Billy looked up at his wife. "I'm sorry, Eliza, I truly am. I was just worrying about you."

"I don't need your worrying any more than you need mine," Eliza said as tears started down her cheeks. "I just . . . I just . . . Oh, Billy, I was so frightened when that mean-looking Pahute man looked at me the way he did! How . . . am I ever going to be a missionary?"

And with more tears Eliza sank onto her husband's lap and buried her face in his neck.

———◦–◦–◦———

"So these are the ones we've been following?" George Hobbs sat astride his mule gazing down at the clustered Pahutes. "Eight, huh? We calculated six or seven, but I reckon the pony tracks fooled us."

"You boys all right?"

"Except for being starved plumb to death."

"Yeah, we're all looking some ganted up."

The three men nodded. "We were only about half a mile away when your search party found us," Adam Robb stated quietly. "We'd run onto the tracks of these Pahutes and weren't exactly sure of their good intentions."

"Otherwise," Jack Robb added, "we'd have been here half a day sooner. I'll tell you what, though. You're a whole lot farther out from Montezuma Fort than Lewellyn Harris said you were!"

"He got through all right?" Platte asked quickly, thinking of the solitary journey to Mexico of the lone missionary.

"He got through sure enough," Adam Robb grimaced. "At least that far. We met up with him a day or so this side of Montezuma Fort. He looked some used up and was mighty hungry."

"That he was," George Hobbs agreed. "Trouble is, the folks at the fort were in nearly the same shape, so I don't know how they could have helped him."

"Things are bad with Sarah and the others?" Ellen Fielding asked quickly.

George nodded. "When I got there near the end of February, those folks were living on seed wheat ground in their coffee mill.

While I sat around waiting for these boys to get back from their ranch in Colorado, we ate up every last bit of food I'd hauled in to them. Harvey Dunton left the same day as us to go live off whatever wild game he could shoot. While he was cleaning out his wagon, he found a sack with a little flour in it, which he gave them. That ought to last them five, maybe six days if they go on tight rations. Other than that, those folks are destitute."

"We've been riding hard four days now," Adam Robb declared.

"And you folks aren't even close to ten days out of Montezuma," his brother Jack added. "Was it me, I'd guess double that, and then only if everything opens up just right. That means the folks at Montezuma Fort will be flat out of food for two, three weeks."

There was deep silence as everyone considered what had just been said. The news didn't seem good for those already at Montezuma Creek, and twenty days seemed more than any of them still on the road could endure. That would bring their journey to very nearly six months—an impossible stretch for people who'd prepared themselves to travel no more than two.

"These look peaceful enough now," George Hobbs declared abruptly as he nodded at the Pahutes, intentionally changing the subject. "'Course, that's hard to tell from a signal fire."

"Signal fire?"

Hobbs nodded. "You remember I said at Cheese Camp how I'd light three fires as a signal on my return? We did that on a high ridge late this morning, and right away we got a return signal from up on Elk Mountain. Well, getting home so soon excited us, so we started toward the fire and got down into a box canyon, and that's when we found the trail. From the sign, these Pahutes were only an hour or so ahead of us, so after that we went mighty careful."

Adam Robb nodded his agreement. "I expected to be shot from every turn in the trail."

"Why?" Platte Lyman questioned. "Are the Pahutes at war or something?"

"You haven't heard about the White River Massacre?" Jack Robb asked. "It was bad, boys. According to the cowboy courier who brought the news to Montezuma Fort, the Utes wiped out the Indian Agent, Nathan Meeker, and a whole passel of others."

"Not to mention a bunch of regular army cavalry," George Hobbs added. "According to that cowboy, the Utes and Pahutes are on the warpath everywhere, and not a soul is safe."

"Both tribes?" Adelia Mackelprang asked.

"They ain't both, Adelia. They're one. Utes and Pahutes are the same folks only with different names. The other night the folks at Montezuma Fort thought they were done for. The dogs started barking and carrying on, and everybody knew they'd soon be under attack. Come morning and they were still alive, Jim Davis and my brother-in-law Henry Harriman took a quiet walk up the river and found where several dozen unshod ponies had crossed during the night. They still don't know why they were passed by, other than the Lord wanted them protected."

"Do you think these people were part of the massacre?"

Adam Robb grinned. "We did earlier, all right."

"But not now," George Hobbs stated emphatically, "not now that we've seen them. Was I you, though, Platte, I'd sure enough put out guards. Only smart thing to do. But to tell the truth, I think the perpetrators of that Meeker killing are still over in Colorado. It was the real big-cheese Utes that did it, you can bet on that—not these frightened, hungry people that hide out here in the San Juan country."

"Ungh!" the loquacious Pahute grunted with a wide smile. "Heap good. Allthesame heap smart hombre." And as he spoke he was looking directly at the confident George Hobbs.

63

○─○─○

Tuesday, March 23, 1880

Beyond Coyote Flat

In agony Eliza leaned on her crutch and pulled one foot out of the sucking ooze that lay hidden beneath the melting snow. With gritted teeth she stretched it forward, planted it gingerly, and repeated the process. Here where the trees were thick, the snow was still quite deep, sometimes up to her waist. Yet the ground beneath it was muddy in spite of still being half frozen, so the going was becoming increasingly difficult. Not only did her crutch sink straight through mud and snow alike, offering little support, but the mud was sticky and sucked at her feet and ankles, constantly pulling her off balance. As if, she thought as tears of pain further wet her cheeks, she was not off-balance enough with her enormously protruding tummy.

But she was not about to ride, not when those poor mules, the cow, and even that fool, glass-eyed mare were teetering on the edge of collapse—all of them giving more than any poor animal should ever be asked to give.

Looking ahead, Eliza grimaced as she watched her darling Billy straining against the rear of the wagon maybe thirty feet in front of her, pushing with what little strength he had left. To the front of the wagon she knew the mules were straining against their tugs, and to the sides their cow Hepsi and the old glass-eyed mare leaned into the worn-out collars and harness Charlie Walton had lent them a few days before. Yet the wagon moved only in slow lurches, sinking in, being dragged out with awful sucking sounds, and immediately sinking in again. And poor Billy, on his face in the mud as often as he

535

was braced and straining against the wheels and sides of the wagon, was so begrimed and mud-covered it was pathetic.

Along the way folks had been chopping boughs off the cedars and junipers that so thickly lined the way, spreading them in the trail to aid their footing. These offered a poor form of riprap for the wagons but no support for the animals and precious little for the people. Yet the larger boughs did help some, and an exhausted Eliza had been doing her best to step from limb to limb whenever they were within reach. Trouble was, they usually weren't, and with the snow anywhere from an inch or so deep on the flats to three or more feet deep in the drifts shaded by the trees, and with the mud churned by hooves and iron-tired wheels eighteen inches and more deep under the snow, the road beyond Brushy Basin was horrible.

For Eliza, however, besides the repulsive mud that caked everything on her body, the worst part of all was the frigid water that had soaked through her worn-out high-top shoes and everything else from her thighs down. Because of the old frostbite, her feet were suffering terribly in spite of the fact that the cold had long since numbed them, her fingers and hands were stiff and throbbing from constantly falling into the same icy ooze, and the rest of her body was freezing from the sweat that had chilled in the cold wind that was now blowing down the mountain. Even the plains of Wyoming hadn't seemed this bad, Eliza thought as she struggled to drag a mud-laden foot out of the ooze and move it forward, for she could remember no such awful mud—

But her poor, darling Billy! Eliza's tears flowed freely as she watched him falling, courageously dragging himself to his feet, and leaning once more into the wheel spokes as he shouted instructions to the animals, and then falling again with the next sudden lurch of the heavily loaded wagon. Ordinarily he wouldn't have fallen so often, but with the mud sucking at his feet and dragging him down—

"Eliza, why on earth are you doing this?"

"Mary," Eliza responded after twisting in surprise, "I . . . I didn't even hear you coming."

"That's because you're making so blamed much noise floundering through this muck. Now answer me, Sister. Why aren't you riding like you should be?"

Turning back and lifting her skirts in order to take the next step, Eliza reached out with her crutch and drove the end of it into the snow. "You ought to know, Mary. Just as you wouldn't burden the horses you were leading a few days ago, so do I refuse to further burden our poor mules!"

Mary looked incredulous. "But . . . but Eliza, there's a world of difference between us! I'm young and healthy and not—"

"Not crippled!" Eliza finished, her expression bleak.

"I was going to say 'not pregnant and within just three or four weeks of delivery.'" Mary's eyes were flashing with anger. "Mercy sakes, Eliza, look at yourself! Every ounce of your strength is going toward pushing and pulling your poor body through this snow and mud. What strength will you have left to sustain your unborn child? Besides that, you've obviously fallen numerous times. Have you done any damage to your baby yet? And if not, when will be the particular fall that will force open your womb and cause the baby to be born before his time?"

In frustration the young woman took hold of Eliza's arm to help and steady her. "What is it about you handcart people? Why do all of you have to be so blasted stubborn?"

"Is . . . is your father stubborn?" Eliza asked, hoping to change the subject.

"Lawsy, yes! He's up ahead of us right this minute, hobbling along through the muck just like you, refusing to ride and probably taking ten or fifteen more years off his life, as if the snows of Wyoming hadn't taken enough away already. Fact is, Eliza, except for not being in a motherly way, he's so much like you it's frightening."

"I doubt that," Eliza declared as she tried on numbed legs to maintain her balance before taking the next step. "But I . . . don't remember him from back then—"

"He was in the Willey Company."

"Oh. That's right. I'm sure I . . . I knew that. Tell me more about him . . . Please?"

Mary smiled grimly. "Well, I don't remember these things, for I wasn't born yet. But Mother tells me they were quite prosperous in Denmark when they joined the Church and decided to emigrate.

Father then sold his home and farm and began using the funds to help others as they prepared to gather to Zion. With many they'd helped, they sailed from Liverpool on the ship *Thornton,* and by the time they reached Iowa, Father had given away all his funds except enough to buy a handcart and stock it with fifteen pounds of belongings per person for his family. That meant himself, mother, their six-year-old son Neils, and a nine-year-old girl named Bodil Mortensen whom Father had offered to take to Utah."

"I was on the ship *Horizon* with more than eight hundred others," Eliza declared as her mind went back. "We were always about two or two and a half weeks behind the people who sailed on the *Thornton.* And once we had reached Iowa and learned that we'd be going by handcart, I, too, remember trying to choose which of my belongings to discard in order to get the weight to fifteen pounds. That's why those two settings of china were so precious to me. I had to discard the rest, along with almost everything else I had left to my name."

"It must have been terrible for all of you." Mary's voice was soothing as Eliza swiped at her tears. "For my father the difficulties really began at a place called Rocky Ridge. He says they'd had nothing to eat in days, the temperatures were usually below zero, and the winter blizzards at that high elevation were unrelenting. That was when Father froze both his feet. Many had already died. In a ravine called Rock Creek they had buried thirteen, including my brother Neils and little Bodil Mortensen, in shallow, snow-covered graves. Yet somehow Father kept going, pushing and pulling all the rest of them across that mountain before he finally gave out and could go no further."

Not daring to comment, Eliza stared straight ahead, her eyes watering fiercely as she continued to force herself through the snow.

"With Father unable to walk another step," Mary continued, her voice quiet, "he pleaded with Mother to leave him in the snow by the trail to die. He wanted her to go ahead and try to keep up with the company so she would live. But Mother couldn't do that. To her, life without Father would have been meaningless. So she said to him, 'Ride. I can't leave you. I can pull the cart.' And she did, Eliza, until the rescuers from the Valley were finally able to relieve her of that burden."

"That . . . is what Jens meant that day when we were riding back from Parowan, when he told your mother he wouldn't bring her on this trek?"

Mary nodded. "That's right. I think he somehow sensed how difficult this expedition was going to be, and he felt that she'd suffered enough."

"So . . . did I," Eliza stated quietly. "I . . . I mean, I sensed that it was going to be very difficult."

"I know you did," Mary acknowledged. "Your journey with the Martin Company must have been just as hard as Father's."

Soberly Eliza nodded. "From the last crossing of the Platte River to the cove west of Devil's Gate on the Sweetwater River, where we finally took refuge until help arrived, is beyond my ability to describe. In my mind it's very much like a bad dream that I can never completely tie together. I saw so much suffering, and so very many perish, that it pains me yet. Father McBride and his wife Margaret I think of, because their daughter Jeanetta and I had become such friends. I remember following Jeanetta's footprints a day or so after her father had died, feeling shocked that so much of her blood was coloring the snow. Only later did I discover that mine and many others' did the same.

"I recollect the day Luke Carter gave up and died. He broke his heart, I believe, helping us girls push our handcart over a particularly difficult stretch of ground when he was too tired to even think of doing so. And John Parkinson was another who was always helping us or sending his son Samuel to help. He, his wife Ellen, their sons Joseph and William, and their tiny daughters Mary and Esther all perished. Yet Samuel, just eighteen as I remember, brought the rest of the children through, and to them and me he will ever be a hero.

"Of course, you know Ellen and Maggie Pucell, and how terribly their family suffered. I recollect that I saw—"

"Who?"

Eliza started. "Oh, pardon me. Unthank is their married name, Mary. They live in Cedar now."

Mary was amazed. "Ellen Unthank, the woman who goes about

on her knee-stubs—the one with all those wonderful children? She was in the Martin Company?"

"That's right. I'm surprised you didn't know that. After their parents froze to death, Ellen had to have both her legs amputated. Maggie needed the same but wouldn't hear of it, though, so they just scraped the frozen flesh clear to the bone, and her legs gradually healed enough that she's still able to walk—a little."

"What amazing faith! And yet—Oh, Eliza, I can't even imagine such suffering!"

"I can't imagine that any of us lived through it. But there were so many good things, too. I'll never forget those three dear boys who carried us on their backs—literally hundreds of us—across the ice-filled Sweetwater and into the cove because they couldn't bear to see us suffer further. George W. Grant is the one who carried me, Mary, and I will love him for the rest of eternity for the tender way he treated me that day. Allen Huntington carried Lydia Hooker, one of the girls who shared my handcart with me, and David Kimball carried both Ann Johnson and Alice Brooks, the other two who were my partners."

Eliza laughed nervously. "You'll probably think me strange for saying it, but after his glorious act of kindness I found myself dreaming of marrying that dear young man. But I wasn't alone in such dreams, I can tell you that. It may be hard to imagine how four such suffering girls, in such desperate circumstances, could fall in love as we did. But in the next few days, had those young men only asked, I know all four of us, and probably a lot of the other single girls in the company, would have married our rescuers in an instant."

"I shouldn't wonder." Mary looked at Eliza. "And I don't find it a bit strange. Did they give their lives, then?"

"Well, they lived, though I understand the freezing Sweetwater crippled every one of them. Billy's father once told him that when Brigham Young heard of the boys' heroic act, he wept like a child, and he later declared publicly that their heroism would ensure all three of them salvation in the celestial kingdom, worlds without end."

Eliza smiled a little at the thought. "Yes, to me they were more than wonderful, and oh, how I loved them. I suppose, now that I think on it, I felt the same way about Ephraim Hanks after he'd cut away my toes and foot and given me a wonderful blessing the week before we got to the Sweetwater. I loved him then with all my heart and soul, and I would most certainly have married him, too, if only he had asked." Quickly Eliza blinked back tears. "Fact is, later on Brother Hanks married one of the girls he rescued as a plural wife— just not me. In spite of my pining after them for so long afterward, isn't it funny how the Lord kept me from both him and George W. Grant—and preserved me to be the wife of Billy Foreman."

It was a statement, not a question, and Mary wisely kept still.

"Oh, glory," Eliza breathed as the tears again started from her eyes. "I've been so blessed in my life, Mary! So incredibly blessed! Even this winter trek will turn into a blessing. I know it will! Yet sometimes I can hardly keep from murmuring—"

"As would any normal person," Mary declared as she helped Eliza avoid another fall. "Yet in spite of those few weaknesses, you've done so much good for others, and your desires to be righteous are so pure in spite of your suffering, in spite of the sacrifices you've been called upon to give, it's no wonder the Lord is smiling on you and Billy so favorably! You're just like my father—"

"Dear Mary, that isn't so! Your father is far more righteous than I am!"

Mary smiled. "Yes, he is righteous. In many ways—in spite of the fact that he takes his hot toddy every night, even though he knows that the Word of Wisdom counsels against the use of alcohol."

Shocked, Eliza looked at her younger friend. "Your father?"

"Yes." Mary's loving smile continued. "My sweet, righteous father has overcome so much, has suffered so much for the gospel's sake, that the very thought of his accomplishments overwhelms me. Yet his nightly toddy remains something he still needs to repent of. And one day he will! I know he will, for the Lord truly loves him and shares his Holy Spirit with him, and through that Spirit the Lord will bring him to complete repentance as rapidly as my father will allow it.

"And that, dear Eliza, is why I look at you with such admiration. In spite of how much you suffer from day to day, you no longer make excuses for yourself. Instead you repent—instantly, if possible—of every sin the Lord chooses to reveal to your heart. I know, for I've watched you and learned from you. Of course you've made mistakes, many of them. But as he did for so many in the snows of Wyoming, including your marvelous rescuers, our Savior has used this journey to the San Juan to purge you, my dear friend, to humble and sanctify you and bring you to him, preparing you for the incredible blessings I'm certain await you."

Again Eliza was staring ahead, not speaking.

"I'm just as sure," Mary said as she aided Eliza with another step, squeezing her frail arm as she did so, "that the Lord is doing the same for Kumen and me and for all the rest of us in this company who want those blessings—my precious father included.

"Now, Eliza Foreman, why don't we give a holler to stop Billy and his mules and get you back up onto that wagon seat—you and this little son of yours I'm trying with all my heart to protect."

And with that announcement Mary waved her free hand and started yelling.

———o–o–o———

Brushy Basin

Tears of pain ran down her cheeks as Eliza leaned back in her wooden rocker, her legs stretched out on a rock before her. Gently Billy was working at her feet, using water warmed in one of the two fires that burned brightly on either side of them as he loosened and peeled away the icy, mud-caked rags that had been dry and clean that morning.

"This is so embarrassing," she declared as she sat with her eyes closed tight against her pain and her hands clenching the armrests of the chair. "What can people possibly be thinking?"

"Whatever it is, hon-bun, it isn't about you." Gently Billy was peeling back another length of rag that was stiff with ice particles, a rag that seemed not to have protected his beloved wife at all. "They have their own frozen legs and feet to worry about."

"Maybe. But my dress and petticoats are hiked all the way up to kingdom come, for pity's sake. And instead of you helping me I ought to be on my knees taking care of you, Billy darling. You're the one who was fighting with the wagon and teams all day, up and down in that awful, half-frozen goo so that there isn't an inch of you that isn't all muddy and iced over—"

"You just sit there and relax," Billy said as darkness closed its grip over the spread-out camp and he arose to replenish the fires. "I'm fine, and you and that little one need caring for mighty badly. I don't want you on your feet again until you go to bed."

"But . . . what will I do about dinner?"

Eyeing the table and chairs that were out but not really in place, Billy did his best to smile. "I've seen you do it enough times, Eliza. I'll set our table."

"But . . . the cooking?"

"Oh, that. Well, I already put some ground wheat in that kettle of boiling water over yonder. In a minute or two I figured to drop in some potatoes and sliced onions, then add some spices and a little fat beef—"

"Billy Foreman, you stop that! You hear?"

"Well, a feller can dream, can't he?"

Eliza sighed. "I suppose so. For me, I just dream of getting to someplace on the river where the ground is flat enough to settle on, and where the weather is warm. That's the only dream I can conjure up any more. Just flat, level, and warm—"

Billy shook his head sadly as he thought of what Eliza was enduring. Every night since they had entered the foothills of Elk Mountain, he and his wife and the rest of the company had been forced to peel away their wrappings and extra clothing, soaked through with freezing water and caked with mud. After hanging these items to dry by the fire, the wearers had then massaged their chapped and frozen limbs with heated snow water and anything else that seemed likely to give them relief, trying to draw the frost out and restore a measure of warmth to their chilled and battered flesh.

A few had crocks of mutton tallow sufficient to anoint their limbs and keep the chapping under some sort of control; the rest used rendered lard or axle grease or anything else they thought might help. And more than a few used nothing at all because they had nothing, and these especially suffered beyond belief.

Thank the Lord, Billy thought, for the generosity of Jens and

Kirsten Neilson, who not only had mutton tallow but knew firsthand how much Eliza was suffering.

Once wrapped in dry rags to keep the grease from soiling their bedding, the chilled pioneers trembled and shivered through the nights, most sleeping on tarps and bedding laid on frozen ground, trying desperately to get warm. With daylight, the dry but greasy rags came off while the muddy wrappings, frozen during the night in spite of the fires, had to be beaten against tire-irons and anything else that was handy just to loosen the frost and get rid of the caked-on mud. Then, heated as thoroughly as possible over once-again roaring fires, the rags were wound over boots, shoes, bloomers, long-handled underwear, and everything else the people could think of to wear as protection against the endless and uncompromising cold.

And thus "protected," Billy thought with deep sadness, they set forth again to do the same thing that had been done the day, or the week, or even the month before!

Thank goodness there had been a more-than-ample supply of firewood. In one sense this thirty-mile forest of trees and snow and mud had been a nearly impossible trial, but for a change there had been plenty of fuel for everyone, and all had used it to the best advantage possible. Roaring fires blazed everywhere of a night, and Billy smiled briefly just thinking of the sight they must have presented.

Still, his numbed mind declared as he forced his stiffened fingers to peel back the last strip of half-frozen factory muslin from Eliza's legs, the whole journey through these trees had been a nightmare, a nearly two-week ordeal tacked onto the most recent end of a never-ending bad dream that had started way back the previous October—

"Eliza," Billy said as he tearfully examined his wife's legs and feet, "this doesn't look very good. I . . . I've found spots of frostbite on your feet and ankles, and it's especially bad where you lost your toes and part of a foot back in '56."

"I'll be . . . fine," Eliza responded weakly. "I survived the frostbite then, so I su . . . suppose I can survive it now."

Billy looked up, his expression bleak with sadness and weariness. "Well, maybe. But then you weren't forty-five and expecting my baby in the next few weeks. You weren't . . . you weren't . . . Oh,

Eliza, what have I done? Forcing you to come on this journey was the cruelest thing a man could ever do to his wife! I . . . I'm so ashamed!"

"But . . . you didn't know!"

Angrily Billy stood and slammed his hand on the table. "But I should have known, Eliza! Can't you see that? I should have known! And because I didn't, I had no business dragging you into this wilderness, making you suffer as you have—as you are!

"The Brethren shouldn't have asked it of us, either! How could they possibly have been inspired when they sent out two hundred and more people, a good many of them innocents, not to settle a country but to starve and suffer and freeze while carving a pathetic roadway through the harshest, meanest landscape on the face of this earth? They couldn't have been inspired, Eliza! They couldn't have! I can't imagine God inspiring anyone to such suffering, pain, and hardship! It has all been a terrible, terrible mistake!"

His tears suddenly falling, Billy returned to kneel before Eliza. "Oh, my darling wife," he wept, "I am so sorry, so very, very sorry—"

"Billy Foreman," Eliza suddenly interrupted, her voice so firm it surprised even herself, "you stop this at once! You are not to blame for my suffering, and neither are the leaders of the Church!"

In amazement Billy looked up into the face of his wife. "But—"

"I mean it, Billy! You must stop criticizing yourself, and you must stop criticizing them, for the spirit of criticism is of the devil and will lead you to apostasy just as surely as it was leading me last summer.

"Instead, my darling husband, we must rejoice and praise the Lord. If mistakes were made, and they surely were and yet will be, then we must rejoice that the Lord allowed us to experience them and live through them. If we've brought upon ourselves long and terrible suffering, and we surely have, then we must rejoice and give thanks that such extremities have more thoroughly acquainted us with God.

"Do I blame you or condemn you for bringing me on this journey? No, Billy, I do not! Am I sorry that I'm here in these mountains, suffering hunger and frostbite and all manner of additional pain! No, not for one minute! When I think about what I've gained through such hardships, Billy, when I contemplate how I've become acquainted with you and reacquainted with my Savior, then despite the pain, I'm filled with joy beyond speaking.

"Mary and I talked about it a little today, and it's clear to me now—more clear than it has ever been. All the suffering in the world would be a small price to pay for such understanding and happiness as I've come to know during this incredible journey."

Smiling sweetly, Eliza drew her husband to her breast. "Thank you, dear Billy, for bringing me along."

64

Wednesday, March 24, 1880

Brushy Basin

"Eliza, old Hepsi's dead."

Looking up from where she was finishing packing the small trunk for the day's journey, Eliza was stunned. "Oh, Billy! When? I mean, how did the poor thing die?"

After helping Eliza to her chair, Billy squatted with his hands out over the last of the fire. It was not yet daylight, but all around them lamps glowed as teams were being harnessed and wagons readied for moving. Eliza had been packing her trunk by the light of such a lamp, and Billy had used another to help him locate their cow.

"This morning when I went to find her, she was down in the snow," he said, "hardly able to lift her head. When I couldn't get her up, I called Platte over, and he told me she looked just like the mule he had to put out of its misery a couple of months ago—all bones and hide and way too scrawny to keep on living. So I asked him, after we'd tried and failed a few times to get her up, if he'd do for Hepsi what he'd done for his mule, and distribute whatever of her that was edible among the company—you and me excluded."

Eliza stared toward the glowing embers. "I'm glad you did that," she breathed. "I could never bring myself to eat that poor thing, not after all we've been through together. Did . . . did you see Platte kill her?"

Shaking his head, Billy did his best to control his emotions. "I . . . I couldn't bear to, Eliza, no more than I could bear taking her life, not with those soft, brown eyes looking up at me so trusting-like. So

547

I just knelt and laid my hand on her neck and told her what a fine cow she'd been, and how much we loved and appreciated her for all the delicious milk and cream she's given us this past year. I told her how sorry we were for wearing her out and starving her to death during this winter expedition, and I thanked her for sacrificing even at the end so some in the company might have a little meat in their pots tonight. Then I . . . I said good-bye and came back to tell you."

"The Lord giveth, and the Lord taketh away," Eliza recited softly. "Blessed be the name of the Lord."

"You know," Billy said after a moment's pondering of the words of the wise and patient Job, "Hepsi was an ornery cuss when we first got her, always putting her foot in the milk pail just when I got it filled, trampling down the garden when the vegetables were just looking promising, terrorizing the neighbors, and so on. Many's the day I've cussed her good. But since we started this expedition last October I've watched her suffer right along with the rest of us. Yet she always gave what milk she could even when feed was too scarce to do her any good. She never dragged against her rope when she was tied to the back of the wagon. And the past few days when I've used her to help the mules and me pull the wagon out of some of those deep mud holes, she gave it all she had."

Eliza wiped at her eyes. "Just like that fool, glass-eyed mare I've so enjoyed making fun of."

"That's right." For a moment Billy thought of the two animals that, with the mules, had become almost like family. "That glass-eyed mare and old Hepsi are two of a kind, all right—useless and ugly as sin to the rest of the world, but boot-leather tough and gritty as sand when them that love them need their help."

"Somewhat like every other member of this expedition," Eliza admitted through her tears, "man and beast included. I suppose, Billy, that losing Hepsi is more of the price I said last night I was willing to pay—to rejoice and give praise to the Lord no matter how extreme my suffering became. I . . . I would never have thought it, but losing that cow is like, well, it's like losing part of myself—far more difficult than putting up with cold and mud and other such temporary inconveniences."

Billy nodded his understanding. "I reckon I feel about the same.

I don't know what the Lord does with such animals as old Hepsi in the hereafter, but I do know this: Wherever they end up I pray to God that I'll be nearby. And I pray the Lord just as fervently that I can fulfill the measure of my creation as diligently and wonderfully as that scrawny, stubborn old cow has fulfilled hers."

"Amen," Eliza whispered softly as she drew her husband to her in the early morning quiet. "Amen, Billy darling, and amen."

65

Friday, March 26, 1880

Double-Ruin Canyon, Whiskers Draw

Holding his new model 1873 Winchester carbine in his hand, the filthy and unkempt Sugar Bob Hazelton couldn't help but grin. He'd been wanting one of these ever since who-flung-the-chunk—wanting one bad enough, even, to kill for it. Trouble was, not only were they scarce as friendly gila monsters, as he liked to put it, but his terrible bout with poverty had continued so that in two full years he'd rarely had more than a few pennies to jingle in his pockets, not enough even to keep each other company let alone purchase a new model 1873.

But now that same carbine was his! And not just the carbine, either. Across the fire from where he sat was a filled cartridge belt and three full boxes of .44–40 cartridges, a perfectly good soogin, an extra saddle and saddlebags, and a full sack of flour and another of coffee. Not to mention, he thought with a grin, two bags of Bull Durham, a small bag of sugar, and a few hardtack biscuits. Yes, sir, Sugar Bob thought as his grin grew even wider, and a hefty chunk of raw silver besides!

It had been a good haul, a very good haul, besides which it had been one of the easiest things he'd ever done in his life! Why, if—

Somewhere outside, a rock rattled down the face of the cliff, and for an instant the man froze. Then with a vicious curse, he scrambled to the doorway of the old Indian ruin, threw himself to the earthen floor, and peered out.

The canyon he was in, a small, horseshoe-shaped alcove surrounded by steep sandstone cliffs, was the perfect hideout, which Sugar Bob had known the instant he had accidentally discovered it. Because it opened to the south, it caught the sun even in the winter, and so it was usually warmer than the surrounding country. In the upper end was a small spring of excellent water that trickled down into a rock tank that appeared to be of considerable size and depth. Of course, it was mostly full of mud and old leaves from the cottonwoods that grew beside and above it. But Sugar Bob knew if he ever cleaned it out, it would make a fine bathing pool. Of course, keeping clean no longer meant as much to him as it once had—

But the best thing about the canyon, Sugar Bob had decided the instant he'd laid eyes on it, were the caves and the ruins, of which there were two. The upper cave and ruin he'd never seen the inside of, for it could only be reached by climbing the cliff by way of tiny notches the old Indians had carved and used. Fool though he might be—and Sugar Bob was quick to admit that in some things he'd been mighty foolish—he wasn't about to climb those notches. Especially since there was nothing up there he figured he'd lost, nothing at all.

The second and lower ruin, in which he now lay hidden, was so perfectly suited to his needs—and the needs of his two horses, which were hidden in the room next to him—that he couldn't imagine a better place for a man to hide. Composed of three rooms built inside the cave, all three of which backed against the overhanging cliff, the ruin was so intact that it gave the appearance of having been abandoned only days, or maybe weeks, before.

Several pieces of old pottery had been stacked about, some of which he was now using; stone arrow and spear points had littered the floor; the firepit had still contained ashes and small corncobs that had been partly burned; two grinding stones had lain where they'd been left turned backward against the wall; and the ceiling of the cave had been black with soot that still came off on his hand when he rubbed it—soot from hundreds or maybe even thousands of ancient fires. Finally, along the back of the cave and painted with some sort of red paint that *didn't* rub off, had been the image of a snake, drawn zigzagged and stretching maybe seven feet across the sandstone wall.

Sugar Bob had no idea what the image of that red snake might mean, but then he didn't particularly care, either. Neither did he care that he was actually poking about in some truly ancient history—history that might have dumbfounded and amazed and perhaps even taught him had he but known or even thought about it with more than a passing glance, rub, or kick. Trouble was, Sugar Bob Hazelton didn't care a lick or a spit about much of anything any longer, not since he'd gone completely and irretrievably insane—

Now, as he peered out through the ancient doorway and down the canyon, his new model 1873 carbine protruding before him, Sugar Bob grinned madly. This was perfect, just as perfect as it had been when that wandering fool of a cowpoke had ridden up to his fire down-canyon the day before, slid off his horse, and offered Sugar Bob the makings. Taking them, Sugar Bob had happened to see the stock of the Winchester sticking out from under the man's saddle skirt, and that sight had sealed the man's doom.

Of course, it hadn't helped that the fool had right away started blabbering about some rich Navajo silver mine he was off to find— *Peshlaki* or some such strange-sounding name. He was even boasting of the chunk of smelted silver in his saddlebags that he'd won in a poker game, and of the fact that all he had to find was this canyon somewhere down off Navajo Mountain.

Sugar Bob grinned at the memory. Practically in the middle of the man's boast, and as he was lighting the smoke he'd built, the sorry fool had looked up just in time to see the blast of flame from the end of Sugar Bob's handgun—that and the mirthless laughter in his bloodshot eyes.

After that the man was dead, so with a kick Sugar Bob had rolled him over and stripped him of everything of value he had on or about him, right down to his long-handled, holed, and blood-stained underwear.

"Easy," Sugar Bob muttered as he lay grinning and staring down the canyon, ready to do the same with his next visitor. "Easy as—"

And that was when the feeling of warmth started spreading upward across his stomach, upward and outward.

Cursing insanely, Sugar Bob scrambled to his knees and looked down, already knowing he'd soiled himself again and that the cat-tail-down packing he'd started wearing in his trousers was too satu-rated to handle any more.

Forgetting the falling rock and everything else, the man heaved himself to his feet and began yelling and kicking everything within reach—the stone walls of the ruin, his new saddle and bags, the large and ancient earthen pot he'd been using to hold and heat water for his futile and increasingly infrequent attempts to clean the evil wounds I. W. Lacy had inflicted upon his groin and nose—

As it dawned on Sugar Bob that his water pot was now in a hun-dred fragments and his warmed water a flood of mud and debris spreading across the floor, his rage grew even greater. His voice was now a shrill scream of utter frustration and fear as he ranted and raved about the ruin and then out the door and down toward the trickle of water that had once been a stream. He didn't think of the possible danger that might be awaiting him. He didn't think of his perpetually soiled clothing and the stench that was always with him now that he'd become incontinent, nor did he think of the festering knife wounds that never seemed to heal. No, those thoughts were always with him, a part of him, praying on his mind and driving him insane with his dreams of all that had been and all that would never be again.

Now, though, as he held his carbine tightly and screamed his frustration against the echoing sandstone walls, Sugar Bob Hazelton's thoughts were only for I. W. Lacy, who had died far too easily; him, Bill Ball, Dingle Bob Beston, and every other sorry mother's son of a human being who'd ever walked the planet. He'd kill them all! Sugar Bob swore viciously. Just as he'd killed that sorry cowboy, he'd kill them all! Now that he'd found the perfect hideout, he'd sally forth whenever he wanted and kill every last man of them! And the women and children, too, he shrieked as his screams turned to cackles. Let them all die! Even those idiot Mormons he'd been hearing for months were heading into the coun-try. He'd kill them, too! Just as old man Lacy had killed him before he'd spilled the old man's guts on that barroom floor, so would he—Sugar Bob Hazelton—spend the rest of his days carrying the pains of death to others—every man-jack one of them!

Sugar Bob cackled again. And while he was at it, he vowed in sudden tears as he looked from his soiled trousers to the new model 1873 Winchester carbine that fit so perfectly in his hand, he'd find that lost Navajo silver mine and become the richest durnfool eunuch from Texas all the way to the San Juan—

———o—o—o———

Snow Flat

"Afternoon, Eliza. Ma says if you'll allow it I can walk beside your wagon."

Eliza, who was riding again after her terrible ordeal in the snow and mud, smiled down at the small girl. "Good afternoon to you, too, Lucinda Nielson. Of course I'll allow it, and be glad for the company."

"It's on account of us finally being out of the snow that she allowed me to come."

"Yes," Eliza nodded, "I thought that would be so. Isn't it nice to have the snow finally come to an end, Lucinda? That's why folks are calling this place Snow Flat, you know—because that's the last of the snow, there at the trees. I am *so* glad to finally get past it and onto relatively dry ground!"

"Lula Redd says old Hepsi died," Lucinda said abruptly. "She says we've all been eating her for supper. Is that true, Eliza? Have we been eating your cow?"

"She did die," Eliza responded carefully, sensing that she needed to be careful. "As to whether anybody has been eating her, I don't know. I've certainly not seen any of the meat."

In silence Lucinda paced the wagon, and Eliza felt hopeful that she'd stopped the unpleasant conversation. After all, Lucinda and the other little girls her age were so filled with questions that had no answers—

"Do I have meat on me?" the child suddenly asked. "Is that what's underneath my skin?"

"I . . . uh—"

"Course you have meat on you," another childish voice chimed in, and Eliza turned to find that Leona Jane Walton and Sarah Rowley were also pacing the wagon.

"Good afternoon, girls," she responded, feeling the old mixture of surprise and happiness that these children actually seemed to seek her out, to want her company. That was almost incomprehensible to her, especially when she'd hardly spoken with a child in years, and she'd done nothing more for these sweet little urchins than show them a little about weaving grass and cattail fronds—

"Afternoon, Eliza." It was Sarah Rowley who was speaking, and for the first time Eliza realized this was an organized gathering of "her" girls—probably set in motion by Sarah or Lula. "Since there isn't any more snow, we thought we'd keep you company today. I expect Delia Mackelprang and Mary Lillywhite will be along shortly, and Lula's right behind that wagon back there."

"That's . . . nice. I'm thankful for the company."

"Lula fell down in that last awful mudhole where Billy—I mean Brother Foreman—is working, and is trying to clean the mud off. That's how come she isn't with us quite yet."

Turning in surprise, Eliza looked back. "Billy isn't behind my wagon?"

"Not anymore. He's back there helping Peter and Harriet Mickelson get their wagon through that hole. It's stuck clear to the hubs, you know, and looks like a frightful mess to me."

"Yes," Eliza said, "I'm certain it is." Then she turned back and gave her attention to the five girls. Little had changed about the sweet little things in the three months since she'd caught them skipping rope to that awful chant about her and Billy, except that they now considered themselves her best friends, and she theirs. And they were probably right, she thought with a smile. For she knew that the whole bunch of them loved her thoroughly, and there was nothing on earth she wouldn't do for any of them.

"Girls, stay out of the ruts if you can, because that's where most of the mud is."

"You mean off to the side of the road, over by the trees?"

"That's right, Sarah. But you'll need to be careful there, too, for the ground is still muddy in places, and your mothers won't appreciate me allowing you to get all smeared with it."

555

"We've been smeared with mud for days now!"

"Yeah, Eliza. It's sort of fun—"

"Howdy, Eliza!"

"Good afternoon, Lula. We're pleased you could catch up."

Lula Redd grinned widely. "I ran all the way. It wasn't even very hard. Pa says we've been eating your old cow. He said she just give out and died, so now she's good for nothing but the meat."

"Sarah says we have meat on us, too," Lucinda declared. "Right underneath our skin."

"Of course we do," Leona Walton agreed. "Ma says we're just human animals, and every animal I ever saw skinned out had the meat right under the skin."

"Girls," Eliza pleaded, desperately trying to change the subject, "we'd better get a move on before that wagon back there runs us over."

"The Mickelsons wouldn't ever run over us!" Lula was adamant. "Besides, they're stuck good!"

"Well, just the same—"

"If I died tonight, Eliza, come morning would I be good for nothing but my meat?"

"What? Why, Lucinda Nielson, whatever gave you that awful notion?"

Lucinda looked stricken. "Leona's ma says we're just human animals, and if folks in our company need the meat from poor old Hepsi to keep from starving, wouldn't they need my meat, too?"

Dumbfounded, Eliza could think of nothing to say as the six tiny girls quickly processed that thought.

"Yuk!" Mary Lillywhite abruptly grimaced. "Ma said just this morning that me and my brother Benjamin was . . . I mean were spoiled rotten, so I'll bet my meat would taste awful!"

"Well, Pa says I'm his sweet little pumpkin," Sarah Jane Rowley declared with a giggle. "Does that mean my meat would taste good, like sweet pumpkin pudding?"

Now all the girls started giggling, Eliza along with them. And as they continued together, Eliza found herself praying that she could get them thinking of something else, something not quite so repulsive.

"Girls, listen to me. I have a game for us to play."

The subject of meat wouldn't seem to go away, and Eliza had suddenly thought of a game that might be helpful for them all to play—a game that would surely divert their minds from their gory subject.

"Can we play it while we're walking?"

"Absolutely, Delia. But we need whomever has the best memory to keep score."

"That's Sarah," they all agreed instantly. "Sarah and her sister Alice Louise can remember everything!"

Knowing that had certainly seemed to be the case with the Rowley girls when they were remembering *her* negative attributes, Eliza nodded. "Very well. Sarah, you be the scorekeeper."

Quickly Sarah agreed.

"We're ready, Eliza. What's the game?"

Turning, Eliza checked on the progress of the tired mules, which continued to plod forward whether she held the reins or not. "The game," she called back, "is to see who can remember the names of the most mothers in the company who have babies two years old or younger. You get one point for the name of the mother, and a second point for the name of the baby. Sarah, can you keep track of who gets how many points?"

"That'll be easy as pie. Can I play, too?"

"Well, why don't you just listen and remember. Now girls, we'll go in the order you arrived. Lucinda, you were here first, so how many can you name?"

"Laura Barney," Lucinda declared instantly, "and her baby, Betsy Maude—"

For the next thirty minutes the girls laughed and complained and continued the game, their minds occupied and the journey feeling a little less difficult for them and for Eliza.

"Are there any more?" Lula Redd finally asked.

Slowly Eliza shook her head. "I don't think so. I've been keeping track as well as I could, and I think you've named them all."

"Which means," Sarah Rowley declared, sounding official, "that the winner and overall champion of great memories in the San Juan missionary expedition is—Leona Jane Walton!"

Eliza and the girls all cheered vigorously while the girls began dancing around each other.

"Now, girls," Eliza said as she leaned down from the wagon bench and handed each of them half of one of her precious few dried peaches as a reward, "which of you kept track of how many mothers and babies there are on this expedition?"

The girls' faces were suddenly blank.

"Well, I did, and this may surprise you. Out of a few more than two hundred and thirty people associated with us, thirty-one are mothers with new babies and thirty-one are the babies themselves. That means, if we haven't forgotten anyone, sixty-two of us—fully one fourth—are young mothers with new babies. No wonder you're all so needed for tending and helping out."

"Yeah, no wonder!"

Eliza smiled. "And because I'm carrying a baby of my own and know how hard it is, I'm amazed by the faith and courage your mothers and these other young women—"

Eliza stopped, staring at the suddenly giggling girls. "All right, what is it? What's so funny?"

"We have some new verses for our song," Lula stated with a wide grin. "That's partly why we wanted to walk beside you today."

"Your song?"

"Uh-huh. The one about you and Billy that you didn't much like. Remember?"

Eliza sighed deeply. "I remember."

"Good. Want to hear it?"

For some reason Eliza's throat had suddenly gone dry. "Will . . . will I like it this time?"

The girls all giggled again, and one or two of them shrugged. "Maybe," Sarah Rowley finally responded. "We do."

Again pulling the mules to a stop, Eliza turned so she could face the girls, doing her best to smile. "Then let's hear it, and I'll tell you afterward what I think."

Giggling again the girls got themselves ready, and then the song began:

Billy Foreman has a wife,
Tall and plump and filled with life.
We all know just what she'll bear,
A lovely child with us to share.

Billy Foreman has a wife,
Our bestest friend for all our lives.
She's taught us things no one could know.
That's why we girls just love her so!

Eliza, her emotions suddenly getting the best of her, climbed down off the wagon seat and knelt in the midst of the girls, hugging them all to her—all of them at once. And for the first time in days she didn't even notice the cold mud that quickly began chilling her legs.

66

The Twist

Billy had never in his life felt so aching, bone-weary exhausted. As he plodded down the rocky, winding descent, it was all he could do to keep from closing his eyes and drifting off to sleep. Behind him, her eyes closed, Eliza sat on the wagon seat, the reins to the two mule teams hanging slack in her hands. But of a truth the mules needed little guiding, since there was nowhere else to go but down the narrow, twisting track.

Without even looking at them, Billy thought with sorrow of the four powerful animals Dick and Parley Butt had loaned him. In wonderful condition at the beginning of the journey six months before, they were now galled, their flesh hung wasted from their bones, and they'd grown so weak from lack of adequate forage and a seemingly endless winter without corn or oats that at times they seemed hardly able to walk, let alone pull the wagon.

But at least all four of them were still upright and trying. Many people in the company had lost part or all of their teams and were now pairing a horse with a milk cow, or a milk cow with an ox, or jerry-rigging three animals instead of the usual four just to keep things moving.

The never-ending journey, through what some of the company were now calling the roughest country God had ever forgotten to create, had also been terribly hard on the rolling stock, the wagons. Broken spokes and shattered felloes were a continual problem, as were splintered tongues and breaks in the running gear. Billy doubted there was a single wagon that was not being held together, in one place or another, by dried rawhide thongs or just plain rag strips wound tightly around a break or splint. In fact, the rags actually worked better on the wheels, which were continually getting wet and stretching rawhide loose. And the carpenters and blacksmiths were kept busy as wheelwrights, repairing the wooden wheels and heating and resetting the iron tires that kept falling off.

With a sigh Billy reached out and patted one of the mules he was stumbling along beside. Thinking back, all he seemed able to remember about the journey was nothing but miles and miles of desperate, unending struggle across a country that was cut with hundreds of arroyos and gulches and so was always either up or down; country that had been either frozen solid and sometimes waist-deep with snow or thawed out and hub-deep in mud. Since leaving Panguitch, they hadn't enjoyed more than a day or two of pleasant, level travel. Instead it had all been grueling, cold, and filthy work, taking such a terrible toll on the already exhausted animals and missionaries that to Billy it seemed almost unbelievable any of them had survived.

Now they were dropping rapidly down the side of Road Canyon, by a rocky, hard-edged road they had dug out that made so many turns and bends they were calling it "The Twist." Once in the bottom of Road Canyon, they would follow it southeastward into a wide wash that was butted on the far side by a massive, serrated sandstone upthrust someone had named "The Comb" or "Comb Ridge" because the top of it reminded them of the comb on a rooster's head. This sandstone ridge or cliff, which rose nearly vertically from the bed of Comb Wash, was over a thousand feet high and extended to the north and the south as far as they could to see. It looked virtually impenetrable, at least for teams and wagons, and so the weary missionaries were turning south down the wash, hoping to find an easy way around it where the San Juan River had cut through.

And everyone *was* weary, Billy thought bleakly. That morning Pap Redd had stopped by to see how Eliza was feeling, and even now Billy thought his words had been particularly instructive.

"You aren't alone, Sister Eliza," he'd growled soothingly. "All about us folks are about as done in as dancehall gals come six o'clock of a Sunday morning. Fact is, I reckon folks feel like they've not only run their string out but snapped it clean, and are as eternally doomed to difficult travel as a bunch of tumblebugs in the middle of crossing a hundred-and-seventy-five-mile-wide pasture flapjack. All but one or two feel like there's no end in sight, never has been nor never will be, and can never again hope for relief."

Of course, that had turned both Billy and Eliza to smiling, after which the man had assured them that the journey was nearly over, and that ten more days would put them at Montezuma Fort. "Then, by jings," he'd continued, "I'll teach you a little jig, Sister, that'll put to shame every step those Perkins brothers ever dreamed of doing—"

Catching his boot on a rock, Billy stumbled, lost his train of thought, and in the process had an instant to see himself as he appeared to others. His boots, new in October, now had rags tied around them to keep the soles in place and his bare feet off the rocks. His trousers, shirt, and coat had been stitched and mended so many times he was no longer sure which was original fabric and which wasn't. His hat, holed in two places by tree limbs, had become shapeless and nondescript. Unlike most of the men, he had shaved his itching beard back near Clay Hill Pass, though his two weeks of new growth since then made it look as if he was starting all over again. His hands and arms were rough and scabbed from numerous injuries, and he was gaunt and thin except in the belly, which was protruding as a first indication of starvation. Unlike some of the others, thankfully, he didn't have lice, though there'd not been a minute since Lake Pagahrit when he'd felt fully clean.

And his poor Eliza, big and awkward with child, was no better off! Her clothing was every bit as stitched and patched as his own, her high-button shoes were nearly as worn, and she was so drawn and thin it frightened him to look at her. Yet despite such things, she seemed always in the best of spirits. Truth be known, Billy had not once seen her truly unhappy since she'd revealed to him her amazing dream. Not in blizzards, not even while wading up to her knees in mud doing her best to help the children who'd gathered around her, had he seen anything but happiness on her face or heard joy in her voice. Even now, as her very pregnant body was being jostled and banged around by the bumpy descent, he could hear her humming the refrain of a popular hymn. It was as if—

"Billy, darling," Eliza suddenly called from behind him, "I . . . I think I'd better walk. The pillows just aren't enough padding under me, and I don't know if the baby can take a whole lot more of this jolting road."

"Or his mama, either one?" Billy asked with a twinkle in his eye.

"That . . . too." Eliza was holding her belly tightly with one hand while the other gripped the seat, her eyes again closed in a grimace against the pain.

"The road's mighty rough and steep for walking, hon-bun."

"I know." Eliza sighed. "And what with me being not only crippled of foot but big and awkward besides, you're going to tell me you think I'd best keep riding."

Billy smiled ruefully. "Of a truth, I do think so. But we're nearly to the bottom of the Twist, hon-bun. Then the road stretches out sandy and smooth—"

When Billy didn't finish, Eliza smiled. "Very well, Billy. I'll ride. But talk to me, please. Help me keep my mind off how perfectly awful this poor old body of mine is feeling."

"Better than that," Billy said as he dropped back and bolted up into the seat, "I'll ride the rest of the way to the bottom with you. Say, did Maggie Sevy tell you that her husband and the other explorers found handholds cut into that cliff yonder that led all the way to the top?"

"You're funning me," Eliza declared as she glanced in awe at the distant cliff.

Billy shook his head. "No, I'm not. They figured the trail had been cut by the same Indians who made the ruins we've been seeing, as the cuts appeared to be mighty old."

"Lawsy, lawsy," Eliza breathed. "I wonder if those old Indians were the true Lamanites, or if they're the ancestors of the Indian folks who are here now?"

"I don't rightly know the answer to either question."

"Well, I'll bet they were true Lamanites. Billy, do you believe those Pahutes we met the other night were actually involved in the killing of that Indian agent over in Colorado?"

563

Glancing at his wife, Billy thought of the Pahute man whose evil grin had so struck him. Of course, the man might have been thinking of anything, anything at all. But the way he'd looked at Eliza—"I don't know," he finally replied, "but I doubt it. None of them looked very murderous to me."

"I . . . I don't think they were the ones, either. And I felt so badly for that poor woman I gave my shawl to—"

"That was your best shawl, Eliza."

"Yes, I know." Eliza smiled. "It felt wonderful to be able to give her something nice, and I—" Suddenly Eliza paused. "You don't approve, do you."

It was a statement, not a question, and for a moment Billy struggled with how to respond. "I . . . just wondered that you would give her your best one," he finally admitted.

Again Eliza smiled. "What sort of gift is something of little or no value?" she asked softly. "Besides, I'll find a way to get another one, maybe even nicer than the one I gave her. What hope would she ever have of doing that, Billy? And what sort of missionary would the Lord have thought me if I'd started right off being selfish with the first Lamanitish woman he allowed me to meet?"

"Well, hon-bun," Billy said, "you did the right thing. I reckon it's just my selfish side coming out and showing itself, worrying about you and worrying even more about me providing for you and the wee one."

"He's certainly been kicking up a fuss today," Eliza beamed, expertly changing the subject. "I don't think baby Will likes bumpy rides even a little, especially inside his lumpy, bony mama."

"You *are* getting awfully thin," Billy stated as he placed his hand on his wife's tummy to feel the baby's kicks. For weeks, but especially since he'd taken over the cooking duties for the two of them, he'd secretly been giving Eliza a larger portion than his own. Yet more often than not she had found a way of giving it back to him, and perhaps some of her own portion as well, so that Billy had no real idea which of them had been eating the least amount of food. "Are you certain the baby is okay?"

"He's fine, Billy. Could be when he makes his appearance in two or three weeks he'll look a bit more scrawny than he should. But he still kicks like a mule and seems to have plenty of strength. For the baby's sake, I still wish old Hepsi hadn't dried up and then died, though. I believe my drinking her milk was good for him."

"I'm certain it was. Trouble is, most everybody's cows have dried up this winter, so there's hardly any milk anywhere. And did you know we only have three chickens left alive? And two of them look almighty weak. I tell you, Eliza, this whole company's right on the edge of starvation! If we don't get to Montezuma Fort soon and get some crops in the ground, then heaven help us."

"Things'll be just fine once we get to our destination, Billy darling, for heaven will help us! You just wait and see—"

—◦—◦—◦—

Comb Wash

"You know, I've been thinking again—"

"Uh-oh." Billy grinned at Eliza as he ladled some gruel into a bowl that he set on the table before her. "When you start into that deep thinking of yours, hon-bun, it's time for me to start getting nervous."

Eliza giggled. "Well, you started it, you know."

"I did? What in tarnation are you talking about?"

"Billy, I swan! Your language is becoming simply awful!"

Smiling, Billy ladled the remainder of the gruel into his own bowl and then sat down across from Eliza while she reverently offered up a blessing on the food. Up and down the Comb Wash, fires winked where members of the company had stopped for the night, the largest group of them close to what would be called Navajo Spring. So there wasn't one camping place but many as the Saints prepared for sleeping and their livestock cropped the new green grass that was starting to spring up everywhere.

Above them the stars hung like tiny lanterns over the Comb ridge, and now and then sounds of laughter, harmonica and mouth-harp music, and the shouts of happy children echoed back from the looming wall of the cliff. For it was warm in this place, warmer than anywhere they'd been since the previous October, and everyone in the company was starting to feel the natural exuberance of spring.

More than that, Billy thought as he stood and took up Eliza's shawl, which he carefully placed over her shoulders, every one of the expedition members knew that by the next day they would finally reach the San Juan. Yes, and within a day or two after that, if all went as expected, they would pull without great effort onto the level bottomland where Montezuma Creek spilled noisily into the larger river.

It was amazing that they were finally so close! It was beyond amazing! It was incredible—

"Billy, I mean it. You started teaching me about the gospel—about the scriptures. I want to ask you some questions about them, and I want to do it now, before any of the children happen to drop by and interrupt my thoughts again."

Grinning, Billy stepped back and once more took his seat. "So," he asked as he eyed the Bible and the Book of Mormon his wife had situated in the lamplight before her, "what is it this time?"

Reaching out and moving the lantern so it wasn't directly between them, Eliza's expression grew immediately more serious. "Remember back when you told me about your own repentance and mighty change, when you were born of the Spirit and so became a son and follower of the Lord Jesus Christ?"

Billy nodded. "I do."

"You said something then, Billy, that went right over my head. But I've been thinking on it a lot the past couple of weeks, and I believe you were right. You said that after the Lord redeemed you from your sins, he began making you aware of their underlying causes. In other words, God had you begin dealing with the reasons behind why you'd sinned in the first place. Isn't that what you said?"

"It is, though I think you said it better than I ever did."

"Only because it's fresh on my mind." Eliza smiled again. "Have you figured out the reasons for your sins yet, Billy?"

"Well, some of them, at least. Actually, what I think I've figured out is that I have certain character flaws, or weaknesses, if you will. Some of them I inherited, some of them I developed through my own choices, and some of them came as a natural consequence of the world I was born into and lived in. It seems to me that all of these make up what king Benjamin called the natural man."

"I remember you mentioning that in prayer a week or so ago,"

Eliza said quietly. "Did you know that Paul used the same term? Listen to this, Billy. I found it in 1 Corinthians, chapter two, verse fourteen. Paul says, 'But the natural man receiveth not the things of the Spirit of God: for they are foolishness unto him: neither can he know [them], because they are spiritually discerned.'"

Billy was thoughtful. "That's interesting, hon-bun, especially considering Benjamin's statement. Here. Let me read your verse again while you look up king Benjamin's address in the Book of Mormon."

Eliza nodded and handed Billy her open Bible.

As a swarm of small insects began diving about their lantern, proving that spring was finally in the air, Eliza quickly flipped through the pages of her copy of the Book of Mormon. "Okay," she said when she had found it. "For the natural man is an enemy to God, and has been from the fall of Adam, and will be, forever and ever, unless he yields to the enticings of the Holy Spirit, and putteth off the natural man and becometh a saint through the atonement of Christ the Lord, and becometh as a child, submissive, meek, humble, patient, full of love, willing to submit to all things which the Lord seeth fit to inflict upon him, even as a child doth submit to his father."

"That's it." Billy smiled as he looked up from his own reading. "So, now that you have references from both books, what conclusions have you come to?"

Eliza pushed the book away, her expression serious. "First of all, it seems obvious that the Lord isn't pleased when we give in to our weaknesses—to our natural or mortal selves."

Billy's smile was wider. "Then why did he give us such weakness in the first place, Eliza?"

"You think you have me, don't you?" Eliza laughed and again opened up the Book of Mormon. "This is Moroni, speaking in Ether, chapter twelve, verse twenty-seven. He quotes the Lord as saying: 'And if men come unto me I will show unto them their weakness. I give unto men weakness that they may be humble; and my grace is sufficient for all men that humble themselves before me; for if they humble themselves before me, and have faith in me, then will I make weak things become strong unto them.'"

"Which means?" Billy pressed.

"That the various character flaws or weaknesses of mortality are given us by God—

"You mean God causes all those awful things?"

"No, silly. I mean that God allows them to form and exist within us as part of our mortality. As you said a few minutes ago, he does this through the traits we inherit from our parents, the circumstances in which we are reared, and the consequences of the choices we make as we live each day. All of these weaknesses, combined together, are what the prophets call the natural man. And the natural man will give us enough grief to humble us, so that we will come to the Lord, exercise faith in him, and accept his holy grace."

"Which is the same message delivered by both Paul and Benjamin," Billy added quietly. "If we do become humble, Eliza, then what happens?"

Eliza smiled knowingly. "God through the grace of Christ will turn our mortal weakness into strength."

Billy nodded. "In other words, we'll have the power to put off our natural man and so become God-like. And since the Prophet Joseph taught that knowledge is power, I believe God makes our basic character flaws known to us through the Holy Spirit, once we have repented and become worthy to hear and learn, so we will gain power over them. In that way only can such weakness become strength.

"In my case, once I began to analyze and pray about it, I realized one day that I'd never in my life committed a sin that didn't fall within the two or three major areas of weakness in my own character. Things or situations outside those areas didn't really tempt me. For instance, I've never been inclined to steal, while someone else may struggle with that every day of his mortal life. On the other hand, I deal continually with the fear of failure, while other folks don't seem bothered by that at all. I believe this means that every person's 'natural man' has been designed for him or her alone and is perfectly calculated to bring about his or her own humility. I know a growing knowledge of my own 'natural man' has made it much easier for me to concentrate on the particular weaknesses I have, seeking to understand where they came from so I can overcome the temptations that so easily beset me."

"And . . . have you?"

Billy sighed deeply. "As you might suppose, I'm still working on it. But with the Lord's help I'm making progress."

"And so am I." Eliza leaned forward, closer to her husband. "For days I've been praying to understand not only why I treated you and others the way I did, but why I was so determined to control my life and my destiny. Well, since yesterday I've been remembering things about my father and mother—hard things they said or did—that I now believe were perfectly though unintentionally calculated to foster my attitude of defiant self-reliance and self-righteousness."

"So you believe," Billy asked carefully, "that what you did was your parent's fault?"

"Oh, no!" Eliza was adamant. "Absolutely not! I believe much of my weakness, or tendency to do those things, came from them. But from as far back as I can remember, I made the choice about my own actions, Billy. That means I was accountable for the injuries I inflicted upon myself and others, not my parents. And that's why I've been carrying such a terrible burden of guilt. Through my own choices I committed those sins, and in the process I wounded Christ terribly. Thus I'm the one who needed to repent, and I'm the one who needed to obtain forgiveness."

"And not your parents."

"No, I don't think so. At least not for my sins. Oh, they're accountable as well, Billy, for the choices they made that went against the light and knowledge they had. But those things, even the bad things they did to or taught me, are between them and the Lord. As for myself, I've freely forgiven them, for that, too, is part of my accountability." Eliza took a deep breath. "That's why I'm finally beginning to understand who I really am—why I choose to commit the particular sins I do."

"Then," Billy declared with a wide smile, "you're not alone seeing your weaknesses turned into strengths, but you're most definitely in the process of putting off your natural man—your natural self.

"You are also, my darling Eliza, one of the most wonderful human beings the Lord ever created. Of a truth, hon-bun, it's an honor for me to be your husband."

67

Comb Wash, Near the Mouth of Snake Canyon

"Well, the news isn't very good."

Billy's voice was weak with exhaustion, for his stomach was no longer accepting the ground seed wheat, and there was simply nothing else left to eat—for either of them. The beans, the jerked meat, even the little bit of fruit Eliza had dried the fall before was now gone, shared with others, especially the children. Eliza, too, was suffering the initial effects of starvation, and she worried that her body wouldn't have the strength either to complete the journey or carry her baby to term.

Now, driving the wagon southward down what they were calling the Comb Wash, she could see from her husband's expression that once again something was seriously wrong. Yet she kept the teams moving while Billy pulled the glass-eyed mare alongside the wagon and wearily stepped from her back directly to the dashboard. As Eliza slid a little to the side, he sat down next to her, rubbed his eyes with the backs of his hands, and let out a deep sigh.

"I never thought that old mare could carry me."

"She's an amazing animal."

"It's amazing that she isn't dead. That's what's amazing."

"What's wrong now, Billy?" Eliza asked, noting the complete discouragement in her husband's voice.

"What else?" Billy responded while he pushed back his hat and stared ahead. "It's the road, Eliza; this blasted, never-ending road! All along we've thought we could work our way around the end of this comb reef where the San Juan has cut through it. I reckon we just assumed there would be some bottomland there. Turns out there isn't, and we can't. The cliff drops straight into the river with no room for a mountain goat, let alone a wagon. I just left Ben and Hy Perkins and some of the others, and to their way of thinking our only hope is to cut a dugway up the side of the Comb just a little this side of the river."

"What does Platte say?"

"He's still back on the trail moving his wagons forward, so he doesn't know about the problem. Kumen Jones and Warren Taylor have gone back to see if they can help hurry him along. Anyway, Ben figures it'll take us three, maybe four days to cut a road up that cliff, and then it'll be as hard a pull as we've encountered."

"They're really thinking of going up over that ridge?" Eliza asked as she looked upward at the impassable-looking reef of stone.

Billy nodded. "They are. Of course, the Comb sort of drops a little into a hump right there, so it won't be quite as bad as if we were to try it along here. Still, it'll be bad enough, especially without any blasting powder. Tell the truth, that road will be so steep I shouldn't wonder if our teams prove too weak to climb it."

"What will we ever do?"

"Use six or eight teams per wagon, I reckon, and then pray a lot. Trouble is, we can't stay there at the river very long, either. There isn't any graze. So Billy Fyre, Wilf Pace, John Topham, and a few of the other herders are already figuring on trailing the herds back and forth across the river. But there's quicksand there, so we'll see how that all turns out."

"How did they know about the quicksand?"

Billy grinned. "Young George Westover decided to give the crossing a try just to show it could be done, and on his way back waded right into some. Way I heard it, he was hollering up a storm when Henry Wilson and Peter Nielson threw a rope around him and dragged him out. But at least now they know which way *not* to go."

"Unless there's more than one deposit of quicksand."

Chuckling, Billy drew a large packet from his pocket. "You're right about that," he agreed.

"Did an express come in?" Eliza asked as she looked at the packet.

"It did." Billy was trying to undo the knots. "Dan Harris showed up with this maybe an hour ago. I guess he's been over into Colorado, to Mancos, and picked up the mail folks have been sending by that route."

"What did you get?"

Opening the packet and reading the only letter, Billy chuckled again. "It's a note from Little Brig—I mean Elder Brigham Young, Jr., wishing us both well on this expedition. He says he wishes he could trade me places. I reckon if he knew our true situation, he'd change his mind in a hurry! He's also enclosed a couple of editions of the *Deseret Evening News* so we won't be too out of touch with— get this, Eliza. He says, 'with what some folks are calling civilization.'"

"Elder Young doesn't sound too enamored with the city his father founded."

"The way I remember it, he never has been." Pulling out and unfolding the newspapers, Billy began scanning the upper edition. "No wonder he doesn't think much of civilization," Billy mused. "Not only have hunters killed off the last of the Southern bison herd down at Buffalo Springs, Texas, but last fall England had her worst harvest of the century, Ireland's potato crop failed, leading to riots, and crops of all sorts failed throughout the rest of Europe. American wheat prices are way up, though, so if we can just get some good crops growing once we get to Montezuma Fort—"

"And find a way to stay alive until then."

With a grim expression Billy looked at his wife. "Yeah," he admitted, "there is that little problem, too."

"Any more news?"

Again Billy began reading. "Well, the U.S. Fish Commission has planted carp in the lakes in Wisconsin, figuring the fish will become a new food source for the country. You know, some of the boys caught some fish back when we were working along the Colorado that were pretty good eating. Maybe a few of us could go to work and do the same here. Goodness knows we need something!

"Oh, here's something else that's interesting. A young chemist back in Baltimore at some school called Johns Hopkins has accidentally discovered a compound made out of coal tar derivatives that he says is three hundred times sweeter than sugar and will be a boon to diabetics. He's calling it Saccharin."

"Out of coal tar?" Eliza was incredulous.

"That's what it says. I'll believe it, though, when I actually taste it. Let's see . . . Here's a story about an attorney name of George Seldon, out of Rochester, New York, who's applied for a patent on a horseless carriage that will be activated by a gasoline-fueled internal-combustion engine. Wouldn't that be a sight to see?"

"It would," Eliza agreed with a sigh, "especially if it could replace these poor, worn-out teams and wagons. I wonder if there'll ever be such a thing as a horseless carriage?"

"Well, they already have trains and ships that are run by steam, so why not carriages?"

"Steam engines I can see. But gasoline fueled? How on earth would they keep them from exploding?" Eliza shook her head resolutely. "You wouldn't catch me riding in such a machine, Billy. Not ever!"

Billy smiled. "It likely won't ever come to that; not, at least, way out here. Now, this is something you can agree with. It seems that retired General William Tecumseh Sherman, speaking to the Grand Army of the Republic in Columbus, Ohio, said, 'War is hell. There is many a boy here who looks on war as all glory, but boys, it is all hell. You can bear this warning voice to generations yet to come.'"

"You're right," Eliza said. "I can certainly agree with sentiments such as those. Isn't he the one that led Sherman's March through the Confederacy back during the War between the States?"

"One and the same, so he ought to know. Here's something else that's interesting. On the seventh of October last, Brother Canute Peterson, president of the Sanpete Stake of Zion, organized the Saints who settled on Huntington Creek, Castle Valley, Utah, as the Huntington Ward. He also organized the Castle Dale Ward for the folks who settled up on Cottonwood Creek. And two days later he organized the Ferron Ward in the same region. That's desolate country, Eliza, for I traveled through it once with President Young. It takes brave folks to settle such a place."

573

"Like this country, you mean?"

Billy smiled. "This country doesn't seem all that desolate. Well, what do you know? In February the state legislature passed an act creating San Juan County, and at the same time the Church created the San Juan Mission, with Silas S. Smith as president."

"Any county officers?"

"It says here they'll be selected by general election once our expedition is settled. Things do move right along, don't they. Here we haven't even figured the rest of the route to Montezuma Fort and already we're both a county and a mission. I should think—"

"Billy," Eliza said as she gripped his arm, "that's Pap Redd coming toward us, and he looks to be in a hurry."

"Yes, and with a pack-mule trailing him," Billy said softly as he lowered the papers to watch.

"Howdy, Pap," he said a moment or so later as the man came abreast of the wagon and Eliza pulled the teams to a halt.

"Howdy and so long, folks." Pap smiled thinly as he tipped his hat to Eliza. Then he turned for a quick glance at his mule.

"Trouble?" Billy asked.

"As ever. Dan Harris brought me word that seven of my children back in New Harmony have been stricken with the diphtheria, so I reckon that for me this expedition is over."

"How old is the letter?"

"Six weeks and a couple of days."

"Oh, Pap," Eliza breathed, "no wonder you're in a hurry!"

The older man nodded soberly. "I've been praying practically every minute since I got the news a couple of hours ago, and I do feel a sense of peace. But I also feel a need to hurry, which means I won't be teaching you that jig once we get to Montezuma Fort, Sister Eliza."

"Do you have enough food?"

"I don't eat much anymore." The older man's expression was bleak. "Just don't feel like it, I reckon. But I did take all the seed wheat Eliza Ann had ground up, and that ought to get me through to the Halls, and then into Escalante. Are you folks all right for food?"

"We're making it," Billy replied quietly.

Pap Redd grinned. "Spoken like a man with true pride, Billy. A little bit ago Alvin Decker killed a calf, and he told me he was saving a cut of it for you folks."

Eliza smiled, and tears sprang unbidden to her eyes. "That's very kind of him."

"No kinder'n you giving all your dried fruit to the children!"

"I . . . we'll miss you, Pap." Eliza couldn't seem to control her tears.

"And I reckon I'll miss you folks, too," the man responded gruffly. "Keep an eye on young Lem and Eliza Ann for me, Billy. That boy has a fire in his belly, and if it's stoked and banked proper he'll end up being somebody a father can be proud of. Sister Eliza, ma'am, my family and I will bless your name forever because of the love you've shown our sweet little Lula. That child's mighty special to her grandpa, I tell you what. Fact is, I hope your little one will be just as sweet."

Abruptly wiping at his own eyes, the man looked northward up the wash. "Well, *adios,* folks. Daylight's a-burning, and Keziah Jane and Sariah Louisa will be needing my help long before I can get there."

"God go with you, Pap. And don't forget to save that tooth for me."

Setting his battered and sweat-stained hat, Pap Redd grinned widely, and after shaking hands with him, Billy and Eliza stood up on the dashboard of the wagon to watch as hc and his pack-mule trotted away up the wash. Alone he was taking the backtrail of the road he had helped pioneer, first as an explorer and then as a road-builder and all-around dentist, doctor, stockman, and handyman.

"You're right," Billy said quietly. "I'm going to miss him."

"So will I," Eliza agreed as she gripped her husband's arm. "But isn't it amazing to think that if all goes well, he'll be in Cedar in about two weeks? Here it seems like we're practically ready to fall off the edge of the earth, and in only two weeks he'll be back where we started."

"It is amazing," Billy agreed as he sat back down and clicked the mules into motion once again. "But not so amazing as if he had one of those newfangled horseless carriages. Of course, it might take him a sight longer, but wouldn't it be something to actually pilot one of those contraptions!"

And while Billy and Eliza Foreman each dreamed their separate dreams, the four ganted and shaggy mules plodded their inexorable way toward the Rio San Juan.

———o—o—o———

War God Spring

It was *tavi-mum-wiski,* late in the afternoon, and the two growing sons of the Pahute called Chee sat silently on the hillside, waiting. Though signs of spring were beginning to appear in the land below them, on the mountain where they sat the buds on *suáy* the aspen had not yet opened, ice still covered the ponds of *pow-inch* the beaver, and even in the daytime one could find great comfort in sitting near *coo-nah,* the fire. But in large measure the snow was gone from the south slopes of the mountain where they dwelt, *tabby* the sun was almost warm now that the morning wind had died, and both boys had grown comfortable enough to become a little sleepy.

"Ho, brother," Beogah said following a huge yawn, "it is in me to think they have all fallen asleep in that wickiup yonder."

Reaching up, the older but smaller of the two adjusted his *katz-oats,* his shapeless white-man's hat. He had also yawned, but now he forced his eyes open wide again so he would miss nothing. "If it is not true of Mike, Suruipe, or our father," he declared, feeling acutely aware that his voice was beginning to change and was jumping from high to low and back again without apparent reason, "it is certainly true of the old one who is called Peeagament. *Wagh!* That one was asleep when we found him, and he seems to be sleeping each time we see him now."

"Or eating," Beogah intoned.

"Yes, brother, that is so. For being so old and so thin he has consumed an amazing amount of that *te-ah,* the deer Tuvaguts brought in not so many days ago. For myself, I believe I would have just left the old man out in the rocks."

"But he is a great chief, O Sowagerie."

Scornfully the smaller youth rose to his feet. "That is no longer how I am called!" he snarled as he glared downward. "To you and all others I am known as Posey, for it is a white man's name that has given me such power over them!"

Almost reverently Beogah looked up at his slightly older brother, knowing that the other's words had the clear ring of truth to them. After all, did he not have the white man's hat? Did he not have the white man's name? And had those things not given him the power to pull the trousers from the very white man who had given him that name? *Oo-ah,* yes! And that even before the foolish white man was *e-i.* And was he not wearing those very trousers now? Truly, Beogah thought as he watched his brother's eyes flash with anger, this one would one day become a great man among the People!

"Well," the angry one stormed, "what have you to say?"

"It is as you say, Posey," Beogah responded humbly. "Your name has given you great power."

Still angry, Posey picked up a stone and threw it far down the mountain, after which he followed it with another, and then a third. "Tell me, my brother," he snarled as he again sat upon the earth, "are we not warriors of the People? Did we not ride as warriors when we went *to-edg-mae,* a great way off, after those two whites? Did we not fight as warriors when they were *puck-ki,* when they were killed? And did I not stare that one in the eyes without fear even though he was not yet dead? Are not all these things true?"

Silently Beogah made the sign that Posey's words were true.

"*Oo-ah,* yes, they are true. Now I ask you, my brother, why it is that two great warriors such as ourselves are not invited into that *at-am-bar,* that talk between the big-mouthed one and the old one who is either sleeping or filling his always-empty belly. *Poo-suds-a-way-ah?* Do you understand this thing?"

Now Beogah made the sign that he did not. Of a truth, though, it did not bother him the way it obviously bothered his brother. That was because he already knew what was being discussed around the fire in the nearby wickiup. He knew, for the old one called Peeagament had been babbling since he had been found that he had been in the encampment of these whites, these mormonee, and had seen for himself their fearful power. More, the old fool claimed to have *no-ni-shee,* dreamed a dream wherein the great *To-wats* had warned him that the mormonee were *nar-ri-ent mo-ap,* strong of spirit, and should be studied carefully but left alone.

On the other hand, the big-mouthed one called Mike had made a *pe-ap,* a big thing of it, that he had taken some of the others, including Posey's and Beogah's own mothers, and had walked without fear into the encampment of the mormonee. There he had eaten of their food and taken of their clothing, which the mormonee had foolishly given not only Mike but each of the others who had braved their encampment with him, thus giving all of them a great deal of power. This thing the big-mouthed one had boasted of for many days, proving to his complete satisfaction that the mormonee were fearful and weak—more weak even than the *nan-zitch,* the young girls of the People.

The talk in the wickiup, then, was between the two warriors, each trying to convince the other of the rightness of his position. Beogah almost smiled at that, smiled at the foolishness of old Peeagament, for well he knew how the talk would turn out. It was only a matter of time, of waiting long enough for the venison in the kettle to be eaten and the *at-am-bar* to run its course—

With an exclamation of anger Posey was on his feet again, his fists clenched at his sides. "This is an insult," he stormed as he stared at the wickiup. "We are not women or children to be cast out! We are warriors, my brother, warriors of the People! *Pikey! Tooish apane!* Let us make a fast riding *mah-bah-quan-do* over the big river to the encampment of these foolish mormonee."

Slowly Beogah rose to his feet. "*Meah-bi-quay,* my brother. It is said they move camp from day to day. How is it we will find them?"

Disdainfully Posey looked at his younger brother. "Are we not men? Are we not true warriors of the People? Come! We will *te-we-ne* to the place where these weak ones were last camped. Then I will follow their tracks, Beogah. *Oo-ah,* yes! Surely I will do it, for now I, the warrior Posey, have much power over these whites! Soon all will see that it is so!"

68

Thursday, April 1, 1880

Comb Wash and the San Juan River

In a stupor of exhaustion Eliza sat in her chair beneath the canvas awning, not rocking but simply staring out across the river toward the country of the Navajos. The fact was, she felt too big and awkward to rock, or for that matter to do most anything else. It had been a month since she'd been able to do up or undo the buttons on her own shoes, and walking was dangerous simply because she couldn't see past her bulging stomach to where she was placing her feet. Add to that the fact that she was weak as a newborn kitten from not eating enough, and—

Eliza sighed deeply, knowing she needed to change her line of thinking. If she didn't, discouragement would set in, and then she'd have real troubles.

The San Juan River, flowing before her, showed the same desolation on both banks. Yet that morning and the morning before, she'd watched the herdsmen and their livestock cross the river seeking at least minimal graze for the animals. So someone thought conditions were better on the other side.

Joseph Woolsey, who had also crossed to help guard against Indian intrusion, had explained the night before how cold the water was, and how it took most of a day to dry completely out, after which he and the smaller herd boys had to soak themselves again bringing the livestock back for the night. This was especially difficult for little Henry John Holyoak, who at nine years of age was among the youngest of those crossing the river to help with the herd.

Yet it had been he who had spotted, the day before, a bunch of cattle mired in quicksand, and his shouts had brought men on horseback who had managed to pull the cattle out and then stop others from getting mired.

Now, as she stared out across the river, none of this seemed to want to stay in Eliza's mind. Instead, she seemed to be in a stupor, so exhausted both physically and mentally that not even the warmth of the afternoon was enough to excite her. She was simply numb, filled with swirling half-thoughts that had no coherence whatsoever.

Of course, the nice cut of veal Alvin Decker had given them two days before had helped immensely, at least for Billy. Even now he was up on what they were calling San Juan Hill, working with the others to construct this last and most impossible dugway up and across the Comb ridge. He couldn't have done it, Eliza knew, without at least a measure of renewed vigor.

Unfortunately, despite the meat and whatever else any of them could scare up to eat, what Billy and most of the rest of the company was accomplishing was now being done through sheer willpower rather than any sort of natural strength.

In Eliza's estimation, therefore, no one could have been more brave than her darling husband and his fellow missionaries, no one stronger or more courageous—

"Good afternoon, Eliza."

Turning, Eliza smiled and returned the greeting. Then, excusing herself from standing, she invited her surprise guest to be seated at the table next to her.

Though Eliza had met the woman and even spoken with her, she didn't know her well. In fact, in practically six months she'd never come near Eliza's wagon—

"So these are your famous table, chairs, and settings?" the woman asked as she fidgeted with her hands in her lap. She was obviously ill at ease, though Eliza hadn't the least notion why. "Folks speak of these things, you know—far more often than one might suppose."

"It's easy for even a pebble to cause ripples in a tiny pond," Eliza responded, still smiling. "But that doesn't mean the pebble isn't still a pebble, if you know what I mean."

"Why, uh . . . why, yes, I suppose I do." Anxiously the woman looked about. "You . . . uh . . . your husband isn't here?"

"Billy's on the hill, working on the road. Is . . . there something I can do for you?"

Now the woman looked terrified. "No!" she practically shouted as she glanced fearfully about, doing her best to avoid Eliza's gaze. "I just came by to . . . to . . . Well, I mean I . . . uh—"

"Yes?"

"I . . . uh . . . Say! Are you enjoying this?"

Eliza lost her smile. "Enjoying what, Sister?"

"Why, you know very well! Enjoying watching me suffer so! But it doesn't matter! It absolutely doesn't. I came here to apologize for my rudeness, and I intend to do just that. Eliza Foreman, I apologize! There, that's done with, and now I'll be on my way—"

"You're apology is accepted," Eliza stated sweetly, sincerely. "But of a truth, I have no idea why it was needed."

The woman was shocked. "You . . . don't?"

"Absolutely not. As I recollect, the last and only time we talked was when I was apologizing to you for the way I'd been carrying on about my husband, saying all those horrible things about him and bringing a spirit of contention into our camp. My sins were quite generally known, which is why I felt it necessary to apologize to everyone involved. But you, Sister? Of course you're forgiven, but I have no idea what you might have done."

The woman, her eyes wide, stared at Eliza. And then, gradually, her tears came, and she buried her face in her hands. "Oh, Eliza," she sobbed, "I . . . I've done exactly what you d . . . did. Almost since the day we met, I've been saying such . . . such awful things about you, calling you names and doing everything I could do to . . . to turn folks against you."

Reaching out, Eliza tenderly took the woman's hand.

"The th . . . thing is," the woman continued, looking up and swiping at her eyes, "after a time I . . . I knew I was wrong! I saw you changing, not just toward your husband but . . . but toward everyone else, too! Why, the way you apologized . . . the way you took over with all those children so . . . so their mothers . . . so *we* wouldn't be so burdened? The way you've reached out to . . . to folks who needed you? They talk about you, you know! Not one but several of them, always singing your praises—

"And that husband of yours? Mercy me! I never saw a man learn so much and change so much in a few short months! Always looking around for things he can do for others. I tell you, he's a man a woman ought to love and be proud of!

"Well anyway, Eliza, I saw it all. I saw every single good thing that both you and Billy did, and it made not a speck of difference to me. I was dead set against the two of you, and nothing was going to change my mind!"

"So . . . what did?"

Again the woman dabbed at her eyes. "I don't rightly know. Well, that isn't exactly true, either. It was seeing how happy you've been, or watching it rub off on my children. I mean, it's been Eliza this or Eliza that, or Brother Foreman something else until I was sick to death of it. But then the night you gave your lovely shawl to that Pahute woman it hit me pretty hard, for I had no such inclination. Yet as those Pahutes walked out of camp I watched you, and I knew you were happy. More important, I suppose, I knew I wasn't. Fact is, I was downright miserable.

"So I talked with my husband—who greatly admires Billy, by the way—and he showed me a whole slew of scriptures about charity and service and love. What struck me hardest, though, were the verses that say God wants us to have joy but Satan wants us to be miserable like he is. And since I was completely miserable while you were experiencing and sharing joy, even with my own children—"

And again the woman broke down and wept.

———o–o–o———

"That's truly what happened?"

Eliza nodded. She and the woman were still seated at Eliza's table, sharing cups of steaming Brigham Tea, which had finally become palatable to Eliza. "It was terribly embarrassing," Eliza continued. "First it was Mary Jones who wouldn't stop being my friend, then it was little Alice Louise Rowley telling me bluntly what her parents had been saying about me. Then Maggie Sevy gave me what-for, after which Mary Jones lit into me again. And all the while

Billy continued to be the sweetest, kindest man in the whole world, never once reviling against me even though he knew the kinds of things I'd been saying about him. Those things all helped."

"But they didn't change you?"

Eliza shook her head. "Not really. True change, I now believe, comes from within, where if we'll allow it, the Lord's Spirit may have dominion to accomplish this change."

"So, it wasn't you?"

"Of course it wasn't. I don't have the power to change me, to take away my guilt or give me peace, either one. Only the Lord has that power. So, with encouragement and guidance from those who loved me, I began inviting his Holy Spirit back into my heart."

"But . . . how?"

"By going back to the basic things that had brought about my conversion to the Lord in the first place—things that for some reason I'd abandoned: Studying the words of the Lord in the scriptures—all of them. Praying diligently and fervently. Listening with an open heart to the Lord's servants as I attended meetings. And most of all repenting—apologizing not just to you and the others but to the Lord himself for my part in his suffering. Finally, I had to endure the humiliation, the Godly sorrow, the broken heart that came with those apologies, and at the same time do all I could to change my behavior.

"After a sufficient time of that," and now Eliza was also weeping, "the Lord forgave me, the Spirit finally came as the Comforter, and now I . . . I, well, finally I feel peace."

"Which is why you're happy," the woman whispered as she dabbed again at her eyes. "No matter how miserable and uncomfortable our circumstances, Eliza, that's why you radiate joy."

"Well, joy *is* God's emotion," Eliza smiled through her tears. "If God is the one who brings about our mighty change of heart, then it only makes sense that we should feel his emotion as we experience it."

And then arising, the two women tenderly embraced, feeling at last the sisterhood that had always been present during their impossible journey through the wilderness but for so long had been ignored.

69

Friday, April 2, 1880

San Juan Hill

With a sense of awe Eliza gazed upward at the bulging sandstone hill that marked the south end of where the river had cut through Comb Ridge. All around her it was quiet, so quiet it made her ears ache from straining to listen to it. No one was saying anything, no dogs were barking from the encampment, not even the animals were moving.

A few yards away the San Juan lapped along steady and sleepy, eddying and back-swirling behind the point where the Comb reef plunged into the water, cutting and digging at the bank downstream where the current ran deep.

Suddenly a chunk of bank broke off and slid into the water, its sound tiny and distant. Yet it was enough, that small noise, to break the spell of silence that seemed to grip each of the company standing at the foot of the monstrous climb.

"As my father might put it," Lemuel Redd said abruptly as he, too, gazed upward, "the notion of that there hill being the best and only road out of here is ringy as a she-bear with sore nipples nursing three cubs. Trouble is, Sister Foreman, she's the only way, and it's yours and Billy's turn."

"Have the others made it okay, Lem?"

Slowly the young man nodded his head. "Yes, ma'am. Four wagons and no accidents. Of course, the boys have been working on the road since Saturday, but it's still taking seven teams to the wagon to get them to the top. If you look, you can see the blood and hair on the rock where the animals have slipped and fallen. Billy, I'd say she looks steeper than the climb out of Cottonwood. Is she?"

Billy nodded. "Platte asked me to measure it when we got here Monday morning. I did what I could, and according to my reckoning only the Hole has been steeper. And then we were going down, not up. I believe this rock runs close to a forty-five degree grade most of the way, which is some steep."

"Yeah," Joseph Barton declared from a few yards away, "with not enough dirt and dust on it to shake the birdlice out of a Barred Rock pullet, let alone give footing to a bunch of horses and mules that stand hipshot in the rear and spraddle-legged in the front at every stop, a sure sign of their exhaustion."

"I know, Joseph. I know."

"Well anyway, Billy," Lem Redd declared, "the teams are all hitched. When you and Eliza are ready, give the word and we'll start the haul."

"We'll be ready soon as Eliza is aboard—"

"Billy," Eliza stated firmly, "I won't ride up this time!"

Billy was stunned. "Eliza, you've got to. You can't possibly think of walking."

Firmly Eliza shook her head. "I won't ride, Billy. I know I rode through a lot of that mud and snow, but this is where I draw the line! I won't add another pound for those poor animals to drag to the top, and that's my final word on it!"

Helplessly Billy looked around. "Well, you certainly can't climb it afoot. Not only is it terribly steep and slick, but in your condition it wouldn't be good for you or the baby—"

"Oh, pshaw! I'll be careful, and it won't hurt either one of us. For goodness sakes, Billy, I'm not an invalid!"

"Pardon me, Sister Foreman," Joseph Barton declared, coming to Billy's aid, "but should you happen to slip and fall you would be. An invalid, I mean. Or dead, more than likely, and your baby along with you."

"I hope, ma'am," Lem Redd chimed in, "that what Brother Joseph just said hits you like a heel-clod from the horse ahead of you in a hard race. Or a whippy branch slashing behind a man you're following too close through thick brush in too big a hurry. Smack between the eyes, and stinging your mind awake. You try climbing that hill afoot, ma'am, especially in your condition, and your and Billy's dream to raise a family in this San Juan country will more'n likely be as down the drain as slime water out of an unplugged stock tank."

"But . . . but the horses and mules . . . my weight—"

"Your weight won't be enough to make a thimble full of difference, ma'am. Fact is, a good part of the blood and hair on that rock comes from bringing these critters back down. Why, every time he comes down, that old mule yonder near the front of the string reminds me of a black bear riding his haunches down a steep talus slope. Hard as it is on rump and tail, that fool mule does the same.

"Now speaking in behalf of my father," and Lem Redd was grinning crookedly as he said it, "you may be saltier than a late summer deer lick, Sister Foreman, ma'am, which I allow you are and then some. But was you to slip and have to try that same fool black bear stunt I just mentioned, you'd fare a whole lot worse nor that mule, and leave a lot more than hair and hide on the rock. Believe me, you would!"

Eliza laughed weakly. "All right, Lem, I get the message. I believe you. And Joseph, I believe you as well. But I'll ride only if both of you promise to call me Eliza instead of that silly 'Sister Foreman ma'am' nonsense."

With sheepish grins both young men nodded their agreement.

"Good. Billy, if you'll kindly give me your hand—"

A moment later Lemuel Redd gave a wild yell and snapped his whip over the heads of the lead team, and with squeals and snorts the animals plunged up the rock face of what was being called San Juan Hill, the rickety wagon straining behind them.

It was a horrible ride that took less than thirty minutes but seemed to last forever, for not only was the road steep but much of it was also sidling, and a good part of the climb Eliza thought they were surely doomed to tip and roll sideways down the hill.

Moreover, it took only moments for her to discover that Lemuel Redd had lied shamelessly about the damage the hill was doing to the animals. Constantly it seemed that one or another of the horses or mules was on its knees and fighting to gain a foothold, leaving blood and hair and flesh to smear the rock where it went down. Meanwhile, the still-erect animals continued to plunge upward against the sharp grade, both Lemuel and Billy whipping the jaded animals into giving all they had.

It was pull and rest, pull and rest, pull and rest, and with each rest Lemuel and Billy were on their knees sloshing water from canteens onto the animals' torn and shredded knees and forelegs. Worse, as they neared the top many of the animals were so exhausted they began to spasm and go into near-convulsions, and as they finally crested the ridge and stood spraddle-legged and frothing with every wheezing breath, Eliza wasn't at all surprised to see Lemuel, every bit as strong as his father, weeping freely while he examined his wounded charges.

Truly the climb up San Juan Hill had been hard enough to take the heart completely out of even the strongest of the exhausted missionaries and their teams.

70

Sunday, April 4, 1880

Between the Comb and Butler Wash

"Billy darling, we're about finished, you know."

Billy nodded as he labored to re-repair one of the wagon wheels that was threatening to disintegrate again. For two days they'd been banging and clattering across the rock that was the backside of the Comb reef, traveling northward and almost exactly parallel to the route they'd taken southward before the horrors of San Juan Hill—the route that was now almost a thousand feet below them. Now they were ready to turn east again, on a route that with only a few short dugways—maybe a good day's work for the entire company—would allow their wagons to descend into the Butler Wash.

"I know we are, hon-bun. Another three, four days and we should be at the fort on Montezuma Creek."

In desperation Eliza shook her head. "That isn't what I mean, darling. I mean, the animals are galled and exhausted, the wagons are wrecks, and I truly wonder if any of us have the physical or mental strength to go the rest of the way."

Dumbfounded, Billy looked up from where he was kneeling on the rock. "Why, Eliza, what are you saying?"

"I'm saying," his wife responded as she sat dejectedly on a rock with her hands locked around her middle to help support her unborn child, "that as far as I am concerned, we've reached the San Juan, and we could stop right here and I would be satisfied."

Amazed, Billy shook his head. "But . . . this isn't even farmland! And where is that happiness that hasn't left you since your dream?"

Eliza sighed. "It never was happiness, Billy. It was joy because I was finally at peace—peace from knowing that I've been begotten of him and have been called a worthy daughter of the Lord. Of a truth, I feel just as much joy right now as I ever have, happy countenance or not. Why? Because I've endured to the end with you and the others. I've come to where I was called to go, the San Juan, and now I'm more than ready to stop."

Billy's smile was filled with love and compassion. "I don't blame you. But we still can't farm up here on the backside of the Comb Ridge."

"Then please take me where we can, Billy—the closest place. I overheard young Lem Redd talking last night, and he said in his opinion we'd walked and slept and eaten and lived on sloping, uneven ground for so long that the thought of any level bottomland, whether at Montezuma Creek or not, was a temptation too sweet to resist. I second the motion, darling. I'm so tired and sore that I can't bear the thought of another step, let alone more journeying."

Tying and securing the knots in the rags he was using to hold together the split felloes and spokes, Billy pulled himself to his feet. Walking to his wife, he gently pulled her to him and held her close.

"This baby's starting to keep us apart," he teased.

"He's doing more than that, Billy. The way he's been making me feel, I'd say your son is about ready to make his grand entrance into this cold, cruel world."

Billy was immediately concerned. "You . . . you mean right now?"

"No," Eliza smiled. "I mean in the next week or so. But of a truth, he is making life a mite uncomfortable for his mother."

Not knowing what he could do about his wife and unborn child, Billy did his best to be sympathetic. "Well," he finally said as he glanced around, "folks are starting to pull into camp for the night, so why don't we camp on that patch of sand down yonder. It looks close to level, and those cedars will give us a bit of protection. Then, once the mules are staked out to graze and I get things set up, you can rest until worship services. You do feel well enough to go, don't you?"

"I haven't missed one yet, have I?" Eliza smiled. "Besides, hearing others' testimonies of Christ does seem to rejuvenate me."

"His Spirit can renew anyone," Billy agreed, and with a slap on Wonder's rump he started the teams forward again, down the slickrock and toward the tiny patch of sand.

———◦—◦—◦———

"Brudders und sisters," Jens Neilson said as he leaned on his cane in front of the assembled throng, "ve haff come a long vay togedder. Ve haff seen de days grow short, und now ve are seeing dem grow long again. Ve haff seen de grass vidder und turn brown, und now already it iss green. Surely de Lord hass blessed us all!"

Quiet 'amens' were heard throughout the congregation.

"Now ve are close to our yourney's end, und most likely dis vill be our last Sabbath day upon de trail. By next Sunday, if de Lord be villing, ve vill partake off de emblems off de Lord's supper at Montezuma Fort. To me, dat vill be a blessed day!"

Again 'amens' were spoken, and Eliza thought of how she felt now whenever she partook of the sacrament. Not only was it a glorious way for her to renew her covenants with the Lord, but on each occasion—both Thursdays and Sundays—she had been blessed to feel the overwhelming confirmation of the Holy Spirit that her most recent sins had been forgiven and she had been made clean through the precious blood of the Lamb. To her the peace and joy of it was so overwhelming, so miraculous—

"Ve haff asked Sister Harriet Ann Barton to bear her testimony off de restored gospel of Christ to us dis evening," Jens Nielson continued, "und she hass agreed. Sister Barton, vill you come forward?"

"Oh," Billy whispered as Harriet Ann Barton made her way around the fire and toward where Jens Nielson was standing, "I forgot to tell you, hon-bun. Maggie Sevy said to say thanks for teaching her how to be happy."

"What? I haven't spoken with her in days and days."

Billy shrugged. "She said you'd know what she meant." He paused, watching the petite Harriet Ann Barton steady herself before speaking. "You know," he breathed, "I wish Harriet Ann would sing. I do enjoy listening to her. To me she sounds just like an angel."

Eliza smiled as she leaned close to her husband. "Maybe that's because she is one. Someone told me she's been feeling poorly, though, so I'm pleased to see she's back up and around."

"I was born in Parowan to Morgan and Harriet Evans Richards," Harriet Ann Barton was already saying. And from the weakened condition of her voice, it was evident why the woman hadn't chosen to sing.

"My parents came from Merthyr Tydfil, Wales, and lost their family when they embraced the Lord's true gospel. With my two eldest brothers they emigrated to Utah and were sent by Brigham Young to Parowan as part of the Iron Mission. That's where I came along.

"Being of a scholastic temperament, I was educated both publicly and privately, and I also became a member of Alfred Durham's choir. Other than that, my life was remarkably like everyone else's—a constant struggle for survival. Our home was built of logs cut and hauled from the nearby mountains, and our land had to be cleared of brush and rocks before ever it could be worked.

"The school benches were made of slabs with oak or birch legs driven into the slab—four or six legs according to the length—and none of them very steady. The floor was made of lumber, and the log walls were chinked to slow the wind, which seemed never to cease its blowing.

"As I recollect, boys and girls were pretty well mixed with each other. There was no attempt to segregate us in our seating. That's the first time I remember seeing my husband, Joseph Franklin Barton. I sat next to him and he pulled my pigtails. He and his family had fled from Paragonah to Parowan because of the Indian troubles and were at that time living in the fort with us. I saw him regularly after that, not always with much enthusiasm."

This drew a chuckle of appreciation from the congregation, Billy and Eliza included.

"Dances and social affairs generally began in the afternoon about two P.M., followed by a community dinner at four after which folks went home to take care of their chores. In the evening all gathered together again to sing and dance until the wee hours. It was at those dances and socials that I developed a little better opinion of Joseph Barton, for not only had he stopped pulling my pigtails but he had grown tall and handsome and was a wonderful dancer with a deep baritone voice to match. And he was willing to ride in from Paragonah just to dance with me, or so he said.

"I suppose that means he also saw something in myself, for after a time we made a trip to Salt Lake City and on May 15, 1876, were married in the Endowment House for time and all eternity. So far, I believe we have each proved satisfactory to the other. And of course you all know that we now have two very lively daughters; Harriet Eliza, who just turned three, and one-year-old Mary Viola, whom we affectionately call little Matty."

Harriet smiled down at her husband and daughters. "As far as my testimony of the gospel is concerned," she continued, "I couldn't have endured these past six months had I not known we were all engaged in the Lord's work, and that his servants the prophets and apostles had called us to it. My heart is afire with that sure and certain knowledge.

"Nevertheless, in times of extremities we occasionally gain our brightest hope, and see most clearly the glory of God shining brightly around us. So it has been for me. In the last few weeks as I have lain in my wagon unable to care for my husband and my babies, two of the Lord's angels have stepped forward to further his work and add to my vision of the Lord. First came sweet young Sarah Riley and then shortly thereafter Maggie Sevy, two wonderful women who willingly shouldered my burdens along with their own. More, each of them exhibited unfailing joy while they were about it, no matter the suffering and inconvenience my illness added upon their already overburdened shoulders.

"Thus has my testimony of God's work been strengthened, brothers and sisters, for if the Lord was not lying when he reminded us that we would know his true servants by their fruits, then I know that I am surrounded by his servants, his mortal angels. How thankful I am that these women and others have somewhere learned to serve with joy, and how anxious I am to do better at the same."

——◦—◦—◦——

"Do you understand what Maggie Sevy was talking about now?" Billy asked as he helped his wife make her way back toward their wagon. "Do you understand why she feels to thank you?"

"I . . . I do," Eliza responded brokenly. "But she is far, far too kind."

"It's fitting that you should feel that way," Billy declared soberly as he opened the side-door of the wagon and helped Eliza up and in. "As for myself, though, hon-bun, I know the truth. I keep my eyes open, and it isn't the least difficult to see the good the Lord is enabling you to accomplish in the hearts of those around us."

"Billy—"

Holding his hand up to stop his wife's protestations, Billy hung the lantern on the hook dangling from one of the bows and reached for Eliza's copy of the Book of Mormon. "Here," he said as he handed it to her, "turn to the eighteenth chapter of Mosiah and read verses eight through ten."

"Very well," Eliza replied as she flipped through the pages. "It says, 'And it came to pass that he said unto them: Behold, here are the waters of Mormon (for thus were they called) and now, as ye are desirous to come into the fold of God, and to be called his people, and are willing to bear one another's burdens, that they may be light; yea, and are willing to mourn with those that mourn; yea, and comfort those that stand in need of comfort, and to stand as witnesses of God at all times and in all things, and in all places that ye may be in, even until death, that ye may be redeemed of God, and be numbered with those of the first resurrection, that ye may have eternal life— Now I say unto you, if this be the desire of your hearts, what have you against being baptized in the name of the Lord, as a witness before him that ye have entered into a covenant with him, that ye will serve him and keep his commandments, that he may pour out his Spirit more abundantly upon you?'"

Tenderly Billy gazed at his wife. "That's you he's describing, hon-bun. Of course you've already been baptized, and so the rest of it just naturally falls into place. Now turn to the first chapter of Alma and read verse thirty."

Silently Eliza did as she was bidden and read, "And thus in their prosperous circumstances they did not send away any who were naked, or that were hungry, or that were athirst, or that were sick, or that had not been nourished; and they did not set their hearts upon riches; therefore they were liberal to all, both old and young, both bond and free, both male and female, whether out of the church or in the church, having no respect to persons as to those who stood in need."

"Do you see, Eliza?" Billy had taken the book from his beloved wife and was now holding both her hands. "Once a person has been born of the water and the Spirit and becomes truly converted to the ways of the Lord, it becomes as natural as breathing to start reaching out and blessing the lives of others. I've been watching you do exactly that since way back in December at the camp above the Hole, and as the days pass your circle of influence for good continues to expand. You reach out to adults, to children, to members of the Church and nonmembers alike, to the Pahutes—Why, given the chance you'd most likely even reach out to those Texas outlaws we've been hearing about.

"But like Sister Harriet Ann said tonight, you aren't alone in this. Much of the camp has become the same."

"That's what I've been trying to say, Billy. It isn't just me—"

"Oh," Billy said, smiling, "I know that. The extenuating circumstances of our journey through the wilderness have contributed greatly to this love we're all feeling for one another. And there are many others in this company whose hearts are just as pure and righteous as yours who have also been reaching out, some since the very beginning of our mission. But nevertheless, you've been a great influence for good, and I'm merely adding my voice to Maggie Sevy's and a host of others when I say I've been honored to have spent the past six months traveling in your presence. I love you, Eliza Foreman. I truly do!"

And tearfully, gratefully, Eliza reached out and drew her long-suffering husband to her.

71

Harris Bottoms

"What's that you're singing, hon-bun?"

Eliza looked up from where she was hobbling beside the creaking wagon, trying with her free hand to ease the pain in her back. For hours she had done the driving while Billy walked, but at last he'd agreed to let her walk a bit, even though he thought it might be too hard on her. As if getting jounced around on that wagon seat wasn't hard, she thought bleakly. Of course, Billy was simply being thoughtful—

"It's a hymn Eliza R. Snow wrote," she replied at length, "called 'The Trials of the Present Day.' The verse I was just singing goes: *'O'er rugged cliffs and mountains high, Through sunless vales the path may lie, Our faith and confidence to try, in the celestial glory.'"*

"Seems appropriate." Billy grinned. "Of course everybody else is singing 'The Latter-day Work Rolls On,' so you're slightly out of step."

Sighing, Eliza stepped around a large badger hole, momentarily wondering why with all the holes she'd seen, she'd never spotted a single badger. "I'd sing it with them, Billy, I truly would. But I'm so confounded tired of this eternal 'rolling along' that I'm afraid I'd burst into tears if I started."

Surprised by his wife's use of slang, Billy could only stare.

"Well, I am!" Eliza defended herself. "The wagons never stop groaning and creaking, the mules never stop plop-plop-plodding and jingling their harnesses, and these squeaking wheels never *ever* stop rolling along! It's . . . almost more than I can bear!"

595

Billy nodded. "I understand how you feel, hon-bun, I truly do. From the beginning this trek seemed like a grand adventure to me, and in many ways it has been. A wonderful work has been accomplished, and I feel it an honor to have been a small part of it. But since Sunday night I've been feeling like you do. I'm powerful ready for the journey to come to an end so we can begin to live again."

"You feel like we haven't been living either?" Eliza asked in surprise.

Billy nodded. "I do. It's like our lives are in suspension or something, and I have this nagging feeling it will never end. I thought after we climbed San Juan Hill that we were nearly to Montezuma Fort. I can't begin to tell you how disappointed I was when I learned we had to build more road down into and up out of Butler Wash. And then this morning when this wash came in sight, I thought surely it was Montezuma Creek. But no, this is only Cottonwood Wash, and who knows how many more fool washes we'll have to cross before we get to the fort. Five days since we climbed that awful hill, Eliza. Five days! And how many more is it going to take?"

"The Lord knows, Billy."

"Yes, he does. But some days that just doesn't seem good enough, at least to me! I've been studying on it, Eliza, and I figure we've come about two hundred and ninety miles since leaving Cedar, blazing a road through what must surely be the roughest, most broken-up country in these United States. Because of that, and because it's taken us just two weeks less than six months to do it, I figure we've averaged about 1.7 miles a day, which is not as far as a normal man can crawl."

"Considering the number of women and children with us," Eliza declared thoughtfully, "that probably isn't too bad."

Billy grinned. "I've been doing a little figuring on that, too. If I have everybody's ages right, and I think I do, then the average age of our expedition when we started out was eighteen years."

"Oh, Billy—"

"Of course that's counting all the little children. If you figure the average age of just the adults, those eighteen and over, the age rises to twenty-eight. Sort of makes you and me look old and decrepit, doesn't it."

Silently Eliza nodded. Of course, she'd felt that way right along. But at least, she thought with a sigh, she was finally going to join the ranks of motherhood—

"Whoa, Nellie," Billy exclaimed as he looked off beyond where Eliza was walking. "Don't look now, hon-bun, but we've got company again."

Turning, Eliza was surprised to see a young Pahute man—a boy, really—riding a scruffy pony along the bank of the wash, exactly pacing their wagon. He was watching her as intently as she was studying him, somehow she knew that. Only the brim from his hat made it next to impossible for her to see his expression.

"I don't see a weapon," Billy said from up on the wagonbench.

"And he's been around white folks before," Eliza added. "The hat's awfully battered, but those Levi Strauss trousers he's wearing look practically brand new. Billy, I believe he's friendly. I think he wants to get acquainted—"

"There's another one," Billy said with a little more urgency. "Back a little, beyond those bushes."

Eliza nodded. "I see him. Look, Belle and Joseph Smith can see them, too. See how the children are pointing? I wonder if these boys live nearby, and if their families are hiding from us? Oh, glory, what if they're both orphans and need our help? I think—"

"The river's ahead!" Kumen Jones shouted back at them from his wagon, the excitement in his voice evident. "Lots of trees, and someone says they can see a cabin!"

"A cabin!" Eliza's heart was already pounding. "Billy, could it be Montezuma Fort?"

"I don't hardly know," Billy said thoughtfully. "What I do know, hon-bun, is that our young visitors have disappeared."

Startled, Eliza looked around. "Why, how very strange! Where do you suppose they might have gone?"

"Here, mules," Billy suddenly shouted as he pulled hard on the reins, "whoa up there! Good. Eliza, give me your hand and scramble on up here. I don't want you walking any more today."

As quickly as she could, Eliza climbed onto the wagon seat. Then, once the teams were in motion again, she rose carefully to her feet, her hand resting on the canvas-covered front bow so she could better peer ahead.

"Lawsy, Billy," she declared, her voice hardly above a whisper, "there are Kumen's trees! It looks like a whole forest of cottonwoods up ahead, and they're all leafed out and green!"

The scattered trees they'd been passing as they followed down Cottonwood Wash were also leafing out, just as fresh green grass was bursting here and there from the hillsides. But no one had paid such things much mind, Eliza thought. Or at least she hadn't—not until her view of the bottom lying before them had opened up—

"I see it, Billy!" she exclaimed excitedly as the mules pulled the wagon out of the mouth of the wash and onto the level bottomland. "I see the cabin away off over yonder, back in the trees! Oh, mercy sakes alive, Billy, darling, I never saw a place so beautiful in all my life! Everything green and fresh and lovely. Over yonder the ground's been plowed, and look how golden those bluffs that line the valley are. I know a lot of it is because of the sunshine, Billy, but I swan if this whole valley doesn't look just like the garden of Eden must have looked—"

"And it's level, Eliza!" Billy declared as he pulled his wagon to a stop next to Kumen and Mary Jones. "There must be hundreds and hundreds of good acres for farming here, and all of it fertile-green and level."

"Well, Eliza," Kumen called from his wagonbench, "what do you think?"

"I think it's wonderful!" Eliza was absolutely beaming. "Is this the Montezuma Creek settlement? Is that the fort over yonder?"

Mary Jones laughed. "That's exactly what I asked, Eliza. But even if it isn't, this is plenty good enough for me!"

"It . . . isn't the fort?" Abruptly Eliza felt tired again, though she had no real idea why.

"No," Mary was shaking her head, "this isn't Montezuma Creek. From what I understand, that's the Harris cabin. My brother Joseph just rode by and told me Platte and Pa are already over there talking with Brother Harris."

"Then . . . where is Montezuma Creek?" Eliza's exhaustion had suddenly turned into a tremendous pain, and without even intending to, she doubled over and plopped herself down on the wagon seat.

"It's about nineteen miles on up the river," Kumen responded as he climbed down and saw to his animals. "Another day, or at the most, two."

"Nineteen . . . miles?" The distance seemed overwhelming to Eliza, especially with the terrible pain in her belly. "I . . . don't think I can go another—"

"Eliza," Billy asked, suddenly concerned with the look of pain on his wife's face, "what is it, hon-bun? What's wrong?"

"I . . . I don't know." Eliza was clutching her swollen abdomen with both hands. "Oh, mercy, Billy, something awful's happening—"

"Mary!" Billy shouted frantically, "something's wrong with Eliza!"

"Wrong? Is she in labor? Eliza, are you going to have that baby right here?"

In agony Eliza could do no more than shake her head. But the pain was growing worse by the minute, and as beads of sweat formed on her forehead, she bit her lip to keep from crying out.

"Kumen," Mary cried as she jumped from her wagon, "go get Belle Smith or Hannah Pace! Them or Mary Ellen Lillywhite. Their wagons are already parked right over there. Tell them Eliza's in labor and something isn't right! And hurry, for heaven's sake! Hurry!"

Holding her skirts in the air, Mary bolted to Billy's wagon and scrambled up. "Billy, we've got to get her back onto her bed, so get your furniture out double-quick and then get a fire going and some water heating. Eliza, you help us as much as you can, and we'll just scoot you back through the puckerhole here—"

"Is she . . . going to have the baby?" Billy asked when Eliza was situated on their seed-grain bed, writhing in agony.

"I hope not!"

"But the water—"

"That's for a tea she needs to drink, a tea that'll maybe slow this labor down. One of those women I sent Kumen after will have the proper leaves to steep—Billy, go get that fire going! And another thing. You won't be moving this wagon anywhere for the rest of the day, not with Eliza threatening like this. So once the water's on the fire, take care of your teams. Kumen'll help you."

Nodding his head numbly, Billy clambered out of the wagon,

and for the rest of the day he wandered about or stood helplessly by while a whole crew of womenfolk busied themselves both inside and outside his wagon. He was amazed at their organization and efficiency, he was thankful beyond belief for their help, and once again he realized how truly little he understood about women.

It was coming dark when he finally had a chance to see Eliza again. And it had been a busy day, too, what with discussions and short explorations and even an official meeting or two for the entire company—him and Eliza and her nurses excepted.

"Are you all right?" he asked, tenderly caressing Eliza's cheek.

"I think so," she replied with a weak smile. "Billy, that was awful!"

"I reckon it was. Belle Smith says the pain was so bad because the baby isn't quite ready. Or you aren't, one or the other. But everybody thinks you'll be just fine now."

"And the baby?"

Billy smiled. "Well, he's still kicking, hon-bun. Right there. I can see it plain."

Eliza smiled weakly. "That's . . . good. But we . . . we'll fall behind now, Billy. They told me I can't travel for a day or two."

"I reckon you won't need to."

"What? But I thought this wasn't—"

"Montezuma Creek." Billy grinned. "I know, hon-bun. It isn't. But it *is* where everybody's voted to stay. Once folks saw how level and green this place is, it was as far as most all of them wanted to go. Platte and some of the others have already negotiated a trade with the Harrises for their claim, and a couple of brethren have started a rope survey to lay out building and farm lots. And come morning they've asked me to go help lay out a ditch so we can get water to the crops we'll be planting."

"Is . . . it true, then?" Eliza breathed, her voice filled with wonder. "Are we really and truly here?"

"We are," Billy responded softly while a cricket began chirping somewhere outside the wagon. "Eliza, hon-bun, you and me and the little one? Well, we're all of us finally and forever home."

72

Wednesday, April 7, 1880

Montezuma Fort

The old Pahute chief known as Peeagament was exhausted—so tired his legs felt like wobbly wooden sticks and a red mist had spread before his eyes. For most of the night he had endured the impossible gait of another nearly useless pony, doing all he could to drive it forward with haste. And when it had fallen dead near daybreak, he had continued the journey on foot, forcing his weakened old legs to run when they could and walk without letup the remainder of the time.

Now, with the two wickiups of the *tsharr,* the white mormonee in sight, it was all the old man could do to keep from falling down in *ow wo-one,* exhaustion. Yet he must not fall, he must not! The *ne-ab,* the chief of the mormonee at the crossing, had entrusted him to carry a paper to these other mormonee in the cabins before him—a paper he had said they must have.

Worse, in the time of darkness he had been chased, he suspected either by Big Mouth Mike or by the two whelp pups of old Chee, and it was only by the best of luck that he had escaped. It was a thing of great sadness to old Peeagament, the way he had been treated by Mike's band and the way his words had been scorned. But this was a new day, and these whites, these mormonee, had treated him more than well. What else was a man of the People to do but agree to carry a paper to these few starving ones who were waiting—

"Ma! Pa!" young Edward Davis shouted. "Someone's coming, an Indian, I think!"

"And he's waving his arms like crazy!" George Harriman added from where he stood beside his friend.

Quickly the doors to the two adjoining cabins opened and the members of the Davis and Harriman families filed out. There they stood agawk while the old Indian ran toward them, his arms still flailing in the air.

"*Wagh!*" the old man gasped as he pulled to a halt before the startled Mormons, doing his best both to breathe and to pull forth his extremely limited knowledge of English so that he might deliver his message. "Many white men, many squaws come big river. Sit down, heap tired, horses no pull. All the time white men sit down!"

"It's the second company!" Henry Harriman breathed. "They've got through at last!"

"God be praised!" his wife Elizabeth cried, and then both women broke into tears.

"Squaws heap glad," the Indian smiled his nearly toothless smile. "All the same like'um more folk come this place."

"That's right," Jim Davis replied as he rubbed his stomach. "White men bring us food." Of a truth, though, he wasn't hungry, or at least not very. Harv Dunton's small sack of flour, blessed by Elder Llewelyn Harris that it would not fail until other food arrived, had inexplicably remained about a quarter full—five or six pounds at most. Yet from that small amount of flour had come slapjacks and bread for all of them every day for nearly a month, and all were well aware of the miraculous nature of the food. Yes, Jim Davis thought, it would be wonderful to enjoy a little diversity.

"Long time no eat," Henry Harriman added for emphasis.

For a moment the old man stared at them, and then with vigor he began shaking his head. "Long time no eat? White man on river long time no eat. Long time! Heap hungry."

"Long time no eat," Henry Harriman repeated, not grasping what the old man had just told him. "One moon, two moons, only little bit bread. White men come, white men bring food to Montezuma Creek."

"No savvy," old Peeagament replied sadly as he shook his head in frustration. "Heap no savvy." Then without another word he pulled a crumpled piece of paper from his pouch and handed it to the hungry white people.

"What is it, Pa?" Edward F. Davis asked eagerly. "What's it say?"

Carefully Jim Davis smoothed out the paper, the old Pahute for the moment forgotten. Quickly he scanned the page, and all watched as his shoulders seemed to sag a little at the news.

"Jim?"

"It's a letter from a fellow name of Platte Lyman," Jim Davis replied, ignoring his wife. "I reckon we'd all better hear what he has to say. Slowly then, he read:

Elder James L. Davis
Montezuma Fort
San Juan Mission, San Juan

Dear Brother Davis:

This is to inform you that this day the San Juan Mission Company reached the San Juan, and, unable to continue on up the river to your location, have designated a townsite here and we have named it "Bluff City." We are very worn out, and our food supply is low. But we are instructed to send a generous portion of what we have to you, at the out post of this mission.

We therefore have dispatched this food supply to you, by those of the company who, having drawn blank slips in the land lottery here, will go on to the Montezuma settlement and live near you.

May God bless and prosper you in your faithful labors.

> *Your brother in the gospel:*
>
> *Platte DeAlton Lyman*
> *First Counselor to Silas S. Smith*
> *President of the San Juan Mission*

"So they aren't coming here?" Mary Davis breathed, a stricken look on her face.

"Not all of them, at least." Jim Davis and Henry Harriman looked at each other, and then at the old Indian.

"Mary, would you and Elizabeth give the old man a drink and a bit of bread? Brother Harriman and I are going to be hitching up the wagon and taking a short trip downriver. You boys keep a sharp eye on things, you hear? We should see you long before tomorrow night."

And with exhausted and faltering steps the two set out to capture their team and harness it to their one remaining wagon.

73

Saturday, May 1, 1880

South Bank, San Juan River

Natanii nééz, the tall Navajo who now carried the *belacani* name of Frank, sat his horse in the gray gloom of dawn staring down off the bluff. Below him and across the big river the canvas tops of the Mormon wagons were just becoming visible, though scattered across the flat as they now were, he knew that many remained hidden by *tíis,* the cottonwoods.

In the far northeast lightning flashed silently—which in the words of Frank's father was caused by the *yei* venting their wrath against the earth. In Frank's mind he believed that this was so, but he also knew it was what was left of a storm that the mountains had not killed during the night. Now the storm's offspring, increasingly less violent, was slowly turning into a female rain that was gently drenching the earth beneath the collapsing clouds, blessing whoever happened to live in that distant country.

Beside Frank, Hoskanini Begay's horse nickered impatiently, and when Frank turned to say something he finally noticed that Bitseel's saddle was empty and that Hoskanini Begay was silently holding the reins to the other young man's mount. Looking further, Frank located the missing one standing on a rise of ground some distance away, blessing the soon-to-be-rising sun with a pinch of pollen from his *jish,* the sacred medicine bundle he wore around his neck.

With a grunt of satisfaction Frank turned back to continue staring off the bluff. These two young men were his relatives, part of his 'born for' clan, which was the main reason he had experienced little

605

difficulty in talking them into joining him. And though he was older and much wiser than either of them, it secretly pleased him that Bitseel was following the traditional way. That meant there was *hózhó,* balance in the young man's universe, and that could only be good for Frank.

Faintly the sound of bawling cattle came to the ears of the three Navajos, and in the growing light they could make out someone on horseback, obviously *belacani* by the way he rode, moving a small herd of livestock eastward away from the wagons. Dagai Iletso, old Yellow Whiskers, had told Frank these Mormon *belacani* had many more cattle than this, yes, and many horses as well, and that all of these animals were being pastured on the sandhills and in the great washes north and west of the crossing where they had camped.

"Do you see them?" Hoskanini Begay asked suddenly, inter-rupting Frank's thoughts. "The *béégashii,* the cows, are being taken toward the bluff." And unconsciously he indicated the direction with a twitch of his lips.

"I see them," Frank responded. "Do you see, nephew, that these *belacani* have come unwanted into *Diné Tah,* the sacred homeland of the People? And do you see that their *béégashii* are now eating all of the new grass that the cloud people and the rain people have grown for our own flocks and herds?"

"It is said that old Yellow Whiskers has many hundreds of his sheep and goats across the river near that place," Bitseel declared as he stepped back onto his horse. "I have not heard it said that they are going hungry."

"But very soon they will be," Frank declared, wanting the young men beside him to understand. "When the sun grows hot and the land turns thirsty, there will be no more grass for Dagai Iletso and his flocks and herds. Why? Because those *belacani* cows will have consumed it all. It is why we must drive these people away from this place."

"We are only three, my uncle."

Frank made the sign that he knew this was so. "There will be others of the *Diné* who will join us," he was quick to add, "all we will need. But at the first, *hazhó o'go,* we must go about this thing carefully. We must see that the *belacani* think we are friends. We must smile and laugh and make a great show of our friendship. In that way we can take from them when they are not aware and become very wealthy, with many horses and many fine things. In this manner our people will begin to recover what Rope Thrower and the army took from them when they were driven to *Bosque Redondo.*"

"Would it not be better just to make a raid?" Bitseel asked quietly.

"If there were more of us, perhaps. But for now there are no more, my nephew, and so this is the best way for us to go."

"It is said that these people are *asdzáán,* old women," Hoskanini Begay sneered as he watched the new settlement in the morning light, "and that even *baa' yázhi,* little warrior girl, could kill them."

Frank chuckled without mirth, thinking once again of the young man he and his friend Peokon had so easily slain so many years before. "What has been said is certainly true," he declared with great arrogance. "These mormonee *belacani* are very easy to kill!"

Yet even as his words left his lips, Frank found himself shuddering, for in his mind, suddenly, was a picture of the hollow, wasted, empty frame of Peokon lying dead in his forked-stick hogan as his woman's people had prepared it for burning. Yes, and also in Frank's mind was a picture of *bináá dootízhi,* the clear-eyed one called Thales Haskell, who Frank knew positively was *yenaldolooshi,* the witch or skinwalker who had stolen Peokon's life.

That one, he thought as he savagely yanked his horse around to ride away from the bluff, was to be avoided at all costs. But if he were not with these others, well then—

And Frank, still riding hard, was once again smiling with the thought of all that he and the men of the *Diné* were about to do.

---o–o–o---

The Sandhills, North of Bluff City

"Howdy, Curly. Mighty purty span of mules."

Curly Bill Jenkins grinned at his former boss. "Howdy yourownself, Bill Ball. They are purty critters, ain't they. Spud figures they belong to the Mormon folks what've settled yonder on the San Juan."

"Must've wandered some, to get to Hudson's range."

"Not likely. I reckon they was took by one of them no-account Pahutes."

"Not Navajo or white man?" Bill Ball asked.

"Naw!" Curly was adamant. "Navajo care for their stock. Was it them took these mules, they'd still have 'em. White man would've sold 'em—that or kept going with 'em clean out of the country. Pahutes, now, they're a rag-tag bunch what either gamble away or just plain lose anything and everything they get their hands on. That's why I figure these critters was took by Pahutes."

"And now you get to return 'em."

Curly's grin grew even wider. "That's on account of we heard them Mormons on the river have some handsome single women among 'em. Being as how Spud allowed I was the handsomest among us, he and the boys figured I had the onliest and best shot at making a little time with one of them women. So clean shirt, fancy rig and all, here I am."

Bill Ball laughed easily. "So I see. Tell me, Curly, how you getting along with Mr. Hudson?"

For a moment Curly stared ahead between the ears of his horse, wondering how best to respond. After all, Bill Ball had been the best trail segundo he'd ever had, bar none, and it didn't seem right speaking good things and so saying something to the man that wasn't altogether true. On the other hand, Spud Hudson had his good points, too, and Curly didn't feel right about slighting him, either.

"Well," he finally drawled, deciding to try and sit both sides of the fence, "besides being one of the most cantankerous, ornery, mule-stubborn sons I ever met, with enough verbal lather when he gets his back up to soap this whole blamed country and still have enough left over to set up a store and sell it, ol' Spud's not a bad sort. We eat well, we sleep regular if not enough, the pay ain't bad, and like you, Bill, he carries his own weight—least when he ain't talking. So I reckon I'm getting along all right."

Shrewdly Bill Ball looked at his grizzled younger riding companion. "You'll do, Curly," he declared at last, impressed by the man's honest loyalty. "You'll do. Had it bin me instead of Mr. Lacy running the LC when we brought that last Texas herd in, you wouldn't have been sent riding the grub line. I want you should know that."

Touched deeply, Curly gulped. "Thanks, Bill. I . . . uh . . . Well dawgone if one of them ornery Mormon mule critters ain't thrown up something into my eye!"

"They'll do that," Bill responded with a soft chuckle while he purposely looked away.

"Where's the rest of the old outfit?" Curly growled after another moment or so of silence while he vigorously rubbed his eyes, making a show of getting something out.

"Most of 'em went back to Texas, Curly, and I ain't heard much since. I did get a letter from the Greenhorn Kid, who said he was riding for Charlie Goodnight out of Palo Duro Canyon and was figuring on the old man turning him into a real hand. I reckon he might, at that. Course the Comanch stayed with me, on account of even Mr. Lacy couldn't have made him go."

"Where's he at now?" Curly Bill asked, glancing nervously around. "That old Indian makes me nervouser'n a chippy in church the way he's always sneaking here and there, popping up out of nowhere and grinning at you with that toothless smile like he'd just as soon cut your throat and could have done it anyhow happen he'd only took the notion. Yes sir, he's one hombre who can make an icicle feel feverish."

"He could," Bill chuckled again, "and that's a fact. Only I reckon he won't, at least not no more. I come on him one morning back in February, maybe March, during that real cold spell we had, and the old man had sloped on up to his happy hunting grounds."

"He died?" Curly couldn't hide his surprise.

"He did, for a fact. Of natural causes, too. But he left a sand drawing for me of a notched horseshoe, which give me to know that no-good sidewinding murderer Sugar Bob Hazelton was still in the country. Mrs. Lacy thought he might be, and she asked me to find him and bring him to justice when she came up with her family the Brumleys after Mr. Lacy was killed. But since she went back to Texas, the Brumleys've been running the outfit with me as segundo, and I just ain't had no time. Then a few days back someone else spotted that notched shoe off west of here, the Brumleys give the order, and I've been cutting for sign ever since."

"You figure he's in Bluff City?"

"Not hardly, not that polecat. Them Mormon folks wouldn't put up with his low-down shenanigans. Thing is, I heard the Mormons'd organized us a county already, with a probate judge, a whole slew of selectmen, and even a tax collector."

"Spud heard that, too." Curly grinned at the memory. "He was fit to be tied just thinking on it, figuring for certain he was about to be taxed plumb to death. I reckon he will be, too, or nearly so. Since then he ain't stopped talking about selling out."

Bill nodded. "It'd give any outfit pause, especially happen they been swinging too wide a loop and maybe have more cows than they think they have. Anyhow, this morning I got to thinking that I ought to drop in on them Mormon folks and find out who the new county sheriff is, if they even appointed one, and maybe invite him along on my hunt for that skunk Hazelton."

"You sure a Mormon sheriff would be up to it?" Curly was obviously dubious. "I mean, Sugar Bob's a sure-enough bad'un who'll come out shooting no matter who tracks him down. Thing is, Bill, I been told sky pilots don't usually hold with gunplay—especially Mormon ones."

"Curly," Bill replied seriously, "if them Mormon folks came into this country the way I hear they did, blasting a road through that rocky land west of here and surviving on the trail through the whole turrible winter we've just endured, well, they've got hair enough on their briskets to satisfy this old son and a hundred others just like me. Happen one of 'em's been made sheriff and wants to go along on this little man hunt, I'd welcome the company and do my best to warn Sugar Bob he'd best start running, pronto."

"It's rough country they came through, is it?"

Bill nodded. "Mighty rough, worse than any I've ever seen, including the *Llano Estacado* or Staked Plains and the *Jornado del Muerto*. And tell the truth, Curly, I ain't even been to the worst of it, where those Mormon folks cut through to the Colorado and out the other side. I've only heard about it, and that sceered me plumb silly."

Curly Bill whistled. "Maybe I'd best have second thoughts about them Mormon women."

"On account of maybe one'd be too much for you?"

Curly Bill Jenkins grinned beneath his mustaches. "Not hardly, Bill. On account of maybe I'd ought to raise my sights and try for two or three. Looks to me like them Mormon menfolk are right as rain about polygamy. Women like that, young and purty and withal tough as bootleather and as hard to wear out, well, a man couldn't possibly have too many."

And with a wild whoop of joyful exuberance, Curly kicked his horse, yanked the mules' lines, and at a lope led the way down through Cow Canyon toward Bluff City, Territory of Utah.

———o—o—o———

Bluff City

"Wagh!" the youth Posey breathed in amazement as he watched the earth being lifted and turned over by George Ipson's plow. The white man was following behind two oxen, expertly working the reins and the two handles of his equipment. Posey had heard of plows, especially those being used to tear up the land under the fool Nathan Meeker's direction before the warrior Canala had put him under the grass, but he'd never seen one in operation. This plow, though he didn't know it, was being used by Ipson to loosen the earth on the last end of the ditch that would bring water from the San Juan to irrigate the newly sprouted and already thirsty crops.

"See, my brother," Posey said without looking at Beogah, "how it *ticki,* how it eats *tee-weep,* the earth?"

Beogah, who sat his bony horse beside the equally scraggly mount of his elder brother, grunted amiably. "Eats and spits it out again, as though it is *puck-kon-gah,* sick."

Laughing at the comparison, Posey kneed his pony and rode toward the scattered wagons that had been parked on what the mormonee were calling their town lots. Posey had heard the words but had absolutely no idea of their meaning. He'd also heard the name Bluff City when Bill Hutchings had suggested it in the white man's *at-am-bar,* his council, many days before, but as yet he hadn't understood it as the name of the white community. In fact, he didn't comprehend community at all but only encampment, and this great encampment of the white mormonee both amazed and troubled him.

His amazement, of course, or at least most of it, stemmed from the great wealth of these people. To Posey, the accumulation of such things as horses, guns, and white man clothing had always meant wealth. But now in every wagon he saw an array of other items, things he understood not at all, that nevertheless denoted such wealth as he could hardly dream of.

He'd seen chickens at Mitchell's trading post, so they were not new. But he'd never seen pigs, and he and Beogah had watched them by the hour since the arrival of the mormonee, laughing at their foolish antics. He'd never seen beehives and was terrified of them, had seen but never paid attention to furniture, and still could not imagine that people would intentionally choose to sit in chairs and at tables rather than on the earth. He was in awe of oil lamps, little fires that could be controlled at will, and of the scattered canvas tents, the white wickiups in which many of the mormonee lived. Even in the wind these were not drafty like the brush and hide wickiups he was used to, and already he was thinking of how he might obtain such a wickiup for himself.

But it was the myriad little things these mormonee possessed that truly gnawed at Posey's mind. Candle makers and holders, quill pens and ink bottles, butter churns, steel chains and tools, combs, hand mirrors, books, paper, tinware, silverware, china, crystal—in fact, many of these signs of great wealth were always on display at one particular wagon beneath a wide canvas cover. Posey could hardly keep away from it.

Now, almost of its own volition his mount moved in that direction, and Posey found himself grunting with satisfaction. There were so many things there that would increase his own wealth, his own power. Already he had taken for himself a silver fork, and though he had no idea how to use it, he considered it a great treasure, one that Beogah and others truly envied. Unfortunately he had lost it to Polk, the old grizzly, in a game of *ducki* a few days before, but even that did not trouble the young warrior. He would simply take another, or perhaps two of them.

Posey broke into a wide grin. These white mormonee were *katz-te-suah,* they were such utter fools. They smiled and laughed all the time, they gave no thought to protecting themselves or their wealth, they went about unarmed and defenseless—this seemed especially true of the tall, bony white squaw of the wagon where all the wealth was displayed—she, her new papoose, and the small man who wore glass before his *poo-ye,* his eyes, and who was her mate. Posey was certain the squaw and her weak mate had no idea he had taken the silver fork from their table, but even so it gave him no concern. Certainly their smiles toward him had not diminished, their kind words had not ended, and their willingness to give him bread or biscuits was just as great. They thought him *tig-a-boo,* a great friend, when all along he was a warrior of the People, an enemy who was gaining power over them—

But now as Posey rode closer to the wagon of the tall woman he lost his grin, for the troubling thing about these mormonee and their encampment forced itself again into his mind. Though he had tried it was not *katz-shu-mi,* it was not forgotten; neither could he *pesuds away,* gain an understanding of it.

Though there were no words in his language for it, what the youth was troubled by was a feeling that came over him whenever he drew particularly near to any of these strange white people. He had thought about it for days on end, and still it made no sense to him. Yet it was there, the sense that despite his personal loathing for the foolish mormonee, despite his disdain for their womanly ways, and despite the fact that he could take their wealth from them almost at will, these people continued to have power over him.

Posey could tell this because he could see it in their eyes, he could hear it in the sounds of their voices. Had he had the words to ask them, even that would have done no good. No, for in response these *tsharr* would have used words such as pure love, or the inspiration and guidance of the Holy Spirit. These words, important to them, would have meant no more to Posey than the word *feeling,* which meant nothing at all.

And as for the feelings themselves, which seemed to Posey more like a weakling's yearning after these mormonee than a manlike hatred of them, he was continually of two minds. Like a true warrior he wanted to take Mike's big gun and put them all under the grass, and yet at the same time he somehow wanted to join them, learn from them, and finally become like them. It was an awful desire that seemed to grow worse whenever he was around the mormonee or their encampment, and so Posey grew more and more determined to come to grips with it, to overpower it, and finally to subject it to his own mighty will!

—◇—◇—◇—

It was hot, and as she wiped her forehead with a corner of the baby's blanket, Eliza glanced out from beneath the canvas awning to see by the shadows how late in the day it was. Somewhere between five and six in the afternoon, she thought—time to be up and out of her chair and seeing to the business of something for her and Billy to eat. Not quite yet, though. Not until her sweet, precious son, whom she and Billy had named William in honor of his father, had finished his own meal.

"Dear God in heaven," she prayed for the thousandth time as she watched her infant child contentedly suckle at her breast, "I thank thee for bringing this little one into my life. I thank thee for giving me both him and my darling Billy. Please bless both him and me that we can be up to the task of rearing little Willy here in righteous-ness—"

"Afternoon, Eliza. How are you feeling?"

"First rate, Mary." Eliza smiled warmly. "I'm just sitting here thinking what a fortunate woman I am. Mercy sakes alive! Have you ever seen such a beautiful creature as this little child?"

Mary Jones stooped and lightly kissed the back of the baby's head. "Not hardly. Look how he has Billy's eyes."

"And *my* disposition. I declare, I never heard such caterwauling as he put out last night. You'd have thought he was starving to death and I was doing it to him a'purpose."

Mary nodded. "I do believe I heard him all the way over in my wagon. It made me think twice about having any babies of my own. Of course, Kumen didn't hear him, so he's still set on having a fam-ily, and I don't know that I can dissuade him."

"Or would want to. So, Kumen is back from cutting logs?"

614

Mary's look immediately brightened. "He is, last night, as a matter of fact. They've cut down dozens of trees, mostly cottonwood, and he feels they'll be able to put up thirty, maybe even forty cabins this summer. So, a good share of us will be able to spend the winter a little more snugly than we did this past winter in these drafty old wagon-boxes."

Eliza glanced at her own, which had once again been removed from the running gears so it could rest directly on the ground. "This lowering of the wagon-box was helpful last winter on the Escalante Desert," she declared sadly. "But now, I don't know. I've never seen so many red ants and scorpions and other pests. Something or other is hiding under everything I move aside in that wagon. I'm beginning to think we'd have been better off leaving things up on wheels."

"Cabins won't be much better, then."

"Not likely."

Mary sighed. "Have you noticed the wind and the dust?"

Eliza grimaced. "Noticed? I swan, Mary. The wind only stops at night, and dust is at least half of what I eat. I remember my father teasing me when I was small, telling me I was eating at least eight tons of earth and rocks every day. It took me years to understand his joke. But in this place I believe he could be taken literally. I keep little Willy's head covered so he can breathe clean air, and then I worry myself silly thinking maybe he's suffocating. We seem to have picked a very interesting place for a settlement."

Mary smiled. "Well, at least Platte hit water with his well, at sixteen feet. Hopefully it will be a little more clear than that river water."

"And better tasting, I hope. Is his well all rocked in?"

Mary nodded. "As of yesterday. He figures we'll be able to start taking water out of it by tomorrow, which will be a great relief. Once that's finished, he plans on returning to the settlements to get his wife and new son."

"I can't wait to meet her. Married to Brother Lyman as she is, I would suppose she's simply wonderful."

"She'll no doubt say the same about you, Eliza Foreman, and it will be the truth. How's work on the ditch coming? Does Billy say much?"

"He's worried, Mary. The ditch is coming along as well as can be expected, but the soil is so sandy Billy thinks it may not hold water. Then too, the San Juan is already dropping rapidly, and Billy says we may not get any water out of it at all."

"I hope he's wrong, Eliza. If we don't get crops this year, I truly don't know how any of us will survive. One winter without food is enough to wear down the strongest of constitutions."

"Mary," Eliza said quietly after a moment or two of silent contemplation, "those Indian boys were here again."

Carefully Mary took a seat on the chair by the table. "I know. I kept Kumen's glass on them the whole time you were feeding them those biscuits. I believe they have a hankering for china and such."

"Yes, and I'm perfectly convinced they're the ones who took my silver fork. But mercy sakes, Mary, what's a body to do? Or feel? I'd be more than happy to give those things to them, but when they simply take them without so much as a by-your-leave, then I get all filled with anger and want to order them to get away and stay away for good! But that's no way to be a missionary, Mary. Is it, do you think?"

"I don't rightly know, Eliza. Kumen feels that we must teach them accountability as well as right from wrong, but that until we do they're innocent of any offense toward God. I suppose that means we shouldn't take offense either."

Eliza nodded thoughtfully. "I'm certain you're right. It's just that—well, I feel awfully excitable when they're around, my heart pounding and my stomach tight with—well, to be honest about it, I'm absolutely terrified! Of course, that makes me feel guilty, for of a truth I ought to be filled with the joy of knowing I've been called to bring the light of the gospel into their desperate lives. But instead I feel fear, Mary, and I don't wish to feel so. They're such nice, quiet young men, watching everything I do, and they're fast learners, too. I've shown them how to eat properly, and the smaller one—I think he says his name is Posey, which seems a perfectly innocent name to me—seems especially adept at it. I believe with a little time I will most certainly be able to develop a friendship, particularly with him."

"Yes," Mary smiled, "I'm certain you will. But do be careful, Eliza, especially when Billy isn't around."

"Oh, rest assured that I will."

Standing, Mary reached out and took Eliza's hand. "Well, I'm pleased to see you up and around. On account of your age and the hard birth, some of the sisters have been worried. But I've been telling them right along how strong you are, and that you'll probably outlive all the rest of us put together. By the by, are you satisfied with your town lot?"

Gathering her baby and pulling her dress back over herself, Eliza took her crutch and pulled herself to her feet. "I am, Mary. I think it's a wonderful lot, and Billy says the acres we drew for farming are some of the best. I hear some of the others are dissatisfied, though, and are thinking of moving along. I hope that doesn't happen."

Eliza hobbled to the edge of the awning and gazed with Mary at the bluffs to the north, now bathed golden red in the late afternoon sun. "Isn't it beautiful? Can you imagine that we're blessed to be able to call this our home?"

"I can't," the younger woman said quietly. "Dust, bugs, bad water, wild Indians—it doesn't matter, Eliza. Already I love this place, and I'm so thankful to finally be here!"

Wiping sudden tears from her eyes, Eliza agreed. "We'll be staying, too," she breathed. "This is the land God called Billy and me to settle. I know it, for even now the Lord, through the Holy Ghost, is giving me a witness of it."

Tightly she pressed her tiny son to her cheek. "Oh, Mary, I've never in my life been so happy!"

Silently Mary nodded. "I think I know how you feel. Look," she said then as she pointed eastward, "here comes Billy!" And then she watched, smiling, as Billy hurried through the dirt and weeds to a beaming Eliza and their little Willy, took them both into his arms, and crutch and all turned them in a joyfully spontaneous jig.

Yes, Mary thought as she turned happily toward her own wagons and tent, Bluff City was going to be a wonderful place to live!

EPILOGUE

Thursday, June 10, 1880

St. George, Territory of Utah

Despite the earliness of the hour it was hot, so hot that Erastus Snow was already pausing in his work to wipe the sweat from his brow. Leaning on the handle of his hoe, he glanced at the azure sky, knowing already that he would see no clouds and knowing too that within the hour he would be forced indoors and out of the oppressive heat. Yet a good portion of the garden was now weeded, and perhaps in the morning he could take care of the rest of it.

Not quite sixty-two years of age, the Mormon apostle's hair had turned white, but otherwise there was no indication of his advancing years. His back remained straight and his mind clear, and he liked to think that he was filled with as much energy and vigor as he'd been on February 12, 1849, the day of his calling to the holy apostleship.

Now, though, as he lifted his hat and wiped his brow, he knew that heat rather than age was about to drive him indoors—there, and in another week or so into the Pine Valley Mountains to the north where the temperatures were cooler and a man could get some decent work done no matter the time of day. After all, it was—

"Brother Snow?"

"Yes, James?" he asked, looking up to see his secretary standing on the stoop.

"I was going through the materials in the packet that came from Salt Lake City during the night, and there's a letter here from Platte

Lyman, marked Bluff City, San Juan County. I thought you'd want to know, sir."

Erastus Snow nodded. "Thank you. I'll be right in."

Moving thoughtfully, Elder Snow walked to the garden shed and put away the hoe, his mind filled with thoughts of the expedition. Of a truth, he'd been aware of their progress right from the day of their departure, perhaps moreso because he knew well most of the missionaries involved. Aware of the difficulties they'd encountered, he'd taken the responsibility for it upon his own shoulders, and he'd spent long hours studying the things that had gone wrong and the dangerous decisions that had been made. He'd also tried to learn from them in case others were ever sent forth in a similar manner. And he'd spent hours in prayer, pleading with the Lord to bless and preserve them and send angels to minister to their temporal and spiritual needs.

The week before, he'd visited half a night with Pap Redd, who'd returned early from the expedition to discover, quite happily, that all his children who'd been sick with diphtheria had recovered. From Brother Redd, he'd learned detail after detail of the struggles and suffering of the company, and at times he'd been reduced to tears just hearing the narration. Yet he'd learned as well of the pioneers' personal growth and increasing closeness to one another. And it was these things, Elder Snow reflected as he removed his boots and entered the rear door of his home, that were his witness to the rightness of the expedition itself, and to the benevolent hand of a loving God who would always bless his children in their extremities.

"Bluff City," he said thoughtfully as he opened the thick letter. "That's a change from Montezuma Fort, all right."

Seating himself, the apostle began reading, and soon his anxious expression was turning into a wide smile. "It seems they didn't make it all the way to the fort, James. Platte writes that though George Hobbs and a few others have joined the Harrimans and Davises or gone on into Colorado and points beyond, practically every last one of the company ground to a halt on the first level bottomland they came to—about eighteen miles shy of Montezuma Creek. They're building their homes there, plowing the ground and digging a canal, and Bill Hutchings of Beaver came up with the name of Bluff City on account of the high bluffs that rim their little community."

Quickly he continued reading. "Well, well. Nathanial and Emma Decker brought forth the first child born in Bluff City on April 12th, just six days after their arrival. They named him Morris. Oh, and Billy and Eliza Foreman have had a baby boy as well, whom they're calling little Will. My, my. And to think of how old Sister Eliza is. Miracles never cease, do they, James.

"They've already had a death in the company, too, on May 4th. Father Roswell Stevens, veteran of the War between the States, is thought to have died from the hardships of the journey. Well then, I say he has secured a place of honor in the realms of glory, for he has sacrificed his life in obedience to the word of the Lord. Platte writes that because they had no nearby timber, Father Stevens's coffin was made from the boards of the very wagon-box that carried his goods to the San Juan. How very fitting, don't you think, James?"

Silently the man nodded.

"Good," Elder Snow declared as he continued reading. "A Sunday School has been organized with James Decker as superintendent. Jens Nielson has been called as presiding high priest, and Kumen Jones has been appointed superintendent of the public schools. Oh, and Captain Silas Smith has finally joined them. He's acting not only as mission president but also as probate judge of San Juan County, which appointment was given him by the state legislature. Platte D. Lyman, Jens Nielson, and Zachariah Decker are selectmen, Charlie Walton, Sr., is the probate clerk, and Lemuel Redd has been appointed assessor and tax collector. Well, they'll all do a fine job.

"Other than that, Platte writes that all are busy planting crops, building cabins, working on the canal, and in general establishing their homes. Oh, and they've already been in contact with representatives of both the Navajos and the Pahutes, and things seem peaceable. In fact, it seems that two young Pahute fellows have practically moved in with them, they are present so frequently, and so prospects for the work of the mission look promising."

Laying aside the letter, Elder Snow leaned back and laced his fingers behind his head. "Well, James," he said as his eyes took on a faraway look and a smile creased his face, "I'd say those good folks on the San Juan are in dire need of a visit from the Lord's servants. Get hold of Brigham Young, Jr., will you, and see if he's willing to accompany me to Bluff City in, say, one month's time." Slowly Elder Snow's smile grew even wider. "No, sir, I can think of nothing I'd rather spend the summer and fall doing than taking up a visit with those dear friends of mine out in the San Juan country."

———o—o—o———

Fall, 1880

To Montezuma, San Juan County Utah September 5th 1880. President Silas S. Smith, Platte D. Lyman and the Saints located and called to locate on the San Juan.

Dear Brethren,

After viewing the facilities for settlement on this river . . . we feel to congratulate you on being the pioneers in opening up this region for civilization; and for the establishing of practical missionary labor among the Utes and Navajos, this being central and neutral ground between them.

While the Indians appear friendly and satisfied with our efforts to establish settlements here, yet with the unsettled condition of Indian affairs in Colorado and New Mexico, with the well known fact that there are small predatory bands of renegade Indians liable to prey on defenseless persons, as well as lawless adventurers from among the whites, we therefore deem it a matter of common prudence that in the incipient stages of your settlement, your temporary dwellings should be in close proximity to each other.

*Wherever practicable we would recommend that you build in the form of a hollow square and close up spaces between your dwellings with a stockade."**

---

* Norma Palmer Blankenagel, *Portrait of Our Past: A History of Monticello Utah Stake (Formerly San Juan Stake),* pp. 33–34. This is a portion of an actual letter to the people of Bluff City from Elders Snow and Young, following their visit in August of 1880.

---o-o-o---

Author's Note

This has been a work of historical fiction. Though all the characters in this work except three existed historically, every one has been rendered fictitious through the construction of dialogue, circumstances, situations, and in some cases even personalities. The characters of Billy and Eliza Foreman are entirely fictitious, as are all circumstances where their lives are interwoven with the historical members of the Hole-in-the-Rock expedition. Sugar Bob Hazelton is a composite of several shadowy outlaws and badmen who inhabited the Four Corners area during the late nineteenth century—and who forgot to leave their actual names behind when they departed or were buried.

That said, the San Juan Mission expedition was a historical event adequately documented by several of its participants as well as the church that sponsored them. So, too, were many of the events participated in by the Pahutes, the Navajos, and some of the cattlemen. The dates used in the story, the various participants, the unbelievable locations, the extreme weather conditions, even some of the dialogue—all these were either recorded by the participants or reflect with as much accuracy as possible what actually happened on those particular dates during the winter of 1879–1880 as the various historical characters converged upon each other in the San Juan country of southeastern Utah Territory. I obtained this information from journals, published texts, interviews, family histories, newspapers, and every other source I and others could track down. From these sources and documents, I have attempted to portray the people as they apparently were, and to reflect, through the fictitious thoughts, feelings, and actions of Billy and Eliza Foreman, the attitudes and experiences of every member of the missionary company as well as the individuals who already lived in the country of the San Juan.

I would like to express my deep admiration of, and appreciation for, the people I have written of. I can't begin to comprehend the sacrifices made by the Mormon people of the San Juan missionary expedition, and I stand in awe of every one of them. I am likewise in awe of the people who already inhabited the country: Navajo, Pahute, and cattleman. As I have studied their cultures, their thoughts, and their beliefs, I have caught a glimmer of what life must have looked like through their eyes. They were peoples already established, with lives attuned to the earth or their work and thoughts geared to more than mere survival in that difficult land. There they prospered when they could, warred with each other when they had to or when opportunities arose, loved and reared families to whom they passed along their beliefs and the traditions of their fathers, and lived richly and even occasionally beautifully.

Who cannot admire such people? Who, having examined their lives, stood on the harsh but beautiful land where they lived, and gazed at their distant and lonely graves, cannot but feel awe and admiration for them and their accomplishments? I do, and I hope it has been reflected in my work.

Book 2 of the *Hearts Afire* series, *Fort on the Firing Line,* will continue the saga of Billy and Eliza Foreman, Posey and his band, Navajo Frank, Sugar Bob Hazelton, and the various other inhabitants of the country of the San Juan.

Annotated Bibliography

Abbott, E. C. (Teddy Blue), and Helena Huntington Smith. *We Pointed Them North: Recollections of a Cowpuncher.* Norman: University of Oklahoma Press, 1982. A very readable first-person account of driving herds of Texas cattle north into Montana, and of subsequent adventures there.

Acton, Zelma. *Oral History.* Interviews conducted by Deborah Fellbaum and Shirley E. Stephenson. Utah State Historical Society and California State University, Fullerton, Oral History Program, Southeastern Utah Project, 1972, 1974. Zelma Acton gives much information about the Utes and their customs.

Adams, Allie, and Lloyd Adams. *Oral History.* Interviews concerning Jens and Kirsten Nielson, conducted by Deborah Fellbaum. Utah State Historical Society and California State University, Fullerton, Oral History Program, Southeastern Utah Project, 1972.

Adams, Ramon F. *Western Words: A Dictionary of the American West.* Norman: University of Oklahoma Press, 1981.

Askins, Charles, *Texans, Guns, and History.* New York: Bonanza Books, 1970. Contains considerable information about the Texans who may or may not have made their way into the San Juan country during their flights from the law.

Baker, Pearl. *Posey the Pahute.* Unpublished manuscript, 1986. This manuscript contains a brief history of anglo/Indian relationships in the nineteenth century, as well as much information about Posey.

Blankenagel, Norma Palmer. *Portrait of Our Past: A History of Monticello Utah Stake (Formerly San Juan Stake), 1882–1988.* Private publication, 1988. This volume contains numerous photographs, historical anecdotes, and summarizations. The interesting format is topical rather than chronological, making the historical flow difficult to follow.

Carter, Kate B., comp. *Heart Throbs of the West.* 12 vols. Salt Lake City: Daughters of Utah Pioneers, 1951. These volumes, as well as all other DUP publications, contain numerous journals, diaries, and reminiscences of the Pioneer West and its people.

Carter, Kate B., comp. *Our Pioneer Heritage.* 20 vols. Salt Lake City: Daughters of Utah Pioneers, 1958.

Crabtree, Lamont J., *The Incredible Mission: The Hole-in-the-Rock Expedition/San*

Juan Mission Story and Trail Guide. Private publication, 1980. Lamont Crabtree uses numerous photographs and maps to describe each portion of the trail as it was in 1880 and then as it appears today. He lists the members of the expedition, omitting some of the names given by David E. Miller but including names Miller does not give. Crabtree also lists the ages of the expedition participants.

Dary, David. *Cowboy Culture: A Saga of Five Centuries.* New York: Avon Books, 1981. Contains some good information on trail herds and the art of driving cattle.

Gottfredson, Peter. *Indian Depredations in Utah.* Salt Lake City: Private printing, 1969. Contains an interesting vocabulary of the Ute dialect as it was understood by early Mormon scouts and Indian missionaries.

Hafen, LeRoy R., ed. *Colorado and Its People: A Narrative and Topical History of the Centennial State.* New York: Lewis Historical Publishing Co., 1948. Dr. Hafen provides excellent accounts of the Thornburgh Battle with the Utes and the killing of Indian agent Nathan Meeker and the Ute capture of his wife, daughter, and others.

Hurst, Michael Terry. *Posey.* Unpublished screenplay, 1977. Written from Posey's perspective, this fictionalized account is based entirely on known historical events.

Jenson, Andrew. *Church Chronology.* Salt Lake City: Deseret News Press, 1899.

Jones, Francis W. *Oral History.* Interview conducted by Pat Whitaker. Utah State Historical Society and California State University, Fullerton, Oral History Program, Southeastern Utah Project, 1972. Francis Jones describes experiences of his parents, Kumen and Mary Jones, at the Hole; discusses some interesting aspects of polygamy; and gives considerable information about his parents' Navajo acquaintances.

Kelly, Charles. "Chief Hoskaninni." *Utah Historical Quarterly,* July 1953. An excellent account of the ways and mannerisms of this powerful Navajo headman.

Lavender, David. *One Man's West.* 3rd ed. Lincoln: University of Nebraska Press, 1977. A wonderful, first-person account of life as a working cowboy in and near the San Juan country of Utah and Colorado.

Lyman, Albert R. *Aunt Jody.* Serialized in the *Improvement Era,* 1958, 1959, 1960. An account of the life and accomplishments of Josephine Chatterly Wood, pioneer nurse and doctor for San Juan County.

———. *Dick Butt, Sheriff of San Juan: Stories of Willard George William Butt.* Unpublished Manuscript, 1957. Details many of Dick Butt's experiences as a Hole-in-the-Rock pioneer and frontier lawman.

———. *History of Blanding, 1905–1955.* Private publication, 1955. Written to commemorate the fiftieth anniversary of the city of Blanding, Utah, this is mainly a reminiscence.

———. *Indians and Outlaws: Settling of the San Juan Frontier.* Salt Lake City: Bookcraft, 1962. It is impossible to say enough about the prolific work of Albert Robinson Lyman. The son of Hole-in-the-Rock expedition leader Platte DeAlton Lyman, he was carried as a baby over the treacherous road by his mother during the summer of 1880. During his ninety-six years of life he not only helped pioneer San Juan County, including being the first white settler of the community that is now called Blanding, but he also knew or was acquainted with practically every resident of the county, Mormon, Indian, or Texan. He authored numerous books and articles about these people, almost all of which have been published.

———. *The Last Fort.* Serialized as "Fort on the Firing Line" in the *Improvement Era,* 1948, 1949, 1950. Written from the Mormon perspective, this is an account of the up-and-down relationship between the Mormons, the Navajos, and the Pahutes of San Juan County.

———. *Man to Man (Voice of the Intangible).* Salt Lake City: Deseret Book Co., 1962. A fictionalized account of the author's youth in wild San Juan County.

———. *The Outlaw of Navajo Mountain.* Salt Lake City: Deseret Book Co., 1963. A somewhat fictionalized account of the life of the Pahute known as Posey.

———. *The Piutes of the San Juan: Shadow of Peogament, Peeats, and Peeogament.* Private publication of three unpublished papers compiled into one by Ky Lyman Bishop.

Lyman, Albert R., and Gladys Perkins Lyman. *Oral History.* Interviews conducted by Charles Peterson, Gary L. Shumway, and Stanley Bronson. Utah State Historical Society and California State University, Fullerton, Oral History Program, Southeastern Utah Project, 1970, 1973.

McLoughlin, Denis. *Wild and Woolly: An Encyclopedia of the Old West.* New York: Doubleday and Co., 1975. An amazing compilation of facts about the varied characters, places, and events that made up the Old West.

Miller, David E. *Hole-in-the-Rock, An Epic in the Colonization of the Great American West.* Salt Lake City: University of Utah Press, 1959, 1966, 1975. Considered the definitive history of the Hole-in-the-Rock expedition. David Miller has brought together every known original document pertaining to the expedition. An extensive list of appendixes contains these journals, letters, and reminiscences. He also lists as many of the personnel of the expedition as he has been able to verify, including the communities from which they departed.

Nielson, Edd, and Ida Nielson. *Memories.* Interview conducted by Deborah Fellbaum. Utah State Historical Society and California State University, Fullerton, Oral History Program, Southeastern Utah Project, 1972. Edd was the son of Joseph Nielson, who came through the Hole.

Palmer, Emma Stevens. *Recollections.* Interviews concerning Walter Joshua Stevens, conducted by Gary L. Shumway and Jessie L. Embry, Utah State Historical Society and California State University, Fullerton, Oral History Program, Southeastern Utah Project, 1973. Joshua Stevens was born December 21, 1856, in Pleasant Grove, Utah, to Walter Stevens and Abigail Elizabeth Holman. With his younger brother David Alma he was called on the San Juan Mission. He married Elizabeth Kinney before leaving, and the trip was their honeymoon.

Perkins, Cornelia Adams, Marian Gardner Nielson, and Lenora Butt Jones. *Saga of the San Juan.* San Juan County Daughters of Utah Pioneers, 1968. In this heavily illustrated volume, the authors trace the history of San Juan County from every perspective, including geologic. The book focuses on Mormon settlement, however, and pays little attention to Navajos, Pahutes, and non-Mormon cattle ranchers.

Peterson, Charles S. *Look to the Mountains: Southeastern Utah and the La Sal National Forest.* Provo: Brigham Young University Press, 1975. An excellent history of the San Juan country, with a strong emphasis on Mormon/Indian/cowboy relationships and their effects on the land.

Pinckert, Leta. *True Stories of Early Days in the San Juan Basin.* Farmington, New

Mexico: Hustler Press, 1964. Gives some details on the Colorado portion of the San Juan country.

Potter, Edgar R. *Cowboy Slang.* Seattle: Superior Publishing Company, 1971. A delightful source of western lingo, with terrific illustrations by Ron Scofield.

Redd, Charles. *Short Cut to the San Juan.* Denver: Westerner's Brand Book, 1949. An excellent abbreviated history of the San Juan expedition written by the son of Lemuel H. Redd, Jr., and Eliza Ann Westover Redd, two of the expedition's members.

Redd, Leland. *Oral History.* Interview partially concerning Jens Nielson, conducted by Louise Lyne. Utah State Historical Society and California State University, Fullerton, Oral History Program, Southeastern Utah Project, 1972.

Shelton, Ferne. *Pioneer Superstitions: Old-Timey Signs and Sayings.* High Point, N.C.: Hutcraft, 1969.

Shelton, Ferne, ed. Collected by Mary Turner. *Pioneer Proverbs: Wit and Wisdom from Early America.* High Point, N.C., Hutcraft, 1971.

Smith, Cornelius C. *A Southwestern Vocabulary: The Words They Used.* Glendale, Calif.: Arthur H. Clarke Co., 1984. Separated into "Spanish Words and Terms," "Anglo Words and Terms," "Military Words and Terms," and "Indian Words and Terms," this is a very helpful glossary.

Tanner, Faun McConkie. *The Far Country: A Regional History of Moab and La Sal, Utah.* Salt Lake City: Olympus Publishing Co., 1976. A topical, intently readable history of the early difficulties in San Juan County.

Watts, Peter. *A Dictionary of the Old West, 1850–1900.* New York: Alfred A. Knopf, 1977. An illustrated dictionary of the common language of cattlemen, frontiersmen, scouts, cowboys, gamblers, miners, and others during the last half of the nineteenth century.

Wellman, Paul I. *Death on Horseback: Seventy Years of War for the American West.* Philadelphia and New York: J. P. Lippincott Co., 1934. Contains interesting information about the Utes and what is known as the Meeker Massacre.

Winslowe, John R. "Gold Canyon, the Most Lied About Mine in the West." *True West,* August 1966. Contains considerable information about the mine near Navajo Mountain known as the "Lost Peshleki."

Young, Otis W. *Western Mining.* Norman: University of Oklahoma Press, 1970. An informal account of prospecting, placering, lode mining, and milling on the American frontier from Spanish times to 1893.

Young, Robert W., and Morgan William, Sr. *The Navajo Language: A Grammar and Colloquial Dictionary.* Albuquerque: University of New Mexico Press. The second portion of this huge, scholarly volume converts English words and expressions into Navajo.

———. *A Family History: Joseph Franklin Barton and Harriet Ann Richards Barton.* Private family publication, 1994. Containing copies of original letters and journals written by two of the Hole-in-the-Rock participants, this volume provides interesting details I have not found elsewhere.